CW01652042

THE
YEW TREE

BOOK ONE

Frankie Franklin

First Published in Great Britain in 2022 by Obelus Publishing

1 3 5 7 9 10 8 6 4 2

First Edition

Thanks to the Methodist church for granting permission for the use of the Morning Prayer.

A CIP catalogue record of this book is available from the British Library.

ISBN 978-1-8384501-8-2 Paperback

Cover design by Obelus Publishing

Typeset in Bembo by Obelus Publishing

Printed by Amazon

This Book is dedicated to 'The Old Man'

About the Author

Frankie is a retired police sergeant, having served over twenty-six years with Thames Valley Police, Frankie was injured in a training accident in November 2011 and retired in January 2019 because of his injuries. He marries his wife in September 1990 and has two daughters. The Yew Tree is the result of many years of writing, and is presented in two books, which Frankie started while still serving in the police, and has now completed in his new home in Dorset, England.

Part One

1850

'Living strongly in the ground
Sad tales oft would be said
Thriving year after year after year
Consuming the flesh of the dead'

No one knew how long it had been in place, longer than the history of the town
A vast, living beast.
No one knows its story.
No one had cared.
Until now.

CHAPTER ONE

The ground is hard and unyielding, frost penetrating deep enough to be walked on without barely a trace, unworkable and seemingly dead, nothing grows, tree branches are nearly naked with just a few brown, dead leaves clinging on in an attempt to keep winter at bay. The Yew remains magnificent. Cold air tries to penetrate the needles that form the flat pointed green leaves, these are protected by the bright red berries that flourish even in the cold of Winter, their flesh striving whilst others around perish, the bark is distinctively thin and scaly giving the appearance of the skin of a huge mythical beast, colours, mixed brown and green live inside and on this protective covering, continually taunting the seasons.

* * *

The hamlet, originally named in the doomsday book as *Vadum Vespertilio,* is three or so miles from the nearest small market town, an old historical town that locals still refer to as 'the village', it is growing in population every year, almost two thousand live here now in just over four hundred houses, many of the poor residents leaving London heading for the country, moving away from those streets paved with gold. The town has one, very large and very old Parish Church, currently it has a curate in charge, Mr Henry Addington, it has a large churchyard and church school, there are other churches, but all are outside of the main town. Shops are open daily, old Mr Thorns tobacconist, Fred Lockhart is the local coal merchant, Mr Batchelor the baker, a small cobbler's shop owned by Mr Davies, Ridleys the iron mongers, there is a new tailor's shop, Freemans's butcher shop owned by Joseph Freeman he is also the local pig sticker and slaughter man. Thomas Wells is the stonemason and William Woods is the carpenter and cabinet maker, he has his barn on the outskirts of town away from the daily hustle and bustle and away from people. Available goods can be purchased from the many market stalls and costermongers that appear every second Saturday, some with vegetables and fruit, some with fish, cockles, whelks, and oysters, one knife grinder and one flower seller appear regularly and these travellers passing through settle on the common for their short stays.

It is a town of mixed wealth and poverty, with the influx of outsiders moving from London to this and other towns, housing is needed to accommodate them, these *new* houses are a few rows of cheaply built terraces, no more than twenty years old, without gardens having just tiny back yards of cobble and dark brick, these small areas quickly became almost forgotten slums, the grass is certainly not greener outside of the city for most that moved here. Small towns as this, cannot accommodate or employ the large numbers of people who moved from the cities, wives and children need to be fed and without any high earning jobs and few low paid jobs, help is expected by these interlopers to the countryside, it is not forthcoming, suffering and slum living is commonplace. The largest Union Workhouse, St Stephens, is situated in St Albans, one of four workhouses in the city, it is full nearly all the time, the parish workhouse in the next village is closed, having been shut down and reopened several times over the previous few years, it now stands empty and unused. Local employment is almost exclusively farming or straw hat making, the town has been well known for this trade for many decades, it supports the main hat making industry in the much larger town of Luton eight miles to the Northwest, the largest town in England at this time without a piped water supply or railway line. Luton had a cholera outbreak in 1848 certainly arriving from London, because of the disease the companies had passed much of their work out to smaller towns during this period, but even so, it isn't a huge employer locally, most of the workers are from families with a long history in the town, these local people don't live in the slum area but in houses and cottages, either tied with their job or passed down to them as these properties have been in local families, most for several generations.

The local families in town are not the poorest around but certainly not the richest members of this society, but all have stable lifestyles and avoid mixing with either the very rich or the very poor in the slums. The wealthy mostly live on the other side of town, away from the poorer housing and slums, not wanting to mix in any way with them, each individual house reflects the status and wealth of its occupants, most are owned by men of industry and business. The families of these wealthy men are well fed and well educated, all having governess teachers to ensure the continued education of their children, the girls being taught separately from the boys, boys being trained to inherit the business that their fathers had also inherited or built up, the girls will only inherit the earth. Disease, having no respect for class, wealth, or status, arrives with deadly conclusion, in 1831 cholera outbreaks in London claimed many lives, London is only twenty or so miles away from this town. Many had died in Hertford and Hatfield in 1839, only eleven years ago, when cholera appeared, these larger towns are only fifteen and nine miles away and the spread of the disease meant some in the town had died, but thankfully the numbers were minimal in comparison, Luton followed in 1848, this outbreak took the lives of many. Typhoid fever is ever present, over the past couple of years it has taken the lives of over a dozen people, mainly from the small slum area, the sanitation there is non-existent, and the resident people drink from the ponds and rivers, which is not unusual but because of these practices the disease is transmitted easily. TB, smallpox, whooping cough, and influenza take the lives of many, rich, poor, young, and old, death is an everyday happening, death has no respect for age or status.

For such a small town, unusually, there are two breweries that serve six public houses and inns, the quiet country inns are so very different to the raucous town pubs that attract visitors from neighbouring villages, especially on market day, money in exchange for beers and wines that the visitors imbibe in quantity. The newest public house, built only three years since, is on the edge of the common and for the past two years is filled to the rafters with visitors at the annual horse racing meeting held on the circular track is on the common, originally started by the Master of the Hounds and several local farmers in 1834, all of whom can be found having a celebration dinner in this very pub after the main event. The horse racing is good for the local dealers and traders, but it is to the annoyance of many of the locals who believe that the influx of 'outsiders' and 'townies', is ruining the reputation of the town as a place of peace and quiet and not one of debauchery, drink, and gambling. The town has no rail link, there are local rumours and grumbles that this may happen soon, several larger towns have railway lines in place, with the great lumbering steam beasts pulling carriages into the city, but this town is not being disturbed by steam, soot, and loud whistles just yet. The common with its open spaces, fern gullies and oak trees is quiet during the weekdays and is always busy at the weekend with families, from all parts of society, taking the air and walking in the countryside. The biannual visit of the Statute or 'Statty' fair, is anticipated by the young and dreaded by the older residents, bringing with it horse drawn caravans with curved rooves, the expertly built roundabout and swings and stalls for the coconut shy and the hoop la, food can be purchased including the delightfully tasting hot horse chestnuts. Smoke is ever present and hangs in the air as the travelling fairground folk bring new life to the open common land, easily seen as you enter the town. New, large houses have been built around the extreme edges of areas around the common over the past decade or so, they are deemed vulgar and unnecessary by those already living in and around the common in their small work tied cottages.

The hamlet is much quieter, with its murmuring, slowly moving stream that meets the brisk barrelling river by the mill, with its creaking, slow moving wheel, built centuries before at the confluence, this is where local grain is slowly crushed, murdered and reborn as life giving flour. Willow cane grows in quantity, mutely and without fear along the banks of the stream at the back of the mill, local women weave the weak canes into strong wicker baskets then to be sold at the markets, they can be seen, skirts and petticoats hitched up as they enter the cold slow-moving water, barefoot, to get access to the tall, spindly branches with their sparse covering of delicate small light green leaves. Farmers work the undulating land, with huge horses to plough the fields and to cut crops, collected by the calloused hands of the farm workers, all of whom live nearby. Farmhouses and barns spot the landscape, tiny brown stains on a carpet of green and yellow, cattle, sheep and pigs are kept close to these farms, they can just be heard through the undisturbed, natural silence.

A change four years previously, the repealing the corn laws, when Prime Minister Peel had sacrificed his position and government to do so, had abolished import taxes on corn, all the local farmers and their families knowing that the good price that they had previously received for their wheat and barley, is reducing and will reduce more over the coming years. Times are hard and getting harder. It is so much quieter here than the town, the few residents, most from families that have been here for generations, live in small cottages, some in alms houses, all stone and brick built, some with rooves of thatch and some with slate, some with whitewashed walls and some left bare, none with running water, but all with enough land to grow vegetables, to feed the family or for bartering with a neighbour, an archaic, deep well provides water by way of an ageing and rusting public pump, firmly fixed in the ground, next to the mill

Francis lives in an old and weather battered cottage in the hamlet.

The cottage, built when Francis' Great-Great Grandmother was a child, stands shabby but proud at the opposite end of the garden to the Yew tree, a stone, wood, and brick built affair with a V shaped, uneven slanted roof that is in desperate need of a new thatch, with parts of it so thin that only the greenness of the moss and foliage growing within it keeps out the ever changing weather. A large chimney protrudes from the west side of the building, it provides strength to the wall on that side to support the structure of the rest of the cottage, thin wisps of grey smoke rise only a short distance from the chimney before flattening out and making its escape, a smaller chimney in the centre of the fraying thatch roof is dormant and appears dead. The east wall of the cottage is a solid, charmless, and windowless stone structure, it firmly holds the cottage in place with its ancient and deep foundations. Aged, strong beams of ancient wood can be seen at the front and back of the building, offering continued support to the bare stone-built walls, unchanged for the life of the cottage, a single gnarled wooden door on this aspect gives access to the kitchen that has four small and uneven windows, three on the front wall and one on the back, bringing light and life to the inside. Unlike some of the big modern houses built up by the common, this building has only one floor, the kitchen is built around the large fireplace on the west wall, a living room in the middle and a single room on the end, added on to the cottage at a time unknown and by persons unknown, originally it was only a barn storage area, then later becoming a second bedroom but now reverted back to being used for storage. The kitchen, a place of warmth and comfort, has a small coal and wood burning cast iron stove standing off centre in the red brick-built fireplace, with a solitary cut oak beam separating the fireplace from the chimney stack, a pair of cast iron fire dogs stand guard in the empty fireplace, waiting for use later in the day. The stove stands at an angle in the inglenook on the right side, the fireplace having lost its grandeur in the room by the addition of the iron stove with its rough iron tubed chimney that forces smoke up and out of the cottage. The left side of the fireplace still has a conventional open fire pit, mainly for warmth but an iron bar running from wall to wall across the fireplace, above the stove and above the firepit is used to hang an old kettle from to heat water above the dancing open flames, standing next to the fire, just inside the door on the floor is a wooden bucket with a rope handle, inside the bucket is a bar of carbolic soap, red as a new house brick, it is well worn and used, a metal pail stands empty and alone by the small door to the back yard. The floor of this room is of old grey stone, uneven and badly laid, even in the heat of the hottest summer day, the floor is as cold as the grave, uninviting and chilling, the walls of stone and wood are marked black in places, evidence of the continued use of the open fire, they support large old wooden beams that form the support to the roof of the cottage, in between these beams are flat planked wooden supports, much thinner than the supporting beams and placed horizontally to the vertical beams, the thatch here is lighter in colour inside than the weather beaten wheat straw seen from the outside, smaller thicker support beams reach between the large beams where they meet at the point of the roof, forming a strong and unbroken triangle. Windows face each other from opposite walls, aged and gnarled wooden frames with old glass that gleans light into the murky kitchen, the solo window on the back wall is window is fixed and never moves, the others that face the garden sit on misshapen stone sills and are held in place with ancient, crumbling mortar, the kitchen window has a single shutter that opens inwards, it has remained closed in recent years with its basic latch working hard to hold the window closed in all seasons and weathers. Wood is stacked haphazardly in the corner of the kitchen, different sizes and structures indicate it has been cut hastily and harshly from its origin of life, one sack containing coal lies on its side with some of the black gold spilling from the open mouth of its container and mixing in with the wood, a jewel amongst the plain browns and greens of the hewn logs. The inside walls are uninviting and bare, the exception being a few roughly placed iron hooks and rings, hung upon these are pots of varying ages and size, some tools and leather straps also hang silently. A few small gaps in the stones contain candles, not homed in ornate holders but sat directly on the stone at different stages of their burnt existence, the faint tainted smell of tallow is ever present, a single oil lamp, as old as the cottage itself, takes centre stage hanging by its handle to a hook fixed to a bare wooden beam. The room has one table, upon which sits a half used and roughly cut yeasty loaf of bread, a large pan containing cold beef dripping, and one, surprisingly clean plate, also here are one knife, one fork and a battered enamel mug, set out ready for use when a meal is cooked. A single chair is carelessly pushed against one wall next to a stable door that leads out to the back of the cottage, on the facing wall is a bench seat, seemingly the only semblance of comfort in this room, with two ornately and faded embroidered cushions, a blanket on the seat so as to offer padding when seated upon, it is placed under the window closest to the fireplace, the wood on the side nearest the fire being very much darker than the wood furthest away from the scorching heat. A small opening takes you through to the next room, before stepping through, standing against the wall is an ancient cupboard, this type of furniture used to be called a 'Scullery cupboard', this cottage has no scullery, it is by far the largest piece of furniture in the room, it dominates the wall without grandeur or stature. It is old and uncared for, a simple bare wooden structure, its base has a battered door with a locking device that has long since been functional, inside, amongst the dust, are a mixture of old cooking utensils and small garden tools, thrown in without organisation or care, many have been unused since before the old King died over a decade previously. The top of the cupboard has an open section, on the top counter of its base, are a few stacked China plates, chipped and old, a faded image of a pheasant can be seen on the top plate, a stoneware jug, plain faded brown in colour, stands empty next to the plates. Above this is another small cupboard, the door slightly ajar as moisture has gradually seeped into the wood and it can't be closed securely, there is no need for security as this part of the cupboard is empty and unused, seemingly bereft of life or love. There are two drawers at the centre of this piece of furniture, one is used frequently to store small items, the other on the right sticks and it takes a huge effort to open it, items in here have been there for an age. Through the small opening, situated where the outside wall meets the inside wall, is a living room, the opening has no door or curtain, there is no need to maintain privacy, this area is smaller than the kitchen, it is colder and shows little sign of care, love or interest being shown to it. The far wall is made of thick heavy stone as it is the original outer wall only, changed when the store room was added at least a century before, it has a roughly struck fireplace, no grace or skill was taken when this was made, almost certainly cut during the Cromwellian era of the Interregnum, it is a hole, teardrop shaped in the stonework made into a fireplace for the chimney, there are no decorative designs or any type of ornamental surround, only a roughly made wooden fireplace mantel, fixed to the wall with large iron nails atop this mantle is a single candlestick, complete with half burnt candle. The fire is not lit, and this adds to the damp, cool feeling within the room, two small firedogs sit unused and seemingly asleep in the fireplace. A single large window manages to give the living room the light it needs to bring it to life, a decaying oak frame, built and fitted into the outside wall of the house has two shutter casement style openings, this fitting gives the room only a small stone sill, the windows have not been opened to air the room for decades and the glass is opaque with grime. Below the window is a bed, big enough for two people, almost of a cot design, with deep raised sides, the foot board being taller than the headboard, it is very old and when made by ancient skilled hands was done so with care, time, and devotion. The headboard rests gently against the wall in the corner of the room next to the fireplace, when the fire is lit it affords direct warmth to the head of the sleeping person when the rest of their body is tucked under an ancient home sewn eiderdown, complete with tapestry and embroidered design now faded and grimy but effective against the worst of the cold. Harsh woollen blankets sit folded at the foot of the bed upon the top of two mattresses, the bottom is just straw filled hessian sacks to pad out the upper mattress, this is thinner, but of better quality and more refined than the straw sacks. Made of thick cotton sheets and stuffed to bursting with the down of geese and ducks, it is home-made and years after its conception it is still soft and welcoming, the bed is completed with a thin pillow, made similarly to the cotton mattress but of poorer quality. A single chair stands on the other side of the fireplace, sitting alone on this piece of furniture is a box of 'Lucifers', white tipped phosphorous matches for starting the fire with a flare of heat when struck and forced to ignite, leaving an acrid stench clinging to the air. A stoneware jug half filled with water sits underneath the seat of the chair, beneath the bed is a chamber pot, earthenware with a faded hoary glaze, chipped and time worn this is used almost every night, the contents of it poured into the pot to remove any aroma that may linger, it is always cleaned and scrubbed with carbolic after use, the contents being taken to the privy to be disposed of in Spring, Summer, Autumn, or Winter. Old rags, used in conjunction with the chamber pot, hang in front of the unlit fire, still damp from being rinsed earlier in the day, they still appear soiled and dirty even after their daily rinsing in the stream at the end of the garden. His Mothers ancient chest of drawers, made of a light-coloured wood, beech perhaps, stands at an angle in the far corner, three drawers, two small ones sitting above one large one, spare clothes, not many and none of them new, lie in the drawers.

A small entrance, roughly hacked in the stone wall stands on the opposite side of the fireplace to the bed, a sack is hung from nails on the wall, creating a separation of sorts to the room beyond. A single window in this room is high up on the outer wall facing the garden, it is small and unopened, the wooden frame in remarkable condition in comparison to the other window frames in the house, it being born long after the others had been put in place, it gives little light, and half used candles placed around the room are evidence of its former use. A harshly made crucifix hangs alone on the far wall. A bed frame is almost in the centre of the room, standing on a dirt floor, covered in straw, straw that long ago lost its golden glint, this room is no longer used for sleeping but as a place of storage, wooden crates, some empty and some housing potatoes and apples stand open to the room, old pots, pans, and clothes have all been put unceremoniously on and around this bed. In one corner of the room is a large hole, dug to a depth of nearly five feet, the soil walls are supported by rough cut wooden planks, this hole contains small shelves and one small table, a homemade wooden ladder can be seen just poking over the top there are large flat stones outside of the hole, these are to be added as the steps down, but for now the ladder will suffice. It is a type of root cellar, unusually this one is inside the cottage, it is used to keep food fresher for longer as the temperature is always much cooler in this underground pit than above ground. On the shelves are storage jars of varying sizes and age, many full and some half used, large chunks of salted meat, beef, pork, mutton, and dried meat hang from hooks below the shelves and there are many jars of jugged meat, hare, and venison, all slow cooked and put in the jars with broth, with their lids on tightly and left to cool. His favourite is the blood pudding, made to a recipe given to him by an Irishman he met when working at the experimental station, mixing pig blood with fat scraped off of the skin, adding oats to it and heating it slowly in a pan on the stove, the Irishman informed him that 'at home' the mixture was then put into pig intestines, making blood pudding sausage, when dried it keeps for many months. Francis puts his into jars and into the root cellar to cool, taking it out by the spoonful when he needs it, either heating it through in a pan or eating it cold are both delights that he enjoys. All the meat stored in the cellar is good, Francis will not buy broxy meat, it always smells bad, the local butcher sells a lot of it without shame to the very poor, Francis isn't a pauper, not rich by any means, but never desperate enough to buy broxy meat. Dried fruit has become easier to obtain, it isn't cheap as it is transported in from London, in his root cellar are figs, raisins, dates and pears, most of which has been given to him in lieu of paid work, he is happy to take food for work, he also has a chicken and two ducks alongside a brace of pheasant hanging from a hook in the wooden walls. On the shelving he has onions that have dried, the flaky skin peeling gently, they are keeping well, sitting next to these is a large jug with a course lip, this is filled with beer from a firkin that lives on the floor of the cellar, payment from a job and part of an ongoing agreement with Dick Freeman, a local licensee. Back above ground, in the corner of the room is a sturdy table with a thick wooden butcher block on top of it, a recently sharpened knife sits next to the block, its blade glinting as the winter sun creeps through the high window, bloody evidence of recent use still lies on the wood, drying to a dark red colour, the only splash of brightness in this dank room. Snares and traps lie dormant on the rough floor, waiting to be charged into action to take the life of a rabbit or hare for his sustenance, spades and other digging tools stand carelessly against one wall, uncleaned and recently used. There is no fire or fireplace, the room was used when first added to the old cottage, as a second bedroom, Francis lives alone now, so no need for this to be wasted as a bedroom, it has been a storage space since his mother had died some three decades ago and he moved from here into the living room.

The small stable door in the kitchen leads to a small back yard, fenced off to waist height, with a small gate to the left, on the right is a slate roofed open fronted woodshed, full of uneven sized cut logs of oak and beech, an ancient axe stands strong with its head buried into a large section of circular wood, used as a chopping block, the now damp sawdust lies leisurely on the cobbled yard floor, a large wooden half barrel and a mangle stand alone on the other side of the yard. Through the gate is a long cinder path that leads past the sty, at this time housing one large sow, to the outhouse, the privy, situated far enough away from the house to be useable it is a battered but sturdy wooden, hand built structure, taller than it is wide, a sloping wooden roof covered with weather damaged pitch that hardly keeps the elements at bay. The double hinged door has gaps both at the bottom and the top, to assist with reducing the smell inside by circulating the air, on the wall hanging from a large nail are pieces of newspaper ripped into small squares, several pieces of soiled rag also hang from other nails and hooks in the wooden walls, a water filled brown pottery jug, like an old cider jug, stands on the floor. A sturdy wide shelf, with a hole cut in the middle is used as a seat and placed across an old wooden barrel that has been half buried into the ground, having its base and lid removed. Below the barrel is a deep hole, the midden, eight or ten feet deep, all human waste falls into the midden, to reduce the smell vegetable peelings, ash from the stove and the fires, charcoal, dry earth, sawdust, and wood shavings are added daily to cover the waste and to dull the aroma, soiled straw and manure from the pig sty is also added on occasion, this helps to break down the waste quickly and effectively, but it is an odious task so isn't done as often as it should be. Francis has designed the barrel above the hole himself and he is pleased with its functionality, the lid of the barrel is placed over the hole in the seat, further attempting to keep the foul smells from below to a minimum. The whole structure can be moved when the midden becomes full or smells so bad that it has to be filled in, this job is done at least once a year, the midden then becomes a compost that eventually will be put onto the vegetable patch in the front garden and used as a manure. This moving process removes the use of, and payment to the night soil man, a local worker and neighbour, who for a fee, will come onto your property at night and remove the waste from the midden and take it away, no doubt dumping it into the river near the mill. Some of the big houses up on the common now have inside lavatories and flushing water systems, the waste still has to go to a midden at these locations, but outside of the house making it easily collected by the night soil man. Francis has no interest in having an indoor privy, it is just him using the outhouse, on his own, he has very few visitors to the cottage. The outhouse is at the far reaches of the rear curtilage of the property, with open fields, ripe with wheat in the summer and deathly bare after harvest, behind it, shaded woodland with bluebell carpets in April and May create a scene of serene beauty when the sun pushes through the canopy above it at first light. An open cart, flat bedded with iron rimmed wheels, stands idly by the fence, there is no horse in this house to pull this cart. The sty, built close to the privy, is fenced off with posts and strong wooden branches, the pig has a shelter built of old wooden planks and posts in one corner, straw lies over the muddy floor of the sty, this is where vegetable peelings and waste meat are thrown in to feed the large sow, the time for slaughter is getting near, this will give Francis enough pork meat to last him many months, all of the pig will be eaten. Francis will not kill and slaughter the pig himself; the local '*pig sticker*' and butcher will do it, taking a small share of the meat as payment, nothing goes to waste. The head will be cut in half and boiled, the soft succulent cheek meat will be a treat, the brawn that is left after boiling, will be put in jars and placed in the root cellar, kidneys, heart and liver will be eaten in stews, cooked slowly all day in the large cooking pot on top of the stove, hams, hocks, shoulders and belly will be salted and preserved, bacon will be cured, ribs, always eaten first are roasted over the open fire, the succulent loin will be air dried and cured in the cellar until solid, then stored alongside the jars of brawn. Trotters will also be boiled, purposely and slowly, these gelatinous tender morsels of meat will also be put into jars to set, ready for re heating whenever needed. Francis never goes hungry.

To the west side of the house is a large vegetable patch, only a few straggling cabbages and hardy parsnips survive at this time of the season, onions are in the ground, but will not see life until late spring at the earliest.

Carrots, beet, potatoes, and marrow have provided much of the food consumed in the cottage over the Summer and Autumn, potatoes stored in the back room continue to be used daily. Wild watercress grows in the chalky waters of the stream, having to be picked, before they flower, in Spring and again in late Summer, the peppery taste changes delightfully with each harvest.

The general enclosures act of 1836 has made it possible for some landowners to enclose their land without parliamentary reference and later amendments have enabled land to be provided and protected and set aside as field gardens for the poor. Francis is lucky to have enough land to have his own plot, he tends it regularly, the soil is fine, and any unwanted weeds are removed almost daily in the Spring and Summer months. Chickens, geese, and ducks take up large portion of the lower end of the garden, rough fencing across its width has only been put up to stop foxes from getting in and to stop the fowl from getting onto his vegetable plot and eating the seeds and vegetables. They are free to swim in the stream and free to leave should they wish to, they never have, they are reliant on being fed daily, Francis has a sack of corn and rough oats for this, these birds have a small, roofed hut to rest in at night. Taking pride of place in the garden is the water pump, with a heavily painted plate at its base stating, '*Bristow and Co 1820*', fitted by Francis several years ago it is situated over an ancient deep well of fresh water, the well is tens of feet deep, and brick lined, his ancestors completing this feat of engineering many decades earlier, the water from deep underground is constant, cold, sweet, and clean. The old bucket and rope were removed when Francis took the pump as part payment for work he completed for the parish, it was an old street, public contraption, having been abandoned in a yard and was rusty and unloved, now it stands over the well, having been given a new life with a lot of care and time, the paint is still in good condition and the pump is serviceable and works well. The force rod that was once iron, now has a sturdy oak replacement, the old iron handle snapped and could not be reused this was the only other part that needed changing, the piston rod and piston inside the cylinder, cleanly connects to the check valve and sealing ring, a clean-up of these parts had shown them to be as good as new. The foot valve and lead down pipe, acquired one very dark night from a locked yard are both in working condition without any signs of leaking, a curved outlet spout on the side of the pump allows the water to be collected from outside of the pump. On the up stroke of the piston the foot valve opens, and suction brings water into the pump head, on the following down stroke of the piston, the check valve on the piston opens and allows water to flow above the piston, finally on the successive up stroke of the piston, water is pushed out of the outlet spout. His is the only house in the Hamlet that had its own water pump, the others have to rely on using a well, if they have one, with a bucket and rope, if not, using the public pump by the mill, and carrying water home is what has to be done to avoid drinking the river or stream water as it is regularly contaminated with human waste. In between the vegetable patch and the fencing to keep the game birds in is the Yew tree. Standing alone with strength and solidarity, low branches stretching out as if to catch a falling object, with smaller branches at its extremity mimicking a human hand, fingers outstretched and taught. Taller than the cottage and easily the oldest living thing in the hamlet, its trunk pulling life from the earth and towering toward the distant sky, the bark is a thin and scaly skin of brown and green protecting the ageing beast inside and covering every inch of the trunk, the giver of shape and strength to the thick branches and smaller twigs that hold tightly to the flat, dark green pointed needle leaves. Deep roots give desired life to the bole, this in turn supports the crown, a magnificent explosion of colour that changes subtly with the seasons, it casts a permanent and foreboding shadow on the ground below. Four men with outstretched arms could not reach around the girth of this living and ancient giant, it has a twin in the churchyard in town, no one knows their history or if they are linked in any way. The churchyard Yew lived before the current church was built, there had been previous churches on the site, but little Is known about their history, places of worship historically tend stay in the same location, with purpose-built buildings of their time, erected for the believing masses to pray and give thanks.

The cottage is probably nearly two centuries old, built long after the Yew first came from the ground, it is the first known building on this site, claimed by previous generations as their own, the ancient Yew is unclaimed and not owned by any man.

Yew trees are known historical symbols of birth, death, and resurrection.

* * *

The Queen, heading toward her thirteenth anniversary as head of the Empire and nearly twelve years since her coronation is known to the local folk but only by name and recent history, the City of London where she resides in Buckingham Palace is a few days travel away, this City is unvisited by most and an unknown quantity to all, rumours of rich life and diseased death seemed to keep the country folk in the country. Francis, now halfway into his fifth decade of life, to an outsider seems at home with his own company, living alone for many years and always without fear or companion, working almost every day from dawn to dusk, a solo working life mirrors the home life he purposely leads. His last work companion having succumbed to typhoid fever many years previously, working alone suits him, the work is hard and physical but for a man of his years, he is seemingly fit, well and disease free, a blessing in these times of death and illness, it is these deaths and illness that keep him in regular work. Living alone suits him also, his mother died when he was a teenager and he has no memory of his Father, he does not know his Father's name or resting place, Mother had never talked about it to him. She died a terrible and uncomfortably death from Scrofula, known to all as 'the Kings Evil'. He has memories, not good memories, of large violaceous coloured swellings on Mother's neck and under her arms that, over time, burst into open wounds, the smell of which was almost unbearable to her, the fevers came then the chills, her general malaise had become a tiresome burden on the young man. Mother had died, he had buried her in the Churchyard in town, Francis is the town and local area grave digger, burying his Mother when he was still apprenticed to the then gravedigger, known locally as John the Spade, was one of his early experiences of death, burial, religious ritual, and the correct way to dig a grave. No stone marks Mothers place of rest, Francis knows where she is buried in the Churchyard but with no other family to visit, it seemed a waste of money to mark a site that no one would ever visit now or in years to come. Francis did have a brother, older than him by over ten years, Jacob left the family home when he was young man, joining as an officer with the Presidency army of the East India Company, travelling from home to London to sign up and join, this was several years before Mother died. He was posted overseas, to lands far so away and exotic that Francis could not even begin to imagine them, Mother died not knowing the names or locations of these distant countries or of the fate of her oldest Son. Francis had heard, only last year through the local priest, Henry Addington, that Jacob had been killed in the war against the Indian Sikh armies in December 1845, Francis had little feeling about this news, the brothers having not had any contact since Jacob signed up when Francis was barely ten years old to work for the East India company. Francis had now been alone for so many years that he rarely thought about his dead brother, buried so very far away, even thoughts of Mother have faded to the closed parts of his mind, he is happy with his own company and rarely has visitors to the cottage, just the way he wants it. With no real close friends, he spends much of his time alone, the exception being when he is working with William, the local carpenter and cabinet maker who is also the undertaker, William has the responsibility to collect all the deceased bodies from the town and surrounding villages, using Francis cart pulled by his horse, taking the bodies in coffins hewn by William at his barn in town, Francis being the unofficial undertaker's assistant attends these occasions with William, they have an ongoing agreement that suits both parties, an agreement that most would fine distasteful and ungodly. Both men have seen death in its many guises, and nothing phases them, except the smell of dead flesh, William is not so good with this. Francis digs the graves, William measures the dead for coffin fittings, William and Francis will then deliver the coffin to the house of the deceased, a local woman will lay out the body, the undertakers returning a week or so later to collect the body in the coffin, they take it to the churchyard for ceremony and burial, in a grave freshly dug by Francis. It is an agreement that suits both men. Francis can, almost daily, be seen walking from the cottage to town, or to surrounding villages, with his trade tools over his shoulder, a mattock, a wide pointed spade and a '*grave bar*', all made for him years ago by the smithy, the grave bar was designed by him it is a long smooth pole, about thirty six inches in length, with a thin, sharp and blade edged spade, perfect for getting the sides of the grave straight and true. Francis never leaves his tools at the churchyard believing that they will be stolen and sold for pennies by thieves, he has several lengths of marked, planked wood, used for shoring up and measuring the depth of the grave as he digs and finally a bucket, the wood planks and bucket are the only tools he leaves in a small lean to shed at the side of the church, this grave measuring wood has never been stolen. Death is an everyday experience for him, death, he knows has no concern or thoughts about the age, religious beliefs, sex or the status of the deceased, death comes, and it takes without consultation. Grave digging and undertaking are unsympathetic employments, he knows most of the people in the hamlet, many in the town and some in the surrounding villages, everyone knows who he is and what he does. Most nod or say 'good day' to him, not many will stop to have a conversation with him, seemingly because of the supernatural superstitions that go with his employment as the digger of graves, there are no purposeful funeral directors in town, some of the bigger towns and cities have this new type of service available, but not this one, Francis and William are the men who are called to deal with the dead. Friendship with either of them is avoided by all because of their deep rooted fear of death, a fear still held within every section of the local community. Francis always digs the graves alone, his work partner, a man he had worked with for nearly thirty years and the son of John the spade had died of typhoid fever years ago, no one had volunteered to work with him after 'young' Johns death and no one has approached him get their son apprenticed to the trade, he is happy with this arrangement, there is never a rush to dig a grave, so one man can happily complete the task, albeit it takes a while longer to complete. The churchyard in town, although large and spread out is very nearly full, for centuries the dead have been buried in this one location and now the stench of decay is ever present, hanging around for all who pass through to witness, sweet, sickly, and unpleasantly identifiable. The smell has no effect on Francis.

Many grave plots are now stacked several coffins deep, families wanting loved ones buried with other loved ones, the original deep pits, many dug by Francis, are no longer deep and no longer capable of taking further burials. On many occasions Francis has removed old and sometimes, rotten coffins, leaving putrid corpses and bones in the bottom of their grave, covering them with a thin layer of soil, leaving just enough room for the newly deceased to be placed in the ground, the new coffin will be covered, sometimes with only inches of soil between the coffin lid and daylight. If the wood from the removed coffins is in reasonable condition it is sold as firewood to those living in the slum, Francis does this as regularly as he can, the extra money is always welcomed, he earns two shillings for each grave he digs, not a pittance but not a fortune either. William pays him a similar amount to work with him, delivering the coffins and collecting the bodies of the dead, on occasion, Francis will take on the role of a *mute* at a funeral service, being paid to attend the graveside to give the impression that the deceased has family and friends, paid to mourn, it is easy money but it means he has to stand with other paid *mutes*, usually the town drunks and ne'er do wells, he never converses with them. The long-term effect of these current and shallow burials has become noticeable in some parts of the churchyard, putrefied bodies frequently having to be disturbed, dismemberment and even destroyed to make room for newcomers, some graves have bones sticking out of the ground, moving as the body decays and the earth and soil sinks and pushes them upward. Clearance of these bones is done by Francis without the permission of the Curate has been done many times, but more are appearing and with monotonous regularity, he believes that the clergyman a knows about the removal and reburial of these sacred body parts, he does not care, the continued burial fees from bereaved families form a large part of the clergy income, so this clearance is necessary for Francis to be able to provide a service and for 'decent' burials to continue. Mother is in a grave of her own, no sharing and no overcrowding for her, she will remain alone, Francis has seen to this.

Overcrowding is not just a local problem, other churchyards that he knows locally have similar issues, but St Nicholas is by far the worst, child mortality is high, disease is rife and uncontrollable, the growing population even in this small town means Francis is kept busy. He is also tasked on occasion by the Priest, to enter the cavernous crypt beneath the church or into vaults inside the church or on occasion, in the church yard to 'tap' coffins, this task is completed by drilling or making a hole in a coffin to allow '*cadaverous vapours*' to escape. Coffins have been known to break open with explosive force due to the build-up of gasses emanating from the rotting corpse within. The coffins in the crypt and the vaults are usually of a superior build quality to the wooden boxes used for the everyday burials of the poor, some of these heavy coffins are sealed with wax and bitumen, meaning that gasses cannot naturally escape. Francis learnt very early on in his apprenticeship that the best and safest way to do this was to strike the side of the coffin with the grave bar, causing a split or a hole in the wooden box, then leaving the area soon after the hole appears, he has experienced as a young grave digger, the cause and suffering from the gas and aromas emanating from a decaying corpse. The smell and escaping putrid air causes pains in the head, heaviness in the limbs and extreme debility, unstoppable lachrymation, trembling throughout the body and violent palpations in the chest, the heart seemingly near to exploding, he has witnessed others vomit during this process although he had not ever been physically sick himself.

Funerals are not usually elaborate affairs, the family of the deceased are invariably poor farm workers or from the slum, they are unable to afford grand final gestures to their dead loved ones, it is not uncommon for Francis and William, after mourners had left the graveside, to remove the body from the coffin, they know it will have been placed into a shroud, usually old sacking roughly sewn together, Francis will then bury the shrouded body in the grave and William takes the coffin away to be re used, William always pays a few shillings extra for this process, they have done this on many occasions. Francis has no time for the outdated superstitions and traditions associated with death, almost every house he attends to deliver a coffin or to collect a body in their coffin, regardless of social status, will have the curtains closed and any mirrors in the house covered, it is believed that if you see your own reflection in a house where a death had occurred, that you also might die. Clocks are stopped at the time of death in the houses, if they have clocks, to prevent any further bad luck; stuff and nonsense as far as Francis is concerned. Bereaved families will also ask for locks of hair to be cut from the deceased, this is usually done by a '*laying out*' woman during the laying out process, but both William and Francis had been asked to do this, when the woman has refused or forgotten, completing the task out of sight of the family, it can then be done without care or finesse. Every family, without fail, insists on the body of the dead being carried out of the house feet first, so that the corpse may not look back into the house as he or she leaves, the coffins made for the poor by William, are not the coffin shaped boxes normally associated with burials, but plain oblong boxes, it is never known by the families which way the body is taken out of the house, Francis and William don't care which way the body faces as it leaves for its final destination. Experience and longevity in their respective trades has made them uncaring and without sympathy, death is death, and it is the end. Francis has recently heard of a new, modern, and somewhat odd procedure, a memento of the dead for the families. Photographs, a relatively new process, are taken of the body, posed after death, dressed in best clothes, with other members of the families present, this new tradition has not arrived in the town yet, but he has heard of it happening in other large towns. He has also heard rumours that some families want mirrors and tubes put into the coffin in case the deceased are not dead, Francis hopes that this will never happened in his town, the dead need burying and if they are not dead, surely, they would have sat up, alive and revitalised in the house they died in, every corpse he has dealt with is dead, he knows this as they have been laid out for the best part of a week. Workhouse deaths are the best for Francis, very little upset or hysterics involved, just a death, infant, child or adult, a hole dug by him in the back yard of the workhouse, jokingly called the cemetery, and in they go, placed in a box built by William, many bodies having to be made to fit by different means if the box is too small, bending the legs, laying the bodies on its side and bringing the knees up to the chest of the deceased, if the cadaver will not fit then the body will be put in the grave as it is, with heavy earth put on top of it, no one will ever know and William and Francis then share the money the workhouse has paid for the coffin. No mourners are ever present, it is rare that a priest will even attend, St Stephens workhouse has kept him busy for the past few years, a pair of local gravediggers had, some years ago refused to dig graves for these '*ungodly*' souls who die in the workhouse, Francis had been summonsed and had kept the employment of the union workhouse since, He does find it a bind at times, having to borrow William's horse to take his cart and tools on the six-mile journey, on bumpy roads, but at two shillings a dig, he is more than happy with this.

Francis also does odd jobs for anyone willing to pay him, either with shillings or with goods and food, most of his work involves digging for others, he is happy to do any kind of work, as long as he is left alone and able to work at his own pace. He has recently been working at the privately funded farming and agricultural experimental station, built outside of the town on open land in 1843, financed by the owner of Rothamstead Manor, John Bennet Lawes, new fertilizers for farming are being developed and tested here, crop rotation and field experiments are also done on this site. It is a huge rural area and for the past couple of years, Francis has been given the job of putting in and repairing fence posts and fencing around the perimeter, the total area of the station and it's farms being over eight-hundred acres, this is an ongoing task that gives him extra money in his pocket, an agreed daily rate of five shillings and sixpence is satisfactory, more than a common labourer and less than a carpenter but the rate is agreeable to both parties and Francis can come and go as he pleases, working as and when he wants or needs to. The site is now completely fenced in, so it is mainly maintenance tasks he has to attend to, enough work to keep him going on the quieter days if he needs the income. Money is of little interest to Francis, as long as he has enough to live on he is happy with his lot, he has very little outgoings, coal for the stove and oil for the couple of old lanterns he has, with no other regular payments for anything else. He buys apples by the crate in the summer, keeping them cool in his storage room and root cellar, other fresh fruit he gets from the hedgerows, he takes great care growing vegetables, these give him enough to eat and enough to store for the winter months. He likes to work and for work he demands payment, fair payment, for the graft he does is often hard and unpleasant, the fence work he does when he wants, if a neighbour or someone in town wants fencing put up or a hole dug for a pond, a well or a midden, he does it at his own pace and when he wants to do it, he never haggles over price, if the person wanting the work done does not agree and wants to haggle, he walks away without a word, it does not bother him at all if he does the job or not, there will be others, there always is. He gets all the wood for the fencing at the experimental station and for those private houses from William, another arrangement between them, Francis gets a good rate for the wood from William and, of course, makes a small amount when selling it on, William will always lend him the horse, knowing that the raw materials will be purchased from him.

Francis is informed about a death in the hamlet or the town by verbal message, usually from the post boy or the constable, Francis has never sent or received a letter as he is illiterate, so this is the only contact he has with the post boy, if not the post boy a messenger boy from town sent by the clergy, on occasion, if appropriate, the constable will be the bearer of news to him. They all know that he will either be at home, at the experimental station or in the churchyard, if he isn't at any of these, he will be working locally at a house or field, his grave digging skills are also used by other small villages in the area, those that have their own parish church and churchyard, he covers four such villages, the furthest being six miles from his cottage. He does not really like going out to the villages, it means extra miles and extra hours for no extra money, still only two shillings for digging a grave, but none of the graves are as full up as the town churchyard or as frequent as those local burials, less people living in these areas means less death, he keeps the work on, mainly because no one else wants the job and it keeps him in good stead with all the parish councils around.

The weather in December last year and now into January is bitterly cold, snow fall has been regular and the ground is as hard as rock with the recent daily temperatures rarely above freezing, messages of death and graves needing to be dug from the surrounding villages and hamlets has increased, the cold is taking many more than the usual cold snaps of previous Winters, this is a particularly harsh spell of cold and he knows his services will be needed. The digging of the graves isn't too bad, the first few inches is always tough due to being frozen, but once through this hard layer the going gets better, the soil is wet and claggy, but he is used to this and in these current conditions it is a good half days work to dig to the required six feet, but much less if the grave is already occupied, it really depends on how many coffins or bodies are previously buried in any space. Village and Parish churchyards are less crowded, therefore he isn't keen on travelling out of town because the churchyards in the villages, although much smaller than the one in town, have less occupants, the digging to six feet or so isn't unusual in these places. He has a strong back, strong arms and powerful legs, all needed to dig graves properly, he knows it would be quicker and easier if he had an apprentice or a partner, he has now been working on his own for so long now that he only occasionally wishes he had someone with him, these thoughts usually fill his mind when it was raining or cold and he wants to go home and sit in front of the stove and fireplace, these thoughts will disappear as soon as they arrive in his mind, getting the job done is always foremost in his thoughts. Most of the small villages have a carpenter who builds the coffins needed, so William only goes with him if required, he is always willing to lend his horse to Francis for the day, if William has use for the horse for his own work, then the digging of the grave will be delayed until the horse is available, the funeral cannot not take place without a grave so waiting is what these people sometimes have to do if Francis cannot get there when he is requested. Grave digging is never immediately required, there is always a few days to get any job completed, if he can't get there when needed, the family will have to dig it themselves, he knows that this does not ever happen, it never has and, as far as he believes, never will, people are scared of churchyards and graves, he isn't and never has been, he has seen too many dead bodies, in varying states of decay, to be worried about what he might or might not be digging up or with any of the superstitious nonsense surrounding the dead and churchyards. The dead are dead, and that is that.

CHAPTER TWO

Francis is awake, hearing the church bells in the distance as the sound carries easily from the town to his cottage, he remembers it is Sunday and the bells are a weekly call to prayer for those who want to attend or for those who are too afraid of their God not to attend, he does not go to sermons himself, spending the time he has with the dead over the years almost has him believing that any God really cannot exist, his faith has been almost but not completely destroyed by visions of the deaths he has witnessed and the inhumane and selfish nature of man when death occurs, he himself has done things he should be ashamed of, he isn't.

His face is outside of the protective covers of blankets and eiderdown is so very cold, the fire in the living room is now a barely surviving collection of glowing red embers he knows that the only way to heat up the room will be to put some small cuttings of wood onto the fire to enable it to spring back to life with yellow jumping flames, his body cocooned inside the warm bedding is rejecting his need to get up and get the room warm, he is hoping that the stove in the kitchen still has a flicker of life in it, he put a large shovel of coal on it last night so, with luck it will have embers that he can stoke and get going quickly. Swinging his feet and legs out of the bed, taking deep breaths in and instantly sees the warm air from his lungs turn into pure white almost smoky clouds that linger in front of him before disappearing only to return on the next outward breath. He avoids knocking over the chamber pot, half full with last night's cold urine, he stands up, stretches his arms high and after adjusting his under shirt and drawers he walks to the small pile of wood next to the fire, the cold from the stone floor piercing the soles of his feet, he looks around for his slippers but cannot immediately see them so he carries on barefoot, he squats down without putting his knees onto the cold floor, picking up several small pieces of kindling before he gets onto his knees, feeling the cold against them he gently but swiftly places the small dried wood on top of the barely glowing embers and blows silently onto them. At first nothing happens, with continued patience and endurance, small flickers of flame come to life from the gentle breaths being applied to them, wisps of smoke appear and are drawn up into the chimney, escaping into the frozen world outside, the kindling takes, and flames appear. Francis slowly and purposely adds ever growing sized logs until the fire has taken, hearing the familiar and satisfying crackle of wood as it heats up to provide welcome heat, it is a small room, and it is soon warm. He stands in front of the new living fire as it begins to remove the creeping cold in his knees and legs that lingers from the short time he was knelt on the floor; he is soon warm. After tucking in his undershirt he re ties the cotton waist string of his drawers then sits on the bed and pulls on his prized, and only pair of soft cotton socks, putting a coarse woollen pair on over the top of them, the wool socks being pulled high up on his calf, the fire is now burning strongly and the warmth is moving freely around the small room, the cold air being forced out by the strong heat. Taking his trousers from the back of the chair he puts them on, feeling the delicate scratch of the tightly woven wool on the small area of unprotected skin below the knees, his drawers, made of linen with an opening at the front are knee length, this stops any further irritation higher up his legs. The braces for the trousers are still attached front and back by large buttons pushed through soft leather strapping, they hang freely at each side of him, reaching to the chair again he grabs his shirt, a smock style linen shirt, now an off white colour, dated and worn, he pulls it over his head, it's loose fitting easily passes his waist, he gathers up the excess material and tucks it inside his trousers. He pulls the trousers to the correct fitting, high above his waist and securing the solo button above the placket, leaving the braces dangling either side of his body, he moves to go through the opening to the kitchen. Seeing his slippers at the foot of the bed, hand stitched by his Mother shortly before she passed, soft leather with woollen interior, probably the most luxurious item of clothing he owns, he takes time putting them onto his feet without bending down, he shuffles through the opening in the wall, yawning loudly, stretching his arms toward the roof beams of the house as he enters the kitchen. It is not as cold in here as the as it was in the living room but not hot by any stretch of the imagination, he checks the grate on the stove, no need to check the open fire as it has obviously burnt out overnight, the fire dogs can clearly be seen in the ashes, he looks inside the stove, the coals from last night are still glowing, Francis puts wood shavings onto the still hot, red embers and they catch almost immediately, then adding dry kindling which also takes easily, he needs the fire to be much hotter before adding any coal, without moving from his crouched position in front of the stove, he reaches to the log pile and selects a couple of smaller, split logs, putting them gently on top of the now burning kindling, he assists the burn by blowing steadily into the opening in the middle of the stove to encourage the wood to catch and start to burn. As it catches, he reaches below the grate and pulls out the ash drawer tray on the stove, standing up, takes the small tray and empties the contents into the pail that is standing by the door to the back yard, this done he returns and puts the tray back into its home, the wood is now burning well and another, larger log can be added. This wood will need to be red hot before any coal can be added, coal burns slower than wood but requires intense heat to ignite, Francis knows that the kitchen will warm up very quickly, but he will need to keep a close watch on the grate if the wood burns too much it will not have the heat required for the coal to be added. Returning to the living room he collects the chamber pot and as the contents are just liquid he considers opening the door to the back yard and throwing it into the yard, knowing how cold it will be to walk outside, he decides that he needs to use the outhouse, so going back into the kitchen he throws off his slippers and puts his feet into his pair of 'winter' shoes, known as Blucher boots. Sturdy and well worn, they fit easily, the thick leather upper of the boots, more malleable than when he originally acquired them a decade or so ago, the soft leather tongue protected by a throat on each side, with three holes on each throat, leather laces are left untied and dangling across the shoe, the sole is made of thick leather with a heel protected by a semi-circle of fitted metal, called a shoe iron, the soles protected by small nail studs hammered into them, a practice that has been used and effective since Roman times. The leather has been protected and waterproofed by Francis himself, using a foul smelling concoction of mutton suet, beeswax and turpentine, a process that he completes every year, over time the cracks and seams fill with this substance and protects the leather. His 'summer' boots, basically the same as the 'winter' boots but without the nail studs in the soles, are treated the same way, the former currently reside under the bench seat, where they will remain until the Winter and Spring have passed bringing weather that he hopes will be much warmer and drier.

With a boot put loosely on each foot, the laces remain untied, Francis opens the back door, the iron thumb latch lifted from its resting place freeing the door to be opened, the front door still has the original sliding wooden latch, basic but functional, neither door can be locked securely from the outside as both only having latch fittings. The freezing air outside easily pushes its way into the warming kitchen, it takes his breath away for a second, he considers putting on his thick outdoor coat, deciding against this he steps out into the yard, it is still not light, but not so dark that he needs a lantern, the sun is just rising slowly in the East, beating the night away and seemingly making the morning colder than the night chill. The cobbled yard is spotted white with frost and the nails on the soles of his boots slip slightly before gaining purchase, through the gate and onto the cinder path, now almost bare in places it is in urgent need of renewing with fresh cinders, the ground below crunches loudly as the frost and these cinders crackle under the weight carried in the boots,

''Damn it to hell!''

Francis curses out loud to himself, he has forgotten the chamber pot, it still sitting on the table in the kitchen, turning about he heads back into the house, lifting the latch from the outside and enters the kitchen immediately feeling that the log on the stove grate is burning well, the warmth is welcoming, although he has only been outside for a few seconds he is chilled to the bone. This year had started cold and now only a couple of weeks in it is still very cold and shows no sign of it letting up, thankfully no snow has fallen yet, the last month of the previous year had also been cold but had been wet, but no snow, this after the unusual heavy snow falling in April of that year. Picking up the chamber pot he exits through the still open door, making sure it closes behind him, hearing the latch engage he walks across the cobbles again making certain not to slip with his pot of liquid carried in front of him, through the open gate again and onto the cinder path that soon becomes a path of well-worn grass as it passes by the sty, the grass is as fragile as expensive glass, covered in hoar frost easily giving way as he walks upon it. The outhouse door is closed, held in this position by a small strip of wood nailed to the outer frame making a makeshift locking device, currently turned on the nail to a horizontal position thus holding the door shut, Francis flicks the latch to the vertical and the door moves open a few inches, assisted to the fully open position by him pulling of the door from the outside, it has no handle and the ancient hinges creak and scream in resistance to being moved on this cold winter morning. Once inside, leaving the door open the lid off of the old barrel is moved from its position covering the hole in the planked wood serving as a seat, as it is so cold the smell from the midden is minimal, Francis empties the urine into the pit, putting the empty chamber pot onto the plank, then picking up the jar from the floor, he tips it and nothing happens, the water inside is frozen and will not be used today to rinse out the pot. Francis curses again, turning around he pulls the door shut as he now needs to use the outhouse, his braces are still hanging by his side, undoing the single button on his trousers he lets them fall without grace to the floor, lifting up the smock with one hand, so that it is held above his waist, he unties the lace on his drawers with his free hand, they also fall down, Francis sits on the plank placing his bottom over the hole in the plank, the wood is surprisingly not as cold as he expects it to be, the door is slightly ajar, staying where it is when not held in place by the basic latch, cold wind blows in through the gaps in the door. When finished, Francis re dresses, this time pulling his braces on, one over each shoulder and adjusting them to a comfortable fit, he picks up the empty chamber pot, pushes the door open, latching it firmly closed and makes his way back to the house, gladly accepting the warmth that the stove is providing to the kitchen, his boots are slipped off and slippers put back on. He rubs his hands together and shivers his shoulders, he goes to the stove and adds a small shovel of coal to the now glowing red hot wood embers, nothing happens immediately but he knows that the coal will take hold of the embers quickly and then burn and smoulder gently providing welcome heat to his chilled bones. The chamber pot is returned to its home under his bed in the living room, a splash of water from the pot is added, he will rinse it properly later. The ash in the fireplace is deep and cold, its flaky greyness now without life, the fire dogs are removed, they are still slightly warm from last night's blazing fire but easily handled, they are put to one side and the ash from the fireplace carefully swept into the small shovel and put into the pail, the small shovel then replaced in its original place standing next to the poker and the fire tongs to the left of the open fire, small logs are put onto the firedogs, now back in their working place, kindling and wood shavings put underneath the logs, he will not light this fire until this evening, the stove is providing heat enough for what he needs this morning.

The coal is picking up heat and the stove will be ready for cooking on very soon, a biggin, white enamel not silver, of yesterday's left over coffee is put onto the top of the stove directly on the hot plate to gently warm through. Francis buys coffee berries from town, the coffee trader, Mr Thorn, is also the tobacconist he has a roaster in his shop, so buying them ready roasted is easy to do thus saving this having to be done at home. The process of grinding is easy enough, using the coffee grinder that his Mother had always had, a small wooden box he thinks it is made of beech, with a pull out drawer, the metal grinder and dish are on the top of the box, the sharp sound of the roasted berries landing in the dish then the satisfying softer noise of the grinding as the handle is turned, the aroma of ground coffee is distinctive and satisfying. The enamel biggin, now ancient and chipped is large enough for one person to have enough coffee for at least one day, by removing the lid and the filter pot, here he has placed a small cut piece of hessian cloth as a filter, it stops much of the newly ground coffee getting into the hot liquid. The ground coffee is put onto the sacking in the filter, he usually puts three small spoons in then putting the filter section back into the pot and slowly pouring boiling water over the ground coffee, not a quick task as the sacking filter slows the flow of water after as it passes through the coffee picking up the bitter flavour as it goes. Once full enough the filter section is removed, the wet and clumped coffee taken out of the filter and put into the pail by the door. He knows of many people who add ground chicory root or finings, which is just burnt sugar, to the coffee to enrich the flavour and colour, this is not for Francis, he drinks it as it comes out of the pot never wasting any, saving it for the next day if necessary, as he has for this morning. It is said locally that coffee should be made fresh every day and not re heated, Francis not wanting to waste a drop always uses the whole pot, re heating if required.

Francis leaves the kitchen, as the biggin gently heats on the ever warming stove, walking through the living room, passing his bed without making it up, the covers haphazardly left in a pile in the centre of the mattress, the room is warm and the fire is burning well, he will let this burn out and re make it before bed tonight. Entering the unheated storage room by pushing the sacking door to one side he feels the cold in this room, so cold that he puts his hands into his trouser pockets in a feeble attempt to heat them up. What he wants for breakfast is in the root cellar, climbing slowly down the ladder he picks up a wrapped parcel from one of the shelves, undoing the string he removes 2 slices of bacon, thickly cut with a good layer of pure white fat on the top edge, wrapping back up the remaining half dozen slices, the last of the bacon from his slaughtered pig, he puts the unused bacon back on the shelf. Francis tells himself that he must go and see the '*pig sticker*' and arrange a visit to the butchers' abattoir to get his pig killed, he wanted to have it done before Christmas but as he had enough cured and salted meat, he has let it drag on, it now must be done. He has already sourced a replacement piglet for next year, his current sow is over a year old, older, and bigger than is usual for slaughter, she now has enough fat on her meat for it to be tasty and succulent, due to her size he will take her to the abattoir rather than have her slaughtered in the sty. The replacement piglet, now eight weeks old, is being delivered to him at the end of January so the slaughter has to be done, Francis tells himself that a visit to Joseph is needed, he also has a small but busy abattoir at the back of his premises as he is the pig sticker and the butcher, he will get the job of slaughter done quickly, it is always a noisy and bloody affair. Joseph will hit the sow square on the forehead with a large iron headed mallet, hard enough to stun her but not enough to kill, he needs the heart to be beating when, with Francis help, the beast will be hooked and hauled into a position by a rope and pulley, then suspended by the hook and rope over a strong wood beam, Joseph always works swiftly slitting the neck of the sow, hitting the artery perfectly allowing blood to freely flow as the still beating heart works hard, until there is no blood left to pump. The precious dark red fluid is collected in buckets, to be turned into blood pudding by adding fat, oats and allowing it to cool and congeal before being ready to be sealed in jars. The dead corpse of the animal will then be lowered into a wooden trough and a few buckets of boiling water, taken from a huge cauldron hanging over an open fire in the corner of the abattoir, will be poured over the carcass, she will then be lifted up once again, Joseph will take a razor and shave the thick, coarse hair from the skin of the pig, any remaining strong hair is removed with a naked flame, filling the air with the unmistakable smell of burnt skin and bristle. The butchery then begins, the body is lowered onto a heavy wooden bench, firstly the head and trotters removed, the head put to one side as it will be kept for brawn, the gristle from the toes of the animal are removed from the trotters and thrown into the street, the near starving children from the slum are hiding and waiting with empty bellies to grab one of these delights to suck and chew on the discarded but free offerings of gristle. The slitting of the body from backside to neck is completed with one swipe from a murderously sharp knife, the rear legs are spread and tied to a smaller piece of wood and then hoisted up again for the entrails to be removed and dumped onto the floor of the abattoir, the dogs and feral cats will soon take these away, kidneys and the liver are skilfully and gently removed, always shared between Francis and Joseph, this prized and tasty offal is never wasted. Francis will then leave, to return after one week as the pig needs to be hung for several days before the final dissection and butchering is completed, Joseph will take his share of the meat, he is always fair and then Francis will have the task of preserving the meat at home, time consuming but it will be worth it when winter hits again in October or November. He will go and see Joseph today, or perhaps tomorrow.

The duo of thick cut bacon is fried directly on top of the very hot stove, bread is roughly cut and liberally smeared with beef dripping, the bacon still sizzling hot is nestled between the bread and devoured between slurps of very hot coffee that warms the cold enamel mug. Francis sits back and enjoys the feeling of having hot food in his belly and savouring the growing heat in the room from the stove, he smiles at the thought of others hastily getting up and dressed in their Sunday finest clothes, he does not have any fine clothes let alone those just for a Sunday, families, hungry and without breaking fast will be visiting a freezing cold church within the next half hour, the bells always ring for half an hour before Sunday services, starting at 6am then again at midday and finally at 6 in the evening, with many attending all three of the services. The clergyman will spout hellfire and brimstone at them putting the fear of the Lord into their very souls and finally taking a few coins from them, most can ill afford to part with any money, the sermon ends quietly and gently, the priest stating, 'Peace be with you all' The shivering congregation shuffle out of the grim, damp church, to go home, poorer than when they arrived, if they are lucky to hot food, if not cold cuts or cold soup from last night, if having no luck at all food will not be available for anyone in the family. Sitting in a cold and lifeless church, hungry and fed up is not for Francis, he is happy enough to eat his food, drink his coffee and stay in the warm.

A yawn is stifled by a large, calloused hand being put in front of his open mouth, the noise he makes is exaggerated and loud, standing up he opens the back door and retrieves a large, full sack from just outside, the sacking and the contents are stiff with frost, having taken several weeks to fill it is time for Francis to visit the slum and sell off the contents of this bag to the highest bidders. Tipping the contents onto the floor in the kitchen he sorts through the items, ignoring the obvious stench of death emanating from the contents now that they have been exposed to the warm air. Clothing is taken by him from the dead, collected in this large sack for onward sale and distribution, much of it in poor condition and often smeared with dirt, human faeces, urine, and blood, most are flea and lice ridden and it all lies on the ground in the kitchen. Francis regularly takes clothing from the bodies of the dead, William does the sam, but not as regularly, William is very choosy about what he takes, clothing of fair quality only, Francis takes what he can, good, bad, ripped, clean or dirty, not that any of it will ever adorn his body but it is to be sold to those who cannot afford new or decent used clothes for themselves or their children. He is a 'picker', one who takes clothes from the dead and sells them cheaply to those still living and poor, most of the children living in the slum will be wearing 'picked' clothing, ill-fitting and barely useful, rags clinging to thin bodies, clearly a representation of the hard life they all have. The poor women, if lucky, will have two sets of clothes, the first being Sunday Church clothing, not of decent quality and a set of hand me downs or clothes from the 'Picker for everyday use, very few of the slum women have shoes on their feet nor do the children, going barefoot is normal, even in the coldest of winters. Men don't fare much better than the women, owning one pair of trousers and maybe two shirts, one for everyday wear and one for Sundays, most men have one pair of shoes, this footwear being torn and usually having holes in the soles.

The clothing that Francis owns is in good condition, all quite old and with few rip and tearing repairs, he occasionally thinks about visiting the market to buy a shirt to add to the three he owns, but all three are warm and still useful, he has two pairs of trousers, both are in serviceable condition so for many years he has not purchased clothing, although he gets filthy whilst working, he rarely washes any of his clothes, leaving any mud and dirt to dry and then taking a hard brush to get rid of any residual muck. He never wears 'picked' clothes, although he does own two long coats that he removed from bodies many years ago, both deceased were wealthy and he stole the expensive outer clothing from the corpses as they lay in the grave in their coffins, this practice, according to him, isn't 'picking'. He has taken garments from many corpses over the years, if they are in good condition he will visit the pawn shop in the larger town of St Albans, having an agreement with the pawnbroker who always takes what he has, these two coats he decided to keep, one for winter and one for warmer weather. The easily identifiable pawn shop with its sign of three golden balls, legend has it that St. Nicholas had saved three young girls from destitution by loaning each of them a bag of gold so that they could get married, is close to St. Stephens union workhouse and is one of many such pawn shops in the town. Both he and the pawnbroker understand that any pledges he puts into the shop will not be recovered by him at any time, leaving the pawnbroker free to sell them on. His winter surtout coat hangs from a single nail on the inside of the back door, double breasted with large buttons to secure it around the body, a capacious, knee length garment made from heavy close woven woollen cloth with a small outer collar and a neat small inner collar to secure the coat snugly around the throat of the wearer, in its original form, it would have been an expensive item for a gentlemen to wear, now it is used every winters day by Francis, it is grimy and well used but still warm and of great use to him since he became its owner some eight winters ago. He had removed it from an elderly man of wealth, his family insisting that he be buried in his finest clothing, the corpse was nearly naked in its coffin when Francis finally buried it. His summer coat, hanging under the Winter coat, his for over a decade, is a single breasted frock style black coat made of quality wool, is also dirty from its daily use in the Summers, its once delicate silk lapels now hardly noticeable due to heavy staining and wear and tear, the satin lining is still the colour of good port, but now thin and shapeless, the deep front pockets empty and unused.

After sorting the rags and clothes, he tightly ties his boot laces, putting the Winter coat on pulling up the short collar in an attempt to fight off the cold he knows he will soon feel, finally he puts his old weather beaten bucket hat on his head, he heads for the front door with the sack of rag clothing in his hand. The early morning biting air attacks the warm exposed skin on his face, he ignores it, working outside he has learnt to work with the elements rather than try to fight them, slinging the sack over his left shoulder, he pats the pocket of the surtout coat takes out his clay tobacco pipe, with its short pipe and curving bowl, placing it unlit into his mouth, the front door is closed and latched, he sets off on the walk to town, to the slum, this will take him an hour or so to do.

* * *

The surtout coat keeps him warm, and he soon feels small droplets of sweat moving slowly down his back, wishing he had fresh tobacco for his pipe, having used his final dusty fragments last night, a trip today to see old man Thorn the tobacconist is needed, it is on his way home so he will drop in and purchase an ounce of loose baccy or a two ounce tin of his favourite tobacco, Bishops Blaze made by Wills and co, two ounces will cost him sixpence, he has this in change in one of his pockets but hopes to have more from the picking sales, he will have to bum a light as the Lucifers he needs are at home on the fireplace, he still enjoys the bitter taste of old tobacco as it fills his mouth. Passing by the smithy and the mills, over a wide section of the river at the Ford he uses the narrow and somewhat unstable wooden bridge, it is called ‘the footbridge’ as it is it is not big enough for even one horse and cart to pass over, the carts are taken directly through the ford, it is not shallow, but certainly shallow enough for a horse and cart to get safely through at most times of year though the river is occasionally in spate and unpassable. The bridge is only used by foot passengers so if the water is too deep or moving too fast the carts have to cross elsewhere along the river. Francis knows that the next mile or so is an uphill walk, he has two choices, take the easier main road, Stakers Lane, this road lies a quarter of a mile to the West of his location at the mill or he can walk up the steep track directly in front of him, taking him through Crabtree orchards, a harder but shorter walk, he heads toward the orchards, slowing his pace a little as the incline gets steeper. Passing the Marquis of Granby public house, up the incline to a row of four cottages, he nods at one of the farm labourers living there, they don't know each other well but are on friendly enough terms, the man is standing in the doorway of his cottage, the far left property of the four, plumes of blue grey smoke lift gently from both the end of his long clay pipe and from the corner of his mouth as he sucks and the blows,

"Morning Francis" says the man

"Morning" Francis cannot remember the man's name,

"No grave diggin' today?"

"I got one this afternoon, in town for a parish funeral tomorrow"

The man nods and Francis walks on wishing he had tobacco for his pipe, walking is always a more joyous experience with a smoke, quite arduous without it, he walks on up the steep incline, past Crabtree fields and the orchards and on toward The Granary, a newly build farmhouse, a large red brick two storey building squarely built with a plain tiled roof, three chimneys, the main one having five pots at this time in use all smoking gently, the central chimney having two pots and the far end stack only having one pot, neither of these have fires lit at this time, no smoke emanates from any of them. The end gable has a shiny black wrought iron weathervane upon it, the dull winter sun catches it, making it glint as it slowly moves in the chilling wind. The farm is part of the experimental station owned by Sir John Lawes, although it is a mile or so from the main farming area it has a recently erected fence around the house and garden, put up by Francis last Summer, it has a large of acreage of arable land surrounding it to the East, also owned by the experimental station. There is no sign of life apart from smoke lifting from the five pot chimney, somewhere on the farm a dog barks suggesting that Francis has been seen and the warning is made by the animal for all to hear, he walks past The Granary and onto a slight downhill path, the upward struggle now eased, toward Lower Topstreet farm, here the common land has a wild appearance, large gorse and furze bushes dominate the landscape, enclosed by areas of heavy fern, in the Summer donkeys and horses can be seen grazing here alongside flocks of sheep, at this time of the year it is a boring plain brown colour with no animals outside, all are being well looked after in large warm barns that stand next to the main farm house. He passes the farm and its scattered buildings, turning left onto Wheathampstead Road, opposite are more large open areas of common land, he walks on toward the slum area known locally as the 'Bowling Alley', no one seems to know how it got this name or how long it had been referred to as this, but the name has stuck. The area has a church school, a small shack of a building owned by the local parish, not many of the Bowling Alley children attend and those that do are not exactly regulars, especially in the Summer months when families all went to work together on the local farms or in the orchards and fruit fields, the pay is a pittance but it is better than having no income at all, if all family members queue for work and are lucky enough to get a day's labour the few pennies and shillings earnt might be the difference between eating some days or not. Many fights happen between husbands and their spouses, the husband often taking the days earnings to go to the local public house, the nearest being a local unofficial brewery known as 'Bennets Butts' an establishment with a skittle alley, many believe the area name may be named because of this, it is popular with the poorer labourers, the Queens Head Inn and the Fishmongers arms area also public houses nearby but not often used by the poor of the Bowling Alley as Bennets Butts is very much cheaper. These public houses are frequented by families from the surrounding area who have lived and worked here for generations, the locals and those from the Bowling Alley rarely socialise together.

When first built the four rows of cheaply built terraced housing were quickly filled, each row having 12 dwellings, it was a reasonably pleasant place to live, originally built by the town council to accommodate the many Londoners moving from the city to the country in search of work and a better life, work that was never available, the lure of living in a clean, quiet country village was exciting for some. Without regular work, the area very quickly became poverty stricken, and now, twenty years after being built, and cheaply built, they are all in a state of disrepair. Employment in the town was then, and still now, is mostly taken by the local people and the '*Alley folk*' find it impossible to get regular paid work, only a few have semi regular employment, this either being at the gravel pits that are now open nearby, long hours worked for very little pay or hazardous work at the Straw Bleaching factory, owned by one Mr William Walker, the work is dangerous, the plaited straw is '*bleached*' by way of sulphur fumigation, working in this chemically poisoned environment burns the nose and throat, many who work there now have such bad breathing problems that they eventually have to leave, any further types of employment not possible due to ill health. In the Bowling Alley there are none of the big houses that are currently being built or have been built recently in the area, so no local domestic related work is available, the only time there is regular work is in the Summer when farmers need labourers, when the harvest is being done or fruit and vegetables need picking, the Spring, Autumn, and Winter months are a barren time for most in the Bowling Alley. All of the dwellings in the four rows are exactly the same, four rooms, with a living room, a back room, none has a kitchen, a sink or a copper, and two bedrooms upstairs, the only fireplace in each house is located in the front room, the chimney stack passes in between the bedrooms upstairs and in Winter the gaps in the chimney have to be stuffed with old paper and rags to block out the wind and to stop the smoke coming into the small airless rooms. Any food available is cooked over this small fire, usually a boiled stew prepared in a single suspended pot, boiled until bubbling hot, the Bowling Alley has a communal oven used for baking bread, this is only ever used when a family can afford flour and have enough fuel to stoke and heat the oven, it lies dormant and cold most of the time. Coal is expensive and if used at all, is used sparingly, coke is the fuel of choice, along with any burnable household waste or fallen wood that is collected by the children from the common and stacked in the small, cobbled yards behind each house, the yards are separated by a low wall, both the terraces on the outside have open land at the end of their yard, this is where the privies are situated. The cess pool closets, only six on each side of the outer terraces, each having to serve 24 houses, are filthy, those living in either of the 'inner' terraces don't have privies nearby and must make their way through several *'twitchell's'* to get to the communal privy. The men are supposed to take it in turns to empty the cess pools at night, dumping the contents into pre dug trenches on the open land, most don't bother, and the cess pits are overflowing with human waste. Large iron boilers are seen in some yards, shared by several houses for boiling up clothes on washday, there is no drainage, all slop water is thrown into the cess pits, adding to the filthy slurry already there.

The terraces are built out of red brick, bought in from Bedfordshire, the floors inside are also brick, any bits of spare old sacking are used to reduce the cold from the floors, the children have to sit on the floor, it is unusual for any of the houses to have more than two chairs, any tables are small and worn. The bedrooms upstairs are divided, all the children in one room and their parents in the other, regardless of how many children occupy the house they all sleep in one room, on the floor if beds are not available, some of these rooms have a curtain made from old sacking taken from the floor, hung up to separate the older children from the younger ones, blankets are old, soiled and do not keep out the cold. Many of the children are without proper beds and sleep in an 'apple pie' formation, a round 'bed' is made on the floor and the children are tucked into it using any available covers or blankets. Some families use tallow candles for lighting, most have rush lights, made from dried rush reeds, and covered in any available fat or grease, mutton fat is deemed to be the best for use as it dries out into a harder and less messy texture than other fats and grease.

The Bowling Alley does have several wells, with excellent and clean water, all the wells are deep and require good strong lengths of rope to be secured to the windlass, water is collected in the attached wooden bucket and transferred into large earthenware pots with wooden lids and taken to the back room of the house for use by the family. Narrow cobbled streets separate the terraces, each house front has a single entrance door and one window on each level, these are the only windows in the houses, none of them have windows at the rear, the women can be seen daily standing in the doorways of their property chatting to neighbours whilst the children play in the small available space and the men, if not working, stay indoors, rarely venturing outside.

This is an area of sadness, poverty, and regular death, all of which bring a sneaking smile onto his weather cracked face as he walks into the Bowling Alley with his sack of rags on his shoulder.

* * *

"The picker is here! The picker is here!"

Several of the local children have seen Francis arrive, he sits on the wall of Bennets Butts, none of the children run toward him, they are all scared of Francis because he digs graves and handles the dead, many a tale has been told about how the grave digger happily deals with death and the dead on a daily basis, the children keep their distance, some of the women appear from the terraced houses and slowly make their way toward him crossing the open ground from where they live to the wall outside of the drinking establishment. Francis sits still, pipe in his mouth and the sack, as yet unopened, standing upright and held tightly between his knees, the women all know that he will not begin the sale by opening up the sack and emptying the contents on the ground in front of him, until there are enough buyers to haggle over the rags and torn clothing. It only takes a few minutes for a small crowd to gather around, but all keeping a short distance from Francis, they are all a little scared of him.

"What you got mister?"

"We all need shoes"

"My Frank needs a shirt; he tore his only one at the gravel pit on Friday"

"What have you got for a tanner today?"

Francis slowly raises a hand to silence all the questions being thrown at him simultaneously, the gaggle of voices come to a halt and the sack is emptied onto the cold hard ground, one woman takes a step forward, Francis remains silent, he stares directly at her making unbroken eye contact. An intake of breath is heard from the rest of the crowd and the over eager customer, fearing the grave digger, stops in her tracks and takes a step backward with a mumbled apology, her eyes averted, not meeting his any further.

"No shoes" Francis says abruptly, load groans come from the crowd, they know that if there isn't any footwear available then the picked clothing had to have come from poor funerals and the clothes and rags will be of poor quality.

"Half a sovereign for the lot" he says without emotion,

"What?"

"I ain't never had half a quid in my life" a voice from the back shouts.

"Bloody liberty!" Another joins in.

Many other groans and insults come from the lips of these women, Francis sits and listens for a while, he then raises his hand slowly and the cacophony of voices slow to silence, he picks out a white man's shirt, not torn or damaged, but obviously stained from the body it was taken from,

"Who wanted a shirt?"

A small, thin, and wispy woman, Betty Franks, raises her hand and steps forward,

"I only got a tanner and an old farthing" Francis looks at the two coins in her open, calloused, and dirty hand, she continues, "The old man can't get work in the winter; I need two and six for the parish rent collector by next Friday and I ain't paid for last weeks"

He knows that her husband, James, is an idle man who rarely works, even in the Summer months when there is plenty of work about, he also knows that her eldest, Jim Franks, currently resides in St Albans Borough common gaol having been caught stealing wood and poaching on the Rothamstead estate, the bailiff and the constable had, unluckily for Jim, been unusually sober enough to be out one clear October night, Jim had climbed over the fence onto the track to Redbourn and had literally walked into both officials, he was carrying two dead rabbits and had a sack full of wood on his back. The next morning the magistrate had sentenced him to three months hard labour at St Albans Gaol, he along with other hard labour prisoners spend 6 hours a day on a large wooden treadmill, working without a break, drink, or food.

Francis remains silent, laying his hand flat, palm uppermost, Betty puts both coins into his huge hand, he closes it quickly and gives her the shirt, she nods a thank you and makes her way through the crowd, going home with a gift for her idle husband, she herself is barefoot and dressed in rags. He sells all the picked clothing, taking a couple of shillings short of a pound from the poor and desperate, he has heard all the moans and excuses before, no work, rent due, no food, he does not care, he always wants to sell the clothes and leaves as soon as he can. He despises the Bowling Alley with its course and rude women, some he knows are prostituting themselves to get food and to get the rent paid, everyone here knows that paid work is scarce in the Winter for labourers and earning a shilling a day each in the Summer and harvest months, means that whole families go to work in the fields, the farmers knowing that the bob a day rate is so much lower than regular labourers get, they know, as Francis does, that these are desperate people who will work for the offered daily rate. Rent, paid to the parish, for the slum houses is two and sixpence a week, £6 10s annually, very low rent in comparison to some but most of the tenant's struggle to find it and hardly ever pay regularly, none of the men, women or children have ever owned new clothing, a tailored shirt in town costs three and sixpence, this for the lowest quality garment. The occupants of the Bowling Alley do not eat daily, it isn't unusual for the whole family to go without food two or three days a week, poaching is rife, but as Jim Franks had found out if you get caught then you will be sent to gaol, meals in most households are thin and weak soups or stews, potatoes are often used to bulk these meals out, they are only a tanner a pound from the farmers, the cheap price reflecting the condition of the potatoes, they are not good and most are blackened and beginning to turn but for the cheap price, they are regularly purchased by the women for their household. Stale bread and tripe are also staple parts of the diet here, tripe at thruppence a pound and stale bread is sold at the end of the bakers working day, a couple of shillings could get enough bread, if used sparingly for most of a week. The crowd has thinned, leaving only a few women nearby talking and gossiping with neighbours, Francis stands up, his legs stiff from sitting on the cold wall, it is only just mid-morning and he has to get to town to the tobacconist, then go home again, get a bite to eat and then, that afternoon go back to town to dig the grave for the parish funeral tomorrow afternoon, he considers leaving it till the morning but decides against it, as he is about to move off he notices a small girl looking at him. He believes she must be about five or six years old; it is difficult to tell as these children are all malnourished and look younger sometimes, her hair is matted and dirty, unusually it is to shoulder length, cut by her mother without doubt he thinks. She is barefoot, her feet are black, cuts and scrapes can be seen through this dirt, radiant streaks of red amongst her stained, unclean skin, her faded, shapeless dress is torn, filthy and ragged, it hangs from her body, a brown shabby wool shawl with bright red edging, hangs limply over her shoulders. She is clutching the front of the shawl to her chest, an obvious attempt to keep out the cold, he stares back at her, she does not appear scared of him as most are, she remains in place, staring at him,

"What do you want?' he asks aggressively, she does not reply but puts out a thin arm with her hand out, palm up. "Begging? From me?" The girl does not speak, nor does she move, staring straight into his eyes without fear, he notices she had piercing light blue eyes, giving her face a sense of cleanliness and innocence. "Go away little girl, I don't give nothing away for free"

She remains in place, disobeying his instruction, Francis takes his pipe from his mouth and rubs the beard on his chin, shaking his head he gets up and leaves, after taking a few steps something makes him look behind from where he has just come from, the girl hasn't moved, still standing, arm and hand outstretched,

"Get away with you girl!" shouts Francis, turning away and carrying on his journey, as he turns the corner, leaving the Bowling Alley and back toward town, curiosity gets the better of him, he turns around, the girl is still there, having not moved, "Bloody stupid slum kids" he says to no one in particular.

Pulling his coat collar up around his neck he makes exit from The Bowling Alley, His journey continues back onto the Wheathampstead Road toward town, passing the old church of St John on his left and then across the common, the wind here bites into his face, the common is an open space of gorse, fern and furze bushes and there is little to stop the cold wind crossing it with ease. He reaches the gravel pits on his left, quiet as it is Sunday and no work is taking place, he crosses the road away from the common and walks past Welcombe Manor House, Francis has worked in nearly all the big houses in town, but not this one. It is a large seventeenth century timber framed building with a recently added, flat fronted three storey section, this part of the building directly overlooks the common with fourteen windows and one door on the façade of the property, it adjoins the original timber framed house making it an oddly asymmetrical and certainly a very large, building. A huge amount of climbing ivy seemingly joins the old timber and stone building to the new brick extension, it easily covers all the front of the original building, including the large imposing chimney as it sweeps onto the newest section, currently covering over a quarter of it, windows here are exposed and free but only by regular cutting and trimming.

In the next plot, to the West side of Welcombe Manor, are four terraced cottages with a red tiled roof, at either end of the terrace these roofs are pointed, facing the road, they enclose a second floor of the property, double opening windows and curtains show occupancy on these top levels, the windows below on the ground floor are bow casement with several latch openers. The middle section has two dwellings and is single storey and has a gently sloping roof, also of red tile, the wooden supports from roof edge to the ground are painted white, each house has a small single window to the front, a wall six feet in height protects the front of the house and substantial gardens. These cottages are owned by the current incumbent of Welcombe Manor and residents come and go on a regular basis, none staying for more than a few months at a time, none are local people, and they always keep themselves to themselves. The family that lives in the Manor House has done so for nearly four years and very little is known about them, they do not attend church, the parish priest recently told Francis this only days after they moved into the Manor House. He was cutting with his tone about them making it known that none of the household were reliant on the belief or existence of God, heathens in his eyes, the family are believed to be Quakers, locals refer to them as 'Spooks', the head of the family is rumoured to be a spiritual healer possessing out of world and ungodly powers according to local and unconfirmed legend. He walks past the house with barely a glance, he has walked past this place on hundreds of previous occasions and has no interest in the occupants or what they are or do, he only listens to the priest because he earns coin from him and from the parish, it would not be a good move to upset the priest.

Looking on the opposite side of the track he sees the Bull inn and stables, owned, and run by the Oldaker brothers, Henry, head of the local hunt, and Robert, a keen and skilled horseman, Francis frequents this inn when working at the experimental station as he knows it always has a cellar full of good beer, wine and cider, the public bar has a large and welcoming fire that is lit most days of the year. Walking onward as he is not far from Mr Thorns tobacconist shop which is situated on the very corner of the High Street and Stakers Lane, he passes another old property, Blakesleys House, a house with a wealthy owner built in the sixteenth century is an imposing site from the main road. With eight large front sash windows, a climbing rose, dormant at this time of the year, hanging on the right hand side of the building, an off centre porch with a small, pointed roof hides an ancient front door, three further windows sit one above the other on the left side of the building with a tall, four potted chimney at the end of the house. A substantial red brick wall surrounds the property, the entrance gate is grandiose, tall, black and locked, wrought iron gates held firmly in place either side by brick gate posts, wider and twice as tall as a man, both topped with white marble spheres held in place by a shaped white marble base, at the height on each of these posts is a large light, held in position by even more wrought iron, on one post, directly below the light, is the name of the house in white letters, made by the smithy and hanging in a central position. The view through the locked gates shows perfectly manicured lawns, even now in January they all appear in perfect condition. This wall replaced fencing that Francis had put in twenty years previously and he had continued to maintain them for the previous owner, a local school master, when he sold it to the current owner the fencing was replaced very soon after it changed hands with the brick wall. For the past decade a gentleman named J.H. Rumball has owned it, previously used as a school and now since Mr Rumball had purchased it, it is a private mental asylum. The patients are from wealthy families and each one has a 'keeper', both patient and keeper can be often seen walking on the common or attending church, the patients are never alone, always attended by at least one keeper.

Francis rubs his hands together, the chill needing to be rubbed out, he knows that he is only a few minutes away from entering the tobacconist shop, it will be warm in there it always is and his sense of smell will be attacked the second he enters, warm vanilla and cherry with strong, fresh tobacco aromas that linger in the air, Mr Thorn also sells the roasted coffee that Francis likes, and the heady mix of tobacco and roasted coffee is desirable to most. He is glad to see that the shop is open, it is only a small shop with a white front door with a glass top panel, the bottom panel is framed in shiny black paint, the window is large and has a display of some of the wares that can be purchased inside, its black canopy is closed at this time, when opened it has the owners name and '*Est 1805'* emblazed upon it with large, clear gold coloured lettering. Entering the shop, Francis inhales the warm and familiar smells, Mr Thorn is behind the counter in his usual high collared pure white shirt, black tie tied tight, waistcoat with a silver chain flowing across from one pocket to another and a clean white pinney apron tied at the waist, he is, as he always is, immaculate.

"Morning Francis" Thorn politely speaks to his customer,

"Morning Mr Thorn, a small tin of Bishops Blaze and half a pound of my coffee"

Thorn busies himself taking the coffee from a jar, he knows which coffee Francis likes, he takes a small shovel and gently places the roasted beans into the tray of the green metal weighing scales, the counterbalance weights on the opposite side, waiting to be moved by the opposing weight of coffee beans, Thorn is absolutely precise, when finished he places the half pound of roasted Ceylon coffee into a brown paper parcel, wrapped tightly so that none of the precious produce can spill out.

"All the way from Ceylon you know, Mr Richard Evans of London roasts it in his very own London premises for me"

Mr Thorn tells him this every time Francis buys it, he ignores the comment as he always does, a tin of Bishops Blaze, made by W.D. & H.O. Wills in Bristol, is handed to him along with the parcel of coffee, he opens it immediately, taking a small amount of the coarse brown tobacco, rubbing it gently into the palm of his hand with his thumb then finally placing the small amount of rubbed tobacco into the bowl, Mr Thorn waits patiently,

"That will be one and six please"

Francis takes the handful of coins he earned earlier that morning from the women of the Bowling Alley, selects three tanners and hands them over, Thorn nods his thanks. Francis then pats his pockets, theatrically some would say, then shakes his head,

"Can I light your pipe for you Francis, you seem to be without a lucifer match"

Nodding and mumbling 'thanks', he accepts the light for his pipe, Lucifers are a shilling a box, the same price as his half pound of coffee, he does not need any as he has nearly a full box at home, he never uses them to light his pipe unless he must, he does this with tapers that he makes, strips of old cloth covered in tallow or animal fat. Mr Thorn takes a single match from a box under the counter, lights it by pushing the end of his thumbnail along the end of the wooden match at the white tipped end, it fluoresces in a blue and white flame, the smell of sulphur is instant and for a second replaces the aromas of sweet coffee and tobacco in the small shop. Francis leans forward as Thorn holds the match at an angle suitable for the tobacco in the pipe to meet the heat from the lucifer, sucking gently on the pipe, the tobacco takes, puffing smoke from his mouth and from the end of the pipe, he stands back and nods again at Thorn, the match is extinguished in a small tin containing sand under the counter. Francis, with coffee and tobacco safely in his deep pockets, leaves the warmth of the shop, stepping into the chilled air of the late morning, the temperature does not seem to have got warmer, if anything it is now colder, the weak winter sun having no heat to share. Collar pulled up, pipe lit he turns left out of the shop and onto Stakers Lane, keeping his head down, pulling his hat lower down on his forehead, he has no mind to speak to anyone, the road is busy with all classes of *townies* dressed in their Sunday best, the working men in aged trousers, flannel shirts with a waistcoat and over jacket, most with a flat cap pulled tightly onto their head, the wives of these men, in drab dresses covered with a clean white pinafore, a woollen shawl and a straw hat, a sure sign of the industry they work in. The wealthy women are adorned in large, flared dresses and petticoats, daring low necklines are given a semblance of decency by the addition of a chemisette worn underneath, large colourful bonnets finish off the ensemble, the men of wealth, all in top hats of varying sizes, long coats opened at the front, showing off a waistcoat over a cotton shirt, wearing either a cravat or a necktie, some in clean pressed trousers and expensive shoes, some in tighter trousers and knee length boots. Francis wants nothing to do with any of them, he will be home in under an hour, the walk takes him away from the town and around the edge of Manland common, when he reaches the bottom of Stakers Lane he turns right toward his cottage, he considers having an ale or two in either the Crown and Anchor, by Pickford Mill or in the Gibraltar Castle nearer to his cottage and where it has been opposite the river for over half a century he knows it used to have its own gaol, he knows he has to walk back to town and dig the paupers grave this afternoon, he heads home and is glad when he can see his cottage and the homely smoke drifting gently out of his chimney.

* * *

After a lunch of cheese and bread Francis puts a pot of rabbit stew on top of the stove, the gentle heat will slowly cook his evening meal, he then returns to town this time taking a footpath from Coldharbour, only a short distance from where he helped dig out a Cist, a Romano Celtic burial site containing a stone coffin, discovered in the early part of the 1820's, at that time he worked on the site on and off for several years, he was present when the stone lid was finally uncovered and broken open, the inside feeling fresh air for the first time in centuries, found inside was human remains, hundreds of years dead, also contained in the coffin was a large green glass jug and four small earthenware dishes. He continues across Manland Common, it is after midday and the sun, pale and low in the sky provides no relief from the cold, hands deep in his pockets with his heavily bearded chin pressed into his chest, bucket hat pulled down low and pipe lit, he passes Bowers House on his way to dig in the graveyard of the parish church of St Nicholas. Bower's house is a large sixteenth century two storey manor house with over twenty sash windows facing the front of the house, every inch of the red brick and black timber beams are covered in tightly formed ivy, its roof of red tile is so large that it seems to go on forever, the chimney at the front of the house is huge and looming with four big pots at its peak, smaller chimneys each with two pots can be just seen poking over the roof from the back of the property. Last year Francis had put fencing up on the boundary of this property, only at the back as the front has a large wall that faces the Cock pond, much used by the villagers, the Old Cock inn on the opposite side of the High Street to Bowers House, the pond is, and has been for centuries, a focal point for local farmers, to water their cattle and sheep, it also has its own host of resident ducks. Francis is still on the footpath that passes the back of Bowers House when one of the servants spies him and calls out over the chest high fence, he is one of two servants who, along with a groom and a gardener, reside at the house, the owner and his wife, Mr James Field and Mrs Eliza Field are wealthy Londoners, the former is now the owner of a large hat factory in Luton, this a new addition to his other business in London, he is listed locally as a '*Merchant of Straw and Fancy goods'*.

He finds Mr Field annoying; he always refers to Francis as "My good man", he stops and speaks to the servant, John, leaning his digging tools against the wall,

"What is it, John?"

"Afternoon Francis" John speaks slowly with a strong local accent, "The Master has asked me to look out for you, will you wait whilst I go and fetch him?" Francis nods in agreement, the servant moves toward the back door of the house, returning a few minutes later, "The Master won't be long"

Francis nods, turning around to look at the open country surrounding him, the back of the house faces open fields, in contrast to the front of the building that faces the ever busy West end of the High Street, he turns back toward the house when he hears Mr Field address him,

"My good man" Francis contains his disagreeable feelings, "My good man, the fence posts around the vegetable garden are loose, could you put them right for me, I would ask the gardener but we both know he will make an arse of the job"

Francis responds gruffly, "Next week alright with you?"

"That would be splendid my good man, whenever you can, John will be here for you as and when it can be done" Mr Field walks away without another word.

John and Francis exchange a look, they nod politely to each other, Francis picks up his tools and heads off making his way around the pond then crossing the road and passing the front of the Old Cock, the 16th century inn frequented daily by locals and often by Londoners, parties of whom take day trips to the town on '*Beanfeast*' day trips from cities on horse drawn *'charabanc'* carriages are a popular past time. The landlord of the inn always provides, at a price, the required and expected sustenance for the day trippers. The inn, being no more than a mile from the racecourse on the west side of the common is very popular with racegoers on race day, they travel in from counties to the North and West, stopping for a few drinks before going onto the races, those traveling from the South and East use the Silver Cup public house. The Old Cock has a small stable used by the Luton to London coach service, this is agreeable to both the landlord and the coach company as the users of the coach always spend money at the Inn, with no railway yet in town the coach is the only way out of town to the larger towns and cities.

St Nicholas parish church, in cruciform shape with its tall square Norman tower on the west side, originally built in the thirteenth century the church has been extended and changed over the centuries, the tower being the only survivor of a fire in the fifteenth century that destroyed the rest of the church. Inside, the church is dominated by large stone arches built at all four sides of the nave, several members of the Cressey family are entombed inside the church, the family are former lords of Rothamstead Manor living there for over two hundred years from the middle of the fourteenth century, it was the Cressey family that built Blakesleys House in the town, toward the end of the sixteenth century.

The parish priest is under strict direction and governance from the Ecclesiastical Parish of Wheathampstead, this small village being the current site of the Abbots Manorial court, although local rumbling is that many, including the Parish Priest want to break from the Abbots in Wheathampstead and make the town a Parish of its own as it previously was in the Middle Ages. The entrance to the church is a short path, leading through a small gate in the waist high, front picket fenced churchyard, another fence that had been erected by Francis, it leads to a small wooden roofed porch, contained within this is a heavy metal studded wood door, to the right of this entrance porch, taking up a proportion of the wall, is a substantial stained glass window framed in ornate carved stone, the churchyard is littered with gravestones, some lying on the ground, some propped up against the church wall, many standing at odd angles, leaning over old, uncared and unattended graves, most of these plots are 'full' and Francis will not officially dig into them anymore, the families of these dead have either all died themselves or moved away from the town, so there is no need for deceased relatives to be buried in these plots with their long dead relatives. Francis has on occasion dug into these ancient burial plots to add other bones to them but only when the need arises.

The Yew tree stands proudly in the shadow of the Norman tower, large, ancient, and ever looming.

The graveyard is situated to the western side of the front churchyard, and carries on around and to the rear of the church building, it is much larger than the front churchyard, the area has many grave and tombstones, old and new, many of these plots are becoming full to bursting but not so many of them have human bones sticking out, bone clearance has become a regular task for Francis since he started as a grave digger, the bones that were originally stacked untidily at the side of the church are now being reburied outside of the consecrated grounds of the church, anywhere he can find, some are buried in and around the experimental station, buried only a foot or so under the grassed topsoil when he was putting up the posts and fencing there. Some are on the common outside of town, also the commons at Batford and Manland have human remains buried by him at several locations, he has even put some in the shadow of the bows of the Yew tree in the church yard, also in and around his Yew tree in the garden at home. He has no time for the fears or superstition associated with the dead, it is his job, he gets paid for it and has no belief that will ever worries him.

Arriving at the church, he walks around the tower and under the Yew tree, its long limbed branches reaching out without cause in the cold of the afternoon, his tools are propped against the tower wall, he walks to the rear of the church, here is his small wooden roofed lean to where keeps his grave planks inside, there is also a large bucket, a lantern, and a small homemade wooden ladder inside this structure. Picking up the bucket and the planks, he makes his way back to collect his tools, todays dig is for tomorrow's pauper funeral, so the dig will not be very deep, certainly not deep enough to need a ladder to climb in and out of. Pauper funerals were once unheard of are now becoming ordinary and routine in the town, many people dying through poverty or incurable sickness, the town's population has grown over the past twenty years or so and it continues to do so, seemingly at an alarming rate, but more dead means more work and more coin for Francis. He has previously buried large numbers that died from influenza, with outbreaks in 1832 and 1849, many died quickly in the town and surrounding areas, cholera struck in 1830, again taking many lives, but poverty is now the ever present cause for the majority of death in town, disease living hand in hand, mainly but not exclusively, with the poor.

Parish, or pauper funerals, are not only for those destitute and living in the slums, many of the farm labourers who live in tied cottages earn very little, they cannot afford to bury their dead, so it falls to the parish to pay the expense, therefore these funerals are cheap affairs without the exorbitance and grandeur of a wealthy person's death and burial. St Nicholas church does not bury the workhouse dead anymore since the closure of the parish workhouse in Redbourn, all the workhouse dead from St Stephens are buried in the grounds of the workhouse, regardless of the town of their birth. The workhouse and its burial grounds also takes those dead that the church will not accept to be buried in the consecrated grounds of a church yard, criminals, prostitutes, unwed mothers and their bastard children, those who take their own lives and non-believers, are all buried outside of any church or religious grounds, this is always the workhouse burial site, the exception being imprisoned criminals, they are buried in the grounds of the prison, these graves being dug by other inmates from the gaol.

It is a regular practice in many towns and cities to dig very deep paupers graves, Francis had heard of some in London that are over twenty feet deep, the bodies then be put in the bottom of the grave and left uncovered, often for weeks at time, until the grave has enough bodies to fill it almost to the top, soil rarely being put in between coffins or bodies dumped in tatty shrouds, unless the deceased had died from disease, a layer of slaked lime is thrown over these corpses, then they are covered with a thin layer of soil. He has heard rumours that grave diggers have died, choking at the bottom of these deep graves, carbonic acid gas from the decomposing corpses causing almost instant death at these depths. The Parish Priest has instructed Francis not to dig very deep pits in his church and graveyards, as the noxious gasses and abhorrent odours in and around the church are already '*most injurious to health*', so pauper graves, deeper when first dug than the usual grave depth, but not so deep as to cause death or harm to the grave digger, after each burial, the coffin or body in the grave is always covered completely with soil, the Priest insists on this.

Reaching the paupers burial area, Francis removes his over coat, although cold out he is sweating having carried all his tools he needs to complete the task, pauper graves are unmarked, the parish is not willing to pay for headstones, the grave locations are marked in the church burial ledger by the curate, Reverend Addington is insistent about this. Francis knows exactly where they are all located, after years of experience and digging in this graveyard he can see with his naked eye the outline of any grave. Selecting the wide spade, he positions it where he wants to begin, the pointed and rounded end of the spade ready to push through the frozen soil, Francis knows the first few inches will be difficult, but the frost should only penetrate half a foot at most, then it will become a normal dig, six hours or so usually, but these pauper digs only take three, four at most.

He pushes the blade into the ground, feeling resistance as the frost bites into the spade, removing the blade without any further digging motion, he moves six inches to the right of the first bite of the spade, he continues with this motion until he has the outline of the grave finished, he does not use a template as some diggers do, he uses his experienced eye to get the task done. He then, with the spade head at an angle, removes the first inch or so of soil, thinly covered with winter dead grass and weeds, putting the spoil clear of the outline of the grave by some distance, he knows that the spoil pile will be substantial when he has finished, and it has to be far enough away so as not to fall back into the freshly dug hole. The uncovered soil is dark in colour and is cold enough with frost to offer some resistance to the digger's tools, once through this the topsoil, still dark in colour, it becomes less resistant and is of a loose granular texture, there are few straggly grass and surface plant roots in the soil, they offer no trouble to the heavy pushing of the large spade. Francis stops to fill and light his pipe when he sees the soil change colour and structure, the grave is now a foot or so deep, the soil is not frozen by frost here but mixed with pure white chalk making it lighter in colour but heavier with moisture, he cares not for the lives of the earthworms, beetles, and woodlice he finds in the soil, he does wonder how these odd creatures live and survive deep underground, he is now over two feet into the grave. He knows the going will be tough as the soil is wet, but as this is at least the third time he has dug this plot, he knows the soil will not be tough and in structured layers as it would be on a fresh dig, the mixture of topsoil, soil and chalk means that the overall balance of the soil is loose and therefore easier to move. The mattock remains unused, but the grave bar will soon be put to work to ensure that the side of the grave is straight and wide enough for the next day's coffin to fit in with ease. He is several inches under four feet into the dig when his spade strikes something soft, the familiar smell of decay fills his nose, the last burial had not been put into the ground in a coffin, Francis had removed the body from the wooden box and William took it away for re use on the next soul that is no more, his spade has ripped through the thin canvas shroud he and William had put this body into before putting it in the coffin and then into the grave, covering it in soil. He uses the spade and his boot to pat down the soil on top of this previously buried corpse, forming a protective covering for the fresh body and coffin to be added tomorrow, this thin covering of soil will keep most of the stench of the rotting body away from the noses of the mourners, if there are to be any, it is also freezing weather so the smell will not be as bad as it might be, in hot summers it is overpowering and makes mourners and religious men wretch. Francis now wishes he had not struggled to the grave with his marked grave planks, he will not be needing them to ensure the grave is deep enough, he is standing head and shoulders above the edge of the grave. He is cross with himself because he should have remembered that this grave would not be very deep, he stops and easily climbs out of the large hole he has created. The sun, now a red and yellow glowing ball is setting behind the trees that live on the far western edge of the graveyard, it will be dark soon, but he knows that he will have enough light to finish the task, he didn't bring the lantern with him he purposely left it in the lean to, mainly because he already had enough tools to carry. He curses as he realises that his pipe has gone out, spitting a brown, tobacco filled goblet of phlegm into the grave he has just dug he takes his grave bar and using the sharp blade he straightens the edges of the grave from top to bottom, leaving any further loose removed soil to fall onto the current inmate of this grave. The hole will remain open overnight and all of tomorrow morning, he has no reason to cover it as the church and graveyard will not have any visitors at night, a place of worship in the day becomes a place to fear at night, grave and corpse robbery had been a minor problem previously but not for many years.

He has seen a few graves that have been disturbed in this churchyard over the years, the marauders of these graves having not been very subtle when digging and happily leaving clearly evident signs that theft of a corpse has taken place. They dig a small hole into the ground, alongside where they believe the head to lay, digging to the correct depth, a tunnel is then dug into the grave, until reaching the coffin. Broad iron hooks are then placed under the lid and pulled forcibly, breaking off a sufficient portion of the lid to allow the body to be dragged out through the tunnel. Clothing is removed from the corpse, they are then thrown back into the hole, in the few that Francis has seen no attempt had been made to put the spoil back into the holes dug next to the grave, he had to do this, much to his annoyance. The last event of this type in the town had been in 1823, in the early hours of a cold November morning, the Finder brothers, Jim and Tom, were on horseback travelling to work, a daily six mile journey to St Albans, they passed a small cart with two men they did not recognise, sitting in it, both brothers noted an offensive smell coming from the cart as they rode past both knowing it to be from a putrid corpse as they had previous experience of this unforgettable smell. The Brothers also believed the two men in the cart to be 'resurrection men', body snatchers who dig up corpses for onward sale to medical schools and privately funded anatomical schools, these resurrection men know that if they are caught, they would only be charged with a misdemeanour offence at common law, the offence being interfering with a grave. The contents of the grave, being dead and therefore not the property of anyone, so theft had not taken place, a fine or imprisonment was the worst that would happen to them. Jim and Tom Finder increased the pace of their horses to create distance between themselves and the cart with its stinking cargo. When they arrived at their place of work, Fowler's builders, and brick company, they informed their boss, Mr Fowler, of their suspicions. The cart driven by the two men duly appeared on the road and Mr Fowler stepped out and demanded that they stop, the demand was refused, Jim, Tom, and other workers took hold of the horse and cart stopping it, then searching under the fresh straw in the back of it they found the body of an elderly man obviously having been dead for some time. The constable was summonsed and the men, both from the East end of London, Mr John Jerome, and Mr John Holloway, were arrested and detained in the gaol. The corpse of the elderly man was taken to St Stephens workhouse, Francis would, eventually, re bury the body, in the unconsecrated burial grounds of the workhouse, the church does not allow the re burial of removed corpses. The resurrection men were held at St Albans gaol until the next sitting of the court sessions, in January 1824, both men were sent by the St Albans court to Bedford gaol, they were later tried by the Bedford Assizes and found guilty of robbing a grave, both received a three month prison sentence, with hard labour. Due to indifferent behaviour, both men spent 6 months in gaol. Grave robbing stopped in 1832, with the introduction of the Anatomy act, this stated that any unclaimed bodies or friendless bodies could be given to the medical schools for dissection, bodies being supplied mainly from asylums, workhouses, and prisons. St Stephens workhouse refused to enforce this continuing to use Francis as their grave digger, to bury their dead in their grounds.

As he is collecting his tools, he catches something moving out of the corner of his eye, on the other side of the fence in front of the church, the sun has nearly set behind him and although not quite dark yet, he cannot make out what has attracted his attention, leaving his tools, he puts on his overcoat and walks toward the front of the church, as he gets to the path he stops, stands still, and looks along the path to the church gate. Standing in front of him is a small girl, the same small girl that stared at him earlier in the day at The Bowling Alley, he is sure of it, walking further toward the gate he confirms his suspicion, it is her wearing the same tatty dress, the shawl is still draped over her shoulders and her bleeding feet are as bare as the day she was born, she looks thinner and paler in the early evening shadows, twilight passing over her face highlighting the tightness and fragility of her skin on her young cheeks. Francis has no idea why she is here; has she been following him? He feels anger rising in his throat, he has no time to be bothered with most folk, let alone a dirty little slum girl from the Alley, taking steps toward her, fists clenched, he shouts,

"Get out of here! Get your skinny arse back to the Alley and don't bother me!"

She does not move, she puts her hand out toward him, palm up, just as she had earlier in the day,

"Begging again! I told you earlier, no one gets anything from me, now be away with you!"

Francis is now standing still because the girl has not moved, not even flinched, and is keeping eye contact with him, tears from her beautiful light blue eyes streak through her dirty skin, these eyes casting a radiant light on this darkening January evening, she has her arm held out toward him,

"I don't have time for you girl" Francis mumbles, almost to himself, turning around he takes a few paces back toward the church, he has to gather his tools, something makes him turn around, he has no idea why, but he turns anyway. The girl is gone.

He walks to the church gate and looks all around, there is no one to see, the girl has vanished, for the first time ever Francis has goose bumps all over his body, all the years working with the dead has left him uncaring and unafraid, until now. He cannot explain why he feels a little scared, it is not the oncoming darkness of the church or the graveyard, it is not the dead lying in graves beneath his feet, he has no reason to feel afraid, but he does, and he does not like it at all. Hurrying to the freshly dug grave he collects all his tools, putting them for the first time ever in the lean to, he leaves the churchyard in a hurry, hands in pockets and head down and starts the walk home.

As he crosses the High Street to go around the Cock pond and to the footpath behind Bowers house something catches his eye, he turns his body to the left, just outside the Inn she is standing there again, arm outstretched, palm up, shaking his head and squeezing his eyes shut to clear his thoughts and to alleviate the instant fear he feels, goose bumps cover his body again, he feels the cold winter wind on his face and opens his eyes.

She is gone.

The feeling of fear will not leave him this time and he sets off, walking quickly, he does not like this feeling, it is new to him, and he wants to be at home, in front of his fire with a bowl of stew.

* * *

The dark leaded sky is dappled with thick grey cloud, it threatens to snow, the wind is strong and cold, forcing itself in from the North, not a pleasant day for a funeral. Francis is walking his way toward

Rothamstead Manor, now part of the experimental station, he has to repair a couple of fence posts and rails that have been damaged by storms, he will have to borrow tools from the gardener at the Manor as he left his in the churchyard last evening, he curses himself for doing this, he despises having to borrow anything from anyone, he also curses himself for letting the little slum girl anger him so much, so much that he felt fear course throughout his body. He has no explanation for how he felt yesterday, he certainly has no such fears today, he knows he will return to the graveyard later that morning and fill in the grave with the dead body in it without any trepidation, fear or any other feeling, his only anger is toward himself for being so damn foolish. The girls dirty face and beautiful eyes still linger in his thoughts.

As he passes Heathfield house, a large almost industrial looking building at Leyton Green, currently owned by Mr James Wyatt, barrister at law, who, according to Francis is just '*another rich city dweller*' that has moved to town from London, he sees William delivering wood to the side of the large house, he has Francis' cart attached to his own horse it is full of cut wood and two exceptionally made cabinets,

"Took the cart s'morning Francis, you were not about, hope that's alright?"

Francis nods at William, "Of course, you could have saved me a walk to town though!"

Laughing, William replies, "You had already gone, you were up with the sparrows this morning I think"

"I was, got a fillin' in to do this afternoon"

He nearly tells William about the girl that frightened him yesterday, but decides against it

"Is that the Bowling Alley woman?" William asks

"Think so, we aren't collecting her, are we?" Francis asks in case he has forgotten about a prearrangement,

Shaking his head, William replies, "No, Fred the coalman is doing it, he is a friend of the woman's neighbour, he's doing it for nothing, I supplied the box, cheap as I could for them though"

"Do you want this one back"

"No thanks, she died of flossy jaw, horrible to look at so I hear, leave her in it my friend" Francis, hides a smile as he knows that William has got the name of the disease wrong, he means Phossy Jaw, he remains silent and nods his understanding, William continues, "Still, that wouldn't bother you Francis, you have seen it all, nothing around scares you!"

Francis feels a shiver down his spine as he recalls the meeting with the slum child on three occasions yesterday, he manages a smile,

"I'm off up to the Manor at Rothamstead, got a couple of posts and rails to fix, is there enough wood up there for me?"

William keeps the experimental station and the Manor stocked with wood,

"Lots there Francis, the posts and rails will be at the back of the barn behind the house"

Giving his thanks, he goes to leave, William stops him,

"Jump up, I have these cabinets for John Lawes up at the Manor, only finished them last night"

Francis accepts and climbs up onto the cart, William clicks, geeing the horse into a slow walk and the cart with the two men aboard gently moves off, "I just got to drop the loose wood off at Pimlico Place if that's alright, they are fixing the privy sheds behind the cottages"

Francis remains silent as they head toward Pimlico place. The row of 16 terraced cottages with a single grey slate roof, only broken in places by the upright double potted chimneys, these are rented labourers cottages except the cottage on the very southern end of the row, this is the common bakehouse for the residents to use, it is the only place that cooking can be done as none of the cottages has a scullery or kitchen. A plaque at the middle of the central pair of cottages states: '*Built by the Benefit and Annuitant society, held at the Blue Boar Inn St Albans 1822*', the cottages are now owned by Joseph Parsons, a local farmer who purchased the whole terrace in 1837. It is well known that he charges two shillings a week rent to his tenants, most of whom work for him, the rent is lower than the slums of the Bowling Alley but the cottages are small, each has a living room downstairs and one bedroom upstairs, only two privy sheds are provided for the whole terrace and water has to be collected from a pump outside the Silver cup pub. Rent is never a problem for Mr Parsons, he takes it directly from their weekly wages, most whom have worked for him for many years, the low rent and low wage agreement seems to suit all parties involved. The wood is to be delivered round the back, the farm labourers are fixing their own privies, Mr Parsons pays for the wood, William delivers it and the tenants fix the old and badly damaged buildings, another agreement that seems to suit all involved, Mr Parsons gets the privies mended, the only cost to him being the wood from William and the tenants get half decent privies to use. William sets the horse off again, the load in the cart now much lighter, only the cabinets and two large beams of oak remain, the oak he tells Francis is for the miller, Edward Hawkins at Redbournbury Mill, an ancient mill situated in between Redbourn and St Albans on the river Ver. Francis tells William that he will not be travelling with him to the mill as he has to get back to St Nicholas Church just after midday, the horse and cart take a slow right turn into Hatching Green, toward the White Horse pub, the innkeeper Joseph Matthews is known to both men, he keeps a good house and the beer is always fresh and clean tasting, they slowly approach the inn passing the open barn with its thatch roof before reaching the White Horse, it appears empty, neither of the men are surprised on this cold January morning, William raises a hand and waves at the pub,

"Just in case Joseph is looking out"

Francis nods in agreement, he tucks his bearded face into the collar of his coat, he knows that when they are past the approaching four terraced houses that are owned by the manor that the cold wind will bite into them as they cross open country on the rutted lane toward Rothamstead Manor, all the tenants work either at the great house or at the experimental station, they are good sized houses with two rooms upstairs and two down, each having its own privy in the garden. They pass by the Rothamstead Lodge entrance and onto the lane, treeless and unprotected, neither man speaks as they travel across the open fields and the land worked on by those employed at the experimental station, the ride is bumpy and uncomfortable, it is freezing in the wind, Francis is glad of the uncomfortable ride rather than the walk he was intending, the journey only takes fifteen minutes or so. They arrive at the side entrance to the estate and are met by a groom who gently takes hold of the reigns to stop the horse, Francis jumps off and sees that the house manager, Thomas Taylor, who is a rather stout and pompous man whom both Francis and William have known since childhood, hurriedly approaching them, as always he is perfectly dressed in starched white shirt and tie, the winged collar seemingly as pointed as an arrowhead, a waist length black coat with tails covers a black and grey waistcoat that is bulging with the strain behind it, he has thinning hair parted sharply to one side, he is clean shaven bar a rather superb set of well-groomed and lengthy sideburns.

"Morning Tommy" Francis speaks with a grin, knowing that Thomas hates being referred to as 'Tommy', he is even happier when he notes the distaste on the man's face,

"William, good morning, I have some staff who will be here abruptly to take the cabinets inside" He looks down his nose at Francis, "Gerald will see to you"

He then turns about face and marches back toward the house, William calls after him,

"Thomas, make sure the cabinets stand empty for a day or so, the wood is cold and needs to warm up again before use"

"Stuck up prig" Francis says to no one in particular.

William chuckles, "You need to stop riling him Francis, you know he thinks Tommy is a name for a small boy and that he hates it!"

Francis does not immediately reply, seeing Gerry the gardener limping toward him,

"See you later William, you bringing the cart back tonight?" William scratches his chin with an ungloved hand,

"Is tomorrow alright with you?" Francis nods in agreement and walks to meet Gerry.

"You got a couple of posts need mending Gerry?"

"Two, and a couple of rails, it's the fencing around the icehouse, a bloody big branch came down just after Christmas and broke them"

Francis and Gerry make their way to the barn to collect two fresh round posts and two half round fence rails, Gerry picks up a tin of nails and a claw hammer, Francis, in addition to the wood is carrying a heavy wooden mallet, similar to those used by the strongman at the Statty fair and a small shovel, they take a slow short walk through the gardens of the manor, Gerry's stiff leg slowing them down, the icehouse is situated in a small area of woodland behind the gardens.

Both posts are in place and just need stone and soil putting in and around their bases to give them a solid footing, both rails are broken beyond repair and will need replacing. Francis completes this task in under an hour,

"Time for a quick tea Francis? I can sort your rate out at the same time"

"Thanks" comes the reply. He always accepts a brew of tea, he does not buy it himself as it is too expensive, he also knows that he will get a bite to eat with his hot drink. Inside Gerry's job tied cottage his wife Eleanor is busying herself making tea, she is a small woman with a rounded bust and wide hips with a tiny waist between, wearing as she always has, a red smock top, a brown floor length skirt, both protected by a pristine white pinafore, a white bonnet covers her hair, a small tightly tied hair bun can barely be seen on the back of her head,

They, like Francis, are childless, both now being well past the age of safely having children, Francis always finds both to be a little sad about this but friendly and happy in every other aspect of their life at Rothamstead Manor. The tea is served, thankfully in robust mugs and not fancy china cups and saucers, his has a print on it of the old King, William IV and his bride Queen Adelaide, a celebratory earthenware mug from the 1831 Coronation, it is chipped in places but serves a good purpose, Francis declines sugar or milk, the steaming cup of black liquid is held by both his work hardened hands, the warmth of the mug gently penetrating the cold callouses on his fingers. Eleanor brings out a dish of bread and butter pudding, Francis gratefully accepts a bowlful, he has an hour or so until he has to make his way to town, it is now heading toward mid-morning and he does not relish the walk in the cold, Gerry gets down to business,

"Now Francis, his Lordship, of course thanks you for sparing your time today" He is always formal when it comes to paying Francis his rate for the work done, "Would you agree that half a day or so would be fair for the work completed today?"

"I would indeed Gerald"

Francis is handed three coins, all shillings, on one side, in a semi-circle around a stamped portrait of the young Queen, is the legend '*VICTORIA DEI GRATIA BRITTANIAR:REG:F:D*' meaning, '*Victoria, by the grace of God, Queen of the British, Defender of the faith*', on the reverse side, the much simpler legend '*ONE SHILLING*', surmounted by a crown, within a wreath of oak to the right and a wreath of olive to the left, at the bottom of all three coins is the date *1840.*

Both men are fully aware that Gerry will when completing his gardening ledger for the household, state that a full day's pay of five shillings and sixpence was paid to Francis, Gerry will take his cut, the remaining two shillings and sixpence, this is an ongoing arrangement between the two men, half a day always added to any work done, Gerry always taking his cut, Francis is not bothered, he has just been paid half a day's money for a little under an hour's work. The tea and pudding are delicious, and the kitchen is warm, the range fire firmly burning a fierce glowing red and giving off luxurious heat to all the occupants, Gerry breaks the silence in the room,

"Francis, have I ever told you about the big house?"

He has, Gerry is a mite absent minded, always has been, and loves telling stories about the history of Rothamstead Manor, Francis does not reply but looks across at Eleanor, she silently raises her eyebrows and smiles at him, Gerry carries on, Francis pretends to be listening intently, but if the truth be known, he is only catching every other spoken sentence, all of which he has heard before, he is thinking about the slum girl, he cannot get her out of his thoughts, and that bothers him. Gerry tells him, once again, that the Manor has been at this location since the 13th century, and the current owner, Mr John Bennet Lawes, had been born in the house in 1804, then inheriting it becoming Lord of the Manor aged only eight years of age following the death of his Father, the family moved out of the Manor following this death and renting the Manor and its land to the very grandiosely named, Mr Maximillian Richard Khymer for the princely rent of four hundred and twenty five pounds a year. The family moved back into the Manor in 1834 following the failure of Mr Khymer's business and bankruptcy.

Lawes had attended Eton college and Brasenose College, Oxford, leaving after three years without a degree, the story about an ostrich that escaped from the grounds of the Manor in 1839 and injured one man whilst it was being recaptured is also re told by Gerry as a side tale, he giggles as he recounts it. The current grounds, since 1843 when the Lawes manure and fertilizer company was formed on site, have been used for fertilizer improvement and agricultural experiments, Lawes, his Wife Caroline and their children spend time between houses in Rothamstead and Hampstead.

Francis hasn't realised that Gerry had finished talking, he becomes aware when he hears his voice,

"Francis, Francis, are you well?"

Francis shakes his head, forcing out the ongoing inner vision of the face of the slum girl from his head,

"Yes, of course, just thinking I will have to make a move to the church"

"As you wish, what were you dreaming about just then?" asks Gerry.

Goosebumps again form on Francis body, even though he is warm and comfortable, he stammers a reply,

"Oh, nothing much, I sort of..."

He does not finish the sentence, he certainly does not want to tell anyone of his very recent feelings of fear, he is the grave digger, not scared of anything, all around know this, he will appear superstitious and foolish if he admits fearing a child. He stands up, directing his thanks at Eleanor,

"Many thanks for the pudding and tea Eleanor, as always both were very lovely indeed"

Eleanor does a theatrical curtsey, at the door Francis politely nods his head to both the occupants, closing it behind him as he leaves, attempting and failing to take some of the warmth with him into the chilled morning outside. When he gets to the lane he takes the left fork, this directs him onto the Coach lane, a less rutted road than the one he had arrived on, again walking across open land, the lane will take him to another of the gated lodges at one of the estate entrances, then onto Leyton Road at the opposite side of Heathfield House where he had met William only a couple of hours ago, it is only just after 11 in the morning, Francis feels unusually tired, the day has been a long one so far, he has vague recollections of a fitful rest and sleep last night, broken and disrupted by visions in his head of the slum girl with her hand outstretched, he rubs his chest with his right hand and moves on.

When Francis arrives at St Nicholas church it is drizzling with rain, he is glad of his greatcoat and sturdy boots both are keeping the wet out, the chill of the day is not as bad now it is raining but it is still cold, Fred the coalman is unloading the coffin from the back of his coal cart, three other men are helping him to lift the plain wooden crate, Curate Henry Addington stands just inside the picket fence gate waiting to receive the body to the consecrated grounds of his church. Standing behind the Curate is the slum girl, she is shivering, the shawl with the red edging she had on yesterday is now missing from her shoulders, she stands wearing only the same shabby, shapeless dress she is still barefoot and is shivering with cold, her blue eyes sparkling like a stream reflecting sunlight on a bright summer's afternoon, they are without tears this time. Francis explodes,

"Get out of here! Go back to the Alley! Leave me alone and get away from this funeral!"

Fred and his three pallbearers turn and look, startled at the outburst from the usually taciturn grave digger, the Curate steps forward and puts his hand on Francis' shoulder.

"What are you doing Francis?" he pleads, getting only a violently gruff response from Francis,

"That bloody girl is following me, haunting my days and nights, she needs to go back to the Alley where she belongs"

The Curate, his hand still resting gently on the shoulder of the red faced, angry man, quietly replies, "That's her mother in the coffin Francis, the child is here to see her laid to rest, her soul heading forth on the journey to Heaven"

The anger subsides from the grave digger, his shoulders slumping, he turns to Fred and the other men, "You men family?"

All shake their heads, Fred is the only one to respond, "Francis, these men are only helping me out, they are neighbours from the Alley, not family, the child has no family now"

Francis realises he has his fists clenched tightly, he tries to relax but his body will not respond to this need, his anger, his fear, taking him to a place he has never been, he does not want or like these feelings he has, hating the lack of control.

"How was I to know, she followed me yesterday and is here again today, I just thought......"

He stops when the Curate takes his hand away from Francis' shoulder and silences him with a smile and a slight nod of the head, he begins to speak soft words of comfort to the girl before reading a short passage from the large leather bound bible held open in his left hand, the pallbearers move slowly into the churchyard, the coffin balanced carefully on their shoulders. They pass Francis and the Curate, the girl now walking alongside them toward the burial plot, dug only yesterday by the now shaking grave digger.

"Will you come to the interment Francis?"

"No" was the short and blunt answer to the Priest.

"Tillie, the young child has no family, it might be nice for her to have mourners for her mother"

"No" is the repeated answer, Francis rubs his chest again, the pudding has given him indigestion, the Curate lets out a long sigh.

"She has no family, no friends, they only moved here a few months ago, less than half a year, no Father to the child has ever lived here in town or is known to any of us, I believe him to be long dead, the child's Mother had worked at one of those new match factories in London, the fumes got to her and she has died of phossy jaw, horrible to see, horrible for the child, who will have to be taken to the union workhouse to be assessed by the relieving officer, I will take her later this afternoon" Francis remains silent, "As you wish Francis, it will be a short service at the graveside, it is raining, cold and I see little point in everyone catching their death, especially the child who is already cold and hungry"

Parish funded funerals, pauper funerals, are never a lengthy or a loving process, the religious ceremony is conducted quickly and only then because the body is being laid to rest in consecrated ground, workhouse and prison burials are just that, bodies buried in the ground without religion or ceremony.

Turning his back, Francis walks away from the Curate, he needs to collect his tools from behind the church, hoping that they have not been stolen, he tells himself that he will never leave them behind again, refusing to admit that it was the immediacy of his all-encompassing fear that made him leave without his tools yesterday. All is exactly as he left it, he only needs the spade, filling in the grave is so much quicker than the digging of it, the grave is only four or so feet deep and the coffin will take up half that depth, less than an hour's work, he has to wait for the graveside ceremony to finish, he does not have to wait long. From his position he can see the four pallbearers leaving the burial site, followed shortly afterward by the Curate, who has his left arm behind the Tillie, gently guiding her toward the church, wiping the soil and ash from his right hand onto his cassock, he looks up and sees Francis, the Curate nods at him, an indication that the burial can now be finished. Picking up his spade, putting it over his shoulder, he makes his way from the back of the church, past the Yew tree, red berries flourishing and ignoring the damp winter conditions, then up toward the burial site, quickly pushing his spade into the spoil heap when he arrives. Taking a look into the grave, the plain wooden coffin now sits just a couple of feet below the surface, this will be the last burial in this plot for at least 5 or so years, when this body has finished decomposing and the coffin wood has rotted away, it is thin cheap wood so the land will consume the body and the box leaving space for further burials, he reminds himself to let the priest know that this plot is full for the register. Francis has never seen phossy jaw before, he has heard of it, a relatively new disease and there have been no cases that he recalls in the town, he lowers himself easily into the grave, there is just enough room either side of the coffin to allow himself to straddle the box containing the deceased, putting his large hands at the head end, he pulls on the lid, it comes away easily, William uses very few precious nails to hammer the lid of a paupers coffin shut, lifting the lid away he sees the body. Francis has seen, handled, and dealt with many hundreds of dead bodies, there is little left to shock him, although this dead lady does not shake him, the way she looks is very unpleasant, macabre, odd, and new to him. Her face is half missing, eyes closed, one of her cheeks and her nose are almost completely gone revealing the bone of the jaw and teeth, several are missing, her gums are swollen, and pus filled, her face seems to be smiling, grimacing, and screaming all at once, this does not bother him, he has seen worse sights. The body of the dead lady is dressed in a thin grey skirt and grubby linen man's shirt, with a shawl draped around her shoulders, her arms and hands are tucked inside the shawl, an odd feeling of déjà vu hits Francis, the bright red edging to the shawl is frighteningly familiar to him, its colour seemingly alive amongst the death surrounding it. Francis recalls that the girl had it on yesterday, he presumes that the girl gave it to her Mother in her dying moments or the lady took it from the child because she was cold in the hours leading up to her death, he leans forward and touches the red edging of the shawl, he has no idea why he is doing this, he stands bolt upright when he hears a noise behind him. Turning his body around, not easy with his feet either side of the coffin in the grave, he sees the child, standing not four feet from the graves edge, he hears a short sharp groan, realising that it is him that is making this fearful sound he stops and becomes silent, staring at the child, transfixed by her light blue eyes, full of tears and sorrow, her hair is wet and clinging to her thin head and face, she raises her arm and puts her hand out, palm up.

"What do you want child!" He shouts angrily, the child changes her hand position from one of begging to pointing a thin and dirty finger at him, he is confused, looking down at his own hands, he is holding the edge of the shawl, the rest of it still partially wrapped around the dead body he is standing over, "Is this your shawl?" he asks quietly.

Tillie does not reply, finger still pointing she takes one step toward him, uncontrollable fear runs through his body, he tries to take a step away from the child, his feet are still either side of the coffin and losing his balance, he falls into the grave, putting his hands out in front of him he is just able to stop himself from falling on top of the body, his face only inches from what is left of face of the dead lady in the coffin. Her eyes now open, dead, and staring at nothing.

For the first time that he can ever remember, he cries out, scared and desperate to get away, he gets out of the grave, thankful it is only a couple of feet deep, the girl is gone, nowhere to be seen. He does not think it possible for a child to run and hide so quickly but she has vanished, his breathing is fast and shallow, he feels as though his heart will burst out of his chest, he swears he can actually hear it beating in the silent stillness of the graveyard, throwing the coffin lid into the grave without fixing it back onto the top of the box, Francis begins to shovel the spoil into the gaping hole, very soon sweating with the speed and ferocity of his exertions. Stopping for a short break to calm down and to gather his thoughts, he looks over to the church, feeling a sharp intake of breath when he sees the child standing under the Yew tree, she is as still as the graveyard itself, staring directly at him, cold shivers run down his spine, this feeling of fear will not leave him, it is not the grave he is filling or the body inside that he is fearful of, it is the child, he takes a few steps toward her, taking in a deep breath, filling his lungs so that when he shouts at her, he is determined to shout at her, she will be as scared of him as he is of her, fists balled and with vile words forming in his throat, he is just about to scream at her,

"Tillie? Tillie, where are you?" Henry Addington walks from the main church door, he notices the child under the tree,

"Tillie, come along now, I have to take you to the union workhouse, they will be looking after you, we need to go so I can return before it gets too dark"

He has an old blanket in his arms, he approaches Tillie and puts it around her shoulders, enveloping her, she makes no effort to pull it tightly around to warm her so very thin and cold body. She allows herself to be guided from the churchyard by the priest, through the gate and toward the pony and cart owned by the church, until she goes from his sight, she does not break her stare, head turned and looking directly at Francis, in return, although he wants to look away, he cannot, his dark eyes remaining locked with Tillie until she is out of his view.

"Bloody good riddance to you"

He quickly fills the rest of the grave, piling the remaining soil up on top until it has formed a mound, taking his spade, he turns his back on his work and walks away, collecting his tools he walks home in the damp and cold that the early afternoon is freely offering.

CHAPTER THREE

February arrives bringing with it a great storm, hours of rain and a ferocious gale, Francis has only left the cottage a few times over the past two days, visiting the privy to empty the overnight contents of the 'po' or to answer calls of nature, on one occasion to make emergency repairs to the pigsty fence, a section having been damaged by a large fallen bow from the overhanging tree, fortunately, his new piglet has not escaped, preferring to stay in the warmth and safety of its small shelter in the corner safe from the ravaging weather outside, the fence will need fixing properly when the storm passes, but for now it will hold. Both the fireplaces and the stove are lit, being at home all day he wants to be warm, and the fires are doing a grand job of heating the cottage, the wind continues to howl across the thatch on the roof, threatening to rip it off at any second, the noise is so loud that thinking rational thoughts is almost impossible, the sturdy door latches rattle making him jump a little, but they remain firmly in place. Francis gets up, looks into the cooking pot on top of the stove, a stew made from the kidneys and liver from his recently slaughtered sow, potatoes and winter cabbage were added a while ago, taking a small sip of the cooking liquor, he winces as the heat of the food burns in his mouth, it tastes good, then gently touching the side of the biggin, he knows that the coffee is not hot enough yet, it is a freshly made brew, having finished yesterday's brew this morning at breakfast, he wants a warm drink with his supper, the leftovers will also be his lunch tomorrow. Tillie has been on his mind and in his dreams. Something about her stare, something about her outstretched begging hand or that pointing finger has taken hold of Francis and he cannot shake it off. His sleep has been fitful and disturbed, dreams awakening him most nights, dreams he has no control over, dreams that haunt his mind.

The door at the front of the house flies open, Francis jumps up dropping the stirring spoon onto the hard floor of the kitchen, he hopes it is the wind but fears it might be Tillie opening the door, his breath is stuck in his chest, he dares not move, he dare not breath, frozen with fear and trepidation, the seconds seem like years.

"Did you not hear me knocking?" William enters the kitchen, pulling the door shut behind him, making certain that the large latch is in place and firmly holding the door, Francis is staring at him, wide eyed and ashen faced, "Francis, are you alright?"

Water is dripping from Williams long coat and large brimmed hat onto the kitchen floor, forming a pool by his visitors' feet, Francis is almost hypnotised watching it, he comes back to his senses when he hears William, "Francis!"

"William?" A silent pause follows, Francis breaks this, "What the bloody hell are you doing here? Scared the life out of me you did!"

"I thought grave diggers don't get scared, you look awful my friend"

Francis tells William that he hasn't slept because of the great gale, that he is tired and that is why he is a bit jumpy, he repeats his question, "What are you doing here?"

"I was just leaving the barn when the constable arrived, can you believe he is out in this weather?"

Francis does not answer the question posed, William continues, "It seems a child died at St Stephens a few days ago and the Workhouse Master wants the child buried, too lazy to do it himself, I was on the way home so thought I would let you know"

"I will go tomorrow if the storm lets up"

"I shall come with you" William states, "That rantallion of a man, the Master Thomas Porter, owes me for three coffins from before Christmas, he won't get another until he pays"

Francis had buried the three dead elderly females from the workhouse that William refers to, the coffins that he has not been paid for were all returned to him, both ladies had been buried in the clothes that they died in, and William knows this, the Master does not know and therefore will be charged. The storm and gale show no signs of slowing,

"You want to have some stew with me?" Francis asks William, who is taken aback, in all the years he has known the grave digger, he has never been invited for food.

"I will Francis, thank you"

"Where is your horse? You can't leave him outside"

Shaking his head, William replies, "I left him at the mill barn, he will be safe enough there"

Francis serves two bowls of steaming offal stew with chunks of bread and the men sit, Francis at the table and William on the bench by the fire, they eat in silence, listening to the glorious violence of the storm outside.

When Francis awakes the storm has broken, outside is a crisp clear morning, lifting the 'po' he realises he has not used it overnight, the fire in his living room is just alive, he dresses without adding fuel to it then goes into the kitchen. William is asleep on the bench seat, covered in a blanket, Francis nudges him with his stockinged right foot,

"What? Where? Francis, what am I doing here?"

"You fell asleep last evening, so I left you"

Francis tends to the stove, the wood taking quickly from last night's embers, offering fresh new heat to the small room, the biggin is put on the hot plate, it is still half full of yesterday,

"Can I use your privy?" William asks

He leaves the kitchen, after slipping on his boots, to use the outhouse, Francis cuts a few slices of bread and spreads dripping on them, the coffee is warm enough to drink, he pours the precious liquid into his mug, retrieving the mug William used last night from under the bench seat, filling this also with coffee. William returns to the kitchen, stamping his feet and wrapping his arms around himself to beat out the cold, gratefully taking the bread and dripping with the mug of coffee, thanking Francis for the sustenance. He leaves William eating his breakfast to use the privy himself. Last night's dreams are mulling over in his thoughts, another night of broken sleep, another night of that child's face haunting him.

William leaves the cottage to go and collect the horse from the mill stable, he will return shortly to hitch on the cart, Francis tends to the stove fire, he needs it to still be warm when he returns from the workhouse later on this afternoon, putting just enough coal on it so that it will catch and burn slowly but ensuring that it does not smother and extinguish the glowing hot wood embers, this done he greedily finishes the coffee left in the biggin, it is not very hot but it is strong and tasty, he eats one piece of bread and dripping for his breakfast, he is unusually not hungry. He feels jaded and tired.

Hearing William return, Francis puts on his overcoat and hat, checking the stove a final time, he latches the front door behind him, positioning the cart so that when the horse is hitched, they can climb aboard and leave without any fuss. The horse, a good natured 18 hand shire, is taller than both William and Francis, does not move when the leather saddle and backstrap are put in place, the back and belly bands are tightened using the tug buckle on either side, the collar is adjusted around the neck of the horse, this must not take any of the strain when pulling, the backstrap is pulled across his huge back, the loin strap and breeching then put in place, the shafts of the cart are gently put into the correct position, secured tightly to the harness, the reins then passed through the back loops and onto the rein terrets on top of the saddle. They are ready to move off. The cart was purchased by his Mother just before she died and is a two wheeled old Hertfordshire dung cart, it had been adjusted and altered enabling it to carry larger loads by William some years earlier, the iron frame with its large wooden wheels are as they were originally, spoked and surrounded with a tight iron band, the changes made are to the flat bed and the front sections, by putting slightly longer planks in and replacing the old and rotten ones that were originally on the bed it now easily accommodates a coffin and longer planks of wood, a basic bench seat has been added, it is an uncovered cart, but it is sturdy and functional and the arrangement for its use suits both men. The journey to William's barn on the outskirts of town is completed in silence, the chill of the early morning not conducive to making either man conversational, Francis draws smoke from his freshly filled and lit pipe, William who does not use a pipe, has charge of the horse, holding the reins in one hand, the other deep and protected in his jacket pocket, chin tucked into his chest and his battered hat pulled low over his eyes. A few trees have fallen overnight, victims of the great gale, many smaller bows from the uppermost heights have been separated from their host and now lie seemingly dead and alone across the road in many places, the horse easily walks through them and the men in the cart only feel gently bumps as the metal rimmed wheels roll over this detritus. The coffin is loaded onto the back of the cart next to the grave diggers' tools, is not newly made, Francis can tell by the smell emanating from it, that this is not the first time this box will have housed a corpse, William notices the knowing smirk on his friend's face,

"It's a bit ripe, I will give you that, perhaps we might leave this one in the ground today?"

The back gate on the cart is latched and secured in place, this design means there is no requirement to tie the coffin down to stop it moving, a gentle slap of the reins moves the horse into a forward momentum, its huge hooves making distinctive sounds as they rise and fall on the damp track that leads them across the common toward St Albans. The common land passes the entrance to Beesonend farm and its associated cottages, then onward past Childwick hall stud and into Childwick Green village, here stands the manor house of Childwickbury Estate, a huge and imposing white painted domicile, the original manor being built on this site in the 14th century, the current 17th century house was constructed for the Lomax family. The current Mr Lomax, a direct descendant of the original Lomax owners, all God fearing men who became lawyers and politicians, this family having owned the house and vast amounts of land surrounding it since 1666, their acreage covering between Redbourn and St Albans. Almost all the staff, domestic, equine, gardeners, farm and otherwise live on the estate in tied houses, all of which are of good quality and better than most in town that other labourers rent. The track widens as they approach the entrance to Childwick Green village, part of the Childwickbury estate, on past Hawkswick farm and stopping at New house farm to let the horse water at the trough on the road, a short distance on from New house farm at the crossroads with Beech Bottom to the left and Sparrowswick tallow works straight ahead they take the right fork, heading toward Oster Hills, a section of land with a large house that was built here in 1827, it was rented to James Quilter Rumball in 1834 who used the property as a private mental asylum, this before he moved the business to Blakesleys Hall, until 18 months ago the house had been occupied by the chaplain of St Michaels,

Reverend Hutchinson, in 1848 it was sold to Mr Abraham Scott, he promptly died leaving the house to, and still now lived in by his Widow and surviving children. Once past Oster Hills their journey is nearly over, a short right turn onto Union Lane, the Union workhouse is situated here, a bleak looking building with only one entrance, this so that the inmates and visitors can be regulated and checked, the Porter who is responsible for signing everyone in and out is a man they both know, he comes out to meet them from his lodge at the entrance, he is putting on his black jacket as he approaches them,

"Warm in the lodge is it, Oliver?"

Oliver James has been the porter at the union workhouse for over 15 years, previously being employed as work master inside the building, a balding rotund man looking every year of his six decade age, he giggles as he replies,

"Don't want to be out here with you couple of *bad luckers*!"

Francis smiles, William continues, "Is the Master here abouts? He owes me a few bob"

"I wondered why you were here William, not like you to attend for a burial" opening the big wrought iron gate to allow the horse and cart through, he continues, "The Master will be in his quarters, he is expecting you, he might be a mite unhappy, he is right miserable today with toothache, but mainly because the child died several days ago and is still not buried, he did contact the Beadle to get a message to you Francis"

The comment is dismissed by Francis with a shrug of his shoulders, William clicks the horse to move on and they slowly pass through the gate into the large courtyard separated into male and female yards by a red brick wall, the master's quarters are immediately on the right as they enter, in comparison to the rest of the buildings these are three luxurious rooms with a sitting room, a waiting hall and an entrance lobby, this area has two small offices for the workhouse staff. To the left of this courtyard is the Men's open living area, cramped dormitories over three floors with beds filling almost all the floor space, each room having a small single fireplace to heat the large space. The ground floor room has one indoor WC, a recent addition, this is used by the hundred or so men living on all three floors, the smell from it is impossibly bad. The women are housed on the opposite side of the courtyard, also in a three story building with similar heating and toilet facilities, they are separated from the men by a wall that is nearly two yards high, the children's ward has only two of its three stories being used for accommodating those under 13 years is in the building next to the men's accommodation. The next building is the dining area, where all occupants eat the three provided meals in silence, gruel and bread each morning at six, lunch at midday is a small bowl of thin stew with meat, usually just gristle fat and vegetables, the evening meal served at six is bread and cheese, occasionally at weekends, a weak soup is served, it is situated next to the women's accommodation against the back wall. The laundry and female working area is in between the master's entrance lobby and the women's accommodation, the workhouse does not have a purpose build chapel or infirmary, there has been talk for many years that these will be built on site but as yet this has not happened. In between the men's accommodation and the children's ward is a large ornately carved archway built of brick and wood, it stands defiant and without ceremony, through this archway is the men's woodyard and work area, this is also the area where the dead of the workhouse are unceremoniously buried. A small wooden structure stands alone in the corner of the burial ground, this is known as the dead house, where the deceased are put until the grave digger can get to the union workhouse and bury the poor dead soul lying in there.

William stops the horse outside of the master's quarters, Francis jumps off the cart and enters the building, the two offices are occupied, the first by the Beadle, the parish constable, a lazy, irresponsible drunk, he is asleep, the second office houses the relieving officer, Mr. Samuel Albert, his responsibility is to evaluate all individual cases of people applying for poor relief, it is on his word as to whether anyone is admitted to the workhouse or not. Francis dislikes Mr Albert, he finds him to be a spiteful individual who seems to enjoy the suffering of others, he uses his position on the Union board of Guardians to put fear into the poor and tries to stamp authority on anyone visiting the workhouse. Francis himself has no cares or thoughts for most people and is happy to profit from death, but he is never spiteful or cruel to those less fortunate than he even when he is taking their coin, Mr Albert looks at Francis over his small round glasses,

"At last, the grave digger arrives!" he says with sarcasm and an attempt to intimidate Francis, he fails, and visibly squirms as the larger man steps menacingly toward him,

"The gravedigger will leave as quick as he arrived if you carry on *Mister* Albert"

Francis emphasising the *Mr*, hissing it at the thin and pale looking clerk through gritted teeth,

"I will fetch the Master for you"

He scurries out of the room, William joins Francis in the cramped office,

"Is that worm getting the Master?

Francis replies that he is, the Master is a man who is responsible for all souls within the walls of the workhouse, registering all births and deaths that take place within the premises, signing certificates stating date and time of either instance taking place. He is a very serious man who lacks any humour, his Wife, the

Matron is responsible for all the women and children is the opposite she is, brash, loud, and full of life, she likes to busy herself with others business, it is she who appears to greet them.

Mr Albert squeezes past William and Francis, who do not move for him, back to his desk and chair, he fakes being busy by dipping his pen in the inkwell and writing on a sheet in front of him,

"Francis" the Matron speaks in her usual loud and high pitched voice, "The Master will be pleased to know you are here, the bodies are in the dead house and they are, well it would be fair to say, without any offence to their souls, they are a bit ripe"

"They?" questions Francis, the Matron nods as she answers,

"We have a dead child, poor soul, accidental of course, fell down the stairs four, or was it five, evenings ago, had to put him in the dead house, then last night we had a stillborn, the mother also passing the poor dear"

"Three to bury then?"

"No Francis, just the two, the stillborn is so tiny, surely that won't be a proper burial"

"Three dead is three bodies to bury, I don't care how big or small they are"

William interjects, "We only have one box Francis"

Francis asks the Matron for an old sheet or large sack to put the extra bodies in for burial, the Matron instructs Mr Albert to carry out this task, he scurries off squeezing past the two men who again don't move for him. The workhouse is supposed to have a resident nurse, they don't, a local nurse is registered to the workhouse but as the pay is so poor she has to work elsewhere to make ends meet, so she is not always on site, the same goes for the Chaplain and the school mistress, both are employed by the Union, both have responsibilities elsewhere and rarely visit the site, none of the inmates get medical, educational, or spiritual comfort with any regularity.

The Matron, seemingly just realising that Francis is not alone, speaks to William,

"May I ask why we have the pleasure of the coffin maker here?"

"You can Matron, I am owed money by the Union, and I am here to collect"

Becoming flustered the Matron looks at the clerk, "The Master deals with all that as you know, how much is it you are owed?"

William tells her it is four and sixpence, adding casually that he never makes any profit from the dead of the workhouse, he is then informed by her that there may not be that much in the cash tin, William stares directly at her, Mr Albert returns and squeezes back into his office, he has with him, a dirty sheet, handing it to Francis as he passes him, William speaks,

"I will take the coffin I have here away then, can't have it if there is no money for me"

The Matron remains quiet but nods at Mr Albert, he reaches into a drawer takes out a locked metal box and opens it with a small key on a chain that is attached to his waistcoat, turning his back on the grave digger and carpenter, shielding the contents of the tin he takes out an old sixpence and four shillings, closing the box, locking it and putting it away. Dabbing his pen into the inkwell, he fills in a transaction receipt for William to sign.

"Six shillings Mr Albert please" the voice of William is clear and loud,

Mr Albert and the Matron look quizzically at each other, the Matron speaks,

"You clearly just said that we owed you four and sixpence, not six shillings"

"That I did Matron, the Union owes me for three coffins, not including today's box that is on my cart, four in total, six shillings"

The Matron began to say, "I am not sure we have that amount…."

A loud and angry voice, that of the Master, coming from the upstairs quarters, is directed at the Matron, "Elizabeth, pay the man and be done with it!"

"The Master has toothache" she informs the men in the room, she continues,

"Mr Albert, please pay in full, it is so expensive running this house for the poor and destitute, I don't know how we will be able to feed them all after paying out all this money"

Workhouse Masters and Matrons are notoriously tight with money, they get a set amount to run the Union workhouse, usually skimping along the way so as to make a few extra shillings for themselves, Mr Albert is going through the same ritual with the cash box and eventually hands over the six shillings to William who happily signs the receipt.

"I need paying" Francis now speaks

The Matron rolls her eyes and in instructs Mr Albert, "Four shillings for the grave digger Mr Albert please"

"Six" Francis insists

"Four, surely it is four" the Matron is losing her usual happy nature, "The stillborn is so small" Francis shrugs,

"Four shillings then if you say so" The Matron sighs in exaggerated relief, "But I only bury two, which one I leave in your dead house will be up to you Matron"

The voice of the Master is heard again, loud, clear, and angry, "Pay the man so they can all bugger off and leave me in peace!"

When all dues have been paid and the Matron looking sad and physically unwell at having spent 12 shillings from the cash tin, William and Francis take leave and walk from the room,

"I will get the Beadle to take you to the burial ground", Matron sounds insistent,

"Is he in his office?" William and Francis both indicate that he is, Matron calls for him, "George, can you take the grave digger to the burial site" No response, she tries again, "George?" Nothing. She raises her voice, usually loud naturally, but this was loud, "George!"

The snorting from the crapulous Beadle clearly indicates that waking him up will take some time, the Master, now screaming at his wife,

"Francis knows where the burial grounds are, he has been coming here for years, now, let him get on and leave me in peace!"

"It's his tooth, poor man" says the Matron in frustration,

Seeing that neither man has any interest in the pain and suffering of her Husband, she bids them good day and makes her was upstairs to tend to the Master. Francis and William take their leave, both climbing onto the cart and making the short journey across the courtyard, through the arch and into the men's work area, to the right is the wood and bone crushing yard, wood is chopped by the elderly men and the younger boys and girls, then sold locally, and cheaper than other traders in St Albans, making the workhouse an unpopular organisation with these businesses, the younger men and older boys crush animal bones to be sold and added to fertilizer. Officially, the Union workhouses had stopped this practice in 1847 when it was banned, St Stephens sell the crushed bones to the experimental station every week, so they have continued with the practice, the Guardians and Governors know of course, but it brings money into the organisation, so blind eyes are turned. Men have been known to become involved in vicious fights, fighting over animal bones that still have some marrow in them, the winners getting to suck the cold but flavoursome food contained within these bones.

Discipline is harsh, if the men or women break the rules, they face going without food for two days, boys are regularly beaten by the Master with a cane, pole or any implement that may be close to hand, fighting is strictly forbidden, but no one from the board or any staff member takes any notice when violence breaks out. Women and older girls are put to work either winding cotton wick for the tallow chandlers at Sparrowswick, or plaiting straw for the factories in Luton, there is little violence in the female workspaces.

Guiding the horse and cart across the unconsecrated burial grounds, neither man has any issue riding right across the top of the buried dead, William stops the horse short of the dead house, they both smell the decaying corpses within, the day old pair should be ok, the smell will be from the five day dead child. William covers his nose, Francis barely registers the odour as he takes his spade and digging bar from the back of the cart, moving to a space close to the outer wall, he begins to dig, there are no set graves in the burial ground so Francis digs where he wants to, the ground is hard, he calls over to William to bring the mattock over to him, he will loosen the ground before digging it. This done, he gets a few inches below the cold surface when the ground begins to soften, he digs silently and efficiently, William watches from the cart making no attempt to assist the grave digger, Francis prefers to work alone and has no intentions of splitting his 6 shillings with the carpenter. He is several feet down, only his head and shoulders showing above the grave edge when he hits the top of an old coffin with his spade, it is deep enough to put the bodies into the grave, he stands up straight, he is just about to call over to get William's attention so that the coffin can be readied to be filled, he looks up and standing on the far side of the burial grounds, someone is watching him intently.

It is Tillie.

He makes a noise that William hears,

"You alright Francis?" he asks getting no reply, the grave digger stands frozen still, his eyes almost bulging from his head, William tries again but gets the same silent reply. The child is standing still, both her hands outstretched in front of her, blood is oozing from many cuts and splinters from her work cutting and chopping wood, children of her age will only chop smaller pieces into kindling,

"Look" one whispered word from Francis, William jumps down from the cart,

"What did you say Francis"

The now pale faced grave digger repeats, "Look"

William is confused, "Look where?"

Francis turns to William, breaking eye contact with the blue eyed child, these eyes as clear as crystal to Francis, even across the open space of the burial ground, he sees them, bright, alive, and beautiful.

"Over there" he points toward the working area, he becomes angry, "Where is she?" he shouts

"Where is who? There ain't no one, just a group of men and children working, as they always are" William shakes his head at the grave digger.

Francis scrambles out of the freshly dug grave with the speed and agility of a younger man, William sees the fear on his face,

"Francis, are you sickening for something?"

"Where is she?" is the panicked reply

Both men look across the burial ground, only a group of men and children working on the far wall can be seen, Francis cannot see Tillie anywhere.

"Francis, you are shaking, this is not like you"

He receives no reply, the grave digger walks across the burial grounds toward the working area, William calls after him,

"Come on, let's get these in the ground and go home, we have been paid so the quicker the better" He walks toward the back of the cart, undoing the latch that is holding the back gate in place, he leans forward and pulls the coffin toward him, he shouts at Francis, "Come on, let's get this done!"

Francis stops his walk, he is about halfway across the burial ground, he turns and makes his way toward the cart to help William get the coffin out. They take the wooden box and place it outside of the dead house, Francis has not spoken a word he still has a fearful look on his face, William has put a dirty handkerchief to his nose and is trying not to gag, the unmistakable smell of rotting human flesh is strong in the air, seeing the man with the small piece of cloth to his nose seems to break Francis out of his silence,

"All these years and you still gag at a bit of a smell"

William replies to him through the handkerchief, "Most are fresh, admittedly they all stink a bit when we collect them from the house, but this is awful today"

Francis manages a smile, "Open the box, I will get the body of the lady, she can go in the box with her stillborn, the child can go in the sheet, I will put him on top of the coffin"

William takes the lid off the coffin as Francis opens the door of the dead house, William turns away as the smell inside hits him, Francis goes inside. He returns only a minute later dragging the corpse of a young female, no older than twenty, dressed in the workhouse 'uniform', grey and black horizontal striped shirt, and a red dress. The red dress in a workhouse signifies that the wearer is pregnant, a yellow dress indicates that the wearer is a prostitute, and a grey dress is for all other women, this is another practice that is outlawed in these institutions, the Master and Matron have kept it in place, as usual without any challenge from the board of guardians. The men all wear trousers and a shirt, grey with black horizontal stripes, children keep their own clothes, shabby and dirty shirts, dresses, and trousers, few, if any have shoes. Clothing is usually stripped from the dead to be re used, it is obvious why this poor deceased lady has been 'allowed' to keep hers, the stillborn has been wrapped and rolled in the folds of the skirt and left lying on the belly of its dead Mother, the tops of her legs are uncovered and bloodstained, she has no underwear to give her any dignity. William helps Francis lift the mother and child into the coffin,

"We can put the other dead child in here as well Francis, plenty of room"

Francis ventures back into the dead house alone, William hears him cursing from inside and is curious as to what has made the grave digger swear, when the body of the child is bought out into the bright cold day, he can see why.

"Holy hell, what has happened?"

Francis puts the body of the small, thin, dead child into the coffin, on top of the dead Mother and child already in place, both men look at the small pitiful body. The child, aged eight or nine, is covered in welts and large bruises, obviously from a beating, a severe beating, the clothes he is wearing are rags, dirty and in places, smeared in blood from the beating,

"Fell down the stairs accidentally?" William asks

Francis shakes his head, "Been dead longer than four or five days I think, nine or ten more like"

William cannot answer, he has seen plenty of death, much poverty and violence, but not as severe as this on child, Francis breaks the silence, "Let's get them in the ground William"

Francis is unmoved by the beaten child, only his initial outburst of swearing being any indication of feeling, the two men carry the coffin to the edge of the grave, after placing it on the ground, Francis jumps into the grave, he takes one end of the coffin and with William assisting him from outside, the coffin is unceremoniously put in the bottom of the grave, Francis stands on the lid to get out. William, already back on the cart, watches as the grave digger becomes grave filler, Francis, every few minutes looks up and across the burial site, expecting to see the blue eyes staring into his, there is no sign of Tillie.

The task completed, the horse takes the cart and the two men slowly from the burial grounds, through the courtyard and to the gates at the porters' lodge, Oliver comes out to open the gates, Francis asks him a question,

"Oliver, have you seen a girl child hanging about here today?"

Oliver laughs, "Lots of 'em! The place is full of children, boys, and girls"

Francis realising what he has just said, tries again,

"What I mean is a girl, would have been admitted here a month or so ago, our Parish Priest would have delivered her"

Oliver rubs his balding pate with both hands,

"We haven't had many new children recently because we are full to bursting" he seems to be thinking hard, "Do you mean Tillie?"

The mention of her name gives Francis goose bumps,

"Yes" he says, "That's her"

Oliver nods as he speaks, "Lovely little girl, polite, really sad life so I hear from the Matron, beautiful blue eyes on her"

"Where would she be now?"

"Working Francis, everyone works here as you know, she should be chopping firewood with the other children, don't agree with it myself, when I was work master I never had children working with the men or the old dears either, men should be chopping wood not the children, we get horrible injuries on these poor children here now" Francis thanks him, he knows that the Master and Matron have put the elderly women and children to work at the wood pile because more profit is made from selling the wood, the more sold, the more profit made, Oliver continues, "The work master has no choice, he has to do what the Master tells him to do and where to put the workers, it's not right though"

The horse and cart pass through the gates, the three men raise hands at each other to say goodbye, Francis hears the gates close as they move off, the large bolts being put in place by the Porter, something makes him turn around. Standing on the inside of the entrance gates is Tillie, he knows it is her by her blazing blue eyes, she is waving slowly at him.

"Bloody hell!" he says as he rubs his eyes, not believing what he is seeing,

"What is it now?" asks William.

Francis opens his eyes, the gates are closed, Tillie is not there, seemingly vanished.

"Nothing" Francis says, "Nothing at all"

"Who is Tillie then?" William is curious

"I don't know" replies Francis honestly.

* * *

The cold winter of January and February has made way for a clear bright March and a warm April, spring arrives bringing with it the bright burst of colour from flowers and hedgerows, the Yew, having survived another of its many lived winters begins to bud, its flowers are white and yellow orbs, very different to the Yew in the churchyard, this having small, scaly, green buds, this is the only noticeable difference between the two trees, both are ancient, magnificent and having huge and dense canopies, easily blocking the bright spring sun from hitting the dark ground below.

Francis is glad about the change in weather, he is still lighting a fire in the kitchen every evening but during the day only the stove is fired up and he has stopped using the fire in his living room, the nights are chilled but not cold enough for a fire to be lit. The root cellar is well stocked with preserved meats, smoked, salted, dried and jugged, the fresh vegetables are nearly all gone, a few straggly winter cabbages and the recently harvested and hanging and drying onions remain in the cellar, half a sack of potatoes is all that is left upstairs, they should last him until the early crop are harvested in a few weeks, early June he hopes, although the half sack he has are starting to go soft and black in places, some have begun to '*chit*'. He has eaten well throughout the winter, the pork from his slaughtered sow will almost certainly see him through until well past the end of spring and into summer, he has also been helping Bert Whittingham at Common lane farm for the past three weeks, new fences and posts put in to replace the aged and rotten ones he had, it was only when his cattle got out and destroyed the lovely and well cared garden of one of his labourers did he contact Francis to come and work for him, farmers are notoriously tight with money, always pleading poverty to Francis. Payment, for this job will be a quarter of a butchered cow and a bucket of butter made by Bert's wife in the farm dairy, a good price for the work he is doing, William, as usual, had supplied the posts and rails to Bert, Francis, as usual, getting a few shillings for putting business William's way. He has a few day's more work to do on the farm, then the job will be finished, payment can then be made, although the beast will be butchered on the farm, he will break the meat down further in the back room to make it easier to preserve, he will eat some of it straight away, he is craving fresh beef and imagines how tasty the first bite of the roasted meat will be, cooked on a spit in front of the stove fire, slowly turning from a red brown colour with fatty white edges to a deep brown outside and a lovely pink in the middle, the fat crispy, juicy and tasty.

Francis is walking home from Common Lane farm, work for the day is done, he has also visited David Holmes at Mackerye End Farm, he has been offered and accepted a labouring job for later in the month, helping David to put up planks of wood on the sides of his new barn, William will not be providing the wood for this one, David will cut the planks on the farm, Sauncy Woods and Holcroft Springs are on his land and both have an abundance of trees that over the past years have cut down. The trees for this task having been cut before December the previous year, they have been stacked and drying so his farm labourers can cut them by hand, into workable planks of thick and strong wood. The evening is fine, Francis feels only a slight chill, the sun has very nearly disappeared over the western horizon, reaching the crossroads he heads directly over instead of turning right to go home deciding there and then to visit Dick Freeman, the landlord of the Marquis of Granby public house, originally a London landlord he moved from the city over a decade ago to take on the 'Marquis'. He owes Francis a few shillings for digging a large cess pit at the back of the pub last weekend, digging graves has now quietened down after the winter rush, he is still regularly digging for the Parish church and the other churches in surrounding Parishes, but it is not as busy as it has been, so he is grateful that the local farmers call on him to work for them, best of all, if a grave does need digging, then he can take half a day from the job he is working on to get it dug in time for a funeral. Crossing the deserted road he passes the smithy, George Lines the blacksmith is obviously busy in his forge, Francis can hear the distinctive sound of a hammer on red hot metal, slow and deliberate strokes, crossing the ford on the wooden bridge he sees the public house in front of him, smoke spiralling from the chimney and paraffin oil lamps in the windows, giving it a welcoming and homely appearance, he enters the public bar. The warmth from the fire casts a different environment to the late spring evening outside, this room in the pub is small with two tables each having two chairs, a bench seat under each of the large main windows are occupied, smoke from working men's pipes is hanging, almost lifeless, in the air of the room, the bar is higher by a few inches than the tables, giving the landlord a clear view of both bars. Standing behind he looks across it into another room, known as the lounge bar, larger than the public bar and is used by the local farmers and landowners, the bar Francis is in is used almost exclusively by local farm labourers and other working men, a small snug sits neatly and hidden secretly away between the two bars, it has its own small fireplace, lit and filling the small room with red, flickering light. Francis catches the attention of Dick, who turns to face him,

"You here for an ale Francis?"

"I am Dick, also for the few shillings you owe me"

Dick looks at Francis quizzically, "You sure I didn't pay you at the time?"

Francis manages a smile, Dick always plays this game, "You did not pay me the ten shillings and I am here to collect"

"Ten shillings!" Dick exclaims, "It is six shillings, and you know it!" Dick realises that Francis has tricked him and has won their ongoing battle this time,

"Six shillings it is then" Francis agrees.

Dick pours Francis a glass of ale, knowing which he prefers, from a large jug he has behind the bar, the ale being drawn from a 34 gallon barrel with XX stamped on the round lid, the barrels are stored in the dark and damp cellar, the fermented hop and malt liquid poured into a pint glass, heavy bottomed with a thick glass handle. This ale is brewed in town at The Peacock brewery, owned by Mr. James House of Wheathampstead, he took over the running of the brewery from his Father in 1843, his Father having started the business in 1820, moving to its site at the East end of the High Street in 1839. The business is doing very well selling its ales to all the public houses in town, the brewery has large stores for aromatic hops and sickly sweet malt, an ancient artesian well is situated in the centre of the brewing barn, the three tun rooms, each housing two huge Tun barrels, these in turn each holding 252 gallons of precious ale, below is a large underground cellar, the barrels, the kilderkins and firkins are stored here, waiting to be filled. Three ales are brewed here, differing only by the strength of the finished fermented liquid, marked with one X for the weak or 'small' ales, two X's for medium strength and three X's for very strong ale or barley wine, some of the barrels and firkins in the underground cellar have the letter K on them alongside the X's, this indicates that this is keeping ale, and it can remain in the barrel or firkin for 9 – 12 months, the taste will change over time, becoming sourer the older it is.

Pushing the full glass over to Francis, Dick says, "Tuppence for that"

Francis raises an eyebrow and rubs his thick beard with a grimy, calloused hand, "On the house I think, for late payment"

Dick picks up the jug of beer to serve a customer in the lounge, speaking to Francis as he walks the few steps to the other side, "You have the cheek of the Irish Francis, go on then, have it on me"

The man being served in the lounge joins in,

"I presume mine is on the house as well Dick?"

"No John" Dick says firmly, "We all know you have plenty of land and money, so you can pay for your ale"

The man laughs and hands over a sixpence, "Keep the change Dick, you obviously need it"

Raising his full glass toward Francis, the man steps away from the bar to a table, he is sitting alone with his newspaper.

"Don't forget my six shillings Dick"

Nodding his head at Francis, the landlord disappears down the steps to the cellar to re fill the jug, when he is out of sight he shouts up,

"Francis, do you need a firkin for home?"

"No" Francis shouts at the opening to the cellar, "Still got some in the last one I had from you"

When Dick reappears, Francis is ready for a refill, Dick, without having to ask, replenishes the glass in front of the grave digger, Francis hands over two pennies and Dick puts six shillings on the bar, this transaction over, Dick says to Francis,

"Did you hear that George has had a '*chavy*' sleeping in his barn?" Francis shakes his head slowly and without interest, Dick continues, "A skinny young girl by all accounts, he thought she was a '*beak hunter*', but he said that she is so thin she ain't got the strength to wring a neck"

Francis grunts, taking a long pull at his ale, without answering. "Chased her away with an iron rod, he never hit her with it, says he felt a bit sorry for her, she had nicked and eaten a few apples from his bucket in the barn though"

A patron in the lounge gets the landlords attention, indicating that a refill of his glass is needed, Dick walks away to carry out this task, filling two glasses of XX ale for the customer then taking the money, looking at it in his hand to ensure it is the right amount, he returns and refills Francis empty glass, he is handed another two pence and he continues,

"Albert reckons she has been in there for a few days, keeping warm in the hay he has for his animals, she looked frightened as she ran away by all accounts, piercing blue eyes on her he said"

Francis froze, the glass of beer only inches from his lips, holding his breath, he asks,

"What did you just say then Dick?"

"The 'chavy' had been helping herself to his apples, sleeping in the barn"

"What else did you say?"

Dick looked confused, "About what Francis"

"The girl, you said something else about her eyes"

Dick nods, now understanding what Francis needs to know, "Piercing blue is what he said"

Francis slowly put down his almost full glass of ale, he feels the colour draining from his face, he feels dizzy, he feels frightened, it cannot be her again, can it?

"Francis, you look awful man, are you sick?"

"What? No, just a funny turn, I must be away home"

Francis, stands up to leave, feels the weight of his body travel through to his legs, they have become uncontrollably unsteady, and he has to grab onto the bar to steady himself,

"Finish your ale at least man, you have paid for it"

Francis indicates that he does not want it, he raises his hand, moving it gently side to side, saying 'No" without using words, he heads for the door, Dick calls after him,

"You sure you are well?"

Francis is gone, Dick takes the hardly touched ale and pours the contents back into the jug under the bar. It is nearly dark when Francis stumbles from the pub, any onlooker will presume he is drunk, he is not, he staggers away from the pub toward the footbridge over the river, stopping on the bridge, he leans over the rotting rail and empties the beer he has recently consumed, from his belly and into the river, even though his belly is now empty he continues to heave for a few minutes, uncontrollable fear fills his every being. He looks over at the forge, the building is quiet now, but he can see a light on, wiping his bearded mouth with the back of his hand, he spits into the river and makes his way over to the blacksmiths workshop, he puts a hand on the latch, hesitates for a second then opening the door, he steps inside, the smithy looks up, he is in his work clothes, a leather jerkin and thick hide apron protecting his clothes and body from the heat as he works,

"Hello Francis, haven't seen you for a while in here, you look bloody awful man, are you sick?"

"No George, just tired, not sleeping so good"

George is wiping his hands with a dirty cloth, "I have just shut up for the day, did you want something?

Francis shakes his head, gathering his thoughts and feeling a bit better, he speaks to the blacksmith. "Dick tells me you had a girl in your barn"

"I did, cheeky young bugger, found her last evening, asleep in the straw next to the pig sty"

"Who is she, do you know her?" the gravedigger asks abruptly.

"I don't Francis, never seen her before, she looked like a slum girl, all dirty, ripped clothes and skinny as my old dog" Francis takes of his hat and scratches his head, "Do you know who she is then Francis?"

"No" was the short reply, then after a few seconds thought, "I might, seen a girl like her around a few times earlier in the year up at the Alley, then at her Mothers parish burial...." He stops as he can hear his voice shaking, "Blue eyes so Dick says"

"Like I have never seen" replies George "Shining like beacons through the grime on her face, she stared straight at me and that's when I raised this iron rod at her" He points to a heavy and lengthy rod of iron leaning against the wall, "I took it with me when I heard noises, the pig was being noisy and had obviously been, disturbed and I thought it was a fox or some sod after my chickens again, when I raised it at her, I saw the fright in her eyes and she ran out, I wouldn't hurt her, but I didn't know it was a child when I went in"

"Where did she go?" Francis growls.

"Not an idea, I went to the straw and found where she had been kipping, a few apple cores lying about that I gave them to the pig so she had been eating my food as well"

"You not seen her since she ran?"

"No, why do you care anyways?'

Francis looks away from George, "I don't really, it might be the same girl that I saw, she is supposed to be in St Stephens"

"The workhouse? Is it still run by that misery of a man, John Haigh, and his fat wife?"

Francis nods,

"That's six miles on the road at least, how did she get here then?"

Shrugging his shoulders, Francis turns to leave, he stops and speaks, "How did you feel when you saw her George?"

Tilting his head to the side, George thinks for a second or two, "If the truth be known Francis, although she is a small and skinny girl, I was a bit frightened if you must know, I can't explain it but those eyes, staring at me, almost pleading"

"Pleading for what?"

"Don't know, don't get me wrong, I was angry with her for being in my barn, but I did feel sorry for her, skinny little mite, but I was uneasy, don't really know why"

The two men looked at each other, Francis opens the door, "See you around George"

He leaves, not waiting for a reply from the smithy who is still rubbing his hands on the grimy cloth.

The evening air is damp and chilly, pulling his coat around himself with his hands deep in his pockets he starts the short walk to the cottage, leaving the smithy turning left onto the road and walking past the river that is on his left side, he breathes in the familiar and unique smell from the almost silent flowing water. The open land around it so far this year has not flooded, on many previous occasions the land opposite the cottages next to the Gibraltar castle public house has been under water so deep that the footbridge cannot be seen, Francis' cottage has always escaped the floods, being just enough distance away from the main river to escape it, the stream will get swollen but his land, so far has escaped flood. Francis likes the comforting, damp evening smell coming from the river, he passes the pub and can see the entrance to his cottage ahead of him and in shadow, he can just make out thin trails of smoke coming from his chimney, he is happy with this as it means that the stove has stayed burning, he will have a warm kitchen and the fire in the stove will not take long to be fully burning again. Something moves by his gate.

The movement in the dark, fleetingly catches his eye, he is certain that he sees something agitating the blackness around him. Standing still, he looks around, there is no one else on the road, the Gibraltar Castle is away to his right, he can just see the lamps burning in the windows, to his left there are no other cottages until you get to Miss Banks-Smyth's cottage next to the public well, it is on the opposite side of the road to the watercress beds, then further down, out of sight even in daylight is Pickford Mill with its four old cottages around it, these are the last buildings, except for the Crown and Anchor, before the next buildings, the nursery workers cottages at Coldharbour, near to the site that the *Cist* was excavated on over 20 years ago, he is alone, but he did see movement, he wants to move forward but his legs will not move, the now familiar feeling of fear returning,

"Don't be a bloody fool" Speaking to himself, forcing forward momentum, he starts to walk toward his gate only a few yards away, he sees movement again, he is certain, his fear now overpowered by anger, "Come here!" he has lost sight of whatever or whoever it was, "When I get you, and I will, your life won't be worth living!"

He enters his garden by kicking the gate as hard as he can, if anyone is behind it he will cause them some injury, this is his intention, his irrational fear, a fear of being scared and not in control, has made him violently impassioned, standing in his garden, fists balled so tightly his fingers are hurting, he looks across his land, the stream running alongside his garden and to the cottage, dark and quiet, he listens for movement but all he can hear on this still night is the beating of his own heart pounding heavily in his chest.

“Must be a fox” he says, walking toward the wooden structure that houses his poultry and game birds, stepping over the fence that keeps them out of the vegetable garden and keeps foxes out, he closes the door, the birds all having made their own way in, they do this at twilight every day without having to be coaxed in.

He stands still and listens. Nothing. As still as the grave.

Stepping back over the fence he moves toward the water pump, picking up the bucket, placing it under the spout he pumps the wooden handle a few times until the clear life giving liquid from deep below the ground makes its entrance and fills the bucket, lifting this by the rope handle, Francis walks toward the cottage, he has convinced himself that it was a fox or some other night animal that he saw move.

What else could it have been?

Another night of fitful sleep, images in his dreams disturb him to the point it awakens him, he lies in the bed, covers pulled up to his chin and staring into the dark abyss of night, after the third, or is it the fourth time he jolts awake, he considers lighting a candle but decides against it, he does not want to close his eyes because if he does, he will see hers, blue, glistening and so alive, stuck in his thoughts and his dreams. He forces his eyes to stay open, blindly staring into the darkness until sleep takes him. Waking up sharply, he instantly knows something is wrong, something is different, but he cannot work out what it is, he quickly looks around the room firmly believing he will see the child, standing in front of him, hands outstretched, blue eyes piercing his soul, he is alone.

What is different? He cannot work it out, getting up he steps over the po, it is empty again, he has an urge to use the privy, putting his trousers on and pulling the braces up over his undershirt he walks to the kitchen, rubbing his tired eyes, the kitchen is as he left it last night, the stove is burning well, he was quite late in bed so it was well fed before he took his rest. Throwing a couple of small logs into the grate, he heads toward the back door, something makes him turn around abruptly, holding his breath as he does so. He is still alone.

It is not until he steps into the back yard that he realises what is different.

The yard and the short cinder path to the privy are on the western end of the cottage, are in shadow for almost of the early part of any day, sunlight only taking over in the late afternoon when the sun crests over its peak and onto this side of the cottage. The sun is high and can be clearly seen in the cloudless blue sky, he is confused, it must be nearly or past midday, but that cannot be so, he is always up even when not working before the cockerel crows. He uses the privy and walks back to the cottage, the sun radiant in his eyes. He has slept all morning, never having done this before, not in his memory anyway he is confused as to why his body, that has always risen early, had refused to do so this day? He is supposed to be working at Mackerye End Farm with David today, not being there will not cause any problems, David will presume that he is digging a grave somewhere in town or elsewhere. The rumbling in his belly tells him that he needs to eat, the stove is very hot and the biggin of coffee sitting atop it will be hot in a few minutes, leaving the kitchen and entering the living room, stopping briefly to tidy his bedclothes, he goes down into the root cellar to get food for his breakfast,

"More like lunch" no one hears him say this.

Selecting a piece of pork from the belly of the sow, thickly sliced with its tell-tale thin streaks of fat and luscious pink meat laying in alternate lines, the layer below the skin is thick and white, thinking for a few seconds, he takes a second piece from the waxed brown paper it is secured in, carefully re wrapping the remaining precious slices. Leaving the root cellar, he looks around the storeroom, taking a pheasant from its hanging place on the wall, he will pluck and prepare the bird for a stew that evening.

She has been hanging for a few days and will be ripe for cooking, she would be nesting about now if he had not have snared her in the fields between Mackerye End Farm and the common land that is free and open to the North side of his cottage.

Back in the kitchen, the smell of the frying belly pork disseminates its joyous odour throughout the small room, mixing with the smell from the mug of hot coffee in front of him, the half plucked hen pheasant lies on the table in front of him. Francis is staring straight ahead in a daydream, he snaps out of it when he hears the cracking and snapping sounds made by the very nearly fried strips of belly pork, he shakes his head and removes the pan from the top of the stove and putting it on a wood block at the end of the table, cutting two thick slices of bread and laying them in the pan with the pork, he sits down and eats the food straight from the pan.

After rinsing the pan with water from the bucket outside, Francis stands at his open front door looking out over his garden, the dusty road to his left and the clear calm stream to the right side, a constant flow across the bottom of the garden, moving onward meeting the river further upstream. A day at home and working the vegetable patch will not go amiss he thinks to himself, the plot needs tidying up, unwelcome weeds have begun to show, he also has beetroot seeds to plant, the potato shoots are bursting through the soil and need re-covering with soil to encourage further growth, the onions are doing well and need little maintenance, the last of the spring cabbage can be picked and the younger cabbage plants have taken and he is hopeful for a decent crop as he had over the last year. Parsnips, in the ground since March have strong shoots, they always take the longest to mature and it will be October at the earliest until they are ready to pick and eat, at least until they have had one frost on them, they survive well by staying in the ground, in fact Francis found a stray parsnip in the ground in February, it was a bit stringy but in a stew cooked slowly for a few hours it added a sweetness to the stock and meat. The two rows of carrots are growing well and will need to be thinned out, a job he hates, this being so difficult with his large rough fingers, but it must be done, looking from the doorway to his right, in an old trough filled with soil marrows are growing, the huge green leaves looking healthy and strong. Firstly, he must go and let the ducks, geese, and chickens out, they have been locked in for much longer than they are used to. Walking slowly from the cottage to the end of his land, he looks at the old Yew tree, with its wide and scarred trunk, strong and weather worn, the shadow cast from the canopy stretches across the garden and stream and will move across to the end of the house before being taken by the darkness when the sun goes down, the shadow covers the bottom end of the vegetable patch in the mornings, the sunshine breathes life into his vegetables for the large part of the day. As he opens the door to the poultry hut he is met with a gaggle of noise from the birds inside, they are venting angrily at him, they all let him know how unhappy they are, the geese are certainly the most vociferous, waddling around in large circles, raising their wings and honking loudly until they are quietened down by large handfuls of corn, grain and oats being scattered on the ground, the chickens join the geese in feeding from the ground, the ducks have all made their way into the slow flowing stream, happy to feed on weeds growing from the bank into the water, small fish and fish eggs will also be taken if they are available. Francis nods at the serene scene in front of him, a few hours in the garden will do him good, but the hen pheasant needs preparing and putting in the pot first, walking back toward the cottage he again gets a feeling that he is not alone, standing stock still he looks all around, he is alone, the gently moving breeze pushing the huge bows of the Yew as it catches the smaller branches and thin leaves, the movement of the bows is almost imperceptible. The only noise in the garden comes from the tree canopy, brought to life by the breeze coming across its highest branches, without deviation or obstruction across the open fields and common land, he goes back into the cottage closing the door and putting the latch in place, this portal would usually be open on a calm sunny day as it is today, Francis wants to be sure he is alone, he wants to be sure that no one is watching him, something is making him wary, after decades of digging graves and burying the dead without fear or superstition he has a nasty feeling of insecurity in his own garden, he has no control over it, he feels safer with the door closed and safely latched. The hen bird is still on the table, some feathers plucked earlier move slowly across the table in the moving air as he passes by, before he starts again he visits the root cellar and fills a large mug with ale from the firkin, he takes a large draw, feeling the slightly sour and bitter liquid move effortlessly down his throat, chilled from being in the cellar, it settles his nerves somewhat, filling the mug back up to its brim he returns to the kitchen and to the task at hand, drinking ale during the day is not usual for him, today does not feel like a usual day.

Taking the pheasant in his hands he continues to pluck out the feathers just as his Mother taught him when he was a child, a quick snap of the wrist to yank out a feather or three, just pulling at the feathers does not work as well, pulling the skin of the bird tight with his left hand and plucking with his right, leaving feathers on the upper neck and wings, no point in removing them, these inedible body parts, along with the feet, will be fed to the pig. Taking a recently sharpened knife, the wings are removed skilfully and quickly, the remaining smaller softer feathers on the thighs are removed, any left will be burnt off over the naked flames from the stove fire, looking across at the stove then standing up, he puts two small logs on to the glowing coals, he needs flames to burn off the feathers and he does not want to light a fire in the hearth to do this. The bird is held firmly in a solid left handed grip on the table, breast side down, Francis makes a cut through the skin, bone and gristly of the neck, separating and then discarding the head, he then makes a cut down the length of the neck, pulling the skin open exposing the neck, this he cuts off close to the body, being delicate and careful so as not to put the point of his knife through the crop, he removes this delicate sack of undigested corn without disruption, he throws it with the wings and decapitated head. Turning the bird over onto its back, both feet pointing upward, a shallow cut is made around both knee joints, separating the skin from the bone and meat, bringing the legs one by one to the end of the table, he uses this edge to bend the feet in his strong hand, twisting and pulling at the same time to pull the small but strong tendons from the legs. Moving the bird around, the vent facing him, the knife is inserted, and a downward cut is made to extend this opening, the knife removed and placed on the table, he uses a two fingered '*draw*', the fore and middle fingers inserted deeply inside the bird, almost to the neck end, feeling for the backbone, he runs his fingers left and right, this releases the entrails from where they sit and he pulls them clear from the inside of the bird, a messy procedure but it needs to be done. Using the tip of the knife, he gently sorts through the insides of the pheasant, separating the gizzard, the succulent liver, heart and kidneys from the entrails, the inedible parts join the other waste meat are destined for the pig sty. He makes a small incision in the gizzard, then cleans out any ground grain remaining inside, the thin translucent membrane from the inside of the gizzard is removed then discarded, what is left is put with the other offal, ready for the pot.

Taking the poker from the side of the fireplace, putting it inside the bird, he uses this makeshift skewer to get to the flames from the burning logs on the stove, then burning off any stubborn or small feathers left on the skin, this takes him less than two or three minutes, the bird is nearly ready for the pot, one remaining task, to quarter the bird, cutting firstly across the spine and then length ways, giving him four good sized portions of pheasant. He takes the cooking pot outside to half fill it with water from the bucket by the door, he looks around his garden, the road and across the stream, he is still alone, going back inside he puts the pot of water onto the top of the stove, a small shovel of coal is added onto the logs, these will provide the precious heat needed to slowly warm then boil the water and its contents. The four quarters of pheasant are placed in the pot, the offal added on top of them, leaving the kitchen and returning quickly from the storeroom with two apples, the same number of onions, three potatoes and a winter cabbage, he sits at the table, cutting the onions in quarters, removing the dried outer skins, not wasting them, the apples get the same treatment, these skins join the discarded meat. Potatoes, not peeled, are cut in half, the cabbage only having the base cut off, the leaves left whole, everything now prepared, apart from one quartered apple, he places four pieces on the table to eat, the rest are added to the pot with the pheasant, the large and heavy cast iron lid put on top, enclosing the stew in darkness to be gently cooked for a few hours.

Picking up the nearly empty mug of ale, he finishes it with one swallow, licking his lips when he is done.

Stepping out into the afternoon sun is a joy, Francis stands with his face pointing up toward the hot glowing ball in the sky, really enjoying the feeling of the late spring heat on his face, then a shiver, cold as the clear stream water in Winter, runs down his spine, goose bumps cover his body despite the heat drenching him from above, opening his eyes he looks fleetingly in all directions, he is being watched, he knows it. He moves to the side of the open door, he grabs a wooden mallet from where he had left in on the ground after its last use, holding the weapon above his head, he purposely walks to the side of the house by the road, no one is there, watching carefully he walks to the back of the house past the cart, now redundant with only a few old sacks in its cargo area, walks slowly toward the privy, he can see no one, the privy door is opened and then reclosed with the makeshift latch secured, he is alone, lowering the mallet he mutters,

"Don't know what is going on with me"

Taking the cinder path back toward the back yard past the pig sty, he remembers that he must put the offcuts from the pheasant, the onion and apple skins in for her to eat, he glances to the far side of the cottage, the stream passes only a few feet from the far end wall, no one can get to there without making a noise or getting wet in the stream, he enters the cottage through the back door, leaving the mallet in the back yard by the door. The feeling of unease has subsided, his anger has not, picking up the offcuts, leaving again by the back door, latching it shut behind him, then feeding the pig the offcuts, the porcine beast is eager to eat and almost lifts its front trotters of the ground in a macabre dance for the raw meat and vegetables. Walking around the side of the house again, still feeling as though he is being watched although alone, insecurity follows him for the first time ever, Francis steps on to the vegetable patch, gets onto his knees he begins to weed the area around the bright green fresh shoots from the carrots growing below the earth, when the parsnips are also weed free and the many rows of potatoes, planted at two weekly intervals so as to have fresh available throughout the remainder of the year after first harvest, have been piled with earth covering the new green shoots from the buried seed potatoes, this will be repeated several times over the coming months to ensure a healthy and abounding crop. Kneeling up, he stretches his back, stiff from being bent over for a couple of hours, his undershirt is sticking to his skin, sweat on his back from the warm sun and toil he has completed today so far, adjusting his braces to a different position on his shoulders he stands, he needs a small trowel to dig a shallow trench, about an inch deep to sow the beetroot, the tool he needs is in the store room of the cottage, he steps inside and although the stove is lit, it is cooler in the kitchen than outside, taking a wooden spoon, he lifts the lid off of the pot using the spoon handle, placing the lid on top of the stove with a dull thud, he stirs the stew, it is bubbling gently and the cabbage has all but disappeared, mixing with the water to make a broth that will continue to cook the potatoes, onions and succulent pheasant, putting the lid back on the pot, leaving the wooden spoon on the table, he walks through to the living room, cooler again than the kitchen, as he moves past his bed to make his way to the storage room, he looks out of the living room window.

Standing at the bottom of the garden, in front of the poultry pen, is the girl, Tillie.

Francis stands and stares back, he can see her and hopes that she cannot see him through the grimy window, she stands motionless, staring back at him locking her sun glistening blue eyes with his. He explodes. Running from the living room, through the kitchen, grabbing a large knife as he does so, throws open the front door, it slams against the wall of the cottage, he jumps when he hears the loud noise, running out into his garden, knife held in front of him,

"You leave me be girl, you leave me be or I will gut you like a…."

His words die off as he looks at the end of the garden, the stream is moving slowly, unchanged, the poultry are pecking, swimming, and strutting, the girl is gone. Standing by the vegetable patch, he slowly moves toward the poultry pen, he realises that he hasn't taken a breath since leaving the house a few minutes ago, standing in the silence, standing still, looking around him with heavy concentration, he breaks the stillness "Where are you!" he yells.

Hearing a slamming door behind him, he turns, eyes wide with fear, knife held tightly in his right hand, pointing it to where the noise has come from, the front door is closed, there is no wind to have caught the door and slammed it shut. His confused mind tells him that it could have rebounded shut after he threw it open,

"That must be it" he thinks aloud, his breathing is heavy and fast, his chest feels tight and the muscles in his left arm hurt, "Calm down Francis" speaking aloud to no one, "The door bounced back from the wall and shut itself"

Breathless and sweating, he stands and listens, hearing only silence and the gentle movement of the Yew branches behind him, his chest is not as tight now, the pain in his arm has gone, breathing heavily he begins to calm but remains standing still, his knife held in front of him. In the continued stillness he hears a distant sound, a metal latch opening, looking at the front door, it is still shut,

"She is round the back!" He roars

Fury rises in his throat, he can taste bile, sour and bitter, he charges at the front door, pulling it open, again banging it against the wall, he enters the kitchen, stillness invades every inch of his space, the back door is closed, sweat forms on his brow and runs into his eyes, he lets it do so without wiping it away, everything is as it was, lowering the knife he mumbles,

"You are hearing things now you damn fool"

Something has changed, something is different. He puts the knife gently on the table, making hardly a sound. Then he notices the difference in the room.

The four quarters of apple are now only two, he is certain he hasn't eaten any, someone has been in here and taken them, perhaps he did hear the back door latch open, slowly, and quietly picking up the knife from its place on the table, he lifts the latch on the back door, opening the door a few inches, he peers out, expecting to be so scared that he will jump out of his skin, he is prepared to grab the girl and show her the knife. He feels the tension in his chest build up again, he looks out, he sees the mallet lying in the middle of the yard, as if it has been disturbed from its original resting place by the back door, he opens the door a few more inches putting his head outside on offer to whatever or whoever may be out there, his body remains inside the safety of the kitchen.

Nothing moves, now holding his breath he steps out into the yard. Nothing moves.

He can hear the pig, snuffling its snout in the ground in a hunt for any morsels she may have left behind, still nothing moves. Taking tentative steps forward he reaches the open yard gate; did he close it earlier? He cannot remember if he opened or closed it during the earlier fruitless search of his garden, moving toward the privy, nothing moves, the crunching of his boots on the cinder as loud as any noise he can recall, nothing moves, his heart beating so hard and so fast it is causing him pain, groaning to himself as he exhales, probably the first time he has breathed in or out since leaving the house, he looks over the fence at this end of his curtilage, nothing but open fields of immature wheat in the middle of its growth cycle, small nodules are forming on the green heads of the plants waiting to be magically turned golden yellow in the sun, this will happen by late July, then it will be ready to be harvested, the strip of woodland with its just flowering carpet of bluebells is shady and calm, nothing moves. Dazed, confused, and trying to relax to get the pain in his chest to leave him, he lets his painful arm drop limply to his side, the knife in the other hand is held in a relaxed grip, breathing deeply he still has the pain in his chest, but it is lessening, closing his eyes he stands by the privy with its serene colourful canvas behind it. His eyes open wide, and he is alert, knife raised when he hears his name being called,

"Francis"

He steps slowly forward, his undershirt stuck to his chest and back from his excessive sweating, caused by pain and fear,

"Francis!"

At the edge of the cottage by the end wall, he peers around, slowly, and deliberately,

"Francis, where the bloody hell are you man?"

He steps out into the sunlight, dazzled for a second as his eyes adjust from the shadow of the cottage into the daylight, putting his free hand over his eyes to see who is calling his name,

"Francis!"

The person calling him moves forward, "Francis, there you are, I have been calling you"

It is William, he continues, "Who are you going to gut with that knife?"

Francis looks down and realises he is holding the knife in a threatening manner in front of him, pointing it at William. He lowers it, unconsciously transferring it from his right to left hand,

"William, what are you doing here?" He continues before William can answer, "I was by the sty cutting up a pheasant carcass for the sow"

William nods," You look dreadful"

"I have been working on the vegetable garden all afternoon, must be the heat"

Both men look at each other,

"I went to Holmes's farm looking for you, he says you didn't turn in today he thought you might have a burying to do, did you?"

"No" Francis gives a short reply

"Why you not working then?" questions William,

Francis hesitates, "I got up late, really late as it happens"

William starts to laugh, "The grave digger is human after all! That must be a first for you!" Francis, feeling better to have friendly company, manages a smile, William asks, "You hurt your arm?"

Francis realises he is rubbing his left arm with his right hand, the soreness in his chest and arm have nearly gone now,

"Just stiff from gardening"

"Well, you got a digging tomorrow, in Wheathampstead" Without replying, Francis waits for William to continue, "Annabel Driver died last week, she has been laid out for five or so days, no coffin yet the local chippy is too busy, I have only found out today that they want one, she is beginning to stink apparently"

"Who told you?"

"The Wheathampstead village constable George Knight, came to my barn requesting I take a coffin over tomorrow for the funeral, he was coming to see you, but I told him I would see you on my way home"

"Is it an afternoon funeral?"

Shaking his head, William says,

"Morning burial, so an early start for you, best you don't sleep in"

"You coming with me on this one?"

Shaking his head again, "Finishing a cabinet for the Lugg family up on the common, they pay well so I want to get it done, why, you don't usually ask me to go"

Grunting, Francis replies, "I don't need you, I was just asking, come around in the morning we can hitch the horse, go to your barn and get the coffin and I will go on from there"

William takes his leave, "Don't you sleep in grave digger!" a parting shot from the smiling carpenter.

Francis is alone again, his breathing and chest pain have gone, he puts it down to the girl, it is all her fault. The sun is dropping rapidly behind the cottage, he goes back into the kitchen, shuts the door firmly behind himself, has a quick look out of the kitchen window, all is as it should be.

He slumps himself into the chair by the table, looking down, the last two quarters of the apple are gone.

* * *

The journey from William's barn on the outskirts of town to St Helens Church in Wheathampstead takes over an hour in a horse and cart as it is just over seven miles. The cart is laden with an empty coffin, the tools of his trade, empty sacks and a brown paper wrap containing bread and dripping for his lunch, he will have this after the burial is finished, the rector of the church, Reverend Thomas Pretyman is a decent sort, Francis has known him since he was first apprenticed to the old grave digger. Rev Pretyman has been Rector at St Helens since 1814, had always been on good terms with Francis' old boss, John the Spade, so a cup of hot tea is always ready for him at the Rectory, a large house on the southwest edge of the graveyard, when the dig is done, and he is waiting for the funeral to finish so he can fill in the grave. Rev Pretyman is also the rector for St Nicholas church in town, but he rarely goes there and hasn't done for several years, were it not for the continued efforts of the sexton Mr George Hawkins, St Nicholas church and its churchyard would be in rack and ruin, so much more than it is already, Pretyman is happy to leave the local curate Henry Addington to take all services in town.

The sun is barely breaking the Eastern horizon as he enters Wheathampstead, he hears the church clock strike five times as the cart heads onto what is called locally, Brewhouse Hill, a steep downward incline to the village, it has the Hope brewery at the bottom of it, owned by a local wealthy family, the Lattimores. He has travelled from town along the Wheathampstead road, through the Bowling Alley, past the deserted gravel pits, it is still too early for the pit workers to be up and about, past Dale Pipers farm and through Down Green to the top of Brewhouse Hill, urging the horse to move on down toward the church, he has seen no one on his early morning trip. St Helens is one of four Parish churches he digs graves for not including his primary role for the parish at St Nicholas in town, up until five years ago St Helens church was controlled by the diocese of Lincoln, a seemingly odd choice as it is so far from the village, it is now under the control and instruction of the diocese of St Albans. The other charges he has are, the church of St Peter and St Paul in Kimpton, only four miles from his cottage, he is not keen on travelling there as the country lanes to get there are notoriously narrow and not maintained at all, the journey can take over an hour and is uncomfortable the whole way, he is thankful that the village has a very small community, and he is not usually called on to dig graves there more than once a month. The small 15th century church has a thin steeply sloping roof with a square tower with a tall spire, they seem small in comparison to the large churchyard, stacked burials have never happened there so all the graves have to be dug to at least six feet, another reason Francis is not fond of working there. The church of St Leonards in Sandridge is another responsibility he has, with its smaller church and a much smaller and enclosed churchyard, the 12th century church with its square tower, this tower only being added and built only 15 years ago, faces the track road from Wheathampstead to St Albans, he likes working there although he only attends when the digger from St Albans cannot or will not attend to the duty of burials, the extra shilling he gets for his trouble is always worth the journey. St Marys church in Redbourn is yet another 12th century building with a steep sloping roof and square tower, although the closest of his outside visits the churchyard is small and requests for burials here don't occur very often many of the dead from Redbourn are buried in the busy graveyard of St Nicholas.

Francis slows the horse to a halt at the bottom of the hill by gently pulling back on the reins, the church and churchyard are on his left, the good sized graveyard is dominated in the middle by the church, a large 13th century cruciform construction with a square Norman built central tower, both the church and its grounds appear still and lifeless, he is as he likes to be, alone. The Rev Pretyman will be in the church early this morning but not this early, Francis grabs his tools, leaving his lunch on top of the sacks in the back of the cart, he walks through the wooden gate into the churchyard, opening the iron studded wooden door of the church by turning the large metal latch, the hinges squeal in resistance to being opened, the sound pierces the silence surrounding him. Opening the old and heavy wooden door he enters the church, as with other religious buildings it is always in a permanent twilight, not dark but not filled with light, he is looking for the grave register, this is where Rev Pretyman will have entered the details of where the burial will take place, although he cannot read or write hardly at all he knows the plot placements and from memory knows where each one is. This one will be a full depth dig as this churchyard has more than enough room to cater for the dead of the village without them having to be stacked as they are in town. Having the information he needs, he takes his leave from the church being sure to close the heavy door behind him he slowly makes his way to the burial site, the dig will be just off the south path at the end of the graveyard, as he is walking away, he hears the latch on the church door open and the atrocious sound of the squealing hinges following quickly after the latch is released,

"The Reverend is early today" he says aloud knowing that no one, especially the dead, will not hear him.

Finding the plot and taking off his outer jacket he begins to dig, it is chilly this early in the morning, he will soon be warm as the dig progresses. The grass and topsoil are removed swiftly, exactly the shape and size required for the coffin to easily fit, it is then he remembers the coffin on the cart, the village smithy, Fred Westwood will be collecting the body of Mrs Anabel Driver, twenty six years old, Mother of five young children and Wife to Alfred, who drives the dray for the brewery, the small cottage she lies in is at the top of the steep hill that leads out of the village toward Sandridge. Francis pushes his spade into the soft soil, leaving his coat he makes his way back toward the chapel to speak to the Reverend, to let him know that the coffin is still on the cart outside the churchyard.

The church is silent as he enters, "Reverend Pretyman" No response, "Thomas, are you here?"

Nothing.

Francis walks down the knave to the front of the church, stopping to look at the altar, feeling nothing, he looks around, the Rector is not in the church, scratching his head he leaves the building to return to the task in hand, the Reverend or Fred will find him when they need the box to put the deceased into. As Francis nears the grave, he sees that Reverend Pretyman is hurrying toward him from the direction of the rectory, his knee length black cassock unbuttoned, the black waistcoat under it is buttoned to the top, a crisp white cravat is tied around his neck, he is carrying his Canterbury cap,

"Good morning to you Francis, I am unusually late this morning, have you seen Fred yet?"

"Not seen him yet Reverend, did I hear you in the church a few minutes ago?"

Reverend Pretyman stops and stares at Francis, "No Francis, I have only just left the rectory, as I said, running late, are there worshippers here already?" He pulls a silver fob watch from his waistcoat pocket, the long chain from the watch to his waistcoat runs across his belly, "No, too early for anyone as yet" the Reverend says aloud,

"I haven't seen anyone, but I thought I heard the church door open; I went to see if it was you, but the church was empty"

A voice carries across the churchyard, "Morning Reverend, are we ready" Fred Westwood appears in view, walking into the graveyard from his smithy at the bottom of Brewhouse Hill, he sees the grave digger standing with the reverend, "Morning Francis, you well?"

"I am Fred, got to get this dug for today, the coffin is in my cart, use the horse and cart if you need, save you hitching yours up"

Fred replies, "I will, thank you Francis, I saw it just outside, in fact I chased a child away from the back of the cart just a few moments ago"

The reverend raises his eyes toward heaven, "These children will come to harm, being out so early, I must speak to Mr Bamford about his lack of parental control"

"Not sure this was one of Bev's children" says Fred, "This 'un seems not to be as wayward as that Bamford gaggle, I didn't recognise her, she is a dirty urchin though, with the most beautiful blue eyes I have ever seen"

Francis nearly falls over, his head spins immediately, his throat suddenly dry and stabbing pain rising in his chest and into his jaw, Rev Pretyman notices the abrupt change in the grave digger,

"Francis, are you sickening?"

Gathering his thoughts, trying to control the crushing feeling in his chest, he shakes his head,

"No, I am alright, just need a bite to eat, I haven't broken fast as yet"

"You look ghastly man, when you have finished go on up to the rectory, Miss Bunnage will have tea made for you"

Fred and the rector leave Francis taking deep breaths and leaning on his spade, his head has cleared and the pain in his chest is subsiding, taking a deep breath, looking carefully around him and not seeing anyone, he knows he is looking for and not seeing Tillie, He carries on digging, controlling his anger and fear by digging hard and fast, the grave is dug to nearly 6 feet in under five hours, quick work even for him, he leans his tools against the trunk of the churchyard Yew that will forever cover the resting place of Anabel Driver, this tree is not as old as the one in his garden but is still a good size.

The church clock chimes eleven times, the funeral is already underway, the family had arrived earlier, and all had followed the coffin into the church when ten chimes from the bells were clearly heard, the church service would soon be over, he puts his tools behind a tree that stands a few yards from the freshly dug grave, putting his jacket over his shoulder he walks to the rectory.

Ten minutes later he is stood in front of the rectory, a mug of tea with a slice of Miss Bunnages superb fruit cake in his hands, the hot drink and sweet cake have made him feel better, the weather is lovely, the late spring sun warming and welcomed by everyone. He can see that the graveside service is ongoing, Rev Pretyman is known for lengthy God fearing services, he is watching as Miss Bunnage calls him from the side door, finishing his tea and cake he walks over, handing the empty vessel to her,

"Miss Bunnage, your fruit cake is so nice, thank you"

Miss Bunnage becomes embarrassed and flustered, straightening her crisp white linen pinney with her free hand,

"Thank you, Francis, shall I cut you a slice for your journey home?" she hands him three shillings,

"With thanks from the Reverend Pretyman for your work today"

"I haven't finished yet; I can collect this later"

"Take the money Francis, I am sure you won't leave without your cake, will you?"

He giggles, something he rarely does, "I will call back when I am done" he assures her.

Miss Bunnage goes back into the kitchen closing the door behind her, Francis turns and takes a slow walk to the front of the rectory down the short driveway to the rectory gates, the grave service seems to be coming to an end, he leans on one of the square red brick gate posts, looking across the graveyard. His breath leaves him suddenly, eyes wide open the pain returning to his left arm and chest, he cannot move. Tillie is in the graveyard, watching the burial, he has seen her but as yet she has not seen him. He does not move, fear helping him to ignore the pain growing in his chest, he sees her slowly turn toward him,

"Do not look over here child" he whispers to himself.

Her eyes meet his, blue as clear summer pools, she will not break eye contact, he stares back at her terrified that she will walk toward him he stumbles backward, tripping over on drive and falling to the ground, lying on the ground clutching his left arm as the pain radiates from his chest into his arm, head spinning the immediate world around him becomes unclear, fuzzy, then black, he is alone.

* * *

"Francis! Francis!"

He feels a gentle hand on his shoulder shaking him, opening his eyes he sees Reverend Pretyman and Fred standing over him, Fred speaks,

"What the hell" looking at the Reverend apologetically, he continues, "What happened there Francis"

He is helped to his feet by the two men, he shakes his head to clear it, the pain in his arm and chest has almost gone, his chest feels tight but more relaxed than it has been today,

"I am fine thanks, I dug the hole quickly today, must have over done it, just a faint from the heat, that's all"

Reverend Pretyman raises his eyes to heaven again, putting his hands together he says a silent prayer of thanks to his God. Francis makes his excuses to leave, he has to fill in the grave, walking away he cannot get the face of the blue eyed girl from his mind, he is shaking, his hands trembling uncontrollably,

"Come on Francis" he says, "Get a proper grip of yourself man"

After retrieving his tools, he fills the grave, taking his time, he has convinced himself that his 'funny turn' was caused by his overly energetic and frantic digging earlier. Stamping the edges of the grave down, he puts his coat on, picks up his tools and walks to the horse and cart on the road outside, he is pleased to see that Fred has put a bucket of water out for the horse, looking across at the smithy he sees Fred at the forge, hammering a rod of iron flat at one end, lifting the glowing white tip away from the anvil, placing it in directly into a bucket of water in front of him, steam rises immediately and a loud hissing is heard as cold water meets hot metal, he looks up and sees Francis.

"Got your bucket here Fred, thanks for looking after William's horse"

"The thanks are mine for the use, saved me time not having to hitch mine up and get the cart out"

Handing the bucket over, the men bid each other farewell, Francis climbs onto the cart and with a gentle tug on the reins, he gets the horse to turn about and face toward the village High street, very small and compact in comparison to his town's main street, the horse moves forward, and Francis sees the rectory, remembering he has cake to collect from Miss Bunnage, he pulls the cart over to the side of the road, pats the horse on its strong flank,

"Won't be a minute now" He walks to the side of the building and knocks on the door, he is surprised when the reverend opens to door to him, "Reverend?"

Seeing the confusion on the face of the grave digger, he replies, "Miss Bunnage is busy washing clothes Francis" Nodding in reply but saying nothing, the priest continues, "Was there something you needed?"

"No, not really, it's just that Miss Bunnage told me to come to the kitchen when I was done to collect a bit of cake for my journey home"

A smile appears on the face of the reverend, "Of course, the famous fruit cake, I won't be a moment Francis, I will go and ask her where it is, do excuse me"

He closes the door, Francis wants to move away, to turn around, but something, a feeling he has will not let him, is he being watched again. Turning quickly and violently to face the gates, with insults and abuse forming in his throat, he prepares himself to challenge this troublesome child, but they die away when he sees that no one is there, the gates are open and he can see into the graveyard, it is serene and quiet, the High street on the far side of the church is busy with its usual daily hustle and bustle, everything is normal, everything except his feeling of anxiety.

"Francis"

The voice of Reverend Pretyman takes Francis' attention away from the graveyard and from thoughts of the child, in his hand is a parcel of brown wax paper, he is glad to see it is quite a large parcel, he walks over and gladly accepts the package,

"My thanks to Miss Bunnage" He pauses, "Thomas, can I ask you a question"

Telling him that he of course could ask whatever he wanted, Francis speaks,

"I saw some child in your graveyard, could have been the same girl that Fred saw by the horse and cart earlier, he didn't know her, do you think you might"

Thinking for a while, in Francis opinion it was too long a pause and done for effect, the reply is given,

"I did not see the child Francis so I cannot give a truthful response, what I can say is that since the Poor laws were changed in 1834, meaning that our parish poor house had to close just two years later, no family here wants to go to the Union house in town so we have a lot of very poor families in the village like the Bamfords that Fred mentioned, most are ill-educated, a trait they share with their parents sadly, they hang around the church hoping for a penny or a morsel of food, I am a poor priest, I cannot offer either to them, they are here all times of the night and day, they are a pest, especially at weddings and funerals, but I didn't see any of them today" Francis is silent, "Why do you ask Francis?"

"I might have seen a child at the Union workhouse last time I was there, it's a distance from there to here, but it might be her"

"Do you want to help the child?"

He indignantly answers quickly,

"No!"

Taking his leave, he encourages the horse to move on, leaving the smithy and the Swan inn behind him, past the large red brick house built in the last century and still owned by the Peacock family, the brewers in his town, Bill Rudd the landlord of the Two brewers is stood outside his hostelry, having just opened, he raises a hand toward Francis,

"Afternoon Grave digger!"

"Good day landlord!" he responds, the two men have been known to each other for many years,

"Time for a glass Francis?"

"Not today Bill, need to get on"

Raising his hand indicating a goodbye, he moves on. Toward the corn mill on the River Lea, the Bull Inn on his right, behind this pub is the 16th century archway, repaired recently by the looks of the red bricks that form the arch itself, this leads to Wheathampstead Place, a large house formerly owned by Queen Victoria's first Prime minister, William Lamb, a man titled Lord Melbourne, he left the house to live at Brocket Hall in nearby Hatfield where he died in 1848, leaving Brocket Hall to his Sister, Emily. Recently widowed this lady was in a relationship with the current Foreign secretary, Henry John Temple or Lord Palmerston as his title is, he also lived in Wheathampstead Place, as did Emily, or Lady Melbourne as she became when she married Henry, they left Wheathampstead Place in 1845 to live in Brocket Hall with Lord Melbourne, selling the large house in the village to a local landowner, Hugh Highby Lattimore, who moved from the nearby, and crumbling, Bride Hall to currently be in residence at the house. Francis had heard the stories about Wheathampstead Hall many times from Bill Rudd, he loved to tell tales of the sordid rumours about Lord Melbourne and his relationship with a married woman named Caroline Norton, also the tales of Lord Palmerston, rumours that he had tried to force himself onto a servant of the Queen, a young lady named Susan Brand during a visit to Windsor Castle a decade earlier, also that the Foreign secretary regularly enjoyed lurid parties with aristocratic ladies. Francis had no interest in stories and rumour, keeping himself to himself was all he wanted to do. Slowly passing Jessamine Cottage on his left, this is the police house and gaol for the village and the home of George Knight the village constable, then carrying on past the mill and leaving the village, up to the crossroads. Easing the horse to the left, the road to the Folly is taken, there are a few other users of the road, some on foot, some on horseback and others in carts of varying sizes and shapes, the Folly is soon left behind him, then on through Cherrytrees, past Caswell Farm and the upper watercress beds and down the short hill toward the mill and smithy, now so close to home. The feeling of unease has not left him, the pain has gone and he is glad of it, sudden and severe pain is not something he has had experience of in his life, this pain is worse than the toothache he had some years ago, Bert the smithy had pulled it out of his mouth with a large pair of snips, that had been painful and had bled like a stuck pig, but this chest pain has no blood, no signs and no reason behind it, he is fearful of the pain returning, he is more fearful that Tillie will return to his dreams and scared she will show up again somewhere.

Pulling up outside of his cottage, he spies William sitting at the front of the house, he waves at Francis, who returns the compliment,

"You been waiting long?" asks Francis

"Hours and hours" William lies, "Can I use the cart to deliver the cabinet I have just finished?"

"Of course, I need to water the horse in the stream before you go, Francis guides the horse and cart into the cool water and the horse drinks thirstily,

"I will get the cart back tomorrow if that's alright with you Francis?"

"That's fine, I am hoping to work at Mackerye Farm tomorrow, as far as I know I don't have any digging to do for the Church"

The horse is quenched, walking from the stream leaving a trail of dripping water behind it, William is now standing by the gate, Francis leans over and takes his tools from the back of the cart, the brown paper wrapped bread and dripping is nowhere to be found, he knows he hasn't eaten it because he had Miss Bunnages cake instead, the other parcel of cake is safely tucked away in his large coat pocket, the bread and dripping must have fallen out somewhere. William looks over,

"Leave those sacks will you Francis, they will be just what I need to cover the cabinet" Francis agrees and jumps down, William gets on board, "See you tomorrow then Francis"

Francis nods without reply, watching as the carpenter makes his way toward Stakers Lane to go back toward town, as he watches the cart move away, he is certain that he sees the sacks in the back of the cart move, not a subtle movement but a heavy and very real agitation, looking again he sees stillness only in the back of his cart, the sacks are as they should be. The cart follows the road as it curves away and out of his sight, he is sure he saw something move in the back of his cart. He immediately thinks of Tillie, this makes him look around from where he stands, he is alone, hurriedly he goes into the cottage the feeling he dislikes again begins rising in his chest.

Could the girl have hidden away in his cart? He hopes not.

Checking the door is latched securely he tends to the fire on the stove.

* * *

Spring had ended with a deluge of rain; late May sun replaced with storms of such ferocity that many said that they could not remember having such bad weather at this time of year in living memory. The river burst its banks ten days ago causing the watercress beds to be completely swamped under fast flowing water that unchallenged and easily across it, the flood is also covering farmland and fields from the stream across to Stakers lane, its forward momentum only being stopped by the gently incline at the bottom of Stakers Lane that leads toward the steeper climb toward town, the ford by the mill is impassable, the footbridge is usable if you don't mind getting wet feet, the river now being several inches above the aged wooden foot boards, the Marquis of Granby has avoided flood by only a few feet, it is still open but getting to it from the mill side of the river was difficult and impossible to do and remaining dry.

His cottage and the usually dusty road has escaped the flood from the river, both are turgid due to the amount of rain that has fallen but not badly flooded, the stream at the bottom of the garden, usually a slow moving, shallow and peaceful stretch of water, is now knee deep with fast flowing water, his ducks and geese are at home in the flooded area of garden by the stream and have made no attempt to move away from their home. Francis had to move the chickens when the water started to rise three weeks ago, putting them in with the ever fattening sow in the sty, several of his chickens are missing, presumed to have been washed away in the flood waters or taken by foxes when the storms first started. His vegetable patch although not flooded by the rising stream water, is soaking wet and Francis fears that his potatoes may be so wet underground that they will rot before maturing and being big enough to pick, the carrots and parsnips, being at the top end of the plot, although in wet ground seem to have escaped the worst of the weather and the sodden earth, his onions may need to be picked, although to do so will be at least two months earlier than he intended, some of the green shoots above ground are turning yellow, a clear sign that they are getting too much water, when the ground begins to dry he will have to check how large the bulbs are by gently pushing a finger into the ground and feeling, they will be small but he is hoping that they will be large enough to pick if he has to, only time will tell over the next week or two if it remains dry enough. He hopes the onions can be left to carry on growing, if the surviving green shoots continue to flourish then he may be lucky, if they all turn yellow and dry, then picking them, regardless of size, will be the only way to save them. Today is dry and sunny, Francis, for the first time in weeks has slept without being woken by the noise of the rain, either banging on the windows in a seeming attempt to get into the cottage and hitting the thatch so hard he feared it would begin to leak through, neither had happened. He managed to sleep last night without the fearful images of Tillie haunting him, waking in the night with sodden bed linen through his excessive sweating has become a regular disturbance for him, last night was a joy, without having the fear that creeps up on him in his dreams that cause the ever increasing pains in his chest, some nights it feels like another person is sitting on his chest, nothing he does lessens the discomfort. Last night he slept without being disturbed by weather, persistent repetitive dreams, pain, or fear.

A breakfast of fresh coffee, thick bacon slices with two fried eggs has given Francis a more positive outlook on his day, he has been busy for several weeks digging graves, mainly in town but he has had to travel to other churches on half a dozen occasions, even in the recent wet weather he has been out on an almost daily basis. The Bowling alley had a late spring dose of scarlet fever with children becoming ill after getting the deadly red rash on their bodies, all with tongues resembling a swollen red strawberry, this illness quickly spread through the slum, several children had died in a few short days, three from one house were all under five years of age and all passed in a single day, their Mother found them deceased in the morning, all three having died silently overnight, they had been collected by Francis and William. They were, at the insistence of their mother, to be buried that same day, the priest denied her this wish stating all deaths had to be registered prior to a Christian burial, the old system of Parochial registration having been removed by the introduction of the General Registry office in 1837, St Albans was the nearest office, and it takes several days to complete this task. The local constable would be tasked to carry this out as it was deemed that the grieving Mother could not or would not get it done, so the three little corpses had remained in her tiny slum house in tiny coffins provided by William. When William and Francis returned several days later to collect the bodies for the parish funeral the front door was open, they let themselves in, the door leading directly into the small living room, the three open coffins nearly filling the whole space, both men covered their mouths with their hands, the smell of decaying flesh is overwhelming in such a small space, even Francis struggles for a second or two with the deeply pungent smell, he recovers quickly, taking his hand away from his mouth, he indicates that William should look in the back room, he can already see that the Mother of the dead children, known only as 'London Lilly', lies dead on the muddy stone floor of the tiny back room. She is lying on her back, which is slightly arched, a puddle of deep brown coloured urine lies on the floor around the corpse, her face is contorted in a permanent grin, eyes are bright red and bloodshot, both men recognise the obvious signs of strychnine poisoning. Not a quick way to take your own life, after ingestion there is no known antidote, the body starts with twitching spasms of the head and neck, as these move onto the body, they become larger and uncontrollable, breathing will become deep and laboured, feelings of nausea and confusion take over and the body eventually dies from asphyxiation after two or three long and painful hours. They take the body, after wrapping it in a filthy blanket taken from the small back room to the churchyard and bury her at the bottom of her children's grave, covering her with a thin layer of soil so as to hide her from the priest who conducts the burial ceremony for the three dead children, he is none the wiser of the extra body in the grave. Everyone presumes that 'London Lilly' has gone back to the city.

Cholera, an ongoing problem in most places, has again reared its ugly head, causing several deaths in the town, one particular house in the 'Alley', a notoriously unhealthy property even by slum standards, is so overcrowded with ten or more people from the same family living in the three small rooms, the accumulation of filth throughout this house and the unsanitary conditions they lived in causing four deaths over two days in this house alone. A few weeks later, an outbreak of smallpox has affected just about every area of town, infecting the rich, the poor, working class and farm labourer alike, with its terrifying fluid filled lumps covering the bodies of those infected, they turn red and becoming painful pustules, this before death finally, and thankfully, takes the victims, it spread through the town with terrifying speed, taking over a dozen with it as it went. Several recent deaths of scrofula, one he buried only last week made him think of his mother, something he has not done for many years, her unmarked grave is still only occupied by her body, he refuses to bury anyone else in her resting place. He had also been kept busy at the Union workhouse, one inmate, Lizzie Bennet, had been delivered of a male illegitimate child in the women's living quarters, she had been seen to take the child to the WC on the ground floor of the building by other women who were present and shortly afterwards the child was found dead, it had fresh red marks around its neck. The beadle, in his usual crapulous state, had forcefully detained Lizzie, viciously tying her hands behind her back, leaving red painful welts on both wrists, before the town constable had been called for. The constable attended, accompanied, because of the serious nature of the offence, by Superintendent Joseph Douglas, Lizzie was arrested and taken to the liberty gaol in St Albans for the wilful murder of her child. Francis had been called to the workhouse to bury the dead bastard child along with two other children that had died recently in the workhouse by way of 'accident', no one had been arrested for these deaths, no investigation had taken place, neither the Master nor the Beadle having any interest in dead workhouse children. Lizzie was placed before the Lent assizes court in Hertford and was found not guilty of the murder of her child, no proof could be offered that she had strangled the new-born, but she was found guilty of, 'concealment of a birth'. She was sentenced by Mr Justice Bolton, a notorious judge on the Assize circuit, to six months with hard labour. Francis buried the dead infant and the three children together in the burial ground, no coffins, just dumped in the grave in the clothes they died in.

He had, only last week, buried three murder victims in Redbourn Churchyard, a local man, Goodwin Spires, had beaten his wife and two children to death at their home, a tied cottage that they had only recently moved into when Goodwin, having moved to town from Radlett, found employment as a farm hand within the experimental station. The bodies, all having been ferociously beaten, were found by the local constable, Pc Frank Young who had been on his beat and passed by the house, he had seen blood splattered on the inside of the windows of the cottage. Goodwin Spires was still inside when the constable entered, he was sitting on the floor with both dead children in his arms, his wife, Fannie, lying face down on the kitchen floor, was described by the constable as being 'unrecognisable' due to facial injuries. Goodwin, who surrendered to Constable Young without words or struggle, is currently in Bedford Gaol; he will almost certainly be found guilty of the wilful murder of his wife and children, he will either be hanged or transported to Australia.

Francis had buried all three victims in the churchyard at St Marys Church in a six foot deep grave, Fannie in one coffin and her two children put together in a separate, smaller box, the children's coffin placed on top of their Mothers and covered with soil.

He is grateful that he has no work today, digging a grave at St Nicholas yesterday in the rain had been dreadfully hard work, for the first time in many years he had feared for his safety when digging, even with his grave boards in place he had noticed that the walls of the grave were at the top two or three feet, very wet and unstable, he had stopped digging at a depth between four and five feet, this being a new grave it should be deeper but he stopped when the feeling of dread had become intolerable to him. The coffins were put in place by the family of the dead after a short graveside service, when he returned to complete the burial, the grave sides have collapsed in on top of the coffin, he quickly filled the remaining space, leaving the remaining spoil pile next to it. Returning home wet, cold, and thankful for his decision to stop digging any deeper yesterday, it could have been him under the fallen soil, he had lit a large fire in the fireplace next to the stove, the first time he has done so for a couple of months.

Today is very different to yesterday, the rising sun is low in the eastern sky but it is already warm, Francis has agreed to help out at the mill later this week, the owner, the oddly named William Freelove Divers, is having new gates put up at the entrance to his mill from the road, Francis, for a good price, has agreed to dig the post holes, George the Smithy, recently finished the two required large wrought iron gates, the posts, each being large single pieces of oak, are to be delivered by William in a few days' time, so he has plenty of time to get the two holes dug. He has decided, as there are no graves that require immediate digging, to stay at home and tidy the garden, the invading water from the engorged stream is slowly receding although the river and the land behind it are still flooded with deep pools in many places, he intends to tend to the vegetable patch and try to drain some of the water from the potatoes and onions by putting in a trench to run away from the plot, not a difficult days work but it would occupy his mind for a few hours.

Pushing his chair away from the table, breakfast finished, he stands and stretches his arms toward the thatch roof, he feels the satisfying cracking in his upper back as his muscles strain against the enforced stretch, he reaches into his coat pocket, still hanging on the hook by the door, takes out his pipe, tapping it gently on the side of the stove to rid it of the burnt tobacco, the grey and black ash falling gently into the hearth the fire in it is alive with hot coal sitting atop burning logs. The fresh tobacco he needs is in his leather pouch, after purchasing it he always takes it out of the tin, preferring to use his pouch, he checks his trouser pocket, it is not there, he finds it in the other pocket of his coat. Taking a pinch of the soft brown leaf, he rubs it in the palm of his hand, flaking it into small pieces before putting it into the bowl of his pipe, gently pushing it down with his little finger. Taking a thin piece of kindling, lighting it by putting it into the freshly lit fire in the stove, he puts the glowing hot yellow flaming wood at the end of the pipe just above the bowl, sucking deeply three, four then five times until he feels the familiar taste of the tobacco rolling over his tongue, finally taking the fresh smoke deeply into his lungs and exhaling a cloud of white smoke into the air of the kitchen, all done without removing the pipe from the corner of his mouth. Francis pulls his braces over his shoulders, he only has his nightshirt on, he has left his day smock in the living room because he will be working in the garden today, he slips on his boots and leaves the cottage by the front door without tying the laces on either boot. The sun is bright, rising as it does at the front of the house and over his garden, the feeling of this early morning warmth on his face satisfies him, relaxes him and gives him a feeling of wellbeing, taking the pipe from his lips and holding it in his right hand he leans his left shoulder on the door frame, he has some other work to do before he can start on the vegetable garden, the sow needs feeding, the chickens can eat scraps from anything left by the pig, he is also running out of wood and coal in the house. He has wood outside the back door in the yard, it has dried sufficiently enough to be cut into smaller logs so as to fit inside the stove hearth, any logs that are to large will be kept for sole use in the fireplace, he reminds himself that the fireplace needs sweeping out and cleaning, the ash will be put into the midden, he will also need to visit Fred Lockhart the brick and coal merchant in town to arrange for a bag of the black gold to be dropped off for him. Fred is easily identified wherever he goes as he always wears an old billycock hat with a large piece of leather sewn roughly onto the back of the hat with an old length of jute twine, so that the leather hangs over his back protecting his clothing when carrying sacks of coal, he also wears '*spankers*' on both legs, straps to stop coal dust and dirt going up his legs. Fred and Francis have a long standing and mutual agreement so he knows a bag of coal will not be difficult to get delivered. Francis has been asked many times, and refused every time, to join the recently formed 'coal club' in town, whereby members can save a small amount of money each week and collectively they are able to negotiate a good price or a discount from Fred. Widows, the elderly and infirm are given preferential rates of sale by the coal club, Francis prefers to deal directly with Fred, it is always best to catch him when a delivery is due in from

Apsley, the coal is delivered by barge on the Grand union canal to this small town, just 5 miles from St Albans, then onto a yard owned by Fred, he delivers it on a huge cart pulled with ease by two enormous farm horses. Fred always instructs his workmen to bag up the last of the old coal in his yard before the new delivery arrives, some small lumps and some large, and also any loose coal left on the delivery cart will be swept up and bagged, these bags of different sized lumps of fuel are sold to Francis, to William and to a few select others who are not in the coal club for a decent, and cheaper price. Fred currently sells a ton of coal to the coal club for ten shillings, who in turn will then sell it to their members and making a small profit, this is cheaper for the members than if they buy it direct from Fred, so selling uneven bags of coal makes Fred a few extra pounds on each delivery day. Fred is a very wealthy man, living with his family in the middle of town in a large red bricked house, locally known as 'Island Cottage'

Francis will visit the brick and coal yard tomorrow on his way to the church, St Nicholas has a double family burial tomorrow afternoon, a Father and son died last week following an accident at the gravel pits, William and Francis had collected the bodies from the pit and delivered them to their family home at the top of Coleswood Road on the far side of the Bowling Alley, the Widow grieving for her husband and son has an added worry, the house is owned by the company that run the gravel pits, she had good reason to fear, the company will only give her a week or so to leave the job tied house now that both the workers from this home are now dead. Francis had walked away leaving William listening to the woman, he is not interested in anyone's sad tales, she was crying and telling William that the Bowling Alley or the workhouse beckoned for her. Francis knows she is probably right; all he cares about is the larger fee he will get for digging just one grave. The parish priest had on one occasion, several years ago when he first started as the church curate, tried to tell Francis that if he dug one grave for two people he would only get the two shillings agreed for each grave dug, Francis then refused to dig for St Nicholas church until the young priest yielded, which was only a week later, agreeing to pay him the usual two shillings for the grave and one shilling for any extra bodies buried in it at the same time, three shillings would be earnt tomorrow and he is pleased about this.

He has some beef left over from last night's supper, putting some unpeeled potatoes directly into the fire in the stove for an hour or so later will provide a suitable accompaniment to the cold beef, turning to go back into the kitchen something moves and catches his peripheral vision in the garden as he turns, it's her he is sure. Turning back to face the garden, swiftly scanning from left to right he sees nothing, frozen to where he is standing, unable to move his legs, holding his breath, his heart pounding quickly and heavily in his chest, looking around again, seeing nothing apart from the geese and ducks that are moving about in the garden, he feels calmness returning to his body and he moves slowly into the kitchen,

"Stop seeing things you bloody fool" his words are barely a whisper.

He slowly and gently closes the door, risking one last peek through the closing gap as the door closes, he is pleased that he sees no one else, he is alone, quietly latching the door leaning his back and shoulders against it, closes his eyes and lets out a long, loud sigh. He is rubbing his left arm with his right hand.

Moving himself away from the door, he goes to the back yard to pick up a hoe and a small fork, he will need both for todays' gardening chores, weeding is not his favourite pastime but first he wants to create a channel alongside the potatoes and onions to try to drain off some of the water that the soaking ground is holding. Walking into the garden and leaving the front door open he makes his way to the vegetable patch, looking around as he does so, the ground is noticeably less sodden than it was yesterday. He digs a shallow trench using the hoe, guiding the trench away from the end of the plot and toward the poultry pen, he notices that the water has receded greatly from this end of his garden, so much so that he might be able to return the chickens to the pen tomorrow, he looks up and over the end of his garden at the fields and water cress beds. He stares as he sees slight movement in the tall reeds on the opposite side of the stream, the stream is still fast moving and thigh deep due to the heavy rains, Francis squints his eyes trying to make out what it is that has caught his eye, it cannot be a fox as that side of the stream is deep in flood water, taking one step forward and tilting his head to the right side, the reeds are in focus and something is certainly behind them, hiding from him. He raises the hoe above shoulder height with both hands tightly gripping the long wooden handle, something is there but it is now not moving, whatever it is, it is still hoping that he will not see it, he realises he is standing in the deep water having walked into the poultry pen and then into the stream, veins seemingly close to bursting, stand out in his neck and on his forehead. He lets out a scream, a primal noise made by fear and anger, rage rises in him that he is unable to control.

Tillie is hiding behind the reeds, he can see her blue eyes looking at him, her dirty face and scraggy hair mostly shielded by the thick and tall river reeds, but those eyes are unmistakable,

"What do you want! Get away from me! I told you I would kill you and I will!"

As he spits the words out, he sees for the first time, fear in the little girls' eyes, wide and filled with tears, his anger unable to see that she is just a scared child, she does not move, she is on her haunches, squatting down, he moves closer and she stands up, still staring at him, she raises both arms straight out in front of her, palms up, tears clearing channels on her dirty face.

Francis flies into a rage he has never experienced before.

"You come here begging, get back to the workhouse, I am going to hurt you!"

He swings the hoe back in a big purposeful arc, pulling it back over his right shoulder, left arm across his body, right arm at a right angle to his shoulder supporting the length of the long wooden handle, with all the force he can muster he brings the garden tool downward, letting the handle slide through his right hand, just as if he were wielding and swinging a wood axe, the tool swings in front of him, hitting the reeds and the metal edge of the hoe slices through them with ease.

Looking down to where he has swung and killed the reeds, his brain telling him that he wants to see the body of a dead child lying there, killed by him, then this ongoing nightmare will be over and he will be able to sleep without disruption, he will get her face out of his head. Will those eyes ever leave him? He wants to be able to live as he always has and to go back to being the grave digger, afraid of nothing or anyone, he looks around. The girl is gone. Sliced reeds lie still on the water as the stream swiftly takes them away, he yells,

"I will get you girl!"

Charging through the stream and up onto the flooded bank opposite he runs blindly through the reeds, hoe held menacingly above his head, he is stopped in his tracks when he falls into a deep pool of water, a flooded water cress bed, he is up to his chest in water. Climbing out of the deep hole he stands only ankle deep on the flooded field, the trees both to his left and on the other side of the watercress beds gently move as one, noiselessly in the breeze, it is silent, not a sound to be heard. He is cold and scared, although the sun is warm and he is seemingly alone he feels uneasy, his ire has calmed, his head bent down with his chin resting on his chest, the hoe held limply in his right hand is no longer a threatening weapon, he walks back across the stream, into the poultry pen, stepping over the short fence and into his garden he throws the hoe away, it lands in the middle of the potatoes, passing the vegetable garden he walks around to the back of the house, removing his wet boots by kicking them off, releasing his braces from their supporting role, letting them drop to his side, he takes off his wet trousers leaving them on the cobbled yard, stepping into the cottage through the kitchen to the living room, then finally taking off his underclothes, leaving them on the floor, a puddle forms around the area they now occupy, he picks up a blanket from his bed he makes his way into the kitchen, sits on the bench next to the stove, puts a large log on top of the still very hot glowing coals, he waits for it to catch and flame, to give him the heat he craves.

The pain in his chest, jaw and left arm is burning into him, his chest is tight, he is struggling to get his breath, for the first time in his memory, he feels a single tear run from his eye and down his cheek.

* * *

The familiar sound of the church bells summoning worshippers to the early service wakes him, he feels the warm morning sunlight moves slowly across his face, not wanting to wake up he turns over, taking the blanket with him, his nose rubs against wood, confused he opens his eyes. Realising he has fallen asleep on the bench and his face is pressed against the back of it, he sits up remembering that he was sitting in front of the stove yesterday afternoon and evening, not moving just staring into the flames and adding coal and wood when he needed it to be warmer, this despite the hot day outside, he has no recollection of falling asleep, the pain in his chest and arm he does remember, they have both gone now.

The blanket falls away from his shoulders, he is naked and shivers a little recalling that he took off his soaked clothes and dumped them in the back yard, they will need rinsing, wringing and hanging out today, leaning over to the end of the bench he puts a few small pieces kindling in the stove hearth, blowing gently brings the nearly spent coal to life, glowing white and red the kindling takes easily, he adds a small lump of cut wood and a few minutes later the hearth is full of flame and heat, adding another log gently on top, he stands covering his nudity with the blanket. His head is fuzzy after what has been a very good night's sleep, the beef he was to eat last night sits untouched on the table in the kitchen, taking the ancient and well used pan he puts a dollop of dripping in it then puts it on top of the stove to heat and melt the bone white fat, this done he puts all the beef in the pan, leaving it to fry gently over the slowly heating pan plate on top of the stove, the biggin, unused but full of coffee from yesterday is placed next to the sizzling pan. Walking into the living room, stepping over his wet underclothes he unceremoniously puts the blanket on the bed, opening the top left drawer of the chest of drawers in the corner and taking out a set of underclothes and putting them on, the drawer, now empty, is closed, socks, his second to last pair are in the other small drawer and his winter trousers are in the bottom drawer with his spare smock shirt, the spare shirt will not be needed, he takes the unworn shirt from yesterday, still hanging over the chair and puts it on, he will have to wear his hobnailed boots until the others are dry.

Once dressed, he still feels empty inside, yesterday's events seemed to have drained him, picking up the wet underclothes he takes them through the kitchen, opens the back door and throws them outside on top of the other wet clothing he had on yesterday, his memory flashes vivid images of running blindly through the stream and falling into a deep pool, chasing the girl, Tillie. He remembers the look on her face, real fear, he remembers his anger, ripe and uncontrollable, he is not a man to get angry, he cannot work out why he had reacted that way, he cannot see why this small, pitiful girl makes him so angry and fearful. His rumbling belly and the smell of the fried beef tell him that he is hungry, not having eaten since yesterday morning he is ravenous, the beef will be welcomed and will certainly fill him up ready to face the day, he will wash then wring out the wet and dirty clothes, hanging them out in the sun will dry them soon enough, he knows he will have to wait a few days for his boots to dry fully. After putting the large, filled kettle on top of the stove to boil the water, he sits at the table, greedily eating the hot fried beef, he is so hungry that most of the food is not chewed it is put hurriedly into his mouth and swallowed quickly to fill the void in his belly, ignoring the rising indigestion in his chest, he is not surprised by this feeling as his has bolted his breakfast. Pushing the plate away then drinking and enjoying the hot coffee, he begins to cough and is surprised as his chest sounds wheezy and crackly,

"That's all I need, a damn summer cold" he says to the empty room.

The kettle is blowing hot white steam into the room, condensation forms on the inside of the window, taking a thick cloth to wrap around the handle he removes the large kettle, goes into the back yard and pours the contents of the kettle into the half barrel, adding a small amount of cold water from a bucket in the kitchen so as to be able to use the carbolic soap to make a small amount of suds in the water, the soaking wet clothes from yesterday are lifted from the cobbles and put into the water, using a short sturdy stick he agitates the clothes in the warm water, leaving them to soak he takes the bucket and the kettle through the kitchen out of the front door and into the garden, both need refilling from the pump. As he steps out of the door, he stops and looks across his garden to the fields and watercress beds on the opposite side of the stream, he can see grass in some parts of the fields and watercress is poking above the flood water, the stream has settled back to a slow moving body of water, it is still higher than it normally is but much shallower than yesterday, the chickens can now be put back in the poultry pen as the water has dissipated completely from this area. As the chickens have not been in the pen for the past few weeks, he hasn't bothered to put the geese and ducks away at night, the honking of the geese tells him that they have seen him leave the house and will want feeding, he obliges them, spreading a good amount of seed and corn onto the still wet but no longer flooded ground, they attack the food greedily. As he fills the bucket and the kettle at the pump, he looks again over the stream some of the reeds are bent over and some are missing from his violent actions of yesterday, he shivers as he thinks of the rage and of his intentions, although the appearances of this child have unnerved him, even frightened him the murderous feelings he had yesterday are now gone and he has no intention of repeating them, dealing with the dead is a simple process, he does not want to add to the numbers he has dealt with over the years, especially that of a child. He has buried hundreds, if not more dead children in over three decades as a grave digger, not one had bothered him, he is a digger of graves and not a murderer. He thinks of Tillie and wonders where she is now. He remembers his real fear of her and has an idea why he might be so scared of her, he likes being on his own, a lonesome sort of man he always has been, the child has invaded his life, as he thinks about this he has a realisation of sorts, perhaps the child has been following him because she knows he has no one in his life, she is also now alone in this world as he is, her pleading eyes and begging arms may just be that she needs food but it may be that she needs someone in her life. But why him?

A brief blustery wind picks up, the Yew canopy speaks in a whisper as the wind passes through it, the noise is almost hushed as it invades the silence he stands in, the wind stops as quickly as it started, he feels a sharp stabbing pain in his chest, bending at the waist and putting his hands on his hips, this seems to ease the pain and the building pressure in his chest.

"You don't need anyone Francis and you can't feel sorry for anyone" he says as he picks up the water filled bucket and kettle, he takes them back toward the house and looks at the vegetable patch, his trench seems to have worked, green potato leaves are poking through the soil will need covering again, the onion shoots are standing tall and green, a few are leaning over with dying yellow shoots, if they are the same in a week or so he will remove them or they will rot in the ground, "The child needs to be in the workhouse with her own sort"

He cannot get the image of the scared girl running away from him yesterday, she was pleading with him and in his anger, he didn't care, he has not had anyone to look after for so long, he needs no one, the uninvited invasion of his privacy angered him it made him feel violence was needed to abate it. He feels shame, his actions against the small child were over the top, after clearing up he decides to walk over to the water cress beds to see if she is hiding there, he knows all the good hiding places, the good trees to climb, he should do he spent enough time over there as a child.

If she is there, he will take her back to the workhouse, to where she belongs.

Putting the bucket and kettle outside the back door, he will need them both later that afternoon to rinse out his clothes, followed by the laborious task of wringing them out will have to be done, he uses a fence post to help him do this then the ancient mangle will be called into use to squeeze out any remaining water, the clothes can then be hung out on the line at the front of the house, he has never ironed any of his clothes. This is a job for later.

The indigestion feeling is still with him and seems to have given him belly ache, he tells himself that he ate too much of the fried food this morning, promising to miss lunch today, this should settle the indigestion and belly pain. Sitting on the chair in the kitchen he removes his dry winter boots and puts on the wet boots he wore yesterday, tucking his winter trousers into his socks he stands up, the ground will be wet in the fields, so getting the wet boots wet again will not make any difference, he will try to keep his trousers as dry as he can. A sensation of dizziness attacks him, and he is forced to sit down again, putting his head into his hands to rub his eyes he realises that he is sweating a lot, he sits up straight and tries to take a deep breath, he cannot, coughing follows, and he is short of breath, the dizziness is joined by a rising feeling of nausea,

"Bloody summer cold"

These words said aloud to make him feel better, after a few minutes the lightheaded feeling passes as does the nausea, he is still sweating and a little short of breath but manages to stand up. Feeling a little better he puts a shovel of coal into the stove hearth then leaves the house, pulling the front door shut behind him. The coughing and wheezing continue as he walks to the bottom of the garden, the geese gather around him as he climbs into the pen, the ducks move away from him and slide into the stream silently, he is just able to take a short run and jump across the stream to the other side, having to stop when he completes this task as he is out of breath and dizzy again. A short stabbing pain in his chest makes him groan aloud in discomfort, then it is gone, he suddenly vomits bringing up the breakfast of fried beef and coffee, wiping his beard when it is over, he stands up straight, now clenching his teeth tightly together as a pain in his lower jaw has started, he mumbles to himself,

"That'll teach you to bolt your food"

Satisfied he has explained the reason for being sick he moves through the reeds and into the field, walking around the watercress beds, he moves across the field toward the trees, on the other side of these is a footpath that leads across the next open field to Stakers lane to the southwest, to the northeast will take him back onto the road his cottage is on, if he carries on he will eventually come out on the road close to the mill. He decides to call into the mill to speak to William Freelove Divers to finalise the arrangements to dig the post holes for him, after the grave dig tomorrow morning he will then start at the mill in the afternoon. The pain in his jaw is getting worse, it is pushing down into his left arm, he shakes this arm in a vain attempt to shake out the pain, he fails so sets off on his quest to check the fields, trees, and watercress beds for the child he scared so badly yesterday. A feeling of melancholy flows through his every being, he reaches the small clump of trees and must rest, leaning against a large oak he struggles to get his breath, the light headedness has returned, and he cannot get rid of it, he sits and rests a while until the gloominess and pain go away. Looking over at the upturned root base of a huge oak that fell during the great storm and gale in February, the tree trunk now lies along the ground and over the river, its huge, destroyed canopy lying on the ground on the other side in soft, marshy land, he can see that the other side of the river is still flooded, the bank on that side not apparent as the water is flowing directly across the land making the river much wider than normal. On this side the water has abated, it being on a slightly higher plain, this is why his garden never fully floods, this area he is resting in when flooded always clears first, leaving behind a few pools sitting in the uneven parts of the fields, he looks again at the upturned root base, taller than a man with its roots exposed to the air, dark soil lies between these roots and the hole that was ripped in the ground when the tree toppled is large and deep and filled with flood water. He sees something sticking out of the water, seemingly stuck to one of the submerged roots, pushing himself away from the tree that has been supporting him he takes several steps toward the uprooted, formerly magnificent oak, as he gets closer, he identifies what it is that is in water, balanced on a root. It is an arm, a small thin arm, the arm of a child, as white as the alabaster on the tomb of Sir John Brokett and his Wife, Margaret inside the church of St Helens, one tiny hand, limp and unmoving can be seen from where Francis stands. Pain in his chest grips him tightly, now so bad it makes him double over, forcing himself to stand, gripping his left arm to control the pain shooting through it he makes his way to the edge of the pool of water currently filling the hole that formerly held the base and roots of the fallen tree. His eyes follow the thin white arm as it disappears under the water, the shape of a small body can just be made out under the water, the mid-morning sun casts a shadow over part of the flooded former tree base making it impossible to see through the dark water, ignoring his pain he steps forward, into the water, his already wet boots letting the cold water through into his socks and feet, the coldness of it is now up his thighs and past his knees, he is in as deep as the hole is, the water is so cold and making his breathing very difficult, Francis feels as though he is about to panic, a feeling he has never had, a feeling he is not comfortable with.

He can see the body, lying just below the water.

A child. Eyes wide open in a dead stare. Stunning blue eyes, dazzling in the murky, cold water. It is her.

Pain surges through his chest, a sensation of pressure becomes all encompassing, he staggers backward, reaching out and grabbing an exposed root in his left hand, pain shoots up his arm causing him to let go, he falls to his knees and the cold water is up to his chest because of the position he has fallen to. He screams out in pain, there is no one around to hear him, moving forward on his knee, feeling the soft, muddy bottom of the pool beneath him, he reaches the child. He can see her mouth is slightly open as if making a worthless and silent plea for help, the sight is one he has seen many times before on dead bodies, but this time, for the first time he is scared and upset by what he is witnessing. Gently putting his arms under her body, he pulls the dead girl toward him, holding her tight against his chest he stands bringing her clear of the water, she is not heavy, he can feel how skinny and bony she it through her thin and shabby dress, the water has washed much of the dirt from her face, she is beautiful. Holding her in his right arm, the left is now too painful, he moves hair that is stuck to her forehead and face, from her eyes, he wants to close the eyelids as he would do on any other corpse, but he is drawn to hers, he knows they are lifeless and cannot see but their colour is so dazzling, he has never seen before or could describe such beauty, even in death they transfix him.

Her body is limp and dead, he notices a large gash on her head, just on the side by her left temple, it is an ugly wound that had bled heavily when inflicted. Francis recalls swinging the hoe into the reeds where the child had been hiding, had he inflicted this horrific wound?

Walking out of the pool, at the opposite end to where he had entered, his attention is drawn to a large root at the base of the uprooted tree, it is as large as his arm, thick and strong, it has jagged edges where it has snapped from its haven underground, these jagged edges are blood stained and he also sees a small amount of hair stuck in the blood. He had not killed this child, he knows she ran away from him, from his rage and anger, running blindly through the reeds, into the trees and probably in her fear and panic has run into the jagged exposed root, then falling into the water, dazed, and hurt, she had drowned.

He has not killed this child, but he is almost certainly the cause of her death.

Pulling her tight into his body he sees foam with a small amount of blood in it coming from her mouth, she also has small trickles of blood coming from both ears, he finds the sight almost impossible to bear, combined with the terrific pain he has in his chest, he is crying, tears rolling down his ruddy cheeks and into his thick beard, he cannot stop them as he walks back toward the stream at the end of his garden, carrying the body of the dead child with him. He sees no one and no one sees him.

The short journey to his garden seems to take an eternity, he is struggling not to collapse from the pain in his chest, somehow he makes it over the stream and through the poultry pen, he is now standing in the shade of the Yew tree, out of the hot sun he is feeling slightly better, even more so when he gently puts the body of the child at the base of the huge old tree in his garden. His throat is dry, he craves water, his mind not functioning because of the pain in his chest and the pain he feels for the dead child, forgetting about the water pump that is so near to him, he walks to the cottage, falling to his knees by the front door looking for the bucket to quench his thirst, he cannot see it and then remembers he left it in the back yard next to the soaking clothes, staggering to his feet he opens the door, leaving it open he falls to the back door, pushing it open he bends down and greedily uses his right hand to get the cold welcoming water into his mouth, laying on his back on the uneven cobbles, closing his eyes and trying to relax, the pain and crushing feeling in his chest is easing, he will rest here for a few minutes.

He opens his eyes quickly, the sun is lower in the sky than it was when he lay down in the yard, it is on the side of the cottage, on his right hand side, the yard is partially in shadow. How long has he lain here?

He has no idea, he gets to his feet, he is unsteady and almost falls, managing to stop himself by grabbing the fence, he feels nauseous again, he walks slowly through the gate hoping to make it to the privy before he vomits, he does not make it, producing only bile as he leans against the door frame of his outhouse. He can see his cart at the side of the house and the road beyond, it is empty, not a soul to be seen, he makes it to the cart, he sees the tools of his trade in the back, he knows what he has to do. Tillie has not been missed by anyone from the workhouse, he knows that no one knows she is here, no one but he knows she is dead, he knows that no one will miss her. Taking the tools he walks, struggling on the short journey to the Yew tree just past his vegetable garden, as he slowly walks he has time to think about her, she wasn't haunting him at all, she was hungry for food, hungry to be wanted and loved, this tiny sad girl had been looking for help and he, the grave digger had ignored her, becoming angry and driving her to her death, smashing her head on a jagged tree root then drowning in the root base pool of the felled oak tree.

He knows that this poor child suffered every day, from her birth to her death, the least he can do is bury her, no one will know, only him, pain takes him to his knees again, crushing his chest as though a belt is being tightened around his body. Forcing himself to stand, he makes it to the Yew tree, he leans down over the still body of the child, he has to close her eyes as they seem to be watching his every move, using two of his thick calloused fingers, he extinguishes light and life from these blue pools of beauty forever.

It is dark when he stops digging, bells signalling the third call to prayer seem to have been many hours ago, it is only a shallow grave, less than four feet deep but he cannot take the pain any more, for several hours he has gritted his teeth and fought against the tide of pain, laboured breathing and the constant unforgiving feeling that his ribs are being crushed, several times he collapsed in the bottom of the grave, each time wondering if this grave will be his final resting place and not that of the dead child, who now sits so very still in the shade of the Yew, peaceful and looking as though she is asleep. Francis is drenched in sweat, dirt covers every inch of his exposed flesh as he finally climbs from the fresh grave and lies on the ground looking up into the canopy of the Yew, he can see the low branches, long and strong as they reach away from the old trunk, looking through these lowest of branches is like looking into a black abyss of nothingness, the incoming darkness of the evening and the dense canopy swallow and devour any available light. Pushing himself up onto an elbow, he is exhausted, and he knows he is only half done, the child needs to be laid in the hole and it needs to be filled in, pain takes him to the ground again, curled in the foetal position he cries out in pain. No one hears him.

Francis has no idea how long he lay under the tree, it is dark when he comes around, the cool wind has dried the sweat on his body and he feels cold, getting to his feet he moves slowly to the child, standing for a few moments to look at her, bending at the knees he puts his arms around the deceased, he has done this many hundreds of times when moving dead bodies, her body is slightly stiff, rigor mortis has begun to set in, he hopes he does not have to straighten her limbs, a task he has also done many times before, but thankfully not often with the body of a child, the rigor never seems as severe in the young. Taking her body to the grave side he lays her next to the opening in the ground, in the moon lit darkness he glimpses the sight of purple staining on the underside of the skin on her legs, he has seen this before when corpses have lain, the blood pools on the underside of whichever way the body has been lying, he lowers himself into the grave. Taking the body of the child in his arms, grateful that the rigor is hardly noticeable as the poor child has little bulk or muscle, he places her on her back at the bottom of the grave, her arms fall to her side, and he leaves them where they fall. His breathing is so difficult that he struggles to get out of the grave, turning to look at Tillie one last time he finds that the thought of putting soil onto her naked face is too much for him, he walks

to the house, takes a blanket off of the bed, the same blanket he slept in last night and returns to the grave, covering the body of the child with the dirty woollen blanket. He tries to think of a few words to say, as the priest does, he has none, so sets about the task of filling the grave, he wants to fill it until it is level with the ground, any spoil left over he will put in the river, he knows there will be very little as Tillie is not taking up a lot of room in her underground resting place.

* * *

The tallow candle gives little light in the kitchen of the cottage, Francis sits in front of the stove, the fire is barely alive and he does not have the strength to bend down to put a log on it, he has managed to eat some bread and dripping, drinking cold coffee to wash it down, feeling nauseas he lies down on the bench, closing his eyes knowing that he will be spending a second night sleeping here, pain courses through his body, he does not care about it, all he can see in his mind is Tillie, eyes shut and dead, lifeless with her blue eyes that will never see the sun again.

It is still dark when the rain wakes him up, for a few seconds he is confused in the darkness of his kitchen, moonlight gives the room a semblance of life, the pain then comes alive, his jaw, his arm and chest, constant and unforgiving pain, he needs to use the privy, he knows he will not make it, managing to stand he opens the back door and urinates onto the cobbles, his clothes still sit in the cold water and carbolic soap, they will need rinsing, wringing and mangling later on, but now he wants to sit down and try to ease the pain. The stove fire has gone out, he cannot or will not light a fresh one, he sits on the bench seat until the moonlight disappears, taking the rain with it, the early dawn of a new day brings light and life to the drab kitchen, he manages to stand, looks through the window to the bottom of the garden, remembering the burial yesterday brings a new pain to his body, in his throat as he tries and fails to stop crying quietly he tastes the salty tears as they drip through his beard to his lips, putting both hands on the back of the bench, head held low, he sobs, alone. Wiping his nose and eyes with the back of his grimy hand he opens the door, the fresh morning breeze invades the cottage, he attempts to take a deep breath of this luscious morning air, the fresh smell of recent rain is still present, a stabbing pain in the middle of his chest stops him doing this, stepping outside he sees his spade, mattock and grave bar lying on the ground outside the door, he has never done this before, he has always put his tools back in the cart when a grave has been dug, last night he just discarded them on the floor, now stepping over them in his stockinged feet, he walks slowly down the garden to the site of yesterdays' digging and burial. The ground is flat and level, the spoil having been put in the stream is now washed away in the slow flowing water, the untrained eye would not know that a grave had been dug here only yesterday, the rain helping the soil under the tree to be virtually the same colour all the around its base including the invisible edges of the grave, with his experienced eyes he can see them. Getting onto his hands and knees he spreads the top soil from under the tree over the grave site finally concealing his secret, no one must ever know what he has done, in all his years as a grave digger, he has taken possessions from the dead, sold their clothes, tipped the dead out of the coffins they lay in to sell the wood to the poor, he has piled body on top of body, he has re buried old bones from the graveyard in un consecrated ground all over town, even under this very Yew tree where Tillie now lies, but he has never secretly buried a body outside of a churchyard and only the once within the bounds of consecrated land, at St Nicholas, he recalls sadly the woman dead from strychnine poisoning. Not ever has he committed such an atrocity, not her nor in any of the other churchyards he works in, not even in the workhouse, a feeling of sadness and dread overcomes him, he has to sit at the base of the tree, he does not have the strength to stand any longer, his back grazing on the rough bark of the old tree, the sun is rising quickly in the east, he can feel the warmth on his right cheek.

Pain grips his every being, putting his arms around his body and hugging himself, he feels the pain take over, taking control, rising from his chest into his neck and jaw, radiating down his left arm, this feels stronger and hotter than any pain he has had before. With his jaw clamped tightly shut, his teeth forced together in an attempt to squeeze the pain from his body, he closes his eyes, finally relaxing his muscles and letting the pain overtake him.

* * *

"Francis!" William is shouting from the roadside of the fence, "Francis, where are you?"

He can see that front door is wide open and very oddly, the grave digging tools are lying haphazardly on the ground, he calls again, "Francis!" Walking through the gate he gets to the open door and sticks his head inside the cottage, "The priest is not a happy man Francis, a double funeral taking place today and no grave dug" The cottage is silent. "Can you hear me man, the Priest is fuming mad to hell with you!"

William enters the kitchen and notes that the back door is also open, he walks through to the living room, the bed is unmade, Francis is not there, he calls out a couple of times as he walks through to the storeroom, after checking the root cellar he makes his way back to the kitchen, it is then that he sees that the stove fire has gone out. Francis always has the stove fire burning, William cannot ever recall seeing the stove so cold, he is about to leave the cottage to check the sty and the privy for the grave digger, he looks out of the kitchen window, with its view over the garden, down to the river with the Yew tree dominating the view.

Francis is sat at the bottom of the tree.

William sighs, without leaving the kitchen or going near to the tree he knows that Francis is dead, he has seen enough death to know.

The constable sits on the cart with William, behind them is an empty coffin,

"Here we are" William informs the constable as they arrive at the cottage.

The coffin is lifted from the cart by the two men, and they take the box through the gate and to where the lifeless body of the grave digger is, Francis' face is blue, and a small amount of blood has dried at the side of his mouth. "Poor bugger" is all William can say.

"Where are we leaving the body William?" asks the constable, who continues, "With no family it seems pointless leaving him in the cottage, you will only have to come and get him again when he is to be buried"

"The Curate has given permission for him to be left in the church until he is buried" William manages a little laugh to himself, "It's funny that a grave digger that don't believe in any God will spend his last night in a church!"

The constable scratches his head, "Who digs the grave for the grave digger?"

"I will" said William quietly, "I will do it this afternoon, at the side of the church under the Yew tree" he pauses for a moment before carrying on, "If I knew where he buried his mother, I would put him in with her, but he never told me or another living soul where she is, so he will have to be buried as he lived, without anyone and all alone"

The constable helps William lift Francis body into the coffin, the corpse is sitting almost upright, the rigor keeping him in the position he died, William nods at the constable,

"Look away young fella, just for a minute"

The constable asks why he has to do this, William explains that he needs to straighten the body and arms, that it is not a pleasant task, the constable assures William that he will be fine.

A few minutes later William is putting the lid on the coffin that now holds Francis correctly postured body, the constable is still vomiting into the stream, William puts a hand on top of the plain wooden box,

"So long grave digger"

Part Two

1914-1918

'Beneath it lies the sleeping child
Under soil and earth and sod
Ever no peace for this long dead soul
Denied a place with her God'

Unchanged by the years, standing as tall and strong as ever.
No questions were ever asked of her
No answers ever given

CHAPTER FOUR

When Francis died he had no known living relatives, William had briefly spoken to him about family, he had mentioned once, and only once that he had a brother, Jacob, who had died in India whilst working for the East India Company, an officer in the army.

William had taken over unofficial tenancy of the cottage, no one else wanted it, tidying it up, throwing away any rotting food and keeping any still usable for himself, no point in waste, he filled in the root cellar with soil from in and around the pig sty, the pig had gone to Bert the Smithy. He wanted to find any relative of Francis to take the cottage on, it would fall to rack and ruin otherwise, he felt he owed it to Francis, who had been his oldest friend, to pass the cottage onto relatives, if any could be found.

Knowing that Jacob had been in the army of the East India company, William had taken it upon himself to investigate to find any living relatives of Francis and Jacob. It was surprisingly, an easy task, especially as he was a literate man. The East India company holds records, including Last Will and Testaments, of all staff both civil and military at East India House in Leadenhall Street, London, William had never been and actually never went to London but with the help of the Priest of St Nicholas, the long suffering Curate, Henry Addington, contact was made and in less than a year they had notification that Jacob had died on 21 December 1845 at the battle of Ferozeshah during the Anglo – Sikh war and had been buried at the

Cantonment in Ferozepur alongside his men. He had been survived by his Wife Julia, they married in 1818 and had a son, David, who had been born in 1825. The East India company kept excellent records, dates of birth, marriage, death, and residence of all employees and surviving Widows receiving pension from them. Julia had died in November 1846, the cause of her death listed as malaria, David, who also worked for the company as a clerk, moved to England in 1848 aged 23.

William had been provided with an address and after he had contacted David they had met in St Albans toward the end of 1851, David was aware of his mother's will but not that a cottage was still in the family and that it had been the home of his Father, his uncle, his grandmother, and others before her. At his request, a copy of Jacob's will had been lodged with St. Nicholas Church in 1820 by the East India company, with instruction that the Church act as executor to his will, David had paid them the two pounds promised, an instruction that was also included in his mother's will. The Church had tried to make more of the situation, suggesting that the will was the property of the Prerogative Court of Canterbury, as all wills in this part of the country are, the East India Company quickly stopped this, the will was written by them under instruction from Jacob and then later from Julia whilst both were serving the company, the Parish Church was clearly instructed only to act as executor of the will, to ensure its instructions carried out.

David had married Anna in the spring of 1850, they had been living in a cottage on land close to North Mymms, belonging to The East India company, Anna was working as a house maid at Brookman Manor house when they moved into Francis' cottage in February 1852, pleased to take it on at no cost to them, their son Alfred being born in the kitchen of the cottage in August of the same year. David left the East India company and became senior clerk at St Albans parish offices, he, along with Anna and Alfred lived a happy life in the cottage, still without running water and the privy still in use, they loved living there. David disappeared in Spring 1854, never to be seen again, no one had seen him on the day he disappeared, and no one has seen him since.

Anna raised Alfred as a widow, although no death pension was ever paid to her by the parish or by the East India company, so times were tough for both. Alfred met and married Annabel in 1870, the wedding party held in the garden under the shade of the old Yew tree. Anna collapsed and died at this event, her only sons' wedding party aged 45, she is buried in an unmarked plot in the churchyard of St Nicholas in town, her grave dug by Francis' replacement, a scrawny miserable man named George Woodward.

Annabel fell with child early in 1871, giving birth to a healthy baby boy, Jeremiah, in September of that year, falling pregnant again before Christmas in 1871. In early June 1872, Annabel went into labour, weeks earlier than expected, Alfred ran to fetch Mary Spratley, the widow of Ted Spratley, the landlady of the Crown and Anchor pub, half a mile further along from the cottage, on the lower road toward Luton, just past Pickford Mill. Mary was needed to help him with the birth, when they both returned to the cottage, only ten or so minutes later, the child, a girl he named Daisy was born, tiny and undernourished, she died within hours of coming into the world. Annabel had died before the child had fully emerged from the safety of the warm shelter inside of her. Alfred was left with a young son to bring up on his own, Annabel and Daisy were laid to rest together, buried only yards away from Anna. At Alfred's request no stone marks their resting place, he knows where they lay, and he visited weekly for the rest of his life. Jeramiah married Victoria, the daughter of Mary Spratley, at St Nicholas church in 1891, Jeremiah was only 19 years old and his bride a year younger, the wedding party was held in the Crown and Anchor pub, many saying that it was the best wedding party ever with Alfred being the life and soul, staying up all night celebrating. In February 1892 Martin was born, as with other members of this family, in the cottage where Jeramiah and Victoria lived with Alfred, a surprise arrival in 1899 was a sister to Martin, Alice. Alfred doted on both his grandchildren until he died in 1903, aged 70, he was buried with his wife and daughter. William died the same year, aged 98, his final resting place is not known. Jeramiah, Victoria, Martin and Alice remained living in the three roomed cottage, the back store room converted by Jeramiah into a bedroom for both his children to share, a new small fireplace and chimney being added to the end wall to heat this room, the old stove has been replaced by a large range, it now taking up the whole space in the fireplace, water is still pumped from the garden, vegetables are still grown, oil lamps have replaced the tallow candles of old and the privy is still in use and is still moved around every six months or so.

The Crown and Anchor had closed in 1899, the pub being sold by the brewery and renamed Crown house and no longer a pub, Mary was moved by the brewery to a different premises on the corner of South View Road, nearer to the cottage, the '*new*' pub was named the Dog and Duck in 1899 and renamed again five years later as 'The Malta'.

The Yew tree remains in the garden, overseeing all life and all death in the cottage through the ever changing seasons.

The cottage still stands where it was built, it's thatch roof still in use, the walls now painted with whitewash on the stone, the exposed beams now black with coal tar creosote, a fresh yellow thatch has replaced the rotten old brown and green mould infested one. The garden still runs to the stream passing the vegetable patch and the ever present Yew tree, with its shallow buried secrets still only known to a long dead grave digger.

* * *

Martin, in February 1910, on his 18th birthday, is leaving the family cottage, handshakes from his father, tears from his mother and hugs from his 11 year old sister.

Service to King and country beckons, he is joining the British Army, he is to join the Bedfordshire regiment, he had no interest in becoming a farm labourer or working on one of the large estates in and around town, he has always craved adventure, wanting to see what life outside of the cottage and its rural surroundings would be like. He signed on for the Kings shilling when just 17, given a starting date, the day he turned 18. He takes the train from the East station, opened in 1860 at Station Road, formerly called Stakers Lane, to Luton Bute Street, leaving the train to catch a train from Luton Midland Road just a short walk from Bute Street, and then travelling to Bedford station. There the army truck is waiting for him and other new recruits, most are like Martin, unskilled and working class men looking for something different in their lives, they all get off the train, standing around smoking cigarettes, a sharp and rude introduction to the discipline of the British army is from the very loud and aggressive voice of a man wearing a peak cap so low over his forehead that you cannot see his eyes. He barks and screams orders at the group, they all board the back of the open truck and are taken to Kempston Barracks.

Three months of basic training follows, Martin hates it initially, the physical training is a breeze for him, a naturally athletic man he enjoys this but hates the bullshit, the army call it *'instilling discipline and obedience',* he calls it bullshit, he soon learns to go along with it, life is easier than trying to beat it, it is a system that cannot be beaten.

The bugler blasts out Reveille at 5am, Martin often wonders who gets the bugler out of bed, the barrack room is shared by twenty of them, it has to be spotless by 6am so all they have time for is a quick brew of tea and then they all get on with making their living spaces spotless, the corporal will be in at 6 on the dot, they have to be standing by the side of their beds in perfect working uniform, ready for inspection. Square bashing starts at 06.30 every morning and continues until breakfast at 8am, then it is back on the parade square for the remainder of the morning, drill practice, learning to march, to form fours and about turning, this is done without a break until 12.15 when all recruits have an hour for lunch, immediately after lunch it is either more drill or physical training, both done on the parade square. The working day finishes at 4.30pm, then, if it is not your platoon's rotation on fatigues or a work party, it is back to the barrack room to get uniforms spotless for the next day, boots need to be bulled and caps brushed, Martin has heard that in larger garrison towns the recruits have mess rooms to relax in, to read in a library or to play billiards, it is rumoured that a buffet is served to the recruits and staff in the evenings. Kempston Barracks has nothing of the sort, most men get their kit cleaned, their bed space made up, eat an evening meal in the canteen and then get as much sleep as they can, many choosing to sleep on the floor under their beds so that they will not have to make it up again the next morning. After three weeks of this bullshit, the training changes, it is still disciplined and hard, but so much better than spending whole days on the parade square, the platoons are being taught the basics of movement in the field, taking part in night operations and route marches, following this, weapons handling, digging trenches and the marksmanship competition. Each platoon corporal threatens every man under his command with pain or death if they fail in the marksmanship competition, Martin later learns that all the training corporals have laid bets with each other as to which platoon member would win the coveted shooting medal for marksmanship. Martin wins the competition, not dropping a single shot, the corporal who screamed at him on his first day is now his best mate, buying him bottles of ale with his large winnings, Martin shares the bottles with the lads in his barrack room.

Three months later, the platoon 'pass out', basic training is finally finished, Martin is now a professional soldier in the Regular army, he signs on of for a total of 12 years' service, 7 as a regular and 5 as a reservist. The Bedfordshire's are made up of two regular battalions, two reserve battalions and one territorial battalion, Martin expects to be posted to the 1st battalion, currently based at Kempston barracks, the 2nd battalion are overseas in Bermuda carrying out guard duty at the Royal Naval dockyard, the British army do not post men aged under 19 overseas, trainees aged 18 remain in the UK and proceed with trade training, cook, rifleman, gunner, clerk, or something else. The 1st battalion are to be posted to Ireland after Christmas, this is not classed as an overseas posting so all the lads in Martins barracks who are under 19, including him expect to be posted to 1st battalion.

After the passing out parade is completed, Martins family are unable to attend, a weekends leave is authorised to all trainees, travel warrants issued and all travel to their homes all over the home counties, Martin arrives at the cottage late on a Friday evening at the start of the first weekend in May. His Mother and Father are in the garden, tending to the vegetable patch, Auntie May, Mothers younger sister is helping out, Alice is sat under the Yew tree with their twin cousins, Jennifer, and Catherine, none of them see him arrive, he stands at the garden gate for several minutes until his Mother looks up, seeing him and screaming, then running toward him, throwing her arms around her son. Not used to displays of affection, the army is not a place for affection, Martin feels a little uncomfortable with his crying Mother hanging onto him, he hears his Father speak,

"Leave the man be Victoria, let him through the gate woman!"

He watches as his Father gently nods at him, taking his pipe from his mouth, he makes his way over to greet Martin with a handshake,

"Good to see you lad, you look smart in your uniform"

Victoria continues to cry as they make their way into the kitchen, Alice, the twins, and Auntie May, join them inside, the young girls are making a fuss of him in his khaki green uniform,

"Girls, lets' leave Martin alone shall we" the pipe is back in his mouth, he continues when the children become quiet, "Shall we go to the pub young man? I'll bet a pint would be welcomed"

Martin smiles at his Father, who has to say "Shush" to his Wife, who is protesting that her boy has only just arrived, Jeramiah is firm with her,

"We will be back for supper, a couple of pints with my soldier son then home" turning to Martin he says, "The Malta or the 'Gib'?"

They decide to visit both, starting at the Gibraltar castle, it is slightly further from home than the Malta, Martin bends down and kisses his Mother on the cheek, promising to be back soon, he then leaves for the pub with his proud Father.

* * *

Arriving back at Kempston on the Sunday evening, he is full of his Mothers very large Sunday lunch, roast chicken, roast potatoes, parsnip and swede followed by Auntie Mays' fabulous bread and butter pudding, her husband, Uncle Pete, who works on the Childwickbury estate, had joined them for lunch, Martin, Pete and Jeramiah had visited the 'Gib' before lunch, much to the dismay of Victoria, who has secretly put several sweet buns and cakes from Ackroyd's bakery into his suitcase for the journey back to Bedford, he has eaten them all. The rest of the platoon all arrive back, all before the cut off arrival time of 9pm, it seems as though most have enjoyed their weekend leave, and all are looking forward to the posting notice that will be on the notice board after breakfast the following day. Martin isn't bothered, he knows that the 1st battalion will be his posting, or if he is really unlucky he will remain as part of the training unit and become the dogsbody to the sergeants and corporals, although this posting is usually reserved for those soldiers that, having completed, and passed training, have only done so by the skin of their teeth, Martin has eased through, so expects to be staying at Kempston barracks, not as a recruit but as part of the 1st battalion.

Reveille is sounded as usual at 5am, but as they are now regular soldiers and not in training, they have until inspection, which is just before breakfast, to get their bed space and kit sorted out, several brews of tea are made and cigarettes smoked outside of the barracks, the butts being put out into the highly polished spittoons that are placed outside of every barrack door, these spittoons being moved out of sight before the arrival of their corporal. Breakfast is finished, all the trainees, over a hundred men, are squeezed into the hallway outside of the canteen, waiting for the company clerk to pin up the postings, the noise of so many men mumbling and whispering nervously carries through the hallway into the canteen where Martin has remained after his breakfast, he is sat with his training 'oppo', 20 year old Jack Bothworthy, a former footman at the Luton Hoo estate, not far from where Martin had grown up, a huge estate owned by a German, Sir Julius Wernher, a man who made his millions from diamond mines in South Africa, Jack tells Martin that he has heard that Wernher has a fortune of twelve million pounds! Jacks' family live in Flitwick village, only a few miles from the barracks, neither man is nervous or worried about where they are to be posted,

"Martin, Jack, you both got posted together!"

'Chummy' Coombes shouts at them from inside the noisy crowd of excited soldiers,

"1st battalion for us then Martin" Jack seems chirpy, "At least I might be able to get home a bit more if we are staying at Kempston for the time being"

Martin nods in agreement, he knows it isn't a training post, if it was, Chummy would not have told them, he comes over to the two seated men, flush faced and out of breath,

"How did you get that posting you jammy git!"

Martin and Jack look at each other, Chummy continues,

"You ain't nineteen yet Martin, must be a mistake"

"What do you mean Chummy?" Martin, now interested, asks his colleague

"You both got 2nd battalion, leaving for Bermuda on Wednesday from Portsmouth dockyard"

Martin stands up,

"Back in a mo' mates, just got to speak to the corporal"

He walks across the canteen to where the training corporals are sat together, he gets to their table and stands to attention, the table of corporals stop talking and look at him,

"Corporal Kenney, may I speak with you please?"

One of the seated soldiers stands, a tall, sturdy man with sandy hair and a moustache to match,

"Speak" he says in a deep Scottish accent,

Martin feels a little nervous, he is standing in front of six regular army corporals, and he is about to question his posting, corporal Kenney speaks before he does,

"I am leaving the training barracks private, no longer an instructor, I am joining the 2nd battalion in Bermuda, I leave on Wednesday"

Martin was confused, all he can say is,

"Corporal?"

"I only request the best soldiers of the training division for the 2nd battalion, to be posted with me of course, good strong soldiers, good leaders, and good marksmen"

He leans forward and whispers in Martin's ear,

"Regardless of age"

Standing away from Martin, the corporal speaks sternly,

"Anything else private?"

"No Corporal, thank you Corporal"

Kenney looks Martin straight in the eyes, winks at him,

"You are dismissed private, now bugger off"

Martin smartly about turns and goes back to the table, Jack looks at him,

"Don't ask Jack, but we are off to Bermuda and corporal Kenney is going with us"

* * *

HMS Brilliant is an Apollo class cruiser, 20 years old with a compliment of 275 sailors and 25 officers of the Royal Navy, the sailors all wearing the same uniform, 'squashed' black cap, with a cap tally stating '*HMS BRILLIANT*' in gold lettering, a stark difference to the darkness of the cap, a blue collar with three white stripes on the edge, a dark blue tunic under which they all wear a blue woolly jumper, the tunic has a black silk bow and a scrubbed white lanyard, with bell bottom trousers and sturdy black boots they all call, '*deck boots*'. Martin and all the other army lads are billeted inside the ship on a large open deck, they are living under canvas for the duration of the journey, 7 days or so to Bermuda, along with his comrades from the Bedfordshire regiment, there are several army engineers and 20 men from artillery regiments. The Bedfordshire's are to join the rest of the battalion, and duties for them are to be security and patrols in and around the dockyard, the engineers and the artillery men are posted to the Bermuda Militia Artillery unit, formed in 1895 and consisting mainly of volunteers from the island, the regular soldiers from the British army are joining to assist with field training and passing on experience to these local soldiers. They will all be billeted at St David's Battery, the Bedfordshire soldiers will be living together at Casemates barracks, a drab two storey building at the southern end of the dockyard. During the weeklong journey across the North Atlantic Ocean, the army contingent has very little to do, all the work parties on board are carried out by the matelots, the army sergeants and corporals, who are supposed to drill the men daily, spend most of their time smoking and playing cards, many of the soldiers are terribly seasick and spend most days lying on their bed roll, trying to keep what small amount of food they have eaten inside their bodies, dry biscuits, the matelots called '*hardtack*' are given to them by the sailors, this seems to be the only food they can keep down. Martin doesn't suffer at all, he and Jack take part in physical training most days, often joined by corporal Kenney, or 'Ken' as he insists they call him when not with the other soldiers, they even manage to get some shooting practice in, firing the army issue bolt action, .303 SMLE rifle (Short, Magazine, Lee Enfield), with its ten round magazine, twenty five inch barrel and detachable seventeen inch bayonet, complete with brass bottle of oil and pull through cleaning kit held in the butt. A competent shot should be accurate up to 400 yards, Martin, with adjusted sights on the weapon, is accurate to distances over double that of the competent soldier. The ship has twelve large guns and two fourteen inch torpedo tubes, Martin, Jack, and Ken get to know a few of the gunners and during practice firing the Chief gunner lets them join in on either the two 6 inch guns, the two 4.7 inch guns or, if they are lucky, on one of the 8 '*six pounders*' placed around the deck. The uniform to be worn on the Island is different to the standard issue of heavy wool battle dress with Brodie helmet, putties and 1908 pattern web equipment, the khaki dress uniform is very similar to the battledress but is lighter, both in colour and weight.

Duties at the RN Dockyard Bermuda are tedious, '*stagging*' on for eight hours, either in the gate house or patrolling the perimeter, then getting eight hours off to eat, clean, shave and sleep, then back on duty again. Time off is a rarity, even then, there isn't a great deal to do, the dockyard is situated on the far Western tip of the Island, barely inhabited by the indigenous Bermudans, the occasional street market will show up and sell local food and goods. When Martin has a day off, he spends it writing letters home, keeping himself fit by running around the perimeter of the dockyard, to the great amusement of his army colleagues, he runs on the outside of the fence rather than the patrol areas on the inside, he spends time every day, cleaning and practicing with his rifle. He finds the weather to be agreeable, sub-tropical nearly all year round, warm in the winter and hot in the summer with very little rain, on many days the humidity level is very high, Martin likes the weather but finds the daily patrolling to be boring, he wants excitement, he has joined the army for thrills, not to walk in large circles following a fence line. He is pleased when he is told that the battalion is to be posted to Pretoria, the state capital of the Union of South Africa in August 1912, the only embuggerance is that they are to travel directly there from Bermuda without returning to England first, he has been away for over two years and wants to see his family, he continues to write to them on a weekly basis.

Arriving at the British Army base of Roberts Heights, Pretoria, in August 1912, the battalion is tasked to carry out Garrison duties, troop parades, honour guards, military funerals and assisting locally with any incidents or disasters and to support the local defence force who seem to spend an inordinate amount of time policing demonstrations and meetings. Martin finds it to be a Godforsaken place, the barracks are some distance from the city of Pretoria, known locally as Jacaranda City because in the spring the amazing purple flowers of the Jacaranda trees flower, bringing the dusty grey and brown landscape to life, there is very little to do, daily square bashing or standing guard at the gate house, with guns held at high port, to show force when on guard duty is at times, is the usual highlight of his day.

The joining together of the four former colonies of Cape, Natal, Transvaal, and Orange River in 1910, has bought about the formation of the South African UDF, essentially a colonial constabulary made up from an amalgamation of the four disparate forces from these colonies, each fiercely protective of their history and protecting whichever of the two languages they choose to speak, neither being English, it has a permanent force of regular soldiers and a citizen force of volunteer recruits. The UDF are tied to the British Armed forces because South Africa, although now self-governing, is still a dominion of the British Empire and therefore answerable to the British Military, they have little time for the men of the Bedfordshire's and the feeling is mutual. Martin certainly has no time for, or any interest in, the difficult politics of the region, the Governor General is a man named Botha, he is supported in government by Jan Smuts, a military man, who fought in the Anglo – Boer wars, he is in charge of the diamond mines, defence and the interior running of the country, the South African policies are complicated and indecipherable to Martin, after the second Boer war, a victory for the British, there seems to be many and difficult ongoing divisions in the country, the Boers, or Afrikaans, are arrogant and overly protective of their way of life and distrusting of anyone outside of their communities, the colonists, have mostly been born in the country, they are loyal to the British King, and seemingly protective of the British army, but from only from a distance. Finally, there are a myriad of indigenous tribes in the area, the Zulu, the Xhosa, the Swazi and the Lemba to name a few, all are known to be relatively peaceable people but, as history has clearly shown, when provoked they will defend, and defend fiercely, their people, their land, and their ancient way of life.

Martin hates the place, hot, dusty and the food is mostly inedible, he has killed a couple of local 'river rabbits' and roasted them so that he can have some decent food, it is almost impossible to keep your kit clean, polished and in muster order, the dust continually blows up and around you by the ever present and unbearable hot winds. Word is received by the battalion, early in July 1914, after nearly two years in South Africa, and over four years since leaving England, that they are to be returned to barracks in the UK, Martin is pleased with this, even the ever present rumblings of a war in Europe with Germany giving assurances of support to the Austro Hungarian nation if they declare war, following the assassination of the heir presumptive to the Austro Hungarian throne a week earlier, war is never a good thing, but this does not put him off wanting to go home.

He is also told, in typical army fashion, toward the end of July 1914, that both his parents have died, he is not given any other details, their cause of death is not known by the army, by the time the message gets to him, they are both in the ground in St Nicholas churchyard in town at home. He is refused permission to travel home early to see his, now 15 year old, sister and to ensure her welfare is in order, no one in the army will give him any information, he understands that they may not know any details as to where she may be, he can only hope that Granny, Aunt May, and Uncle Pete have done the decent thing, he is certain that they will have taken Alice into their one of their homes. It is pointless writing to find out, he will almost certainly be home before a reply will get back to him.

The battalion leaves Pretoria in August 1914, heading home to Britain, arriving at Southampton docks, early afternoon on Saturday 19th September, the unit march to a camp at Lyndhurst, ten miles from Southampton, spending a night under canvas.

Martin is allowed to go directly home on Sunday morning after a night at the camp, he will be on bereavement leave. He manages to jump on transport vehicle going to Southampton, he then takes the train from Southampton to London Waterloo, then across to St Pancreas, boarding a train that takes him to the East station, less than a mile from the cottage, it now, he realises, is his cottage.

1914

CHAPTER FIVE

War is imminent, Archduke Franz Ferdinand, in June, the heir to the Austro Hungarian throne, and his wife, Her Serene Highness Princess Sophie of Hohenberg, had been assassinated by Gavrilo Princip in Sarajevo, countries in Europe are divided into two coalitions, the main protagonists being the triple alliance of Germany, Austria and Hungary on one side and the triple entente of France, Britain and Russia on the other.

Germany declared War on Russia on 1st August, then did the same with France on 3rd August with Britain declaring War in Germany on 4th August, these 3 days were to change the history of the world and the lives, and deaths, of millions.

* * *

Monday September 21st

Martin steps off of the train at the East station, it is just before eleven in the morning, having missed last night's connection and having to sleep at St Pancreas, he has taken the first train he can get on this morning. Putting his soft peak cap with the regimental badge on it, on the back of his head in a relaxed style, he puts his 'valise', a large military pack, and his rifle on the station platform, he takes his 1908 webbing, slinging it loosely over both of his shoulders, leaving it hanging loose at the front, not bothering to fasten the buckle, the buttons on his khaki serge tunic are undone, revealing his khaki green army under shirt.

"Tidy yourself up soldier, you are a bloody mess!"

Martin looks up and sees a police constable, smartly dressed in blue uniform, collar buttoned tightly at the neck, shiny numbers, three two one, are attached on each side of the constables' high collar, Martin replies,

"Who are you then?"

The constable steps toward him.

"Constable 321 Neville Reid, G division, and you?"

Martin does not identify himself but replies,

"What happened to Ernie Pond? He was the bobby around here before I left"

The constable seems to relax a little,

"You know Ernie?"

Martin nods,

"It was him that really got me interested in the army, he fought in the second war against the Boers, getting over there for the last few months of fighting back in 1902"

"Ernie got transferred in November last, back to C division at Watford, I hear that he has been recalled as a reservist and has been sent to France with the artillery"

Martin begins to button his tunic,

"How long have you been in town then Neville?"

"Only six weeks here, I started in July, training at Hatfield, I was then posted to St Albans for a month or so, and well here I am"

Martin extends his right hand, it is taken by Neville and the men shake hands,

"Constable Herb Ward was also here before me, he got moved to Tring in July, he has also been called up as a reservist, did you know him?"

Martin shakes his head,

"Have many had their army reservist status activated?" Martin asks

"Yes" says Neville nodding as he does so, "That's why I am here, the way things are looking, we will all be looking to join up"

"You lot are in a reserved occupation aren't you?, anyway there are hundreds volunteering now and I haven't heard any rumours about call up or conscription yet, there are plenty of regulars and reservists in the army to deal with this mess for now, did you hear that the first big battle was won by the British Expeditionary Forces at Marne last week?, it is rumoured it will all be over soon, I have to say that I am not so certain"

"Will you be going to France?" the constable asks Martin

"I am sure it will happen, but I am just back from South Africa, got a bit of leave because my parents died in August"

"Sorry to hear that Martin" Neville says to Martin

"Then I get off the train and you are busting my balls!" Martin is smiling at the police officer, tunic now buttoned up and webbing secured at the front, the young constable blushes a little,

"A sergeant from St Albans, Sergeant 55 Beckwith has been in town today, visiting some French government fella who lives in town"

Martin laughs,

"Is he still living in Station Road?"

"Sergeant Beckwith?" asks the confused constable, Martin laughs out loud,

"No! The spy, Esterhazy, he arrived six months or so before I left and was at 140 Station Road, his lady and himself calling themselves 'Mr and Mrs Fitzgerald'"

"Sounds like him" replies the constable, "But he moved from Station Road to Milton Road now, has lived there for a few months, Daniel Skillman from the post office told me that he had also changed his name at the same time, he now calls himself Count De Voilement, I thought it was a bit of a secret about his shady past"

"Everyone in town knows!"

Martin put out his hand again,

"Must be off Neville, good to meet you"

Returning the handshake, Neville asks,

"You live near here?"

"I do" Martin replies "My family has the cottage by the water cress beds"

"The one with the huge Yew tree in the garden?"

"That's the one, so not far to go, take care Neville"

"I was there when your parents were taken out for burial"

Nodding his understanding, Martin walks away from the train station, rifle slung over his right shoulder, every other step he takes the rifle bangs against his Brodie helmet that is slung on the webbing at his hip. Walking past Mr Ackroyds bakers' and grocery shop on the lower road to Luton, Martin waves at the owner as he passes by, he walks toward the cottage, the Malta pub is open, he decides to have a lunchtime pint before going to the cottage, although a few might be needed to give him the nerve to go home to the empty cottage. Walking up the few steps to the door, he pushes it open and hears the mumble of conversation and smells the cigarette and pipe smoke that mysteriously hangs in the air, a few regulars look up as he walks in and then carry on with their conversations, dominoes or cribbage games, the one bar pub, with the bar in semi-circle against the far wall, hasn't changed in the four years since he left,

"My word, is that young Martin in my pub!"

The landlady, still Mary Spratley, now in her early 60's, appears from behind the bar to give Martin a hug,

"Hello Granny"

Mary stands back from Martin,

"Let's have a look at you, my soldier Grandson, such a smart uniform, how long have you been away?"

"A little over four and a half years now, it is good to see not much has changed"

Hugging him again Mary whispers, "So sorry about your Mother and Father" Mary has tears running down her wrinkled cheeks, between quiet sobs she says, "My poor Victoria"

Wiping her eyes, she stands us straight, brushing and straightening her pinney, she addresses one of the patrons, "Walter, can you watch the bar for a while?"

The man she spoke to, doesn't look up from his game of dominoes, but raises a hand indicating that he has heard the request.

"No free beer to anyone" Mary points threateningly at Walter, to Martin she says "Come on love"

Mary walks behind the bar, Martin follows her, through the bar and the curtained doorway into a small hallway, he leaves his valise in the hall, the doorway in front of him leads to the back kitchen, Mary is already a few steps up the steep staircase that lead to the living room, small parlour, spare room, and the bedroom his Grandmother lives in above the pub, as he begins the climb himself he hears a voice from inside the pub,

"Get your arse into gear Wally, I need a pint!"

Martin enters the familiar living room, as tidy and organised as he remembers, putting his cap on the small dining table, then leaning his rifle gently against the brick surround of the unlit fireplace, undoing his webbing and slipping it off his shoulders laying it on the floor next to the rifle, Mary approaches him, hugging him very tightly,

"Martin, my Martin, it is so good to see you"

Martin, unused to emotional greetings, especially from his Grandmother, although she has always been loving toward him and Alice, she hasn't ever been an emotional woman. She had been widowed for over 20 years, her Husband, Thomas, also known as 'Ted', dying from consumption just weeks before Victoria was born in 1873, Mary had taken over the pub as licensee and has to be, and is, as tough as her customers, emotional outbursts were not her at all!

Holding her in his arms he said,

"Come on now Granny, I must ask, how is Alice, where is she?"

Mary steps out of Martins arms, "

She is fine son, since your Mother and Father passed, our May has taken her in, she is doing really well, they will be here in a couple of hours or so"

The relief shows on Martins' face,

"What happened to Mother and Father?"

They both sit down, Martin in the old but comfortable single armchair, Mary on an upright cushioned double seat by the fire.

She tells him that both his Parents had quickly become ill in early July that year, both suffering severe breathing difficulties with a heavy and continuous dry cough, both had complained of bad chest pain, after a few days of this, both having a high fever, they were taken to their bed to rest. The headaches they were both suffering had become unbearable, neither would take food due to the almost continuous nausea they suffered, the sweet putrid stench on their breath could be smelt strongly in their small bedroom, the *living room* as the family had always called it, that they shared. Alice has gone to stay with Aunt May, having her own room, her twin cousins share another at the compact but three bedroomed, 2 Maple Cottages, the tied house that comes with Uncle Peter's job on the Childwickbury Estate. The local doctor, William Blake, had been informed that both Victoria and Jeremiah had been taken ill and required a house visit, he arrived on his pony and trap, having travelled from his surgery, at Bowers House, three days later. Dr Blake quickly diagnosed advanced diphtheria, sadly by this time both of them were struggling to breath, both having huge swelling of the neck, Jeremiah was also suffering with large puss filled ulcers, all covered over with a grey membrane of skin, on his legs, no cure or proper treatment could be given, Dr Blake made both of them as comfortable as he could, as he left he told Mary that death would be the best outcome for her Daughter and Son in law, both were struggling to breathe and both were bedridden and unable to move without pain, he gave them a few days. On their last day, both Jeremiah and Victoria had refused or been unable to face the chicken stock soup made by Mary, she had left them, it was midmorning, both were in bed and barely alive.

Mary had returned that evening and their bed was empty, both Victoria and Jeremiah, who seemingly earlier were unable to move, had managed to get out of bed, she ran to the front door to search for them, she found them both sitting under the Yew tree, the early evening sun just beginning to dip toward the Western horizon, orange and red light shining on both of them, sitting side by side, holding hands and very obviously dead.

The 'village' constable, a new bobby at the time, Constable 321 Neville Reid had arrived the next day with the death certificates, signed by Dr Blake, the bodies of Victoria and Jeremiah had been moved a day earlier from under the Yew tree with help from a few regulars of the pub, all with scarves covering their faces. Both were put into basic wood coffins, supplied by Mr Wright, the undertaker from town, they were both 'laid out' in their kitchen and there they stayed until collected by Mr Wright on the day of the funeral, he had known Jeremiah well as they had grown up together, as a favour to the family he provided his services at cost only. The funeral costs were one pound and fifteen shillings for each coffin and burial, four shillings to the grave diggers, George Hawkins and his brother Geoff are now working together as the diggers of the graves, one shilling and threepence for each death certificate, Mr Wright had given assurance that he would give the priest 'a drink' to conduct a short service in the church and at the graveside. Husband and Wife are buried together in St Nicholas churchyard under the Yew Tree, in the next plot to Ted Spratley, Father to Victoria and Mary's husband, the funeral went without pomp or procession, the coffins were collected from the cottage and put onto two horse drawn funeral biers, it is usual for coffins to be transferred onto a grand horse drawn hearse, they did not for this funeral, they remained on the funeral biers for the three mile journey to the church. Mary, May, Peter, and Alice travelled in the local horse drawn cab, the cabby, Mr William Hogg, providing this service for free, out of respect to the family. The procession, only consisting of the two funeral biers and the family in the cab, took the deceased from their cottage home, along the lower road to Luton, past the Almagam Mill, all the way to Westfield junction, turning left and travelling slowly through Westfield ford and past the Red Cow pub, the locals respectfully removing hats and caps, bowing their heads as the dead went by, past the entrance to Westfield Common Nursery, where Jeremiah had worked for nearly a quarter of a century, former colleagues standing thoughtfully and peacefully outside, then over the railway bridge and onto the track across Westfield common, travelling through the open fields on either side of Sun Lane, turning left onto the High Street, past, the now stinking and stagnant, Cock pond, Dr and Mrs Blake were stood outside Bowers house as the coffins passed by, then turning right to be met at the church gates by the Reverend William Wingfield Colley, curate of the town, a short service inside the church followed. Mary makes a point of mentioning that the church had recently been gifted a large painting of the nativity by local artist Frank Salisbury, when Martin who is not really interested does not respond to this statement, Mary continues by telling him that his parents are buried in the graveyard, no headstone has, as yet been ordered.

"Don't get one, they didn't want one" he said

"Are you sure Martin?" quizzed his Grandmother, he continues,

"They both told me this when I joined the army, I told them if I was killed, I would like to be buried in town, but not to mark my final resting place, they both agreed and then told me that neither of them wanted any form of grave marker"

"As you wish" Mary answers but is visibly upset by this, Martin gets up and kneels in front of her,

"You know where they are Granny, Alice knows and when I am shown, so will I, no one else needs to know"

She nods in agreement,

"Are you hungry lad?"

He was but told her that he wasn't, he needs to go home,

"I will be going to the cottage if that's alright with you"

Mary stands up, walks to a chest of drawers, takes a large key from a pot on top of it, hands it to Martin,

"You will need this"

He thanks her as he picks up his kit,

"Don't tell Alice I am here yet please Granny; I will surprise her"

"She will go to the cottage with May before coming here, they go a couple of times a week to open the doors and check the garden, May has a key"

Martin collects his rifle and valise, he smiles at his Grandmother,

"I didn't get the pint I came in for!"

"Come back later with May and Alice, you can have a pint then, I will have tea ready, the pub closes in an hour or so, then I don't open until after six tonight'

He nods and leaves the room, exiting the pub the same way he had entered, turning left, he walks past the Methodist church, now nearly a decade old, he crosses the road, and a short distance later, he is by the gate to the cottage.

It all looks the same, but he knows it will never be the same again for him and for Alice,

"Hello Martin"

He turns to see who the voice belongs too, he doesn't recognise the speaker, a woman, about the same age as him, slim and attractive, stunning dark eyes, with jet black hair, tied at the back in a tight bun, a long black skirt, showing off her slim waist, a white lacy long sleeved top with a high necked collar, set off with a thin necklace on the outside of it, she is carrying a black jacket and a small black hat.

"Hello" is all he can say, the silence screams at them both until she speaks,

"You don't remember me, do you?"

He shakes his head, she is familiar, but he says "No miss, I'm sorry I don't"

She laughs out loud, he adores the sound of her laugh, a happy, pleasant, and free sound,

"Grace, Grace Wilson, we went to '*St Nicks*' school together, you sat in front of me"

Martin looks quizzically at her, then a memory comes alive inside his head,

"Your family used to live in Salisbury Road, your Father worked with mine at the nursery at Westfield"

She smiles at his recognition, he cannot take his eyes off her smile, she notices he is staring at her, he blushes, she speaks first,

"My Dad is still working there and we all still live in the same house, Dad, Mum, Me and young Patrick"

Martin is entranced by her beauty and her smile,

"You married now?" he blurts out clumsily, she laughs again, delightfully throwing her head back as she does,

"No Martin, still very single, I work in the school at the National Children's home"

Martin seems confused,

"What is that then?" he questions

"How long have you been away?" she asks,

"Since early 1910, I came home once that year for a short leave, then left for Bermuda then on to Pretoria in the Union of South Africa, I haven't been home for over four years"

Grace explains to him that the National Children's home opened a sanatorium for 64 patients at Elmfield house in 1910, for London children suffering from consumption, to be treated with lots of fresh air and physical therapy, in 1913, at Highfield, also on Ambrose Lane, just around the corner from the sanatorium, a children's home had been established as the successor to the original home, formerly in Bonner Road, Bethnal Green.

"Is that up where Ambrose wood is?" Martin asks.

Grace tells him he is correct,

"The wood is still there and forms part of the home"

"That must be close to the Nickey line railway then?" Martin cannot think of anything else to say, the short, 7 mile railway line from town to Hemel Hempstead is one thing he remembers about the area, although he has never ridden the train on this line.

"It is right next door to the home" Grace replies excitedly,

She continues to explain that the children's home, although still being built, is taking in numerous orphaned, abandoned, homeless or suffering children from London and the surrounding areas, she had been a school mistress at the sanatorium but now teaches in the new school within the grounds of the children's home.

Martin takes out his pocket watch, checking the time,

"You must be late today; school must have started a couple of hours ago!"

"I work alternate mornings and afternoons, today is an afternoon for me"

She looks at her own watch, "I must hurry, or I will be late"

They look at each other for a few seconds, Martin blushes again.

"Goodbye Martin, nice to see you in your uniform, very handsome!"

Still blushing, he says, "Lovely to see you Grace"

She walks off, turning to face him she asks, "Why are you home now?"

His head drops, "Oh, I was in Pretoria when my Parents passed, this is my first time home, I have to ensure my little sister is safe and well before I set off again"

She runs back to him, taking his hands in hers,

"Martin, I am so sorry, I heard about your Mother and Father, it had slipped my mind, accept my apologies and condolences"

"Of course," he replies "No apology needed"

Grace is still holding his hands in hers, her skin soft and warm against his tough hands,

"I must go" she says, still holding his hands

"Of course," he replies

She gently pulls her hands from his and begins to walk away, he musters up some courage, calling after her,

"I will be in Grannies pub later this evening if you would like to come in?"

He hears her laugh again, she answers him as she walks away,

"A young lady in a public house on her own? What do you take me for Martin!"

He laughs with her, and shouts back,

"You won't be on your own, you will be with me"

He hopes she has heard him, he stands watching as Grace walks off toward the Electric Hose and Rubber company, just on the other side of the East station, this is also new to him, had had seen it for the first time from the railway station platform, he remembers it was Pickford Mill when he left, this new rubber factory had apparently replaced the old mill in 1911, the large sign outside it clearly states, '*Electric Hose and Rubber Company Est 1911*', Granny had referred to it as the Almagam Mill, he presumes this is a local nickname for it.

So much has changed around here he thinks to himself, Grace is now out of his sight, he turns to the cottage,

"At least you look the same old girl" he says to himself, looking down the garden he stops and looks at the huge and magnificent Yew Tree,

"And you, old tree, you haven't changed a bit, still as scary as you ever were"

Opening the gate, Martin enters the land and property he now owns, for the first time in over four years, tears begin to form in his eyes, and he makes no attempt to stop them as they fall slowly over his cheeks.

Everything is almost as he remembers it, he is glad of the familiarity, as he was when he entered the pub earlier, he expects there to be other changes in the local area, the rubber works, the Almagam, replacing Pickford Mill was certainly unexpected, he has never heard of the national children's home or the sanatorium, all these changes have happened since he left and he has had to take all this in since he arrived, only a couple of hours ago, he hopes the inside of the cottage hasn't changed too much and it is as his memory recalls. Turning to look down the garden again, he is surprised to see that it is in good order, the vegetable patch seems weed free with onions growing, soon ready to be harvested, he can see parsnips and cabbages also growing well, he presumes that Alice has been busy keeping the garden tidy since their parents' deaths. At the other side of the plot stands the Yew tree, he smiles to himself as he feels a bit silly having spoken out loud and directly to the tree just a few minutes earlier. The stream at the end of the garden, just past the water pump, still very much in use, moves as slowly and as gently as ever, Martin smiles again as he recalls spending a lot of time as a young boy standing in the stream trying to catch sticklebacks, small fish with spines across their backs, he looks across the stream to the watercress beds. They are a commercial enterprise, the land being owned, since he can remember, by a commercial watercress grower, Edward Mizen from Mitcham, on the borders of Surrey and South London, he has two sons, both also called Edward, the younger of his boys being known as 'Ernest' to avoid any confusion. The beds across from his cottage are and have been since just after the turn of the century, managed by a local man, who Martin knows well, Fred Wood. Martin met Fred when they were both boys, Fred is 2 years older than Martin and from Whitwell, a small village 5 miles north of the cottage, Fred had been apprenticed in the mill by the river, cycling daily from his family's tiny cottage to his work, in rain, wind or shine. In 1901, Fred left the mill to be employed by the Mizen family to run the watercress beds for them and he still does. Martin can see Fred in the beds, knee deep in the fresh spring water that the watercress thrives on, raking the vegetables toward him, then to be bunched by the *watercress ladies*, who put the harvest into large reed baskets, still made locally, to be taken directly to the nearby East station for onward transport to the London markets, he shouts across the stream,

"Hello Fred!" Fred looks up and waves back, "How are Helen and the boys?" asks Martin

"All good thanks Martin, good to see you home" a pause,

"Sorry to hear about your Mother and Father, sad times indeed"

Martin thanks Fred and waves to him again.

Fred and his brother have been raised by their single, unmarried Mother, Charlotte, so both had grown up to be tough, bastard children are often vilified and shunned by society especially in small villages, it has never bothered Fred, he is happy with his life, Martin is just about to put the key in the lock when Fred calls over again,

"I will be having a pint when the pub opens, before cycling home if you are about Martin?"

Martin tells Fred he will be in the pub and will see him there, Fred gets back to work, Martin takes the key from his tunic pocket, a single key with a ring at one end and the flat single barred key at the other. The green panelled metal rim lock on the front door stands out against the plain wood of the door, a single keyhole on the left and a knob next to it, the key makes a distinctive sound as it goes into the keyhole, turning it to the right he hears the deadbolt come free from the strike, turning the knob clockwise, the latch bold releases and the door opens into the kitchen, he steps in, removing the key from the lock and putting it on the kitchen table. Leaving the door open he stands for a minute or so, eyes closed and breathing in the smells he remembers so well, dominated by the ever present aroma from the thatch above him, still firmly held in place by its original strong ancient beams, with flat wooden planks nailed in between them holding the thatch sturdily where it lies. He fondly recalls Donald Shelley, the master thatcher from St Albans quickly taking off the old thin and rotting thatch, replacing the bad wooden planks, putting many more in than had been previously in place and then the seemingly painstakingly slow task of re thatching the cottage roof, the courses being held in place with twisted wooden pegs, known as *sways.* This had been in 1909, the 'new' thatch was now over five years old and holding well, Martin looks up and can see the light yellow thatch in a few places in between the flat planks. The room, although familiar to him, seems airless, Martin turns around to open the kitchen window to let the late summer afternoon air in to circulate and clear out the still stale air in the cottage, smiling again at another memory as he undoes the latch and opens the sash window. These windows were fitted in 1905, about the same time as the new Post office on the High Street in town was being built, his Father, Jeremiah, had met in the Old Cock pub in town, one of the foremen from the building site, the son of the owner of the building company, a young man named Ernie Jarvis, originally from the East End of London, known to everyone as 'E.C.', he is now living in town at Moreton End. E.C. was not a happy man on the day they met, one of the newly apprenticed builders on site had been tasked with measuring the space for the window frames in the new post office, after the measurements were taken the hardwood frames had been ordered and made in town by the local carpenter from Rothamstead Manor, Mr Claude J Walter, a master of his trade and, with the permission of Sir Charles Lawes Wittewronge, son of the founder of the experimental station, Claude had made the hardwood frames in his work shed at Rothamstead, to the exact size that the apprentice had given to him. The sizes had been wrong, and Claude had to re make them all, good news for him as he was to be paid again, E.C. had been fuming, the wrong frames were to be wasted as they had been made specifically to measure, Jeremiah offered to take them off him, the cottage at that time needing three new windows, the ones in place at that time were ancient and rotted. E.C. had five frames so they came to an agreement, Jeremiah would purchase all the frames at just below cost, E.C. was glad to be getting some of the money back that the company had paid out for the incorrectly sized frames, so long as Jeremiah collected them from the work shed at Rothamstead. They were actually being *stored* at Claude's house at number two Cravells Road, he was of course, he told Jeremiah, only storing them for safe keeping. E.C sent one of his builders from the post office site to work for Jeremiah, he set to work, replacing the three old windows on the front wall of the cottage, and putting two new ones in on the back wall, knocking holes in the substantial kitchen wall and the wall facing the back yard in the living room. Fitting the new windows had been straight forward, the new holes were made to measure, that could not be said for the front windows, the old kitchen and bedroom windows came out easily enough but the new frames were smaller than the old ones, the builder, James Williams, left the old stone sills in place then fitted the new windows and filled the gaps on either side with cement and stones, above both windows he fitted an arch of red brick, bricks 'borrowed' from the post office site. The window in the back bedroom had originally been high up on the front wall, this was removed and the gap it left, was filled with the stone that had been taken out from the wall in the gap made to accommodate the new window. George 'the glass' Gardner, the local glazier, had cut and fitted the glass for the windows, all of the local men working at the cottage were members of the quoits club at The Malta, founded and run by Claude, so the work was done for a decent price, friends doing friends favours.

Martin swallows hard as sadness fill his body, remembering how happy his Father had been when the work fitting the windows had finished, his Mother loved the influx of light that the new windows on the back wall gave to the inside, he himself had loved having the carpenter, the builder and the glazier in and around the house, having been thirteen years old then, the workman had treated him well, getting him to help to fetch and carry tools that they needed, then going to the pub with them and his Father at the end of the day and drinking beer shandy, his payment for a day's work well done.

The range in the kitchen, stands unused and cold, it is clean and the hanging brass pans above it are shiny, more evidence that Alice and May have been keeping the place clean, Martin walks through the kitchen, running his right hand gently on the top of the family dining table as he walks toward the door, to what was, his parents' bedroom, always known as 'the living room' for reasons no one knows, he glances at the Longcase clock standing proudly next to the dresser. The clock, a wedding present to Victoria and Jeremiah, is known as an eight day clock, with two cable suspended weights hidden behind the door on the front panel with a small key lock, one weight drives the pendulum and the other the striking mechanism, this clock has a small chime that sounds on the hour, its large painted dial face is housed in a mahogany veneer, it has two holes, one on each side, to wind the weighted movements. He hears two gently struck chimes, taking out his pocket watch, he looks at both, to ensure that the shown time is correct, it is, he carries on. The dresser, always described by Mother as a '*Welsh*' dresser, proudly displays two rows of plates on its racks, the row of small drawers below the racking, are all closed, two ceramic jugs stand on the top of the base, three drawers and two doors below are also closed tight, keeping the jars of pickles, jugged meat and tins containing tea and sugar safe and secure. Pulling the door to his parents' bedroom open, inwards toward the kitchen, the door catches on the door frame as he does this causing yet another familiar and welcoming sound, he steps into the living room, he is happy to see it looks as it did when he left, the whitewashed painted walls are still clean and bright, but he feels sad that the room is now so unused and still, the small fireplace, the shape of a teardrop cut into the robust stone wall, with an small but ornate red brick surround built by his Father before he was born, lies dormant, evidence of its last fire still sit in the grate. A small chest of drawers, made of walnut, stand below the 'new' window on the back wall, neatly placed on top of it is a sterling silver hollowware vanity set, in '*Repousse*' style, a large hairbrush sits brush side down, next to it an identical but smaller hairbrush, a clothing brush with single handle and longer bristles than those on the hairbrushes lies on its side, a boot button hook and a smaller corset hook, both with exquisitely designed handles, lie dormant and unused. Sitting on top of the chest of drawers is a small dressing table mirror, it's frame also made of walnut, with its square, flat base. Mounted in the sinuously carved brackets on either side, is the framed mirror, the pivot pins allowing variable tilt for the user, nothing of his Father is placed here, this was his Mothers domain, her clothes, he knows, will be clean and neatly folded within these drawers, he cannot bring himself to open any of them at this time.

The bed, seemingly as old as the cottage itself sits below the other window, it is almost a cot design, with deep raised sides, the foot board being taller than the headboard, it was obviously made with care, time and devotion, the metal sprung mattress is thick, sitting snugly within the frame of the bed and on strong wooden slats. A tick cover, made from heavy cotton, protects the mattress and anyone sleeping on it from feeling the springs as they rest, a heavy, handmade, and embroidered bed rug covers the blankets and sheets below it. A simple double doored wardrobe stands against the wall shared with the kitchen, he opens it, the door hinges quietly squeaking as he pulls both doors open, inside are the few pairs of trousers and shirts that were owned by his father and several dresses of his Mothers, he recognises the strong chemical smell from the mothballs inside the wardrobe, gently closing the doors he sees the small three drawered bedside table, wedged between the bed and the wall on his Father's side, without looking inside the drawers he knows it will contain, socks, underwear and a shaving kit, amongst all the other nick knacks owned by Jeremiah, it is made from a dark wood, possibly mahogany, it strikes Martin that none of the furniture in this bedroom matches, it all possibly being picked up from house sales or more likely, from Charlies second hand furniture shop on Vaughan Road.

Moving on from the 'living room' and into the bedroom he shared with Alice until he left in 1910, a lifetime ago or so it seems to him, pushing the door open he steps in, it is unrecognisable from the room he remembers. The two rough wooden beds he and Alice had are now gone, replaced with a splendid metal framed bed covered in a light blue and white striped eiderdown, pink flowers fill the white sections with bursts of colour, a dressing unit with a vanity mirror and two large drawers stands in the corner in between the fireplace and the blue curtained window, the fireplace has a beautiful dark wood framed tapestry screen in front of it, the tapestry an explosion of colours depicting tulips and roses both with vibrant bright green leaves and delicate stems, a short brass fire guard fender sits in place in front of the screen, the fireplace, clean and ash free, is surrounded by a white painted wooden frame, two dolls and a porcelain lady sit on the mantle, one pair of ladies' boots stand to the right of the fireplace. The whole room has been wallpapered, and quite recently it would seem, the bare stone walls and the brick fireplace and chimney he remembers, have seemingly been covered with handmade wooden laths and horsehair lime, gypsum or Portland plaster being put over the wooden laths. These walls are now covered by bright floral paper, from the high supporting roof beams to the floor, an old wardrobe stands in the right corner, opposite the door, tall and made of oak with a single door.

Nothing of his remains in the room, it is clean, fresh, and very feminine, he has to admit, a much better room than the stone and brick walled, two wooden bedded room with an unprotected fire that he had shared with Alice until he was eighteen, feeling as though he is intruding in his sisters' space, he leaves, closing the door behind him. Going back into the kitchen he takes some kindling and lights a small fire in the grate of the range, also taking a wild woodbine cigarette from the packet in his breast pocket, noting that he only has one left, the pack had originally contained five, he has enough change in his pockets to buy another packet or two, they only cost a penny for a pack of five, inhaling deeply, he looks around for the kettle as it is not on the range, spotting it on the floor by the side of the range, he picks it up. Leaving through the open front door, he makes his way down the garden to fill up the kettle at the water pump, walking to the Yew and rubbing his hand on the rough bark, he has no idea why he does this, he is just finishing pumping the water into the kettle when he hears laughter, female laughter from the road, looking up he sees Alice and Aunt May approaching the gate. Both stop suddenly when they see the front door open, he sees the anxiety on their faces, they must think an intruder has been here or even might still be inside,

"I left it open to get some air inside" he shouts across at them.

Aunt May puts her hand to her mouth, Alice looks for a few seconds, then realising it is her big brother, she screams his name and runs toward him, he puts the kettle on the ground,

"Martin! Martin! It's you!"

She runs into his arms, he takes her in his, he can feel her sobbing deeply and holding him tight, he responds and squeezes her tightly, making her feel safe from everything and anything. The three of them enter the kitchen, Alice hangs onto Martin's arm, not wanting to let her brother go, the kitchen is full of smoke, coming from the chimney,

"The chimney must be blocked" says Martin "May, would you open the back door please"

May does as she is asked, Martin lifts the burning kindling from the stove fire with a small ash shovel, taking the glowing wood outside and leaving it on the shovel out by the front door, he returns to the kitchen.

"No tea or coffee here today!" he exclaims, Alice and May laugh at him

"I will have to clear the blockage, or the chimney could set on fire"

"Don't you make a mess soldier!" May jokingly says to Martin "Come on Alice, no point in cleaning and dusting today, your brother will make a terrible mess here"

Alice begins to complain that she has only spent a few minutes with Martin and wants to stay, Martin places a hand on her shoulder,

"Alice, go to the pub with May, Granny has invited me for tea, I will clear this blockage, get washed up and then come to the pub, I will be an hour or so"

Alice runs and hugs her brother,

"I have missed you too little Sister, go on now, I will catch you up"

Alice looks directly into her brothers' eyes,

"Mother and Father…"

He hushes her gently,

"I know all about it Alice, Granny told me, we can talk later"

Letting Martin go, Alice and May leave to go to the pub,

"Remember soldier boy, no mess in here"

He smiles and watches as Alice and May walk toward the pub arm in arm.

Taking off his army tunic and shirt he walks through the back door into the yard, the wood storage is still as it was, there is a change here though, the old rotten shed that was made from bits and pieces of wood and planking has been replaced with a new purpose build wooden shed, bigger than the old one and certainly of a more solid build, a ladder sits on the pitched roof. It is not locked so Martin opens the door, as he looks inside he notes that every inch and every being of this shed is his Father, tools hanging on the walls, clean and in order, old tobacco tins containing nails and screws stand neatly against the back panel on a waist high bench, underneath this bench he can see a chimney brush with several extension pieces, he will only need a couple, the cottage is single story and the chimney is on the outside wall and not very high, he recalls seeing the ladder on the roof of the shed, going outside he removes the ladder by sliding it off of the wooden runners screwed into the roof, in place to stop the ladder falling off, it is a double extended ladder with round wooden rungs supported under each one by a strip of iron, two iron brackets at the top of the base section enable the fly section to slide through, then to be secured in place by two iron rung locks, he doesn't need to fully extend the fly section, only six or seven rungs higher will be needed. With the ladder in place, the feet safely pushed into the soft soil, the top gently placed against the roof to the right side of the chimney stack he climbs up and gets onto the roof, standing next to the chimney, being careful to stay on the stone edge of the roof so as not to damage the thatch, taking the brush he attaches an extension rod to it, then inserts it into the top of the open pot on top of the chimney, pushing it down, it moves easily and freely, he attaches the second extension rod and pushes again, a few inches further down, about halfway inside the chimney, he meets resistance, using a little force he manages to push the blockage down the chimney with ease. The brush is removed and he climbs down the ladder, putting it back in its rightful place on top of the shed, Martin enters the kitchen, thankfully now clear of smoke, he goes over to the range and removes the flue plate, as he had often seen his Father do, he expects the blockage to fall into the fire grate, but nothing happens, Martin puts his arm into the flue, glad he took off his uniform shirt as he expects the metal chimney stack to be full of soot, he is surprised when his arm goes up through the flue and into the open space of the stone chimney, confused he removes his arm. He inspects the chimney by looking up it from the stove, angling a newly lit candle to be able to see into the darkness, the metal chimney rising from the stove is only a foot or so long, stopping just after as it disappears through an iron damper that has been placed in the chimney, removing his arm from inside the flue he stands with his left shoulder against the front of the chimney breast, leaning down he puts his right arm up the chimney until it reaches the damper, only a few inches above the top of the fireplace and out of sight, it comes free easily, he manages to remove it by turning it on its side and carefully taking it from its home inside the chimney, as he does so an amount of debris falls from inside the chimney onto the stove. He quickly identifies it as an old bird nest, a large nest that has obviously been causing the blockage, looking inside the stone chimney breast he can see that the iron chimney from the stove does not go the full way up inside the stone chimney, it passes only a few inches above the damper, through a hole made for this, this is why the bird nest had not come down into the stove but had landed on the damper. Mystery solved, he is just about to put the damper back in place, it will fit snugly over the ranges iron chimney, when something inside the chimney catches his eye, even with a lit candle he cannot make out what it is, putting his arm into the chimney he can feel the straight, flat ledge of the smoke shelf, where the damper usually sits snugly, toward the back of this shelf he can feel a gap, as though several stones and brick have been removed, investigating the space with his fingers he touches something, he thinks it is a piece of old sacking. It takes several attempts to get his fingers to move it, gripping it with the ends of his fingers he manages to move it a few inches, enough to get some purchase onto it, removing it from the soot encrusted chimney, bringing it into the kitchen and into daylight, he sees that it is an old hessian sack wrapped like an parcel around an object, taking it over and putting it on the kitchen table, he sits in a chair and begins to unwrap the strange parcel, the hessian sack is filthy with soot and is falling apart in places, inside is another layer of wrapping, it is old sheets of newspaper, on the first layer he removes he can clearly read the banner heading below a coat of arms,

'The London Gazette'

Below the name of the newspaper it reads,

'Published by Authority'

'From Saturday January 4 to Tuesday January 7, 1794'

Much of the remaining print is indecipherable, worn away by time and the soot from inside the chimney, only two words at the bottom of the page can just be made out,

'Price eight'

Martin attempts to make out other words from the one hundred and twenty year old newspaper, he fails, putting this piece to one side he removes the next piece, again it is ancient and faded, nearly the whole page cannot be read, bar one small section that he reads aloud to himself,

'Turin December 18'

By Accounts received from Barcelona, dated the 11th Instant, it appears, that intelligence had arrived there from the Camp at Roussillon, that the Spaniards and Portuguese had obtained a compleat Victory in a general Adion over the French, in which the latter lost between Seven and Eight Hundred Men killed or drowned in passing the River Tec , above 600 taken Prisoners, 46 Piecces of Cannon, Two Howitzers, One Mort?'-, a great Number of Muskeis, with Tents, Cloathing, Ammunition and Stores. The Loss of the Spaniards and Portuguese amounts to 200 Men.'

It means nothing to him, the wording and spelling from a time so long ago he cannot even begin to imagine, putting this piece of newspaper on top of the other, ripping it as he does so, almost certainly because of its age and fragility, he makes sure to carefully unwrap the remainder of this ancient parcel, he stops suddenly, he takes a huge intake of breath, looking again to make sure he had really seen what he thinks he has, remembering to exhale, he takes a closer look at what is inside the remaining, carefully wrapped newspaper.

The tiny bones that are sticking out of the old newspaper are that of a left hand, obviously of a child, carefully he peels back the layers covering the contents, the newspaper he either removes or folds away gently from what is inside.

A skeleton, a tiny fragile skeleton, so small it cannot have lived for very long, if at all after birth, the body is wrapped in an old piece of material, many parts of it have rotted away with time, through these gaps, some bones of the long dead child can clearly be seen. The body lies with its arms at its sides, the left arm can clearly be seen as it is not covered by any material or newspaper at all, parts of these bones have dried flesh hanging from them, the corpse has been partially mummified by the heat and dryness of the chimney, it is undamaged as the body was tucked away in the nook inside the chimney, and from any direct heat source, the right arm, apart from a few finger bones in view, is covered with the material. The bottom half of this tiny body is partially covered, both legs can be seen protruding from the material, thin, birdlike leg bones with the tiniest and most delicate feet attached at the bottom of each, the main body of the corpse is wrapped in the material, no bones can clearly be seen but the material is a shabby, misshapen, and stained mass across this midsection. Finally, he looks at the skull, Martin wants to look away, it is beautifully hideous, his eyes are drawn to stare at it, the lower jaw is toothless and has an obvious underbite, the nose cavity still has aged and dried flesh attached to it, giving the corpse a semblance of life, the eye sockets are empty, the pits as black as the depths of hell, a large forehead of bone is the final part of this hideous and ghoulish puzzle. Martin believes that this is possibly the remains of a stillborn child, brought into the world dead and then wrapped in the material, then wrapped again in a newspaper, before being put into a piece of sacking, he presumes the paper could not have been that old when the child was wrapped inside, this being the case, the tiny body, no bigger than the palms of both Martins hands, had been placed inside the chimney on the ledge and has been there for the past 120 years.

What does he do with this corpse?

What can he do?

He asks these questions of himself and has no answers, he tells himself that he should call the police, but what can they do? There will almost certainly be no record of the birth, he knows that his family, in various guises, have always owned and lived in this cottage, so the child must be somehow related to him, maybe not by blood but certainly by marriage or as a cousin many times removed. His Mother had, when he was a child, kept a written list, in a small black notebook, of the family tree and the known history of the cottage, she noted as much as she could find out about, but Martin has no idea where it may be now. He does remember, from conversations with his Mother many years earlier, that it is believed that the cottage had been built around 1680 and hadn't, as far as she had known, changed much since then, thinking and speaking aloud, he works out that if this dead child had been born in 1794, the year printed on the old newspaper, the child would have been born to his Great Great Grandmother, so had he or she lived, he or she would have been his Great Grandparent. Mother had told him, years before, the names of all his Grandparents, but he cannot recall the name of any of them, especially that of his Great Great Grandmother, but he does remember tales, told to him by his Grandad, Alfred, whom he does remember and who died in 1903 aged only fifty one, tales that had been handed down through the generations of his family, including a story that Alfred's Great Grandmothers son, who had been the local grave digger, had died whilst sitting under the Yew tree in the garden of this very cottage.

He suddenly looks up, eyes wide, he has an idea.

He decides to bury the child under the Yew tree, the child had been born on the family land and therefore should be buried on it, he will not need to dig very deep as the skeleton is so tiny, there is no point in reporting it, the body will only be taken away and disposed of, so he will see to it himself.

Half an hour later, Martin is standing in front of the small hole he has just finished digging on the edge of the dark soil under the huge canopy of the Yew tree, a hole no bigger than the size of a box that new shoes would be put in, he has dug down to a depth of a couple of feet, the grave is no more than twelve inches wide by eighteen inches across, taking the spade he walks back toward the house to collect the tiny corpse that currently sits on his kitchen table. Halfway up the garden, just before the vegetable patch, he suddenly turns, an awful feeling of being watched has come over him, goose bumps rise involuntarily all over his flesh and his senses, now on full alert, tell him that he is not alone, staring at the Yew tree he sees nothing, just the gently moving bows and branches of the old tree, the whispering noise they make as they move in the wind, transfixes him for a moment or two,

"Bloody fool" he says to himself "It's the tree, no one else is here"

Checking around again to make sure, he makes his way to the house.

Gently carrying the tiny skeleton of the child in his hands, Martin walks back to the small freshly dug grave, getting on to his knees he places the re wrapped body of the child into it, Martin is not a religious man, the only prayer he knows is the Lord's prayer, without hesitation and although having no real belief in any God, he begins,

"Our Father, which art in heaven, Hallowed by thy name, Thy kingdom come, Thy will be done, in earth as it is in heaven: Give us this day our daily bread, And forgive our trespasses, as we forgive them that trespass against us; Lead us not into temptation, But deliver us from evil, for thine is the kingdom, the power and the glory, For ever and ever. Amen"

He had learnt it in Latin at school when he was five or six years old, he tries to recall the words,

'PATER noster, qui es in caelis, sanctificetur nomen tuum...'

He cannot remember any more that the first few words, he realises that he has taken the spade back to the house so he uses his hands to push the spoil on top of the skeleton, he feels nothing, no sadness, no grief and no attachment to the long dead child, he has no idea of how the child lived, if it had lived at all, or died, he has only just come to terms with the death of his parents, so the death of a child, who may or may not be a relative, over one hundred and twenty years ago, has little or no effect on him.

As he stands, he wonders if he is near the spot where the grave digger died over forty years before he was born, he nods to himself as he realises the similarities, he is now a grave digger as well, he pushes the soil that is slightly raised up over the grave flat with his army boot, he walks back toward the house, time to wash up and go to see his sister.

The Malta is locked when he arrives, knocking on the door he takes two steps back knowing that the door opens outwards, Alice is the one who opens the door, she says nothing but throws herself into Martins arms, sobbing uncontrollably.

Lifting her up he carries her into the pub, Aunt May and Granny are standing behind the bar, Mary is polishing pint glasses with a tea towel, after May has cleaned them in the sink, both look at Martin, he places his sister gently onto one of the bench seats by the front windows, pulling up a chair he sits in front of her, holding her hands in his,

"Alice, it's alright, nothing to be afraid of, I am here now"

Alice looks up at him, tears fill her eyes,

"But you will go away again soon won't you Martin, the war will take you away I just know it"

Martin tells her that it will take him, he has to fight, it is his job,

"But what happens if you get killed, Martin I will be all alone!"

Mary speaks up,

"You will always have us Alice, me, Aunt May, Uncle Peter and your cousins, Jenny and Catherine, you will always be safe with us"

Martin pulls his sister toward him, hugging her, he whispers into her ear,

"I won't be killed little sister, but I will have to go away, probably to France, but I will come back, I don't know when, but I will come back to you"

Alice pulls herself away from him,

"You promise?"

"I do promise"

He hugs his sister again, Mary speaks to them both,

"Come on you two, upstairs, wash your hands, I have pork pie and sandwiches, corned beef, and cheese, upstairs waiting to be eaten, Uncle Peter will be here soon, so we had best save him some, put the bolt across the door Martin please!"

The four of them make their way upstairs to the front room, Martin stops,

"I won't be a minute" he says "Just getting the beer I was promised earlier"

He hears his Grandmother tut from upstairs; he smiles.

Turning back and going to the bar, he takes a clean straight pint glass and pulls himself a pint of Glover and Sons pale ale, Richard Glover, a London brewer, is the owner of the brewery in town having purchased it in 1897, he had immediately demolished the old brewery leaving only the large residence, Brewery House, on site and rebuilt the whole brewery, in 1902 his brewery combined with Pryor Reid brewers of Hatfield, it is Glovers pale ale that is Martins choice of beer.

He downs half a glass with one swallow, licking his lips

"By God that is good"

He is stopped from taking a second pull on his drink by a hefty knocking at the front door,

"I will get it" he shouts upstairs.

The top bolt is the only security currently in use, he pulls this back and pushes the door open, Uncle Peter is stood on the step,

"Now then boy" he says to Martin in his deep Hertfordshire accented voice, "How have you been?"

Martin steps back and Peter enters, the men shake hands, Peter points at Martins pint of beer,

"If you are having a sly early one, then maybe I should join you"

He pats Martin on the shoulder and the pair go upstairs, after refilling Martins glass and pulling a fresh pint for Pete.

The pub is open, regulars fill the bar on both sides, smoke hangs in the air and there is a murmur of low sound as the men talk to one another after a day's work, Martin is sat at the bar, he and Alice have had a long chat about their parents, everyone else present remained sympathetically silent for them, Martin assures Alice that he will return from overseas, although not ordered back to barracks yet, he knows it is coming. Martin thanks Peter and May for taking Alice in and for keeping the cottage and the garden in good form, both say that they are happy to continue with the arrangement, Martin insisting, and they agree after a long argument, that he will pay toward her keep. Martin and Alice are to visit their parent's grave tomorrow, Alice is staying with their Grandmother at the pub for the night, Martin had politely declined, telling them he wants to stay at the cottage, Alice does not want to stay there at all, she has made that very clear to Martin, he understands her reticence to stay in the cottage overnight, but he feels fine with it. Martin has not mentioned his find of the child's skeleton in the chimney breast to anyone, he has decided that will be his secret and his to keep forevermore. He is just finishing the pint that Fred Wood had put behind the bar for him, Martin had not managed to catch up with him earlier, when he hears a voice,

"You see the troops on the common?"

Martin turns to see who it is that is speaking to him, the elderly man's face is familiar, but he cannot put a name to it,

"Troops?" Martin enquires

The old man, slowly nods, sucking on his pipe and inhaling deeply before answering, smoke leaving his lungs as he does so,

"Hundreds of them, been here a couple of weeks now"

"Do you know which regiment they are from?" Martin asks

Nodding again, the man answers,

"The Notts and Derby regiment, Brian has got four staying with him at Cravells Road"

Martin has no idea to which Brian he is referring too, but knows of the regiment, known as the 'Sherwood Foresters' and the 'Robin Hoods', the man continues,

"Some army medics as well, they have set up a tent hospital at Rothamstead Park"

"I will have a walk up tomorrow and speak to the R.S.M, a few of the lads could stay at the cottage, it seems odd to leave it empty, let's face it, I am going to be called back soon, so I won't be in it"

"Army are paying sixpence per man per night, so it would be worth your while"

Martin thanks the man, shakes his hand, and introduces himself,

"I know who you are young man"

Martin looks confused, the man is familiar, but he does not know his name,

"You might know my boys, Cyril and Hubert, from Wheathampstead"

Martin thinks for a second,

"Hubert Wren! I did weekend work at the mill with him when we were boys, you must be Mr. Thomas Wren, the wheelwright?"

A smile forms across the rugged lined face of Thomas Wren,

"That I am boy, good to see you, I thought you would be in France"

"I am waiting to be posted Mr Wren, don't think it will be long now, how is Hubert?"

The smile left the face of the old man,

"He went to Australia at the beginning of August, emigrated, Cyril is working with me now"

It is clear that Mr Wren does not wish to continue talking about Hubert, the sadness is written on his face,

Martin and Thomas chat for a while until the old man states that it is time he was getting back to Wheathampstead, explaining that he has been in town since that morning to help his old friend, and the local wheelwright, Mr George Course, to fix a large broken wheel on a cart at Bowers house,

"It was a 'bit of a bugger but I owed George a favour" he tells Martin, he also says that he should have been back home hours ago, he laughs as he tells Martin that his wife will be furious. The men shake hands, "Stay safe boy"

"I will Mr Wren, thank you"

Several other locals come over to chat to Martin, most asking if he knows any news about the battle in France that is ongoing, Martin has very little he can tell them, he is aware that there is a battle and that it is in and around the river Ainse and has been going on for several days, Field Marshal John French of the 19th Hussars is leading the BEF and French forces, against a huge German force taken from the 1st and 2nd German armies, there was chat within his regiment before he left that the fight was not going the way of the BEF or the French. One of the pub regulars has a battered copy of the Daily Mirror newspaper, it has a photograph on the front page showing British soldiers firing a huge gun, the report suggests that all is going well for the British Expedition forces, Martin does not want to suggest otherwise to the men in the pub, although from what he has heard before coming home on leave, it isn't the good news the local men believe it to be. His attention is drawn to the door when he hears a slurred and loud voice shout,

"Hello Gracie, not used to seeing a lonesome lady in this pub, not the done thing at all, you won't get served girl, you best come sit with me"

Martin looks across and sees that Grace has entered the pub and one of the patrons, a quite drunk man is shouting at her, he stands up and walks over to her, speaking to the man who had raised his voice at her, he is also standing, but only just,

"This lady is not alone; she is with me" he tells the man calmly.

The drunk man opens his mouth to protest, Martin leans forward and points a finger at him,

"The lady is with me, do you understand?" this time stated firmly and clearly,

The drunk man sits down with his cronies without another word, they are laughing at him for making a fool of himself and being put in his place by the young soldier.

Martin knows that any licensee has the right to refuse service to a female, the pub is a 'male domain', his Grandmother is the licensee and more often than not, she is the only female in the building, he knows that by law females can be refused service.

Offering his hand to Grace, who accepts, they walk around the bar,

"Shall we get away from the noise?" he asks her, she nods in reply

"Good evening Grace" Mary pipes up as she serves beer.

"Good evening Mrs Spratley, are you well?"

"I am, thank you" turning to Martin, Mary continues

"Alice is asleep upstairs love, could you stay down in the bar, I wouldn't want her disturbed"

Martin nods,

"Could you walk me home instead Martin?" Grace asks

"Of course," turning to Mary, "Gran, I will see you tomorrow"

Martin kisses his Grandmother on the cheek, she throws him a scalding look but smiles at the same time.

Martin and Grace leave the pub, it is early evening and the sun, low in the western sky, has almost set and it is just beginning to get dark to the east, a slight chill fills the air, they turn left and walk toward the Methodist church opposite Martin's cottage,

"We could have turned right and gone up South View Road then into Salisbury Road Martin"

He apologises to her,

"I haven't been home for so long; I suppose this way to the cottage is so familiar and it has taken me this way toward my home and not yours"

He stops and attempts to turn around, she takes his arm and continues toward the Church,

"We can cut through using the footpath at the back of the Gib" she says to him "If I didn't know better, I would think you were trying to get me back to your cottage!"

Martin is initially shocked by her comments, then he looks at her face, she is smiling at him,

"Stop pulling my leg Grace!"

They continue to walk, as they pass the church Grace stops and looks across at the cottage, now in darkness, a slight wisp of smoke can be seen coming from the chimney,

"Will you keep the cottage Martin?"

He nods but is silent, Grace, still holding Martin's arm, suddenly pulls him across the road toward the cottage,

"Let's go and see your property shall we soldier boy!"

Martin lets himself be led across the quiet road, he opens the garden gate for her and using the key from his tunic pocket, he opens the door to the kitchen, it is warm inside, Martin had lit a fire in the range before he left earlier the glow from this is the only light in the room. Martin lights an oil lamp and puts it on the table, Grace sits on the ancient bench seat under the window, it has cushions and several crochet covered pillows, Martin adds a shovel of coal to the fire,

"Shall we have a brew of tea?" he asks Grace, she accepts.

It is only when the clock strikes ten times that Grace realises how late it is, the couple of hours since they arrived, have passed quickly and so easily, just two people talking and occasionally holding hands, Martin is initially reticent, almost scared to do so, but after a little encouragement from Grace he finds himself enjoying her company very much and also enjoys gently touching her hands with his.

Martin walks her home, offering to explain to her Father why she is so late, Grace smiles at him, grateful of his chivalry but tells him she will be just fine, outside of her parents' house, she kisses him on the cheek,

"See you soon Martin, I had a lovely evening"

Martin hears himself hurriedly speaking to her,

"Tomorrow?"

She looks at him, before replying,

"As it so happens, school is closed tomorrow, the army are using the school buildings, so, yes, I would like to see you tomorrow"

They bid each other good night, Martin realises that he hasn't set a time to meet her, he then also realises that he has already promised Alice that they will visit the grave of their parents at St Nicholas, cursing himself, he walks home to the cottage, he spends the night on the floor in the kitchen, he cannot bring himself to sleep in his parents' bed and he wouldn't dream of sleeping in Alice's room.

* * *

Tuesday 22nd September

Martin wakes suddenly to a loud banging, it takes him a few seconds to realise that he is on the floor of the cottage, lying on a thick blanket with a crochet covered cushion under his head, he can hear his name being called,

"Martin, Martin are you there?"

He recognises the voice as that of Grace, he looks up and sees her pretty face at the window,

"Come in" he shouts, wiping his eyes "The door is not locked"

Grace enters the kitchen, seeing Martin dressed only in his army trousers and shirtless, she turns her head away, blushing, he puts on his army shirt and pulls his braces over his shoulders,

"What time is it?" he asks

Grace has no need to answer, as just then the longcase clock chimes seven times, he looks at her,

"You are early"

She shrugs and smiles at him,

"I need to have a wash" he says, adding some wood to the range fire, he then pulls the kettle across to the hot plate,

"That's for tea, I will wash outside, please Grace, sit down" he says sleepily,

He indicates a free seat at the table, Grace sits and Martin steps into the back yard, she watches him through the kitchen window that looks directly into the yard, he shrugs off his braces, takes off his shirt and lifts a bucket onto a wooden bench, taking handfuls of cold water he splashes his face and under his arms, taking a small bar of red carbolic soap he washes his face and body with the small amount of suds made from the soap, he then leans forward and slowly tips the whole bucket of water over his head, with his hands he moves the cold, fresh water over his body to rid himself of the suds. It is then that he realises he has no towel with him,

"Grace, sorry to be a nuisance, could you pass me a towel, they should be in the dresser on the back wall" he shouts

Less than a minute later, the back door opens and an arm holding a towel appears, he steps forward and takes the towel, the arm disappears and the door shuts,

"Thank you!"

He thinks he can hear a muffled "You are welcome" from indoors, smiling to himself he dries his face and body with the thin towel, finishing with a quick rub of his hair, what little of it he has, he keeps it short, almost shaved. He rubs his chin, he should shave, but decides against it, putting his shirt back on he goes into the kitchen, Grace is pouring tea,

"I hope you don't mind, but I have made the tea"

He sits at the table with her, unashamedly looking into her dark and beautiful eyes,

"I don't mind one little bit"

The tea is drunk in silence, Martin breaks this after a few minutes,

"I do have a bit of a confession to make Grace"

She puts her nearly finished tea down on the table,

"It's you, isn't it, you are married!" she teases him,

He laughs, telling her that he is also very single,

"I promised Alice that I would visit our parents grave this morning with her, I forgot last night when I asked you out"

Alice looks straight at Martin,

"You asked me out, did you?"

Martin blushes and becomes flustered, he clumsily attempts to answer and make excuses, he then sees that Grace is bursting to laugh at him but is holding it in,

"You are pulling my leg again Grace!"

She laughs out loud and Martin loves the sound of it, feeling goose bumps rise on his skin, he does not know what to say next, Alice speaks first,

"Martin, it is not a problem, I can finish my tea and go home, we can do this again some other time"

"Will you come with us?"

Martin almost whispers the words, he is scared of her rejection, he sees a fabulous smile appear on Graces face, showing her pearl white teeth,

"Are you sure Alice won't mind?"

Martin assures her that his sister won't mind one bit,

"In that case, I would be happy to accompany you and Alice today"

Martin puts on his tunic and cap, leaving his valise, webbing and rifle in the living room, his belly is rumbling but he knows that there isn't any proper food in the cottage, opening the front door, offering Grace to go first in a gentlemanly manner, she does so, he steps outside with her, realising that the key to the door is on the table and that he hasn't locked the back door, he goes back inside the kitchen, as he puts the bolt across the back door, he says to himself, very quietly,

"For God's sake Martin calm down, it is only a girl"

Locking the front door, the pair leave the garden and turn left toward the Malta, Martin is overjoyed when Grace slips her arm through his, she is wearing a white frilled collar shirt, laced at the front and at each cuff, a smart light blue linen jacket over it, an ankle length skirt with a double hem at the bottom, its colour is a shade darker than her jacket, he can just see pristine white stockings and white shoes that have a slight heel, finally a glorious wide brimmed hat, the same colour as her skirt, he can see her shoulder length black hair cascading from the back of the hat, she is as pretty as anything Martin can ever remember and he feels very proud to be walking with her arm in arm.

They reach the pub, Mary is outside, wiping down the windowsills,

"Morning Granny"

Mary answers without looking at him, carrying on with her chores,

"If you want breakfast, you are too late, Alice is just clearing up now"

He was hoping for breakfast, but replies,

"Breakfast? No thanks, I have had tea, can I go up and let Alice know we are here"

Mary turns to face them when she hears Martin say 'we',

"Good Morning Grace love"

"Hello Mrs Spratley"

Mary puts her cleaning cloth in the front pocket of her pinney,

"I think we can dispense with the 'Mrs Spratley' now Grace, Mary is fine"

Grace thanks her for this courtesy.

"Go and get your sister Martin" Mary sharply tells him, he does as instructed and enters the pub, both the women outside hear him shout up the stairs,

"Alice! Are you ready?"

Alice appears in the bar and hugs Martin,

"Morning little sister, how are you today?"

She doesn't answer but continues to hug him,

"Alice, do you mind if we have company with us today?"

She looks into her brothers' eyes, then looks out of the door and sees Grace chatting to their Grandmother, she pulls herself away slightly from him, playfully poking him in the chest,

"Grace Wilson? Martin, she is so lovely, is she your girlfriend now?"

Martin blushes and laughs at his sister,

"Don't be so cheeky or so forward young lady"

He hugs her again,

"Come on you, let's go"

He sees tears in his sisters' eyes,

"It will be fine Alice, I promise"

They walk outside, Alice speaks to Grace,

"Hello Grace, you look lovely"

"Thank you, Alice, I hope you are fine with me accompanying you and Martin today, I will of course understand if you want to be alone"

Alice puts her arm through Graces and they both start to walk toward Station road, Grace looks back at Martin,

"Come on then slowcoach!" Alice calls to him.

"Granny, I don't know whereabouts in the churchyard Mother and Father are buried, will Alice remember?"

Mary wipes a single tear from her cheek,

"I don't think she will ever forget son, go on with you, the ladies are walking without you"

He looks up and sees that Alice and Grace have both crossed the road, almost immediately as they left the pub, he knows why and smiles to himself. On the other side of Southview Road, opposite the pub and next to the public well, is a patch of land and a shack made of corrugated iron, the land is well cared for, and vegetables are obviously being cultivated on the site, a local eccentric called Jack Bright lives here. Mr Bright also owns large swathes of land and property in and around Church green in town, his wife lives alone, in one of his houses that is close to St Nicholas church, local rumour has him to be wealthy but choosing to live in the shack on his land opposite the pub, this he has done for some years now. Martin remembers him as an angry and cantankerous man, he, and his friends when they were boys used to throw lumps of wet mud at the hut, Mr Bright would chase them shouting threats and obscenities as he ran, he never caught any of them. Martin doesn't cross the road, he walks past the front of the land lived on by Mr Bright, he looks over and sees the old man is working in the garden,

"Morning Mr Bright" he says cheerfully, he gets no response, Mr Bright looks up at him, lifts his head slightly as a greeting and then gets back to his gardening, Martin runs across the road to catch up with the ladies, still arm in arm.

"Wait for me you two please!"

Alice and Grace stop outside of Mr Trustram the harness makers workshop on the corner of Station Road, Martin catches them up, passing Mr Ackroyds bakery and grocers, his nose catches the delicate aroma of baking bread and cakes, this reminds him that he hasn't eaten breakfast and is hungry,

"I need to get some food ladies, anyone for cake?"

Both, at the same time, reply, 'Yes please' and both seem excited by having cake so early in the day, Martin enters the bakery, Mrs Ackroyd is standing behind the counter, her full length white pinney is spotlessly clean, her hair tied tightly in a bun on the back of her head,

"Good Morning Sir" she says as he enters,

"Good Morning Mrs Ackroyd" he replies as he takes off his cap, putting it under his arm,

The baker's wife looks quizzically at Martin, he steps toward the counter,

"Martin?" she asks

He nods at her,

"Yes Ma'am"

Mrs Ackroyd reaches over the counter and touches him gently on the cheek,

"So sorry to hear about your parents Martin, are you home for the first time since"

He tells her that he arrived yesterday, just before lunch, explaining to her why he missed the funeral, he asks after her husband, Thomas, and sons, Ernest, who is the same age as Alice and 'Tiny", who must now be seventeen. Martin and Mrs Ackroyd chat for a minute or so, she tells him that Ernie is in town selling bread and cakes from a tray and that he best not return home until they are all sold, Tiny, she tells him, is busy in the stables tending to the horses,

"Oh, just listen to me going on, you must be busy yourself Martin, what can I get for you"

Martin points to the iced buns nestled together behind the glass counter,

"Three of these please"

As Mrs Ackroyd puts the cakes into a bag, telling him that they are a ha'penny each,

"You must be hungry!"

Taking the cakes, now safely inside a brown paper bag, he hands over two coins, a one penny bit and a ha'penny, both with the profile of George V on one side and a seated Britannia on the other,

"Thanks Mrs Ackroyd"

Looking outside the shop, Mrs Ackroyd sees Alice and Grace waiting for Martin, she waves and both of the ladies' wave back,

"Have a lovely day Martin" she says to him with a glint in her eye and a wry smile on her face,

"I will, thank you, please pass on my regards to Mr Ackroyd and to 'Tiny' and Ernie"

They say 'goodbye' at the same time, as he leaves Mrs Ackroyd says to him,

"Nice to see you home Martin, stay safe"

He nods thanks to her, puts on his cap and leaves the bakery, opening the bag he takes out a bun for himself and hands the bag to Alice, the three of them walk away, eating the sweet tasting bread each with its own strip of luscious and sticky icing on top, they make their way toward Coldharbour Lane, they begin to walk up the very long and very steep Ox Lane, passing the nursery at the bottom of the hill and under the railway bridge, they continue on, heading toward town and to the burial place of Jeremiah and Victoria.

Grace respectfully waited outside of the churchyard, both Alice and Martin had insisted that she was welcome to join them, she politely declined, watching the young soldier and his sister stand at the unmarked graves, standing close to the huge ancient Yew tree in the large churchyard, she can clearly see that Alice is upset, Martin has his arm tightly around her shoulder and her head is buried into his chest. Grace walks toward the pair as they leave the churchyard, she can see that Alice has been crying, her eyes are red and still wet, she puts her arms out and Alice gratefully accepts the embrace from her in silence, Martin is looking away from them both,

"I need to walk to the common, the Sherwood Foresters and the Robin Hoods are there and I need to speak to the Regimental Sergeant Major"

He explains to Grace, having already told Alice, that he intends to let four soldiers use the cottage after he has left, he sees a slight look of disappointment on Alice's' face, he hurriedly adds,

"Not just yet though, I will be staying there until then"

Grace smiles, she gives Alice a gentle squeeze on her shoulders,

"Shall we go and see the soldiers with big brother Alice?"

With a broad smile, Alice replies,

"I think we should" she looks at Martin "To see how proper smart soldiers' dress!"

Martin chases his sister across the green in front of the church, easily catching her, they laugh as they wait for Grace to catch up with them. They take a route through Leyton Road, instead of walking along the busier High street, crossing over Rothamstead Avenue, Steabben the butchers' shop on the corner is open, its window displaying cuts of beef, mutton and pork, several pheasants and rabbits hang from S shaped hooks, the gold lettering of the shop sign proudly displays in large capitals, the name of the family that own and run the shop, the glass red bricks on either side of the shop are, as they always are, highly polished. Walter Steabben can be seen inside, wearing his white work coat with his black and white striped waist apron tied tightly around his thin waist, Martin looks up Rothamstead Avenue past the shop, he sees the large and impressive Ivy Cottage, also owned by the Steabben family, Mr and Mrs Steabben and their three daughters all currently live there, they then walk past Batchelors row, three terraced and beautifully thatched late 18th century cottages, then on toward and past the Methodist chapel, with its very old and very deep public well in the grounds behind it, just a little further on they are passing the green and crossing onto the common land in between Leyton road and St Albans road, in front of them, to their right, is the impressive house known only as 'Bennets', with majestic Elm trees in front of it, the towns public hall is slightly further on, it being situated just before the entrance to Rothamstead park, with its glorious double line of Lime trees standing guard either side of the route into the park. It is not open today to the public, Sundays being the only day the general public can be admitted onto this land. Past this entrance, there stands the former public house, the Bull inn, now known locally just as 'The Old House', it stands alone before the Silver cup public house comes into view, opposite this pub are the '*Baa lamb trees',* a group of elm and oak trees growing on a raised section of the common. The name is unusual and is believed to have come from a family that historically owned property in the area, for a period that has lasted over two hundred and fifty years, they are the Balaam family, a local farm in Redbourn had originally been called *'Bailam Farm* and is now called Byland's Farm, also on the land near to this farm, a map from 1753 shows a building called '*Bear Lambs',* it is possible that the cartographer had misheard the strong Hertfordshire dialect and accent, and Byland had been written as Bailam and then again as Bear Lambs.

The group of trees has been known as the Baa Lambs for as long as anyone in town can recall.

They cross over the St Albans road in front of 'Bennets' and onto the common on the opposite side, Harpenden Hall can be seen from where they stand, its red brick wall running around the house on the edge of the Wheathampstead road. This piece of common land is busy with military movement, hundreds of soldiers, some working on wheeled artillery being pulled by a single horse, others, lying flat on their bellies, each with a Lee Enfield rifle pointing in front of them, practicing drills with an irate sergeant shouting almost constantly at them, others are just hanging around outside of what seems like a myriad of expertly pitched tents, the sheep that have been on the common for generations are still there, living alongside and ignoring the soldiers.

"Wait by the Railway Hotel for me, I won't be long"

Martin walks into the disciplined commotion of the Army encampment on the common, he is almost immediately approached by a young Lieutenant, he stands to attention and smartly salutes the officer, who returns the salute,

"Lt Piggford, 46th North Midlands division, Sherwood Forrester's, can I help you private?" He looks at Martin and at his unit cap badge, "You are not one of mine?"

Remaining at attention, Martin introduces himself, giving rank and name,

"2nd Battalion Bedfordshire regiment Sir, currently on compassionate leave, I live near the town"

Lt Piggford instructs Martin to stand at ease, then to relax to stand easy,

"What can I do for you Private?"

"I am looking for the R.S.M Sir, I have a small cottage near the East Station, and I won't be needing it shortly, my Battalion is awaiting orders to move to France, I have been made aware that some of your lads may need a billet"

The Lieutenant calls over to a private who is standing nearby,

"Private, can you come here please"

The young private marches smartly to the officer and salutes him,

"Private 1545 Beeson, Sir, 1st/5th Sherwood Foresters"

The officer returns the salute and also tells Beeson to stand easy, after a short conversation, both privates salute Lt Piggford and he leaves them, they then turn to each other and shake hands, Pte Beeson has been tasked by Lt Piggford to find the RSM for Martin,

"Robert Beeson, mates call me Bob"

"Martin, mates call me Martin!"

This brings a smile to the face of the visiting soldier,

"You are a long way from home Bob" states Martin, "I see you are a territorial, what was your real life work?"

"I was a labourer on the Midlands Railway, I am from Moss Street in Derby, it's a bit different to your little quiet country town, how about you Martin?"

Martin laughs,

"Career soldier, that's me Bob, joined the day I was eighteen, so I really don't know anything else, I was born and raised not three miles from here in a little hamlet outside of town, my now not so quiet town!"

"You on leave then? I only ask because none of us are allowed any leave at all, we expect to be in France by November, bet that won't be as nice as your little town"

For the first time since arriving home Martin feels emotional, he holds back tears of grief,

"My parents died when I was overseas, I missed the funeral, I have been back only a day or so, I need to make sure my younger sister is going to be safe and well before I go"

"I hope all is going to be well for you and yours mate, condolences about your parents"

Before Martin can reply, the two soldiers are interrupted by a bellowing voice,

"I will find you work if you don't have anything to do privates!"

Bob and Martin look across to the owner of the voice,

"Bloody hell" Bob says "That is the man we were to look for, Regimental Sergeant Major Westerman, I think he might be shouting at us"

Both men return to attention, both shout "Sir" at the same time.

The RSM approaches, his slashed peak cap almost covering his dark eyes, his moustache is small and trimmed perfectly, the Sam Browne belt horizontal from right shoulder to left waist, joined perfectly to the vertical part of the belt, his tunic is pristine with its distinctive crest of rank on each sleeve, the trousers and puttees look almost new they are so clean and tidy, his black drill boots are so very highly polished on both caps that the sun is reflecting on them, a pace stick made of polished dark wood with brass tips at each end, is tucked tightly under his right arm.

He stands in front of the men, he growls,

"Bugger off Beeson, I am presuming you have something to do?"

Beeson replies, "Sir!", turns smartly to his right and doubles away, leaving Martin with the formidable RSM Westerman,

"And who might you be sonny?"

Martin introduces himself again, name, rank, number, and regiment.

"And what might a professional, regular soldier, who needs a bloody good shave by the way, be doing here with this territorial regiment?"

Martin explains, for the second time, that he is on compassionate leave and also that he has a small cottage near to East Station that will be vacant in about a week or so and could possibly be suitable for four soldiers,

The RSM calms a little,

"Follow me private"

He turns on his heels and sets off at a quick pace, Martin follows behind, they reach a tent and the RSM enters, he waits outside, waiting to be invited in.

"Come on in private"

Martin removes his cap and steps into the tent, the RSM is sat at his desk, he points to a chair and Martin sits down,

"Relax private, this is my office, for the time being anyway, I am going to ignore the very real fact that you have not shaved today, I am certain I will never see you unshaven again"

He looks up at Martin, a wry grin on his face,

"No Sir" Martin replies, still sitting bolt upright

"Relax" the soldier says, "Martin isn't it?"

Martin nods, relaxing a little, the RSM continues,

"I am Regimental Sergeant Major Edward Arthur Westerman, 8th Battalion Sherwood Foresters" he pauses. "Your little cottage might be just what we are looking for, I need to have a corporal and three soldiers at the East Station most days, all our troops and equipment arrive through there, do you, by chance, know the Station Master, the porters, or the signalmen at the station?"

"I have been away for over four years Sir, but I might"

The RSM looks at several reports on his desk, finding what he needs he reads the names out to Martin,

"Mr E Jones is the station master" he looks up at Martin, eyebrows raised,

"I knew the former station master, I have been to his house at the station Sir, but I am sure I don't know Mr Jones"

"Messer's Woodward, Chapman and Gammon are the signalmen" he again looks at Martin,

"If one of them is Stephen Gammon, then I went to school with him Sir, he was a boy porter at the station when I joined up in 1910"

The RSM continues,

"The porters are" Westerman shuffles paper again, "A Mr Lord and a Mr Clements"

"I know both of them Sir, they have been working at the station since I was a boy"

RSM Westerman repeats the word 'good' at least four times,

"We have had to look for billets for over 4500 officers and men, some are still living in tents here on the common, I would like to get them a few comforts before deployment"

"Any news on when you are going Sir?"

Shaking his head, he replies,

"Soon I think, how about your lot?"

"Nothing confirmed Sir, when we arrived at Southampton a couple of days ago, the NCO's told us that deployment would be within the month"

Westerman takes note of Martins address and tells him that he will arrange to get the sanitary inspector to view the cottage, purely procedure he insists, also that he will inform the station master, the signalmen and the porters that they will have the permanent military presence they are supposed to have on a daily basis, but of course, only after Martin has been posted. Martin agrees but tells the RSM his men will need army camp beds because he is going to put all his families' possessions into the back room and lock it, this will leave two rooms, the living room, and the kitchen for the men to sleep in and use, Westerman agrees to this. Martin has a few more points to raise, firstly that any monies payable to him must go to his Grandmother, Mary Spratley at the Malta pub, this to pay for his sisters keep whilst he is away, the RSM agrees to this, stating, with another wry grin, that he will visit the pub and see to it personally, Martin then asks that the soldiers keep the garden and vegetable patch in good order, using whatever vegetables they need and finally, if his sister needs to visit the cottage for any reason that she should have free access, again this all agreed.

The meeting is over.

Martin stands up, cap smartly tucked under his left arm, Westerman puts out a hand,

"Good luck over there Martin"

The handshake is accepted,

"You too sir"

Martin turns to leave,

"Private?"

He turns back,

"Sir?"

"Shave, you horrible little bugger!"

Martin nods and leaves with the RSM laughing out loud, several soldiers standing nearby look confused as he leaves, he shrugs his shoulders at them with a smile.

Putting his cap back on, he makes his way on the short journey to the Railway Hotel where the girls will be waiting for him for the walk back to the cottage

* * *

Wednesday 23rd September

The following morning Martin is up and out early, it is only eight thirty, he has already walked Grace to the school at the National Children's home, he will walk back at lunchtime to meet her to escort her home, they both very much enjoyed each other's company yesterday, it is obvious that there is a spark between them, and he is glad that Alice and Grace get along so well, Alice making it hugely obvious to him that she now *loves* having a new 'big sister'. After visiting his parents grave, alone this time, he stops at Whitehouse newsagents at 24 high street, near to the White Lion pub,

"Morning Mr Whitehouse"

Henry Whitehouse, a gentleman in his mid 40's with thinning hair, a second generation newsagent, who had taken over from his Father, Levi at the turn of the century, his Mother and Father had originally started the newsagents in 1858, they had previously been school teachers in a tiny school, run from their cottage near to Church green, this had been demolished to make way for the building of the National school, Mr Richard Lydekker from The Lodge had provided them with pencils, string and stationary, with which they started their newsagents.

"Morning" he replies, there is a pause "My word is that you young Martin?"

"It is Sir" Martin replies,

Henry using his head to point toward the common says,

"Are you with this lot?"

"No, I am with the 2nd battalion Bedfordshire's, I am home to look after my sister for a short while"

Henry passes on his condolences and accepts the ha'penny from Francis for the newspaper,

"Bad business that is"

Henry points at the front page of the newspaper, Martin opens the paper fully to see the front page, above the banner declaring the name of the newspaper, in bold capital letters it says,

'THREE BRITISH CRUISERS SUNK BY GERMAN SUBMARINE'

The front page is dominated by photographs of three ships, all armoured Cressy class cruisers, along with photographs of 6 officers from the ships, above these photographs it says

'BRITISH NAVAL LOSS IN THE NORTH SEA: THREE SISTER CRUISERS SANK BY GERMAN SUBMARINES'

The three ships, mainly crewed by inexperienced reservists, HMS Aboukir, HMS Hogue, and HMS Cressy, had been on home water patrol with other naval ships in the North Sea off the coast of the Netherlands, a huge storm had driven the destroyers back into port, the cruiser squadron stayed out on patrol. At 0620 on Tuesday 22nd September 1914, a German submarine fired a single torpedo into HMS Aboukir, she sank in under five minutes, then at 0700, two torpedoes hit HMS Hogue, fifteen minutes later she also sank, finally at 0720, two torpedoes were fired at HMS Cressy, one missed but one hit its target, followed by a third fired torpedo and the second to hit the ship at 0725, she immediately capsized and finally sank at five minutes before eight o clock that morning.

1,459 officers and men from the three ships had perished.

More sailors had drowned in the sixty minutes it took to sink these three ships than had died in the whole of Nelsons fleet at the Battle of Trafalgar. Martin looks up from the newspaper at Henry, saying nothing, he folds the Daily Mirror and puts it under his arm and turns to leave the shop, he hears Henry speak,

"Good luck to you Son"

Martin leaves, quietly closing the door behind him.

The war is now in full swing, men from his country are dying on the battlefields and in the sea, Martin knows it will be a matter of days before he is recalled to his unit and then onto France to fight alongside the other soldiers, he also knows that the recruiting offices of the British Army have been constantly busy with young men '*signing on*', it seems to him that these young men really believe in the alleged excitement of war, he knows it is going to be hell on earth.

Taking a look at his watch, he begins a slow walk back toward Ambrose Lane and to the NCH at Highfield, he tells himself to cheer up before meeting up with Grace and most certainly he must not show her the Daily Mirror, he puts the newspaper in the first dustbin he sees, in a side alley of the Red Lion pub, without reading another word from it. He crosses the High Street onto Sun Lane, turning left just before the railway bridge, onto Tennyson Road, following this road to its end, he crosses over Hollybush lane and into Ambrose Lane, over the Nicky line bridge, stopping for a minute or two to see if a train is due to pass, it is all quiet, so he carries on the short walk to 'Highfields', finally into the grounds of the National children's home. He sees Grace leave the school building from the wooden bench his is sat upon, he is just off the centre on the oval shaped green that is in the middle of the establishment, the school buildings sit to the left side at the bottom of the oval, four terraced white fronted buildings with dark tiled roofs, they stand alone, the administration building to the right of the school is the nearest other completed building, all around the oval other houses are finished or very close to completion. Martin finds the area to be peaceful and although he had no idea that the land had been built on until 2 days ago, he likes the place, he smiles as he thinks that the reason for this might be Grace. He returns her wave, he cannot take his eyes off of her as she walks toward him, the white long sleeved blouse she is wearing has a high collar, a delicate dark coloured brooch, pinned to the middle of it stands out against the pristine whiteness of the blouse, a gentle lace frill flows down the centre of it from the neckline to just above her waistline, here, there is a thick black silk band attached invisibly to an ankle length plain black skirt, clean black lace boots can just be seen below the hem, Grace is carrying a straw boater hat with a dark ribbon tied into a bow around the crown, her dark shimmering hair, is tied in a bun at her neck, she is beautiful.

He stands as she gets near to him,

"Hello Martin, thank you for meeting me"

Before he can answer, Grace leans in toward him and kisses him on his cheek, he hears children, who are now outside and on the oval having just left the school, they whistle and cheer as he is kissed by their teacher, Grace gently laughs and places both her hands onto Martins chest, he takes both her hands in his, more whistling and jeering from the children, Grace turns and looks at them, without a word from her, the children stop making their noise and quietly make their way to their houses, the boys turning left and the girls to the right.

"Remind me not to get on the wrong side of you Miss Wilson!" he exclaims to, she throws her head back and laughs, how he loves her laughing, she notices him staring at her,

"Come along soldier, lets walk" , Grace puts her straw hat onto her head, puts her arm through his and they set off on the walk to their homes.

Arriving back at the cottage after walking Grace home, Martin feels a sense of loneliness that he hasn't felt since arriving back home, he is missing his parents, he is missing Alice, who is meeting him this evening, and, although he only left her at her parents' front door not ten minutes since, he is missing Grace.

He adds fuel to the fire in the stove, taking a large pan, he puts it on the hot plate, half filling it with fresh water from a jug on the floor, he will be adding a rabbit that he picked up on the way home from Graces, by luck he had bumped into Joseph Freeman, who had obviously been collecting captured game from his snares, taking a rabbit off of him, for a good price, it is to be for the evening meal for him and Alice. He will skin and butcher the rabbit in the back yard, he hasn't done this for a while, a couple of times in Pretoria, mainly because the food was so bad that he set snares and roasted the local Riverine rabbits on a spit over an open fire, they tasted about the same as the ones at home. Putting the rabbit on the wooden bench outside in the back yard, taking out his penknife, he keeps the blade very sharp, he uses it to make a small incision in the hide of the rabbit, putting the knife down and then inserting two fingers from each hand inside the small hole he pulls in opposite directions, this easily tears the furry skin away from the hide, he pulls until he works the front and back legs out of the hide, a quick sharp pull on each leg tears the skin away, leaving the carcass left with four furry shoes. Turning to the rear end he pulls the hide completely off, the tail remains, it does this sometimes, other times it will come off with the hide, turning the rabbit around he pulls the skin over the head of the rabbit until the neck meat is exposed, the feet, complete with furry shoes are easily snapped off at the ankles with a sharp bending motion, he then cuts the tendons and muscle with his penknife to detach all four feet, the head is then removed, his blade easily cutting through the muscle, tendon and bone. He then carefully cuts a small incision in the belly of the animal, being sure not to nick the bladder or intestines, using two fingers of his left hand and inserting them in the small hole, he lifts the skin away from the intestines and cuts it from the ribcage to the pelvis, then gently cutting into the chest area he removes the thin membrane that separates the small chest cavity from the intestines. The intestines are quickly removed, he remembers to put to one side the heart, liver and kidneys from the animal, these will add richness and flavour to his stew, he then takes his time to remove the skin from the remainder of the animal, he has eaten rabbit with the skin left on before but prefers the taste if it is removed, he cuts the front legs off, leaving plenty of meat on them from around the shoulder, this is easily done as the front legs are not attached to the main body by bone, the back legs are cut through to the hip joint and then snapped off by hand, again leaving plenty of meat on the small joints, next is to cut the ribs from the carcass, there is not a lot of meat on them, but they will add great flavour to the stock, the belly meat is then removed in two pieces and the loin section is cut into three. The rabbit is prepared, he washes the meat to ensure it is clean, taking it inside the cottage and putting it in the pot of hot water, adding carrots and onions from the garden, finally adding four huge leaves of greens to the pot, they will almost disappear into the stock, helping to flavour and thicken it.

This done, he has other jobs to finish, the stew will take three or four hours to gently cook. He sets about moving the personal family items into Alice's bedroom at the back of the cottage, his sister won't be needing much, it has been agreed that when he is called back to barracks Alice will be living at Maples cottages during the week with Aunt May and Uncle Pete, then with Granny at the pub for weekends, this makes sense to Martin, May and Pete's twin girls attend St Nicholas Church of England school in town, formerly named the 'National school', it had been renamed St Nicholas school in 1906, Martin had been a 14 year old pupil at the school when the name changed, to all the children after the change and since, the school has been nicknamed 'St Nicks'. Alice is in the same class as her cousins at the school, her teacher Mr F.R. Smith, is a strict disciplinarian, but he also has a lovely manner with the children, he has been good to Alice since their parents passed, always having time for her, and letting her cousins know to tell Aunt May when, at times, being at school had become difficult. The school currently has a headteacher called Mr Francis Saunders, a surly man who always wears a flat cap, his jacket buttoned up over his collarless shirt, he has a huge, healthy, and full moustache, Aunt May has assured Martin that the head teacher is also aware that Alice may become withdrawn when Martin leaves town to return to army duties.

Moving his parents bed is a hard task for Martin on his own, it is old and made of hard and heavy wood, it takes him an age to get it through the door into Alice's room, taking three attempts to get the angle correct for it to go through, he is again bare chested with his braces over his naked shoulders, he is sweating because of the hard manual labour moving more and more furniture into the room, he has left the dresser in the kitchen but has put the contents of it into wooden crates, the pots and pans, buckets, shovels and a few other tools are to be left in the kitchen, he is sure that the soldiers will need to use them. A large iron hasp and staple he purchased that morning from Ridleys in town is now securely in place, he locks the door with a large, brass Yale padlock, the keys for this will be with Granny at the pub if Alice ever needs them, he has decided to sleep on the kitchen floor for the remainder of his time in the cottage, he can't sleep in his parents living room, it just doesn't feel right at this time. As he puts the shackle into the main body of the lock, pushing it firmly into place, he hears his sister calling him,

"Martin! Where are you?"

"In the '*living room*' little sister, I have just finished putting everything away in your room"

Martin walks into the kitchen carrying his khaki army shirt in his right hand, the keys to the padlock are in the left, his skin is flushed and seating from his afternoons work, and he needs to wash himself over, as he enters the kitchen he says, "Alice, can you fill the kettle, I need to wash and shave"

He is through the door when he sees that Alice is not alone, Grace is also standing in the kitchen, he stares at her, again, then remembers he is shirtless, he lifts his shirt up in an attempt to cover himself up, he drops the keys as he does so and as he bends down to pick them up he bangs his head on the dresser, the ladies present find this hilarious and both are laughing with tears rolling down their cheeks,

"Very funny ladies" he says rubbing his head, "Very funny indeed!"

His head is very sore, he keeps rubbing it in a vain attempt to rid himself of the discomfort the bump has caused him,

"Sit down Martin, let me have a look at that bump" Grace speaks to him, he does not react, she speaks again, sternly, "Sit!" she points at the chair by the kitchen table, he does as he is told, elbows on his knees, "Sit up properly Martin!" Grace is stern again; he complies and smiles at her. She stands in front of him, gently moving her hands over his short hair, he can smell the freshness of soap and gentle perfume coming from her body, which is perfectly placed not six inches in front of him, he closes his eyes and forgets about the pain on his head.

"I think you will live soldier boy"

He opens his eyes and Grace has moved away from him, having taken a seat on the bench under the window, Alice sits next to her,

"Granny is doing clothes wash tonight, I have to take any dirty clothes you want cleaning to her, do you have any?"

Martin nods,

"I did wash some yesterday, they are outside in the yard drying off, but I have got a couple of army shirts that need a rinse out"

Martin looks at the ladies, they are both looking at him,

"What?" he asks quizzically,

"Where are they then?" asks Alice

"Where is what?" Martin asks back

Alice tuts at him, "Your dirty shirts silly, I can take them to Granny now and then come back to sit with Grace and you"

Martin gets up and opens the top of his army duffel bag, taking out two shirts and two undershirts, all khaki green and handing them to Alice, she takes them, pulling a face as she does so,

"Martin, these all stink!" Alice exclaims to him,

Grace puts her hand over her mouth to silence another laugh,

"I won't be long, what are we eating this evening Martin?" she lifts the lid on the slowly cooking stew with a cloth,

Martin looks at his sister,

"We?"

She nods at him,

"I called on Grace and invited her to eat with us tonight"

"Oh, did you now?"

He looks at Grace and winks,

"I saw that Martin!" exclaims Alice

Martin looks sternly at his sister, then runs at her, grabbing and tickling her,

"Now look here young lady, you take my washing to Granny or there will be big trouble!

Alice is laughing uncontrollably, Martin stops and speaks to both of them,

"It's rabbit stew tonight with fresh bread, Alice could you pop into Mr Ackroyds, he should still be open if you hurry, and get a loaf please?"

He takes a penny from his trouser pocket and flips it toward his sister, she does not catch it and it clangs as it hits the stone floor,

"Martin! I wasn't ready for that!"

Alice picks up the penny, puts it in the front of her pinafore dress, tells them she will be back soon, takes the washing, leaving Martin and Grace alone.

"Rabbit stew?" Grace asks, Martin points to the pot on the range, she goes over and lifts the lid, using a piece of cloth from the side of the range, the room fills with the smell of the deeply aromatic stew, "That might just do for us" she says, putting her hand on the side of the kettle, "This is warm enough if you want to wash"

Martin thanks her and stands up to get the kettle, Grace is standing in his way, she doesn't move,

"Grace?" Martin says

She steps forward, puts her soft and gentle hands on either side of his face, moving in she kisses him, he feels the softness of her lips on his, the kiss is soft and lingering, Grace has her eyes closed, Martin has his wide open, she pulls away from him, keeping her hands on his face,

"Wash and shave soldier boy, I agree with your sister, you stink!"

Using the cloth, Martin lifts the kettle from the range, takes it into the back yard, taking the bucket from the wooden bench, he throws the water he cleaned the rabbit with over the yard fence, he re-enters the kitchen, through and out of the front door to go to the pump to fill the bucket. As he heads back to the cottage, he sees that Grace is stood in the doorway looking at him, he realises that he is still shirtless and that Grace is looking at his half covered body, she does not move as he passes through the door, their bodies gently rubbing against each other as he goes into the kitchen, he stops turns his head toward her and kisses her on the lips, a short meeting of their skin,

"Shave!" she says to him.

He takes the bucket of cold water to the back yard and adds the hot water from the kettle, going back into the kitchen he retrieves his army issue haversack that contains his wash kit and '*housewife*', these are both canvas rolls secured with a strip of canvas tied in a bow, he takes out the '*housewife*' as it is near the top of the haversack, then he lifts out the wash kit, leaving the small King James bible, his *'four by two'* rifle cleaning cloth and his pocket service book inside the small bag. When the wash kit is unwrapped he can see its familiar contents laid out, the *housewife* he leaves rolled up and puts it to one side, inside it are spare cord laces, buttons, needles, cotton and a packet of lice powder, turning his attention to the wash kit, he takes his boar hair bristle shaving brush, the bar of solid shaving soap and his cut throat razor, it is only then that he realises that he has stored his Mothers mirror in the padlocked back room, he decides to manage without, he has shaved 'blind' plenty of times before, the wash kit roll also contains shoe polish brushes, he won't need these until he returns to barracks, a knife, fork and spoon, a brass button polisher, used to keep his dress uniform clean when shining buttons, a bar of carbolic soap and a wooden toothbrush with natural bristle, all these remain in the roll. Martin splashes warm water on his face, dipping the shaving brush into it, he works up a foamy lather on the brush with the bar of shaving soap and applies it to his neck and face, this done, he carefully angles the razor in his right hand, with his left hand he pulls his skin taught and begins to shave. The shave finished, with only two nicks in his skin, he cleans and puts away the shaving kit, he needs to wash his whole body, taking the carbolic soap out of the roll, he slips off his braces, undoes the puttees on both legs, rolling them neatly as he has no intention of putting them on again today, his boots are off then his socks, lifting them up and smelling them, immediately deciding to change them, as he does this he hears laughter from inside the cottage. Martin looks up to see Grace watching him through the window, he is embarrassed that she had just seen him smell his own socks, but thankful that she has laughed, reminding him that she is in the cottage, if not he would have been naked in the back yard, washing and tipping the bucket over his head, the back door opens and, as with yesterday, Grace's arm is in view and is holding a towel for him,

"Thank you, Grace," he says as the takes the towel, the door shuts and he is alone again. Martin decides to stand behind the shed, he will be out of view of the cottage and the road, carrying the bucket to this location, he strips of and washes in the still warm water, towelling himself as dry as the thin towel will allow.

Martin is sat at the table, dressed in clean underwear, socks and shirt, his khaki trousers are fine to wear again, Grace is stirring the stew,

"I am supposed to be doing that Grace, I am certain that Alice didn't invite you just to stir my stew!"

Alice, puts the lid back on the cooking pot, she hangs the stirring ladle on a hook next to the range, she walks over to Martin and touches his face where two pieces of tissue are helping to stop the bleeding from his shaving cuts, leaning forward toward him as he is still seated, she kisses him again, he responds, the kiss becomes passionate and Martin pulls Grace onto his lap, keeping his arms firmly around her waist, she puts her arms around his neck, the kiss ends and they both look at one another, neither wanting to let the other go, they kiss again, the embrace is exciting for both of them,

"I'm back!"

They both hear the gate open and Alice's' happy voice, Grace quickly kisses Martin on the lips and stands up, straightening her dress, when Alice lifts the latch to open the door, Grace is stirring the stew again,

"Grace! What are you doing? Martin is supposed to be making our tea!"

Alice looks at Martin, puts the loaf of bread onto the bench and crosses her arms over her chest,

"Martin!"

He smiles gently at his sister,

"Alice, I had the stew made even before either of you got here today, you know that, so Grace has just been stirring it because I had to wash and shave"

"So I see" says Alice "You look like you have been in a fight" she giggles, picking up the bread and handing it to him.

"Two little scratches, not bad considering I did not have a mirror"

He puts the bread onto the bread board on the kitchen table,

"Shall I get plates and cutlery?" asks Alice

"Bugger it!" says Martin,

"Language" says Grace, exactly at the same time as Alice says,

"Martin!"

He puts his hands up to surrender to them both, he then explains that he has locked the plates and cutlery in the back room with everything else, he stands up,

"Back in a minute"

He finds the items he needs and returns to the kitchen, his sister and Grace are sat together in a huddle, whispering to each other,

"What is going on here?" enquires Martin

They both assure him that nothing is 'going on', just 'girl talk' they inform him, Alice takes the plates and cutlery and lays the table, Martin sits where their father used to sit, Grace at the other end of the table, where Mother used to sit with Alice on one side in between them. The stew is a success, even if Martin had forgotten to get any butter for the bread, but even so, it was tasty and succulent, Martin is sucking on a hind leg bone, the ladies both looking at him with some disgust, he puts the bone down, looks at Grace and Alice and shrugs his shoulders at them. The clearing up is finished, the dishes washed and put back into the back room, the padlock is put back in place and the three of them are getting ready to walk Alice back to the pub, Uncle Pete will be there waiting to take her back to their house at Maples cottages, she has school in the morning,

"Can I stay at Granny's tonight Martin?" Alice asks "I don't need to go to school anyway, I know everything that I need to know"

Martin, firmly but politely replies, "No, school is important, and you need to go" he ruffles her hair gently, "Come on, let's get you to Granny's, then I can walk Grace home, I might even have a pint after that!"

Ten minutes later the trio are standing arm in arm outside of the Malta, Uncle Pete is also outside, waiting for Alice, she is reluctant to go,

"Alice" Martin speaks gently to her, "You need to go with Uncle Pete, I will see you tomorrow, I am coming to Maples cottages for tea, so you get school done and I will see you tomorrow afternoon"

She hugs him,

"Is Grace coming with you?" Alice asks

Martin and Grace are put on the spot by Alice's questions, they are stumped for a reply, Pete helps the situation,

"Alice, if it gets you up on my cart, Grace will be very welcome to come and eat with us"

Alice looks longingly at Grace, "Please come Grace, it will be marvellous, Aunt May is the best cook" Alice looks at her brother,

"No offence meant about the rabbit stew Martin; it was nice"

Grace accepts the offer, Alice is safely sat on the bench seat of the cart holding the reigns to Pete's horse, Dapple, Pete comes over to Martin,

"Can I have a quick word with you my boy?"

Grace, hearing this, walks over to the cart to say goodbye to Alice,

"What's up Pete?" asks Martin

Pete rubs his chin with his right hand,

"There is a sergeant or something in the pub, he is talking to your Gran, he was asking for you"

Martin puts his hand out to Peter, they shake hands,

"Don't fret Pete, it will be about the cottage, you know I am letting four soldiers stay there after I have gone"

Peter raises an eyebrow, he puts his pipe into his mouth,

"Alright then Martin, go in and find out, I will see you tomorrow" he pauses "Please bring Grace, she is lovely you know that don't you?"

Martin tells his uncle that he does know, then they bid each other good evening, Grace stands with him until the cart turns into Station Road and then out of sight.

"Will you come inside with me Grace?"

"I don't know Martin; will your Granny be fine with you and me being in there together?"

"Yes, she will, anyway, Pete has just told me that an N.C.O is inside asking for me"

Martin explains to Grace what an N.C.O is as they enter the pub together, a few regulars lift their heads up from their beer, but most ignore them as they enter, Martin sees RSM Westerman standing at the bar talking to Mary,

"Sod it" he says, Grace asks him what is wrong,

"I am not correctly dressed, no cap and no puttees on, the RSM will go mad"

Mary beckons them over, Martin walks to the bar, stands to attention, and addresses the RSM,

"Sir, good evening, please excuse my state of dress, I was just walking my sister to the pub"

"Relax Martin" Westerman says, turning his attention to Grace, "Good evening Miss, I was unaware that this young soldier had such a lovely sister"

Grace blushes,

"Good evening sir, I am not Martin's sister, we have just dropped Alice off here to be collected by her uncle"

Westerman looks at Martin raising a knowing eyebrow toward him, he speaks again

"Mary, Miss, will you excuse us for a moment, I need a quick word with the private"

Grace nods quickly, Mary says,

"Go and sit down Eddie, I will bring you and Martin a drink over in a few minutes"

Westerman thanks Mary and turns to sit at a table toward the back of the pub, Martin turns to his Granny and mouths silently to her, "Eddie?"

Mary waves him away, looking unamused at her Grandson but with sadness in her eyes, as he walks to sit with Westerman, he hears Grace say, "Is everything alright Mary?"

He stands next to the table, Westerman looks up at him, "Sit down son, we can relax in the pub don't you think?"

"Thank you, Sir,"

Westerman looks at him, "We are both regular professional soldiers Martin, you can call me Eddie in here"

"Thank you, Sir," Martin replies, he then feels foolish, Westerman smiles.

He reaches inside his tunic and takes out a folded piece of paper, the smile now gone from his face, he hands the envelope to Martin, who asks,

"What is this?"

"I think you know what it is Martin"

Without opening it, Martin quietly curses,

"I am glad the army has taught you some good old fashioned English lad" Westerman says. Martin, still hasn't opened the folded paper,

"When do I have to be back Eddie?"

Without hesitation, Westerman answers, "Friday"

The shoulders of the young soldier slump, he has been expecting this telegram, but wants to stay with Grace, he does not want to leave her. "Bloody hell, I only have one more day"

"Open the telegram Martin, we had it delivered to us by the Postmaster, Mr Skillman, he received it today through his telegraph office and thought the news might be better coming from a fellow soldier rather than being delivered to you by the telegram boy"

Martin opens the paper, he sees the familiar crown crest in the centre of the telegram form, with the words 'Post office' left of it and 'Telegram' on the right, the date, '23 9 14' is written in pencil in the top left corner, below this are the handwritten capital letters 'O.H.M.S'.

Without looking, he knows that the address of the sender will be 'Beds Rgt, Kempston Barracks', Bedford.

He sees his name and number and reads the message, written in Daniel Skillman's neat print,

'*Recall to Kempston Barracks, 0900 Friday 25th September 1914*'

Martin puts the telegram down on the table in front of him, Westerman says, "You knew it was coming son"

Mary arrives and places 2 pints of freshly pulled beer in front of them, Martin looks at her, he is about to thank her when he sees tears in her eyes, she leaves them, looking across to the bar at Grace, she is silently crying, staring straight at him.

"I hope it was in order for me to tell you Grandmother, I thought it would be easier for me than from you"

Martin is still looking at Grace, it is obvious that Mary has told Grace that Martin will be leaving in less than 36 hours. "Yes sir, thank you sir"

"Drink some beer Martin, I know it's not the best news, and by the look on your face, the timing is not good"

Martin is still looking at Grace, "Yes sir, thank you sir"

Eddie Westerman puts his pint down, he gently shakes Martin on the arm, quietly he says, "Private, get a grip man"

Martin snaps out of his dream state, he looks at Eddie, "Sorry sir, I have been expecting it, things are just getting good here"

Still looking at Eddie, Martin continues, raising his glass, "All good health to you Eddie, and to your comrades"

Eddie taps his glass to Martins, "And to you son, it will all be good, mark my words"

Martin takes a long draught from his beer, "I had better get ready for the move then, I will have to go tomorrow, I won't be able to get to London by train in time to get to Bedford for transport if I leave it till Friday"

Eddie scratches his head, "I have an idea, if you can come to the camp tomorrow morning, see the company clerk, he will have a rail warrant for you"

"I travelled free from Southampton, all across London and to the East station when I arrived"

Eddie waves a hand at him, "I know that, but since the trains were nationalised a couple of weeks ago there has been a bit of chaos with some of the troop movements, let's not risk it, I know that the early mail train from Welwyn gets in at just after 3am at the East station, then you can go to Luton Bute street and walk across the road to Luton Midland Road, then on to Bedford, you should be in Barracks by seven or eight in the morning"

"Blimey Eddie, you are a fountain of knowledge!" Although Martin knows the route of the train, he had no idea a train left so early in the morning,

"I need to be" Eddie says "I had to send half our deployment to Luton Hoo by train last Friday, His Majesty King George was visiting, and we had to be inspected, best way to get there was on the train, it was a waste of time in my opinion"

"Keeps the senior officers happy Eddie"

"It does" agrees Eddie "But it takes my young men away from training, and believe it or not, Kitchener is visiting Luton Hoo on the 29th and we have to do it all again!"

"I'm sort of glad I will be in France by then!" Martin smiles.

"On that subject soldier, you best go and see to your young lady, I hope to see you tomorrow, if not, the paperwork will be with the company clerk, I need to get another pint from your grandmother"

Eddie finishes his beer, taps his empty glass on Martins,

"Good luck Martin, I hope we bump into each other in France"

Martin raises his glass as Eddie walks back to the bar.

Grace is still standing at the bar, her huge dark eyes are glistening with tears, Martin stands and walks over to her, he takes both her hands in his, gently squeezing them he steps into her and quietly says, "It will all be fine, I promise"

She takes one hand from his and removes a handkerchief from her skirt pocket, patting her eyes dry, she replies, "You can't promise me that Martin, this is war, this is absolute insanity, and you will be in the middle of it!"

Mary puts a large brandy on the bar in front of Grace,

"Drink love" Mary says, Grace replies,

"No thank you Mary"

The glass of toffee coloured liquid is pushed toward her by the landlady, they look at each other, Mary puts one hand on Graces hand on the bar,

"Drink love" Mary says again, this time nodding at Grace. Grace picks up the brandy glass, a slight tremble can be seen from her hand, the drink is taken in one gulp, there are a few murmurs around the bar,

"Women drinking in our pub"

"Did you see that William?"

"It's not right, shouldn't be allowed"

Mary, seeing that Martin is getting angry with the comments aimed at Grace, speaks to the whole pub in a loud and commanding voice, "Gentlemen, this is my pub and has been for many years, I choose who I serve and who I don't, if any single one of you wants to challenge that then speak now, then we will see who gets served, speak now or forever hold your peace on this subject"

Every man in the pub hunches his shoulders forward and suddenly becomes very interested in their beer,

"I thought so" said Mary.

Eddie is stifling a laugh, he is impressed with the strength of this landlady,

"Gran, we are getting out of here, I will see you tomorrow before I go to Pete and Mays, then" he pauses "Then I will be off early the next morning" He looks at Eddie, "Sir, thank you sir"

Ernie moves his head, indicating that the young soldier should leave, Martin and Grace leave the pub,

"Another pint please Mary" Eddie puts his second empty glass on the bar.

Martin and Grace turn right from the pub and immediately right again, to walk up the steep hill of South View Road, they will be turning right into Salisbury road toward Graces house, the walk to the top of South View Road would take them directly onto the Common, it is nearly dark and both know that walking on the common in the dark, with its uneven ground and spiky thorn bushes is not to be done, they reach and turn into Salisbury road, neither has said a word to the other since leaving the pub. Grace stops and puts her arms around Martins neck, putting her head on his shoulder she begins to sob gently, Martin returns her embrace and they stand together, Grace lifts her head from his shoulder, his arms are around her waist, she now has both hands flat on his chest,

"You have to go on Friday, don't you?"

He nods in response, he sees that her tears are almost uncontrollable, he takes his handkerchief and says to Grace, "Wait there I will be back in a moment"

She watches as Martin walks to the public water pump, situated outside of number 20, he pumps the handle a few times until water comes out and he soaks his handkerchief, he walks back to Grace with the now wrung out handkerchief,

"Here you go" he says gently, he wipes her tears with the cool cloth, she takes it off of him and wipes her face with it,

"Thank you Martin", she hands the handkerchief back to him, he smiles,

"Keep it, I don't want a wet hankie!"

Grace hits him playfully in the chest, smiling at him as she does, he says to her,

"That's better, I adore seeing you smile"

She leans in and kisses him passionately on the lips, a door opens and a lady stands looking at them, arms crossed over her ample bosom, she coughs loudly and theatrically. Martin looks and recognises the lady, he has known her since childhood,

"Good evening Mrs Nette, I hope you and Mr Nette are well"

He is still standing with his arms around Grace, the middle aged lady puts on her spectacles, they are hanging from a chain around her neck, she looks for a second,

"Martin? Who are you with?" Mrs Nette looks for a moment, "Grace Wilson is that you as well?"

Grace is embarrassed and doesn't reply, Martin speaks for both of them,

"It is Mrs Nette, I am walking Miss Wilson home", Mrs Nette looks sternly at him,

"Can I suggest, that in the name of decency, you both walk faster than you are at this moment"

Martin nods, "Good night" They walk away, arm in arm, Martin turns back when Mrs Nette addresses him again, "Martin, my condolences to you and Alice, prayers were said in church for them"

He knows that Mrs Nette is a member of the congregation at the Methodist church and has been since it opened on the lower road to his cottage in 1905.

He thanks her and they walk away, hearing the door close and the latch being put across the inside of her door.

"Martin, what will she think of us?"

Martin tells her that he doesn't care what people think, he assures her that Mrs Nette is a 'good sort' and will not gossip about them. They arrive outside of Graces parents' home, she turns and looks around, to make sure that her parents, or anyone else for that matter, are not looking at them in the street.

She again kisses Martin passionately, holding his face in her hands, silent tears fall across her cheeks, he can feel them gently falling onto his face from hers.

"Good night Grace"

"Good night Martin, are we still going for tea at your Aunt and Uncles tomorrow?"

"I will call for you at about four if that is fine with you"

She pulls away from him when the front door of her home opens, her Father stands in the doorway,

"Good evening Mr Wilson" Martin stands almost to attention when addressing Graces Father. He is a man in his late forties with a bald pate, gold rimmed glasses, dressed smartly in matching trousers and waistcoat complete with fob watch chain from middle button to the left pocket, a light brown shirt with faint stripes, he is tieless, his shirt is undone at the collar, he has a large pipe in his mouth, removing the pipe he exhales smoke, Martin knows that he is a relative of Edward Wilson, the famed polar explorer and confidant of Captain Scott.

"Grace said you were home young man; our family sends condolences to yours"

Martin nods, Mr Wilson continues,

"Say good night Grace" He says sternly whilst looking at him "I appreciate you walking her home Martin"

"Sir" Martin replies, Grace looks at him,

"See you tomorrow Martin"

He nods, watching intently as Grace leaves him and walks the short distance to her front door, she turns and looks at him as her Father closes the door, he lifts a hand to say goodbye.

* * *

Thursday 24th September

Martin wakes from a dream, vivid, colourful, and beautiful, as soon as he opens his eyes, he cannot recall any of it, something has woken him from his dream, from his state of slumber, he hears the long case clock chime five times, then another noise, faint, but he is certain he hears something, holding his breath he continues to listen.

There it is again.

A tap at the front door, he jumps up, dressed only in his underwear, he goes to the front door,

"Who is it?"

A whispered reply, he thinks he has misheard, but opens the door anyway, hopefully and with his heart beating so very fast. The sun has not yet risen, golden shafts of light are rising slowly in the east, fighting the darkness for dominance of the morning, it is light enough for him to see the person standing at his door,

"Grace?"

He steps aside letting her into the kitchen, he again says, "Grace?"

She takes something from her dress pocket,

"I didn't want you to be without your handkerchief"

She looks at him, neither are embarrassed or ashamed of his near nakedness, a few seconds silence between them is broken as she moves quickly toward him,

"Oh Martin, I know it is silly, but I cannot bear to be apart from you"

Martin takes her into his arms,

"Our timing, and the Germans timing is lousy" he says, he moves her away slightly from him so that he can address her directly,

"What about your parents? They will wonder where you are won't they?"

She shakes her head, explaining that she is always up and out of the house before six when on 'mornings' at the school, her day should start at seven thirty, he pulls her back into his arms,

"You will need to be away soon then; it is a good forty minutes' walk from here, give me ten minutes to have a quick wash and dress so I can walk with you "

"I am not working today" she says quietly, "I am not going in, they can and will survive without me for a morning"

Martin looks at her quizzically, "What will you tell them tomorrow?"

She kisses him on the lips, "I will tell them that my boyfriend is a soldier and that he is returning to barracks to go to war"

He feels joyous at being described as her 'boyfriend', they embrace again and her soft lips find his, they sit on the bench seat under the window, gently and intensely they explore each other.

When the clock strikes seven chimes, Martin and Grace are lying on the floor of the kitchen, blankets underneath them for comfort and a sheet of cotton covering their naked bodies, they lie in each other's arms, Grace with her head on Martins chest, she speaks without looking at him,

"Martin, how should we feel at this moment"

He kisses the top of her head, "Not shamed, not embarrassed and not scared"

"Thank you" she says lightly,

"What for?" he asks

She kisses his chest, "For being you, for not being pushy, for being gentle and for being caring and understanding"

"Grace?"

She looks at him, her dark eyes wonderous jewels that he cannot, at this very moment in time, imagine ever taking his own eyes from, he continues before she can answer, "That was my first time as well, so we were both gentle and both caring and understanding"

Grace lifts herself up onto her right elbow, Martin's hand is on her left hip, he is gently stroking this area with his fingers, he lies on his back, and she climbs on top of him, leaning down toward him, they kiss, his hands now on her lower back, "You are just perfect" he says to her.

Just as morning becomes afternoon, Grace and Martin are sitting at the kitchen table drinking tea and eating toasted bread, dry as Martin forgot to ask his Gran for some butter, Grace sits covered only by the thin cotton sheet and Martin now has his underwear on, the range is lit and the room warm, the kettle has steam coming from its spout, Martin lifts it from the range, using the cloth to do so, opening the back door, he pours the boiling water into a bucket on the wooden table, it is half filled with cold water and the addition of the boiling water make it just right, not to hot and not too cold, to wash with.

After a few minutes of playful argument about who is going to wash first, Martin eventually pulls the sheet from Grace and runs into the back yard, he hangs it over the washing line, Grace stands unashamedly naked in the doorway looking at him,

"Your private bath house my lady" he bows to her, she steps into the yard, the stone floor of the yard is cold on her bare feet, taking Martin in her arms she pulls him toward her, she quickly pushes down on his underwear, they fall to the hard yard floor,

"A shared bath house" she whispers in his ear.

He responds with animated fervour.

* * *

Martin stands alone outside Graces parents' house, it is just after two thirty, the two of them arrived there as though Grace has finished teaching for the day and Martin has walked her home, the front door opens,

"Come on in lad"

Graces Father beckons him to come inside, Martin removes his cap and steps toward the house,

"Thank you sir"

Mr Wilson addresses him in an old fashioned stern manner, "Grace tells me you are returning to barracks tomorrow morning and then onto France"

"That is correct sir, although I don't know when we are departing for France, it won't be long I am sure"

Mr Wilson extends his hand toward Martin, "Take care then lad"

He nods toward the kitchen as Martin accepts the handshake, "They are in there"

With that he is gone, the living room door is closed behind him, Martin is left in the hallway of the house, only the lingering odour of sweet pipe tobacco has left any trace of Mr Wilsons recent presence. Martin walks into the kitchen, Grace is standing in front of her mother, who is sitting at the kitchen table, Grace puts her hand out toward Martin, he takes it and lets himself be guided to stand with Grace,

"Mother, you know Martin"

Mrs Wilson stands, Martin bows his head, "Good afternoon Mrs Wilson"

The lady of the house nods an acceptance,

"Grace tells me you are both taking tea at your Aunt Mays house this evening?"

"If that is in order with you and Mr Wilson Ma'am" Martin respectfully replies

"It is, I have spoken to Mr. Wilson and we would like Grace home by ten thirty this evening, can you ensure this happens please"

Martin, stifling a smile, assures her that he will abide by this, thanking her for allowing Grace to accompany him. They leave the house and walk arm in arm in the late sun of this September afternoon, as they enter the Malta, Mary is stood behind the bar, clearing up as she had just recently closed,

"Granny, we are just off to May and Pete's for tea, I take it you are staying here?"

"I am" she replies curtly, "I have got to open up later"

"Granny, I, well, I… " he stammers,

Mary comes from behind the bar, hugs her Grandson, "I know son, I know"

He can hear the pain in her voice, she becomes curt again,

"Now you listen to me Martin, I will look after Alice, but you make sure you come home to us" she grabs his tunic with both hands, "Do you hear me?"

"I do Granny" she hugs him quickly then goes back behind the bar,

"William Hogg is outside, probably looking for a fare if you are quick"

Martin blows her a kiss, they both leave the pub, for the first time Martin feels a little frightened about the war, he wonders if this will be the last time that he will be inside this pub. The local cabbie, Mr Hogg is outside, his horse and hansom cab, immaculate as always, they both greet him, he lifts his top hat to the couple,

"Could we be taken to Maple Cottages on the common please Mr Hogg" Martin enquires, Mr Hogg looks at his pocket watch,

"Of course you can young man, Maples cottages it is", this makes Martin smile, it is not uncommon for Maple cottages to be referred to as 'Maples Cottages', this is because a former owner of Childwickbury estate, Mr. John Blundell Maple, who was also the member of parliament for Dulwich, was a very wealthy man with an avid interest in horse racing, his stud farm on the estate at one time was the largest in the country with two hundred and twenty horse boxes, he also owned more mares than any other thoroughbred breeder in the country, the estate still has its own stud to this day. In the early 1880's, Maple had many of the old and tumbledown buildings on the estate demolished and had them replaced with newly built cottages, for the staff working on the estate the 11 cottages were only a small part of the changes made on the estate, they were named after him, so Maple cottages is correct. John Blundell Maple died in 1903 and Childwickbury was purchased in 1906 by another wealthy man, a diamond and gold merchant originally from the East end of London, Mr Isaac 'Jack' Barnato Joel, a man who also had a keen interest in the racing and breeding of horses, Jack is still the owner of Childwickbury, Martin only knows him by reputation, his Father had met him a few times when working on the estate with Pete and had always talked about him in a positive manner. Joel also invested heavily on the estate, but he kept all the names of the buildings and cottages as they had been originally, he always referred to Maple cottages as 'Maples cottages' and so, many locals, mainly those that work on the estate, also call the cottages 'Maples."

Hogg jumps down from his cab and opens the side door,

"Young lady" Hogg offers his hand to Grace to assist her into the seat inside, she accepts, she and Martin are inside the cab in under a minute, Mr Hogg, who locally is known as '*Long Oats*', referring to a large stick or broom handle that is carried by some horse owner, and is used to '*belabour*' a horse, it has always seemed a strange nickname to Martin, as he knows that Mr Hogg has always carried a large, elegant whip and he has never been seen to beat his horse,

"Giddyap!" Mr Hogg says to his horse and with a gentle shudder, the cab moves off,

Martin and Grace hold hands whilst sitting next to each other, no words are spoken, they both watch as the landscape, that is familiar to Grace but has changed a little for Martin. The cab slowly turns left onto Station road, over the River Lea on the old wooden bridge, taking the sharp left corner by the watercress beds, still on Station road they pass the East Station, over the bushes Martin can see the back of the station building with its grey slate roof and three large chimneys, one on each side of the main building and one more slightly lower than the others as it sits on a single story building, they can both hear loud hissing and can see white clouds of steam rising from the engine on the tracks, although they cannot see a train they know one is in and waiting to depart, they move on. Toward the right hand bend, passing a row of small and twee red brick cottages, built for the railway workers, Station Road post office North is on the corner opposite the Great Northern Inn, a pub used daily by the railway workers. Then on up the hill, still on Station Road they slowly pass the houses built on Manland common, still referred to by the locals, *the 'new' houses*, even though some of the houses have been standing for nearly three decades. Further on they pass Cowper Road, a dominant and visually stunning water tower can be seen rising up over sixty feet into the sky, then past Devonshire road with its late Victorian and early Edwardian houses, next on the left is Milton road, Martin knows that Shakespeare Road, with its two water towers, runs between Cowper and Milton roads and that Spencer road connects the two together at its Easterly end, this is an area known as 'Park View estate', all were built toward the end of the Victorian era and at this time is the largest estate in town. The cab passes under the railway bridge as they enter the town, the main railway station is to their left, he glimpses across to the station, he sees two of the half a dozen ornate Victorian lamps that bring dim light to the two platforms. Martin leans in and kisses Grace, she responds and they both miss the remainder of Station road, stopping only when the cab turns left at the Railway hotel and onto the St Albans road, Martin has a sense of déjà vu, he had purchased his padlock, hasp and staple from Ridleys which is opposite the hotel, as they pass the army encampment on the common he smiles to himself as he sees the soldiers drilling on the common, three perfect lines of men and weapons, carrying out the instructions that are shouted to them by the drill sergeant, Martin knocks on the cab roof and asks Mr Hogg to stop,

"I won't be a moment Mr Hogg; I have to collect some travel documents from the clerk"

Martin returns five minutes later, he thanks Mr Hogg and they set off again,

"That's that then" Martin says as he taps the top pocket of his tunic that now contains his travel warrant for tomorrow morning. They pass the gravel pits, the Silver Cup pub, the baa lamb trees, one of the entrances to Rothamstead park and its research facility are on their right as is Pimlico Place, now nearly a century old. They cross the quiet common land the Red Cottage is on their right as they pass the junction to Hatching Green, then onto the entrance to the brick works, the racecourse at the west end of the common seems quiet and unused. Maple cottages can be seen on the right, the cab turns onto a track that used to be named Female Lane and stops at the first cottages. There are eleven cottages in all, each dwelling being semi-detached to its neighbour, the double fronted cottages are identical each of them having red tiles on their roofs, there are three chimneys, one large in the centre of the roof, to draw the smoke from fires both the cottages its four pots standing proud atop it. At each end gable of the cottages there is a smaller chimney, this one is used only by each cottage that it serves, for the fireplace in the living room and for the range in the kitchen, to draw smoke from its almost constant use. Each cottage has a white painted pointed gable with white painted wood beams coming from it, creating the illusion of a white triangle, with its inside space containing three horizontal and two curved vertical beams, below this is an upstairs window, a treble glazed large frame with lattice on the glass, below is the green front door, hidden under an angled porch and tiled with the same materials as is on the roof. Two white painted posts support this porch, to the left of the porch is another large window, this one has four panes of glass but is different to the upstairs window as it does not have lattice design on it but instead has a criss cross of painted stiles, mullion, and meeting rails. To the left of this prominent part of the building, is a small, connected outhouse, also with a green painted door, to the right and set back from the front part of the house, the ground floor and upper floor have exactly the same windows as the prominent part of the house. Mr Hogg steps down and opens the door for Grace, offering his hand that she accepts to assist her out of the cab, Martin steps out and hands Mr Hogg several copper coins, the cabbie touches the front of his top hat and turns to leave, he is stopped when Grace asks him,

"Could you tell me the time please Mr Hogg?"

Obliging the request, he looks at his pocket watch, "It is five and twenty past three miss"

Grace thanks him, she adds, "Would it be possible to collect us from here at seven please?"

Mr Hogg tells them that he will be there promptly at seven to collect them both, advising them that the fare home will be slightly raised due to the time of the evening, with a "Giddyap" the cabbie is gone.

Martin asks Grace why she has done this, she simply replies, "I want a couple of hours for just us tonight Martin" He looks at her for a moment, she speaks again, "Please"

He nods in agreement.

"A little white lie won't hurt, we will tell May and Pete that you are on mornings tomorrow, anyway I have to be up before sunrise to get to the station in time" He looks at her,

"I am on afternoons tomorrow" is all she can say, desperately trying to cover the feeling of sadness enveloping her every being.

He nods again, "Anyway, and I don't mean anything by this, I need to get my goodbyes with Alice done and dusted, I don't want it to linger on"

They both turn as the door to number 2 Maple Cottages opens, Aunt May is standing in the porch,

"Hello you two, such good timing, Pete will be home in a bit, he will want a glass or two with you Martin, tea will be at about five, is that good with the both of you?"

Martin replies that is all fine with him and Grace, agrees he is about to explain that they will be collected at seven and the reason why, he does not get the words out as Alice runs from the house,

"Martin, Martin!"

He walks up the path to meet her, scooping her up in his arms, lifting her off the ground, she is crying again, "Aunt May has told me, it's just not fair, you have only been home a few days!"

She is angry, not with Martin or Grace, but with the situation, he puts her down onto the lawn,

"Alice, I have no choice, it comes with the job of soldiering" He squats down in front of her, "I promised you, and I meant it, that I will be safe, and I will come home to you"

Alice looks at Grace and puts out her hand, Grace steps forward and takes it in hers,

"Alice" she says quietly "You and I will be the best of friends whilst Martin is away, he has also promised me that he will be safe, so he had better do as he says!"

The three of them hug on the front lawn.

"Uncle Martin!" two voices shout at the same time, he looks as his nieces, Jennifer and Catherine barge past their Mother and join in the group hug,

"Hello girls, how are you both?"

Both insist that they are well, May speaks over all of them,

"Alice, Jennifer and Catherine, please leave Martin and Grace be and lets all go inside, the neighbours will be looking I am sure"

The group of five walk into the cottage, arm in arm until they get to the door and the chain is broken allowing them all to enter. Inside the cottage it is so much cooler than outside, the front door leads directly into the living room, the furniture that comes with the cottage and supplied by the estate is slightly shabby but comfortable, a couple of ancient prints in thin ancient frames hang on the walls, the small iron fireplace is unlit but has kindling in it ready to fire up should it get chilly. There is a '*best room*', just off of the living room to the right, Martin, in all his many visits to the cottage has only been in this room on a handful of occasions, he recalls it being a tidy but sterile room, with two seated comfortable chairs both with handmade lace doilies laid over the back of them, this room has no fire, so it is the cold that Martin remembers. The kitchen is off of the end of the living room, it is similar to his cottage, it has a large black, cast iron range that is giving off huge amounts of heat into the room, pots and pans hang from the mantle above the range, the kitchen furniture, a table with six chairs and a large dresser, are all old but functional, the smell of a pie cooking fills the air,

"Now that smells good Auntie, what is it?"

"That will be a venison and mushroom pie"

Martin moves forward to open the range oven door to have a look, May scalds him,

"Get out of it, nosey young man!"

He looks wounded, May smiles at him, hitting him on the arm with a long wooden spoon, "Make yourself useful, go and get me some water please"

He takes off his cap, puts it on the table and picks up the bucket and opens the back door, there are two wells that serve the cottages, he makes his way to the nearest, the garden is wide and long, chickens and ducks move freely about but have no access the vegetable plot that is securely fenced off from them. Martin leaves the garden through a small gate, this end of the garden has a pig sty and inside is a large sow and eight noisy piglets, they ignore him when it is clear he is not feeding them, he turns right out of the garden to get to the well and water pump. When the bucket is full, he begins to walk home when he sees a familiar form running toward him, he puts the bucket down and gets down on one knee,

"Hello Sheba!"

A large German shepherd dog nearly knocks him over, "Steady girl!" he says playfully. He spends a couple of minutes fussing over the dog, a voice from behind him says,

"Bloody hell boy, don't make the dog go soft on me" Uncle Pete comes into view,

"Sheba" he says "Home"

The dog instantly responds to his command and Martin watches as she runs toward the garden, easily vaults the fence, and disappears from sight, they hear the cacophony of noise made by the chickens and ducks as the dog charges through them.

"Now then boy" his pipe now in place at the side of his mouth, "I hope you haven't opened any of my beer yet?"

"I wouldn't dare Pete"

The Uncle and nephew shake hands and walk to the cottage, smoke trailing behind them as Pete puffs on the pipe, getting the last of the tobacco in the bowl to burn without any waste. The venison and mushroom pie is excellent, served with potatoes and carrots, Pete and Martin having finished three bottles of Benskins I.P.A each, are now halfway through the fourth, both savouring the golden coloured beer, Pete tells Martin that he is on good terms with the drayman from the brewery yard in St Albans, he continues to tell him that Benskins although a brewery company from Watford, the firm had purchased the old Kingsbury brewery from St Albans sixteen or seventeen years ago, and work from the old brewery yard situated just off of the Verulam road,

"And just how did you come by this very decent beer Pete?"

Pete winks at Martin,

"As I said boy, the drayman and I are on good terms, he might want a rabbit or a pheasant from the estate at times and these might be traded for bottles of beer"

Nodding and smiling Martin finishes his last bottle, looking across to Grace who is engaged in deep conversation with Alice, Jennifer, and Catherine, he looks at his pocket watch, it tells him it is now five minutes to seven, Mr Hogg will be waiting outside, he knows it is time to say goodbye to his family, he also knows that Alice will be inconsolable.

Martin stands up and shakes hands with his Uncle Pete,

"Stay safe boy" Pete speaks quietly to Martin "We will take care of Alice so don't fret"

Nodding his thanks, he looks over to his sister, she has disengaged from Grace and the twins, she stands open mouthed looking at her brother, "No" she says "No Martin, stay a bit longer"

Martin walks over to his sister and puts his arms around her shoulders, gently pulling her head into his chest, bending down he whispers in her ear,

"I need to go Alice" he has to swallow hard; his throat is burning, and tears are forming in his eyes, "Remember that I love you dearly, I want you to be good for Uncle Pete and Aunt May, they will take great care of you"

He stops talking for a moment, taking a deep breath he looks up to the ceiling and closes his eyes, he then continues to whisper to Alice, "Granny will always be here for you, and you can go to the cottage anytime you want to" He kisses her on the top of her head, "Don't ever forget me Alice, you will be in my thoughts every second I am away"

Martin stands up, squeezes Alice gently, she is standing still and not moving, Pete steps in,

"I got her now boy"

He takes over holding on to Alice as Martin moves away from her to hug his Aunt and his nieces, he picks up his cap from the table and puts it on his head, Grace is squatting down in front of Alice, he hears her say,

"Alice, I will come and see you on Saturday at the pub, we can spend the day together down by the river, would you like that?"

Alice does not answer, she breaks away from Pete and throws her arms around Graces neck, she is sobbing quietly,

"Come now Alice" Pete speaks gently to her and takes her back into his control; Alice lets herself be separated from Grace. Martin is standing by the front door, Grace joins him and they both leave the cottage, they can see Mr Hogg in his cab waiting for them, Martin turns to face the house as he reaches the front garden gate, he lifts his right hand to wave at the family, who are now all gathered by the front door, Alice is looking directly at him, silent tears run freely down both of her cheeks, he smiles at her and mouths to her, "I love you."

He turns and walks away with Grace, getting into the cab without another look back, he knows this is hard on Alice, but he also knows that he has to go, going back, even for another hour or two, will only make things worse.

The cab jolts as the horse moves off,

"Alice will be fine Martin" Grace puts her hand on his arm as she speaks, "I will spend as much time as I can with her"

Martin can't speak, he nods and looks out of the window, taking in as much as he can from the common and the town not wanting to forget anything, knowing that he may never return.

* * *

Friday 25th September

Martin hasn't slept, it is two in the morning and he is almost ready to go, with the front door key in his hand, he has to put it through the door of the Malta as he passes on his way to the station, the kitchen is tidy and clean, the blankets and pillows from the floor now stored into the back room, which is locked and secure.

Grace had left him at just before ten the previous evening after they had spent a couple of hours alone together, she had insisted that she was not to be walked home, wanting to say her goodbyes to him at the cottage. In that instance in time, Martin had thoughts that her leaving was the worst thing that had ever happened to him, leaving him with a momentary pang of shame for these thoughts, thoughts of love and emotion for Grace, his parents had not been dead more than a few weeks, he feels genuine sadness for their passing, but Grace leaving the cottage last night had been so much harder to deal with, ashamed, he said a silent prayer of apology to his Mother and Father. He followed Grace home, she did not know he was just behind her as she walked the short distance to her parents' house, he wanted to make sure that she got there safely, he also wanted to have one last look at her, he could see her as she steps through the front door, she is crying when the door is answered and she is let into the house by her Father, Martins last look at the girl he has fallen in love with is her being consoled by her Mother as the door closed.

He walked slowly back to the cottage, arriving back at the soothing and familiar sight of his family home, he stands by the fence and gate, feeling the weight of terrible loneliness crushing him, he sits on the ground outside of the back door for an hour or so, just sitting quietly in the dark and staring at the Yew tree. Its huge presence is silhouetted firmly against the dark night sky, its gentle movement in the September breeze hardly noticeable, the almost silent sound of its boughs straining within the giant canopy and groaning gently, combines effortlessly with the mellow noise as the branches and twigs stir in the silence of the night.

Martin checks his uniform is correct and smart, his boots are clean, his puttees have been put on with care, his trousers are dust free, for now, his tunic is straight, the pockets are empty all bar one that contains his pocket service book, in it is recorded his personal and army details, service record and kit issued, the brass buttons are shiny and bright, his 1908 pattern webbing is dirt free, assembled and fitted correctly enabling him to remove it as a single piece, slipping it on and off like a jacket. Martin has assembled his webbing in '*battle order*', the valise is not attached, if it were, he would be dressed in '*full marching order* ' and the haversack would be attached to the webbing on his hip. The two inch wide braces pass through the epaulettes of his tunic and cross diagonally at the back, his haversack is securely fixed to these diagonal straps, this ensures that the weight of the haversack is evenly spread out. The three inch wide belt is secured at the front, the brass D shaped buckles are as shiny as the buttons on his tunic, the two cartridge pouch sets, each containing five ammunition pouches, are attached to the belt at the front, each pouch holds three five round 'stripper clips', a total of a hundred and fifty rounds of rifle ammunition, seventy five on each side, can be carried, Martin has none with him, the pouches are all empty. Also attached to the webbing is a bayonet 'frog', this is a tubular canvas carrier that connects the scabbard to the belt, the bayonet is inside the scabbard and hangs in front of his left hip, his water bottle, full of water as it is a military offence not to have it filled and its carrier hang from his right hip, finally, attached at the back of the belt are two carriers for his entrenching tool, one for the head and one for the helve. He hasn't worn full kit for nearly a week and his body has forgotten how heavy it is, fifty pounds in battle order and nearly seventy pounds when the valise is attached, the webbing is designed to spread the weight, but it is still heavy, on top of all this carried and attached kit, he has his rifle slung over his shoulder.

The door is locked, he puts the key in his trouser pocket, turning to leave he has one last look at the garden, it is in darkness as the sun hasn't begun to rise as yet, he opens the gate, quietly closing it behind him as he leaves the cottage, heading for the station and into the unknown. As he approaches The Malta, he can see three people standing outside, as he gets closer he can see that his Grandmother is standing on the top step, at the bottom of the steps Grace stands with her Father, his heart nearly beats out of his chest at the sight of her, she is holding her Fathers left arm very tightly, as he reaches the front of the pub, he puts his valise down,

"Do you lot know what time it is?"

The three smile weakly at him, he approaches Mr Wilson, shaking his hand he says,

"Sir, I thank you for being here to wish me well and for bringing Grace to see me"

Mr Wilson nods toward Martin but says nothing, Martin looks at Grace and then to Mary.

"Granny I have the key to the cottage and to the padlock"

He walks past Grace, gently touching her hand as he does, he hands the keys to Mary,

"Remember what I told you Martin; you look after yourself"

He kisses her on the cheek and steps back, she then speaks to Mr Wilson,

"Henry, may I have a word please"

"Of course, Mary" he looks confused, especially when Mary continues,

"Inside the pub please"

Mr Wilson takes the two steps up into the pub,

"I won't be but a minute" he says to Grace.

Mary and Henry Wilson enter the pub, Martin hears the bolt being put across from inside, he knows that Mary has bolted the door so that when it is unbolted, it will give him warning as to when Mr Wilson is about to make an appearance. Grace and Martin embrace on the steps of the pub, they kiss each other slowly and with passion, Grace stops and looks at Martin, he can see tears welling up in her beautiful dark eyes,

"No tears Grace, there has been more than enough crying"

She wipes her eyes with the back of her right hand.

Martin kisses her quickly on the lips, "Just know that I am in love with you Grace Wilson"

He steps away from her, picks up his valise as he hears the bolt on the door being pulled open, Mary and Henry step outside,

Grace stands in front of Martin as he begins to walk, she leans into him and whispers in his ear, "I am in love with you soldier boy"

Henry moves to intervene, Mary stops him by putting a hand on his arm, he looks at her and she slowly shakes her head at him, Martin kisses Grace on the cheek then walks away toward Station road, turning the corner without looking back at any of them.

He arrives back at Kempston barracks, just after seven in the morning to immediately be told to 'stag on', gate duty for the next twelve hours, most of the regiment are still at Lyndhurst, preparing for transport to a ship at Southampton docks.

He and forty two other soldiers have returned to barracks, most of whom have been home on compassionate, bereavement or hardship leave, they are instructed to be ready to move at very short notice, even a quiet tour of duty in the guard house can't take his mind off of Grace, he knows that he is not unwell but he has a continuous sinking feeling in his gut, the worst of it is that he has no idea how long it will be until, if ever, that he sees Grace again.

* * *

Saturday 26th September – Tuesday 6th October

Martin and his comrades have spent all day completing preparatory tasks prior to leaving barracks, stacking, and loading large wooden crates that are full of blankets, ammunition, and other such kit, when not working the are almost continually shouted at by Sgt Oakes, who is described, behind his back, by all the privates as 'a horrible little man', he demands bulled boots and spotless personal kit at all times, he happily takes up the rest of the day for them with more incessant bullshit. The food at the barracks is surprisingly good, the privates are eating with the NCOs in the mess hall and as there are less than a hundred of them on base, the cooks, or 'cabbage mechanics' as the soldiers call them, are having to supply meals to a fraction of the numbers that they have been used to, therefore the food is decent, sadly, although none of them know it, the good food will last less than 36 hours for them.

At 0600 hours on Monday 27th September the remaining soldiers of the 2nd battalion are mustered on the parade ground, the message delivered to them by the senior ranking officer at the barracks, Captain Charles Foss, he demands complete silence as he reads to the gathered men from a telegram,

7th Division Routine Order No. 22, 27th Sept 1914. WO 95/1635

Mobilisation of 7th Division at Southampton

All Battalions of the 20th, 21st, 22nd, 23rd, 24th & 25th Infantry brigades

21st Infantry brigade – 2nd Beds Rgt - SS Winifredian & SS Cornishman

2nd R Scots Fusiliers – SS Cymric & SS Lake Michigan

2nd Yorks Rgt – SS Caledonia & SS Victorian

2nd Wilts Rgt – SS Cestrian & SS Turcoman

Embarkation Southampton	*4/10/14*
Sail 0600hrs	*5/10/14*
Dover docks	*6/10/14*

Disembark Zeebrugge 0600hrs 7/10/14

God Save the King

All the soldiers shout 'God save the King!' with great gusto in response to Captain Foss oration,

Foss continues and tells them that they are to join their '*brothers*' from the 1st Battalion in Belgium and France, he reports to those present, that the 1st Battalion has been, and still are involved in heavy fighting near to Mons, a town in Belgium, they, alongside soldiers from the Northumberland fusiliers, the 1st West Kent's and the 2nd Battalions of the Kings own Yorkshires and the Duke of Wellingtons, had defended a village, Wasmes, from large and overwhelming numbers of attacking German forces. The BEF had taken heavy artillery fire from the enemy, killing many during a firefight, they had then followed orders to strategically and successfully retreated to St. Vaast. Murmurs from all the men clearly shows that they don't believe in reports of a 'strategic, successful retreat'

"Quiet" Sergeant Oakes shouts, his one word order starts quietly but quickly rises to an amazing crescendo of sound, the men settle. Captain Foss finishes by reporting that BEF deaths are believed to be in excess of one thousand six hundred men, he quickly adds that he has no figures for deaths suffered by the Bedfordshire's during the battle. The small number of men present remain silent, the war has just become very real to them, reports of British soldiers dying in such large numbers shakes them all, some look visibly scared. Foss brings the muster to a close, Sergeant Oakes brings the men to attention, Foss orders his soldiers to be ready to move at ten, giving them less than 4 hours, most, if not all, are already ready to go, kit is stowed correctly and letters to home have been written and posted, Martin has written his will, completing it last night, it is neatly folded and tucked inside his pocket service book.

He hopes no one will ever read it.

Mobilisation to Southampton is tedious, the train from Bedford to London Waterloo is without doubt, the slowest train Martin has ever travelled on, it is supposed to be a direct train and the trip, they had been informed was to last just over 2 hours, but it has stopped at half a dozen stations to allow more and more soldiers to get on, every inch of the train is taken up with military men and their kit, Martin is thankful that he has a seat, he and five other colleagues who had been amongst the first to board the train have managed to get into a first class compartment near to the front of the second carriage, it is a squeeze for all of them and their kit in the small space, but with their valises stored on the high luggage rack, the six of them are as comfortable as they can be inside the dark wooden panelled compartment. The bench seats on either side are straight backed, covered in a material that is a plush red velvet, worn out in places, but comfortable none the less, certainly more comfortable than the other soldiers who have not managed to bag a first class compartment. They smoke woodbines, play cards, and fitfully sleep on the journey, it takes over double the original estimated time to get to their destination, they are all glad to see the train pull into London Waterloo. The station is packed solid with soldiers and sailors, the former although seemingly in disarray are not, they are lying on the platforms with their kit stowed on the ground, they have managed to remain disciplined, in between the rows of soldiers' rifles have been stacked in a tepee style, stocks to the ground and barrels resting together at the top of the stack, each soldier has his valise under his head as he sleeps or rests. The sailors are not as disciplined, most are standing in groups, their squashed caps balanced on the back of their heads, smoking cigarettes, and pipes, some have bottles of beer in their hands, none have any rifles with them. Martin and his colleagues are directed to platform four, here they find a space and set up as all the other soldiers have done, at this time none of the NCO's can tell them what time their train will be arriving and when it will be leaving. Martin lies on his back with his head resting on his valise, his rifle is stacked with others behind him, he has a woodbine in his mouth, removing a swan vesta match from its box, he strikes it on the platform igniting the red tip into a bright yellow flame, he brings the match toward him his hands cupped around it to stop it being blown out by the strong breeze that is gusting around platform four, the match and the cigarette meet and with encouragement from Martin inhaling on the end, it takes, he can immediately feel the freshly burnt tobacco being sucked into his lungs, he exhales a large amount of smoke, blowing the match out at the same time, discarding the small stick of burnt wood by flicking it onto the rail track, he pulls his cap down over his eyes, closing them in the semi darkness caused by his cap.

"2nd Battalion on your feet!"

Martin is still waking up when his mate, Jack Bothworthy, nudges him in the ribs,

"Get your arse up Martin, the horrible little man is shouting at us"

Martin lifts the cap off of his eyes, the brightness of the afternoon sun shines through the glass roof of platform four making him squint, he quickly realises that he has fallen asleep with the cigarette held in his fingers, it has burnt out, he flicks the stub away, checking his fingers for burns, he thankfully finds that he is unburnt, the woodbine had stopped burning before reaching his skin.

"Do you two need a fucking personal invitation to join us today!"

Sergeant Oakes is screaming at Martin and Jack, in unison they both jump to their feet and say, "No Sergeant"

They collect their kit and rifles and follow the rest of their unit to the train that has arrived at the platform whilst Martin was sleeping, it is not at the station end of the platform and has stopped further down, they walk a couple of hundred feet before they are directed onto a carriage. This carriage is certainly not first class, more like a freight truck with huge sliding doors and only an open area to sit in, Martin sits in the back left corner with Jack both using their valises as seats, the carriage slowly fills with other soldiers, it soon becomes cramped and the jollity they shared at Waterloo is becoming aggressive with threatening words being spoken between many of the men. Martin hears a shouted order from outside the carriage, he cannot see who speaks the words as the carriage is now too crowded, all he can see in front of him is the uniforms of his colleagues from the Bedfordshire's and from other regiments who are also in the carriage with him.

"Calm down. Now!" the words are authoritative and commanding, the resounding voice continues, "We have men in France being shot at in trenches by the Hun, that gentlemen, is certainly an uncomfortable place to be" the voice pauses, Martin believes the pause is for effect, it works the carriage quickly becomes quiet, "Being mildly uncomfortable for a couple of hours on a train to the seaside is a doddle in comparison, now bloody well shut up with your whining!" another dramatic pause before he finishes, "All of you!"

The double doors are slammed shut, the light in the carriage is cut down by half, the murmur of quietly talking men fills the air, Martin can still feel an uncomfortable, but now an almost scared atmosphere in the carriage, he and Jack agree that the words from the unknown NCO have struck a chord with everyone, including them, they get as comfortable as they can for the remainder of the journey.

The train arrives at Southampton West railway station just before nine that evening, Martin stands as the carriage slowly empties out of the cramped men, his body is stiff from sitting in the same position for several hours, he stretches his arms in an attempt to release some of the tension in his body, he looks down, Jack is asleep, he kicks him gently,

"Come on sleepy head, how do you manage to sleep in these conditions?"

Jack opens his eyes, yawns, and replies, "It is a talent I suppose"

They collect their valises, rifles and kit and leave the carriage and step onto the platform, the scene in front of them is similar to London Waterloo, military personnel fill the platform, the station is much smaller than its London cousin and with the amount of soldiers and sailors moving around there isn't much room to move, there is much bumping and nudging as each person tries to get to where they need to,

"2nd Battalion Bedfordshire's, to me!"

The voice of Sergeant Oakes rings out true and clear above the hustle and bustle on the platform, Martin and Jack make their way to where Oakes stands, they can see that it is nearly dark outside,

"How the hell are we going to get to the camp?" asks Jack

"One guess mate" Martin replies

Neither have time to continue their conversation, Sergeant Oakes interrupts,

"Fall in men, over here!" he indicates that his soldiers move to the outside of the ticket hall and into a large open space in front of the station building, the tired and aching soldiers slowly move into formation,

"Snap to it lads!" shouts Oakes

This sharp order from the Sergeant makes the men wake up and they fall in, three deep, fourteen across, Oakes brings them to attention,

"Shun!"

The short sharp sound of forty two men stamping their boots simultaneously resonates from outside and into the ticket hall, other units are doing similar with their sergeants bellowing at them, Oakes stands them at ease, then to stand easy, he tells them to remain where they are, he walks over to the entrance where he meets with several other men of his rank, they shake hands, they all stop when an RSM from the Royal Artillery appears from inside the ticket hall, the group have a short conversation with the RSM, when he is finished, uniformly, they all shout,

"Sir!"

Oakes walks to his men, he growls, "Be ready lads"

The voice of the RSM shouts loudly,

"Parade!"

The large group of soldiers, as one, bring their chests up smartly, hands held together in the small of their backs, the RSM continues,

"Parade! Parade shun!"

Martin has no idea how many men lifted their left legs then stamped them down to the position of attention, but it is done together, exactly at the same time, the RSM seems pleased as he has the smallest of grins on his face. He is obviously a long service regular soldier, the medal ribbons on his chest show he has seen active service, probably in the second Boer war, his uniform is immaculate, the buttons on his tunic glisten even in the near dark conditions, his trousers, different to the infantry uniform in that they slightly flare at the thighs. The RSM waits a few seconds, with his thin stick under his right arm, his perfectly trimmed and waxed moustache twitches from side to side as he prepares to give further orders, making sure he drags the words out slowly, he shouts,

"Parade, stand at" pausing for two or three seconds "Ease!"

As one, the parade complies with the order, he leaves them in this position and does not order them to 'stand easy'. The RSM explains to the parade that he is from the Hampshire Yeomanry, C squadron, he ensures that every man knows that he is in charge, giving a small lecture on behaviour, no soldier is permitted to enter any licenced premises at any time, every soldier must have his kit ready to move at a moment's notice and that they are to march to 'the Common' where tented billets will be allocated.

"Parade!" the soldiers although already standing at ease, lift their chests again awaiting the order, it comes quickly,

"Parade shun!"

The parade now at attention, the RSM instructs the sergeants to be ready to move in a matter of minutes, Oakes returns to the small platoon of soldiers from the 2nd Bedfordshire regiment, standing them easy, he instructs them quickly and succinctly,

"Kit on lads, full marching order, we form up outside in five"

Most of the platoon have not organised their kit in marching order, including Martin, they remove their haversacks from the webbing and attach the valise using the two valise straps, the haversack is then connected at the hip, all are ready in under the allocated five minutes. Over two thousand soldiers now line the street outside of Southampton West railway station, three rows of uniformed men from many different units and regiments await the instruction to march the one and a half miles to the common, they don't have to wait long,

"Parade, by the left, quick march!"

They set off, at standard marching pace, 116 beats a minute with a step of 2 feet six inches, left foot first they march for just over half an hour, they enter a huge area of common land that has been roped off, large white pointed tents cover huge areas of the common. Martin and the Bedfordshire's are split from the main group of soldiers, Oakes explains that as they are only going to be here for a few hours, they have been allocated four 'transit' tents, they are to march to White Moor, Lyndhurst at first light to re-join their regiment and the other regiments that form the Brigades of the 7th Division.

Martin wakes up to the tent being shaken, he firmly believes that he has only just shut his eyes,

"Up and at 'em lads"

Martin has no idea whose voice is coming from the outside of his tent, Jack, as usual, is still asleep, Martin nudges him, "Here we go mate"

The tent he is in, with nine others, is cramped, they had all decided not to leave any of their kit outside last night, they know that although soldiers don't usually pilfer, they will 'replace' any lost kit, so the tent is filled with ten soldiers and all their kit, there is not an inch to spare. Martin looks at his pocket watch, it is five thirty, looking outside of the tent he sees that it is just getting light, but the sun has not risen as yet,

"Where are the latrines mate?" he asks a passing soldier,

"Up there" he points "Follow your nose"

Martin laughs,

"I mean it mate; you can't miss it"

He returns ten minutes later, Jack asks him where the latrines are,

"If I was you Jack, I wouldn't bother" Martin holds his nose,

"Is it that bad?"

Martin nods, Jack disappears into the tent, returning with a few sheets of newspaper and his trenching tool,

"Back in a jiff lad's"

Martin watches as Jack disappears into a small clump of bushes, he rubs his chin, he needs to shave, or he will face a disciplinary, a corporal Martin knows walks up to him,

"Morning Corp" Martin greets him "Just going to get a quick shave, any chance of a bit of scran before we set off?"

Upon hearing the word 'scran, Martin is quickly joined at the front of the tent by the remaining eight soldiers, they all greet the Corporal,

"Who is missing here?" he asks.

The nine men look at each other, Martin answers,

"Private Bothworthy Corp, he is using the latrine"

Jack appears from the bushes, the Corporal stares at him, "I hope you have not been shitting in the bushes Bothworthy?"

"Me Corporal? No Corporal" Jack replies with a smile on his face

The Corporal tells him to stop grinning like a fool, he does as instructed

"Make sure that trench spade is spotless for inspection Bothworthy, do I make myself clear?"

"Corporal" replies Jack

The group of men listen as the corporal explains that they will be marching to Lyndhurst, to a camp at White Moor, a ten mile march, leaving at seven o clock, food is being served at the mess tent,

"We have priority as we are the only unit leaving today" Explains the corporal, "So you best get your arses over there, you have less than an hour till we march"

They are excused shaving, for today only by the NCO, they grab their mess tins and cutlery from their valises and go for breakfast.

At five minutes to seven the forty two men are in formation, ready to march, Jack is complaining that breakfast had been a 'bloody' disgrace,

"Two bits of bread and a couple of slices of bully beef with a brew of piss poor tea, and they expect us to march on that" he moans. He is told to 'button his lip' by the Sergeant, they set off on the long march to White Moor, the day is overcast but dry, 'Good marching weather' according to Sergeant Oakes, most of the men don't agree, a train to Lyndhurst would have suited them better, the thought of a three or four hour march does not appeal to many, if any of them. They march past the railway station at Southampton West, in the opposite direction this time, its ornate clock tower with its four white clock faces and a pointed spire sit atop the red brick tower of the station building, they march onto Millbrook road and follow this road until they reach Redbridge, through this area, they march into Totton at the north end of Southampton water, here they stop for a ten minute water break near to the railway station, some groan that a train from Southampton would have been so much quicker, they shut up as Sergeant Oakes walks past them, looking at the moaners without saying a word. Marching again into the open land of the New Forest they pass an ancient sign for Handsowne and keep on going, as they pass under a railway bridge the same men are moaning again, becoming silent when the sergeant growls at them, they pass Lyndhurst Road railway station and continue over the open heath land. Before they reach the town of Lyndhurst, they meet a group of four soldiers standing at country crossroads, supposedly on direction duty, they are loitering and smoking, Oakes brings his men to a halt, he approaches the four soldiers, none of them react to the sergeant approaching them.

"I you don't put that fag out sonny I am going to shove it where a qualified doctor won't be able to stub it out"

The four soldiers, not sure which one the sergeant is addressing, put their cigarettes out on the floor, Oakes points at the NCO with them, a young Lance Corporal,

"You sonny, come here"

The lance jack approaches Sergeant Oakes, stands to attention,

"Lance Corporal Much, Sergeant, 2nd Wiltshire's"

He looks terrified as Oakes steps in to almost be nose to nose with the soldier, Martin cannot hear what is being said as Oakes is whispering to the Lance Corporal, who's face turns grey then takes on a white hue,

"Yes Sergeant!" he shouts

Oakes turns to his men, "2nd Bedfordshire's, Shun!"

The forty two men come to attention, Oakes continues, "March over gentlemen, we are following a track cross country to White Moor camp" he takes a huge breath in,

"Turning right, dismissed!"

The platoon turns smartly to their right and with a stamp of their feet they are dismissed and can relax, "Smoke 'em if you have 'em, ten minutes we are off again" Oakes instructs his men, he looks across at the Lance corporal, who is standing with his three colleagues, he points at them, "Don't dare light one Lance corporal, don't you dare"

The men from the Wiltshire regiment move a short distance away, the Lance corporal stands his men in a line, at ease and avoiding any eye contact with Sergeant Oakes.

The men arrive at White Moor camp in single file, Sergeant Oakes, in an unusually good mood, orders the men to take off their webbing and 'take ten', Martin takes off his cap and his webbing, the feeling of relief on his back is instantaneous, he can feel that his shirt is stuck to his back with sweat. Jack is already sitting on his valise, he offers Martin a cigarette, he accepts, noting that Jack is smoking Redfords Navy cut, its packet a distinctive red, white, and blue colouring with a depiction of a sailor hitting a union flag with a hammer is easily recognisable, '*5 for 1d*' is printed in the bottom right corner, big white letters against a blue background,

"Where did you get these Jack?" Martin asks as he lights both their cigarettes with one of his swan vesta matches,

"Won them last night whilst you were snoring, playing three card brag"

Martin inhales deeply, "Who was your victim?"

Jack feigns insult and pain, he points to himself, "Me? Cheat? How dare you!"

They both laugh, Jack then says, "It was 'Window' Sills if you must know"

Martin looks incredulously at his pal, Jonny 'Window' Sills is one of the youngest deployed with them, only just nineteen and as green as they come, it is obvious that Jack had been cheating at cards. When they are halfway through their smoke, Oakes appears, walking toward them, the men all stand but are waved at by Oakes to remain seated,

"Bothworthy, could I have one of your smokes that you cheated young Window out of last night?"

Jack looks at the sergeant and is about to deny the allegation, Oakes is pointing at him and smirking, "Nothing goes on that I don't know about private" Sergeant Oakes says as he accepts a cigarette from Jack, he uses Jacks half smoked cigarette to light his own, "Thanks" he nods at Jack with a wink, "Gather round the rest of you" he says in a voice loud enough to be heard by all, the men slowly and stiffly get to their feet, leaving their kit on the ground they huddle around the Sergeant. "I have some good news and some bad news for you all boys" he says, the group remain silent,

"The bad news is that we, along with most of the other 15,000 men that now form the 7th division, will be practicing trench warfare, that means digging, sleeping, and shitting in ditches gentlemen"

He silences the moans and groans, men complaining that they are tired having not had much more than a few hours' sleep in the past two days,

"The good news is, because we have been on the go for nearly forty eight hours, we are excused digging and training tomorrow so that we can get our kit in order, ready for the off"

"When will that be Sergeant?" a high pitched voice from the middle of the group asks, Oakes looks for the owner of the voice, nodding when he finds the man,

"'Patsy' Palmer, it had to be you" the men laugh quietly, 'Patsy' so called because he has the high pitched voice of a woman, is a thirty year old career private and excellent soldier, Oakes continues, "You will be going when the powers that be tell us when you will be going, until then, I have a list of allocated billets, it will be pinned up outside the clerks' tent, get your kit stowed, get some scoff and get some sleep"

"Sergeant" they all say together,

"One more thing" Oakes speaks again, "You are not to go off camp to visit the local hostelries or to annoy the local ladies"

The men laugh quietly again,

"Am I clear lads?" Oakes raises his voice,

"Sergeant" they all repeat again

"The corporals will be round to check you all later and to inform you of any changes we have to our itinerary, remember, most of your mates have been here for nearly two weeks, they may not be as happy and joyous as you are"

The men all look at him,

"Dismissed" Oakes gives the final order.

The last day of September comes and goes, Martin had enjoyed his day off, managing to catch up on some sleep, getting his kit is in order, his old blanket exchanged for one without holes in and a new great coat have been added to his valise. After a few days of trench digging, or field practice as the NCO's call it, Martin is lying in his tent, writing to Grace, reading the letter back to himself he realises that it is probably the most boring letter anyone has ever written, nothing that he really wants to say has been put onto the writing paper in front of him, Jack sticks his head inside the tent, holding the flap around his neck to give the impression that his head is floating, Martin looks up, "Idiot" he says to Jack,

Jack opens the tent flap fully, "The horrible little man wants to see you"

Martin looks confused, "Me? Why?"

Jack shrugs, "Don't know, but he wants to see you now"

Martin thanks Jack, he stands and puts on his tunic that is hanging from a pole inside the tent, he quickly checks that his uniform is correct, puts on his cap and makes his way through the camp to find Sergeant Oakes. Five minutes later he is standing outside of the senior NCO's tent, it is open at both ends and Sergeant Oakes is sitting at a makeshift desk that he is sharing with Colour Sergeant 'Barnie' Barnes,

"Get in here private" Oakes instructs Martin, he enters the tent and addresses the NCOs in rank order,

"Colours" then turning to Oakes, "Sergeant"

Barnes does not speak, instead he puffs smoke from his pipe, Oakes speaks,

"Paddock has a broken leg"

"Brian Paddock?" asks Martin

"How many Paddocks do you know private?"

Martin does only know one, Brian Paddock, he is their Lance corporal, he is in their tent and is the NCO for their platoon that consists of himself, Jack, Jacob 'Alf' Rivers, nicknamed 'Alf' by Sgt Oakes, and described by the same as one 'Annoying Little Fucker', and William 'Posh' Miles, he sees the look on Oakes' face and decides not to answer, Oakes continues,

"The stupid bugger fell whilst climbing out of a trench, I have heard of soldiers falling into trenches but not out of them" Oakes looks at Barnes, who in return takes his pipe out of his mouth and shrugs.

Oakes gives Martin two single V shaped stripes, Martin takes them,

"Sergeant?" Martin asks quizzically, Oakes looks at him, stands with both fists on the desk and leans forward,

"It appears that you are the chosen man, do you want them or not private?"

"Yes sergeant, thank you sergeant" Martin can feel the stripes in his left hand, he is looking at Oakes, neither say anything, Colour Sergeant Barnes breaks the silence,

"Lance Corporal, I think you had better go and sew on your stripes, neatly mind you, then take your pocket service book to the company clerk to be updated, you are now a tanner a day richer"

Martin looks across to Barnes, who says to him, pipe still in his mouth,

"You are dismissed Lance Corporal"

Martin hurriedly replies to both men,

"Colours, Sergeant"

He turns on his heel and leaves the tent, now a Lance Corporal. It is the 3rd October.

The following morning, the 4th October, Martin, with his perfectly sewn single chevrons on each arm of his tunic, is writing another letter to Grace, he had posted the previous letter but it was a boring factual account of his days, this one he hopes, is a declaration to her of his passion and love for her, the tent shakes,

"Martin come on mate; we have been summonsed"

He looks up and sees Lance Corporal 'H' Lord talking to him, he gets up, as he puts on his tunic, he asks,

"What's afoot then 'H'?"

"No idea, but all the NCO's, including us lowly Lance jacks have been called to the clerk's tent"

The RSM calls the crowd of officers and NCOs gathered in front of the clerk's tent to attention for the Commanding officer,

"Officers and NCOs of the Bedfordshire's" a pause for the men to be ready, "Shun!"

The RSM salutes the Commanding officer, Major John Murray Traill leaves his tent and stands on a box to address his officers and NCO's'

"Thank you Regimental Sergeant Major Thurleigh, stand easy men please" Major Traill looks at the back of the crowd, "Can you men hear me at the back?"

These men, including Martin, all say that they can, Traill continues,

"Firstly, LtCol Coates is unwell, so I will remain as CO for now, I will be made up to LtCol today"

Cheers from the crowd,

"Good, thank you men, I am happy to tell you that we are to leave White Moor camp today, starting at 3pm"

Murmurs grow in the crowd of men,

"Settle Gentlemen please" growls the RSM

"The men need to be ready to go in the next two hours, we are part of the 21st Brigade which in turn is part of the 7th division and we are all going today, along with the 20th and 22nd Brigades, fifteen thousand men in total, we are first alphabetically so we will be mustered and leaving first"

The crowd of men remain silent, "We muster at 3pm, march to Lyndhurst Road railway station, trains are being laid on to transport us to Southampton, we march to the docks, and we have been allocated two transport ships, company commanders will have these details for each of their companies'" He looks at his men. "Good luck all, God save the King"

The men reply together, "God save the King!"

He looks across at RSM Thurleigh,

"Officers and NCOs of the Bedfordshire's, Shun!"

The group of men stand to attention, the RSM salutes the Major as he leaves, the RSM turns to the group of men,

"Company commanders report to the clerk's tent when dismissed"

He pauses,

"Turning right, dismissed!"

Martin and 'H' look at each other,

"Here we go mate" Martin says, all he gets in reply from 'H' is,

"Bloody hell!"

Martin looks at his pocket watch,

"Bloody hell indeed, two hours to get everything sorted, catch you later 'H'"

Martin runs to his tent to tell his section the news.

It is minutes after five in the evening when the first train leaves the small railway station, Martin is standing by an open window, all the seats are taken by the time he and his section embark onto the train, he isn't bothered about standing the journey is going to be less than an hour, they feel lucky as they have just heard that the 20th and 22nd Brigades are marching to Southampton, he has already marched one way, he feels it only fair that he rides on the train for this journey. A great cloud of steam passes his window, the whistle on the train sounds as the train chugs away from the station, plumes of black smoke billow from its funnel, Martin sees the sign for the railway station, in large black letters against a white background, pass him as the train pulls out of the station on one side of the two available tracks, under the large iron footbridge and into the open countryside of the New Forest, the train passes through Totton station without stopping, then through Redbridge and Millbrook before terminating at Southampton West railway station. The disembarkation of the several thousand troops from the 21st Brigade, strewn across several trains that arrive within half an hour of each other, takes over two and a half hours, Martin is in the group that is the first off of their train, they have been hanging around outside of the station, sitting on their kit and smoking cigarettes, Martin has finished his letter, happy that he has bared his soul to Grace, he has not mentioned to her that they have been deployed, that can wait until the next letter.

"Sergeant Oakes, can I leave to go and find a post box, I would like to post this letter before we sail"

"No" is the surly answer "No one leaves, I would hate to march off and leave you behind"

Martin has no time to speak to the sergeant because he has walked off,

"Horrible little man" Martin mutters under his breath, he turns to Jack,

"Mate, I am just going into the ticket office to see if the station has a post box"

Jack nods at him and raises a thumb, all without opening his eyes, Martin takes the letter from his haversack and walks the short distance to the ticket office, it is busy with military men and civilians all crowded together, he looks for a member of the station staff to ask about a post box, he sees only one man in uniform, he is standing on the platform, Martin approaches him. The man in uniform is in his mid-fifties, with greying hair and a large moustache, his uniform, a blue hat has a silver badge on it, a white shirt with a barely noticeable pinstripe with a blue tie, a fully buttoned waistcoat that bulges at the belly, a large watch chain hangs from one pocket to the middle button of the waist coat and then across to the other pocket, his jacket is also blue, Martin notes medal ribbons being worn over the man's left breast pocket. His work badge, pinned on the right side of the jacket, reads, *GUARD.*

The man's left arm is in a sling.

"Excuse me sir" Martin asks the guard,

"Don't call me sir young man, I was a gunner in the artillery" The guard has a strong cockney accent, he puts his hand out ,"Alfie Smith, former gunner with the Royal Artillery, what can I do for you mate"

Martin explains his predicament,

"Follow me" says Alfie

Martin follows him to a green door, they both go through it and the world of noise and chaos outside is gone, the room is small and is obviously the staff rest room,

"Do you want a brew mate?" asks Alfie

Martin explains that he had better not, he has left his group and they are awaiting deployment to the docks, Alfie smiles,

"Plenty of time for a cup of 'Rosie' mate, there is still one train load of soldiers waiting to disembark, they are currently held at Millbrook, by my reckoning, you have an hour at least to wait"

Martin takes off his cap and gladly accepts the offer of a cup of tea, Alfie takes off his jacket slowly, his left arm appears useless, Martin stands up to offer him help to get his jacket off,

"Don't fret mate, I am used to this" raising the injured arm slightly he says, "Did this in '95 whilst working at the Royal Arsenal, got it crushed in a bit of machinery, its bugger all use now"

"What is a London boy doing in Hampshire then?"

"I am back up to the 'smoke' on the last train tonight, we came down yesterday in an empty train to get you lot picked up, I will be back home in Plumstead by the early hours I hope"

He hangs his jacket on the back of the chair to Martins right, he glances and notes that the medal ribbons are old, one has three blue and two white stripes, the other is crimson with a small bronze cross on it.

"Bloody hell Alfie, have you got the Victoria Cross?" asks Martin, Alfie looks over,

"Yes mate, do you want milk and sugar in your tea?"

Martin replies that he would like both, surprised that Alfie has almost dismissed the medal ribbon he wears,

"What's the other ribbon for Alfie?"

Alfie sits down and hands Martin a chipped enamel mug full of steaming hot, strong, and sweet tea, he cups his hands around it and takes a tiny sip,

"That one?" Alfie asks pointing to the blue and white ribbon "That's from the Mahdist war, I was in the Artillery with the British Desert Column, made up of officers and men from the Army and the Royal Navy"

Martin sips his tea, not speaking, he hopes that Alfie will continue, he does,

"I fought for '*us*' during the Gordon Relief expedition, the battles of Abu Klea in January '85 and at Kirbekan in Feb '85"

Martin knows nothing about the conflict to which Alfie is referring, he looks over to the guard, his cup still held in both hands,

"You want to know about the VC don't you Martin?"

Martin nods, "Only if you want to tell me Alfie"

Alfie takes a huge swallow of hot tea,

"It was nothing really, one of our '*Ruperts'* got into a spot of bother when he was sorting his gun, and I helped him out by waving a hand spike at a few of the Sudanese and frightened them off, we lost 76 of ours that day, more were wounded, we did get over a thousand of theirs though"

Martin realises that there is so much more to this tale than Alfie is letting on, it is the guard who changes the conversation"

"Give us your letter young Martin, I will post it in London when I get back"

Martin hands him the letter, Alfie looks at the address, "Don't know the town, but I presume Grace is someone special to you?"

"She is Alfie" Martin finishes his tea "And I hope she continues to be so after this German nonsense is sorted out"

Alfie stands when Martin does, the men shake hands,

"Good lucky Martin" says Alfie "Don't do anything stupid over there"

Martin smiles, "Stupid enough to get a Victoria Cross Alfie!"

"Get out of here you!" Alfie feigns anger but he is smiling.

Martin puts on his cap and leaves the small office, his love letter to Grace now entrusted in the hands of a man he met a little over a quarter of an hour ago, he walks back to where his kit is, pushing his way through the soldiers, sailors and locals, Jack is still asleep. Martin sits down, takes out his packet of woodbines, removes a cigarette, puts it in his mouth and strikes his match on the ground, as he is lighting it, Jack speaks to him, his cap still over his eyes, "I'll have one of those please mate"

Martin, takes the lit cigarette from his mouth, takes another from his packet and lights it for Jack using the lit end of his cigarette, he nudges Jack with his boot and passes him the lit cigarette, putting it into his mates outstretched hand, Jack puts it in his mouth without removing his cap that still covers his eyes.

"Thanks mate" he says to Martin.

It is just turning eight o clock when the restless group of men are ordered to get their kit together and to muster on the road outside, Martin falls in with the men of his section, at eight fifteen the long column of men march off, arriving at the dock gates at Southampton thirty minutes later.

The troop carrier Martin is embarking onto is the SS Winifredian, some of the other Bedfordshire's are to sail across to Zeebrugge on the SS Cornishman, the embarkation of the Cornishman will not start until tomorrow, the men selected to sail on this ship will be spending the night in one of the huge sheds by the dock. Both ships are huge grey hulks, with a tall mast at either end and a single funnel at their centre, the Winifredian looks old and tired, and Martin has concerns that it may not make it across the Channel to the Belgium port at all. Martin, Jack, 'Posh' and Jacob find a space near to the funnel, the open deck area is rammed to bursting with the men from 2nd Battalion Bedfordshire's, loading is completed by eleven that night, but the Winifredian and the Cornishman are not going to set sail for at least another seven hours, time spent by all the soldiers on the cramped and cold deck of the ship. The ship is due to leave at six tomorrow morning. It doesn't, men and horses on board the SS Winifredian are all restless and uneasy

It is 10pm on 5th October, the ship sets sail, heading for Calais and Dunkirk, the seas are rough and at a time unknown to Martin, he feels the ship turnabout, he knows they are headed back to England.

It is 6am, the 6th October, the ship has been stationary off Dover for over an hour, the port of Dover is in their view, the men on the deck are tired and restless, none of them really want to go to Belgium, to the war, but none of them want to stay on this ship any longer, many have been seasick on the short journey from Southampton to Dover, not pleasant for their 'oppo' next to them if they can't get to a rail. Martin doesn't feel seasick at all, he has managed to eat a few dry biscuits and two tins of sardines, he had earlier swapped a tin of bully beef for three tins of sardines with 'Posh. They are not allowed to leave the ship, no one seems to have any idea why they have docked at Dover and when they are leaving again, tempers are getting frayed in the cramped conditions with an amount of shoving and pushing going on, the NCOs are quick to stop any real fights breaking out.

Finally, at nine o clock on the evening of Tuesday 6th October 1914, the SS Winifredian leaves the port of Dover, headed for Zeebrugge and right into the middle of the ongoing war.

Martin is not scared of war; a little afraid maybe, but he is scared he will never see Grace again.

* * *

Corporal Abraham Bragg, regular army, currently serving in the Notts and Derby regiment, known as the Sherwood Foresters, stretches out in his army camp bed, he is several inches over six feet tall, the lower half of his legs fall easily past the end of the canvas bed,

"One of you put a brew on" he shouts from his room into the kitchen, he looks at his watch, it tells him it is a quarter past seven,

"Will do Corp" a voice calls back.

Bragg swings his long legs to the side of the bed and sits up, he rubs his face and attempts to smooth down his unruly short hair, standing up, he waits a few seconds for his head to stop spinning, he walks through the open door of his room to the kitchen, three more army camp beds take up half the space in the kitchen, with the table, the bench seat, and the dresser also in this room, there is not much manoeuvring space.

"Jump to it lads" Bragg says, none of the three men in the camp beds move, Bragg grabs the first bed and lifts it up tipping the blankets, pillows, and the soldier onto the floor, "Don't let me ask again lads" he say angrily

The soldier on the floor, Private Jake Stevens is a 21 year old territorial soldier, a resident of the city of Derby and had worked in a grocer's shop until, he, along with all the other territorials in the UK, had been mobilised in early August. He has been posted to this country town, with the 4,500 other soldiers, nearly all of whom are territorials, since August 21st, four battalions from the Notts and Derby regiment forming part of the North Midland Division, are now living in town, many have been billeted to live with local residents. Jake, along with the other three occupants, were initially living on the common in a tent, the cottage is now their temporary home.

Jake, with Cpl Bragg, Private Bob Beeson and Private Dave Shafford had been amongst the last to be billeted, luckily for them, their section, with Bragg as NCO, had been tasked a few days ago with patrolling the East station, a role they were initially given for a week, they have been living and sleeping in the waiting room, cramped and uncomfortable for all of them. When Martin was posted to the war with his regiment, the cottage became available for them, they were in the right place, in the right job at the right time.

Bob Beeson picks himself up from the floor, "Morning Corp" he says brightly, "Shall I put a brew on then?"

Bragg smiles at Bob, he opens the back door, "Great idea Bob, I am off to use the facilities" He steps through the door but stops before he completely leaves, "Jake and young Dave"

The two men, now sitting on the side of their camp beds look up,

"Yes Corp" they both say,

"As Bob is now making the brew, you two fine young soldiers can have a tidy up and stow all the camp beds and get some water"

Both men begin to complain, Bragg puts his hand up, palm toward them, they both stop, Bragg smiles, "Thank you, let's get it done"

Bob picks up the kettle, gives it a shake and decides that there is enough water in it, puts it on the hot plate, he then feeds the fire in the grate of the range, it takes him a few minutes of careful nursing, the fire is very nearly dead, to get it going again, he succeeds, and more wood is added to get the range plate hot and the water in the kettle to boil. Jake Stevens, who like Bob, is twenty one years old, begins to fold the army camp beds up and tidy the blankets and pillows, storing them in the bedroom used by the Corporal. Dave Shafford, the youngest in the section, is eighteen years old and has only been in the territorials for ten months, he had been working at a flour mill in his home village, Borrowash, only joining the territorials for some excitement, having lived in Borrowash all his life and until now, has never travelled outside of his home county. He has no real memory of his Father who was killed in a pit roof collapse in 1900 at Highfield colliery, Dave had been just four years old, his Mother moving back to her home village of Borrowash with Dave, shortly after being widowed. His Mother had died, at home in 1910, it had been Dave that had found her, he has a vivid memory of her sitting bolt upright in the kitchen of their tiny cottage, sat in a chair directly in front of the stove, he had forced himself to touch her stiff body, her face was a red colour, as bright as a cherry, this is, sadly, how he remembers her. He had lived with a spinster Aunt in the village after his mother's death, never returning to school, instead working in the flour mill for the miller, a loud and obnoxious drunk, William Tester, the army had been his release from the tedium of village life and from the abusive Mr Tester, joining the Notts and Derby regiment had given him the comradeship and family that he had always desired, compared to many of his army colleagues, he is a quiet and thoughtful young man. He has only recently finished his six months full time training and had only been back at the mill a number of weeks when the regiment was mobilised, Mr Tester was not happy, Dave was secretly pleased to be leaving his job at the mill. The three other soldiers he currently lives with treat him well, although they do wind him up on a daily basis, being the youngest he always gets allocated the worst jobs and is the butt of all jokes, because he is a naturally shy and nervous man he rarely retaliates, but he doesn't mind, he likes being part of this small team.

Jake says to Dave. "Water or tidying up?"

"I will get the water Jake, is that alright with you?"

Jake tells him that it is fine, Dave puts on his trousers and boots, pulling his braces up over his under shirt,

"Dave lad, can those thin arms of yours carry two full buckets?" Bob teases,

"Yes, of course Bob" Dave replies quietly, Bob playfully punches him on the arm,

"Good lad, tea won't be long mate"

Dave opens the front door and walks out into bright morning on this the last day of September, the sun is rising over the fields and arable farmland that spread out behind the smithy, stretching his chest and back muscles, he looks across the garden, the vegetable plot still has onions lying on the top of the soil, parsnips and greens are still growing in it, half a row of carrots remain to be picked, they had a few in a stew last night and they were sweet and full of flavour. A row of tomato plants at the top end of the plot are looking sad and aged, a few red fruits still cling to life on the ever bending stems, he is sure that it is only the stakes tied to them that hold them up, a few yellow flowers, that will never bear fruit, hang limply from the shoot tips at the tops of the plants. They had, on their first morning in the cottage only four days ago, dug up the onions and laid them out to harden and dry, he looks at the sky, it seems as though it will be dry today, the onions can be moved to the shed, also several rows of main crop potatoes had been dug up by the men the day before yesterday, they have been left in the shed, and will need to be put into the hessian sacks, also in the shed, two of these sacks will need to be filled as they are to be taken to Mary at the pub this morning. This will make space for the two wooden boxes given to them yesterday by the congregation at the Methodist church, apples, plums, strawberries, and even a small pumpkin packed into them, to be put into storage in the shed. Mr Ackroyd, the local baker, has also been very generous, supplying them bread and tasty, sweet cakes, all in all, Dave is feeling content, and safe, with his life at the cottage. The huge Yew tree toward the end of the garden stands tall and defiant, Autumn is approaching, he knows it will remain unchanged through the seasons, the oak and beech trees across the stream next to the water cress beds are already showing signs of change, the former greenness of their leaves now turning a vivid, eye catching red or a soft lazy bronze colour, very soon all of them will turn brown and eventually take their final gentle journey to the ground as the grip of life from the tree lets them go. Losing his life terrifies him, war terrifies him, pain terrifies him, a painful lonely death terrifies him. A wave of panic surges through his body, from his toes to the top of his head, a familiar sinking feeling returns to his gut, he can hear his breathing increasing, panic is returning to him again and he cannot stop it,

"Dave, are you getting the bloody water or not? Don't tell me you are scared of that big old tree as well as everything else"

Dave turns to the speaker of these words,

"No Jake, I mean yes Jake" he stammers "Yes to water, no to being scared of a tree"

He picks up two buckets and makes his way down the garden, he hears laughter from inside the kitchen, he knows Jake and Bob are having a laugh at his expense, he doesn't mind really, he approaches the water pump, passing under the huge canopy of the Yew tree, it seems to talk to him as the gentle breeze moves through its bows and twigs, he shivers. Jake is correct about one thing, this big old tree does make him feel uneasy and a little frightened, he fills the buckets and quickly makes his way back to the cottage. He sees a bicycle leaning against the outside of the garden fence next to the gate, it is an old cycle that seems to have had a recent re paint, the frame is a very green colour, the leather seat, with its large springs set underneath it is very worn, dipping at its middle, seemingly regularly used, a new silver bell shines out against the dull rusted handlebars, obviously not re painted with the rest of the cycle, the brown rusting lever brakes sit a few inches below the handlebars, the cycle has worn rubber pedals, he can see that the chain could do with oiling, Dave thinks that it looks similar to the bicycle he has at home in Borrowash when he used to ride to the mill, a Rover Meteor number 2, he smiles at the happy memory of being free from home and from the mill, when riding his bicycle. As he goes back into the kitchen, he notes that Jake has cleared up the beds and presumes they are now stored in the bedroom, his three colleagues, Corporal Bragg has now returned from the outhouse, have been joined by a fourth person, Dave has not seen this man before,

"Private Shafford please meet Mr Lord, one of the porters from East station" Bragg introduces the men to each other, Dave politely says,

"Good morning Sir, I had the pleasure of meeting your colleague, Mr Clements on Monday"

"Morning to you, I have been away for a week or so visiting a sick Aunt in Chiswell Green, I left Mr Clements in the lurch a little"

A mug of hot black tea is handed to Dave by Bob, he gratefully accepts it, Bragg explains why Mr Lord is visiting them this morning. A trainload of supplies, ammunition and kit is arriving at the East station this morning at eleven, Mr Lord assures them that there are no other military transports due in before eleven and there will be a total of three military trains arriving throughout the day, the last being at five in the afternoon, Bragg continues,

"Mr Lord has kindly offered the services of the porters and signalmen to let us know of any arrivals for military purposes and to give up plenty of notice so that we don't have to hang around the station all day"

The men all thank Mr Lord, stating that they are all grateful to him and to the other staff,

"The point is gentlemen" Lord tells them, "Is that we really want our waiting room back, so coming to inform you is not a hardship for any of us, we are hoping that we will have advanced notice to tell you about any arrivals the day before, so we can all have our days planned"

"I will have to clear it with the RSM, but I am sure it will all be in order, thank you Mr Lord"

Mr Lord nods at the Corporal, he reaches into his canvas bag, "Do you gents need any milk?"

He takes out a small jar, the type usually used for preserving and pickling, it is full of milk,

"We are lucky enough to be on good terms with Mr. Cooke" the four soldiers look at each other, they have no idea who Mr. Cooke is, Lord continues, "We have a surplus of milk most days and wondered if you chaps would be able to use it?"

They thank the railway porter for his kindness and accept the jar of milk,

"We will be at the station in good time for the arrival of the first military train Mr Lord" Bragg tells him.

Lord turns down the offer of tea and leaves the four men in the kitchen, Jake hurriedly opens the jar of milk and puts a drop in each man's mug,

"I think it is going to be a good number here at the cottage corp"

"It is" replies Bragg "But I will square it off with the RSM, we don't want to get caught out do we"

An hour later, the four soldiers are in uniform, shaved, and clean, they are standing outside of the Malta pub talking to the landlady having delivered two freshly filled sacks of potatoes to her from the vegetable garden, a voice they recognise calls to them,

"Afternoon soldiers"

As it is only twenty past eight in the morning, the men realise that the man speaking to them is throwing sarcasm their way, it is RSM Westerman,

"Morning Sir" Corporal Bragg greets the RSM

"Bragg, I have just been to East station and you aren't there are you?"

Bragg thinks for a second or two, "No Sir, we are here"

Westerman looks at the four of them, then at Mary, he touches the peak of his cap,

"Good morning Mary, I hope all is well and that my men are not attempting to purchase beer from you at this time of the day"

Mary giggles, "No Eddie, they have delivered to me a couple of sacks of potatoes from the garden, these boys harvested them for me and I am grateful"

The RSM looks at the soldiers without speaking to them,

"Would you have time for a cup of tea Eddie?" Mary asks

RSM Westerman accepts the offer, he looks at the four men,

"Work you lot, I will drop into the station on my way back through"

"May I have a word please Sir?" Bragg asks him

Mary tells Eddie to come inside when he is finished talking Bragg, she disappears into the pub, Westerman speaks to Jake, Dave, and Bob, "Bugger off you three, I am sure you don't need the help of the Corporal to cross the road do you"

They all reply "No Sir" then make their way across the road toward the bakers, leaving Bragg to speak to the RSM.

Bragg shortly re-joins the three privates at East station, they are in the staff area having been asked by Mr Lord not to use the waiting room, yet more tea is being made and they are all eating cake, a brown bag is thrown at him, he catches it,

"From Mr Ackroyd, Chelsea buns he calls them"

Bragg looks inside the bag, he has not seen a bun like this before, swirling pastry with raisins and sugar on the top, he takes the pastry out and bites into it,

"Oh, that is so nice!" he exclaims with his mouthful, he accepts a mug of tea from Jake, the other soldiers all look at him, they are also enjoying the sweet pastry.

"RSM Westerman has sort of agreed to our plan"

The three privates, put their mugs down and listen intently to the Corporal,

"He agrees that us being at the station when there is no military movement is a waste of time"

Jake, Dave and Bob have beaming smiles on their faces,

"Don't look so happy too soon chums" Bragg tells them, "Westerman knows, that apart from the early milk and post trains, the first passenger trains start arriving here at seven in the morning, at least one of us needs to be patrolling here from this first arrival until the last train leaves at seven" he takes a sip of tea "The RSM will have to clear it with Mr Jones, the station master, but he doesn't foresee any problems, we, all four of us, have to be here for any military arrivals and departures, he has made it very clear to me that he knows that we are on a good number here, and that this job we have, is, in his words 'Better than delivering bread, drill practice and ceremonial duties in town', if any one of us screws up, we all get moved back to town" he looks at the three men one at a time, "Do I make myself clear?"

"Yes Corporal!" all three reply

"We can take it in turns to be here early, should be a doddle between the four of us Corp" Bob pipes up, Bragg looks at him, squinting his eyes with menace,

"The three of you private, I will not be patrolling, it is my job to ensure the correct movement of arriving and departing military troops and equipment"

Bob remains silent,

"Is that clear private?"

Bob nods his understanding,

"One of us needs to be on one of the platforms at all times" he looks at Bob, who responds,

"Shall I go first Corp?"

"Now that is a fine idea Private Beeson, carry on"

Bob puts the remainder of his Chelsea bun into his mouth, he swallows it with a mouthful of tea, he puts on his cap and steps toward the door, Bragg puts his arm out,

"Bob, there is a war on mate, best you take your rifle with you" smiling, he hands Bob his rifle,

"Sorry Corp, thanks Corp"

The other three remain indoors, they watch as Bob walks up and down the platform a couple of times, then crosses to the other platform, using the wooden walkway across the single track to get to the other side as there is no over bridge at this station.

"This will be a cracking job for us until we get orders to deploy to the war" Bragg says aloud, "Also, the RSM has said we can use the pub in the evening should we wish, best behaviour though, I think he is friendly with the landlady"

"Sounds good to me Corp" Jake responds.

Dave doesn't say a word, upon hearing the phrase, '*orders to deploy to the war*', he has another wave of panic overcoming him, Bragg notices that Dave seems to have turned pale,

"Are you all right Dave?"

He gets no response, Dave is staring out of the window, eyes wide open, Bragg raises his voice, "Private Shafford!'

Dave jumps, shaken by the Corporal shouting at him,

"Yes Corporal?" he says meekly

"Did you hear what I said?" Bragg seems impatient, Dave's subconscious has heard what was said,

"Yes Corp, the pub Corp" he blurts out

"Are you sure everything is all right with you?"

Dave, who is calming a little, lies to Bragg and Jake,

"Yes, fine thanks, just a bit tired that's all"

Bragg tells them to finish their tea and to get out on patrol with Bob.

* * *

Alice and Grace are walking arm in arm toward the cottage, it is the first Sunday in October, the weather is dry, but the sky is a deathly grey and menacingly threatens rain, the Methodist church is emptying out after the morning service with members of the congregation standing outside chatting to one another,

"Do you go to Church Grace?" asks Alice

"Father and Mother attend St Nicholas every Sunday" she replies, "I used to go when I was a child, but I stopped when I turned eighteen, I do go once a month to Highfield chapel at the children's home as part of my teaching responsibilities"

"Granny doesn't make me go" says Alice happily, "Because I stay with her at weekends, I don't have to go with Aunt May, Uncle Pete and the girls, they go to St Johns over the common from their cottage"

Alice lets go of Graces arm as they cross the road, as they are approaching the fence and gate of the cottage, Alice slows down, almost stopping,

"Alice?" asks Grace "Are you feeling unwell?"

She puts her arm through Graces again,

"No, I am thinking about Mother and Father and that Martin won't be here, I know he has only been gone for a few days, but it seems such a long time since he was here with us"

Grace holds Alice hand with her free hand,

"I am sure he is fine; I received a letter just yesterday and he seems to be in good spirits" Grace then realises that Alice may not have heard from her brother and that mentioning the letter might be upsetting, she is relieved to see Alice smile,

"You get a letter and I get a post card, with only a few words written on it from a place I have never heard of called 'Lyndhurst', you have a letter with lots and lots of words"

Alice pulls Grace a little nearer to her, "A letter for you and a post card for me, I wonder which one of us he really likes now!"

"Alice!" exclaims Grace. "Your brother loves you and you know that!"

"I think he loves you as well Grace, and I think you know that!"

Grace blushes a little, she manages to reply, "Alice, enough now"

Both are smiling at each other as they reach the gate of the cottage, they can see four soldiers in the garden, two are on their knees tending to the vegetable garden, one is leaning on the wall by the back door smoking a cigarette and the final man, obviously the youngest, is filling a bucket of water at the pump,

"Hello" Grace speaks to them, "I hope we are not intruding?"

The man smoking the cigarette steps forward,

"No miss, are you Alice?"

Grace smiles and Alice giggles,

"No, I am Miss Grace Wilson, this is Alice"

Bragg nods his head respectfully to both of them,

"I am Corporal Abraham Bragg ladies, in charge of this bunch for my sins!" he points to the two soldiers gardening,

"Those two are Private Jake Stevens and Private Bob Beeson"

Both men raise their hands as a greeting, Bragg points to the soldier at the pump,

"That ladies, is Private David Shafford" Dave is oblivious to the visitors,

"Dave!" shouts Bragg, "Say hello to our guests"

Dave waves and says hello, his voice so quiet that it hardly carries, Bragg continues,

"I suppose young Miss that we are actually your guests as this is your cottage"

Alice responds shyly,

"It is my Brothers cottage really; he is in the army as well"

"I know" replies Bragg, "Our RSM met him before he left town, we are grateful to you both for the use of the cottage"

Members of the congregation from the Methodist church pass the cottage, chatting noisily amongst themselves,

"All our boys billeted in town will be in all the churches this morning, St Nicholas, St Johns, at the Methodist church in town, not this one, the Catholic tin shack church in town and the mission hall on the common by the row of cottages, for a little place you certainly seem to have plenty of religion "

"Do you go to Church Abraham?" asks Alice

Bragg shuffles his feet and becomes a little uncomfortable,

"No miss, my day of worship is a Saturday and as there are no places of worship for me nearby, I get by without"

Alice seems confused, but continues, "What about the others?"

"Alice!" Grace exclaims, "You can be so rude" she turns to Bragg, "I apologise for Alice and her forward ways Corporal"

"It's not a problem miss" replies Bragg "Please call me Abraham or Abe, whichever you are comfortable with" he turns to Alice, who has become shy again,

"Alice, these lads work hard every day of the week, Sunday is our quiet day, not much movement at the East Station, so they choose to relax here rather than get dressed in full uniform to walk into town for church"

Dave walks toward them, stopping by the gate and staring at Alice, she in turn, stares back,

"Dave, take the water in and leave the young lady be" Bragg instructs him, he ignores the corporal, still staring and smiling at Alice,

"Private!" Bragg exclaims, making Alice and Grace jump, "Take that water, inside, now!"

Dave nods and moves away,

"My apologies ladies" He opens the gate for them, to Alice he says, "Do you need something from the house miss?"

Alice nods but remains silent, Grace helps her out,

"We need a pair of shoes for her Abraham, we are hoping that Martin has put them in the back bedroom"

Bragg shouts at Dave for the second time, "Private Shafford, get out here, make way for the ladies please"

Grace laughs out loud, Alice giggles from behind Grace, Bragg smiles looking at Alice,

"He is used to it Miss, this is the army, I should think your Brother has told you all about the army and our way of life"

Grace looks at Alice, who seems to have been struck dumb,

"Martin was only home for a few days, this after being away for over four years, there wasn't a lot of time for him to tell Alice all about his travels"

Bragg, seeing that Alice is becoming upset, changes the subject as Dave exits the house, "All yours ladies, if you need any assistance please shout and I will get one of the lads to you"

They both thank Bragg and make their way to the house, as they pass Dave, he and Alice share a look at each other, Dave nods his head slightly at her,

"Miss"

Alice giggles and replies "Hello" she then walks to the front door with Grace.

The door is open and they both step into the cool kitchen, it is tidy, the soldiers kit is stacked in one corner next to the dresser, their tunics are hanging on the back of the kitchen chairs and caps are sat in a line on the bench seat under the window, the kettle is on top of the range and the fire is glowing nicely and slowly heating the water, a large kitchen pot stands on the other side of the range, inside this is a chicken stock made from the bones and skin from yesterday's meal, two halved onions, a few carrots and a sliced courgette are also sitting in the stock, waiting for heat to be added so as to be cooked,

"Some bloke called Freeman gave us a couple of rabbits last night" Bragg has his head through the kitchen door, "Rabbit and vegetable stew for us tonight, Bob is a half decent cook so it should be good"

Neither of the ladies answer him, "Excuse the intrusion, I wanted to check the kettle hasn't boiled yet, Dave will be making a *mash* of tea in a bit, I will come back in a few minutes"

"You are not intruding Abraham; this is your cottage for now" Alice replies

Grace looks at Alice and can see huge tears welling up in her eyes, Bragg has also noticed, he makes his excuses and leaves them alone,

"Alice?" asks Grace "Whatever is wrong?"

Alice can't answer, she is so choked with emotion, Grace takes Alice into her arms and holds her tightly, "Grace, it's not fair, first Mother and Father die, then Martin comes home and leaves almost straight away, what happens if he…" she doesn't finish her sentence, they both know what is worrying her, the same thoughts have been in Grace's mind, she puts them to one side, stroking Alice's hair she says,

"It's been a tough few months for you Alice and you have dealt with it all so well"

Alice looks at Grace, "Thank you, Grace"

"What for?" asks Grace

Alice hugs her tightly, "For being here with me"

Grace and Alice walk from the kitchen into the living room, the army camp beds are stacked up against the wall by the fireplace, blankets and bedding are folded neatly on the floor, the padlock is quickly undone, Alice looks into the very nearly full room, Grace starts to laugh,

"How are you going to find the shoes you need in here Alice!"

With a shrug of her shoulders, Alice enters the room and begins to climb over the stacked furniture and boxes. Half an hour later they both emerge from the room, Alice has a small box with the items she has decided that she cannot do without, including her shoes that she found next to the fireplace, the door is padlocked again and they both go into the kitchen, Dave is pouring hot water from the kettle into a large teapot that neither Grace or Alice have seen before, Dave looks up at them, he speaks to Alice,

"Sorry Miss, I have to make the tea, I hope I am not disturbing?"

Alice remains silent, Dave is staring at her, Grace answers for them.

"Not at all, but if you pay attention to what you are doing then you won't spill anymore water on the floor"

The teapot is overflowing, Dave jumps back, lifting the kettle to stop any more water spilling on the floor,

"Bugger it!" he says, then, with wide eyes, looks at Grace and Alice,

"Ladies, I am sorry for the language" he puts the kettle back on the range, taking a cloth he begins to mop up the mess, Alice steps in to help him,

"I'm fine thank you miss; this is my mess; I will clear it"

Bragg, Jake, and Bob knock on the door,

"Is it alright if we come in ladies"

Both say that it is,

"Bloody hell Dave, you have gone and made the floor all *clouty* after spilling all that water"

Dave is still mopping up,

"Sorry Corporal, I got distracted a little" he looks over at Alice and they both smile,

"Best that tea ain't *caded* young Dave" Bragg says, he turns to Alice and Grace,

"Would you like some tea ladies?"

Both decline the offer with thanks,

"I don't blame you really, Dave would probably throw it at you anyway" Bragg playfully throws a cloth at Dave who catches it with a smile,

"Tea will be *mashed* in minute Corporal"

Bragg looks at Alice and Grace, "You don't mind if we have a cuppa whilst you are still here, do you?"

"Of course not Abraham, we are leaving now anyway" Grace replies to him "Come on Alice if you are ready"

Alice is staring at Dave as he clears up, she hasn't heard Grace, the other three soldiers and Grace all look at each other and stifle laughter,

"Alice" Grace says gently, putting her hand on Alice shoulder, "Shall we go and leave these gentlemen in peace"

Alice stops looking at Dave, her face is flushed, "Certainly, goodbye"

With that Alice leaves through the kitchen door, Grace follows, bidding the soldiers a good day. As they get to the gate, they can both hear jeering from inside the kitchen,

"Go on Davey boy!"

"Young and in love Dave lad!"

"Whey hey!"

Alice looks embarrassed but smiles at Grace, they both hear Dave, laughing as he says, "Bugger off you lot, leave us alone!"

As Grace and Alice walk toward the Malta, Alice asks Grace a question,

"Do you know what a *mash* of tea is, or what *clouty* and *caded* mean?"

Grace puts her arm through Alice's, who is holding her box with both her hands,

"I haven't a clue at all what any of those words mean"

Grace stops talking but is laughing,

"What is it?" asks Alice, Grace, still walking next to Alice says,

"Young David is a nice boy, isn't he?"

Alice stops walking and looks at her friend,

"Grace!"

Both finish the short walk to the pub, laughing and giggling together.

* * *

Wednesday 7th October

It is raining as Martin waits to disembark from the SS Winifredian, his pocket watch tells him that it is six thirty in the morning, standing on the open deck, webbing and kit in full marching order is being worn by every soldier, the small space each man had occupied is now so much smaller than it had been, Martin prays that they will be able to get off this boat soon. They are all aware that the German army have invaded and taken many parts of Belgium, Liege had fallen in August, despite great bravery from the Belgian army, who also eventually fell as they were hugely outnumbered by the invading forces, the strong German army advanced into France, it is believed by the British army hierarchy that the bravery shown in Liege gave the British and French troops time to prepare and to fight well and succeed at Marne and stopping the Germans advance to Paris, Martin and all the men of the 2nd Battalion Bedfordshire's are told that 'most' of Belgium will be under German control when they arrive.

Tensions rise as the men stand hour after hour in the rain, Martin has the feeling of being a caged animal stuck in one position with nowhere to go, it becomes claustrophobic for some. Martin and Jack have to lay hands on a young soldier standing next to them his fear and panic is infectious and others around are having similar feelings but venting in different ways, some verbally, some physically and in the case of this young man, being so scared that he attempts to push or climb his way out of the situation,

"Steady on young fella" says Martin taking a firm grip on the soldiers' arm

"Let me go! Let me go! I can't stay here a minute longer" panic is rising in his voice, Jack steps in and takes his other arm,

"We have got you lad, stay calm and stay with us, you are safe here and we will be off soon enough"

Martin nods at Posh and Alf, indicating that they may be needed to help shortly.

The young soldier cannot control his panic, he struggles against Martin and Jack, the men standing around them begin to get anxious by his behaviour, pushing and shoving him as he is held firmly by Martin and Jack,

"Listen here soldier, if you don't calm down, this crowd is going to get angry with you, then the sergeants will be informed and you will be taken off of this boat but not in a way you will like" Martin shakes the man hard, "Snap out of it man, that is an order!"

The soldier sees the single chevron on Martins sleeves, he calms a little,

"Sorry Lance corporal, sorry, but I feel trapped, closed in, sorry but I can't, sorry"

Jack lets go of the man's arm, he is no longer struggling,

"We are all a bit nervous lad, but losing your mind will spread to others and panic in this environment will be unhealthy for all of us"

"Yes, Lance Corporal"

"Stand in between Jack, Posh, Alf and I, it won't give you much more space, but it won't be as crowded for you"

Jack asks the other men standing around to try to give the lad a few inches of space, most are fine as they can see very real fear on the face of the young man, a few moans from some and one refuses to move,

"Stupid boy shouldn't be in the bloody army if he can't take a bit of discomfort"

Jack steps in between them, he knows this man,

"Don't be like that Johnno, you know how some get sometimes" Jack speaks up.

Johnno laughs,

"Piss off Jack, who do you think you are, the saviour of all cowards?"

Jack grabs Johnno by his webbing, in such a confined space, men get pushed and shoved, several punches are thrown, no one is injured by tempers are frayed, Martin shouts at all of them,

"That is enough! Stand back all of you"

All of the men, bar Johnno stop pushing and jostling, Johnno continues,

"Bloody yellow streak in that boy's spine"

Martin stands in front of Johnno,

"Johnno, I may only be a Lance corporal, but you are a private, stand down, that is an order"

Johnno looks in dismay at Martin,

"Or what" he pauses then says sarcastically "Lance Corporal"

Martin thinks for a second or two,

"Well Johnno, a couple of things will happen if you don't, firstly I will let Jack here carry on with what he was going to do to you, and you know he will bust you up"

Martin points at Johnno,

"Then, when the sergeants turn up, and they will turn up, I will tell them you started it and it is you who needs locking up, they will believe me Johnno because not one man standing here will be on your side because you, as usual, are out of line" He stares Johnno in the eye,

"Stand down private, I won't tell you again"

Jack still has hold of Johnno's webbing, a familiar voice calls out to Martin,

"Lance corporal, is all well in that area?" Sgt Oakes is standing on what would have been the ships promenade in better times,

"No problems here sergeant, just making a bit of space for the young lad here, he is feeling a bit queasy" Martin steps toward Johnno, through gritted teeth he says,

"Back off now private, I have already ordered you to do so"

Jack lets go of Johnno's webbing, who says,

"Give a man a stripe and he becomes the coward's saviour"

Martin, who by now is prepared to lose his stripe, is just about to swing at Johnno when Oakes speaks in a clear loud voice,

"Johnson, you have one second to do as the Lance corporal has ordered you or I will have you in chains my boy"

Johnno steps back, men make space for him to move away,

"Not another word lad" Oakes commands, "Lance corporal, we should be disembarking within the hour, there has been some issues getting the artillery guns and horses off, spread the word please"

"Sergeant, yes sergeant" Martin replies

Johnno is being jostled and jeered by the men surrounding him, Martin speaks to them,

"Steady lads, leave it be, it's finished now, let's be calm for a bit longer, save your fight for the Germans"

Finally, the order comes to disembark, Martin shuffles along with the rest of the men of the 2nd Bedfordshire's, all are weary and stiff from being on the ship in very cramped conditions for over two days, the walk down the long and thin gang plank is slow, the bottle neck of men from both sides of the ship has reached a point whereby movement is almost non-existent. Martin is glad when his boots touch the hard soil of Zeebrugge, he is stopped by a sergeant from the Corps of Military foot police,

"Lance Corporal, I want you to take this first group of soldiers to the railway station just outside of the docks" he points in the general direction of the station, "The trains will take you to Bruges where you will be met and directed further, do you understand?"

"Yes sergeant"

Martin raises his rifle and instructs a group of a hundred or so soldiers to follow him, they form two lines and march, a short distance as it turns out, to the railway station.

Martin looks at his pocket watch, it is four in the afternoon, the rain has thankfully stopped, and he is standing on a platform of what looks like an old cattle station, a wide open space unprotected from the elements, the train is an old steam engine with at least two dozen flatbed carriages trailing behind it, the men shuffle on, once again crowded together, but at least this journey, a little over ten miles into Bruges, will only be a short one. They are all ordered directly off of the train at Bruges Saint Pierre and form up in three lines outside of the railway station, the large group of men set off on a march just after five in the evening, arriving at *Sint Kruis*, a small town to the West of Bruges, Martin, along with another large group of men, they are directed toward a large granary barn, this is to be their billet for a short time.

Martin takes off his webbing and dumps it unceremoniously on the floor, sitting down next to his kit he feels fatigue taking over every sense he has, he really wants to smoke a cigarette, but he is just too tired to bother, shutting his eyes he lets sleep take him easily.

* * *

"Bloody hell a food wagon!"

Martin is woken by Jack who has spotted a field kitchen wagon pull up outside of the barn they are in, Martin smiles, only the army can have a food kitchen set up quicker than the artillery that they will almost certainly need, he realises that he is very hungry indeed,

"Come on Martin" shouts Jack as he walks off "I don't want to be at the end of the line"

Martin retrieves his mess tin and mug from his valise and jogs over join the line with Jack, there are twenty men in front of them, he looks around, most of the soldiers are still asleep or too tired to get up for food, the army cooks are setting up and nearly ready, the sergeant in charge of the food stands on a box and shouts,

"Look lively men, all of you, food in five"

The men who have not yet moved, slowly get up and join the queue, all knowing it is a disciplinary charge if you purposely miss a meal, the line of men is now getting longer, Martin is thankful that Jack got him up quickly. The kitchen is a large, two wheeled horse drawn carriage, one of three that are now on site, it has a tall chimney in the middle of it, smoke is freely pouring from the top of it, it has four large lid covered containers, in front of it a low trestle table stands with an old metal urn and trays of roughly cut bread sitting on it.

Martin hears Jack say, "What is the scran sarge?"

The kitchen sergeant looks at him, "Veg and meat stew"

Jack thanks him for the information, then continues,

Again, the sergeant looks at him, answering with two words, "It's meat"

Jack, realising he won't be getting any more information, decides to shut up and thanks the private who is now serving the stew to him. One large ladle of stew is allocated per man, the urn contains strong black tea, Martin fills his mug and takes two slices of the bread, he and Jack return to the barn and sit to eat the meal.

It is surprisingly good, the meat is tasty and not covered in fat or gristle and the stew is thick with potatoes and carrots, they both agree that this is better than the field ration packs that they all have in their valises. A tin of bully beef, a tin of the hated Maconochie beef and vegetable stew, a packet of Huntley and Palmers no.4 biscuits, these have to be dunked in tea to make them soft enough to eat, a small amount of wrapped cheese, a couple of wrapped lumps of sugar, a small box of loose tea, Martin is certain that the army cannot function without tea, a tin of jam and finally, a tin of 'ideal' condensed milk. Each man also has small tin of 'Tommy's cooker' fuel, containing solid methylated fuel that stinks to high heaven when ignited, a small metal frame stands over the top of the tin and an enamel mug or a mess tin can be put over the flame to heat food or tea.

When their food is finished and they have rinsed out their mess tins and mugs in the trough of water in the corner of the barn, they go in search of the latrine tent, they soon find out that there has not been any provided or pitched, both men have to resort to finding a quiet spot to relieve themselves, the bushes and backs of the buildings are unsanitary due to the amount of men using these places as a toilet.

Martin lies on the hard stone floor of the barn, using his great coat as a blanket, sleep easily takes him, he is oblivious to the discomfort of not having a bed or mattress

* * *

Thursday 8th October

Just after midnight, the soldiers are woken and ordered to get ready to march in full marching order, all men are told to muster outside in ten minutes, Martin is ready in under five minutes and is outside, it is dark and drizzling rain, he is told by a corporal that they are to march to a town called Klemskerke, a distance of ten miles, here they are to join the 2nd Yorkshire regiment and await orders, the battalion are ordered to 'stand to arms', rifles made ready and bayonets fixed, they remain in formation for over two hours in the cold drizzle, eventually the order to 'stand down' is given, then shortly after 'forward march is ordered, the long line of tired, wet soldiers set off.

Arriving at the small village of Klemskerke, the soldiers easily outnumbering the residents, they march through the town and set up 'camp' in a field on the outskirts, they are ordered to set up bivouacs, each man has a canvas tarpaulin with them as part of their kit, Martin and Jack button their canvas sheets together and using a stake of wood at one end and tying the other around a tree they have their '*bivvie*' or as the army call it, *the Mark 1 shelter,* set up in only a few minutes, the inside gives them just over eight feet of cover, there are no flaps at either end, so cover is from above only, this is why Martin has chosen to use a tree at one end, this affords a small amount of cover from the elements. Jack gets a brew of tea on the go; they both know it will be bully beef, biscuits, and a brew for scran tonight. Jack falls to sleep early, just as the men of the 2nd Yorkshires are given the order to 'stand to', it is getting dark and Martin is sitting at the open end of the *bivvie*, he can see the village across the fields, the church dominates the skyline, with its tall spire covered in grey lead, below the spire he can see three of the vented windows of the bell tower, the slate grey roof of the church stretches to the left of the spire, the houses in front of the church have bright white walls with red tiled roofs, the trees, standing to the right of the church, sway gently in the early evening breeze, it is a beautifully serene scene, he is sure that this will not continue, he lies down, closes his eyes and thinks of Grace, he hopes that she has received his letter.

* * *

Friday 9th October – Saturday 17th October

'Stand to' is called at four thirty in the morning, Martin, Jack, and their comrades, stand in silence, weapons at the ready with bayonets fixed, the army theory is that most enemy attacks will be mounted just before dawn or just after dusk, either using the cover of darkness, half an hour later the order to 'stand down and breakfast' is called. During breakfast, which is more tea and biscuits, Martin meets and chats to a Corporal from the 2nd Yorkshires, Archie Basher, he tells him that they will all be marching to a town called Assebroek, he pronounces it '*Arsehole brook*', where the rest of his battalion are billeted. He explains to Martin that his whole regiment have been '*pissed about*' by the senior officers, after arriving in Belgium they marched to Assebroek and billeted there, then they were split up, some remaining in the town and the others, including him, were ordered to march toward the city of Ghent, but for some unknown reason they have completed a series of marches that eventually took them to the coastal town of De Haan, they were immediately 'about turned' to set up bivvies' here at Klemskerke and tomorrow to march back to Assebroek, right back where they started out!

The men shake hands, stating to each other that they, no doubt, will meet up again somewhere, Martin walks back to the bivvie and takes it down, Jack arrives back from his morning ablutions,

"What are you doing mate, no order has been given to break camp"

"It will Jack" he replies "It will, believe me"

At seven in the morning, the order is given to 'break camp', Jack looks at Martin,

"How the hell did you know?"

"Doesn't matter mate, what it does mean is that we can have a quick brew and a smoke"

He hands Jack a woodbine and they both light their cigarettes at the same time, making sure that the flame of the match is covered in the cup of their hands.

At eight thirty the 2nd Bedfordshire's set off on the right flank of a column of moving artillery, with the Yorkshires taking the left flank, marching through Bruges and to Assebroek, when they arrive the local signposts show that the town is only a mile from where they set out 2 days ago from Sint Kruis. Many of the men are billeted in barns and houses, Martin and Jack are unlucky and have to bivvie on the outskirts of town, the rain is incessant throughout the night, Martin sleeps intermittently and dreams of Grace, his only sanity at this time.

The next week is tedious for all of them, not a sight of the enemy on the ground, there was a little excitement on the 12th of October whilst billeted at a pea canning factory, a German 'Taube', a reconnaissance plane, flew over, the pilots of these aircraft have the capability to throw bombs from the cockpit and the soldiers take cover as it flies over them, but no bombs are dropped by the pilot. Most of their days are spent marching to towns that are supposedly occupied by the Germans, this has not been the case at any of them, at Steebrugge, along with nine others, Martin is lucky enough to be billeted with a local family, albeit in a barn where they all sleep, and sleep well in clean warm straw, they are able to wash and shave with hot water and best of all, they are all given a hot meal, a stew called 'carbonnade flamande', pork and onions cooked in beer and herbs, served with the thinnest chips Martin has ever seen, each man is also given a bottle of brown beer from the farmer they are staying with, strong tasting and very bitter, they all enjoy the few hours they spend at this farm. Marching onward and stopping in several towns and villages, Koolskamp, Boulers-Beuern, Menin and finally meeting up with the rest of the 21st brigade, after a long and tedious march, at the large town of Ypres on the morning of the 14th of October, then only stopping for only a few hours rest before setting off again at five in the evening to take up billets southwest of the town on Bailleul Road. News reaches the battalion that Bruges has been occupied by reserve troops of the German 4th Army, also unconfirmed reports that unarmed civilians have been subjected to brutal force, over a million Belgians, to escape the violence from the German invaders, have crossed the border into the Zeeland-Flanders area of the Netherlands.

Martin is exhausted and at 8pm he is asleep in a shared billet in a tiny house belonging to a local cobbler and cordwainer, he doesn't eat when offered food as he is too tired.

Moving on early the next morning to take up entrenched positions on the Menin road to Zillebeke, the 2nd Bedfordshire's relieving the soldiers from the French 80 regiment on the front line and digging in trenches started by these French soldiers, digging and reinforcing continues until dark, the men are ready to rest and sleep but are ordered to march on, arriving at the village of Gheluvelt that had until they arrived been under German control, they march in at nine thirty on the 16th arriving without meeting any enemy. Martin and the rest of the exhausted Bedfordshire's are billeted in the village, they are made Brigade reserve and therefore do not move for over twenty four hours, they are fired upon in the afternoon of the 16th, no one is injured and no one has any idea where the shots were fired from or by whom.

Most don't care, they have been in Belgium for ten days nearly and haven't, as yet met the enemy, the rumours of a horrific trench war have not arrived, it has so far been easy, lots of marching and sleeping under canvas, but no enemy contact and no casualties.

* * *

Sunday 18th October – Sunday 25th October

The battalion is formed up on the Menin to Ypres Road between Gheluvelt and Gheluwe, facing southeast, toward Menin, six miles from the town, they are all in full marching order, rifles are slung over shoulders and bayonets are not fixed. The order is given to advance, not marching, remaining in file, but not marching, the men set off on the road, it is more of a rough mud track than a road, wide green and yellow fields stretch as far as the eyes can see on both sides of them, occasional groups of rustic stone farm buildings are dotted alongside the route, the men are almost silent, the only sound is from the uneven crunching of stones under their boots. They are a mixed group from the 2nd Bedfordshire's', the 2nd Wiltshire's, the 2nd Royal Scots Fusiliers and a small company from the 2nd Yorkshires, the remainder of the Yorkshires have been pulled back to a small village called Becelaere, A and B companies having been the first into Gheluvelt and following minor contact with the enemy, who were at that time busy retreating, prisoners have been taken from these German units, so because of this they have been pulled off of the line for today.

As the column of men climb a gentle slope and over the rise they are bought to a halt as the officers and sergeants are checking the maps, looking for landmarks across the damaged landscape. Martin hears what he initially thinks is wood splitting, standing still he hears the same sound again and again, something whistles past his face, so close he can feel the moving air as it passes him, someone screams, a high pitched and painful scream,

"Attack front! Take cover!"

Martin has no idea who shouts the order, but he comes to his senses and throws himself onto the muddy track, he tries rolling away, to get into the fields either side but his valise stops him from doing this. He hears more screams, the sound of rifles firing seems to be travelling only one way, and that is toward him. He knows that the German infantryman carries the Geweh 98 rifle, it has a five cartridge magazine, they use different ammunition to the British army, the Lee Enfield fires .303 and the Geweh 98 uses 7.92, with a shorter and wider bullet, crawling, he makes it to the side of the track, he can see his colleagues doing the same on both sides of this road, he lies as flat as he can and, for the first time, points his rifle in anger directly down the track, he cannot fire over the other side of the track as other soldiers from the 21st brigade are also trying to take cover from the increasing attack from an enemy that he cannot see.

"Keep down lads" sergeant Oakes sounds calm "Report from the front ranks!"

Martin hears a reply but cannot make out what is being said, he realises that some of the lads at the front of the column are now returning fire, he looks left ,then right, the track is empty bar one British soldier who is lying on his front, arms by his side with his rifle still slung over his right shoulder, he is only about six feet from Martins position, but as bullets are flying over his head he has to take his eyes off of his comrade because if he keeps his head up it will almost certainly be shot off. He is angry and frustrated because he has no idea where the enemy is so cannot return fire, this, his first contact with the enemy and he has not fired a shot.

Somebody shouts from the front,

"They have stopped Sarge!"

Oakes replies, "Stay down lads, for a couple of minutes"

Martin looks across at the soldier lying on the track, he can see red mixed in with the mud around the soldier, he shouts out, he begins to stand up to go to the aid of the man,

"Sergeant Oakes! one of ours has been hit"

Oakes sees him moving and screams at him, "Stay where you are soldier, that is an order!"

Martin fights every instinct he has not to go and help his colleague, but he knows that Oakes is talking sense, he lies down again and remains in position. As he is lying on the ground, in a slight dip in the land at the side of the road, he feels for the identity tag tied around his neck, it is there, the small, pressed metal disk attached to a length of string, it has his name, army number, regiment and religion on it. These were only issued to them a couple of weeks ago, he wasn't allowed to have 'none' stamped on it where the religion is written, he opted for Church of England, this was not questioned by anyone at the time. Martin shouts at the soldier lying in the road,

"Hey mate!" he gets no response, "Oy mate, move if you can hear me"

Alf is lying next to him, "I don't think he can hear you Martin"

Alf is shaking, Martin puts his hand on Alf's shoulder,

"Are you alright mate, are you hit?"

Alf shakes his head, "No, but I am bloody frightened, I can tell you that"

Martin nods in agreement even though he didn't feel any fear at any time during the attack, a voice from the front rank rings out,

"No further fire sarge, I think they have moved on"

He hears Captain Bassett shout, "Men, remain where you are, Sergeant Oakes, with me"

Martin looks to his right, he sees the officer and the Sergeant stand up slowly and move to the middle of the track, Basset has his service revolver pointing in front of him and Oakes has his rifle at his shoulder, they reach the front of the column, both lower their weapons. After a few quiet words to each other, Oakes shouts an order,

"Stay down men but you can relax, smoke 'em if you have 'em"

Martin sits up, he sees Oakes point at him from the track, "Lance corporal, take one man and tend to the wounded on the track"

He nudges Alf and they both stand, with their rifle stocks in their shoulders and the barrels pointing toward the ground they run to their stricken colleague.

Martin kneels next to the obviously bleeding man, with Alf's help they turn the man over, both of them take a deep breath in, Alf rolls over and throws up onto the track, Martin can see that the man is dead, the right side of his face is missing, the left eye is open and staring straight through him, the stare of a dead man, Martin sits back on his heels.

"Lance corporal, who is it? Is it one of ours or from the other regiments?" Bassett is approaching him, Oakes is one step behind him,

"One of ours' sir" Martin replies weakly, Oakes moves in front of the Captain, stopping as he reaches Martins side,

"God help us" Oakes says in a whisper, Bassett arrives,

"Who is it Lance Corporal?"

Martin stands, he cannot speak, he cannot move, he takes off his cap and stares at Oakes,

"It is Private Bothworthy Sir" Oakes speaks for Martin, he puts his hand on Martins elbow and whispers to him,

"Are you alright son?"

Martin nods his head, "Yes Sergeant"

Oakes moves back, looks at Alf and becomes officious again, "Lance corporal, will you take Private Rivers for a smoke" he points to the side of the road "Down there will do"

A young Lieutenant appears from the side of the track, he is from the Wiltshire's, he addresses Bassett, "Sir, we have one dead and six injured, all bullet wounds"

Bassett thanks the young officer, he addresses Oakes,

"Sergeant Oakes, sent someone up and down the track, I need to know how many casualties we have"

"Sir!" Oakes replies, he looks across to the Bedfordshire's, "Palmer, grab one other, quick smart up and down the track and report to me if we have any other injured or dead"

Patsy stands up and takes Posh with him, Martin and Alf are standing in a ditch at the side of the track, Martin is smoking a woodbine, Alf has one lit in between his fingers but isn't smoking it, the grey smoke twists, and twirls from its glowing end,

"I was only talking to Jack seconds before it all started, he was fine, talking and everything"

Martin takes a deep drag on his cigarette, he doesn't reply to Alf, letting him talk,

"I heard the shots fired and threw myself into the ditch, I thought Jack had come with me, I didn't look because I had my head down, I should have done something, anything, something"

"Mate" Martin speaks firmly even though he is choked up at the death of his friend, "Nothing you did was wrong, there is nothing any of us could have done"

He looks up as Patsy and Posh return, Oakes is removing the identity tag from around Jack's neck, putting the small disc, still attached to a length of string into his tunic pocket, Patsy speaks to him,

"Sarge, we have two walking wounded up at the front, one has a bullet to the shoulder and the other has been shot through the hand"

Oakes nods, Captain Bassett is walking back toward him, he stands, "Sir"

"Be ready for the off in ten minutes sergeant" he looks at the corpse of Jack Bothworthy,

"Leave this to me sir" suggests Oakes, the Captain nods and walks back to the front of the line.

"Ready to move in ten men, finish your smokes and have a slug of water"

He points at Patsy and Posh, "You two, move Bothworthy to the side of the road and bury him"

Posh looks like he is about to faint, the sight of his dead mate is getting to him

Martin steps forward,

"Posh, you go stand with Alf, Patsy and I will bury Jack"

He indicates to Patsy that they will move Jacks body to the side of the road, they take an arm each and begin to pull, the body is heavy and as they lift his arms, Jacks lifeless head falls back onto the track,

"Bloody hell" says Patsy

"We have to lift him under his arms mate" instructs Martin

They are joined by three others from the battalion, between them, they lift the body and place it at the side of the road, then, silently taking out their trenching tools, they dig a quick and shallow grave for their friend. His body is put into the hastily dug grave and covered with a thin layer of soil, the three soldiers that joined in and helped, stand silently with Patsy and Martin as they stamp the earth down on top of their dead colleague.

"Men, fall in on the track!" Oakes' voice carries easily in the quiet.

Alf and Posh are watching as Martin puts Jacks rifle, barrel end, into the ground at the head of the grave, putting Jacks cap on the upstanding rifle butt.

The four of them get onto the track, stepping aside as the wounded make their way back in the direction they have just covered, eight men with hurriedly applied bandages walk away from their comrades, accompanied by one uninjured man, they will have to walk all the way back to Gheluvelt to be treated. Martin knows both the injured Bedfordshire's,

"John, Robert, how are you both?"

Both men tell him that they are doing as well as can be expected in the circumstances, one of them points at the grave, Martin looks at him and says,

"Jack, that's Jack Bothworthy lads"

Both shake their heads and move on, away from the war.

The command to move comes from sergeant Oakes, "21st Infantry brigade, advance in two ranks!"

Martin has moved forward, near to the front of the column, he finds himself standing beside a Captain from the Royal Scots Fusiliers, who introduces himself,

"Captain Croker, how are you doing Lance Corporal"

"Not so bad sir" lies Martin after introducing himself,

"I see you lost one of your laddies just then"

"Yes sir" replies Martin, "A good friend of mine"

Captain Croker pats him on the back,

"Sorry to say this Lance Corporal, but get used to it, we have been over here for six weeks now and we have lost a lot of good men"

"I am sorry to hear that sir" is all Martin can think to reply.

"This is war lance corporal, it's a bloody mess and none of us are safe, officer and soldier alike, a bullet has not a thought as to whether you are a private or a Colonel"

"So, what do we do sir?"

Croker thinks for a few seconds,

"We carry on, we fight the enemy and try to kill them, not an easy thing to do at first, but if you don't fight back and kill, then you will be killed"

"Sir" Martin says glumly, Croker carries on talking to him,

"There will be times when this fight brings a smile to your face, remember these moments, they will keep you sane"

"Really sir, funny moments?" Martin really can't comprehend any funny moments as his friend has just been killed, Croker puts an unlit pipe in his mouth,

"I saw our Lt Col have his horse shot from underneath him a couple of weeks ago, not funny on the face of it, but I saw the look of disgust and unhappiness on the man's face as he hit the floor, for some reason I found it funny at the time"

"Is the Lt Col your officer commanding here sir?" asks Martin

Croker takes the pipe from his mouth,

"No Lance corporal" he pauses "That will be me for now, I am the most senior officer from the Royal Scots left alive on this front line"

Martin looks across at the captain,

"Must be getting back to mine, damn nice to meet you Lance corporal"

"You too sir"

"Remember what I said, laugh at the funny moments"

Captain Croker moves to the left of the column and re-joins the men from his regiment.

Martin is thrown to the ground by an explosion, he feels blood on his face, he puts his hand up and feels wetness on his left cheek, another explosion and he throws himself into the ditch at the side of the track,

"Take cover men!" An order is shouted.

Men are crying in pain, men are shouting for help and men are sitting silently bleeding as the shrapnel bombs explode around them, Martin feels something hit him from behind, he is not hurt though, he is sure of it. Martin has experience of the British army shrapnel bombs, he is sure that the Germans must have a similar projectile, they are thirteen pound weighted shells, fired from over a mile away and they contain spherical bullets, much like a shotgun cartridge except the cartridge and the bullets are much bigger, the rear section of the shell, the brass, is packed with cordite, when fired this propels the head to its final destination. The front section, or the head, has a nose fuse and it is this that is filled with the lead balls, each about half an inch across, with a tube through its centre, this conveys the ignition flash from the ignition fuse to a small gunpowder charge in a cavity in its base, when ignited, the gunpowder charge explodes and propels the deadly lead balls, over forty in each shell to be expelled out in all directions causing injury and death to those nearby.

Many of the shells are missing the column, hitting buildings on the roadside, or exploding in the fields, creating small craters in the soft earth with ease,

"Find hard cover!" the order is shouted from the front of the line,

Martin looks around, to his rear is an old barn, it does not have a roof and one of the side walls is missing, Martin has no idea if the wall and roof have been damaged in the recent fighting near here or if it has been like this for some time, he doesn't care, he shouts as loud as he can,

"Barn on the right flank, moving now!"

He stands up and runs, taking cover behind a wall, he is joined by at least a dozen other soldiers, they all fall to the ground, Martin looks around, "Is everyone all right?"

He sees Colour sergeant Barnes putting a pipe into his mouth, his left arm is a bloodied mess, his three chevrons with the crown above then are crimson,

"Bastard mess" is all he says, lighting his pipe with his uninjured arm.

The shells are dropping all around them, men are screaming, and Martin can see bodies on the far side of the road, he assumes they are men from the Wiltshire's or Yorkshires, as his regiment and the Fusiliers are on this side. There are ten of them behind the wall of the barn, a horse without a rider walks into view, one of the soldiers jumps to his feet and brings the horse to cover and safety, oddly, the horse seems unaffected by the noise and carnage going on around them, the shelling continues, some of the soldiers are sitting with their backs to the wall, they have removed their webbing, most are having a smoke and are calm, their rifles leaning nonchalantly against the red brick wall, colour sergeant Barnes is having a field dressing put onto his injury, the white bandage turning red almost instantly when it is applied to his damaged upper arm,

"Perhaps a bit tighter lad" he says to the young soldier tending to him.

Three of the soldiers are lying on the ground, one on his side propped up by his right elbow, his cap on the back of his head, he still has his webbing on although he appears to have ditched his valise, the remaining two men are lying on their backs, one has no headgear on and is silent and wide eyed, he is uninjured, the final soldier, a soldier Martin cannot identify as the man is holding his cap firmly over his face and is obviously crying with fear, Martin can just about hear him whisper,

"Help me Mother, help me"

"You are bleeding Lance corporal", one of the men sitting at the wall observes, Martin rubs his left cheek and looks at his hand, a small amount of blood is transferred from the cheek wound to his hand,

"It's nothing Mike" he says to the man, taking a handkerchief from his pocket, then pouring a little water from his canteen onto it, he cleans his face, he looks across at Mike, who says with a smile,

"Beautiful Lance Corporal, absolutely beautiful"

The shelling seems to have slowed and Martin is just about to give Mike an answer when he hears a shout from further down the line,

"The buggers are running!"

Martin looks around the wall, he can see, a hundred yards to his right and from an area a few yards in front of their column, running down the slope are a large group of German infantrymen, heading for the river to the south of their current position and west of Menin, they are making good their escape, he knows that they are German by their distinctive spike helmets, or '*pickelhaube*', these helmets have green canvas covers on them with numbers printed in bright red on the front of the cover, Martin cannot make out the numbers as the men are just too far away, they are all wearing grey/blue woollen tunics with red piping around the turned up cuffs and the same red piping on the outside of their trousers, these are tucked into black leather jackboots. The men are struggling to move quickly as they are all carrying the Geweh 98 rifle and a large, cumbersome backpack, the ammo pouches they carry can be seen on the front of their belts at waist level, some are falling to the ground as they try to escape. Martin feels anger and revenge take over his every being, he stands out in the open, puts a round in the rifle chamber by bringing back and then replacing the bolt action, lifting the butt of the rifle into his shoulder and bringing the rifle to eye level, he takes aim, not a specific aim, but at the group of soldiers fleeing, he puts his finger on the trigger, feeling the gentle curve of the trigger sit firmly on his right index finger, he pulls the trigger back to take up the small amount of slack in the spring, taking a deep breath in, he slowly exhales as his index finger puts tension through the trigger and the rifle fires its first round in anger. He has no idea if he hits any of the enemy, his anger over the death of Jack is consuming him, the bolt on the rifle is rapidly pulled back and then forward, bringing another .303 cartridge into the breech, he fires again, this time he sees a man go down, is this his first kill? He is unsure as his 'oppos' are now also firing at the fleeing men. Martin pulls the trigger and nothing happens, the five round magazine is empty, his training kicks in, without looking at the rifle he removes the magazine, drops it to the floor, takes a fresh loaded magazine from his ammunition pouch on his belt, he pushes it home into the magazine housing, quickly pulling the bolt back and then forward he fires again into the middle of the fleeing men,

"Cease fire lads, that's enough" Colour sergeant Barnes yells above the noise,

Martin still has his rifle at eye level but has stopped firing,

"Stand down Lance corporal, they are now too far away to hit" Barnes is insistent.

Martin slowly lowers his rifle, bending down he retrieves his empty magazine and puts it in a pouch.

"Those bastards used the shrapnel shells as cover to escape as they let us get too close to them" one of the men exclaims, Martin nods slowly at the man,

"Is anyone injured?" asks Barnes.

None of them are but the soldier who had his cap over his face and calling for his Mother, is now lying in the foetal position with his arms covering his face, Barnes nudges the soldier firmly with his right foot, "Get up soldier, its over for now"

The soldier uncovers his face and looks up at the colour sergeant,

"Sorry colours, I couldn't help it, I didn't think I would be scared but I was, I was so scared"

Martin looks across at the soldier who is now sitting up, it is 'Johnno' Johnson, the man who had berated the young soldier on the SS Winifredian for being scared, Johnno looks at Martin, he hangs his head in shame, Barnes leans down to Johnno,

"Best it doesn't happen again Johnson, we are all scared boy, but we must do our bit"

He nudges Johnno again with his foot, this time with some firmness behind it,

"Am I clear son?"

Johnno nods and gets to his feet, he is looking for his cap, Martin sees it lying on the ground and kicks it toward him, Johnno picks it up,

"Thank you, Lance corporal" he says

"Fuck off Johnno" Martin replies and walks away and back onto the track to join other soldiers, to help with the dead and wounded.

He walks past three privates from the Yorkshires, they are carrying the body of an obviously dead soldier, Martin can see that the dead man is a corporal, the two chevrons on each side of his tunic are still intact, the middle of the tunic is not intact, it is a mass of guts and gore, Martin hopes that death was instantaneous, he nods at the Yorkshire soldiers as he passes and sees that the dead man is Archie Basher, whom had been speaking to only a day or two ago when bivouacked at Klemskerke.

The soldiers of the 21st Brigade are ordered to move back a few hundred yards, the officer giving the order, sitting astride a dark brown horse, is Lt Col Traill, Martins commanding officer, he seems unphased by the recent eruption of violence, he directs men away from the carnage and organises the officers, NCO's and soldiers to take up positions in the trenches they had passed by earlier, the Lt Col is obviously not happy with the lack of protection offered by the depth of these trenches, he orders a sergeant from the Wiltshire's to take charge and to get '*Every soldier, regardless of rank, digging for their lives'*.

The men of the 21st are joined a couple of hours later by officers and men from the 20th Brigade, made up of 1st battalion Scots and 2nd battalion Grenadier guards, the 2nd Border regiment and the 2nd battalion Gordon Highlanders, who are easily identified as they wear Glengarry caps that have a red, white and black check band around them, their large silver regimental badge is on the left side of the cap, they are also all wearing kilts, a tartan that is patterned with dark blue squares each being surrounded by light green edging and a thin yellow line passing through the green, they look and sound fearsome to Martin. The soldiers are told to remain in position, with the 20th taking the left side along with the Royal Scots fusiliers, the remainder of the 21st taking the right side, all dug into newly deepened trenches, it is raining, and the trenches are filling with water and liquid mud.

Sergeant Kirby, patrols the trenches, his lit pipe is a constant with him, and it is he who informs Martin and the four or five men nearest to him that 2nd Lt Bell has been killed in the shrapnel attack, also dead is Sergeant 'Buster' Crabbe and one other private, who at this time, due to the level of his injuries, cannot be identified, two other soldiers from the Bedfordshire's are missing and nineteen others have been wounded,

"Bloody hell" Martin looks across at Lance Corporal Taylor,

"What's up Wilf?" asks Martin,

"This is going to get worse before it gets better Martin"

Neither man speaks after this, Martin sits on a small ledge he has entrenched into the side of the steep trench, reaching into his jacket, he takes out a small note pad and a pencil, he starts writing a letter to Grace.

After a long and cold night in the trench the division receive orders to attack Menin, a town on the Belgian border with France, the remainder of the Yorkshires have arrived overnight and are back in the trench system with their colleagues, whilst waiting for the order to move off, all the soldiers are tasked with the ongoing improvement of the trenches, a difficult job as the rain continues and the mud is almost impossible to move out.

The town of Menin has been under German occupation since late September when a reconnaissance unit from the 20th Uhlan regiment, all on horseback, had moved in and easily taken the town, quickly raising the German flag from the town hall, it is known that the residents from the town have been taken prisoner and many are locked inside the town hall. The 22nd brigade are moving in toward the town, men from the 2nd battalion Queens Royal West Surrey regiment, the 2nd battalion Royal Warwickshire's and the 1st battalions from the Royal Welsh Fusiliers and the Wiltshire's have been ordered to take the newest German trench system, they have moved under cover of darkness and are entrenched to the east of where Martin and the men of the 21st are waiting for their orders to move. News filters through to the men in the trenches that the 22nd have been unsuccessful and are under sustained attack and they are hard pressed to move and need help to withdraw, the 21st are ordered to advance, using sustained fire they are able to ensure the successful withdrawal of the soldiers who have tried and failed to take the trench system at Menin from the Germans. Martin stays in the trench for the remainder of the day, at dusk he is preparing for a second night of discomfort when they are ordered to leave the trenches and return to the village of Gheluvelt, here they will be billeted, fed and the wounded treated. Activity on the road back to the village is busy, although Gheluvelt is a tiny place with less than 1000 residents it is situated on the direct road to Ypres, surrounded by heavy woodland, it is strategically important and at this time, the BEF has control of the area, although Martin can clearly see signs of a recent massive artillery attack on his walk back. There is huge water filled holes and ditches in the fields, he and few of the Bedfordshire's stop to help soldiers from the 2nd battalion Worcester regiment, who are struggling across the muddy fields with several stretchers that contain injured men, some of the Worcester soldiers are knee deep in the soft mud, they are grateful for the help in getting the stretchers from the fields, across the roadside trenches and onto the road. Many of the craters created by landing bombs have dead bodies of British army soldiers lying in them, the wounded are getting priority treatment at this time, the dead will have to wait.

Martin gets five other privates from his regiment and they take over carrying the stretchers from the exhausted men of the Worcester regiment, they carry the wounded to an aid station that has been set up in an old barn on the outskirts of the village. The Bedfordshire's are placed on battalion reserve and stay in the village overnight, hot food made on the mobile catering units is welcomed, the other soldiers of the 21st remain on the Menin Road, spending another night in the soaking trenches, they will be eating cold bully beef and biscuits.

During the next three days, Martin and his mates in the Bedfordshire's are moved almost constantly, moving to support the 22nd at Zonnebeke, where they are shelled heavily by German artillery, this bombardment continues to smash and destroy the landscape around them, fields and buildings are becoming indistinguishable from one another as the heavy bombardment continues to level everything around them. The battalion remain in this town for a few hours and are involved in heavy fighting with the Germans, who are quickly repulsed and make a hasty retreat. Martin and his section of five privates are directed to move a two miles to the northeast toward a small hamlet named Broodseinde, here they are to attempt to locate a platoon from the Royal Welsh fusiliers who were sent out two days ago, leaving at early evening to scope the area for enemy movement, it has been reported that there has been a skirmish to the North of Broodseinde and that the Royal Welsh may have been involved, if found, they are to be ordered to retreat to Zonnebeke.

A little over an hour later, Martin and his section arrive at Broodseinde without having any contact with the enemy, the hamlet is tiny, a few locals look through the windows of their homes, but do not venture outside, none of the Bedfordshire's speak Flemish and they get no response to their shouted questions to the locals in English. They travel through the hamlet in under five minutes, they continue toward another small settlement, Tyne Cothoek, Martin guides his men around the outside of this tiny place, skirting around outside as he has no information as to whether they are in front of or behind enemy lines. At a road junction stands a tree, it is over a hundred yards from where they stand, but Martin recognises it easily, it is older and bigger than the tree in his garden at home, but it is certainly a Yew tree.

He looks at it, a huge, gnarled trunk holds up a huge and ancient heavy canopy, many of the lower branches almost touch the ground before curving away from it, he stops and looks again,

"Move off the road" he whispers the order to his men.

Sitting under the tree are six or seven German soldiers, some with helmets on and others without,

"Are they asleep Lance corporal?" asks a soldier,

"I have no idea George" replies Martin "Rifles up lads"

The six men slowly and quietly put a round into the breeches of their rifles,

"Slowly lads, move forward, remain off of the main road if you can" he indicates that three of the men should move to the other side of the road, they do without bringing attention to themselves, they move forward slowly. Suddenly, one of Martins men, from the other side, opens fire on the Germans, everyone else, bar Martin, joins in, rifles are firing and being reloaded, Martin raises his hand,

"Cease fire" the two men with him stop shooting, the three on the other side continue, Martin repeats the order, this time in a voice that carries over the sound of the rifles being reloaded, he is angry, "What the hell was that?"

A voice carries from the other side,

"One of them moved Lance corporal"

Martin knows that the man is wrong, he can see that the German soldiers were already dead before his section started firing, the soldier who started it has had an attack of the jitters and the others followed, he doesn't blame him, their actions are an instinctive reaction to the first shot being fired.

"They were already dead lads" he says without emotion. They approach the Germans and sure enough, it is obvious that they have been dead for at least a day. They all have bullet wounds to the body and head; all have dried blood around them indicating that death wasn't recently for these men.

As they get closer, large rats run from under the bodies and scurry into bushes nearby, the Yew tree groans as the wind moves through its canopy.

Martin feels a shiver run down his back as he speaks to his men,

"Let's get back to the battalion"

The men all agree, and they move away from the horrible scene.

They arrive back and report to Captain Basset, Martin explains that they did not find the Welsh fusiliers and detailed the six dead Germans under the Yew tree,

"Good work Lance corporal" the Captain says, "I apologise that you and your section were sent out and put in danger, but the men from the Welsh arrived back here at Zonnebeke only a half hour after you left, unscathed, they got bloody lost, I believe it was them that shot the Germans"

Martin raises his eyebrows; the men accept the dismissal from their Captain and set off to make a brew and to have a smoke, their rest is to be short lived. Martin and the regiment are ordered back to the trenches at Gheluvelt, shelled heavily again as they move away, the platoon from C company has to remain in the trenches at Zonnebeke as the shelling has destroyed large parts of their trench system and for now, as escape is impossible, they are stuck there. 2 platoons from D company have been sent to the front line, to reinforce the trenches with the Royal Scots Fusiliers, heavy shelling takes the lives of Lt Fernandes, several NCO's and ten privates, the remainder of the battalion, including Martin, are now in a steep sided trench on the outskirts of Gheluvelt, they are to remain in position to repel any German attack on the village.

* * *

Friday 23rd October – Saturday 7th November

In the early hours of 23rd October, a company from the regiment are sent to fill a gap that has appeared in between the positions of the Royal Scots and the Yorkshire's, the company, led by Lt Wright, are attacked at a bend in the road, the young Lt is killed and casualties amongst his men are heavy. Martin is part of the company that is ordered to fill the gap that is still open and will allow free enemy movement if it is not plugged, they move from the West end of Gheluvelt, to advance, under heavy shell fire that kills many men, before getting within sight of the position they are to take, the remainder of the regiment, including Martin, continue the advance and come under heavy rifle and machine gun fire, many more are killed and injured. The officer in charge of the platoon Martin is in, is wounded during this advance, Captain Patron, carries on and leads his men from the front despite his wounds. The men are ordered to advance into a wood, they make it to the location without further loss, Martin, along with Sergeant Oakes and handful of privates, are tasked to move along the edge of the wood, in a short time they meet up with the Yorkshire soldiers, this end of the gap has now been filled, they take up positions in the trenches and wait. An hour or so later the regimental commanding officer, Lt Col Traill, arrives at their location, having ridden from Battalion HQ along the Becelaere Road, to speak to the officer commanding the Yorkshire regiment, Oakes informs the men that the gap is now filled, and that the Bedfordshire's are to remain in the trenches at this, the front line, for the time being and overnight, they are told to be prepared for a possible long spell at the front line. Martin remains in the trench for the next thirty six hours, the letter to Grace is now finished, he will have to wait to get it posted, the regiment have not had any mail received or sent out for a week or so, if they get a break from the front line, he will then be able to get it sent off, he is sad that he has not had any mail at all from Grace or Alice since he has arrived, but he remains hopeful that he will hear soon.

Sporadic rifle fire from the German positions, over half a mile to the south, is not responded to from the British positions, it has stopped raining at last and they are allowed to brew up during daylight hours, cooking and smoking is forbidden when it is dark, the smallest light at night will give away their position to the enemy.

An evening attack is ordered on the town of Becelaere, currently held by the Germans, the men from the Guards regiments, the Bedfordshire and Yorkshire regiments are to advance to this town, they have strict instruction not to lose touch with each other and that gaps must not appear in any part of the Allied line. The regiments advance from their trenches at five in the evening, they all wheel to the right and contact is lost almost immediately with the Guards, the allied forces are on the receiving end of heavy artillery and machine gun fire, although the men behave with strength and steadiness, and despite heavy casualties, the order to retreat back to the trenches is given after three failed attempts to take ground and advance. Martin is back in the same trench he had left only a few hours earlier, behind him, in the town of Gheluvelt has suffered from heavy artillery fire, at least three buildings, including the Battalion HQ, are on fire and beyond saving. Martin despairs at the damage to property and for the loss of life,

"And for what?" Martin says aloud, "For us to return to exactly the same position as we were in before" he looks at Posh, "This is bloody madness mate"

The following day, the 26th October, the Guards regiment advance forward, past the trenches that Martin and his mates are in, again toward Becelaere, the Bedfordshire's are to follow after them, but the Guards don't get more than a few yards past Martins trench before they are forced to retreat under consistent gunfire, taking heavy casualties, in the confusion, two officers from Martins regiment are shot and killed by German snipers, Captain Hall and Lt Bastard, shot within a few minutes of each other. Both are buried by Martin and his fellow soldiers, at the edge of the woodland, they are laid to rest close to each other, the digging and burial is carried out under the orders and guidance of Captain Thom, who insists that the two men be buried and not left where they have fallen.

Officers and men are dying in huge numbers, it is only a week since these battles around Ypres started, already Martin has seen many hundreds die and the numbers of men in the 21st has depleted massively.

It is now the 28th October, shelling from the German lines into the BEF trenches is continuous, battalion HQ has been hit again, it will have to be moved as the building is almost beyond use, Martin remains in the trenches, Posh and Alf are both within a few feet of him, conversation has to be shouted during the shelling, it has become almost normal to raise your voice as you hear the approach of the incoming shells.

'A 'company, situated twenty yards from Martin and his mates, take a direct hit from a shell, the old redoubt they are in has collapsed and men are buried, panicked shouts for help can be heard from their position, Martin, Alf, and Posh break from their positions to go and help. The redoubt that has collapsed, is one of the first that had been built in this area, the raised front edge and platform have been reinforced with sandbags and tall staves of wood and wicker fencing, the trench is several feet below the level of the raised platform, it is now all one level, the wooden staves, some seven or eight feet long, stick out from the wet mud by only a foot or two. Lance Sergeant William Peggs, from the grenade section, is the temporary sergeant for 'A 'company following the death of Buster Crabbe a few days ago, screams at Martin,

"Five or six are still under here Martin, some of the lads have dug themselves out and are in no fit state to dig, help mate please"

Martin shouts across to soldiers on the opposite side of the collapsed trench,

"Jonesy!"

Private Matthew Jones looks across,

"Yes, Lance Corporal"

"I need six soldiers to dig here, take every other man from your side and get them over here!"

Jones doesn't answer but Martin can hear him shouting up the line,

"Alf, Posh, we have to dig with our hands, if we use our entrenching tools, we are going to hurt these men who are buried"

Jonesy arrives with five other soldiers and without being told they all begin to dig down with their hands,

"Got one!" Jonesy has uncovered a hand, three others join him, and the man's face is quickly exposed, allowing him to breathe, he coughs and splutters as he feels air filing his lungs,

"Gerrard is underneath me, get me out quick I am right on top of him"

The men dig quickly and have the man out in minutes, the soldier underneath him is unresponsive,

"Can I help lance sergeant?"

Martin and William look up and see the battalion 2nd in command, Major Robert Stares standing over them, William is out of breath from digging frantically, Martin replies,

"Sir we have at least another three of four mates buried here" The second man has been pulled free, he is breathing but is not conscious, he is passed to men in the trenches to be cared for.

"Another one here!" Alf screams, Major Stares runs over to him, his once neat and clean uniform is now covered in the sticky mud from the trenches, he gets on his hands and knees next to Alf and begins shifting huge clumps of mud away from the trapped man with his hands.

"Two here lads!" Martin runs over to help, the two trapped men are head and shoulders above ground already, one Martin knows very well, it is Johnno, who is screaming for help,

"Calm down Johnno, we will have you out in a few seconds" Martin says to the frightened man. Martin, William and one other have Johnno and the other trapped man out in a couple of minutes, Johnno is crying and screaming, Martin grabs him by the tunic,

"Johnno!' he shouts at him "Listen to me and listen good"

Johnno becomes suddenly quiet,

"Yes Martin"

Martin wipes mud from Johnno's face, he still has hold of his tunic,

"Listen, go down there" he points to his position in the trenches, two other soldiers that were buried are already there, blankets over their shoulders and sipping mugs of tea, a loud whistling from overhead makes them all cover their heads,

"Get down men!" shouts Major Stares

The German shell lands short of their trench system but covers them in flying mud and debris, Stares shouts again, "Is everyone all right?"

Several men shout, "Yes sir!"

"Need another few hands here men" Stares speaks with authority to the men.

Alf and Major Stares have uncovered the buried man's head, it is Corporal John Franklin, he is conscious and breathing but he is being held under the mud by a large seven or eight foot long wooden stave that lies across his chest.

"How many are out?" Martin asks William, who has a quick head count,

"Four out, Private Marks is now conscious, the lucky beggar has no recollection, but he is safe and uninjured, it will be five when we get Corporal Franklin out of the mess he is in"

Martin and William join Alf and Major Stares, the removal of the large piece of wood has to be completed slowly so as not to cause any further collapse,

"Lance Sergeant what on earth are you doing?"

William and Martin look up and see 2nd Lt Bates standing over them, he is the newest and youngest officer in the battalion, not liked by the men because of his attitude toward the rank and file, William answers him, "Digging out our buried friend's sir, what does it look like?"

Martin tries to suppress a smile and fails, Bates is not happy, "Something amusing you Lance corporal. That stripe you have can be taken back you know"

Major Stares stands up, looks Bates directly in the eyes and says, "Fuck off 2nd Lieutenant"

Bates is turning a deathly hue of grey; it is obvious that he had not seen the Major,

"Sir?" is all he can say,

"You heard me, go to my hut and stay there"

Bates has no answer to the Majors instruction, Martin helps out, "Sir, the Major has his hut about a hundred yards further down the trenches" he points in the direction of the trench HQ hut, a hastily built bunker with wooden walls and a roof that the officers use to read maps and prepare battle orders. Bates leaves without another word, the digging continues, the wooden stave has been cleared enough for three men to lift it clear of the man trapped in the mud,

"You will do anything for a day out of the trenches won't you Corporal Franklin?" the Major quips as he and Alf pull the corporal free from his muddy grave, Franklin smiles, "Can you and Alf continue to dig please Sir; my bloody pipe is buried hereabouts somewhere!"

"Did you hear what I said to the 2nd Lt corporal?"

Franklin smiles again, "I did Sir" he replies,

"You have my answer then don't you corporal?"

"All accounted for sir"

A private confirms that all men who were buried are now free and accounted for,

"Good news, top work men, the five who were trapped, report to my hut please, I have to write a report and need your names and numbers etc, bring a mug of tea with you" He looks at John Franklin, "You Corporal, bring one for me as well please"

"I will sir" the smiling NCO replies.

Martin returns to his position in the trenches, Johnno is still there, a mug of tea held in both hands, he looks at Martin, "Thanks Martin, I thought I was a goner"

"Take your tea and go see the Major please Johnno"

As he walks down the trenches, Martin calls after him,

"Johnno!" He turns back, Martin continues, "Been a hell of a couple of weeks hasn't it?"

Johnno manages a smile, "Yes Lance corporal"

The morning of the 30th October arrives, beginning much the same as the other mornings have started over the past fourteen days, heavy shell fire is landing all around the battalion who have all jumped into shallow ditches on the Gheluvelt to Zandevoorde road, a couple of miles SSW of Gheluvelt, in all the time the battalion has been in Belgium with all the men that have been killed and with the destruction of the landscape, Martin knows that although he and the battalions are covering miles every day they are still only less than two or three miles from where they started at Gheluvelt on 16th October. The enemy occupy the town of Zandevoorde, Martin and his fellow soldiers have been ordered to protect the recently established Battalion HQ, at this time in an old farmhouse, trenches have not yet been dug and therefore the only cover that they have from this morning's barrage are shallow water filled ditches at the side of the road. The 7th cavalry brigade are driven past the Battalion HQ in open wagons, from trench positions they had been in near to Zandevoorde, this leaves the whole right flank exposed, as the cavalry units pass through, it becomes clear that the Germans have advanced out of their trench system outside of town and from a position out in no-man's-land, they open fire from 900 yards out with machine guns, Martin and the Bedfordshire's are pinned down as are the 7th cavalry, any movement from their position will mean certain death, the machine guns continue to enfilade the Battalion HQ. The order is given to move from their positions and to form two lines and to attack the German machine gunners by flanking them from either side, Sergeant Oakes makes it very clear that his soldiers must shoot forward and not to the side, shooting to the left or right, depending on which side you are positioned on, will mean shooting each other,

"If you are going to get shot, let a German do it and not a fellow British soldier" is Oakes final comment.

The attack is a success, the German machine guns are silenced very quickly, the soldiers from the 2nd Bedfordshire's fired hundreds of rounds from rifles and machine guns into the German positions, Oakes orders the men to take positions in the empty German machine gun trenches, they have advanced a good nine hundred yards toward the occupied town of Zandevoorde, the men are elated, no casualties from any of the advancing soldiers and the cavalry are now able to move into position. Martin sits in his new trench and lights a cigarette; he has no idea of the brand having taken them from a fellow soldier in a card game a few days ago. He has just finished and is about to light another when he hears Sergeant Oakes approaching, angry and swearing,

"Men, orders have been given for us to retire back toward Battalion HQ, the trenches on the far side of this town have been taken from the Welsh fusiliers, this has exposed the trenches of the Scots fusiliers, who are also retiring back, we are to provide cover fire for the retirement of these units"

He takes a cigarette from Martin and continues, "I know you are all disappointed to give up this land we have advanced on, but our countrymen are having difficulties and we are to help them, they will do the same for us one day I don't doubt that"

The men from the Bedfordshire regiment move back toward Battalion HQ, to provide safe passage for the soldiers who are being overrun by stronger German forces, as they move in front of the farmhouse they are passed by officers and men from the South Lancashire regiment going toward the location they have just vacated, Oakes speaks to a captain from the other regiment, who is seated on a fine white horse,

"Sir, we have just left that area, we had taken it but have been ordered back to cover the retreat of the Welsh and Scots fusiliers"

The captain stops his horse, "Typical army orders sergeant, we have been tasked to come in this way to support the fusiliers, we are to go through here and occupy the land in front of them"

Oakes shakes his head,

"Good luck sir, from what I have heard, the place is crawling with the Hun, that's why the retreat has been called"

The officer puts his heels into the sides of his horse to encourage it to move forward,

He touches the front of his cap with his swagger stick, "We must follow orders sergeant, no matter how bloody stupid they may seem"

The Bedfordshire's stand at the roadside to let the Lancashire officers pass, they move on toward Battalion HQ. Oakes is ordered, as they arrive at HQ, to take all his men and to re-join the rest of the officers and men from the Bedfordshire's who are digging trenches in a line behind the Gheluvelt to Zandevoorde road, only a few yards from where Martin had laid in a ditch a few hours earlier as the Germans shot at him and his mates, another day of danger, another day of being attacked and another day of moving back to almost the same place they had started. Martin, as he is digging again with his entrenching tool, is beginning to wonder if the senior officers have any idea what they are doing and if they care how many men they lose, of course he keeps this to himself. It is raining heavily, Martin settles in as best he can, fully prepared for another wet night in the muddy trenches.

The final day of October is an early start for the men of the 2nd Bedfordshire's, at two thirty in the morning, Captain Lemon takes two platoons to a small fir tree wood, situated about two hundred and fifty yards in front of the line held by them, the North Lancashire regiment are already situated at this location and are taking heavy shell fire from two sides, the bombardment carried on all day yesterday and it is expected to begin again at first light. The sun has hardly cleared the east horizon when reports of the enemy advancing on the wood are being passed down the line, Martin is lying in a shallow ditch, eyes firmly open and watching the fields directly in front of him, a shallow trench system runs parallel to the front of the wood, Martin and seven or eight others are on watch duty, looking for the enemy but outside of the relative safety of the shallow trenches. An adjutant arrives at the front line with orders from the Brigadier at Battalion HQ for part of the battalion to move back, Captain Lemon is ordered by Lt Col Traill to take half the men and return to Gheluvelt where the German army are attacking the small village, Traill also leaves the wood and returns to the battalion hut in the trench situated on the Gheluvelt to Zandevoorde road, taking Major Stares with him, Martin remains in the wood, he watches as Captain Lemon and a group of soldiers make their way out of the partially protected area.

As they reach the end of the line of trees they are attacked by a large group of German infantrymen, Martin and others leave their positions to help their colleagues who are being overwhelmed by this attack, this is Martins and many others, first experience of hand to hand fighting. Martin runs along the edge of the wood, soldiers from Captain Lemons platoon have fixed bayonets, rifles are being fired at close range by both sides, he runs at a German soldier who is pushing his bayonet into a young private from Martins Battalion, he hears the young man cry out in pain, Martin charges at the German soldier screaming as he runs, the German infantryman looks up at the raging British Tommy running at him. Martin sees instantaneous fear on the Germans face, a young man who looks to Martin to be no more than eighteen or nineteen years old, he pulls his bayonet from the body of the dead British soldier but not quick enough, Martin with his rifle and bayonet out in front of him runs into the German soldier hitting him in the chest with his bayonet, he keeps running making the enemy soldier move backwards with Martins bayonet now in the front of his chest, through the rib cage and out of his back.

"Hilf mir Mutter" screams the young German, Martin continues to push his rifle and bayonet into the soldier, as he moves forward the German falls to the ground, putting both his hands helplessly around the bayonet that has pierced his body,

"Nein, hör bitte auf!" the young man screams with fear and pain in his voice. Martin is raging with anger, he pulls his rifle and bayonet from the young man's body, he is preparing to stab the enemy soldier again, the rifle held squarely in front of him, ready to be pushed into this body again, he stops when he sees the fight to stay alive leave the eyes of the young soldier. He stands for a second, staring at the man he has just killed,

"Martin! Over here!" he looks over to Posh who is shouting at him, he runs over, Posh is pointing to a group of German soldiers who are retreating,

"They shot Captain Lemon and have taken him prisoner!" yells Posh,

Martin can see their Captain being dragged across the field by four enemy infantrymen, he shouts at a group of Bedfordshire's who have their rifles trained on the fleeing men,

"Don't shoot! Don't shoot! they have Captain Lemon!"

The men raise their weapons, but as soon as they do, a further group of German soldiers are quickly approaching,

"Line of fire!" Martin orders, the men throw themselves onto the ground, they have an advantage as they are partly covered by the shallow ditch that they now lie in, Martin and Posh join them,

"Fire at will" Martin commands, the noise from the rifles is deafening, smoke rises from their position and Martin is joined where he lies by Lt. Gott, he looks at Martin,

"Good decision Lance Corporal" Martin looks at the Lt, he has blood seeping through his tunic, he notices Martin looking at him,

"It's nothing Lance Corporal, really, a flesh wound"

Martin nods, Lt Gott orders the men to continue to fire at the enemy, some of the Germans have made it to the top of the ditches, the men of the Bedfordshire's repel the attack, they move back through the wood to the trenches and to relative safety.

The Germans have retreated, they have also attacked Gheluvelt with two battalions of men, in an attempt to re take the village from the allies the enemy meet with the 2nd Battalion Worcester's, who have only 350 men left at this time, the Germans break the line and take the village, using their superior artillery to shell the BEF lines, the Worcester's supported by the Welsh regiment, advance back into the village and surprise, the celebrating German units, the village is re taken and German casualties are high. Martin helps Lt Gott back to the trenches, they arrive to horrendous scenes, the trenches have been held by the Bedfordshire's, but losses are severe, countless numbers injured and dead, Martin is assigned to lead a patrol to return to the wood and check for British survivors, it is deemed a safe place to return to at this time as the Royal Garrison Artillery are now bombarding the German lines with constant shelling, the enemy has retreated to higher ground, the BEF have held the village and the lower ground and importantly, they have held the heavily wooded areas of this countryside that will afford them cover.

In the small wood, Martin and his patrol find Captain Botfield, severely wounded and barely alive, Lt Dixon is also found and assisted back to the trenches with a leg wound, Captain Lyddon and Lt Anderson are reported to be missing, presumed captured or dead, they find Lt Patterson dead a little further on.

"No!" Martin hears Alf scream out loud, he runs to where Alf is standing,

"Alf? What is it?" He looks into the shallow ditch at the edge of the wood, Posh is lying face up, he has bullet wounds all over his body, his pallor is dull and grey, he is dead.

"Damn it" Martin says "Posh wasn't quick enough when the Hun over ran our positions"

He pats Alf on the shoulder, "Come on mate, we will come back for him in a bit, we must help the wounded"

Alf, head hanging low, follows Martin along the tree line.

The dead are buried in shallow trenches at the edge of the wood, Martin has also learnt that Lt Col Traill and Major Stares have both been killed, shot in their trenches as the Germans came over the top, Posh is laid to rest alongside his commanding officer and the second in command. Captain Charles Foss is the senior ranking Bedfordshire officer and takes command of what officers and men he has left.

Three other officers, Captain (QM) Cressingham, Lt Mills and 2nd Lt Waddy are the only surviving officers from the 2nd Battalion, they have only three hundred and fifty men that have survived this the first battle of many in the southwest corner of Flanders, in the areas surrounding Ypres.

Martin and the remaining men from the Bedfordshire's spend another six days and nights on the line, living in the trenches before they are finally relieved, they make their way to billets, to sleep, to eat and to sleep some more before returning to the line.

This battle is over, nearly sixty thousand men from the British Expeditionary force lie dead, in Mons, in Marne, in Aisne, Menin, Gheluvelt, Langemarck and Ypres to name but a few.

The French dead is higher than the BEF and Belgium have lost over ten thousand men.

German losses are also higher than the BEF, the French and Belgians combined.

The Battle of Ypres continues for another month, many thousands more will die.

* * *

Sunday 8th November - Saturday 14th November

It is early on Sunday 8th November, the day arrives with unseasonably bright and sunny weather, Alice is excited because Grace is calling in a short while and they are walking to Sauncy Wood to collect sweet chestnuts and some hawthorn berries, Granny wants to make soup and jam, Alice had mentioned it to Grace last week and to her delight Grace has agreed to accompany her. Alice has dressed accordingly, she wants to be warm on the walk but smart in case she meets up with David Shefford, the young soldier staying at the family cottage, she has noticed him looking at her when she passes or visits the cottage, the other soldiers mock David gently, Alice knows it is because of her and she admires David for taking the joshing from his mates so well. Standing in front of the mirror, she combs her hair and begins to braid it on either side, she joins the long braids together, they hang beautifully from the back of her head and to below her shoulders, she looks smart, her strong black boots are perfect for walking in the woods, thick stockings, held in place by elastic garters below her knees, a plain black skirt with three large buttons at the side of her waist, this falls to just below her mid-calf, giving her enough freedom to walk and covering enough of her legs for modesty and acceptability, her sheer white blouse is secured just above her bust with a small brooch, the navy blue and grey heavy knitted cardigan made by Granny, will keep her warm as well as looking nice, she is also wearing knee length thick cotton knickers and a thick cotton chemise, both of which are covered by a light cotton petticoat.

"Alice" shouts Mary up the stairs, "Grace is here"

Alice picks up her knitted hat, Granny also made this, it is the same colour as her cardigan, it sits on the back of her head leaving a little of her fringe free and allows the remainder of her upbraided hair to be tucked away,

"Alice, are you coming down, or shall I send Grace away?"

Alice makes her way down the staircase to the bar, "I am here Granny" Mary looks her up and down, "Hello Grace" Alice continues excitedly, Grace replies,

"Alice you look lovely, you put me to shame!"

Alice has on a brown waist length jacket, with two buttons at each cuff, it is secured by two horizontal buttons at the waist, a plain white blouse, also secured with a brooch, but higher up than Alice has hers, a black waistcoat, buttoned from top to bottom, an ankle length brown dress, black boots, and a simple black short, brimmed hat. Alice warmly hugs Grace, who returns the hug, Mary says, "I take it you are off the Paris fashion show dressed like that young lady and not foraging for your old Granny"

Alice moves to where Mary is standing, she puts her arms around her Grandmothers waist and rests her head on her bosom,

"Granny, I am sixteen in January, I am not a baby, you know I will do anything for you, I promise to get berries and the sweetest chestnuts for you!"

Mary tuts at Alice, who laughs and releases her hold from Mary,

"If you can, go to Whitepightle wood, the best chestnuts are there"

Alice moans, "That is the other side of Sauncy wood and Holcroft spring Granny!"

Grace speaks, "Mary, of course we will go to Whitepightle wood, I know the very group of trees you speak of"

Mary thanks her, "Have you heard from our Martin at all?" she asks Grace.

Both Alice and Mary look at her, not wanting to tell a lie or to upset anyone she says,

"I have, yes, two letters arrived together over a week ago, and one further arrived yesterday" she looks at Mary, "How about you Mary, I do hope he has written to you and Alice"

“He has” Mary says sternly, “But not three times”

Alice smiles and looks at Mary, “I have had two letters, so between us Granny, we have had three as well”

Alice runs out of the door shouting ‘goodbye’ to Mary.

“Grace” Mary says, Grace turns back as she holds the door open, “Thank you for spending time with Alice”

“Of course, Mary, I love being with her”

They nod at each other, and Grace leaves the pub, Alice puts her arm through Graces and, turning right from the pub, they cross the road to avoid any confrontation with Jack Bright, they can both see him sitting under his Elm tree smoking his pipe, they walk past without speaking to him. They reach Pickford Pond, it is at the front of the Almagam factory but named after the old mill, they turn right onto the footpath that will take them over the common to the Dell, this is a steep section of the field that has a white chalk face, it stands out in stark comparison to the grey and brown fields of this November morning.

“I remember sledging here with my Father in the winter of 1907 and into the early part of 1908, it was such fun” Grace tells Alice,

“I wish it will snow this year Grace; I would love to go sledging”

“It is fun, but you do get very cold Alice, I remember that winter being so very cold, but we had snow that was so deep I could hardly walk across the field and I was nearly sixteen!”

They climb the steep chalk face of the Dell and rest at the top,

“Shall we go to Whitepightle wood first Alice, we can walk along the track at the edge of Sauncy wood and go through Holcroft spring to the track to the wood?”

Alice groans, “It is such a long way!”

Grace stops, puts her hands on her hips and says, “Alice, you promised your Grandmother”

“Grace” replies Alice,

“Yes Alice”

Alice starts to walk away, “You look so old standing like that!”

Grace picks up her skirt and runs toward Alice, who runs away from her pursuer, laughing so much she has to stop when a coughing fit takes her breath away.

They reach the edge of Sauncy wood and take the track that runs between this wood and Holcroft spring, the sun is almost behind them and is low in the sky, shafts of faded golden sunlight breaks free through the gaps in the trees, the fallen leaves on the floor of the wood glow red in the shaded light, Alice breaks the silence,

"What did Martin write to you about?"

Grace doesn't answer immediately, she walks on up the track before saying,

"That he is fine and well, that he is missing us all and that we are not to worry about him"

Alice thinks about this for a minute, before saying, "That is very boring!" she looks at Grace for a reaction, Grace gives nothing away, "He should be writing romantic love letters to you Grace, not boring everyday stuff"

"What does he say in your letters from him?"

"Seemingly the same as you, boring stuff about marching and digging holes in fields"

Grace puts her arm around Alice's shoulders, "He will be fine Alice; you know that don't you"

Alice nods, the walk on in silence.

Grace does not mention the details of the last two letters from Martin, she smiles and shivers as she recalls his beautifully worded letters, his declaration of love and promises of better times to come, how he thinks of her every second of every day and knows that one day, they will be alone again. She understands every word he has said to her on the writing paper to her, she knows she should feel shame but doesn't, the time she spent alone with Martin before he left were special to both of them and will remain their secret forever more. Grace wants nothing more than to be alone with Martin again and she will wait as long as it takes. Her concentration is broken when Alice shouts, "Oysters!"

Grace is momentarily confused, then she sees that Alice is standing near to a fallen rotted tree, growing on the aged soft bark are a cluster of white stubby stalked mushrooms with a light brown cap that cover and protects the fine white, hairless gills below. Alice has put down her basket and is gently picking the mushrooms and putting them into the basket before covering them with a tea cloth,

"You seem to have plenty there Alice"

Alice nods, "More than enough for Granny to make soup with"

Alice goes on to tell Grace that the soup is thick with potatoes, onion and carrot all cooked in a lovely homemade chicken stock, the mushrooms giving the soup a distinctive, almost a nutty liquorice taste, Grace admits to Alice that she has never tried them in a soup or in anything else.

"You must try some of Grannies, it is super delicious!" Alice says excitedly,

"Come on Alice, let's move on"

They are both back on the track, Sauncy wood has been left behind them, Holcroft Spring with its thin woodland is on their left and open fields to their right, the fields are undisturbed until they reach Turnershall Farm and Hollybush cottages, both can just be seen in the distance. The sun is still behind them as they head north on the track toward Whitepightle Wood, it feels warm on their backs, not summer hot but autumn warm, it is before midday and long shadows lie in front of both of them, mirroring their every move but always ahead of them on the quarter of a mile walk to the wood. They leave the bright autumnal sunshine and enter the small wood, the temperature drops significantly and both Alice and Grace pull their cardigan and jacket together at the front, toward the centre of the wood behind a group of grand oak trees that are surrounded by fallen acorns, stand three tall grandiose sweet chestnut trees, the high branches still clinging onto some of the delicious nuts, concealed within the ball like cases covered in tiny spikes, it has been windy over the past few nights so a large crop of freshly fallen fruit lies on the ground, both carefully remove the sweet fruits from their casings, being stuck by the spikes more than a few times.

"We should roast these in front of the fire at Granny's this afternoon"

"I recall you saying that these were for chestnut soup?"

Alice thinks for a moment, "I did, but we have mushrooms for soup, so we can roast the sweet chestnuts"

"Let's see what Mary has to say first"

The fruits collected, and a large amount at that, they leave the small woodland, passing by 3 tall and graceful ash trees, the canopies of these trees seem as one forming a huge dome at the top of their tall and strong trunks, the small, single winged fruits of these trees lie on the ground. Back on the track they head in an easterly direction, toward Raisins Farm, stopping on the way to collect the blood red coloured berries from Hawthorn that grows freely in the hedgerows either side of the track.

"Granny makes jelly with these berries, it is lovely, but I have tried them before she boils them, and they are nasty to taste" Alice pulls a face as she says this.

They pass Raisins Farm, the farmhouse is a mid-17th century timber framed building, the walls of old red brick with thick old timbers exposed to the elements, a plain tiled roof has two chimney stacks, both have black smoke coming from them, the smoke rises straight up into the midday sky, the farm is as quiet as the grave, the only sign of life being the two smoking chimneys. They climb a low fence and walk into a field, following the hedgerows that lead them past Turnershall farm, this is as quiet as Raisins farm only the gentle sound of cows lowing in the barn carries across the quiet fields, they pick up a footpath that takes them from the farm to Hollybush cottages, Grace tells Alice that she knows one lady that lives here in one of these cottages, Mrs Smith, her son, curiously named Dolphin, farms both Mackerye End Farm and Castle farm, the latter having originally been called both Causwell Farm and then Cresswell farm at different times over generations, he took on both farms when his father, also called Dolphin, had died in 1902. They carry on, walking past Mackerye End Farm, it has a large red brick and timber framed farmhouse with ageing brown tiles on its sunken roof, the farmhouse is surrounded by long barns, these are much younger than the farmhouse, they have red tiled roofs with strong wooden frames and walls, they see a man in the yard pulling a bale of hay on a cart from one barn to another.

A short distance from the farm is Mackerye End House, a large 14th century manor house, Grace points out a date plaque that is placed on the east gable end of the house, 1665, this is when the large pointed 'Dutch' wood gable was added to the front of the building. This building is also built of red brick with prominent projected wings at either end of the house each having a small window and a large Tudor style chimney stack at their end, they have three octagonal shafts with the centre shaft patterned by the bricks being laid in a different style to the outer stacks. At the centre of the large red tiled roof, standing in between a pair of casement windows, is a bell turret made of wood with its round grey roof coming to a point, it is here where a large weathervane stands proudly atop it. The middle floor has a total of seven windows, two large sash windows in each wing and five smaller sash windows stand uniformly in a line between the wings, the ground floor has two identical sash windows on each wing, two windows stand each side of the central porch with a brick arch surrounded by a square brick frame. At the back of the house and out of view is a huge, shorter chimney stack, said to be the oldest surviving part of the house and believed to have been built during the reign of Henry VII. The grounds are vast and are protected by a tall brick walls surrounding the sides and rear of the property, to the front is a long drive and at the entrance are large iron gates, thick, perfectly topiarised yew hedges stand proudly protecting the front side, two tulip trees stand guard on each side of the gravelled track to the house. They walk past the grand manor house, following the track as it bears to the right and past the chalk pit, here they pass two men both Alice and Grace know them, Frank Catlin, and Arthur Todd, they are Ploughmen for Dolphin Smith and they are heading in the direction of the farm, both touch the front of their flat caps and say,

"Good af'noon ladies"

"Good afternoon Mr Todd, Mr Catlin" Grace speaks to them, Alice remains silent,

"What you got there then?" asks Mr Catlin, Grace, a little shy, answers,

"Horse chestnuts, mushrooms and hawthorn berries"

"Bet you got those chestnuts at Whitepightle wood" Catlin says, Alice nods and the men bid the ladies a good day and walk toward the farm. Just a short walk on is where a footpath begins and takes them toward the common and onto the lane commonly used as an access route to the Lower road that, depending on your direction of travel, will take you to either Luton or Wheathampstead, here they cross and walk past the three terraced thatched cottages with its low roof beams and old windows, each having a diamond shaped window lattice, the walls, built from faded old red brick, are supported by heavy wooden beams. The forge door is open, Mr Bingham is busy at work, his wife runs the small grocery store and post office near to the Malta pub he looks up and waves at the ladies, they wave back, looking through the large doors of the smithy they can see that Mr Bingham is wearing his usual leather apron, a heavy hammer in his right hand, his left holding a glowing white iron bar with a pair of huge tongs, he is hitting the burning hot end with the regularity of a ticking metronome. They reach the foot bridge, stopping in the middle of it to look at the river as it flows slowly away from them, tickling the lowest branches of the weeping willow trees that hang at water level,

"Shall we walk along the river Grace?" asks Alice,

"Yes, let's do that" is the reply.

They step off of the bridge and follow a thin track that runs alongside the River Lea, they are walking in the opposite direction to the flow, the water is deep and clear, long green weeds can be seen stretching out as the water tries to take them but they cling onto the stones on the river bed, ahead of them are two men sitting on small folding seats, both are flicking their cane fishing rods in and out the fly and line lifting and landing on the moving water with absolute ease and perfection, Grace can see trout in the river but none are biting on the men's fly hooks. The men are of similar age both in their early sixties, Alice has seen them both in town before but doesn't know them, Grace does, the men stand as the ladies' pass, both lifting their caps to them,

"Good afternoon gentlemen" Grace speaks to them,

"Ladies" both men bow slightly toward them, Alice giggles, both men notice and smile.

"Is that you young Grace?" asks one of the men.

He has pure white hair with a sharp parting just off centre, his hair is unfashionably long in comparison to many of the men in town, it is brushed smartly at both sides over the tops of his ears, his large moustache is perfectly trimmed and as white as his hair, he is dressed in a dark three piece suit with a clean light blue shirt with an open collar and a navy blue cravat, his soft cap is still in his hands, Grace replies to him,

"It is sir, may I introduce my companion, this is Alice"

The gent bows slightly toward Alice again, Grace continues,

"Alice this is Mr Richard Lydekker from the Lodge House in town"

"Very nice to meet you Alice" he points to his fishing partner, "This is my younger brother, Captain Arthur Lydekker" who also bows ever so lightly toward Grace,

"Nice to meet you Alice"

He is a slightly smaller man than his brother, his hair is darker but not as thick as Richards, his is thinning slightly on top, he also has a thick brush moustache, but it is not as exuberant as his older brothers, he is also wearing a dark three piece suit, it has a feint pinstripe, he is wearing a crisp white shirt with a tie secured tightly at the starched winged collar. He turns to Grace, "Lovely to see you Grace, how are your mother, father, and young Patrick?"

"They are all well sir, thank you"

Alice speaks to Arthur, very quietly and softly, "Are you in the Army Captain Lydekker?"

"I was Alice, a long time ago, the Bedfordshire regiment, I served from '71 to '82, that is where the 'Captain' title comes from, I now live at Tollgate Cottage in town with my good lady wife"

"My brother is in Belgium with the Bedfordshire's" she whispers, "He is now a Lance Corporal"

"That is marvellous" replies Arthur, "Both Richards boys are in the army, waiting to go" he looks at his brother, who continues,

"My youngest, Cyril, has just joined the 5th Battalion Bedfordshire's as a Subaltern, he is commissioned from the 1st Hertfordshire Royal Artillery, my eldest, Gerard, is due to be commissioned to the same battalion as his brother in the Bedfordshire's at the end of the month, he is also with the 1st Hertfordshire's at this time"

Alice answers, "Martin is with the 2nd Battalion"

Captain Lydekker smiles at her, "The Bedfordshire's are a superb regiment, your Brother will be fine with them, I assure you"

"Thank you, sir," replies Alice, tears are forming in her eyes, both Richard and Arthur can see this, Richard tugs his brothers' sleeve,

"Come on Captain, we have trout to catch" both men replace their caps and retake their seats, casting lines in opposite directions, Alice and Grace bid them both goodbye.

"Are you all right Alice" asks Grace, Alice nods and wipes her eyes with her sleeve, they walk on in silence, arm in arm, under the low overhanging branches of the trees on the riverbank, they cross over the river using the two footbridges that pass over the main river and the freshwater spring stream that runs alongside the river lea from the watercress beds, they reach the Lower Luton road and turn left, the cottage is a few hundred yards in front of them, Grace knows that Alice is looking at the cottage, she nudges her young companion,

"Are you looking for David by any chance?"

Alice puts her hand up to her mouth, "Grace!" she exclaims, "I don't know what you mean!"

Grace throws her head back and laughs, with arms still linked they cross the green in front of the Gibraltar castle pub, walking toward the cottage. In the garden the four soldiers are relaxing outside, they have just returned from the East station,

"Corp, do you think that there was more movement this weekend than on any other Saturday or Sunday since we have been here?"

Bragg nods, "I do Jake, things are afoot I think"

"What does that mean Corp?"

"Well Dave", replies Bragg, "With the amount of movement of vehicles and munitions from our little station, I don't think it will be long before we are moving from here and off to the jolly war"

Dave, stares, wide eyed his face becoming paler, "I heard that the war will be over soon anyway, we are winning, aren't we?"

Bragg looks across at Jake and Bob, both shrug their shoulders,

"I don't know where you got that from" Bob talks to Dave, "Did you hear that us and the French have now declared war on the Ottoman Empire, the Russians are currently fighting in the Caucuses, there is also fighting in Iraq, Africa and even in China, the bloody Germans are everywhere mate"

Dave looks shocked, "Are you sure Bob?"

"I am, this won't be over anytime soon Dave"

"Hello boys!"

The four young soldiers look over the fence and see Grace and Alice waving at them, they all wave back, Dave instantly has colour returning to his face, he shouts,

"Hello Alice, how are you?"

His three companions jeer at him, Alice blushes, Bragg speaks firmly to the others, out of earshot of the ladies, "Not a word about the war and the fighting, not a single word" He points at each of them, and they nod in understanding, Grace and Alice are standing by the gate.

"Cup of tea ladies?" asks Bob, they look at each other, Alice nods, almost imperceptibly, to Grace,

"That will be lovely Bob, we have walked miles today"

Bob looks at the basket that Alice is carrying, "What secrets are in there Alice?"

"Mushrooms, sweet chestnuts and hawthorn berries for jam"

Bob rubs his belly theatrically, "I love sweet chestnuts, cut a cross in the top, chuck them in the hot coals on the fire and take them out when they go black, lovely"

Alice speaks to him, "Would you like some, we have plenty here?"

Bob looks at Dave, "Is that range fire going well Dave?"

Dave tells him that it is.

"Make a mash of tea young man, the ladies must be gasping after their walk" he opens the gate for Alice and Grace.

Dave looks at Alice, "Hello Alice" he says quietly, she replies,

"Hello David"

She hands him a small handful of chestnuts, their hands touch for a second, both look at each other, Jake whistles,

"That's enough Private Stevens" Bragg instructs, "Alice, would you please help young Dave with the tea?"

Alice doesn't reply but nods,

"Thank you" Bragg says, he looks at Dave, "Off you go then Dave, cut those chestnuts and throw them on the fire mate, they won't take long"

Dave turns to the Corporal, "Corp, can I break out the Huntley and Palmers please?"

"Of course, anything for these ladies"

Dave and Alice enter the kitchen, when they are out of earshot, Grace smiles at the three remaining soldiers,

"You rotter's!" she looks at all of them, "Leave them alone, they are both embarrassed!"

They all laugh, Bragg asks Grace, "Have you heard from your fella?"

It is Graces turn to blush a little, but she tells them all about Martin, they all listen intently, knowing it will be their turn soon enough. They are still talking when Alice and Dave appear from the house, Dave is carrying a tray with a large teapot, mugs, sugar and milk balanced on it, Alice has a tin of biscuits, with the words '*SUPERIOR READING BISCUITS*' inside a red circle on a blue background, ornate gold swirls are at each corner or the tin, in the middle part of the tin, are the words, again in white letters but on a blue background, the words, '*HUNTLEY & PALMERS*', in the very centre of the tin, in a red oblong banner in white letters it says '*RICH TEA*'.

Grace and the three soldiers are finishing a conversation, it is Bragg that is speaking when Dave and Alice appear,

"So, reports say that the Irish MP, Arthur O Neill was killed two days ago in Belgium, it's not in the papers, Westerman told me this morning, news travels fast these days"

Dave, hearing this information stands still, the deathly greyness returning to cover his face,

"Dave, stop buggering about and get that tea on" Jake shouts at him, he then turns to the ladies, "Apologies for the language ladies, but he is a bit slow at times"

Dave walks slowly to where the group are talking, he puts the tray down on a large piece of circular wood that they use as a seat, Jake ruffles his hair,

"Good lad Dave, you will do all right"

Dave nods, Bragg sees that Dave looks frightened, "Dave lad, get those biscuits out will you" he turns to the ladies, "Another present from the Methodists"

Dave looks at Bragg who winks at him quickly, "Serve the ladies first Dave" he looks at Jake and Bob, "Leave the other two till last"

Dave manages a smile, "Yes Corp" he turns to Alice, "Would you like milk and sugar Alice?"

* * *

The final train on the evening of Tuesday November 10th has just left, no passengers alight or embark, only military machines and artillery are on this train, none of them has any idea where the final destination for all this kit is but they all know it will almost certainly be France or Belgium,

"Cup of tea then back to the cottage lads?" Bragg asks the others, they all agree,

"Shall I make the brew corp?"

"Dave, you already know the answer to that one" he nods toward the room used by the staff from the station, "Go on" Dave walks away, Bragg calls after him and he turns to face his corporal, "Good lad"

Dave walks away smiling.

"Belay that tea making order lad!"

The voice of RSM Westerman carries across the platforms, they all look across as Westerman crosses to their platform using the wooden walkway over the tracks, Bob looks at the others, confused, "How the hell did he know that tea was being made?"

"Don't ever question the RSM Bob" Bragg replies, the men all stand to attention, "Sir"

Westerman looks over at Dave, "You too lad, get your arse over here"

"Yes sir" Dave breaks into a run, lining up with the other three.

"Pub gentlemen, ten minutes"

"Sir?" questions Bragg

"Did you not understand Corporal?" the RSM growls, "I want you all in the pub in ten minutes, not nine, not eleven, but ten" he looks at the four soldiers, "Is that clear lads?"

"Sir!" the four voices uniformly reply as Westerman marches away.

"What is going on?" asks Dave

"I have no idea Dave, but whatever it is, it can't be good" Bragg replies slowly,

"Best we make a move my lads, caps on and none of the usual slouching home"

The four men set off for the Malta pub, all of them hoping that Mary doesn't tell the RSM how often they are in her pub and how much ale they sup. Bragg enters first, followed by Jake, Bob then Dave, caps are removed as they enter, a voice rings out from across the bar,

"Now then Abe boy, I do believe we have a rematch to get done"

Bragg looks across at Ernest Almond who is sat with his brother Jack, they own a horse and cart and deliver anything that needs delivering locally, Bragg quickly steps over to Ernest and Jack, "Not now Ernie, the RSM is in, best behaviour and all that mate"

Ernie takes a long pull on his beer, putting down the empty glass, "Dawn is expecting me home soon, so lucky for you boy!"

Bragg thanks him and they agree to rematch next time they meet, Brag returns to the others, Westerman is sat in the corner of the pub, cap off and a pint of beer in front of him,

"Mary, my lads are here if you please" he says, Mary looks at the soldiers, "What will it be gentlemen?"

They look at her, puzzled, "I have no idea either" she fibs, Westerman has already told her the news, "Eddie came in and said you would be here in a few minutes and that you were to be given a pint each"

They again look at each other, Mary asks again, "What will it be?" quietly adding, "The usual?"

Bob steps in, "Yes, please Mary, Corp, you and Jack go sit with the RSM, Dave and I will carry the pints over"

As the corporal and the private walk to sit with the senior NCO, Mary is busy pouring four pints, Dave turns to Bob, "Should we be worried Bob?"

Bob picks up the first pint, takes a sip, leaving a healthy creamy white moustache on his upper lip, he lifts the second pint, indicating that Dave should pick up the others,

"Yes" he replies, "We should all be worried"

They walk over to join their fellow soldiers, RSM Westerman is halfway through speaking as they arrive,

"...so good work at the train station lads, no complaints at all, in fact the station master has been very complementary about your punctuality, politeness and professionalism" he looks at Bob and Dave as they arrive and hand out the beer, Westerman raises his glass to the soldiers,

"Cheers men, very well done"

They touch glasses and all say 'Cheers', Bragg speaks up first, "What is this all about sir?"

Westerman drinks half of his beer before putting it down on the table, "We are leaving town; deployment orders are in"

They all look at each other, Dave looks horrified,

"Calm down Dave" says Jake, "We all knew it was coming"

"Like death, you know it is coming, you just don't know when!" Bob joins in,

"I know" is Dave's short reply, Jake continues,

"When are we off sir?"

"The 16th, next Monday we will all muster in the town on the common"

Bragg, Bob, and Jake look at the RSM, Dave is silent, Westerman speaks,

"Don't worry lads, I won't make you walk to town to march all the way back again, you four will muster at East station at 0600 hours on Monday morning, I will arrive shortly after, the train from Luton Hoo will arrive loaded with kit for our transfer"

"Where are we going to be based now sir?" Bob asks

"Bocking, Essex, wherever the hell that is" Westerman finishes his pint with ease,

"The Battalion are marching there, a two day over land march, setting off at 0900 hours on the 16th to march to Harlow, a distance of twenty six miles" he looks at the soldiers, they remain silent, "Overnight in

Harlow then another fourteen mile jaunt to Dunmow, before you ask, I have no idea where that is either, an overnight there and then onto Bocking, arriving sometime on the 18th, tents and bivouacs will be used for the overnight stays"

He looks at Bragg, waving his empty glass, Bragg nods, he looks at the bar and Mary lets him know that she has seen him,

"Thank you corporal, now for the good news, you lucky four will not be marching with the battalion" he looks at them for a reaction, smiles from three of them, one of them, Dave, still looks terrified, "You are to get on the military supply train, it will stop at Welwyn, you are to make your way from there on the next train to London and then on to Bocking, once there you are to locate the convent" He looks at his paperwork, "The Chapel of the Immaculate Conception, an order of Franciscan Sisters reside there, we will nearly all be billeted there for the duration, in tents and such like" He hands Bragg a few sheets of paper and a map, "That corporal is your tasks to complete before we arrive on the 18th, you will locate and liaise with the Royal Engineers at three locations" he points on the map, "Here at Panfield, 2 miles from our billet, here at Marks Farm, 3 miles from out billet and finally, here at Black Notley, 4 miles from our billet"

Bragg responds, "What is required of us at these locations' sir?"

"Trench digging lad, under the supervision of the Royal engineers, we are digging a series of trenches and defensive lines near to the Essex coast, just in case the Hun fancy a trip over the channel"

Dave is still quiet, he has hardly touched his beer,

"Drink up Dave lad" says Bob, "It might be your last chance to have pint or two"

Dave responds quickly, with fear in his voice, "What do you mean, my last chance?"

"Once again Dave, you need to calm down, all I meant by it is that we will be back in billets with the rest of the battalion by this time next week, I don't suppose we will get visiting access to the local pubs in Essex"

"You certainly will not private" Westerman replies.

Dave sips his beer,

"Or we will all be dead, killed by the invading Hun!" Jake laughs as he speaks, Bob and Bragg also laugh, Dave is obviously mortified by Jakes words.

Mary arrives with a tray laden with five pints of beer,

"There you go gentlemen" she looks at Bragg, "That will be one and three Abe"

Bragg puts a shilling and three pennies into her waiting palm, he raises his glass,

"Cheers and long life to all" he says, Jake and Bob laugh out loud,

"Bloody hell Corp, you must be joking! long life indeed"

They all laugh, with the exception of Dave who sips at his beer.

Westerman finishes his beer in one long pull and stands up,

"Remember lads, we will be deployed to France or Belgium, it's a case of when, not if, so prepare yourselves" The four soldiers stand as the RSM puts on his cap,

"Corporal, a word please" He nods at his soldiers and takes his empty glass to the bar,

"Another one Eddie?" Mary asks,

"No, thank you Mary, I have work to complete in town, they have changed our webbing from the familiar 1908 pattern to a new leather thing, type 1914 the army call it, the lads are having problems with it, so it needs sorting"

"Will you be back before you leave town?"

"I will" he tells Mary "Wednesday or Thursday, to check on this lot"

Mary walks away, speaking as she takes the dirty glasses to be washed, "They need checking, that's for sure"

Westerman turns to Bragg, "Corporal, the whole Battalion is required to attend church on Sunday, a sort of farewell, most of us will be at St Nicks or St Johns, one of you will have to represent us at the Methodist chapel" he nods his head to the side, indicating he means the chapel opposite the cottage"

"Yes sir, no problem sir"

"I will be back on Wednesday or Thursday, to have a final pint in here and to make sure you and your lads are ready for the off"

"Will that be Wednesday or Thursday sir?"

Westerman grins at Corporal Bragg, "Good try lad, good try, be on your toes I might visit on both days, it may be earlier, it all depends on what takes my fancy"

Smiling, Bragg replies, "Yes sir, of course sir"

Westerman puts on his cap, "Corporal"

"Yes sir?"

"Don't let the others rag Shefford too much, that boy is shit scared"

Bragg opens his mouth to protest, Westerman lifts his pace stick and cocks his head,

"That is not a request Corporal"

Bragg tells him that he understands, Westerman speaks as he is leaving, "He will get used to the idea of war" he straightens his cap, "He will have to"

He leaves and Bragg goes back to the others, Bob and Jack are laughing like hyenas, Dave is almost in tears,

"What's going on lads?" he asks Bob and Jack, the former wipes his eyes,

"Sorry Corp, we are just ribbing young Dave about going over the channel to scrap with the Hun, we say that it all sounds bloody marvellous, sadly Dave does not agree" he playfully punches Dave on the arm, "You don't agree, do you mate?"

"Enough Bob" Bragg instructs, Bob begins to protest,

"But Corp, it is only a bit of fun"

"I said enough Private Beeson" he looks at Jake, "Same goes for you Stevens"

Both men stop laughing and do as instructed, Bragg sits down, he speaks to Dave,

"Are you OK Dave?"

"Yes Corp" he replies, "Bob and Jake are only having a bit of fun, I am sure of it"

Bob and Jake move in closer to Dave and put their arms around him, both kiss him on the cheek, Dave smiles for the first time today, Bragg rolls his eyes and says out loud, "May Yahweh help me with you bunch"

* * *

Sunday 15th November

Alice and Grace are out walking along the river, they are arm in arm,

"It is not fair" states Alice, "They all leave tomorrow and we won't see them again"

Grace gently pulls Alice closer to her as they pass the mill,

"Don't say that Alice, they are only going to Essex and from what Abe tells me, they will be back this way for weapons practice at Luton Hoo regularly"

Alice brightens up a little, they stop at the double gated entrance to the mill, a large farm horse towing a long trailer is approaching on the road, they both know it will swing across and through the gates, the driver waves at them both as he passes,

"Morning ladies", he lifts his flat cap off his head,

"Morning Mr Titmuss" they say together as they wave back at him then walk on, toward the three thatched cottages, turning right the forge is in front of them its doors are shut and it is silent, even the blacksmith has a day of rest on a Sunday. They cross the river, deciding to walk across the open area toward the watercress beds and past the cottage, the overnight rain will have made the track alongside the river very muddy, they reach the Marquis of Granby pub.

"Early start this morning ladies?"

George Parsons, the landlord is sweeping leaves up from the courtyard of the pub,

"Hello Mr Parsons, just out for a stroll before Alice goes back to Maple cottages for the week"

"Please give my regards to your Grandmother Alice, I am certain to see her at the next licenced victuallers meeting"

Alice tells Mr Parsons that she will be pleased to pass on the message, they say 'Good morning' to each other, and the ladies walk onto the green grass past the parish boundary post, clearly marking the two parish boundaries, they remain in the Parish of Wheathampstead as they walk back toward the river. They can see George Titmuss in the large courtyard of the mill on the other side of the river, he is unloading sacks from the back of the trailer, holding the main bulk of the sack on one shoulder and gripping the top of it with a strong, straight arm then walking slowly with the heavy load across to a nearby barn, they walk to the footpath leading down from Station Road, they turn onto it and cross the river using the footbridges to get to the road that will take them to the cottage. As they approach they can see one soldier standing by the gate, Grace hears Alice take a deep breath,

"Is that David?" asks Grace, Alice nods quickly in response, Grace releases herself from Alice's interlocked arm, "I will cut through by the Gibraltar castle and get home that way"

"But..." Alice begins to say, she is interrupted by Grace,

"But nothing Alice" she says firmly but with a huge grin on her face, "I will pop back to the pub in an hour or so to see you before you leave for your Aunt and Uncles"

Alice hugs her, "Thank you, Grace, you won't forget to come and see me will you"

"Of course, I won't forget" she walks away and crosses the road, "I will see you later, good luck"

Alice is confused, "Good luck Grace, what for?"

Grace laughs and walks away, Alice continues toward the cottage, Dave is opening the gate and stepping through to the road, he is in his khaki tunic, buttoned all the way to the collar, his cap is under his arm, trousers are clean, and puttees are fitted correctly, his ammunition boots are clean and polished,

"Hello David, you look very smart this morning"

David mumbles a thanks to Alice, "I have to go to church this morning, the other lads are in town at the churches there"

The pair remain in an embarrassed silence for a few moments, Dave breaks it,

"It is a shame we don't have our number two dress uniforms here; they have been left at barracks; we all look smart in that"

"Is it very different to this one David?"

He nods at her with enthusiasm,

"The tunic is scarlet red with white collar and cuffs, it has seven shiny metal buttons down the front, each one bearing the image of the Royal Arms, our trousers are dark blue with a thick scarlet strip down each leg" he emphasises this point by running his right index finger down the side of his khaki trousers, "A bright white belt with metal buckle and a dark blue round forage cap, with scarlet piping around the crown" he again uses his finger to demonstrate, "The badge of the Notts and Derby regiment in the middle of the cap has to be shiny and clean"

Alice takes one step toward him, "What time are you leaving tomorrow David?"

"We have to be at the station before six in the morning, then travel onto London" he looks at Alice, "What about you?"

"I will be back at Maple cottages by mid-afternoon today"

She ventures one step further toward him, he shuffles his boots on the ground, covering the shiny caps with a delicate layer of brown dust, she suddenly steps close to him and takes his hands in hers, crushing his cap under his arm, she whispers,

"You will be careful won't you David, you will look after yourself"

He stutters his words, she can see his eyes glistening,

"I will Alice, I have to, I will do what I have to do, it needs to be done"

She lets go of his hands suddenly when a voice speaks from behind them,

"Good morning Alice" she turns to see the Reverend Wesley Woolmer, a man in his mid-thirties, dressed in a black coat and waistcoat with the thick white ministerial collar underneath, pin striped dark trousers and sturdy black shoes, he has a small round hat sitting squarely on his head, he has a round face and round glasses,

"Reverend Woolmer, good morning"

"May I introduce Mr Henry Salisbury" Alice, Dave, and Henry all nod at one another,

"Mr Salisbury is a member of the congregation at Leyton Road, but is here with us this morning to deliver a sermon"

Alice stands back, "Reverend Woolmer, this is David…" she struggles to continue as she does not remember Dave's surname, he takes over,

"Private David Shefford, 8th Battalion Sherwood Foresters, 46th Midlands Division"

Both men shake his hand, Rev Woolmer continues, "Splendid, are you the young man attending chapel this morning, I had the pleasure of meeting your Regimental Sergeant Major last Wednesday as he was leaving the Malta public house, he mentioned one of you chaps would be in the congregation, representing your Battalion"

"Yes sir, that is me sir"

"Shall we walk, the chapel is just over the road" he indicates toward the chapel with his right hand, Mr Salisbury sets off, followed by Rev Woolmer, Dave turns to Alice,

"Goodbye Alice, it has been so nice to meet you and to know you"

He hurriedly walks to catch up with the two men who are now entering the grounds of the Methodist church, the Reverend and Mr Salisbury shaking hands with members of the congregation as they arrive and pass through the small metal gate onto the sloping path up to the chapel door, he turns around before he enters, smiles at Alice, and lifts his hand to her, she gently waves back, then he is gone.

Alice runs from the cottage to the pub, tears streaming down her face as she passes the church on the opposite side of the road, she is so upset that she doesn't see Dave standing on the path outside of the church, nor does she hear him say,

"Goodbye Alice"

Just over an hour later, Alice is heading back to the cottage with the keys in her hand, she has told Mary that she needs to collect some warmer clothes from the room at the back of the cottage and that she hopes to meet Grace who has promised to come and see her. The congregation is leaving the church, she slows her walk, Henry Salisbury approaches her, "Hello, it's Alice, isn't it?"

"Yes sir" she replies

"If you are looking for the young soldier, he left the church soon after the service started, he did not feel too well apparently"

Alice thanks him for letting her know, she moves off hurriedly crossing the road toward the cottage, she arrives at the gate, it is open, she notices that the front door is also wide open, something makes her look down the garden. She can see David underneath the Yew tree, he is on his knees and appears to be praying, she smiles and walks through the gate, "David, what are you doing?" she asks as she walks toward him.

It is then that she sees that he is not praying.

She screams, loud enough that men from the church run across to where she stands, frozen to the spot, unable to move. Her screams are replaced with sobbing, uncontrollable sobbing, she falls to her knees, one of the arriving men kneels next to her, Rev Woolmer arrives, "Alice, whatever is wrong?" he asks,

She cannot answer, she points to the Yew Tree, several of the men run down the garden to the base of the tree and to where Private David Shafford is. He is on his knees, leaning forward, a rope tied tightly around his neck stops him from falling onto his face, his arms hang limply by his sides, the rope is looped and tied around one of the lowest branches on the tree, it is taut between the branch and the neck of the young soldier. His face is contorted, seemingly taking in a final agonising view of the world he feared so much, his bulging eyes with vivid red lines showing clearly against the whites are open, as is his mouth, his lips and tongue are blue and grotesquely swollen. The men lift him gently but quickly, one of them produces a knife and cuts the rope, David is laid out and the rope around his neck removed, Alice can see that his body is limp and lifeless,

"Alice?"

She looks up and sees Grace entering the garden,

"Alice" she repeats, "Whatever has happened"

Alice falls into her arms as Grace kneels beside her, Grace looks at Rev Woolmer, a voice calls from the Yew Tree,

"Reverend Woolmer!" He looks toward the man speaking to him, "I think you had better come down here please"

Woolmer looks at Grace,

"What is going on Reverend?" she asks.

He stands up and Grace can see the body of David Shafford lying on the ground, a length of rope lies next to him,

"Oh my" is all she can say, she holds Alice tightly and can feel the girl's body moving as she sobs uncontrollably, she strokes her hair gently,

"My poor Alice, my poor Alice"

1915

CHAPTER SIX

The year starts very much as '14 had finished, the men from the 2nd Battalion Bedfordshire regiment are hugely depleted in numbers both in officers and from the rank and file, since arriving in Belgium just under three months ago so many have been killed, many more injured, some of these later proving to be fatal wounds, men known to each other, who fought alongside each other, now lie with each other on the battlefields of the Western Front.

January brings snow and sleet in the trenches, the men are cold and having spent New Year's Eve and New Year's Day in the wet and cold knee deep mud, it is of great relief to them all on Saturday the 2nd of January when the 1st Wiltshire's arrive to relieve them. The battalion leave the trenches in cold sleeting rain to march to billets at Pont de la Justice, no one cares what the billets are like they just need to be dry and warm for the two days they will spend there before returning to the front line.

The remainder of the month is spent on the front line or in billets at Pont de la Justice or Fleurbaix, shelling by the enemy is rapidly becoming a normal routine for all of them. Five high explosive shells land near to A and B companies on the 26th, one man is wounded in the shoulder by shrapnel, it is a miracle that no one is dead let alone wounded by this ferocious attack. It is two days later when the regiment is joined by its newest officer from the 3rd Suffolk regiment, acting Captain Shapter, a nice young man with a clear thinking head on his shoulders.

He is dead three days later, on the 31st, the month finishes just as it began.

February might as well have been January, the same trenches, billets, rain, sleet and snow, the only new development is the arrival of four officers from the 5th and 7th Canadians, who arrived at the billets on the 28th having recently arrived in France, they visit the trenches on the evening of the 28th, the conditions, the mud and cold are a huge shock to them.

March begins with the Bedfordshire's again spending days in the trenches, moving back and forth to billets at Estaires or at Laventie. Estaires is the preferred location for the battalion as it has a full army field kitchen permanently based there, the French people that the men billet with are very generous with the little food that they have but most of the men are not keen on the French grub, they also want to eat their evening meal at five or five thirty in the evening, the French hosts usually eat after nine in the evening. The army kitchen is always alive with activity, men watch the meat being butchered, no one ever asks what the meat is and as long as it isn't bully beef they will eat any cooked meat, huge urns of boiling vegetables, picked and taken from the fields surrounding them, those that haven't been subjected to the daily, constant, and fearful bombardment from the enemy, wood is chopped for open fires to roast the meat on and potatoes are peeled, lots and lots of potatoes are peeled. The 2nd regiment Bedfordshire's are grateful for any hot meal the army gives them, a decent brew of tea is what they all want most of all, tea in the trenches is made with water that isn't the cleanest, it has a strange tang to its taste. Estaires is a small town, busy with buildings at its centre and rural at its furthest outskirts, the British Expedition Forces have easily trebled the number of residents living in town, many are billeted with locals, many in barns and outhouses of the numerous farms with their beautifully thatched roofs, ornate windows, and wooden boarded walls. What most of the men like and also hate about this town, is the many trees that surround it, at this time of year they are tall thin, bare trunked with only an occasional branch here and there that stick out at angles. The trees are loved and hated because it is these trees that they pass by as they march into town, to see the farmhouses, the family homes, and offices of the Mairie at is centre, the 15th century town hall is always a striking and welcoming sight for the men returning from the trenches only a few miles away. It is also these trees that the men pass through on their way back to the trenches, leaving the relative safety of the town that has been held by the BEF since war began, back to trenches that sit in vast areas of open land that has been flattened and ruined by artillery shells that smash into its very heart, taking the life from the soil, leaving huge water filled holes, bodies float lifelessly in these waters and bodies lie all over the battlefields, it is not safe to go and move them for burial. Any of the towns they are billeted in, be they destroyed, damaged, even burning, are always preferred by all of them to the hell of these trenches in France. The battles in Flanders seem a lifetime ago although these battles in France the same, the trenches are the same, the noise of the shells landing is the same and your mates getting killed and wounded is the same.

It is hell.

It is going to get worse, and they all know it.

* * *

Martin is awake, it is just after midnight on Wednesday 10th March, having left his billet at Laventie a few hours ago he is having a cigarette and a mug of cocoa with Corporal Ernie Haines, they know each other having grown up in the same town, although Ernie lives at Cravells Road, a few miles from Martin's cottage, in the area of town known to both of them as 'the Bowling alley',

"You will never guess who I saw the day before yesterday" Ernie speaks, Martin shrugs without answering, Ernie takes a long drag of his cigarette, blows out the smoke and carries on,

"Herb Ward"

Martin looks at him with wide eyed astonishment,

"The policeman from town?"

"The very same" he blows more smoke out of his lungs, "He is with the Royal Field Artillery, they are working with several divisions of the Indian artillery, they are lined up a half mile or so ahead of us, just behind the front line"

Martin finishes his cocoa, throwing the dregs away, "Must be something to do with today's movement" he looks at his pocket watch, "We will know in a couple of hours; I will go and muster my lads in a few minutes or so"

Ernie scratches his head, "I wonder what Haig, Rawlinson and the rest of them have in store for us this time"

Martin again shrugs, he puts his cigarette out on the ground and slings his rifle, "Catch you later Ernie, stay safe today"

"Will do Martin" as Martin walks away, Ernie calls after him, "Congratulations"

Martin looks at him, confused,

"The promotion Corporal, well done mate, who is the new lance jack?"

"Another one of us boys from town, Albert Bandy got the stripe"

"That young sprog from Coldharbour! He isn't old enough to shave let alone be an NCO!"

"Young yes, but I have to tell you Ernie, he is a very fine soldier, gutsy and fearless"

Ernie smiles, Martin thanks him and waves as he walks toward where his lads are billeted, it is nearly time to start getting them mustered.

It is 0200 hours, the men are mustered, lined up quietly and nervously, Lance corporal Bandy is the NCO in charge as Martin and Sergeant 'Charlie' Chandler, who joined the 2nd battalion a month ago, replacing Sergeant Clibbon, who had been killed last month, they are being briefed with the other senior NCO's, the commanding officer. Lt Col Onslow is dishing out the roles and responsibilities for the regiment in today's push, the men are nervous, not knowing what they are expected to do today is worse than being on the front line, at least there everyone knows what to expect, shelling, machine gun and rifle fire is a certainty during any spell in these trenches, but standing here, not knowing if they are off to intercept the enemy, or to try and take a village back from the enemy or to be sent over the top for yet further attempts at gaining small amounts of ground.

Martin and Sergeant Chandler arrive back, the men are shuffling their feet and smoking cigarettes, they are told to gather round and listen carefully. The task for today is a huge one, two divisions of the German Jäger infantry are holding a small town called Neuve Chapelle 4 miles south of the battalions' current location, this will take them further into France and further away from the Belgium border some ten miles to the northeast. Four divisions from the BEF will be taking part in the assault, Lt Generals Haig's' first army, consisting of Lt General Rawlinson's IV corp, the 7th Infantry division with Brigadier General Watts in charge, the Bedfordshire regiment is part of the 7th, it also includes the 3rd Cavalry division, then the I corp, part of the 1st army, consisting of the 1st, 2nd and 3rd brigades and finally the 1st division Canadians with 4 divisions of Indian Gharwall soldiers who will support the attack providing artillery and machine gun support from a position to the northeast and the southwest of the town. Nearly forty thousand men are to move into and try to take the German trenches, this is the first deliberately planned offensive and direct attack on German lines and trenches that has been attempted since the outset of the war. The attack will begin with artillery fire from the Canadian, India and the BEF cannons, there are over five hundred of these shell firing beasts currently pointed at enemy positions in the town, and toward the outside of town, the German trenches are good targets as they are not very deep, only about three feet at best, they are stacked four feet high above ground with wood and sandbags. The attack trenches the BEF soldiers will be in to begin with are of a similar depth but don't have the added security of sandbags and wooden frames, these shallow firing positions in front of the main British army held lines and trenches are unprotected and dangerous places to be.

Sergeant Chandler tells the Bedfordshire's that they are to be the reserve battalion for the first wave, they will be taking up positions in trenches behind the Royal Scots Fusiliers who will make their first advance to the firing trenches, the 2nd Wiltshire's, the Princess of Wales Yorkshire's, and the Gordon Highlanders will be in positions a few hundred yards to the north, the Worcester's and a company from the Northern regiment are to the south of the Bedfordshire positions. Artillery will start just after first light, coming from the Canadians in the northeast and the Garhwalls to the southwest, the Indians are to be supported by a regiment of Ghurkhas and the men of the 3rd London regiment. To the northwest of the town, are the 23rd and 25th infantry brigades, made up from men of the West Yorkshire regiment, the Devon regiment, a company of Royal Engineers, the Irish Rifles, and the 13th London. In front of these men, also in trenches, are the 2nd Royal Berkshire, 2nd Lincolnshire, 2nd Middlesex and 2nd Rifle regiments.

At 0230 hours the Bedfordshire's begin their march from Laventie to their assembly positions, four miles to the south, to the other side of a town called Mauquissart, the march is completed in silence and at 0500 hours Martin and his men are in trenches just a hundred yards or so behind the Royal Scots Fusiliers who have now left the security of the deep trenches and are in the shallower firing trenches, even in the early morning darkness Martin can see the heads of the Scots easily above the trenches, rifles in front of them pointing across no-man's-land toward the enemy positions, there are enemy trenches almost everywhere surrounding their position, although in reserve Martin knows that they will be called into action at some point. Daybreak happens very slowly, starting at 0630 hours; the weak morning sun has no heat, and its bright winter light is highlighting the advanced positions of the BEF soldiers in the firing trenches.

Martin is standing next to two men, both from his hometown, Private Ernie Harris, born on the same day and the same year as Martin, is from Kinsborne Green a mile or so to the northwest of town, they had never met until they both joined the regiment, and Private Reg Pearce, two years younger than Martin and Ernie. The three men have their backs to the walls of the large trench, standing in between the tall, triangular wooden frames that strengthen these steep front walls, the frames are filled with logs, the triangular supports are set up a few feet apart and it is in one of the small gaps, in between the frames, where the men stand. Across from their position is a small structure, build in a similar fashion to a garden shed, but made from round logs and planks of wood, its roof is reinforced with several layers of sandbags, this is the battalion headquarters for the Bedfordshire's, as they look over they see another Kinsborne Green man, Corporal Henry Barnes as he leaves the HQ, he notices the three men looking at him, he walks over to them through the wet mud that swallows up the floor of this trench,

"What do you know Henry?" asks Ernie,

"That's Corporal to you Private" he smiles as he speaks to Ernie, they grew up together and know each other well,

"Any news for us Henry?" asks Martin, Henry shakes his head,

"Artillery will be going off at some point, but as to when that will be, no one seems to know, either that, or they are not telling us"

"I have had a little look over the top" Martin indicates above his head, "I can see the Scots fusiliers ahead of us, they are out of the main trench and in firing positions, I bet we move forward to their trenches when it all begins"

Martin shakes a cigarette out of a nearly full packet, he offers the others a smoke, Ernie and Henry accept, the three light their smokes at the same time, all three covering the flaring match with their hands as it is struck, it has become habit to cover any lit match even outside of the trench systems, especially at night, lighting a cigarette can give away your position to the enemy, so even though they are protected by a tall front trench wall and it is now light, they cover the naked flame out of habit. At 0730 hours the artillery starts, over five hundred guns firing constantly, the Indian battalions firing every one of their ninety cannon, eighteen pound shells land directly into the German lines and into positions in the town, the Canadian artillery regiment have howitzers, wheel mounted cannons that fire 4.5 inch and 6 inch shells, these are fired and reloaded at impressive rates of speed, the larger guns from the field artillery can be heard, but not seen, the distant rumble as they fire is followed a few seconds later by the devastating sound of the huge shells landing and destroying whatever target they have reached. The shelling lasts for over half an hour, thousands of shells are fired into the enemy positions, Martin assumes that the damage and loss of life is enormous. At 1030 hours, the battalion receive orders to move forward to the front line trenches, as they move out from their trench system, they are caught out in the open on a road, they come under intense shell and rifle fire, men are injured but Martin cannot see how many and how bad their wounds are due to the intensity and longevity of the attack, the battalion cannot advance to the trenches they are heading for, neither can they retreat to the rear trenches they have left, if they move they will be exposed and more men will be wounded or killed, they are all ordered to remain in file, lining the road either in ditches or squatting next to any cover they can find. They remain in this position for over six hours, the men are stiff and cold and when finally told to advance forward to support the Royal Scots Fusiliers, many are so cold and stiff that they find it difficult to get moving, Martin and the other NCOs encourage their men to get up and get moving and quickly, they all move as one and enter the old German trench system, on the right flank of the Scots fusiliers, they are almost immediately subjected to enemy shell fire.

"Take cover and remain in cover!" an order is shouted down the line, the Germans have left these trenches and have retreated back toward Neuve Chapelle, supported by intense artillery from the German cannons, the accuracy of their shell fire is astounding, even as they retreat the shells are hitting the trenches and surrounding areas, Martin throws himself to the bottom of his trench as a shell explodes only a few yards from where he is advancing forward, men lie all around him, they are all moving and seem to be alive, Eddie Odell and Arthur Darts are both sitting up, obviously dazed but seemingly unhurt, 'E.G.' Waller has his arm around Ernest Summerfield who is holding his cap in front of him, Martin can see a hole in it, he hears Waller assuring Summerfield that he has not been hit and that a bullet has gone through his cap without hitting him, Waller is laughing as he tells his friend that all is well, Sergeant Sid Fensome, who Martin believes is the man that issued the 'take cover order' is telling Corporal George Stringer and Private Horace Preece, a great football player and a supremely fit man, to run back to the Battalion HQ hut and report contact, the phone lines that have been extensively laid throughout the trenches are not working, they both run off into the trench system with the reports for the officers commanding. Martin asks if anyone is wounded, he is happy to get no injury reports from any of the men, another shell screams toward them, he watches as it explodes to his left where the Royal Scots Fusiliers are, it is a direct hit in the trench, he hears men screaming and orders being yelled, he cannot make out what the orders are over the noise surrounding him, he risks a quick look over the top of the trench. All he can see is vast areas of destroyed land, there are only a few trees remaining standing and they are stripped of any life, standing without branches or leaves, another shell is incoming, Martin dives to the bottom of the trench, landing in a pool of water and liquid mud, he feels the foul tasting fluid enter his mouth, he gags and lifts his head out of the mud only to be pushed back in as a soldier lands on top of him, he is winded and as he kneels up he looks and sees Eddie Odell standing over him,

"Sorry Corp" he says, his hand is outstretched, offering to help Martin to his feet, he accepts and is pulled to his feet, he wipes the mud from his face and eyes,

"You injured?" he asks Odell,

"No Corp" he replies, "But I am fed up being knocked onto my arse!"

Martin manages a smile, and he moves on further into the trench system with his fellow soldiers, Lt Wilkins calls the men to stop and rest, he and Sergeant Fensome call Martin over, he runs, keeping his head down as the trenches are not as deep here,

"Corporal, get the men to dig in here, we are to entrench here for the remainder of the day and probably the night" the Lt gives him the order and then moves back along the line, presumably to give other NCO's the order to get their men to dig in for the night.

Sergeant Fensome arrives and calls Martin over to him,

"Sid, what is it?" asks Martin,

"I need you to put a patrol together, Lt Wilkins will be taking a team and advancing to that tree line" he points northwest of their position, "It seems that the enemy has retreated from the trenches, but some have taken position up there, we need to know how strong their numbers are"

Martin immediately gets twelve others to join him, they wait for Lt Wilkins to arrive back at their position, Sid and Martin allow the chosen men to stand easy and have a smoke and a brew.

Lt Wilkins arrives fifteen minutes later, apologising to the men, telling them that the telephone system the British Army has in the trenches is a 'bloody disgrace', he had to run to Battalion HQ at the far end of this trench system, he also informs the men that the attack on the German trenches has, so far, gone well, trenches and areas in the town have been taken and held, but casualties are believed to be high, the initial battle only lasted a couple of hours, but here in the north sector there are several pockets of German soldiers that are holding strong in areas in and around the town, the line of trees at the high level is believed to be one of these areas, the Indian Garhwal brigade are to carry out similar raids to the south west of their position. He finally tells them that HQ are baffled as to how the enemy is being so accurate with its shelling despite the fact that they are retreating, many men, especially the Ghurkhas and the Irish rifles, have been injured and some killed by these high explosive shells that are landing directly into the trenches. The men are ready to move off, it is still light, the weak daytime sun still has little heat, but its winter light forces itself across the battlegrounds of Neuve Chapelle.

Lt Wilkins and Sergeant Fensome lead the patrol, Martin is at the rear with Lance Corporal Albert Bandy, making sure that no man is lagging or left behind, they pass through trenches held by the Royal Scots fusiliers, Martin is not shocked to see tens of bodies laid out ready for burial, many men have been injured, some of whom will not survive their injuries, the area surrounding these trenches is barren, smashed to pieces by the artillery from the BEF and from the Germans. Martin can see up ahead some of the damage caused, not one building remains fully standing, piles of charred wooden beams and sections of brick walls lie smouldering, many of the houses that have not been completely shattered are on fire, in the distance to the south, Martin can see the remains of the church, half of its tower is still standing but the building is aflame, and it will no doubt topple before darkness falls. Shells are still falling in and around the town, thankfully not where the men of the Bedfordshire's are, the German shelling is seemingly centred in this specific area of town, at the crossroads, close to the burning church, Martin can see from his position, that Lt Wilkins is correct, the shells are hitting the recently taken trenches with great accuracy, men are dying and unable to advance or retreat, the Bedfordshire's move on toward Layes Brook, having to go away from the main battle to avoid the shelling, they move slowly through the small settlement until they reach the bridge, it is being guarded by men from the 2nd regiment 2nd battalion Ghurkha Rifles, fearsome soldiers, short stocky men, all wearing the same uniform, a distinctive slouch hat, four large ammunition pouches are on the diagonal strip of webbing across their chests, all are carrying the famous curved Kukri knife on their hips, they all also have their bayonets fixed to the end of their rifles, Martin wonders if these soldiers actually prefer hand to hand combat to this shelling and long distance warfare, as they all seem ready to defend their position or attack the enemy at a moment's notice. Lt Wilkins speaks briefly to a Ghurkha captain before they move on again, along a road that will take them to the extensive entrenchment at the east and south of the town, it is raining when they reach the trenches being held by the 1st Sherwood Foresters, who are in reserve for the 8th Division, hence they are static at this position. Martin immediate recognises the cap badge of the regiment from his time spent at home with the 8th and 6th Battalion reservists, who, were when he left, still training on the common in town, Lt Wilkins calls for a ten minute break, he disappears to find his opposite number in the Sherwood Foresters. The area held by this regiment is partly trenched and partly track roads, the roads are wide open as almost every inch of bush and foliage has been destroyed, many of the Sherwood Foresters are lying in shallow ditches at the side of the road. At the entrance to the trenches, Martin and his colleagues are having a breather, Martin takes a smoke out of his top pocket and is patting his pockets to find his matches,

"Here you go Corporal" a Private from the Sherwood Foresters is lighting his own cigarette and offers the match to Martin who gladly accepts. Martin introduces himself and tells the private about the men from the Sherwood Foresters he met when last at home, the man, who introduces himself as Jacob Rivers, Martin smiles as he tells Jacob they have a 'Rivers' in their battalion, his mate, Alf, Jacob then tells Martin that he had originally served in the Royal Scots Fusiliers for seven years, beginning in 1899, serving overseas in India and Burma, leaving in 1907 and leaving the military to work on the railways in his home town of Derby, then he had volunteered for service recall at the start of the war in August last year

"I met one of your lads earlier this year when I was home on leave, he also works for the railway in Derby" Martin tells Jacob,

"What was his name?" asks the Sherwood Forester, Martin has to think for a few seconds,

"Bob, Bob" he scratches his head, "Bob Bees something or other"

Jacob laughs, "If you mean Bob Beeson, then yes, I worked with him labouring on the ballast trains" Martin points excitedly at Jacob,

“That’s him! That’s the very man!” he stops to inhale smoke from his cigarette, “I also met an RSM, a scary chap named Edward Westerman”

“I don’t know the man” replies Jacob, “But I have certainly heard of him”

Both men fall to the floor as they hear the boom of artillery being fired,

“Down! Everybody down!” a man shouts from inside the trenches, the shell is followed by another, then another, then at least four more in quick succession, they fly over the position Martin is lying in, landing seconds later with an excruciating screaming sound, at a location toward the town, Jacob sits up, dusts his tunic,

“Are you ok corp” he asks, he then puts a thumb over his shoulder, “They are landing where the 1st Irish rifles are, down by the crossroads near to the town”

Martin looks up, “I think that’s where we are heading for in a bit, we have to go through their position to get to that treeline” he points without looking.

The men shake hands, wish each other good luck, Martin follows the rest of the Bedfordshire’s as they all enter the trench system and follow it for a hundred yards or so until they get to the edge of the wood, looking up, they can all see the tree line and small wood that they have to clear.

“Listen in lads” Sergeant Fensome commands, “Lt Wilkins is checking to see if we can do anything to help these Irish rifle lads, they have taken a beating today, shells hitting them directly in their trench positions” he pauses, “If they don’t need our immediate service then we will be going up the hill” he points to his right.

“Corporal” Martin steps forward,

“Sergeant”

“I want you and Lance corporal Bandy to take three others and begin to move up the South side of the wood, there are a few ruined farm buildings next to the road to Armentieres that need to be cleared before we can all go through”

Martin points at three soldiers, they step forward with Albert Bandy,

“I will take the front Corp” offers Bandy, Martin nods at him, they are just about to leave when Lt Wilkins arrives back. He tells them that the Irish rifles have taken huge losses, many are injured but they are coping, Fensome tells Wilkins that Martin and his small platoon will be moving as advance party to clear the farm buildings, Wilkins, turns to Martin,

"Eyes open corporal, there are Hun here abouts, trapped and surrounded by us, they will be keen to get out"

Martin takes his platoon away from their position, and they walk through the Irish Rifle's trenches, the wood is up a small hill to their right and he can see the three farm buildings in front of them, one has been levelled and is a smouldering pile of bricks and wood, the second has three walls still standing, the front wall facing them is gone and what remains of the roof is on fire, the five of them crouch down in cover behind a roadside wall,

"I think it is safe to presume that those two buildings" he points at them "Are not hiding any enemy" he points at the third, he can see, that apart from its roof, the rest of the building seems to be intact "There is our immediate problem gentlemen"

He knows that the only option they have is to approach it, he spreads the platoon out in a staggered line, Albert Bandy is on the far right flank nearest to the barn, Martin who is at the other end of the line, indicates that they will all fix bayonets and move forward. The men stand and slowly move forward, rifles at the ready, to fire or to stab with the bayonet, they get to within thirty feet of the farm building, shots ring out, lots of them, Martin throws himself to the ground, lying on his front, he points his rifle to the only window on this side of the building,

"Fire at will!" he orders, he can hear rifles being fired up the line to his right, after a minute or two of constant fire he orders them to cease. He props himself up on his elbows, the window they were all firing at is no longer there, only a few splinters of the wooden frame remain, he reaches for a pair of old binoculars he carries with him, slowly and carefully he studies the building, looking for any movement, it seems to be still and silent. He shouts down the line,

"Are we all uninjured?"

Three voices return his question, one remains silent, Martin asks the men to name off, they do this, Albert is not answering,

"It's the Lance corporal, he has been hit corp!"

Martin hears the panic and fear in the man's voice,

"Steady Bernie" he tells the man "Can you see him?"

"Yes corp, I think he has copped it"

Martin stands up and runs in a crouched position along the line, he passes Bernie, tapping him on the head as he does so,

"Good lad Bernie, keep your head down lad"

He reaches Albert, he is lying face down in the mud, his arms are by his side, his legs bent slightly, Martin turns him over,

"Holy God" he says at the sight of the bullet ravaged body of the Lance Corporal,

He rolls Albert back onto his front, he feels rage welling up inside of him, he stands and walks toward the barn, rifle in front of him, firing five rounds through the hole in the wall where the window used to be, still walking he changes the magazine, the remaining three soldiers are following him, also firing, he stops and looks at one of them,

"Have you got a bomb with you John?"

Private John Warren nods at his corporal,

"Put one through that window" is the order he gives.

Warren takes out a number 2 MKII grenade, he unravels the cloth streamers wrapped around the seven inch wooden throwing handle, the streamers help the flight of the grenade when it is thrown, a five inch brass cylinder sits atop the throwing handle, inside it is a detonator, a brass needle percussion pellet, with a one and a half inch long conical headed steel needle that pierces the percussion pellet when it lands on its target, this detonates the half a pound of tonite, an explosive made from equal weights of barium nitrate and gun cotton, when it explodes it creates high temperature gasses and noxious fumes, anyone near to the grenade when it explodes will be killed or seriously injured. Warren removes the safety pin and with skilled accuracy he throws the grenade, it passes through the hole in the wall and explodes with a loud burst of air, a quick bright flash and smoke immediately follows, they hear screams from inside the barn,

"Advance!" Martin orders, the men stand and move forward swiftly, they reach the barn in less than half a minute, Martin sends two, Bernie Breacher and Jimmy Brown, around the building ,he and Warren put their rifles through the window space. Martin sees instant movement as a German infantryman runs to escape through the door at the far end of the building, Martin fires three rounds in quick succession and hits the man who falls instantly to the ground, in the gloom of the barn interior he sees that three other Germans are lying on the ground under the window, two have obvious fatal bullet wounds to their necks and faces, the third is lying face down and has no obvious injury, he looks over to the door, another German jumps up from a dark corner and makes a break for it, Martin and Warren fire at the same time, taking the man down, Bernie and Jimmy, shout as they enter the building, Martin and Warren raise their rifles into the air and away from the back door, Bernie sees the German soldier lying by the door, Martin's bullets have found their target but not fatally, Bernie steps into the barn, shouts in English that the injured German soldier should stay on the floor, he is trying to reach for his dropped rifle, Bernie stops the man from trying to get his weapon by putting his ammunition boot on the chest of the German, with wide eyes and without a sound, he pushes his rifle forward, easing the long bladed bayonet into the chest of the enemy soldier, who attempts to pull the blade out with his bare hands, an impossible task with Bernie forcing it into the man and through him, with a twist of the bayonet he finally kills the young soldier,

"Any more corp?" asks Bernie

"Check this one here, the other two are dead"

Bernie puts the butt of the rifle to his shoulder and nods at Jimmy to move forward to check the last German, he is rolled over by a push from Jimmy's boot, it becomes clear that this infantryman has been killed, probably instantly, by the bomb thrown by Warren, he has severe burns to his face and upper body.

"Move out lads" Martin says coldly.

The platoon return to the trenches, Martin reports to Sergeant Fensome,

"Albert Bandy is dead Sid, the Germans were in one of the damaged barns, there was nothing any of us could have done"

"What happened Martin?" asks Sid

Martin takes off his cap and runs both hands over his shaved hair,

"They were in the last barn, we approached slowly and in staggered formation, they opened up on us from a window, we fired back, Albert took the full force from three or four rifles, he was the closest man"

Sid Fensome remains silent, waiting for Martin to continue, he takes a cigarette out and hands one to Martin, who continues when he has accepted a match from his sergeant,

"Once we had seen Albert get killed, John Warren, at my order, threw a bomb through the window of the barn, after it had exploded I sent Bertrand 'Bernie' Breacher and Jimmy Brown around the outside to the back of the building, John and I walked toward the front, looking through the window we saw one of them running toward the back doors, I fired and hit him, he was dead, John and I then fired at one more who was running out of the barn, he went down and Bernie finished him with his bayonet"

Sid has his hands in his pockets, his cigarette dangling from the left side of his mouth, he inhales and exhales slowly,

"Good lads, are you certain that there are no more enemy there?"

"The buildings are clear, we haven't been any further, but to that point, we are all good"

Sid tells him that he will need to report the details to battalion HQ, about the enemy contact and the loss of Lance Corporal Bandy when they return to their trenches later, he calls for the men from the Bedfordshire's to get ready to move off, he signals to Lt Wilkins and they move off in file toward the barns, Martin who is walking near to the front instructs the two men at the very front to go around the outside of the barns, he does not want any of them to see Albert lying dead. The group of soldiers cross the road to Armentieres and advance up the slope to the tree line reaching the top without any further contact with the enemy, Lt Wilkins orders the group to rest at the edge of the treeline but out of clear sight, the men all step a few yards into the small wood, realising it is actually an orchard although none of the trees bear fruit or flowers, all the men are quietly nervous, Martin and Sid are with the Lieutenant, they are standing at the tree line, looking down over the town, it is a smouldering ruin.

"Sir" Martin takes his binoculars from his eyes to talk to the officer,

"What can you see corporal?"

Martin explains what he can see from their viewpoint,

"Well, I'll be damned!" exclaims Sid, "That explains the accuracy of their guns!"

Standing upright, amongst the desolate devastation that was once Neuve Chapelle, at a crossroads is a large figure of Christ on the cross.

Standing out amongst the hell surrounding it, the crucifix with Christ on it is untouched, the enemy have either left it in this position or have moved it so as to use it as a marker for their gunners to fire shells, this is the reason the Ghurkha regiment, the Garhwalls, the 1st Irish rifles and the 2nd Leicester regiment are having such a horrendous day with shell after shell hitting them, wounding, and killing many.

"Sergeant, send two men back to the trenches, find the Captain from the Irish rifles and explain why they are getting hit so badly" Lt Wilkins orders.

Fensome quickly instructs two soldiers to carry out this task, shelling starts again,

"That's ours I think, it is coming from the southwest" Martin speaks as he puts the binoculars to his eyes, he can see the Indian battalion moving forward, toward an area they had shelled that morning, large swathes of German defensive lines with barbed wire defences up to fifteen yards deep in places has been destroyed, leaving a huge gap for the soldiers from the BEF to advance through, protected by the cover of artillery cannon fire.

"Time to move off men" Lt Wilkins instructs, the men stand and are just about to move off when they are re-joined by the two soldiers sent off to report the crucifix marker,

"All done sir" reports Private Charles Rogers, "They are going to move it after dark, hoping that the Hun will still aim at it tomorrow as it will be a hundred yards into no-man's-land"

An explosion causes Martin to fall to the ground, dazed he looks around, smoke fills the air around him, he can just hear Sid Fensome shouting, the ringing in his ears is so very loud, he sees the men around him taking up positions, lying in the natural ditch around the edge of the wood, or behind trees, all are firing into the wood, he clears his head in time to hear Sid give him an order,

"Martin, get Lt Wilkins out of here, he has taken a blast!"

Martin gets up into a crouch position, he can see Lt Wilkins lying on the ground, he is alive as his legs are moving, his left arm is a mess, a large wound is bleeding heavily,

"I got you sir" Martin says as he drags Wilkins into the wood, the young officer screams in pain, "Sorry sir, but you were in the open"

Martin quickly looks at the wound in the arm, shrapnel from the German grenade, he also has a wound to his chest, he is severely injured and is losing consciousness.

"Sid!" Martin shouts, "The lieutenant needs a medic and quickly"

Martin has to lie on the ground next to Lt Wilkins as bullets fly over his head,

"Stay where you are Martin, we are going forward to get these bastards" he orders the men to stand up and advance toward the enemy fire, every single man does as instructed, despite enemy bullets being fired toward them. Martin crouches up again, reaching into a pouch on his webbing, he removes a field dressing, these have only been issued to the battalion for a couple of weeks, he hopes they are the same as the old ones, he is in luck, he quickly reads the print on the front of the brown cotton wrapped package,

WAR OFFICE MEDICAL DIVISION

FIRST FIELD DRESSING

TO OPEN – Outer cover: pull tapes apart

Inner waterproof cover: Tear apart the uncemented corners as indicated by the arrows.

CONTENTS. – Two Dressings in water-

proof covers each consisting of a gauze pad

stitched to a bandage and a safety pin

DIRECTIONS FOR USE.- Take the

folded ends of the bandage to each hand, and

keeping the bandage taut, apply the gauze

pad to the wound and fix the bandage. One
dressing to be used for each wound.
DO NOT HANDLE THE GAUZE OR WOUND
ARTHUR BERTON, Ltd, London, January 1912

"Bloody hell, that is a lot of instruction, why doesn't it just say, 'put gauze on the wound', I would still understand!" he says angrily, Lt Wilkins is unconscious, so he is talking to himself. He presses one bandage onto the upper left arm of the officer, ties it around and secures it with a knot, the second he puts onto the outside of the injured man's tunic, over the top of the chest wound, he then reaches under Wilkins and ties the bandage firmly around his chest, he looks up as he can hear noise coming toward him, dropping the now empty field dressing packet, he picks up his rifle and points it in the direction of the noise,

"Hold up Corporal!" Martin recognises the voice, "It's me" he lowers his rifle as Jimmy Brown comes into view, followed by the others from the Bedfordshire's,

"Where is Sergeant Fensome?" asks Martin

"Charlie Rogers has been killed corporal; the Sergeant is dealing with him"

"Are there any other dead?"

"No corporal, a few of the lads have minor wounds, Horace Preece has a hole in his hand where a bullet went straight through it! The Germans are either dead or have legged it"

Martin thanks the private, Sid Fensome comes into view, Martin explains that Lt Wilkins needs to be taken to the medical area, Fensome orders three men to take Wilkins down the hill and get a stretcher bearer from the Irish rifles trench to get him the help he needs, they are also to contact battalion HQ, tell them the hill and wood line are both clear, they are to use the trench phones if they are working, he sends them on their way. The remainder of them spread out along the tree line, giving them an advantage over any enemy that might venture up the slope toward them, it also gives them a view of the ongoing battle below, it is getting dark, the only voice heard is that of Sergeant Fensome.

"No bloody smoking"

It is an over an hour until one of the privates sent away with Lt Wilkins returns, he reports to Martin and Sid,

"We are to report back to the battalion trenches sergeant" the out of breath private gasps as he talks,

"What is your name private?" asks Martin

"Private George Haggar Corporal" he replies.

Martin puts a hand on his shoulder,

"Take a breath George, you have done well to get the message back to us amidst all this chaos"

Private Haggar thanks Martin, Sid speaks,

"Carry on with the message private"

Private George Haggar tells them that they are to report back to the battalion trenches, when asked who was relieving them, his answer is simple,

"No one sergeant"

Sid Fensome is angry,

"They send us up here to take this small wood, we do exactly that, I have lost two men, our Lieutenant is severely wounded, and half of the lads have been hurt" he takes out his cigarette packet, it is empty, Martin takes his out and offers them to Sid,

"Smoke 'em if you have 'em lads, cover your Lucifers and cover the glow" he looks at George,

"Bloody well done private, go and have a smoke and a rest for a bit"

"Yes sergeant" Haggar responds and is gone to sit with his mates. Sid looks at Martin,

"I don't know why we bother Martin" he has a couple of deep drags on his cigarette, the glowing tip hidden inside his cupped hand, "Do you think the Generals and Field Marshals have any idea what the hell they are doing?"

Martin shakes his head, "No" is his simple response.

He looks down at the town of Neuve Chapelle, in the darkness the fires can clearly be seen from his elevated position, houses, farms, barns, churches, orchards and farmland are all now destroyed, where there was once a thriving French town is now a mangled mess of bricks, burning rooftops and without any doubt, casualties of war, British and their allies, French, German, military and civilians, all killed so that one side can gain a small advantage, and for how long? Martin thinks back to Sid's vicious venting a few minutes ago, he is sure that the Generals and Field Marshals have no idea what is going on here on the battlefield or what the hell they are doing.

Cigarette finished, Martin organises the remaining soldiers to help their injured colleagues, those that need assistance, from the relative safety of their small wood on the hill back into the hell of the trenches.

* * *

During the early hours of Friday 12th March, Martin is awake in the trenches, it is a cool and misty morning, everything is damp, and he is chilled to the bone and watches as his breath freezes in the air as it leaves his mouth, he wonders if it may give away his position to any keen eyed German watching from their trenches. He has spent much of the night digging new trenches with others from the battalion, these being at right angles to the existing trenches and opposite the area of the high tree line he had been at yesterday, following this adjustment to the trenches, a company from the Royal Scots fusiliers have been moved to the right of their line in the trenches.

Voices become raised, shouts and screams, rifles being fired, orders being shouted, Martin realises that the voices he can hear above all else are German, he looks around at his area of trenches, his platoon are all looking at him,

"Steady lads" he reassures them, "Eyes open on both sides of our trenches, if anything gets past the wire and over the top, then shoot it" He studies the men around him, standing against the sides of the trenches in the near darkness, they all look worried but not terrified, most are veterans of this lousy trench warfare, most have been in this position before,

"Am I clear lads?" he asks,

"Yes corp" is the answer they all give.

Sergeant Fensome appears in the trenches from around a blind corner,

"Martin?" he asks

"Over here Sid"

Fensome joins him, backs against the back of the trench, he is breathing heavily,

"The Hun have attacked the Scots lads, they are taking a terrible beating, lots wounded and many dead and the trench has been lost"

Martin stares at Sid, "Bloody hell that trench is next to ours"

As he says this a large number of Scots Fusiliers come through the Bedfordshire trench system, injuries clear to see, many are severely injured and have to be carried, Martin organises help from his platoon and others from the Bedfordshire's whilst keeping the trench covered with rifle fire, Sid puts a hand on his shoulder,

"We are vulnerable here Martin, stay put, fight if you have to"

He nods at Martin, who nods back to him. Martin barks out orders to his men around him, they could be next in line for a German attack, and it seems to him that the Germans that attacked the fusiliers trench came from the high tree line that they took yesterday, costing them two dead and many wounded, only to leave it uncovered and as has seemingly proved, the Germans re-entered and took it back without resistance overnight. For the next three hours, the war remains calm, no Germans try to take the section of trench Martin is in charge of, one of his men whispers that a small platoon are coming toward them, Martin looks up as Major William Denne, Captains Cumberledge and Baird, two sergeants, one corporal and eighteen soldiers are with them, eight of them are from the 2nd battalion.

Major Denne addresses Martin,

"Corporal, this is the end of our trenches, we are going over to attempt to regain what the enemy took from us a few hours ago, if we need to retreat, we will come back this way"

"Yes sir" Martin replies,

"Don't bloody shoot at us corporal!" the Major smiles at him,

"No sir, wouldn't dream of it"

Martin sees the assembled men, the men from the 2nd battalion are Company Sergeant Major Joseph Horne, Sergeant Tom Hutchin, Corporal Henry Green and privates, George Nottage, Ernie Allen, 'G' Mutimer, Percy Boness, Bertie Breacher, Joe Clark, Bill Curtis and Walter Dennis, apart from Walter Dennis and Bertie Breacher, he doesn't know the others very well, but he is on nodding terms with all of them.

"Martin"

Martin turns to face Walter Dennis, "Walter, how are you?"

Walter looks to where the trench corners and out of sight, "Been better mate, this should be fun"

"You will be fine Walter" Martin assures him, Walter smiles,

"If I am not corporal, will you name your first child after me!"

"Bugger off" replies Martin.

It is 0700 hours, the mist is still hanging heavily throughout the trenches, the morning light gives it a feel of eeriness and a false sense of calm, Major Denne calls the raiding party to him, they leave and are out of sight as they pass the corner of the trench. It is a short few minutes later when all hell seems to be letting loose in the next trench to Martin, he orders the men around him,

"Be ready, be sharp"

He can hear rifles being rapidly fired, he can hear grenades exploding and he can hear men dying, his mouth is dry, and his heart is beating fast and hard.

He can hear movement coming from the German trench toward his own, "Rifles up lads, eyes open"

The men around him all put their rifles to their shoulders, Martin sees Major Denne enter his trench system, he quickly orders the men to lower rifles, Denne is dragging an injured man with him, Martin runs over as they come around the corner,

"Sir, you are hit!" Martin can see blood coming from the Majors tunic,

"Take him Corporal" Denne orders, Martin helps the severely wounded man and Denne runs back toward the enemy trench, Martin looks down at the man he is now holding in his arms, it is Walter Dennis.

"Hang on Walter, you will be ok mate" he shouts at a private to get a medic, he looks down at Walter, who smiles at Martin, he sees the life leave his friends eyes, his body is now limp in Martins arms.

Walter Dennis is dead.

Martin looks at his pocket watch, it is 0725 hours, only twenty or so minutes ago the three officers and eighteen soldiers had left this trench, none have returned alive yet with the exception of Major Denne, who has gone back into hell. It is another five minutes before Captain Baird and Captain Cumberledge appear, they are helping Major Denne, who appears to be unconscious, both the captains are wounded but able to walk, two medics appear, Denne is put onto a stretcher and taken swiftly away, Martin speaks to Captain Baird, who is holding his bleeding right arm

"Any more on the way to us sir?"

Baird replies, "I don't think so corporal, it was a bloodbath in there, I was with four soldiers, I saw one killed as soon as we entered the trench, the other three are wounded, but terribly so, there is no hope for any of them I fear"

Martin looks across at Captain Cumberledge, he is about to ask him the same question when Baird addresses him, "Leave him be corporal, none of his lads made it, all wiped out"

The captain walks away, taking Cumberledge with him.

"Are we next to go in Corp?" one of the lads asks, Martin shrugs his shoulders.

British army artillery begins to fire, Martin and his lads all fall to the floor as the shells pass at low height over their trench, he hears the shells hit their mark, he has a very bad feeling about this, he stands and gingerly climbs the ladder up against the trench wall, he reaches the top just as another barrage of artillery flies over the trenches, he peers over the top of the trench, clearly seeing the shells land, directly into the trenches held by the Scots fusiliers.

Sliding down the ladder he grabs the nearest soldier to him,

"What is your name son?"

"Private William Simmons corporal"

"William, run down the trenches, grab the first officer you see and tell him that our artillery is killing the Scots lads in the trenches next to the Germans!"

Simmons nods and runs away down the trench.

"Bloody hell" says Martin to anyone who is listening.

The shelling stops, Martin and others listen on this misty morning, to men screaming from trenches near to them, Martin knows it is their own shells that have killed the men from the Royal Scots.

"Should we go across corporal?" Simmons is back,

"No" Martin is blunt, "Crossing no-man's-land without orders is not only a death sentence, the Germans will cut you down, or our own bloody gunners will get you, also, our orders are to hold this end of the trench, we are the last line before the Germans"

Simmons tells Martin that he understands, and he goes back to his position on the trench wall.

It is not long before another officer appears, Martin is fully aware who this man is,

"Captain Foss sir, what brings you here?" he asks

Captain Charles Foss, adjutant to Major Onslow, is well liked by the soldiers of 2nd battalion, he is a fair but firm officer,

"Well corporal" he says "I have been sent down here to assess the situation, I can say without fear or favour that the British trenches are a veritable shambles, I think that some direct action is needed to sort this out"

He looks at Martin, "Corporal, you were on the party that went to the high tree line yesterday were you not?"

"I was sir, it is a small orchard, it overlooks the trenches that have just been lost" Martin replies

"Jolly good" Foss looks around the trench, "I will be back in a short while, are you and yours all good for now?"

Martin tells Foss that he is fine and so are his men, Foss disappears back into the British trenches, Martin looks across at one of his men and shrugs his shoulders. Ten minutes later Captain Foss returns to the end of the British trench line with eight men, Martin recognises the as the men, nearly all long serving regular soldiers, from the Bedfordshire's grenade section, the NCO, Sergeant Bill Peggs, a happy go lucky, ever smiling Londoner, from the East end, had served in South Africa with Martin, he joined the Regiment only a few months after Martin. Another London lad, this time from the North of that city, Bill Eade, is standing next to him are Stan Scrivener and Phillip George Cogan, smoking cigarettes, behind these two are George Freshwater, Joe Lovette and Harold 'H' Barnett, the final duo of this tough octet of men are Fred Brown and Herb Smith, Fred has joined the battalion straight out of basic training and arriving in France two days after Christmas 1914. Herb had originally been a special reservist in the fourth battalion, joining in 1911, he joined the 2nd battalion on November 11th, 1914, being drafted in with George Cogan, he has proved himself to be a distinguished bomber and a vital part of this small team.

Foss approaches Martin,

"Are you ready then corporal?"

Martin replies, although a little confused by the question,

"Ready for what sir?"

"To come with us of course" Foss points his right thumb over his shoulder in the direction of the eight bombers,

"I am not a bomber sir"

Foss smiles, "I know that corporal, but you know the area in and around the high tree line, I need your knowledge to get into those bloody trenches that the enemy took from us"

Martin thinks for a few seconds, "I think your best bet will be the way we came back down from the trees, it is to move left out of the end of this trench" he points in the general direction he is talking about, "There is large, flooded ditch to cross, but the Germans will not be in this area as it is a soaking wet swamp, I doubt that they will be covering it either for the same reasons"

"Good, thanks corporal" Foss stands looking at Martin,

"Sir?"

"Come along, show me and my band of bombers the way"

Martin realises that Captain Foss is adding him to his attack platoon,

"Yes sir. Of course, sir" he replies.

He looks over at his eight comrades from the grenade section, they are all smiling at him, Bill Peggs speaks from the other side of the trench, "Come on Martin, we might even let you chuck a bomb or two!"

"You buggers' knew the captain was going to tell me to go along with this, didn't you!"

"I can't possibly answer that corporal" says Peggs with a huge smile on his face, "That is a grenade section secret" Martin shakes Bill's hand as he joins them, "I think you know most of the lads here Martin"

Martin acknowledges that he does, Foss joins them, he has a small trench map in his hand,

"Corporal, show me on the map"

Using his left index finger, Martin points on the map where the Germans took the trenches from the Scots only a short time ago, the orchard at the high tree line is directly above the trenches, the map shows the amount of ground taken yesterday during the battle, the battalion having fought their way through open land and through a large farm, named on the map as Farm Vanbesien, the bomber team refer to it as '*The Moated Grange Farm',* Martin has no idea why but goes along with it. Foss indicates where the Germans are entrenched, although they are almost surrounded by the BEF the trenches they have taken will easily give access for more enemy soldiers to advance into the British front lines. Foss puts the map away inside of his tunic,

"Lead the way corporal"

Martin picks up his rifle, tells the man next to him in the trench what he is doing,

"Best of British with that corp" the man says.

Martin walks to the end of the trench line and stands still, he points to an area in front of them, an open area, "Just ahead of us is the ditch that is full of water, we will be exposed but as I said, it is so wet and almost impassable, that I doubt the Germans will have it covered at all"

"Let's hope you are right corporal" Foss says as he walks out of the trench system and into open land, he, and the rest of them are moving in a crouched position, the mist helps with their advance to the edge of the ditch.

"I am not wading through that" Bill says, "Nothing worse than wet puttees, that will make our legs freezing cold"

Foss agrees, he sees the amusement on the faces of these tough, experienced soldiers,

"They don't want to get wet sir" Bill replies happily

"Cover me" says Foss, who stands up and with a run and leap, he is across the ditch, dry and safe, this method is repeated for all the soldiers, once on the other side, Foss gathers his team and talks to them almost in a whisper,

"The German trench is twenty or so yards over this mound, he points to the team in the order they are to follow him, Eade, Scrivener, Cogan, Peggs, Freshwater, Lovette, Bennett, Brown, and Smith last, Foss tells Smith that he is aware of his skill as a bomber and expects his grenades to be thrown over him and the others, not amongst them!

They all smile,

"What about me sir?" asks Martin,

"Remain here corporal, there will be a backup party advancing toward us after we have entered the trenches, point them in the right direction as they leave our trenches, tell them to bloody hurry up when they hear the ruckus begin" he turns to the grenade platoon, "We will be on open ground men, there is every chance that they will see or hear us approaching, move quickly"

Martin watches as Foss, followed by his team, clambers out of the mound, and runs toward the German front line, Foss has his service revolver pointed in front of him, firing it as he crests the top of the trenches, the eight men with him are all carrying grenades their rifles are slung across their backs. Bombs are thrown by the men, this causes the Germans to be stirred into activity, heavy rifle fire ensues but the Germans in the first section of trenches almost immediately stop firing when the grenades land in their positions, killing several and wounding more, surrounding Foss and his men with their hands in the air, Martin hears Foss shout,

"No more bombs, or we will be blown up as well!"

Martin hears noise behind him, it is the backup party from A company, he joins them and as the bombers did, he leaps over the ditch and runs into the trench system, passing Foss and the bombers who have taken one German officer and several dozen soldiers' prisoner, Martin reaches a blind corner at one end of the trench he and others are in, there has been no sight of any Germans as yet. Martin signals for the men to stand behind him with their backs against the trench wall. Slowly he moves away from the wall, giving him a slight view without exposing too much of him to be shot at, he sees three German soldier's standing against the far wall, rifles pointed to the junction where Martin and the other are standing.

"Corporal, what have we got?"

Martin turns to speak to Sergeant Oakes, who he hasn't seen for a couple of weeks and presumed he had been wounded or killed, Martin whispers and puts three fingers up,

"Three enemy, standing with guns pointing toward this corner"

Oakes nods, he confirms with Martin, "Standing?"

Martin nods back, Oakes in a hushed voice says to Martin, "Can you lie down and shoot from a low position? They will be expecting us to barrel around the corner and shoot at us where we stand, not on the floor, do you get my meaning?"

Martin nods again, he indicates to the two soldiers behind him, Albert Pressland and Tom Richards to move back to give him some space, they do this and Martin lies, body flat, on his left side, head low in the sticky and wet mud, he has his rifle in a firing position, his left arm is crooked and taking most of the weight, the butt of the gun is at an angle into his right shoulder, his right arm is gently over the stock of the gun and his finger is on the trigger, he knows he has a full clip of five rounds in the gun, cocking the bolt action back slowly and forward quietly, he hears the first round move into the breech. He takes a deep breath in, as he exhales, he rolls slightly away from the wall, the barrel of the rifle is clear of the corner and his head is now exposed, he has both eyes open and has a clear sight picture, looking through the half oval shaped back sight with a small sight pin at its base, he lines it up with the barrel sight, the German on the left is looking above where Martin is lying, he feels himself pulling the trigger. The first shot off, he cocks the bolt action again, moves the rifle a few inches to the right, finds the second German who has been taken by surprise and is just beginning to lower his rifle toward Martin, the trigger is pulled, moving the rifle again as he re loads the empty chamber he can see the third German, the enemy soldier has his rifle at his eyeline, and it is pointing directly to Martins low position. Martin rolls out into the open as a bullet slams into the ground where he had been only a second ago, he picks up the German in his sights and fires three quick shots off, cocking the bolt action lever quickly and smoothly between shots. Albert Pressland is standing next to him, his head just around the corner of the trench,

"That is some good shooting Martin"

He looks up and sees the three men lying on the ground, three men whose lives he has just taken from them, from their family and from this war. These are not the first men Martin has killed, but he is amazed at how unafraid he was and how calm he felt throughout. Tom and Albert are the first two into the area where the dead enemy soldiers now lie, they approach them carefully in case they are not dead, but they had need not worry as every one of Martins five .303 rounds have found their target. Martin gets to his feet, his uniform is covered in the mud from the trench floor, he sees his two colleagues approach another corner, they disappear from his view. A volley of rifle fire is heard followed by an explosion from around the corner in the trench system, Martin looks at Oakes,

"Where are the shells coming from Sarge?"

"No shells Martin, the artillery has been told to lay off and the Germans have not had time to know we are here yet" Oakes replies.

Soldiers are passing Martin to go and investigate the fate of their comrades,

"Sergeant, Corporal, come quick, we have got two down!"

The voice carries its dark message to Martin and Oakes; they can both hear the fear it conveys; both run around the first corner and see Tom and Albert lying prone in the mud, they all have injuries to their bodies that both Martin and Oakes recognise instantly as having been caused by grenade shrapnel.

"How are they?" asks Oakes hopefully

"Both dead" is the response, one of the soldiers at the front of the platoon, shouts at Martin and Oakes for them to move to his position, both men step around the two dead Bedfordshire men and around the next corner, more bodies lie in the mud. Five German soldiers, all with bullet wounds are dead,

"Looks like our lads let loose with a volley of shots, killing these five, sadly it would appear that a grenade or two was also sent by these men"

Martin agrees with Oakes, "Bloody hell Sarge, our two lads must have continued to fire at these bastards even when they had grenades thrown at them"

Oakes nods slowly and purposely, "Brave men Martin" he looks at the sky, "They paid the price for it though"

Martin, although shocked at the death of two men he knew very well, knows that the trenches have to be cleared, he moves to the front again,

"Let's get this job done and go and have a brew lads, shall we?"

He follows the line of the trench, and they all follow after him further into the trench system.

* * *

Alice had her sixteenth birthday three months ago, she left school in November of last year, the Government stating that any child over the age of fourteen could leave school to assist with the war effort. She, almost immediately upon leaving St Nicholas school signed up for a series of classes and lectures on Home Nursing being run locally by Dr Violet Kelynack, another local medical man, Dr Blake, had arranged and ran the first aid courses, her cousins had also left school and were both on the same courses as Alice. She passed the courses with flying colours and in January, following a request from the Commanding officer of the 1st North Midlands field ambulance for local volunteers to help with caring for the wounded soldiers, Dr Kelynack formed the voluntary aid detachment of the St Johns Ambulance brigade and Alice, Catherine and Jennifer, although not aged twenty three, which is the age requirement to be a VAD, all joined together as helpers but not as nursing assistants, their age is being ignored because so many military nurses and VAD's have been posted overseas to work in the field hospitals, so although only sixteen, this is overlooked because their help is needed. Catherine is working out of the Golf clubhouse on the common, her jobs include serving meals, reading to the patients, and cleaning, the field hospital has been moved to this location from its previous home at Rothamstead park just inside the gated entrance at Hatching Green, the tented hospital station is still there, but it was deemed to be too cold to use in the winter. Jennifer is based at the town's main railway station, helping the nursing assistants with the arriving wounded soldiers, giving them a hot drink, and helping them from the trains to the waiting ambulances. Alice had originally started at the Golf clubhouse, but in January a detachment from the military field ambulance unit moved to the lectures institute and reading rooms, Alice was asked by the Matron if she would like to continue her work with them at this new location.

The Institute, as it is called locally, is a row of cottages formerly owned by the family that had lived at Welcome Manor, a family of local Quakers. The manor house and the cottages were purchased in June 1866 by a local benefactor, Mr Henry Tylston Hodgson, 24 hospital beds are available in this hospital. Mr Tylston lives in Welcome manor and is the Vice Chairman of the Midland Railway company, he owns most of the properties from Station Road to Crabtree lane, just on the outskirts of the Bowling Alley, a distinguished and well-dressed gentleman with a neatly trimmed moustache and beard cut in a similar style to King George V. The cottages had been rented by the Lectures institute until March 1912, since then they have been used sporadically by locals for minor events and meetings, the North Midlands field ambulance had gratefully accepted Mr Hodgson's offer to use the buildings as a field hospital and have been in residence since February of this year.

Alice works long hours at the hospital, her roles and responsibilities include making and serving meals to the wounded, reading to them if asked, helping them out of the building either in a wheelchair or on crutches, to take in the fresh air of the common. She takes great pride in her work and always looks smart and clean in her uniform. All of the volunteers, who are of age, wear the same uniform, a stiff white hat similar to the floating veil hat worn by qualified nurses, a blue dress, light blue for the assistants and dark blue for the qualified nurses and a white apron with a large red cross at the centre of the breast, Alice and her twin cousins are not allowed to wear the nurses hat or the apron with the red cross on it, they are neither qualified nurses or 'official' nursing assistants so their 'uniform' is the same light blue dress as the nursing assistants, but they wear a plain white apron. The hospital receives patients injured on the battlefields, all will have had some treatment at a casualty clearing station situated a few miles behind the front lines, these stations provide initial treatment, surgical support, and a degree of convalescence to the soldiers before being evacuated back to the UK. Uncle Pete also works for the VAD as an ambulance driver, he is also a volunteer with the Hertfordshire voluntary reserve, posted to number 3 company, 3rd battalion volunteer training corps, his employer at Childwickbury, Mr Jack Barnato Joel is very generous allowing his staff time off with pay to help with the war effort, Joel is also friendly with the commanding officer of the Herts voluntary reserve, Lt Col Edward Wighley Braithwaite and is happy to allow his staff to join the voluntary reserve.

The town has soldiers back living in local billets and training on the common again, the 5th Prince of Wales (North Staffordshire) regiment, the first death in the Institute hospital was not a wounded soldier from the war, but a young solder from the North Staffordshire's, 16 year old Private Stanley Woodward, 6th reserve battalion, he fell ill with influenza and died in the hospital shortly after it opened, he was buried in town with full military honours, he had served only eighty days. When the young soldier passed away, Alice was in the room with him, memories flooded back to her about the death of David only a few months ago, but with the help of a senior nurse from the VAD and a military nurse from Queen Alexandra's Imperial military nursing service, she had been able to deal with the death. She had placed the young man's service cap on top of the wooden coffin when his body was collected, she clearly remembers the cap badge, a Prince of Wales fleur de lys with the Latin 'ICH DIEN' inside banners below the feathers, a knotted rope motif is below the fleur de lys and the dead man's regiment name at the base of the badge. Since this first soldier's death, Alice has dealt with men dying and injured, Major Arthur Clay from the 6th battalion North Staffordshire's died of pneumonia on 18th February, a funeral was held again at the parish church, he is not buried there though, his body was sent to his family for burial in Staffordshire. Many men have wounds that are life changing for them and they will never see active military service again, most of the patients sent to the hospital are expected to make a full recovery, then to be returned to the front line, one of these men is Alice's current patient, a 21 year old officer from the 1st battalion Bedfordshire regiment, 2nd Lt Charles Gray. 2nd Lt Gray, a friendly, good natured man from Wheathampstead, has told Alice the story of how he had been injured, he was at town called Bailleul on the French side of the border with Belgium in a front line trench system, trench number seven, alongside soldiers from the 1st battalion Dorset regiment, when shelling from enemy guns at Messines, some 10 miles to their north east, started a heavy bombardment in the morning of Friday 19th February, the Dorset's had earlier fired a large amount of mortars into the German trenches and the response was that large enemy shells were landing in the trenches held by the Dorset and the Bedfordshire regiments. One of the Dorset trenches had taken a direct hit and men were heard to be screaming for help, Charles, with two platoons of his men, ran a short distance across open ground to help their stricken colleagues, he had dragged an injured young Corporal from the Dorset's back across the open ground, under heavy shelling, machine gun and rifle fire, to the Bedfordshire trenches and had treated his leg injury. The Corporal, James Duffy is only eighteen, luckily his injuries were not bad, shrapnel in his leg that was removed at a casualty clearing station, Charles had not been so lucky, although at the time he helped Duffy he had no idea he had been injured, one of his corporals had pointed out to him that his tunic was covered in blood at the right shoulder, further investigation revealed over a dozen shrapnel wounds, some needed surgery to remove them and he had been sent back to the UK for further surgery, treatment and to convalesce, he had asked to be sent to this hospital as it is only a few miles from his home village. Cpl James Duffy was killed the following day, shortly after returning to the front line.

Alice and Charles have become close, following several successful surgeries, the injuries to his shoulder are very nearly healed and they both know he will be leaving to be posted back overseas in a week or so.

Saturday 10th April, 0600 hours, Alice arrives at work in time to get the breakfast trolley ready for breakfast to be served to the men she helps the nurses with, it must be ready to be taken from the kitchen and served at 0700 hours, as usual her 'uniform' is spotless and clean, she walks into the staff area and takes off her cloak,

"Early as usual Alice"

She turns to see the nursing Sister from the QAIMNS addressing her,

"Morning Sister Janes, I like to be early so as to get everything ready for the soldiers"

Katie Janes smiles at Alice, "I wish all my nurses were as prepared as you, young lady" she studies a clipboard before carrying on, "You will be preparing 2nd Lt Gray for his discharge"

"Is there a date for him to leave Sister?" asks Alice,

"Yes, this Friday, his response to treatment has been first class, please check with your military nurse, who today is….." She again consults her clipboard "Julie Smith"

Alice acknowledges Sister Janes and sets off toward the kitchen to be given her duties for this morning. Julie is already in the kitchen, two army officers are also there,

"Morning Julie, you are early today"

"Not like me to beat you in is it Alice" Julie responds to Alice, "This is Captain Smith and Lt Barratt from the South Staffordshire regiment"

Alice acknowledges both men who are having a hot drink, Julie is quiet, she seems a little sad, Alice enquires, "Is everything alright with you Julie?"

Nurse Smith forces a smile, she tidies her hair by twisting the bun at the nape of her neck, it did not need adjusting, it gives her something to do at that very moment.

"Private Steele passed away late last night, I wanted to get his effects in order nice and early this morning"

Alice remains respectfully quiet as she can see that through the tough professional exterior being posed by Julie, that she is upset and trying to hide it.

43 year old Private Alexander Steel of the 2nd / 6th battalion South Staffordshire's had been found unconscious the previous day on the Lower road to Luton, by the Folly, he had a severe injury to the back of his skull, it is presumed from an accident, he never regained consciousness. He had been billeted with other men from his regiment, staying with Mrs Collier at Dorset Villa, Shakespeare Road, Captain Smith, and Lt Barratt are at the hospital to collect his personal belongings, they will then attend the Shakespeare Road billet to collect his personal and army effects from there,

"I am sorry to hear that Julie"

Julie thanks Alice and makes her excuses to leave,

"It's a real shame" the captain speaks to Alice,

"What is sir?" she responds

Captain Smith finishes his drink, he puts the mug into the sink,

"Private Steel, terrible thing to happen, his Wife and five children are being informed this morning of his death"

"Five children!" exclaims Alice "That is so terribly sad"

Nodding in agreement the captain continues, "We are hoping Mrs Steel can be bought to town for the funeral, it will be a full Military cortege"

"Will he be taken to his hometown for burial?"

"No miss, sadly not, he will be buried in the parish church here in town, a full military funeral for the lad"

Alice does not have time to answer as Julie re appears,

"Gentlemen, we are ready for you now" she looks at Alice "Please excuse us Alice"

Alice remembers that Julie has not given her any duties for this morning, she calls after her,

"Julie, I am sorry to stop you, but I need to know my duties for this morning please"

Julie stops at the kitchen door, she has a smile on her face,

"After you have served breakfast, can you please concentrate on 2nd Lt Gray today Alice, he needs to be ready in four days as he is leaving us" she leaves with the two officers. Alice knows that it only takes a few hours to prepare any patient for discharge, Charles is not leaving until Friday, Julie obviously knows that the two of them are fond of each other and is trying her best to give them time together before he leaves the hospital. She steadily pushes her trolley with the breakfast prepared by the cook, for the four men on the ward she is working on, Charles is one of them,

"I understand you are looking after 2nd Lt Gray this morning Alice" Matron meets her in the hallway,

"Yes Matron" Alice replies quietly, she is a little afraid of the Matron,

"Remember please, you need to call one of my nurses or one of the nursing assistants for any medical issues, you are not allowed to be involved in dressing changes, cleaning wounds or handing out medication"

Alice acknowledges the Matron, who gives her the same lecture every day she is here,

"Yes Matron" Alice says again, the Matron, just for a second, loses her hard exterior and sharp face, she becomes gentle and her face is no longer stern,

"2nd Lt Gray is a fine young man isn't he Alice?"

Blushing heavily, Alice can only nod, the Matron quickly returns to her former strict self,

"Remember what I said Alice"

With that she was gone, Alice makes her way to the small ward, the men are all awake, three of them are chatting to each other, the fourth is lying on his side, facing away from the others,

"Morning Alice" the three answer together, the fourth does not speak or move.

The first bed on the left is 2nd Lt Gray, he smiles at Alice,

"Hello Alice" he says quietly to her,

"Good morning Charles, how are you today?"

He tells her that he is fine, she serves him a bowl of oatmeal, two sausages and scrambled egg and a cup of tea, he thanks her, she says to him,

"Was there anything you wanted to do today?"

"A walk on the common would be nice, would that be in order?"

"I will check with Matron or Julie, but it should be fine"

She moves onto the bed next to Charles, it is next to the window overlooking the common and toward Leyton Green, the soldier in the bed still does not move, he remains lying on his side and staring out of the window.

"Good morning John" Alice says brightly to the man, she gets no response, he remains still, she continues to talk to him,

"I will put your tea and breakfast on your bedside table John, I will be back in a few minutes to help you to eat it"

He does not move, does not speak and stares, seemingly without blinking, out of the window.

He is Private John Freeman, 1st Battalion Bedfordshire regiment, part of the 15th brigade, II Corps, his right arm is missing from below the elbow and his face and neck are a mass of vivid red scars and still healing wounds, only eighteen years of age, he had only been in the regiment a few months when he found himself on the front line with the 1st Bedfordshire's, firstly at the Battle of Mons and then at the Battle of Le Cateau, they had only been in Belgium just over a week, when the battalion were involved in heavy fighting at Mons, the German army easily overpowered the BEF, forcing them to retreat to Le Cateau, France. In less than a week he had been in Ireland, France, Belgium and back into France. The regiment had been in Ireland when they were mobilised for war, leaving Mullingar on 14th August by train, arriving at Belfast the following morning and embarking on the SS Oronsa, a single funnelled cruise liner that was being used as a troop carrier, this ship sailed out of Belfast at two that afternoon, arriving at Le Havre, France later that night. The regiment marched to a soaking wet and muddy BEF camp on high ground at Le Havre and staying for one night only, moved off and marched to the railway station, eventually onto a train to take them to Le Cateau. Upon arrival, no rest was authorised and a march to billets at Pommereuil commenced immediately, here John and his colleagues had a few hours rest whilst they waited for the remainder of the 5th Division to arrive. The following two days consisted of marching and billeting, firstly at Gomminies and then into Belgium to Boussu Bois, respite was short lived for the Bedfordshire regiment, because at midday on Sunday 23rd, the men were sent to Wasmes to dig trenches, the senior officers assuring them that no immediate fighting was expected, it was whilst digging the trenches that the soldiers were shelled heavily by the enemy, men were killed and injured, John received a wound to his right forearm, a piece of shrapnel hit him and a mate had pulled it out for him as they took cover in the bottom of a muddy trench, a field bandage was put over the large gash. Even when the shelling stopped, they were ordered to remain in trenches, until they were eventually recalled to another position, another trench but nearer to the front line, the enemy attacked almost as soon as they arrived, John and the soldiers he was with, were all trapped and unable to disengage or retreat from the enemy soldiers, fighting was fierce and at times they had no idea who they were firing their rifles at. Only when nightfall arrived and under cover of darkness, were they able to move back toward Paturage, taking up defensive positions in houses, farm buildings and around the bridges. The Germans attacked again at first daylight, the Bedfordshire's held their line until the houses and bridges in the area around them had all been destroyed by enemy shells, there were no viable buildings left to afford them any cover. John was inside an old farmhouse when it was hit by a German shell, he and four others were trapped under the rubble of the building as it collapsed with them all inside. It took over 3 hours for him and his mates to be dug out, for all of that time he was unable to move, unable to scream for help as his chest was being crushed by the weight of the stones around him, he remembers being grateful for the miniscule amount of light that penetrated the small gaps in the stones he was trapped in. The regiment retreated, along with the rest of the BEF, to Bavay, some 10 miles to the south of Paturage, they were all tired, scared and defeated. The great retreat of the BEF took John and the 1st Battalion Bedfordshire's back to Le Cateau, 18 miles to the southwest of Paturage, the men immediately set about rebuilding and strengthening the trench system there, Johns wound to his lower right arm was very painful at this time, his torn tunic covering the dirty bandage that is still tightly covered the wound.

In the early hours of Wednesday 26th August 1914, John was in trenches at Le Cateau, the enemy attacked with heavy artillery but the trenches, due to solid rebuilding, withstood the barrage, but they had to retreat, again, when German infantry soldiers compromised the trenches to their right, John was one of the last out of the British trenches, fighting hand to hand with the enemy until the trenches were lost. The regiment retreated to give the retiring British artillery cover as they were forced to leave their positions, this was when the gun he and his mates were covering suffered a direct hit from a German shell, the ammunition and the gun exploded, causing a cataclysm of events that meant that all but John and Lt Wagstaff were killed, Wagstaff was wounded, both his legs suffering severe shrapnel wounds, when the German infantry attacked this position, Wagstaff ordered John to leave him and make good his retreat, he had refused but Wagstaff threatened him with court martial if he did not follow the order, John, who was injured himself made it back to the battalion muster point, this is where he collapsed. He had shrapnel wounds to his face, neck, chest and back, and when he was taken to the casualty clearing station, he was not expected to live as his wounds were so severe. But he did survive, two days later when his regiment marched away toward Eaucourt, the surgeon took his right arm from below the elbow, infection had made the limb unsavable. John was sent back to the UK, initially to a Red Cross hospital in London, but had been sent to the field hospital in town, just after Christmas 1914 as it was nearer to his family home at East Hyde, near Luton, he had been in the Institute since the first day it had opened, he had not said a single word since arriving.

"Leave him Alice, the 'bullet wind' has got him" the voice is from Private Freddie 'Knocker' White of the 1st Battalion Worcestershire regiment. He had been advancing toward the town of Neuve Chapelle from their position in the northwest sector when he had been shot, he thinks probably from machine gun fire, he has wounds to his chest and legs, all are healing well. The final soldier, Private Charles Bigg, a local man whose family live on the Lower Road to Luton, next to the Almagam rubber works, where he worked before enlisting in the 1st battalion Hertfordshire regiment in 1914, replies to Knocker,

"I still want to know what a boy from Islington is doing in the bloody Worcester's and is now lazing about in this lovely hospital"

Knocker smiles as he replies, "You, Charlie, should be at home with your Mummy, you only live a couple of miles from here, that bed should be taken up by a proper soldier, not a country boy like you!"

Both men enjoy the banter, it has been a constant between them since they had both arrived, Charlie had been injured in a French town called Cuinchy on 7th February when he was in one of two platoons of men from the Hertfordshire's, they joined soldiers from the 3rd battalion Coldstream guards and attacked a German fire trench, the attack was a disaster, the information that they had been given was that the trenches had all but been abandoned by the Germans, this was incorrect and they had met with large numbers of German infantrymen armed with a huge amount of small arms in the trenches. The Hertfordshire men that survived were all wounded, one officer and a lance corporal were killed in the trench, another private had died that evening from wounds received, Charlie has been shot through his left shoulder, he is recovering well and along with Charles and Knocker, he expects to be posted shortly, back to the war and back to France or Belgium.

"Bugger off Knocker, at least I am allowed to carry 'bombs' in my job, I am surprised that they let you have a rifle mate"

Knocker is about to fire back a response, Charles beats him too it, "Gentlemen, shut up and eat your breakfast"

They both pretend to salute and say "Yes sir" in a sarcastic manner.

He smiles as he looks at Alice, "Ignore them Alice, they are idiots"

Alice is cutting a sausage into small pieces and feeding it to John, he accepts the food, slowly chews it and swallows, all without looking at her, his stare continues out of the window.

"Charles old man" Knocker is still being sarcastic, "Did you tell Alice your news?"

Alice looks up from her feeding duty, "Charles? What news do you have?"

The 2nd Lt looks both angry and embarrassed, "It's nothing really"

"Bloody hell Charles, it is amazing" Charlie joins in "You will be the talk of Wheathampstead"

Knocker looks confused, Charlie helps him out,

"Wheathampstead is a small village a few miles from here, it is where the Lieutenant is from"

"There is nothing but small villages around here" Knocker quips,

"Charles?" Alice asks again, he wrings his hands tightly together,

"It is nothing, I have to go to London on Monday to collect an award"

Charles, who is looking directly at Alice, does not see Charlie sneak up to his bedside locker until it is too late,

"Charlie put that back!" he insists, laughing Charlie hands a newspaper he has taken from Charles to Alice, she puts the fork down on the plate of food, taking a cloth from her dress pocket, she cleans her hands and takes the newspaper, the London Gazette, from Charlie,

"Please Alice, it really is nothing, don't listen to these fools"

Alice reads the page that the newspaper is folded back to, it is dated 2nd April 1915, a few paragraphs down she sees Charles name,

Awarded Military Cross

2nd Lt Charles Gray. 1st Battalion Bedfordshire regiment.

For conspicuous gallantry and devotion to duty under close enemy machine-gun fire. This officer took forward two teams and succeeded in moving off two guns, He displayed great courage and determination in laying a line under very heavy fire. One of the teams was shot down, but he, although seriously wounded, succeeded in rescuing injured soldiers and in bringing in the other gun. His gallantry and devotion to duty during recent operations is most marked.

Alice looks at Charles, "That is a little different to how you explained it to me Charles"

"And to us Alice" Knocker speaks but points to Charlie as he does so,

"What we have here lads, is a proper hero!" Knocker and Charlie break into spontaneous applause and cheering, Julie appears in the doorway,

"Be quiet you men" she instructs angrily, "You will have the Matron on my back for this"

Then men stop what they are doing and apologise, Julie speaks to Alice,

"Please let me know when you are done Alice, then I can see to the dressings and medication for these men" she looks at Charlie and Knocker, "Bath time for you boys this morning"

They both begin to protest but stop when they see the look on Julie's face.

"Would it be in order for Alice to walk me across the common this morning?" Charles asks Julie,

"I should think that will be fine Charles" she says sternly, "Congratulations on your citation 2nd Lieutenant" said not so sternly.

Charles, embarrassed by the attention, climbs out of his bed, "Shave and wash for me" He leaves the room with his washbag clutched under his arm.

Just before lunchtime, Alice and Charles are walking on the common toward the Baa Lamb trees, it is a warm and sunny April day, Alice is pleased when, as they left the institute, Charles had offered her his arm, on his non injured side, she accepted it and they remained arm in arm until they reach the clump of trees on the common opposite the Silver Cup pub, they sit on a wooden bench.

"Would you accompany me to London when I get this medal Alice"

Alice looks shocked, "In London?" she asks

"Yes" is his simple reply.

"I will have to ask Granny and Aunt May; I have never been to London before"

"It is a big and noisy city Alice; the countryside is a much more peaceful and beautiful place"

"Why do you want me to go with you then?" she asks

He looks into her eyes,

"So that you can bring a little of your peace and a lot of your beauty to the city"

She blushes heavily and can't speak, her breath is taken away when he carries on,

"The ceremony is at Buckingham palace and the King is presenting the medals"

That evening, Alice is sitting in the cottage waiting for Grace to meet her there, the regiments in town have not asked to use the cottage as a billet this time and Alice is happy about this, it has become a regular meeting place for her and Grace for the past few weekends, she is still staying with May and Pete during the week even though she has no schooling to attend to anymore, their cottage is much nearer to the Institute and she can get a lift with Pete in his ambulance most days.

With Graces help she has returned the cottage to a state of normality, when Abe, Bob and Jake had left she had not visited the cottage at all for a few weeks, the visions of Dave lying dead under the Yew tree are still raw and she could not bring herself to go anywhere near the place, only over the past four weekends with gentle nudging from Grace has she entered the garden and the cottage, they have both taken all the cottage furniture from the back bedroom and put it all back in its correct place. Alice feels better now that the cottage looks more like the home, she remembers rather than the military rooms it had become when the Sherwood Foresters were billeted there. For her own peace of mind, she had to remove all signs of them having been there, her memories of the boys, especially David, remain the same, although some are frightening and tortured at times, but now the kitchen, the living room and her bedroom are full of furniture and life, she feels safe, even content, with being there.

The fire in the range is burning and glowing red hot coal is heating the large kettle left behind by the men of the Sherwood Foresters, steam is flooding from its large spout, Alice takes a heavy cotton cloth and removes the kettle from the heat, the steam stops almost immediately, tipping the kettle she pours a small amount of boiling water into the teapot she has prepared and ready, putting the kettle back onto the range she then swills the hot water around inside the teapot to warm it up. This done she adds two heaped teaspoons of Lyons loose leaf tea, the tin has the brand name in large white letters, each letter having an orange border that stands out against a blue background, this background has a white border, next to the white the tin is edged with more orange, also surrounded with a white border, the words, '*Always the best*' are in black lettering at the bottom of the tin, set in the middle of the orange border, the lid is put back on the pot and she lays the cotton cloth over it, Alice is sure that they used to have a proper tea cosy but she has no idea where it is. She checks that the teacups and saucers are neatly presented on the kitchen table with the tea plates, each contain a fresh iced bun from the bakers, Alice had just caught the grocery store as Mrs Ackroyd was closing up this afternoon, she very generously sold Alice the last two buns for a low price. The grocery store is very well stocked, Mary told Alice only that morning that she believes that the war may cause a huge food shortage and also that German owned bakeries in London are being attacked by locals, even though the families that own these establishments have lived in Britain and supported communities for decades, Alice thinks the attacks are outrageous and the war is hardly the fault of families of German bakers who live in London. She jumps up when she hears the gate open, she runs through the open front door and sees Grace walking up the garden path toward her,

"Grace!" she excitedly exclaims, "I have missed you so"

Grace accepts the hug Alice gives her, "Come along Alice, I only saw you last Sunday!"

She puts her arms around Alice shoulders, "I do like your dress Alice, is it new?"

Alice steps back from Grace and laughs, "No, I wish it were, this is an old thing"

"Well, I think it looks splendid" Grace replies with a smile that brightens the day.

Alice is wearing a green ankle length dress, it crosses over her bosom and is tied at the waist with a matching belt, underneath she has on a high necked white lace blouse, she looks at Grace,

"You always look so glamourous Grace, so pretty in everything that you wear"

Grace tells Alice to stop teasing her, she straightens her dress, it is light blue with a delicate black flower pattern all over it, the plunging V at the front has white cotton frilled edging and a mauve waist band is the same colour as the frilled chemise she wears underneath it.

They walk arm in arm up the path to the door and separate as they go through the door,

"Iced buns, my favourite, thank you Alice" It is Graces turn to sound excited.

They sit down and Alice pours the tea, Grace leans forward, her elbows on the table and her hand placed under her chin,

"So young lady, how is the soldier?"

"Which one Grace? I help several of them" Alice replies coyly, Grace throws her head back and laughs, her dark hair cascades over her shoulders and down her back,

"You know very well which soldier I mean Alice!" she says, "Now tell me, please!"

Alice enthusiastically tells Grace all about Charles, his military cross award and the presentation at Buckingham palace,

"You must go Alice, you simply must, Buckingham Palace indeed!"

Alice becomes distant and gloomy,

"Alice? What is it?"

Alice turns to her friend,

"Granny doesn't want me to go, Aunt May and Uncle Pete are just fine with it, Pete has met Charles and knows he is a decent sort, but Granny has said she will think about it"

"Do you want me to speak to Mary for you, I am sure I can persuade her to let you"

Alice's eyes light up, "Would you do that, for me?"

"Of course, I will Alice, one thing I must know though"

"Anything, anything at all!" exclaims a newly invigorated Alice,

"Well," Grace says playfully, "I presume it is just for the day, there won't be any overnight stop involved?"

Alice stares at her friend, eyes wide and mouth gaping, "Grace!" she almost screams, "Certainly not, how could you think such a thing!"

Laughing out loud again, Grace winks slowly and purposefully at Alice, who protests again,

"Grace! stop it now!"

Grace picks up her teacup, puts the rim to her lips, she gently blows on the surface of the blood red tea, she is still looking at Alice who is frowning, Grace raises one eyebrow, and both fall about laughing, Grace just has time to put her teacup down before she drops it. Tea is finished and buns eaten, Alice tells Grace about the three other men in her care, Grace is interested in John Freeman, even more so when she realises that she knows some of his family,

"If he is from East Hyde, then I think I might know his sister, she works in the infirmary at the children's home" she stops and thinks for a few seconds, "Janine Freeman, she is a couple of years older than me and engaged to a Captain from the Sherwood Foresters"

Grace tells Alice that Johns father works for the Great Northern railway and that they live in a tied cottage under the viaduct at East Hyde, Grace recalls that Mr Freeman works at the station in the ticket office. It is a tiny station at Newmill End, a quarter of a mile or so from the hamlet of East Hyde, also close to the Midland railway station at Chiltern Green, a much bigger and busier station than Newmill End.

"Well, he keeps going missing" says Alice "He has been found at the East Station on several occasions, I suppose he might think he is near to home or looking for his Father"

"Have his family been to visit him?" asks Grace,

Alice nods a reply, "Yes, a few times, they have another son in the Royal Navy, he is a gunner on HMS Triumph, I believe Mr Freeman said that the ship is involved in fighting off the Turkish coast, he is so very worried about both of his sons and for very different reasons. The cottage is tidy, both have cleared away the cups and saucers they used,

"What are you doing tomorrow Alice?" Alice becomes embarrassed and shy, Grace laughs,

"Oh, I see, you are seeing Charles tomorrow, aren't you?"

Alice giggles, "I am, we are taking a walk into town together, he is leaving on Friday to stay with his family in Wheathampstead for a day or two and then he is off to London to get his medal"

Alice stops talking suddenly,

"Alice, whatever is wrong?"

Alice has tears in her eyes when she answers, "Then he is off to the war"

Grace puts her arms around Alice, quietly, she says, "Then we will both have men away fighting wont we"

They leave the house, Alice walks to the fence line and picks a few wood anemones and bluebells, she walks down the garden and puts the flowers under the Yew tree, against the knotted and gnarled trunk, "For David" she whispers, turning around she walks back up to where Grace is standing by the gate, they link arms and walk toward the Malta pub to go and see Mary.

Alice and Charles meet the next morning, not at the Institute but outside of John Irons bakers on the high street, Charles has a paper bag in his hand,

"I hope you like apple cake, I thought we could walk, I need to go to Robert Jones the tailors, he is adjusting my tunic to make it more comfortable with this" he points at his shoulder, "His shop is just a little further up the High Street, then perhaps we could sit and eat the cake"

Alice agrees and is again ecstatic when Charles offers her his arm, she takes it, and they walk slowly from the bakers toward the tailors. Alice is silent as Charles tells her all about himself and his family, he is not from Wheathampstead as she had thought, he lives at the Folly, his father and mother are at Cherry Trees cottages, next door to his Uncle George and Aunt Mary, George is his father's older Brother. His Father and George both work on the railway, originally as labourers, but George now also works on the engines as a stoker, Charles Father still works with the labouring gang on the tracks. George and Mary have one son, Francis, or Frankie as Charles calls him. Charles and Frankie are both in the army and write to each other regularly, they have been close since childhood, Frankie is currently a Lance Corporal with the Oxford and Bucks light infantry, he arrived in France at the same time as Charles, they had met by chance on the battlefield at Mons, this is when they promised to write to each other. Frankie has been in the thick of it, fighting on the Ypres salient at Mons, Passchendaele and Nonne Bosschen wood, where his regiment had defeated the elite Prussian Guard. Frankie had moved away from the Folly in 1911, to reside at Green Lodge Stables in Bovingdon with his wife, Florrie and their three children, where he was employed as a coachman, the family moved to Caversham just before the war, he had enlisted at Binfield Heath in Oxfordshire shortly after the declaration of war against Germany. It is obvious to Alice that Charles thinks the world of Frankie and because he is a few months older than his cousin, he is very protective of him.

They reach St Nicholas church, they walk into the churchyard and sit on a bench that is positioned in a sunny spot next to the huge and ancient Yew Tree, Alice shivers a little when she sees the tree looming in front of her, Charles notices the look on her face,

"Are you feeling alright Alice?" She tells him that she is fine and that he must continue with his tales of the Folly. Alice smiles when Charles tells her all about his group of friends, 'The Folly boys', they had all joined up within a few days of each other in 1914, he has a photograph of all of them sitting on a cart, he takes it from inside of his tunic and shows her, Alice can't see Charles in the photograph and he explains that he is the photographer, he wanted a picture of all of his mates to go with him to war. Alice looks at the photograph, the men are all smiling, some are waving their caps excitedly in the air, some are leaning casually against the cart and a couple of them are sitting very formally, she looks at Charles,

"Do you all keep in touch; do you know how they are all doing?" she asks

He pauses for a moment, Alice notices his hesitation to reply,

"Charles, I am sorry if I have made you sad thinking about your friends, please don't carry on if you don't want to"

He puts the photograph on his knee and points to the men one by one and tells Alice about them,

"This is Cyril Carter, he was a Royal Navy sailor, sadly killed when the ammunition store on HMS Bulwark exploded in November last year in the harbour at Sheerness, nothing to do with the war, it was a fearful accident that killed over 750 men"

Alice can only reply, "That is so awful"

Charles raises his eyebrows but carries on,

"That is Frankie, you know about him already, standing next to him is Sid Bandy, then Horace Wilson, who at the time I took this photo, had moved to The Hill, Wheathampstead with his wife Louisa, they have two children, but he came back to the Folly to be photographed with us all"

He takes a small bite from his apple cake,

"Sitting on the cart is George Robins, a few years older than most of us, he is a Captain with the East Yorkshire regiment, he has been in the army since 1901, he was at Magdalen College in Oxford and left to join up, he has been all over the world but returned before the war to The Folly with his wife, Beryl, he is on the Western Front at this time, another one of us right in the middle of it all"

Alice touches Charles hand gently to encourage him to continue,

"Horace Izzard, Bertie Lawrence, George Minall, Albert Munt, who also lives in cottage at Cherry trees" he moves the photograph slightly and points to the last two men, "those two are Cyril Pearce and Bert Odell"

He puts the photograph away, he finishes by saying,

"One of our old gang, not in the photo, now lives in Bedford somewhere, Murray Harrison, I haven't seen him for a while" he looks at Alice, "That is my lot! a great bunch of men, we all had such fun growing up"

"It sounds as if you have good friends there Charles, proper heroes, all of you"

Charles looks at the ground, a little uncomfortable at being called a hero,

"One of our chaps is a real life hero, he has recently been awarded the Victoria Cross"

"A soldier from your battalion?' asks Alice

Charles shakes his head, "No, actually from your brothers' lot, the 2nd Battalion, Captain Charles Foss led a bunch of men into enemy trenches at a town called Neuve Chapelle, nasty business apparently, it was listed in the London Gazette last month"

As he looks across at Alice, he sees fear on her face, realisation hits him that she is terrified for her brother,

"Alice, have you heard from Martin in the last week or so?"

She replies that she has, in fact she has had a postcard and a letter from him in the last few days, Charles takes her hands in his, gently squeezing them, he says,

"There you go, Captain Foss led the men into the trenches in the second week of March, if anything had happened to Martin, with Foss or at any time during that battle, he would not have been able to write to you, would he?"

"Do you think he is safe Charles?"

Charles knows that nowhere on the Western front is safe, even when behind the lines billeted in towns and villages, enemy shells strike hard and lives are lost, he decides to answer her question with a safe answer,

"He wrote to you twice in the last week, so he can't be very busy, can he?"

Alice doesn't answer, she frees one of her hands from his and wipes her eyes,

"Tell you what Alice, if I can, I will try and look him up when I go back, his battalion is in a different part of France to mine, but I will try, then I will write to you immediately"

As he finishes, they both look up and see another soldier standing in the Graveyard, underneath the Yew tree, looking at them, Charles stands, faces the soldier, and puts his cap on,

"Can I help you Lance Corporal?"

The young soldier with a single stripe on each of arm of his uniform tunic, stands to attention and salutes at Charles,

"Beggin' your pardon sir" Charles returns the salute, and the soldier continues, "I am a friend of the young ladies' brother, Martin, we both played football for the towns first eleven"

Charles looks at Alice, she also stands, the Lance Corporal takes off his cap,

"My name is Albert Weston" he looks at Alice, "Everyone calls me Bertie though"

Alice face lights up as she realises who the young soldier is,

"Bertie! I did not recognise you in your uniform"

"I am in the 7th East Surrey regiment, we are off to France in five weeks, I am home just for two days, to say my cheerios' to Mother and Father"

"Do they still live at Coleswood Road?"

Bertie is pleased that Alice remembers his parents,

"Yes Alice, they do, I am going to see them, I am just in town hoping to see the quarter master from the North Staffs regiment, hopefully to exchange some kit of mine that are the wrong sizes"

Alice and Charles both nod, it is Alice who speaks first,

"You may bump into Martin; he is over in France now"

Charles smiles, he knows the chances are slim and that there are hundreds of thousands of British men at the Western Front, but he had bumped into Frankie at Mons, so it isn't impossible, Bertie replies.

"May I ask how he is doing, none of us in my regiment know what to expect"

Alice tells Bertie that Martin is doing well, that he writes to her every fortnight or so and seems to be fit and well, Bertie seems a little anxious, Charles removes his cap and speaks to him,

"Bert, I have been over in France and in Belgium, took a little knock" he taps his shoulder, "You will be fine, it is a bit frightening at times, it is really not too bad, remember, your comrades will all be scared, each man always looks out for the man next to him, so you will never be alone"

"Thank you, sir"

Charles steps forward and shakes Berties hand,

"Good luck Bert, see you over there perhaps?"

Both men put their caps on, Bertie salutes the officer standing in front of him,

"Bye Bertie be safe" says Alice.

He thanks her and walks away,

"That was a nice thing to say Charles"

He looks at her quizzically, she replies,

"It must be so very awful over there, you told him that it was a bit frightening, but everything will be alright, such a nice thing to say to him as he is obviously scared"

Charles shuffles his feet and looks at the ground,

"It will be alright wont it?" asks Alice

"Everything will be fine Alice" he takes her hand and puts it in his, "I promise"

* * *

It is dark when Alice and Grace alight from the train at East station, Alice is beaming, her smile is so bright, and she is so happy,

"Thank you so much Grace for taking me to London to be with Charles"

Grace smiles at her young friend,

"It is my pleasure; it was an exciting day, wasn't it?"

Alice nods enthusiastically, "I do wish you could have come to the Palace with us Grace, it is so grand and beautiful, and it was so nice to see Charles get his medal from the King!"

Grace smiles, this is the fourth or fifth time she has heard Alice enthusiastically talk about the ceremony, she is happy to listen and is glad that her young friend is smiling again,

"I had a very nice time walking in Green Park and around St James Park Lake, I even had a peek at Downing Street, I was hoping to see Mr Asquith or Mr Lloyd George but alas the street was empty and quiet!"

They reach the Malta pub, stopping outside to say goodnight to one another, Alice hugs Grace,

"What's all this for?" asks Grace "We have had a lovely day, no need for tears"

"Charles goes back to France tomorrow" Alice looks at Grace "I know everyone will think I am silly, but I will miss him so much"

The two embrace for a few seconds in silence,

"Are you at the institute tomorrow?" asks Grace

"I am, we have a new soldier on the ward, Lance Corporal Charles Parr, he was billeted in town with the $2^{nd}/6^{th}$ battalion Staffordshire regiment, they only left in March, he was injured having been in France for only a few days"

"How is he?" Grace enquires

Alice shakes her head, "His injuries are just awful Grace, when he arrived on Friday, we didn't think he would make it through the night, he has been at the St John and St Elizabeth hospital in London for over a week, he has been sent back here as some of his regiment are still training in town"

"I am sure he will be fine in your capable hands Alice" Grace stands back from Alice "Shall I see you next weekend Alice?"

"Yes, please Grace, my weekends are not the same when we don't meet"

They embrace quickly, Grace walks toward the Gibraltar castle pub to take the cut through to Salisbury Road, Alice climbs the steps to the pub slowly, she is drained and emotional after today's events, she sneaks a quick look at the cottage, all is quiet, she can see the top of the Yew Tree dominating the skyline of the garden. She shivers and enters the pub.

* * *

Martin spends most of the early parts of April in stinking wet trenches, patrolling or behind the lines, for some reason the division is insisting on a lot of practice attacks and parades, lots of high ranking officers visiting the regiment to inspect their troops, Martin had an inkling that a parade was in the offing when, on the 2nd of April, the men were given an order to take bath and to present their kit!

Sure enough the next day the Brigadier General arrived and inspected the division and told the Major that he is very happy at how clean and tidy the men are, it is sad that only 22 officers and 643 other ranks, Martin included, from the 2nd Battalion Bedfordshire's were able to parade, all the others, over 500 at this time, are either dead or injured, Martin is sure that it is no coincidence that 75 other ranked soldiers arrive from Battalion HQ in Bedford the following day. Some of the lads have been transferred from the 4th Battalion, but most of the new lads are volunteers with only minimal training, they will have to learn the hard way how to get on and survive trench warfare.

Field Marshal Sir John French arrived on the 12 April to inspect the Brigade, Brigadier General Watts addressed all of the men, thanking them for their service and bravery at Neuve Chapelle, the Commanding Officer, Major John Mackenzie V.C, leads the salute and takes the handshake with the Brigadier General.

Martin is bored, he scarcely dares admit it to himself, but he would rather be in the trenches at times than be taking part in pointless ceremonial parades, he keeps his opinions to himself as his colleagues may think him barmy, but he does wonder if some of them are having the same feelings.

In the middle of the month the battalion move to Fauquissart, a tiny village near to Laventie, they have been here a few times before, billets are allocated, and they are warned of more parades during this period of rest and relaxation. Martin is happy when the mail arrives, Private 'C.C.' Harding the regimental postman is the most popular man for the few minutes he distributes the mail, those who do not receive mail are always upset and angry and take it out on poor old C.C.

Martin walks away from the crowd around C.C. and away from the centre of Fauquissart, the small village where some of the battalion are currently billeted, it is no more than a ribbon development of buildings built along the main road, the whole surround of the village is made up of trenches, some large and spacious but most are hardly wide enough for two men to pass and taller than every soldier who walks through them. The buildings in the village have taken some shell fire and many are damaged, some beyond repair, but where Martin now walks, the Rue de Bois on the south side of the village, it is remarkably untouched, as he looks around, he thinks that it will not be long before every building he can see will be reduced to rubble, as has happened to every town and village he has visited, passed through, or been billeted in since arriving. It is unusually quiet, no shells are being fired and only the occasional spate of rifle fire can be heard in the far distance, he knows that the front line trenches are occupied by the 2nd Battalion the Queens Royal regiment, he knows that this quiet spell will be a relief for those soldiers. He walks until he gets to a low wall, with short spiked green painted iron railings, he follows the line of the wall, running his right hand along the railings as he walks, listening to the gentle noise it makes as he moves along, he reaches a gate, painted the same colour as the railings, looking down a path he sees a church in front of him. The path is in shadow from the building to its left side, a 2 storey house that leads to a double opening barn doors, also painted green, he can see that they open on a slide rail at the top of each door, twenty yards from this building and set back from the road is the church, it has an almost triangular frontage with a large studded wooden door at its centre and has a large stone cross on the peaked roof above the door, standing tall and symmetrically behind the front of the church is a tall square bell tower, with louvres on each side, the spire is tall and at its peak stands an elegant weather vane. To the right of the path are two large trees, they dominate and almost cover the view to the front of the church, Martin opens the gate and enters the church yard, he takes a seat on the ground under a large Yew tree, he is drawn to it by familiarity with the similar tree his garden, the other tree is a wild and untamed Cypress tree, so unlike the elegantly topiarised Cypress trees at Hatching Green he vividly remembers, this is an unkempt and very tall tree. The Yew gives him shelter from the warm and sunny day, it has been raining almost constantly for the past week or so, the warmth from the sun is welcomed, the shade of the Yew gives him solitude and peace, a break away from the army and from everyone is something he craves at times.

He has two letters each from Grace and Alice and one from Granny, he smiles as he opens the letter from Mary first, he knows it will be a very short and formal letter, 'hope you are well', 'we are all fine', 'keep your chin up' and other such short formalities. He is not disappointed, the letter is just exactly as he thought it would be, he treasures it none the less. Alice's letters are full of life and expectations, she likes to write about what they will do when he is home again, her hopefulness is just what Martin needs to hear, he is surprised to hear that she is volunteering with the field ambulance and the VAD, he is momentarily scared that she could be posted overseas to the medical clearing stations and field hospitals that are situated all over the Western front, his fears are soon gone when he reads on for a few more sentences, Alice explains that she, Jennifer and Catherine are only volunteers as they are too young to serve with the VAD, he is very proud of her for doing this and he will express his pride when he writes back to her. Alice has never mentioned Private David Shafford to him, Grace has explained to him in a letter that Private Shafford had taken his own life in the garden of the cottage by hanging himself from a low bough of the Yew tree. He has not mentioned in his return letters to her, Grace asked him not to bring it up, Alice will one day tell him about the experience and her feelings about it, he knows Grace is right, emotions like this cannot really be expressed on postcards or notepaper. He always leaves letters from Grace till last and today is no exception, Martin looks at the two envelopes, the neat script handwriting has beautifully formed letters and words, making it easy to read, the black ink she uses stands out against the light blue of the envelope, he puts them both to his nose and takes a deep breath through his nose, he is sure he can smell her perfume on the envelope, closing his eyes, just for a few seconds, he imagines lying next to her and smelling the same perfume on her body. He opens his eyes when he hears some of his mates howling and whooping with joy from the next street over from the church, parcels have also arrived and gifts and food from home are always welcomed, Martin has received a few goodies from home, mostly from Grace, but this time he has received letters only. He reads the envelope again, his name, rank and number have pride of place at the top of the address, the stamp in the top right corner has been turned clockwise slightly, Martin smiles, he understands that this means 'a kiss' using the secret language of stamps, this form of silent communication has become popular with the soldiers and their loved ones.

He reads the address,

'2nd Battalion Bedfordshire Regiment

British Expeditionary Force'

He is always amazed, and pleased, that such a simply addressed letter can find him at the Western Front as he and the Bedfordshire's move around regularly, the mail reaches them with amazing regularity, even when they are in trenches at the front, the R.E.P.S and the lads working in the field post offices certainly work hard to get the mail to and from the front.

He looks at the date stamp, so as to read the letters in the correct order they were sent to him, the stamps are illegible, he knows that Grace will have put the date she wrote the letters at the top of her note paper. Opening the first letter very carefully, not wanting to damage the neatly addressed envelope, he takes out the letter and looks at the date, the 17th of April, only four days ago, this must be the later letter, he takes the other, spends time again looking at the handwriting and smelling the envelope,

"Describe in detail what you can smell will you Corp!"

Martin looks up and sees Private Alfie Cox walking toward the church and past where he is sitting,

"Bugger off Coxy!" Martin smiles as he talks to the soldier he knows well, "What are you up to?" he asks Alfie

"Just showing young Richard Hemmings here around our delightful but temporary home"

A young private step forward, standing upright,

"Private Richard Hemmings Corporal"

Martin puts his letters down next to where his is sitting,

"Welcome to our world Hemmings, when did you arrive?"

Richard Hemmings shuffles his feet, unsure if he needs to stand to attention when talking to a corporal, Martin helps him out,

"Relax Hemmings, this is our day off" he looks at Alfie who is smirking, "Take that smile off of your face Alfie, I hope you are showing young Hemmings how things are done?"

Alfie nods, Martin turns back to Richard,

"So, when did you arrive Richard?"

"Just yesterday Corporal, with twenty other lads and three officers"

"Where are you from lad?"

"Codicote Corporal, a small village in Hertfordshire"

Martin smiles, "I know it well, it's only five miles from where I grew up, I hope to return there very soon"

Richards face lights up as he hears Martins words,

"I served in Pretoria with a lad from Codicote, Ernie Ginger, I think he is with the 6th Battalion now, he was transferred from the 2nd in August '14, just before we were sent over here in October, the 6th was put together with men from all different battalions of Bedfordshire's"

"I think I might know his younger brother, George, it is just the two of them and their mother, I believe their father died some years ago"

Martin shakes his head,

"I will have to take your word for that Richard, Ernie never talked about his family much" Martin looks over at Alfie and raises his eyebrows, Alfie talks to Richard,

"Come on then Richie my boy, lots more to see today, I think a trip to the trenches will be nice"

"Nice to meet you Richard, keep your head down and don't listen to a word that Alfie says to you"

They all laugh, and the two privates move away from Martin, Alfie throws a mock salute at Martin, they set off, walking through the churchyard toward the small, wooded area behind it, heading for the trenches on the East side of the village.

Martin picks up his letters and selects the letter he was smelling before the arrival of the other two soldiers, he puts the other letters into his lap, he reaches into his trouser pocket and removes a small penknife, opening the blade he cuts carefully through the envelope and removes the precious letter from inside. It is dated 28th March, Grace is, as usual, very gracious about others, telling him all she can about home and the people he knows, he reads in the letter that Albert Bandy had been killed in battle, Martin has not mentioned in any of his letters that he was with Albert when he was killed, in fact he hardly mentions the war in his letters, strange as it may seem, he doesn't want to tell those he loves how terrible it can be over here, he reads on. Grace speaks fondly of Alice; Martin is so glad to hear that she is coping with the death of young David Shafford and that she is very well thought of at the Institute and that she approaches her responsibilities with a maturity beyond her sixteen years. She assures him that Mary is fit and well, as she always is and that they speak regularly and discuss the letters and postcards that Martin sends home, he is very glad to read that Grace only speaks to his grandmother about certain parts of his letters, she assures him that the private content will always remain so. Her last paragraph, as it always is, contains words written from the heart, her feelings toward him and how much she misses him and that all she wants in her life is him, she signs off as she always does, '*Your ever loving Grace'*.

He carefully puts the letter back into the envelope, sitting for a moment and taking in her words of love for him, taking the second letter from Grace, he opens it, again with care, and reads slowly, taking in all the details and words. His eyes are opened wide when he reads that Alice has become close to one of the men in her care, Grace, who knows that Martin is overprotective of his Sister assures him that all is above board, Martin reads on, she tells him that the man is 21 year old 2nd Lt Charles Gray from the 1st Battalion Bedfordshire regiment, Martin puts the letter down for a few seconds as he tries to recall if he knows this man or not, he decides that he does not and carries on. 2nd Lt Gray had been injured on the Western Front and had been sent to the Institute as it is the nearest army hospital to his home, his family live at the Folly, Martin again puts the letter down as he racks his brain trying to remember if he knows the family, this Charles Gray is only a year, or less, younger than he is, their paths must have crossed at some point, he is unable to put a face to the name so carries on with the letter. He is shocked and a little angry to read that Alice will be accompanying Gray to London for a medal ceremony, he calms a little when Grace tells him that she will be going along as a chaperone and that Alice will be visiting Buckingham palace and hopes to be close to the King when the medal is presented, Grace has not mentioned what medal that Gray is getting, he smiles to himself finding it amusing that Grace was very detailed about the plans for the day, about what they are both going to wear, but fails to mention what medal 2nd Lt Gray is receiving from the King, he presumes that it is a bravery medal, most are dished out in the trenches or behind the lines, the young officer was lucky to get his from the King at the palace, he realises that the medal ceremony was two days ago on Monday the 19th April, his little Sister going out to London with an officer from his Regiment!

His concentration is disturbed by a voice addressing him,

"Corporal"

He looks up,

"Private Hemmings, did you enjoy your tour of the trenches?"

"Yes, thank you corporal"

Martin looks at the young soldier, he remains silent,

"Corporal, Alfie says I am to tell you that all the NCOs are to muster at 1600 hours for a briefing"

Martin knows that Alfie will have been tasked with getting the message to the NCO's, he has sent Hemmings to do his work,

"Thanks Richard, how many more have you to find?"

"Three Corporal" he looks at his list, "Sergeant Oakes, Colour Sergeant Hutchinson and Sergeant Hubbocks"

Martin puts his letters inside his tunic and stands, stretching out using the tree to balance,

"Follow me Richard, I have a good idea where the three of them may be"

Martin knows where all three senior NCO's will be, Len Hubbocks had been injured very early in 1915 when he was attached to the 1st Battalion, he has recently returned to the front and joined the 2nd Battalion during the first week of April, the son of a publican and a dab hand at playing cards, he enjoys taking money from Oakes and Edward Hutchinson.

"They will be playing cards at the back of the barn being used as our temporary HQ"

He leads Hemmings from the peaceful churchyard, and they walk toward the rear lines, the wind picks up as they leave their peaceful surround and Martin turns to look at the Yew tree, it whispers to him as the wind passes through its branches, he shivers and walks away from the churchyard.

Shortly after 5pm, Martin is sat with a few other NCO's eating a meal of pea soup with meat chunks, probably horse meat, there are a few sliced carrots and turnip mixed in,

"So, what do we think about the rumours about the Germans using gas on us?"

During the briefing, they had been given information relating to intelligence about the use of Chlorine gas by the Germans, they are all having a hard time believing or accepting it,

"Sod chlorine, those useless cabbage mechanics have put tins of *Maconochie* in this broth" Sergeant Oakes is lifting the soup out of his tin with his spoon and letting it drop back in again,

"They ruin a decent horse and pea broth by adding tins of that rubbish"

The others, including Martin, quietly laugh at Oakes as he plays with his food, their amusement is cut short when an officer approaches them, they all stand, using his hands he insists they sit and finish their meal, Len Hubbocks knows the officer,

"Hello sir, you all better now then?"

The officer looks at Len and has a realisation that he knows him,

"Hello Sergeant Hubbocks" he steps in and the two of them shake hands,

"I am fine now, and you? I hear you took a hit in January"

Len nods,

"Just a flesh wound Sir, nothing much really"

"How long have you been with the 2nd Battalion?" asks the officer,

"Only a few weeks Sir"

Hutchinson pipes up, "Enough time to fleece us of our well-earned pay sir!"

The officer looks across at Edward, he laughs, "From what I hear Colours, directly from my lads in the 1st, it is best to steer clear of Sergeant Leonard Hubbocks and his card school!"

The men all laugh as Len pleads his innocence, assuring the others that no cheating goes on, the officer turns his attention to Martin, "Could I have a word with you please Corporal?"

Martin stands after putting his nearly empty mess tin on the ground, "Sir" he says

"If you need to finish your food, I can speak to you then"

Martin looks at his tin, "No, it's alright Sir, I think I have had my fill"

The officer points to a canvas shelter that is twenty yards away, "Perhaps we could sit over there Corporal"

Martin nods and steps out of the circle of men he is with, Len speaks to the officer,

"Sir, not one to speak out of line, but if you don't wear your medal ribbon on your tunic, the C.O will bollock you" he pauses "If I may make that gentle observation Sir"

The officer nods at Len, before he can answer, Martin speaks,

"After you sir" He points at the shelter and follows as the officer makes his way toward it, these makeshift shelters always remind Martin of the home made tents his Father used to put up in the Garden for Alice and him to play in during the hot summer months, a sheet of tarpaulin with tall pole at either end, a strong centre pole lashed with string between the two, the outer edges of the tarpaulin held firmly in the ground with homemade wooden tent pegs, he and Alice had spent hours playing in the garden, the stream and under the shelter when the days were long and hot,

"Corporal?"

Martin realises he is daydreaming, "Apologies Sir, I was just thinking about home" Martin is standing outside the shelter and the officer is sat down on a long wooden bench,

"Please relax Corporal and have a seat, it's Martin, isn't it?"

Martin sits opposite the 2nd Lieutenant, he is a little concerned how this man, who he thinks is about the same age as him, knows his name,

"Martin my name is Charles"

Martin does not reply but looks quizzically at the officer, who continues talking,

"Charles, Charles Gray, I have the pleasure of knowing your sister, Alice"

It takes Martin a second or two to gather and process the information he has just been given,

"2nd Lt Charles Gray? I have just been reading about you in a letter from home, from my lady"

Charles grins,

"Grace is so lovely Martin, Alice adores her"

"Yes Sir" is all Martin can think to say.

"I promised Alice that if I had the opportunity to find you I would, she was very concerned when we talked about Captain Foss getting his V.C., she was so scared that you were involved in that little scrape"

"I was sir, I led Captain Foss and the bombers to the German trenches"

Charles raises his eyebrows, "I didn't realise you are part of the bombers team Martin"

"I am not Sir" Martin pauses "I had been on patrol in the area before the Germans took the trenches from us" He swallows deeply "My Lance Corporal, Albert Bandy, was killed on that patrol, anyway, Captain Foss took me along to show him and the bombers the safest way to get to the occupied trenches"

"Sounds like you deserve a gong along with Foss and the others Martin" he doesn't wait for an answer and continues, "Albert Bandy? From Coldharbour?"

Martin nods, "Yes Sir, only eighteen but a good soldier"

"His Uncle, Sid, lives around the corner from my parents at the Folly, Sid joined the army the same time as me, young Albert worked at the nursery at Westfield common didn't he, his Father is also Albert if memory serves me correctly?"

"Yes Sir, he was an errand boy, volunteered as soon as he was old enough, his father is Albert, and his mother is Lizzie"

Both men are quiet as they reflect on the death of a man that they both knew from their lives outside of the service, if only fleetingly in Charles case,

"I understand you took my sister to London Sir?"

Charles puts his hands up in front of him, palms toward Martin,

"All above board, I assure you, Grace travelled with us Mrs Spratley insisted, I had to visit her pub, she gave me a right going over"

Martin giggles, "That's Granny alright"

"You have my word Martin, Alice and Grace travelled to London on the train with me, Alice accompanied me to Buckingham palace for the presentation and then I had to almost immediately travel to Southampton for transport over here, Alice and Grace took the train home"

"What did you get Sir?"

Charles looks confused, Martin tries again, "What medal did you get?"

Charles blushes and becomes visibly uncomfortable, "It is the Military Cross actually"

"Impressive" says Martin,

"Team effort Martin, I assure you, nothing like what you did for Foss and the bombers"

"Congratulations anyway Sir"

Martin stands and puts out a hand, Charles stands and accepts, the men shake hands,

"Thank you, Martin you can drop the 'Sir' I think, Charles is just fine"

"If it suits, I will remain official when others are about, it's only fair I think Charles"

Charles sits down again, Martin follows suit,

"It won't be for long Martin, I am re-joining the 1st tomorrow, they are scrapping for Hill 60, and they are taking a bit of a bashing, so I hear"

"I am sure we will bump into each other again Charles, this battlefield isn't as big as some think"

Charles agrees with Martin, then he says,

"Speaking of bumping into people, I met a chap that knows you Martin, what was his name?" Martin stays silent as Charles thinks, "Bertie, Bertie, I don't remember his surname, he played football with you for the Town team"

Martin beams with a huge smile, "Weston, Bertie Weston!"

"That's the very man Martin" Charles says excitedly, "Alice and I were out for a walk, and we bumped into him, I didn't know him at all, but he knows you"

"How is he doing?"

"He is with the East Surrey's; they are deploying in the next few weeks to join us on this summer holiday we are currently enjoying!"

They both laugh, Martin asks Charles, "Did you play for the Folly team, we played there a few times, on that bloody awful sloping pitch by the allotments"

Charles laughs out loud, "No, football is not a game I am any good at, a few of my friends played in the team, I used to watch the games and have a few beers in the Rose and Crown afterwards"

Martin nods in agreement, "The Folly were not a great team, but they did have one cracking player, a fella by the name of Izzard"

Charles claps his hands with excitement,

"Horace! Horace Izzard, we are great mates Horace and I, he joined the Duke of Wellingtons, he was only seventeen when we all attested together, I remember the Justice of the peace from town was a very serious man, that was in May '14, I haven't heard anything from him since I left" he pauses, becomes very serious, puts his right hand on his heart and says,

"*I* Charles Edward Gray, swear by Almighty God, that I will be faithful and bear true Allegiance to His Majesty King George the Fifth, his heirs and successors, and that I will, as in duty bound, honestly and faithfully defend His Majesty, his heirs, and successors, in person, Crown and dignity against all enemies, according to the conditions of my service"

"Bloody hell Charles" laughs Martin, "No wonder you are an officer, with a brain that can remember that! I don't even remember where I attested!"

Charles smiles, Martin speaks, "I used to like the Rose and Crown as well, even though I was only sixteen then, Mr Burrows was always happy to give me a pint!"

Charles slaps the table with both hands, "Me also! He left in December '09 and Amos Smart is back as licensee now"

"Can't say as I know him, I left when I was eighteen in February 1910 and haven't been back much since" reflects Martin.

He looks at his pocket watch, "I had better go Charles, I have to be at the factory near to the drawbridge or '*Pont-Levis*' as the Major calls it, using that bloody awful accent as he does, it is at Estaires and is a good hour's march to get there"

The men stand, it is Charles that puts his hand out this time, Martin takes it, "Goodbye and good luck Martin, I hope to see you again"

Martin pulls Charles a little closer to him, he has a broad grin on his face, "Look after my little sister" he says, adding "Sir" at the end of the sentence.

Charles puts his right hand on his heart, "On my life Martin"

* * *

At 8pm, located just North of Fauquissart at a tiny hamlet called, Le Fort d'Esquin, it is really nothing more than a crossroads and a few houses, Martin is with his platoon, Alfie Cox and Richard Hemmings are amongst his men, he notices Johnno standing with another platoon, he calls over to him, "Johnno!"

'Johnno' Johnson looks up and see Martin waving at him, he comes over to him and the men shake hands, Martin turns Johnno's arm during the handshake, he points at the single chevron on his arm,

"Well, Lance Corporal, who would have thought that a few months ago" he lets go of the man's arm,

"Fresh on today Martin, our platoon leader was shot and killed last night, as senior man they have given the stripe to me"

"Who got killed, did I know him?"

Johnno nods, "Yeah, I thinks so, Frank Payne, about the same age as us, he was a Surrey boy, Guildford I think, that is where he worked before all this, at the railway station"

Martin rubs his chin,

"Bloody hell, what happened"

Johnno sighs,

"Lt Ramsey took a patrol out last night, Ramsey took a bullet to the head, luckily for him a nasty wound is all he got, Frank wasn't so lucky"

"Good luck to you mate, who is the Corporal in your platoon"

Martin turns when he hears a familiar voice say,

"I am"

"Hello Georgie!" Martin says, "How are you?"

George Titmus and Martin served together in Bermuda and Pretoria,

"I am good Martin; I was loving life in Aldershot before this all kicked off"

"I thought you were still in St Albans?"

George shakes his head, "Beatrice and I moved to Aldershot just a few weeks before mobilisation"

Martin passes on his condolences for the death of Frank Payne, George doesn't say much in reply, a few mumbled words of thanks.

"Fall in, ready to move!" the voice of Colour Sergeant Hutchinson carries through the early evening stillness, George, Martin, and Johnno shake hands and go their separate ways to their platoons.

Operation order number eight is underway, the German army are believed to be sending small parties of infantrymen to the areas in and around Estaires, the shelling is ferocious, they can hear it from their starting point some five miles to the South at Le Fort d'Esquin, Martin has been to Estaires a couple of times since arriving in France, it is still held by the BEF, the Germans have not yet advanced on the town with a serious attack although there have been several skirmishes between the enemy armies, shells, fired from miles away, land on a daily basis in and around the town. The long column of soldiers set off, marching toward Les Rossignols, a small town south of the village of Laventie, Hemmings tells anyone that will listen that

Rossignol is the French word for a nightingale, Martin knows Richard Hemmings is nervous and says to all of the men around him,

"No talking in the ranks"

They continue to march toward a change in the road, leaving Les Rossignols behind them, it is a huge T junction, with Estaires two miles to the West and Armentieres eight miles to the northeast, steep sided deep trench systems are visible on both sides of the junction, trees cover the view of the river Lys on the far side of the junction, the battalion slows as it reaches the T and begins a left turn, this is where the column of men are attacked. Machine gun fire from both sides of the road hits the column from Germans who are hiding in the trenches, the men at the front of the column have to run forward as jumping into the ditches is not a safe option, men in the middle section and the end section take cover in the trenches, orders are barked out and men that have left the open road and dived into bushes and trenches for their lives take up defensive positions, the Germans need to be stopped but it needs to be coordinated. Martin is in the front section almost at the junction and taking the left turn when the firing starts, he shouts for the men near to him to run forwards toward a group of trees in front of them, he has no choice, even if the enemy are in the trees, it is their only option. He hears the bullets from the machine guns hit the road around him, he reaches the bushes at the front of the tree line, and he throws himself into them, sharp thorns dig into his arms, legs, face, and body, he continues to push himself through the hawthorn bush, ignoring the pain from the thorns as much as he can, he reaches the trees and takes cover behind the trunk of the nearest one to him. Martin shouts for soldiers to report to him, voices nearby confirm that the men that ran with him are miraculously uninjured from the machine gun fire, all have deep scratches and puncture wounds that they can all live with. Martin looks across the junction, hoping to see the remainder of the battalion taking the trenches back from the Germans, he can hear heavy gunfire but cannot see where it is coming from, he presumes that the Germans are firing down the length of the trenches to stop the British getting to them, something moves to his right, the Germans from the trenches that were on his left when they were marching are making a break for it, Martin shouts an order, "Rapid fire on the right, all of you!"

He raises his rifle and fires into the group of Germans running toward the river, he doesn't aim at any person in particular as he fires all five rounds quickly, he sees enemy soldiers fall from the hail of rifle bullets that are thudding into their bodies,

"Cease fire lads!" rifles still continue to fire at the Germans, all of whom are now lying on the ground, "Cease fire!" his command is loud and aggressive, the rifles stop, most of the enemy are lying dead on the ground, two are still moving, unable to stand but still alive. Martin looks at the road junction, he can see four Bedfordshire soldiers lying on the ground in the middle of the junction, two are very still and two are screaming in agony, the Germans are still in the trench system to his left, he looks around where he is standing, there are at least a dozen soldiers hiding in the trees with him,

"Johnno, get four lads, make your way toward the enemy we have just stopped"

Johnno nods, Martin stops him before he leaves, "They got four of our mates"

Johnno nods again, he points at four privates that are taking cover behind trees, they follow him along the tree line toward where the dead and injured Germans lay, Martin points at three soldiers near to him, two privates and one Lance Corporal, "Any one of you got a bomb?"

One of the privates puts his hand up,

"Give it to me private" The lad starts to protest, Martin stares at him, "Now!"

The bomb is handed over to him, he then tells the Lance Corporal to take the two men along the tree line toward the occupied trench, if they can they are to remain in cover and fire into the trench, they are to draw the Germans fire toward them and away from their colleagues currently trapped in the trenches,

"What are you going to do Martin?" asks Lance Corporal Dan Masser,

"Use this bomb" Martin replies coldly.

The remaining soldiers in the trees are instructed by Martin to keep a sharp look out for any Germans making a run for it, he has no need to tell them what to do if this happens. Rifle shots crack through the air, Martin looks over, Johnno and his platoon are making sure the Germans on the road are dead, no screams are heard. He quickly refreshes him memory on how to use the bomb, although not a bomber he has used them in training, but not for a while, he unravels the streamers from the number 2 MKII grenade as he remains in cover, the safety pin still firmly in place on the grenade, he waits, seconds tick by, he feels sweat running down his face, the salty water stinging as it rolls over the many puncture wounds on his face, the enemy guns stop, he can hear orders being shouted in German, rifle fire from the tree line to his left is steady and continuous,

"Good lad Dan" he says to himself, with his rifle in his left hand and the bomb in his right, he breaks cover, pulls the safety pin from the grenade, and runs as fast as his legs will take him toward the German trench, machine gun fire starts again in the trench, they are now firing toward Lance Corporal Masser and his small patrol of men, Martin runs, bent low, the trench is now twenty yards away, fifteen yards, ten. He hears a scream from the trench, he presumes from a German, he hopes one of the patrols rifle bullets has found its mark, he runs forward his right arm raised, he throws the bomb when he is only five yards from the trench, his momentum taking him forward, the bomb explodes in the bottom of the trench, he feels the air pressure from its explosion hit his body, he has no option but to go into the trench himself it is too wide to jump over seconds later he is in. Hitting the bottom of the trench as hard as he does momentarily disorientates him, he jumps to his feet and lifts the rifle to his shoulder, the trench is full of acrid, bitter tasting smoke, he walks into the smoke, vision is not good, he fires his rifle, again and again until the magazine is empty. He reloads quickly, he hears voices,

"Don't fire Corp! It's us!"

Martin keeps the rifle at his shoulder but lowers the barrel, so it is pointing toward the ground, the smoke clears, and he sees that he is standing amongst five dead enemy soldiers, one is alive but only just, he is sitting with his back against the trench wall, his face is hideously burnt from the explosion, he has a rifle in his right hand but makes no attempt to lift it, his left hand is raised toward Martin,

"Bitte, bitte" the enemy soldier says, Martin looks at him.

"Bloody hell corp, that was insane!" one of the privates from the patrol speaks to him,

"Bitte, bitte" the enemy soldier says again, Lance Corporal Masser looks at Martin,

"He is saying 'please, please'"

They all stare at Dan Masser, he shrugs,

"My grandfather was German, we used to speak it at his house when I was a kid" he adds hastily, "He is dead now"

"Bitte, Mutter, Mutter!"

"He is asking for his mother now Corp"

Martin replies, "Dan, take the lads out of the trenches, check the four wounded on the road and get the rest of the column up here quick smart"

"And you Corp?" asks Dan.

Martin doesn't answer but just indicates with his head that the Lance Corporal should take the other two and leave the trench,

"Right lads, David, run down the trenches and let everyone know it is safe to advance, let them know you are coming, loud and clear, do you understand?"

The private tells him that he understands, he runs past Martin toward the British troops shouting his name very loud, Dan speaks to the other private, "Let's go Mark" they scramble out of the trench, within seconds Dan is screaming for a medic and help with the men on the ground, the German looks at Martin,

"Bitte Tommy, bitte"

Martin walks and stands in front of the dying young German soldier, he can see several holes in his grey wool tunic, blood is seeping through freely, Martin thinks that they are almost certainly bullet wounds, the German is crying for his mother, he pleads with Martin, saying 'please' over and over again. Martin steps in and puts his hand toward the Germans face, the young enemy soldier flinches, "Shhh now lad, nice and quiet"

He closes the eyelids of the soldier, the skin feels crisp and burnt under his fingers, he puts the barrel of his rifle gently into the man's chest, placing it directly over his heart, the enemy soldier keeps his eyes closed, he is calm and says,

"Danke, bitte"

Martin puts pressure on the trigger of the rifle,

"Mutter!" cries the soldier, it is the last word he ever speaks as Martin pulls the trigger, he feels the gun recoil into his shoulder, he looks at the German, he is dead.

"You alright Corp"

Martin looks up to the top of the front edge of the trench, Dan has his rifle in his hand, "All good Dan, how are the injured lads?"

"You better get up here Corp"

As Martin scrambles up the trench wall, he is approached by Captain Shearman, on his first day back with the regiment after being hospitalised through illness, he has clambered out of a trench on the opposite side of the road,

"Bloody fine work Corporal, I saw it all, are there any more enemy?"

"No sir" replies Martin

"I will report to the Captain Corp, I really think you should go to where Johnno is with the injured lads" Dan is looking at the officer whilst he speaks to Martin, the Captain nods and Martin thanks him and runs over to the middle of the junction where the four men are laying, the road is filling up with men from the battalion who are climbing out of the trenches on both sides.

"Johnno, who is it that is injured?"

Johnno looks at Martin, he is fighting back tears,

"It's George, he is dead, also Alf Ansell and the new lad, sorry I don't know his name"

Martin looks at the bodies of George Titmus, Alf Ansell and the third is Richard Hemming,

"Bloody hell" Martin curses out loud, he looks over when he hears his name being called, it is Oakes, he is cradling another man's head in his lap on the ground.

It is Alfie Cox.

He kneels down next to Oakes, Alfie has been shot in both legs and in the belly, he looks at Oakes who shakes his head, just a little so that Alfie won't see.

"Martin?" Alfie speaks in a hoarse whisper

"Yes mate" replies Martin

"The boy did good, so brave" he has a coughing fit and small amounts of blood are forced from his mouth, "Let everyone know, how brave he was" he grabs Martins tunic, "When the shooting started, I got hit straight away, Hemmings ran toward the trench firing his rifle, he hit one German in the chest, killed the bastard, then I saw him fall" he coughs again, more blood foams at his mouth, "Tell them, tell them the boy did so very well"

He falls back into Oakes' lap, Martin puts his hand on Alfie's chest, he smiles at his friend,

"Shut up Alfie, you never stop yapping do you" he says gently,

"Tell them Martin"

Martin assures him that he will do just that, a stretcher appears, and he helps the battalion medics lift Alfie onto it,

"See you later Alfie, I will check on you when we get to billets"

Oakes takes Martin to one side, "You alright Martin?"

"Yes Sarge, all good" The men look at each other, "Alfie looks like shit Sarge"

Oakes nods, takes his pipe out of his tunic pocket, he doesn't light it, Martin takes a cigarette from his tunic pocket, he strikes a match, lights his cigarette, and then holds the flame over the bowl of Oakes pipe, a few deep puffs and the pipe is lit and going well,

"Belly wound, think he might have taken one in the lung as well, I have seen it before" he looks at Martin "It will be touch and go if he is lucky"

Martin swallows hard, Oakes looks over Martin's shoulder,

"I have to go Martin, the Captain wants to speak to me, you sure you are alright"

Martin forces a smile, Oakes leaves him. Martin walks slowly toward Johnno, the rest of the Battalion are forming up in a column again, they have a mile or two to march to the drawbridge.

The Bedfordshire's are relieved from protecting the drawbridge by men from the Grenadier guards and from 6 company the Gordon Highlanders, they march to their billets in Estaires entering the town on a straight cobbled road with trees, tall thin trees line both sides, Martin realises that he marched this way into Estaires only a few months ago. Once dismissed he asks Johnno to find out where his billet is to be, he sets off to find out how Alfie is doing. He knows that Estaires does not have a casualty clearing station so he stops a private he can see has the distinctive red cross emblem of the Army medical corps on the left arm of his tunic, "Excuse me mate"

"Yes Corp, what can I do for you?"

"I had a mate that got shot today, where is the nearest casualty clearing station?"

The medic takes his cap off and scratches his head, "It's at Merville Corp, four miles West of here"

Martin thanks the man and begins to walk off,

"But Corp, we haven't sent anyone today, all the arrivals here have either been dead or died soon after"

Martin stares at the army medic,

"Sorry Corp, didn't want you to have a wasted journey"

Martin steps back to speak to the medic, "Where are the dead now?"

"Which unit are you with Corp?"

Martin tells him, the medic points to a brick built barn, it has signs of a very recent shell attack,

"In there, three were dead on arrival and one died within minutes of arriving"

Martin thanks the man and walks toward the damaged building, as he steps around the rubble on the ground and into the interior of the barn, he sees a man bending over the dead body of Private Richard Hemmings, he recognises the man as Captain Parslew from the Army Chaplains department and attached to the 2nd Bedfordshire's,

"Sir" Martin makes the Chaplain aware that he is in the building, Captain Parslew looks up,

"Can I help you Corporal?"

Martin takes off his cap, "I know these men Chaplain, I have just heard that the fourth man carried in on a stretcher has also died, I just need to know"

The Chaplain stands, "These pour souls are to be buried tonight, along with the dead from several other regiments, it has been a tough day for all Corporal, I am taking the identity discs so that I can register where these men will lie"

Martin steps in front of Hemmings corpse, "Eighteen years old Chaplain, just eighteen" Martin looks up, the roof of the building is gone so he is looking up at the darkening sky, "Richard Hemmings, I met him just yesterday for the first time, he was new to the unit" The Chaplain listens as Martin continues, "I am looking for Private Alfie Cox" he pauses, "Sorry Chaplain, Private Alfred Cox, he was alive when I last saw him, I know that George Titmus and Alf Ansell are dead, they both died at the crossroads with young Hemmings"

The Chaplain puts a hand on Martin's shoulder, "I have the discs for Alfie here Corporal, I am so sorry, he died within minutes of arriving here"

Martin puts his cap back on, "Thank you, Chaplain, I will leave you to your business, thanks again Sir"

"It's a horrific journey we are all on Corporal, we all deal with it in different ways"

Martin nods, he opens his mouth to speak, the Chaplain smiles and puts his hand up to stop Martins words from being uttered, "Before you ask Corporal, I have no idea why my God lets this happen, I have no idea what mankind did to my God for him to allow this carnage, what I can tell you is that my God has kept hundreds of thousands of men safe, including you Corporal"

"For now, Chaplain, for now" replies Martin "Thank you Sir"

Martin leaves the Chaplain to his grisly task, he walks toward the field kitchen he is sure that Johnno will be there and he will have Martins billet details, his mind wanders from death and from the war, he thinks of Grace, seeing her today is what he really needs, he knows it is impossible he will be without her until this mess is over if he survives, Johnno is waving from the queue of soldiers at the field kitchen, he waves back and walks over to join him.

Martin wakes up in a sweat, it is dark, he tries to look around to get his bearings, having no idea where he is panic begins to rise throughout his body, the taste of bile is at the back of his throat, he shivers as he feels warm sweat run down the middle of his back. His eyes adjust to the darkness, he is in the factory at Estaires it is being used as a billet for the men of the 2nd Battalion, the large space he is in is lit only by the moon from outside, a window behind him allows the night light to gently pierce the darkness, he can hear men around him sleeping, there are two or three red glowing areas in the space as some men are having a cigarette in the darkness, sitting quietly alone and smoking. He feels a familiar gurgling in his belly, an urgent visit to the latrines is needed, Martin stands up and carefully makes his way to the door, making sure that he does not stand on any of the sleeping soldiers, pain and cramps in his belly and bowels makes him stop and bend over at the waist for a few seconds as he waits for it to pass. He has had violent bouts of diarrhoea for two days since returning from the trenches, he is unsure as to what has caused the affliction, it could be a number of events over the past week or so the trenches they are in at Aubers, a couple of miles South of Estaires, are sodden, it has been raining since the 1st May and hasn't stopped or so it seems, the ground is so wet it is impossible for anyone to dig a trench toilet to use, the waterlogged mud is impossible to dig a hole in. He and everyone else have kept a few bully beef tins and this is what they use to defecate and urinate into, the contents, mostly liquid for all of them is then thrown over the top of the trench into even more mud and filth, the engineers have supplied bags of lime that is thrown over the top to cover the human waste, many a man has had to crawl out of the trench when the order is given to advance, when machine gun fire is aimed toward you as soon as you leave the trench the best option is to get on your belly and crawl, even if this means crawling through liquid mud and human waste, the lime helps to soak up some of the horrendous liquid mess but not all of it. Some of the lads that also have diarrhoea blame the daily delivery of hot tea they get when in the trenches, fires cannot be lit due to the sodden conditions, so the hot tea arrives most days in two gallon petrol cans, no matter how many times the tea is cooked, boiled, and heated in these cans, it still tastes of petrol, Martin and his colleagues always drink it as it is the only hot drink they get when in the trenches. Worst of all, and in Martins opinion the reason for the violent diarrhoea and dysentery cases, is the lack of fresh water in the trenches, fresh water is supposed to be delivered daily to those in the trenches under cover of darkness, it is not unusual for water not to be delivered for days, sometimes more than a week at a time, this is when you either have to go thirsty, which is never an option, or drink the available water that is to hand. In and around the trench systems there is a huge amount of water, shell craters are filled almost to the brim, the trenches themselves are several inches deep with water, the shell crater water is stagnant, and mud filled, the men, including Martin, will drink this rather than go thirsty, it is not boiled as the trenches are too wet to light any fire to heat water or to cook, so it is consumed straight from its location, cold and disgusting. On more than one occasion, men have reported finding dead animals and dead humans at the bottom of the stagnant pools they have been drinking from. Gas gangrene is also common, nothing is dry in the trenches, clothing is sodden twenty four hours a day, it never gets a chance to dry out, boots are left on feet for days or even weeks at a time, the skin of the soldiers' hands and feet are permanently wrinkled and trench foot is common amongst even the cleanest of the men. Gas gangrene, also known as wet gangrene in the trenches, hits you hard and attacks the body very quickly, the RAMC doc, Lt Watson, has given the men a lecture on trench hygiene, he told them that the bacteria that causes gas gangrene thrives in wet conditions and any soldier with an open wound, and most do have some form of injury, is at risk from the bacteria getting into their body, if so, the results are horrific for the individual. A fever quickly develops, joints ache and blisters appear under the skin, pain around this area is awful, the skin will become pale but very quickly, in a few hours, become dark red, purple or black, the blisters will discharge a brown pus that is so foul smelling, anyone nearby will gag if they smell it, the victim will vomit and has to be taken from the trenches for treatment, surgical removal of the infected and dead skin, debriding, is brutal, on occasion a limb will have to be removed because of the gas gangrene. Martin is sure that some have purposely infected themselves, they would rather risk amputation or death than spend another night in the hell of the trenches. Some trenches have 'Good water filling stations', the water at these locations is fresh and clean, but of course all the men are doing is filling their water bottles that have recently had filthy, infected water in them, so the 'clean' water will be contaminated, albeit only slightly. Martin leaves the factory and makes his way to the latrines, unlike the trench latrines, if there are any, these are purpose built, they are in the open air and there is no privacy, they are a line of eight large galvanised metal boxes, each with a wooden lid to keep the smell in as much as possible, when the lid is lifted a roughly cut hole in a sheet of wood is your seat, the metal boxes are situated over a deep trench, lime is occasionally dumped into this trench to help with hygiene. Martin is used to the lack of privacy especially at time like this when a visit to the latrine is urgent, this is not the first time he has suffered with a belly upset, he has been seen Lt Watson and has been assured that he does not have dysentery, he has given Martin some powders to take, with water of course and offered him a couple of days bed rest, either in the trench aid station or at the aid station behind the lines, Martin refused. He arrives at the latrine area set some way behind the factory and close to the river, he lifts the lid on the first metal box and the smell immediately takes his breath away, it is dark, but the moonlight reveals to him that he is alone, it makes no difference, he has to use the toilet regardless of who else might be there. He lights a cigarette, ensuring to keep the flame of the match hidden in his cupped hands and he keeps the glowing end of the cigarette inside the cup of his right palm, it is then that he realises that it might not have been belly ache that awoke him, a dream is flooding back into his memory, he tries to block it out, but it remains vivid and real. He is back at home in the garden and is looking toward the stream and the Yew tree, he sees movement at the base of the tree, the ground is moving, the soil is breaking open and he sees a tiny, skeletonised hand lift through the soil, the arm follows then the body until the tiny skeleton of a child stands beneath the low boughs of the tree. The child points a bony finger toward him, nothing else, it just points at him, suddenly the ground around the tree is moving, not just in one place but in many, soil is being lifted and thrown to one side, graves are being dug out from the inside, the tiny child still points at him, he hears a laugh, a cackle that is not human, he believes that it is the tree laughing at him, as he looks above the child, still pointing, a rope with a roughly tied noose sways in the breeze, the ground is still moving and he can see what he thinks are the bodies of the dead coming out of the ground. This is when he awoke, covered in a sweat, he has no idea why he is dreaming about the tiny skeleton he buried last year under the tree, he is also confused, and a little scared about the other graves opening up in the ground around the tree, the noose must be for the lad from the Sherwood's that took his own life in the low boughs of the tree.

"Morning Corp"

Martin shakes himself away from remembering the dream, he looks, and Bill Bartlett is sitting next to him using the latrine, the other metal boxes are unused,

"Bloody hell Bill, couldn't you sit at the other end!"

Bill laughs, "Sorry Corp"

Martin smiles as he says, "Bill you are a Corporal as well, you don't have to call me Corp anymore!"

Bill looks at the stripes on arms on his tunic, "I can't get used to it, I was a lance jack for so long, last week's sudden promotion hasn't sunk in yet"

"Same rank as me or not, take your arse to the other end of the latrine will you!"

"Yes Corp" Martin throws him a stern look, "Sorry, I mean yes Martin"

Bill slides off the box, leaving the lid open and holding his trousers around his thighs he shuffles to the far end of the latrine, "Shall I shut the lid on this toilet then Bill" Martin shouts at him,

"Oh, yes please Corp"

Martin shakes his head in the darkness, the dream is almost forgotten but he can't understand why he had such a strange and vivid dream. The sun is beginning to rise to his left, morning light is pushing the darkness away and another day is beginning, Martin gets off of the latrine, closes the lid and makes his way toward the field kitchen, he is hungry for the first time in days and wants to take advantage of an early, and hopefully, hot breakfast.

He is soon back in the trenches, they have been told to expect a long stay this time, another huge battle in and around Ypres has started, an attack on the town of Festubert is going ahead, the BEF offensive has already begun. For the past two days the artillery have constantly been bombarding German held positions and trenches between Neuve Chapelle to the North and the village of Festubert to the South, Martin and the rest of the 21st brigade are in reserve positions to the West of the front line, in front of them are the 20th Brigade and the 22nd Brigade, the 1st Battalions from Staffordshire, Queens, Royal Welsh Fusiliers and the 2nd Battalions Warwickshire, Gordon Highlanders, Scots Guards and Borders are all at the front line in allied trenches very close to the German trenches. They are to wait until the Indian Corps to the North, the Garhwal and Sirhind Brigades, together with the 5th and 6th Brigades from the BEF, attack the enemy trenches further along the line and then they are to make their way through the German lines, then to about turn and attack the enemy from the rear, when this happens the 21st Brigade, including the 2nd Bedfordshire regiment are to move forward and occupy the trenches vacated by the 20th and 22nd brigades. Martin, and he is not alone, thinks that the plan is a bloody awful one, General Haig has ordered the first night attack of the war, insisting that the BEF soldiers will have the element of surprise and the cover of darkness to assist them, Martin and his fellow NCO's believe this to be a load of rubbish, the two day artillery bombardment will eventually stop and this will give the enemy some idea that an attack is imminent, using the darkness as cover will work both ways, the enemy will also make use of the conditions, a problem will be that soldiers may not know who the hell they are shooting at when the shooting starts. Although the brigade is the reserve for this attack, they all know that they will be called to the front at some point, all of them are scared about a gas attack they have all been told about the Germans using chlorine gas last month on a battlefield between Langemarck and Gravenstafel, they have heard that over a hundred and fifty tons of chlorine gas was released by the enemy from their position when the wind picked up and was blowing death toward the allied lines, in the way were the 45th Algerian division of the French army. The attack was witnessed and documented by Major General Snow from the 27th Division HQ at Potijze, he described greenish-yellow clouds of smoke coming from either side of the German lines, turning into a heavy mass of blue-white mist when they came together, moving slowly along with the wind, men complain of burning in the throat and lungs, breathing becoming almost impossible, blurred vision and blindness due to the burning in the eyes, vomiting and spitting blood, men begging for water with purple blotches on the skin. Hundreds had died from the gas attack.

The artillery is slowing, and Martin can hear whistles blowing further up the line, just as darkness falls Major Mackenzie passes the order for all to be ready to move, Martin speaks to his platoon and assures them that all will be well even if he doesn't believe it himself, the order comes down the line that they are to move into positions at the front line trenches, this to stop any Germans that may get through when trying these Allied positions. The 2nd Battalion Bedfordshire's are to occupy positions vacated by the Welsh Fusiliers and the Warwickshire's, approaching through an area North of Festubert, known as the 'Indian Village', called this because in November 1914 the Indian Corps had lost the area to the Germans and were ordered straight back in with instructions to take it back at all costs, they did just that and have held it ever since. Martin and his platoon move through the area unchallenged and take up a position in trenches close to the road, the Rue de Bois, the trench, compared to some he has been in is relatively dry and has sections cut into its wall, each of these sections has a length of corrugated iron fixed above it, giving the occupier a small space to keep dry or to sleep in, although there will be no sleeping today for any of them. Martin looks to his right and then to his left, the trenches either side of him look similar, a gap of five or six yards of open space is in between some of them, he sees Johnno and raises a hand at him, he gets the thumbs up in return. Arthur 'Netherfield' Beardsley, nicknamed Netherfield as this is his hometown in Nottinghamshire, speaks to Martin,

"Do you think we will be going over the top today Corp?"

"Yes mate, I do" replies Martin emotionlessly.

Machine gun fire is heard from in front of them, not far in front of them either, he sees the looks on the platoons faces, "Easy now lads, let's hope that the machine guns are ours and pointing at the enemy"

He has no time to add to the sentence as he hears his name being shouted from the trench to his left, he looks up and sees Sergeant Tom Eustace calling him, Martin shouts back, above the continuous noise from the battle in front of them, "What's up Tom?"

He cannot hear the reply as the noise is getting closer to his position and is drowning out whatever Tom is saying to him, "You lot" he speaks to the platoon, "Stay here"

He runs across the gap between the trenches and makes it without being dragged into the war,

"You called Sergeant!" he says to Tom, the men shake hands, Tom introduces the man standing behind him,

"This is Lance Corporal Coleman from the 2nd Border regiment"

Tom and the Scotsman nod at each other, Tom continues, artillery shells begin to fall close by,

"His platoon has been driven back, the Germans are much stronger than anticipated, lots of his comrades are lying wounded in no-man's-land, most have shrapnel injuries and cannot get back"

"Shall we go and get them?" Martin asks almost flippantly,

"Coleman and I will go from here" Tom points to the gap in between the trenches, "If you can go from the other side of yours, take one man with you, grab who you can and get back here"

Martin nods a reply and runs back across the gap, "Netherfield" he speaks to Arthur "Get your brave boots on lad, we are off to rescue some of our Scottish colleagues"

Arthur puts a thumb over his shoulder, "Out there Corp?" he asks

"Yes" is the simple reply,

"OK then" is the just as simple response from Arthur.

Martin looks across at Tom and Coleman, they are ready to go, he nudges Arthur, and they step out from the relative safety of the trench into the gap directly into the open space that leads toward the German lines, they don't need to go far, they quickly reach three wounded men, keeping low they drag the three men between them pulling on their arms to get them to the trenches. They arrive and put the men down in Johnno's trench and turn to go back out again, Johnno is standing next to Martin, he taps him on the shoulder and the three of them move back out into the open space, high explosive shells are landing all around them, some of the injured men from the Borders regiment are being killed by these shells, as they move forward a shell explodes very close to them, Martin is thrown into Johnno and the two of them land in a heap on the floor, Martin looks up to see where Arthur is, he is nowhere to be seen, "Netherfield!" he shouts, he gets no response, he tries again, and then for a third time,

"He's had it Martin" shouts Johnno over the ever increasing noise surrounding them, they move forward and find four wounded men, one has an arm injury and could have walked to safety, he had bravely decided to stay with his mates on the battlefield. Martin, Johnno and the wounded Borders soldier take the three other men to safety, they get back to their trenches and the injured men are given the urgent first aid they need. Martin looks across and sees Tom indicating to him to go to his location, Martin runs across to the Sergeant,

"That's enough, the shelling is too heavy, no more attempts to be made" They both duck down as a shell explodes on the other side of the trench, "We got twelve back, how about you?"

"Seven, but I lost Netherfield, I have to presume he is dead, there was nothing left of him"

Tom nods, Martin turns and returns to his platoon, they are sitting in the dugouts of the trench, cigarettes are passed around and they all sit and have a smoke. Orders are passed down the line that the Bedfordshire men are to advance forward and take up a position in a trench that the Germans have recently left, they are to consolidate it and make it an Allied fire trench, this means making the shallow trench deeper so that they can fire at the enemy whilst standing up, the usual method for this is to build a fire step a few feet from the bottom of the trench so that the soldiers on firing duty can stand comfortably and behind some cover and point rifles and machine guns toward the enemy. Major Mackenzie and Captain Hutton-Williams take the 2nd Battalion across the short distance to the trenches that have been taken from the Germans by the 1st Berkshires, they have taken heavy losses and are happy to see the lads from the Bedfordshire's arrive. Martin and his platoon take over a trench from two Berkshire soldiers, the rest of the platoon have been killed or wounded, Martin sends both men back to the rear lines, they protest but he orders them to leave, they do so with thanks.

The next few hours are taken up with digging down over three feet into the bottom of the shallow trench and adding fire shelves and strengthening the trench with the more than ample amount of materials left behind by the retreating Germans, sandbags are filled and placed on top of the trenches, with gaps for the rifles to be put through, the Germans have already used high lattice fencing on the back wall of the trench, supported every six feet with a strong vertical wooden beam. The final task is to re-lay the yards of wooden boards that the enemy had put on the floor of the trench to lift them above the mud, this done the soldiers are very pleased with their work, the trenches are deep, solid, and dry. The shelling is going on around them, some of the recently taken trenches have taken direct hits and Martin knows that the battalion will have casualties, probably heavy casualties, the whole of the 21st Brigade and the 7th division will have lost hundreds of men today, he puts the thought from his mind and takes up a position on the fire shelf, it is almost one in the morning, the only light across the battlefield is the bursting and exploding of high explosive shells from the enemy, allied shells soar above him, bound for the German trenches and beyond, it has been a tough day for all of them, but the results are good for every one of them, trenches have been taken from the enemy and modified for good use by the BEF. Just over an hour later Martin receives orders that the men of the 2nd Bedfordshire's are to withdraw from their position and to return to the reserve trenches that they started in, the soldiers in his platoon are furious and he doesn't blame them, he has to make sure the orders are obeyed, he puts his hands in front of him, the soldiers are still venting their anger,

"Stop!" Martin orders, the men settle down, "Do you want me to disobey this order?"

"No Corp" they all say at once,

"Well let's do as we are being told, frustrating though it is, we are moving backwards" he pauses, then adds, "Again"

The platoon gathers their kit together and leave the trench they worked so hard to make it into a decent fire trench, they are all moaning the Germans will come and take it straight back and make use of their hard graft, Martin lets them moan, mostly because he agrees with every word they are saying, they leave the trench at about 0300 hours, and they make it back to the reserve trenches without meeting any enemy. The reserve trenches are small, only about two feet wide and about five feet deep, the platoon put their kit at one end of the trench on top of the back section, this sits a couple of feet lower than the front wall,

"Shall we dig into the walls and make trench beds again Corp?"

"Lads, I wouldn't bother, have a smoke, brew up and get some sleep, the way things are we will be off again soon, best we get some rest for the time being" Martin sits on one of the firing platforms, at least this trench isn't flooded, he takes a cigarette out of his tunic pocket and lights it without covering the flame of the match, he leans back, inhales the smoke, and closes his eyes. He has to go and register the death of Netherfield, he has no identification discs or a corpse, but Martin knows he is dead, nothing was left of him, he decides to finish his smoke and take the trip along the trenches to Battalion HQ, find the Chaplain and register the death, sleep finds him very easily.

He wakes with a start, immediately he looks around where he is, it is just getting light and the patrol, bar one man, are all asleep,

"Morning Corp" Harry Moule, a cheerful man from Aspenden, he is about the same age as Martin,

"Was anyone screaming my name Harry?" asks a confused Martin

"No Corp, it is a quiet as the grave and it is one bloody big grave out there"

Martin takes another cigarette and gives one to Harry, he lights both with one match,

"I think you were dreaming Corp, something about a tree and burying something under it"

Martin must have looked shocked as Harry asks if he is alright, he assures him that he is and tells him to wake the others as he is going to register Netherfield's death.

He walks nonchalantly between the trenches smoking his cigarette, he walks for five minutes until he arrives at the small HQ that has been cut into the side of a trench, it has a corrugated roof and wooden sides, Martin can see weak light coming from under the tarpaulin that is being used as a door, as he arrives Johnno and Corporal 'Chalky' Chalkley leave,

"Martin" Johnno says

"Chalky, Johnno, is it busy in there?"

They both shake their heads, Johnno speaks to Martin,

"John Gilbert and Harry Palmer got it last night during the shelling"

"So did Alfred Hetherington" adds Chalky "What about your lot?" he asks Martin

"Netherfield took a direct hit from a shell; I take it the Chaplain is in there taking details?"

They inform him that he is correct, Martin tells them both he will catch them up later on and makes his way into the HQ, he pushes the tarpaulin to one side, he sees Lt Col Thorpe and Major Mackenzie sitting at a table, they are both looking at a map and are deeply engrossed in conversation, Mackenzie looks up at him,

"Did you want me Corporal?"

Martin stands to attention,

"No Sir, I need to register one of mine with the Chaplain"

"Who Corporal?" asks Mackenzie

"Netherfield Sir" Mackenzie looks at him without answering, Martin corrects himself,

"Private Arthur Beardsley Sir"

"Terrible Corporal, how are the rest of your men?"

Martin tells him that they are all in good spirits, he has absolutely no doubt that Major Mackenzie has no idea who Private Arthur Beardsley is, or was, but it is decent of him so pretend that he does, the Chaplain speaks to Martin,

"Do you have his identity discs Corporal?" The Chaplain looks very tired and haggard, Martin thinks this must be hell on earth for a man of God,

"No Chaplain" he replies,

He sees a look of distain come onto the face of the Chaplain,

"Well how do you know he is dead then Corporal" snaps the Chaplain

"Chaplain?" Martin replies, a little confused by the way he is being spoken to, the Chaplain sighs and takes a cigarette out of a silver tin and lights it before replying to Martin,

"It is very easy Corporal, if you don't have the discs from the poor man's body, how in God's name do you know he is dead?" The Chaplain is becoming irate, so is Martin who replies, with more than a little aggression,

"Because I was stood next to him when a fucking great big German shell landed on him and blew him to bits!"

The Chaplain is taken aback by Martin's response to him,

"Corporal" Mackenzie says sternly,

"Sir" Martin turns toward the Major, the Lt Col still has his head down over the map,

"We are all tired Corporal" he looks at the Chaplain "Including the Sky pilot here"

The Chaplain puts his hands up in front of himself as a form of apology,

"Corporal, could I have the name of the soldier again please"

"Private Arthur Beardsley" pauses, "Number 13787"

The Chaplain nods,

"I see you know the man's army number"

Martin replies slowly and coldly,

"I make it my business to know all the lad's details in my platoon"

Mackenzie, who is holding in a laugh, says to Martin,

"That will be all Corporal"

Martin turns to both officers,

"Sir" he says smartly and turns about to leave the HQ,

"Oh, and Corporal" Mackenzie calls him back,

"Sir"

Major Mackenzie taps the map with his right hand,

"Have a brew and a bite to eat, but don't get too comfy in these trenches Corporal"

Martin says that he understands, thanks him, and leaves the tiny space.

At three that afternoon, Martin and the other NCOs from the 2nd Battalion are called to muster outside of the HQ trench, Martin knows most of them, there are a few newly promoted Corporals and Sergeants amongst them he is not familiar with, most will have been transferred in from the 1st Battalion to cover the losses the 2nd have suffered, Chalky manoeuvres into a position next to him,

"Bloody hell Martin, there ain't many of us left is there?"

Martin takes a look at the NCOs around him, "No mate, we must have taken a hammering for these lads from the 1st to get sent to us, they are having a bad time as well, so I hear"

Chalky looks around again, "Our officers' numbers are getting less and less every day"

Martin can see the officers standing in front of the HQ, Lt Col Thorpe, Major Mackenzie, Major Onslow, Captains Hutton-Williams and Huntriss, Captain Foss, Lt Kuhn, Lt Parker, Lt Boys who is standing next to two very young looking 2nd Lt's, he has not seen them before, Chalky tells him that they are 2nd Lt's Lardner and Grover, known in their section as 'Boys' Boys" because their section commander is Lt Boys. There is only one more officer, Martin has seen him around the trenches only recently, he is a 2nd Lt, in his late twenties or early thirties, he is wearing his khaki field service cap at an angle on the right side of his head, the one pip to symbolise his rank is on the front crease of the folding cap, the badge of the Royal Flying Corps can be seen on the left side of the cap, all the other officers are wearing the usual service trench cap with a peak on it. He has a thin black moustache, and his short black hair can be seen on his head, his tunic is different to the Battalion officers, it has only two pockets at either side of the waist and no visible buttons on the tunic, he has the wings of the Royal Flying Corp at his left breast, above his medal ribbon. the Sam Browne belt looks the same as the other officers,

"That fly boy has the Distinguished conduct medal" Martin observes, "He must have been one of *us* at one time"

He cannot speak any more as the Lt Col calls the men to gather round in an informal manner, Company Sgt Major Hutchinson calls for quiet, his words are followed quickly by all ranks.

Lt Col Thorpe starts off his commands with an apology, the officers and men from the 2nd Battalion are to go back to the old German fire trenches that they occupied that morning, Hutchinson quells the murmurs of discontent from the gathered soldiers, the attack will be in conjunction with the officers and men from the 4th Cameron Highlanders, who will move in from the left side of the allied trenches, the Bedfordshire's are to move in from the right, Lt Col Thorpe and Captain Huntriss will take a company of men and lead the attack, Major Mackenzie and Captain Hutton-Williams will be in support of the advancing companies, before he dismisses the officers, he instructs the Lt's and the 2nd Lt's to prepare their men for short notice deployment. His final words are to introduce 2nd Lt William Stonier; he will lead a platoon of bomb throwers to the far right along the communication trench, supported by a platoon from 2nd Battalion.

Martin can see Capt. Foss talking to Lt Col Thorpe and 2nd Lt Stonier, they call Sgt Oakes over to speak to them, after a few seconds, Oakes turns and points at Martin and Chalky,

"One of us has got a shit duty coming our way" Chalky says gloomily,

Martin's name is called out by Oakes, Chalky smiles,

"Looks like it is you Martin" he slaps Martin on the back firmly, "Off you go mate"

Martin makes his way through the NCO's, Oakes has stepped away from the officers to speak to him,

"Martin, these officers have got a job for you and your platoon"

Martin looks over at Stonier, "Fire support for the bombers Sarge?"

Oakes smiles, Martin can see his pipe tobacco stained teeth, two of his central bottom teeth are missing, Martin is sure that he hasn't noticed this before,

"You got it in one Corporal, we might make a soldier out of you yet my boy"

They walk over to where Thorpe, Foss and Stonier are talking, he stands to attention, Oakes does not but tells him to stand easy,

"Corporal" The Lt Col addresses Martin, "Captain Foss tells me that you are a dab hand at supporting the bomb throwers"

Martin looks at Foss who is smiling like a Cheshire cat, Thorpe continues, "I also have it on good authority from Captain Shearman that you are not a bad thrower yourself" he does not wait for Martin too answer, "Your platoon are to support 2nd Lt Stonier and six bomb throwers, you will advance ahead of the bombers to ensure that they get a clear run at the German trenches" He stands up straight, "Is that understood Corporal?"

"Yes Sir"

Foss nods at him and leaves with Thorpe,

"Good luck Martin" Oakes speaks and leaves Martin with Stonier.

"Corporal, I am William Stonier" the officer puts his hand out, Martin takes it and introduces himself, "Not much more to say really, we will all move off when the Lt Col moves off with his company, I am hoping that they will create a diversion for us to be able to get a surprise on the enemy, the bombers will do their stuff and we can, hopefully, take the trench from this end" Stonier is direct and to the point,

"May I ask one question Sir?" Martin enquires,

"Of course," Stonier replies

"I see you have the DCM ribbon" Martin points at the officer's chest, "You were rank and file at one point in your service, that medal is only for other ranks and not officers"

Stonier smiles, "You are very perceptive Martin, I joined in 1908, with the 1st Battalion Bedfordshire's and made Sergeant in only a few years, when the Central Flying School was established in May 1912 I applied to transfer to the RFC, I was already a qualified pilot, a hobby of mine"

Martin does not answer and waits for the officer to continue, "I passed my training in good time and had 25 hours solo time as war broke out, it was then I was returned to the 1st and sent over here" He taps the DCM ribbon "This was from a bit of a scrape at Mons in August last year, I was a bomb thrower. I got through it without a scratch, I took my commission in February of this year, I have just been transferred to the RFC as a 2nd Lt, I have only flown three missions, when I was sent back here a few days ago to lead a bomb throwing party, we throw the same bombs from the planes onto the enemy"

Martin is impressed, "It's good to have you with us Sir"

"Get the chaps ready Martin and bring them here, we need to be ready to roll as soon as this starts" he looks at his wristwatch " I will get the bombers and meet you back here in fifteen minutes"

Martin returns to his platoon, the six men are sat drinking cups of hot tea,

"We made it Corp, hope that is ok, couldn't stand any more petrol tea!"

Martin nods, "Drink up lads, you have about ten minutes to get your kit together, we are off to the front to support the bombers" he turns to his Lance Corporal,

"Nimrod, bring the lads up when they have finished their tea, don't dawdle, we meet the bombers in fifteen minutes at trench HQ"

Lance Corporal Nimrod Oakins, a 23 year old Hertfordshire lad from Apsley End near Hemel Hempstead, turns to the rest of the platoon,

"Bill, Frank, Harry you three will be with me front left" he turns to the other two men, "Jake, Barney, you will follow the Corp on the right, are we all clear?"

They all say that they understand, Martin turns and walks back to the trench HQ, he passes through a trench and spots a familiar face, a friend of his and fellow career soldier, Bill Pearson,

"Corporal Pearson" Bill turns and smiles when he sees Martin, who continues, "You have been a Corporal for as long as I can remember Bill, is a promotion looming?"

Bill laughs out loud, "You must be bloody joking Martin, my arms are not strong enough to carry another stripe!"

The men shake hands, Martin notices that Bill's platoon is down by one man, it has no Lance Corporal, Bill sees Martin looking,

"Ernie Stone was killed yesterday mate, machine gun cut him down as soon as he left the trench, he was the first out and the first killed"

"Sorry to hear that Bill"

"It has really shaken the lads" he points at his platoon, "A couple of them are newly arrived, the first bit of action they see is their Lance Jack taking full machine gun to his body, and to cap it all, we are with Major Mackenzie's unit today, so although in a reserve position, I know that at some point we will be right at the front"

Martin looks at one of the men, he stands immediately,

"Private John Crew Corporal" he says

"Relax Private, this is the trenches, not a parade ground"

Bill is smiling, "John has been with us for a week or so, he did us all proud yesterday, he went out with Harry Mockridge" He points to another young soldier, "They pulled Ernie back into the trench, sadly there was no hope for him despite the bravery of these two lads"

"Good work lads" Martin says as he introduces himself,

"Could I ask you something Corporal?" John Crew is half standing to attention,

"You can of course John, just take it easy"

Crew relaxes, "I don't want to sound impertinent Corporal, but is your younger Sister called Alice?"

Martin looks sternly at the young soldier,

"Yes, what of it?"

"Nothing Corp" Crew answers quickly "My Father and Mother know your grandmother"

"How so?" asks Martin, now interested, Crew looks terrified as he answers,

"My Dad has on occasion delivered pheasants and rabbit to The Malta"

Martin thinks for a few moments,

"You are not James Crews lad, are you?" he asks

"I am Corporal, I had the pleasure of meeting your sister a few times at the pub, I was there just before I finished training"

He looks at Martin who has raised one eyebrow, a look of fear comes across his face again,

"Nothing bad Corp, honest, its only that Alice was the only person anywhere near my age in the pub and we only talked a bit"

"Martin, stop winding the lad up!" Bill says, Martin laughs,

"Sorry John, I am only messing with you, I know your father well, you live at the cottages at West Hyde, don't you?"

"Yes Corp!" Crew is now smiling, "Father is the gamekeeper for Graves Wood, Calvery Wood, Birch wood and Tumble grove"

Martin smiles as he remembers his childhood, spending days with his father and James Crew in the woods beating the pheasants out so the men could shoot them.

"I need to be off" Martin says, he shakes Bill's hand, "Good luck Bill, see you later"

He turns to John, "Look after Bill will you John, he is getting on a bit and might need help!"

"Will do Corp, thank you" Martin shakes his hand and leaves the trench heading for HQ.

Martin is with his platoon when 2nd Lt Stonier arrives with his six bombers, he laughs when he hears a familiar London accent,

"Bloody hell, is he really being allowed to lead us into trouble again!" Sergeant Bill Peggs shouts across. Martins platoon look at him, he assures them that all is well as he knows Sergeant Peggs, he walks across and shakes hands with all the bombers, Corporal Herb Smith, Lance Corporal George Freshwater, Privates Bill Eade, Harold Barnett, whom Martin had served in South Africa with and finally Joe Lovett,

"A strange reunion" Martin says, "With a few promotions I note" he points at George and Herb's stripes, "Where are the others?"

The bombers all look at each other, Martin guesses that there have been casualties, Bill Peggs speaks first,

"Stan and Phillip were both killed in trenches the day after the expedition with Captain Foss, shell got them both at the same time, Freddie Brown has been promoted, he is still with the 2nd Battalion, now as a Sergeant, he couldn't be spared for today's outing"

"Sorry to hear about the lads getting killed" Martin doesn't finish the sentence as 2nd Lt Stonier interrupts,

"Sorry to butt in men, we need to go through our job for today and then we will be off"

"My platoon has been briefed Sir; Lance Corporal Oakins has designated taskings"

Stonier nods, he looks at Bill Peggs,

"We are all good Sir; we will let Martin's lads lead the way then when the time comes, we will do all the brave stuff!"

The men all laugh,

"As you wish Sergeant" the 2nd Lt says sarcastically,

"Will, are these soldiers ready?" Major Mackenzie has joined the group,

"They are Sir, as soon as you give us the word, we will move along the communication trench to the right and then across to the enemy trenches"

Mackenzie looks at the bombers and at Martins platoon, "Be careful with this lot 2nd Lt, they tried, and failed, to bump off Charlie Foss a few months ago!"

"I will watch my back Sir" Stonier smiles at the men

Mackenzie looks at his watch, "Two minutes 2nd Lt"

They all say "Sir" as he walks away toward his group of soldiers, Martin can see John Crew amongst them, they look at each other and Martin nods across to the young man, who raises a hand in response. It is time to go, Mackenzie and his group move off to their position in the old British trenches, Capt. Huntriss with Lt Col Thorpe move at the same time, the whole of the 2nd Battalion is involved in one way or another in this offensive,

"Lead the way Corporal" Stonier says to Martin, who in turn nods at Nimrod Oakins and they all set off along the communications trench, slowly and carefully, they know the Germans are less than fifty or sixty yards away.

A German bombardment has started, it is as heavy and continuous as any of them can recall, machine guns can be heard firing from all over the battlefield, Martin is moving forward in a crouched position on the right wall of the trench, behind him is Private Frank 'Jake' Jakeman and Private TW 'Barney' Barnard, Martin has no idea what the TW stands for, a couple of yards in front of him, on the left wall is Lance Corporal Nimrod Oakins and behind him are Privates Bill Addington, Harry Moule and Frank Payne, he presumes that the bombers, led by Sgt Bill Peggs are behind him with 2nd Lt Stonier amongst them. The noise above them from the sharply dropping and exploding shells is deafening, Martin stops when he sees Nimrod and his three soldiers drop the kneel, Nimrod raises his right hand indicating that the whole group needs to stop and get into cover, Martin moves over next to his Lance Corporal so that he can hear what he has to say and also to have a look at what is in front of them. Stonier arrives next to them, Nimrod points across an open space in front of them, the remainder of the trenches giving them cover have been destroyed leaving little or no cover for them to get to their objective,

"Trench K4" Nimrod points at the map Stonier is holding, "Is about fifteen yards or so in front of us" he points at the map again, "The trenches shown here are no longer there, the heavy shelling has destroyed them"

As if to prove his point, a shell lands in between their position and the German trenches, it forces them to move further back into the communication trench, Stonier takes over,

"Charlie Brewer and his lads are coming in from the opposite direction, we have to hope that they will distract the Germans enough for us to get into their trench system and the bombers can do their stuff"

All three nod, Martin shouts above the noise, "We wait for my signal" He turns to Stonier, "Sir, if you and the bombers can be ready to move in an instant, we can cover you from the German trenches if we go first"

The plan is agreed, they don't have to wait long, they hear a confrontation in the trenches in front of them, Martin presumes that 2nd Lt Brewer has arrived, he indicates to his platoon to move, Stonier takes position at the edge of the trench as the platoon run across the open land toward the trenches. Bullets from a machine gun land all around them,

"Keep going!" Martin yells, they all arrive at the German trenches together and Martin is pleased to see that they all jump in and land on their feet, turning immediately toward the enemy who at this time are advancing further into their trench system to confront the men let by Brewer.

"Covering fire!" Martin shouts and the men all stand and fire from the trench toward the German line, Stonier sees what is happening, and he and the six bombers run across the open land, all reaching the trench without injury. Martin hears rifles being fired, he knows it is the familiar sound of the Lee Enfield he can hear, he looks around a corner of the trench and sees Oakins, Addington, Moule and Payne firing at a group of Germans in the trenches, he can see Brewer and his men advancing from the opposite direction, he watches this carefully as he does not want the men from the 2nd battalion to fire upon each other. He moves forward, rifle in his shoulder, he sees the Germans running away from them, he fires and hits one enemy soldier in the shoulder, they advance and after a few seconds he hears a loud shout,

"Lt Brewer 2nd Battalion advancing!"

Martin responds, "Sir, we are with 2nd Lt Stonier and the bombers, also 2nd battalion"

The shooting stops, several Germans lay dead in the trench, Brewer and Stonier meet and have a short talk, Stonier returns and calls Martin and Bill Peggs to him,

"Charlie Brewer has seen the Germans take a secondary trench from here into another system" He turns to Bill, "Sergeant, we will now advance and bomb that trench, everyone else is to remain here"

They all hear a scream from a position a few yards North from where they are, the Acting CSM from the 2nd Battalion had been leading a group from the reserve positions, having stepped out of the top of the trench he has been shot and killed instantly, they know that this means that the enemy are close by, probably in large numbers, they are definitely still in their trench system and seemingly heading toward them. Brewer speaks to Martin,

"Corporal, can you and yours take the top cover from here, we will move back ten yards and so the same from just around the corner"

Martin barks orders to his platoon, they all take up high positions near to the top of the trench, the bombers and Stonier pass them and enter the secondary trench,

"Enemy to the front!" Oakins shouts

Martin looks around and sees a group of about twenty German soldiers leaving the trench system adjacent to theirs, almost certainly flushed out by the allied soldiers attacking them from behind, no orders are needed, his platoon and Brewer's platoon begin to fire, the Germans fall like skittles in a bowling alley, none of them make it to the trenches. Loud explosions can be heard from behind them, the bombers have made it into the German trenches and are throwing their grenades, they all turn when explosions start going off in front of them, Martin shouts,

"Take cover, mortars from K5!" He is thrown to the bottom of the trench and covered in a light dusting of soil, he can taste it in his mouth, shells begin to land close to their position, the shelling and the mortars could trap them if they stay much longer.

He turns when he hears Stonier and the bombers coming back from the enemy trenches, "That's it, we are out of bombs" he turns to Martin, "Report Corporal"

"We are taking heavy mortar and shell fire Sir, the Germans must still be in, or have retaken K5, it is 300 yards or so from us, we are in direct line of their fire, and we are running out of ammunition"

He pats Martin on the shoulder and runs toward Brewer, only a minute or so later he returns with Brewer and his small party of soldiers,

"We need to get back to the communication trench Corporal" They all duck down as a mortar hits the edge of the trench a few yards to their right, "From there we can regroup but I feel we may need to hold our position there and certainly not here"

Martin calls to Oakins, "Nimrod! Withdraw to the communication trenches, you take your three men and give cover fire when you get there"

Oakins nods and he, Bill, Harry, and Frank climb out of the trench and run toward the communication trench, only a few yards away.

He hears the sound of many trench mortars, small double wheeled and very portable mortars, they are firing their three inch shells, each with its weight of ten pounds easily carrying it over the 300 yards to their position and beyond, he knows that a good crew can fire a mortar every ten seconds, he also knows that there is several trench mortars firing toward their position simultaneously, Nimrod, Bill, Harry and Frank are only yards from safety when they are hit by mortars, more than one landing on their position as they run, all four are cut down immediately, Martin jumps up to the edge of the trench, "Nimrod!"

He is pulled back down by 2nd Lt Stonier and Bill Peggs, it is Bill who speaks to him with firmness in his voice, "They are dead, no point us all going that way Corporal" he gives Martin a little shake and carries on, "Martin, we all know how you feel, but getting yourself killed won't help them or us"

Just for a second Martin falls back and sits in the trench, he is angry, but he knows that Bill is right, they are being overwhelmed and need to get to safety, he is bought back into the war by Stonier,

"Corporal, we need to get to that communication trench" he looks around at the small band of soldiers, "All of us"

Martin stands, "2nd Lt Brewer Sir, can you and your party provide as much cover fire as you can toward K5, I know you won't hit anything but it may just give us enough time to get across, we can then do the same for you" he turns to Bill, "If you and yours fire a few yards to the left, then leave seconds after us, we may get enough cover to make it to safety"

Without answering Martin, Brewer sets his men up and they begin to fire,

"Sir" Martin says to Stonier, "We all need to go, and it needs to be now!"

Martin and his two remaining platoon members climb up and out of the trench, followed by 2nd Lt Stonier, Bill Peggs and the five other bombers hang back for a few seconds, firing rapidly toward the enemy, the mortars have stopped, the cover fire is working, Martin runs, his chest is sore and his legs heavy, but he makes it across, he is pleased to see that everyone makes it. Bill Peggs and his bombers have arrived, he is shouting orders to the soldiers, Martin takes his position, standing in the communications trench with his rifle aimed toward K5, he sees Stonier kneeling next to him, he is looking at Brewers patrol,

"Fire!" orders Peggs, the deafening sound of nine rifles being fired at the same time begins,

"Now Charlie, now!" shouts Stonier.

Shells land very close to their trench, the noise and smell is almost unbearable,

Out of the corner of his eye he sees the small party of 2nd Battalion soldiers running toward him, they all make it to the trench, the men shooting stop, and all take cover in the communication trench.

"Arthurs been hit!" a voice that Martin does not know screams, he moves over to where the scream came from, 2nd Lt Brewer is on his knees, kneeling next to a solider that Martin knows, Private Arthur Loan, an Essex lad who is always smiling.

"Easy now Arthur" the voice of Brewer is quiet and calm amongst the noisy surroundings he and the others are in, Martin kneels next to Brewer who puts his fingers to his lips indicating that Martin should be quiet.

"Is that you Dad?" asks Arthur taking the hand of 2nd Lt Brewer, he has wound in his back, red hot shrapnel has hit him as he ran across the open land, he got to the trench carried by momentum, Brewer, who is about the same age as Arthur replies to him,

"Yes Son, it is me"

"I can't move Dad, everything is dark"

"I know lad, close your eyes, everything will be just fine" Brewer puts his free hand onto Arthur's chest, he takes two or three deep breaths, his chest rises and falls, rises and falls again, then it is still. Brewer closes his eyes and whispers a quiet prayer, he takes the identity tag from around Arthur Loans neck, removes one and puts it in his pocket, leaving the other around the dead soldiers' neck for later identification. Martin stands and walks across to where Stonier and Bill Peggs are talking, Stonier addresses him as he arrives, "Corporal, your platoon and the remainder of 2nd Lt Brewers party are to remain in the communication trench, but nearer to our lines" He points at Bill, "Sergeant Peggs and his men will return to our original position and report to HQ in our trenches, 2nd Lt Brewer and I will return and make our report, I will register the dead" He looks Martin straight in the eye, "I will return to you and let you know what we are to do next" Martin remains quiet as the young officer finishes his sentence, "God only knows what carnage has happened out there today, if what we have been through is anything to go by then it won't be good news"

Martin looks across at Bill, who puts his thumbs up and mouths the words, "Are you alright?" to him, Martin nods in reply, he turns when 2nd Lt Brewer speaks to him, "Corporal, I have told my men that you are in charge, I will also come back with 2nd Lt Stonier"

With that they are all gone, Martin is left in charge of six men, two of his and four from Brewers party, the shelling continues around them, and the mortars have started up again, he has a quick peek over the top of the trench, the open ground is clear, apart from the fallen dead, there are no advancing enemy soldiers at this time, he points at his men, "Jake, Barney, take covering positions" he points at a firing shelf in the trench wall, "You other lads, have a smoke and we will do fifteen minutes about in the firing positions"

They all do as they are told, Martin sits a short distance from the others, takes a woodbine from his top pocket, lights it without offering the others a cigarette or a light, they are lighting theirs from one match. He inhales deeply, holds the bitter tasting smoke in his lungs for a few seconds and then exhales it, he repeats this time and time again until the woodbine is finished.

It is dark when Stonier and Brewer return, Sergeant Oakes is with them, Brewer takes his men back to trench HQ for further deployment instructions, it is much quieter now, the shelling and mortars have stopped, only the occasional burst of machine gun fire breaks the silence of the night.

"Lt Col Thorpe has put a stop to the advance for now, everyone, except you and your two men, are being re deployed, you are to stay here for now, more soldiers will be sent to you"

"I take it we will be going back into those trenches?" Martin tries to sound positive.

Oakes nods and says, "Nothing official as yet, the Lt Col has ordered every patrol and platoon back to our original positions" he takes out his pipe, puts it into his mouth unlit, he continues to talk with it in his mouth, "We have taken huge losses today; Major Mackenzie was killed when he and his patrol moved out of reserve positions to help Captain Huntriss who was in dire straits"

Martin speaks to Oakes, "What about the Majors patrol, how did they fare?"

Oakes takes a match, lights it and puts the flame to the tobacco, when it is lit, he continues, "All dead, it was a massacre"

Martin takes in a deep breath,

"Did you know some of them Martin?"

"I did Sarge" he takes a woodbine out, taps it on the cigarette packet and holds it in his hand, "Bill Pearson was a mate of mine" pausing as he accepts a light from Oakes, "And I met Harry Mockridge and young John Crew just before we went into action earlier, his family live near mine"

Oakes raises his eyebrows, "I also heard that the 4th Cameron's have gone back in and taken a trench back from the Germans, I also hear that several of them have fallen into flooded shell holes and drowned"

Martin exhales his smoke. "When will this be over Sarge?"

Oakes doesn't reply and both men sit in silence and smoke.

* * *

Lance Corporal Charles Parr had been laid to rest in St Nicholas churchyard in the first week of May, Alice was at the service, standing at the back of the church with the other volunteers and VAD nurses, the church was packed with soldiers from the South Staffordshire regiment. Lance Corporal Parr had died at the Institute on 25th April, not much is known about him, only that he was thirty three years old and from Liverpool but had been living in Birmingham prior to joining the army as a territorial in 1914. He had, along with the rest of his battalion, landed in Le Havre early in March 1915, by mid-April he was back in town and in the Institute as a patient, it is not known how he came about his horrific injuries, but it is presumed that he was injured on the Western Front only days after landing in France. He had succumbed to his wounds on the afternoon of Sunday 25th April, only that morning he had seemed chipper and happier than he had been for some time, Alice and Joan, her VAD nurse colleague had served breakfast to the men in their care and Charles had been awake and eaten some breakfast, only a few hours later he died without warning. Joan was very upset; she had spent a lot of time caring for Charles and they had talked about him returning home after he had healed. The funeral had been a grand affair, a full military turnout, the RSM at the head of the procession with his rifle held under his left arm with the barrel facing the ground behind his and the rifle butt facing front, behind him to his right were six soldiers from the South Staffordshire's, marching in file, their rifles held in the same position as the RSM, to the left was a Captain from the regiment, also holding his rifle in the odd position. Alice had heard the RSM call for 'Reverse Arms', this is when the soldiers at the front had placed their rifles in this position, she presumed as a mark of respect for the dead soldier. Behind these men at the front marched a full military band, behind them were officers on horseback and the coffin of Charles Parr pulled on a strong wooden bier, behind this were the remainder of the battalion, a huge spectacle for the town on a cold May morning, the column of soldiers marched from the common parading on the patch of green land behind the Railway hotel, then marching along the High Street, passing the various shops, newsagents and public houses, the soldiers finally being bought to the halt and forming up in three straight lines that went from the Cock pond outside of Bowers house to the far end of Church Green, a sad and fantastic sight for the people of the town. The coffin had been carried into the Church by six capless colleagues of the deceased, a short service of thanks followed and then Lance Corporal Charles Frederick Parr was laid to rest in the churchyard in a quiet place at the far left corner of the graveyard, many miles from his family and home.

The early weeks of May had also bought news of the death of Harold Pearce, he had been living and working in the mill just along from the cottage, his parents live at Coleswood Road, Harold was only a couple of years older than Alice and she recalls speaking to him regularly when she had walked along the banks of the River Lea, he had died in France following the gas attack on the Western Front by the German Army. The month of May couldn't finish soon enough for Alice, the only good points for her had been hearing from Martin, although they are less frequent now and sometimes only a few words on a postcard, Charles writes to her every week, she tingles and burns with excitement as she waits for the postman to deliver the mail to her at The Malta, Aunt May and Uncle Pete collect it for her during the week as she still lives with them and her cousins, she only occasionally stays at the pub with Granny because of her hectic volunteer commitments at the Institute, although one letter she received from him during the second week of May informed her that his friend, George Robins, had been killed, ironically on the same day as Harold Pearce, both men having family living only a few miles from each other, both men dying on the same battlefield, fighting for a piece of land called Hill 60. Alice had read the letter from Charles several times, she had never met George Robins, but she could feel the hurt in Charles written words, and this had upset her more than she had imagined it would have.

June arrives, bringing with it summer sunshine and warmth, windows are open on the ward and three of the wounded men are sitting outside, smoking cigarettes, drinking coffee, and reading newspapers, only one man, John Freeman, lies in his bed staring out of the window, he is not looking at the three other soldiers, he stares past them looking across at the common in front of him. Alice sits next to his bed reading to him, she loves Charles Dickens and is reading aloud '*David Copperfield*', she has not had any sort of reaction from John who still remains silent as he has been since arriving. Alice has just finished chapter fifteen, the title character has been taken to the home of the alcoholic Lawyer, Mr Wickfield and his daughter Agnes by his Great Aunt, Miss Betsy Trotwood, they have been introduced to the Wickfield's by his clerk, the flame haired, sycophantic, and obsequious character of Uriah Heep, a boy who makes frequent references to his own '*umbleness*'. Alice despises the character of Heep but loves to read about him and his syrupy humility, having read the book several times she knows that Heep will eventually get his *come uppance*, but at the end of this chapter he and David have met as Heep is closing the office for the night, David finds Heeps hand to be cold and clammy and wipes his palm on his jacket afterwards, Dickens descriptive writing is, in her opinion, as yet unchallenged by any other author. Alice closes the book at the end of the chapter, she is smiling as she enjoys reading to John, he has not moved throughout despite Alice speaking in a slow, quiet, and soothing manner, she looks up and sees Joan entering the ward, she is with Mr and Mrs Freeman, Alice is surprised as they had only been in to see him during the last week, she is beckoned over by Joan, she puts her book on the bedside table and walks over to the entrance to the ward,

"Alice, Mr and Mrs Freeman would like a few moments alone with John"

Alice turns to Johns parents, "Good afternoon Mr and Mrs Freeman, I hope you are both well"

They both nod and move away from both women, Mrs Freeman sits in the chair recently vacated by Alice, Mr Freeman remains standing,

"What is going on Joan?" asks Alice

Joan hands Alice a folded piece of paper, she opens it carefully, it is a Post office telegram, the date stamp on the right hand side reads ' Portsmouth 29 May 15', Alice reads on, the telegram says,

'*OHMS Portsmouth*

Mr John David Freeman, 2 Viaduct Cottages, East Hyde, Luton, Beds.

Regret to report that your son David James Freeman Gunner 1st class J001236 is missing presumed killed on war service

Commodore Naval Barracks Portsmouth'

Alice takes in a breath and looks at Joan, "Oh no" is all she can say.

Joan puts her hand on Alice's arm, "Let's leave them be for now Alice"

They both leave, Mrs Freeman is sobbing as Mr Freeman talks to his son.

Alice finishes her duties, she has a few days off, including the up and coming weekend, she is staying with Mary during her time off as she is meeting up with Grace tomorrow lunchtime, they will be catching up and both writing letters to Martin and Charles, as she is getting ready to leave, she is approached by Dr Kelynack, the Commandant of the VAD, "Alice, may I have a word before you leave, please?"

"Of course, Ma'am" Alice follows Dr Kelynack to her very small office at the far end of the building, Alice is offered a seat and sits down, she is nervous,

"You look terrified young lady" Dr Kelynack says, "You have nothing to worry about, I only want to pass on my thanks to you for your excellent work with Private Freeman"

Alice lets out a sigh of relief, "Thank you, Ma'am, have you heard about his brother being killed in action?"

The Doctor nods "I have, terrible business, the parents are here, aren't they?"

Alice tells her that she left them with Private Freeman only a few minutes ago,

"Alice, I only wish you were old enough to join the VAD, your work with these injured men is so good, I struggle to remember you are only sixteen sometimes"

Alice blushes, Dr Kelynack continues, "Especially your dedication to Private Freeman, it is very difficult to continue when it seems that there is no hope and no real healing, your tenacity is to be admired, I understand that he has not spoken since he arrived here?"

"That is correct Ma'am, not even a sound when the nurses changed his dressings on his wounds, thankfully they have all healed well, he is heavily scarred, but healing has been good"

Dr Kelynack pauses, she leans forward on her desk, "Alice, Private Freeman will be leaving us very soon, as you say, his wounds are healed but he is wounded of mind, do you understand?"

"I do, what will happen to him?"

A long sigh is let out by the doctor, "He cannot go home to his family Alice, although not a danger to anyone, he is certainly a danger to himself" she shuffles some papers on her desk "He has been missing from here on no less than eight occasions, being found more than once at one of our local railway stations, walking on the line itself once" she looks again at the documents, "He got as far as St Albans on one occasion" She puts the papers down on the table

"So where will he go when he leaves here?" Alice asks again

"He will have to go to a facility or institution that can care for his condition, he cannot go back to the war, his physical condition will not allow that, even if he had not lost the arm, he would be shot for being a coward or for malingering"

Alice has a look of shock on her face, "Can they treat his wounded mind Ma'am?" asks Alice.

Dr Kelynack sits back in her chair, "There are varying views on that Alice, many believe that these men, John Freeman is one of many thousands suffering similar mental symptoms, should face up to their fears, shaming them is a popular form of treatment, the hope is that if they are shamed for their 'behaviour' that they will 'snap out of it" and be able to return to the war"

"That is so nasty!" exclaims Alice,

"I agree, some believe that strong physical training and exercise helps, Private Freeman cannot participate in this form of therapy, electricity is used by some practitioners" she stops for a moment, "Alice, are you sure you want to hear this?"

Alice tells the Commandant that she needs to hear it,

"Electric shocks to affected areas is believed to stimulate recovery, men who don't walk have electricity passed through their spine, men like Private Freeman who are mute will have electricity passed through their pharynx"

Alice puts her hands to her face to cover her open mouth, "No!" she exclaims, "Surely that is torture?"

"No Alice, these are medical treatments, another treatment means that the men are deprived of what they need most, in an attempt to get them back to normal"

Alice looks confused, "I don't understand"

"Well, for instance, if a man is educated and likes to read, he will be deprived from going to a library or to read a newspaper or a book, men that seem to fear noise will be put in rooms near too busy roads so as to subject them to what they fear the most, some who fear begin alone are forced into isolation" she can see the shock on Alice's face again, raising a hand she continues, "I know it seems harsh, but if it works then it is best for all concerned"

"Does it work?" Alice asks bluntly

"No, not in my opinion" replies Dr Kelynack, "I think these men need respite, care and attention and they will need it for long periods of time, if not for the rest of their lives, all we can do here Alice is to help heal the physical wounds, damaged minds cannot be fixed here" she pauses again, "If they can be fixed at all"

"When will John be leaving us?"

"I hope in a few days, there are not many places for men suffering as he is, I am hopeful a bed can be found for him locally, perhaps at the county asylum in St Albans?"

Alice stands, "Will that be all Dr Kelynack"

"Yes, thank you Alice, please don't take it to heart about poor Private Freeman, we don't have the facility here to help him any longer, you have done fantastic work with him"

Alice thanks the Commandant and heads for the door,

"Alice" she turns to face Dr Kelynack, "How is Lt Gray doing, have you heard from him at all?"

Alice beams a huge smile,

"I have, thank you Doctor, he seems to be coping just fine, I am expecting a letter any day now"

Alice leaves the small office, exiting the building at the front, she waves goodbye to the three soldiers who are still sitting outside enjoying the late afternoon sun, she smiles at them even though she does not feel at all happy, she can also see that Mr and Mrs Freeman are still with John.

Leaving the grounds of the Institute and turning right onto the Wheathampstead road, she decides to take the back road to Station Road, this road takes her around Blakesleys House and away from the High Street, she wants to get to the Pub to see Granny and not to be distracted by the many shops that will still be open, especially Mrs Austins sweet shop with its many delights. Alice remembers that she used to sit on the floor when she was younger and stare at the penny sweets on the lowest shelf, she would also stand outside of Dudmesh the saddlers shop, the smell of leather emanating from the workshop was so exotic to her, other smells in town also remind her of her childhood, Sampson's fish shop at Church green, Mr Busby in his chemist shop, he always wears a black skull cap and has been known to act as the towns dentist at times, and Ackroyds bakers and Irons bakers always smell sweet and exciting to her, even now as a sixteen year old. She waves at Old Tom Lovett, the Rag and bone man, he is the proprietor of the Marine store dealers at Church green, a small wooden building where he keeps and sells on the second-hand goods, he collects from those who do not need them or want them anymore, he is the local cricket umpire, town crier and valued member of the choir, he waves back and shouts 'Good evening Miss" in his booming voice. She walks onto Station Road, past Salisbury the iron mongers, then stopping for just a minute to look in the window of Watsons shoe fitters, the town has another shoe shop, Gibbons the bootmakers, further along the High Street, Valentines stationary shop is closed, she turns as her name is called, she sees a boy she went to school with, Cecil Rolt, he is riding an old bicycle, he is riding toward Chirneys bicycle shop where he has worked since leaving St Nicks. As she passes under the railway bridge she sees, on the opposite side of the road, a gentleman dressed in Victorian style clothes, it is Mr Pellant the clock maker and jeweller, he tips his hat at her as he passes, she knows that he is doing the evening rounds he does every day, visiting the larger houses in town to wind their clocks. Passing Milton Road and Cowper road, there are only a few houses on each road, these were built before the war and building has now stopped, she continues on her way toward the Malta, further on she passes Overstone and Dalkeith Roads, then Manland Avenue on her left, as she heads toward the bottom of Station Road toward a right turn that, if she continues on it, will take her toward the Marquis of Granby pub, passing Carisbrooke Road, but she crosses into the open parkland that leads toward to the river, the footpath taking her over the two bridges, one over the stream and one over the River Lea. A few farm workers and men from the mill are sitting outside of the Gibraltar Castle pub, one of them waves at her, it is Charlie Edwards the dairyman, she waves back and walks past, toward the cottage, she slows down as she wants to have a good look at the cottage, it seems cold and unused, the chimney is silent and smokeless, the garden is in need of some work, she tries to keep on top of the vegetable patch but she has been so busy lately that it is looking somewhat neglected. As she approaches, she promises to tidy it up tomorrow, she sees something move from behind the Yew tree, stopping to look again she can see nothing, only the big gnarled old tree, it is still, there is no breeze, she steps to the gate and leans over to try to get a view behind the tree, she is unable to see anything from where she is, she can hear the stream moving gently as it always does, was that a splash she heard? Alice sees definite movement in the watercress beds, she hopes it is a dog or a rabbit, looking at the tree she feels a shiver run down her back and decided to move on to the pub to see Granny. It takes only a minute to get there, and she pushes open the door, as she does so she hears the familiar low sound of men talking to each other, she has a quick look at the cottage, all is still and silent, she sets off quickly toward the pub.

"Hello my dear Alice"

Mary is standing behind the bar and seems very pleased to see her Granddaughter, Alice steps into the bar, letting the door close behind her, she walks around the bar, gives Mary a kiss on the cheek,

"Hello granny, what do we have for tea?"

* * *

Grace arrives early the next morning at the pub, Mary answers the door to her,

"Good morning Grace, I thought you were meeting Alice at lunchtime at the cottage?"

Grace hugs Mary, who seems shocked by the sudden show of emotion,

"Oh Mary, I have such good news!"

Grace takes the newspaper she is holding and places it on one of the tables in the bar, it is the London Gazette dated 1st June 1915, the newspaper is over ten days old,

"Whatever are you doing with the London Gazette Grace, that is not a paper that is sold around here?"

"It was left at the children's home by one of the visiting officers from the Staffordshire regiment, I picked it up out of interest and was reading all the citations for bravery, when I came across this"

She points to a section in the newspaper, Mary takes her spectacles from her apron pocket and shrieks as she reads the name above the citation"

"Lord almighty, that is our Martin!"

Grace, still excited tells her to read on,

"I can't Grace, read it to me will you please"

Grace picks up the newspaper, under Martin's name and rank she reads the citation,

'*Distinguished Conduct Medal*

2ND Battalion Bedfordshire regiment.

For conspicuous gallantry and devotion to duty on 21st April 1915 at Estaires, France

During an enemy machine gun attack on a column of Allied soldiers, he, in a most gallant manner directed his men and led an attack into enemy held trenches, under fire he entered the enemy trench on his own and used grenades to inflict many casualties on the enemy.

He showed bravery, courage, and leadership'

Mary is wiping tears away from her eyes and hugging Grace when Alice enters the bar, she heard voices from her room and has come down to see what is going on, she sees her grandmother crying and hugging Grace, she puts her hands to her mouth, she screams, "What has happened, its Martin isn't it?"

Grace and Mary look and see a shocked Alice standing by the door, Grace realises that Alice thinks harm, or worse, has happened to Martin, she lets Mary go and runs to Alice,

"It is Alice, but it is such good news" she holds the newspaper up and points to the citation, Alice reads and then bursts into tears,

"I thought..." she cannot finish her sentence as emotion and relief flood over her, Grace puts her arms around her and cuddles her, then lets her go,

"I am so sorry Alice, I didn't think, I am sorry"

Mary steps over to them, she is back to her usual stern self,

"A lot of fuss over nothing" she looks at her Granddaughter, seeing the tears and the fear on her face ,"Oh Alice, you didn't think Martin was hurt or worse, did you?" Alice bursts into tears again, Mary takes Alice into her arms, "You silly thing, he is fine, he is a hero, certainly by what this newspaper reads" Alice hugs her Granny back, "Now then Alice" says Mary, "I have things to do, the pub needs cleaning before I can open, why don't you take Grace to the kitchen and have a cup of tea" Alice looks at Mary, "Go on now, the pair of you, don't be getting under my feet"

Grace and Alice leave the bar and to the small kitchen at the back of the pub and behind the bar area, it is a remarkably quiet room considering it is so near to the public bar, they both gently sigh as they enter, the coolness of the air in the kitchen is welcomed, even with the range fire lit and with the large windows open it is still cooler than the rest of the building. The walls are whitewashed and spotlessly clean, the brick floor is swept free of dust and everything is neat and tidy, on the back wall is the wood burning range stove, jet black in colour, it dominates the space on the wall it occupies, its back plate made of cast iron is surrounded by a huge wooden frame, similar to the fireplace in the living room but much larger, sitting on the right side of the high shelf on the frame is an old casement clock, set in a beautiful dark mahogany box, its original white face with large roman numerals is now faded and stained, Mary must have to stand on the edge of the stove to turn the keys to wind it, three old china plates stand upright against the wall, each having a faded red pattern around the edge, three cups with identical patterns sit in front of the plates, a silver candelabra with three candle cups, there are no candles in it, completes the line up on the shelf, it sitting on the far left side. The lever for the damper sits centrally on the back plate, it is currently nearer the closed position than to the open, below this is a small hood that sits directly above the fireplace, a small fire is burning in the hearth, a log is almost half burnt through, to the left of the fire is the small oven, its door firmly closed, and the kettle stands on the hotplate above it, steam rises from the spout tells them that the water is boiling. The large oven to the right has the door latch firmly in place, sweet smells emanate from this oven, Mary is cooking a cake although they are not sure what sort of cake it is, an old stone hot water bottle sits on top of the stove and a heavy pressing iron sits on the metal shelf that is away from the main heat of the range. To the left of the range, in the far corner of the kitchen, is the built in washing tub with its separate fire below to heat the water in the '*copper*' above it, a large circular wooden lid is currently firmly in place over the top of the tub, various pots and pans sit neatly on the free space on top of the wash tub. Moving round the kitchen there is a wooden unit with a sunken ceramic fireclay Belfast sink sitting perfectly in the middle, it has perfectly square, inch thick slate tops either side of it, the only tap in the room sticks out of the wall above the sink, directly below the sink are two outwardly opening doors and either side of these is a larger door, each has small brown rounded wooden handles, the unit has been hand painted light green. In the centre of the kitchen is an ancient heavy wooden table, its top is bare and uncovered wood, several inches thick and resembling a butcher's block, at each corner stand ornately carved legs, their beauty in stark contrast to the basic and obviously regularly used tabletop, a high backed Windsor chair is pushed in at each side of the table, Grace pulls out one of these chairs and sits.

"Do you want a cup of tea Grace, or shall we wait until we get to the cottage"

"Let's wait" replies Grace

Alice is pacing around the kitchen,

"Alice, whatever is wrong?" asks Grace

Alice pulls out a chair and sits, her elbows on the table and her chin in her hands, she mumbles,

"I haven't had a letter from Charles this week"

Grace puts a hand over her mouth to smother a laugh, Alice notices her do this and smiles,

"Have you heard from Martin?"

Grace nods, "I got a letter yesterday, the first for a couple of weeks, but he did not mention anything about a medal or anything at all to do with what he did"

Alice does not answer,

"Have you had a letter from Martin Alice?"

She takes her hands away from her chin, pulling a face she says,

"Only a postcard last Wednesday, I bet he writes more to you than, 'Hope you and Granny are both well, everything is alright here', that's about all I get"

Grace does not hide her laughter this time, she takes Alice's hands in hers, "Charles will write, he is very busy you know, I am sure that he is fine, his family are still living at Cherry Trees at the Folly, we would certainly have heard if anything had happened to him" Grace says these words even though she does not fully believe them, many men from neighbouring villages and hamlets had been killed and news only filters through to the locals in days, if not weeks afterwards.

"Postman has delivered!" Mary shouts from the bar, Alice jumps out of her chair nearly knocking it over as she runs to the bar from the kitchen,

"Alice!" scolds Grace, she gets up and follows her young friend slowly and in a more serene manner.

"I have a postcard from Martin" Mary is trying to read it without her glasses,

"Put your glasses on Granny" says Alice impatiently. Mary slowly takes her glasses from her pinney, deliberately slowly, Alice moans, "Come along Granny! Do I have any letters or postcards?"

Mary fans out the mail as you would do with a deck of cards, "Take your pick young lady"

Alice steps forward and takes a letter, looking at the name and address, she sees that it is addressed to her and is in Charles neat handwriting, she holds the letter to her breast and smiles, Mary speaks again,

"Try again"

Alice looks at her, mildly confused, she steps forward and looks at the items in Mary's hand, one postcard and one letter, she takes the letter and yelps with glee, it is another letter from Charles, Mary hands her the postcard, "One for you from Martin"

Alice takes the postcard, "It will say the same as yours Granny" she turns to Grace "I do hope my brother writes better letters to you than he does postcards to Granny and me"

Grace does not reply but tilts her head slightly and smiles,

"Shall we go to the cottage and open the letters?" asks Alice

Grace spreads out her empty hands, "No letters for me Alice"

Alice runs to Grace and takes her by the arm and leads her to the door,

"Shall we go and catch the postman and see if he has any mail for you Grace"

Mary looks sternly at Alice, "Slow down Alice, Mr Skillman has a job to do, and he won't thank you for stopping him and asking him to meddle with deliveries of mail"

"We can walk to my parents' house; he may have been before he came here"

As they leave Mary asks Grace, "Will you be taking tea with us this evening?"

"That will be lovely, thank you Mary, what shall I bring?"

"Nothing at all" Mary exclaims "James Crew was in the pub last night, you know the gamekeeper from West Hyde" she continues without waiting for an answer, "I have some fresh rabbit, so its rabbit pie if you would like"

Grace tells Mary she would very much like to have tea with them and that she will inform her parents not to provide for her this evening, she knows that the cake in the oven will be baked and decorated for them to eat after dinner, they leave and head toward Grace's home.

An hour later they are sat in the cottage, the fire in the range is burning well and the kettle is still hot from the tea they made a short while ago, they are both sat at the kitchen table, Alice has her two unopened letters and Grace has one from Martin, they arrived at her home the same time as Mr Skillman and had taken her letter from him, it remains unopened in her lap.

"This letter from Charles is dated the 3rd of May!" Alice sounds annoyed, "I have had others since then, this one appears to have been lost!"

"It happens all the time with the military mail, they have millions of letters to sort and deliver from the war, so if one or two goes missing, then we have to live with it"

Alice opens the envelope carefully, taking out the letter she greedily reads every word written to her, "Oh my!" she puts the letter on the table, Grace looks at her, "Charles and Martin have met!" Grace fakes her reaction, Martin has already told her that he had met Charles, but she decided not to tell Alice, knowing that Charles would almost certainly tell her in one of his letters,

"Charles says he and Martin had a brief chat before he was sent back to the 1st Battalion" she reads a little more, "And that Martin is a fine man and a fine soldier!" she looks at Grace, "How exciting!"

"It seems as though they hit it off" Grace replies with enthusiasm she hopes is not over the top, Alice hasn't noticed,

"What does Martin say in his letter? Perhaps he will mention Charles?"

Grace takes her letter from its envelope and reads, tears fill her eyes as Martins words of love and affection pour out from the cheap paper and into her mind, as usual, he hardly mentions the war and there is no mention of Charles in this communication, she folds it up and puts it back in the envelope,

"Well?" asks Alice

She decides that a white lie won't hurt, "He says that he and Charles met just after Charles arrived back in France, they had very little time together, but he likes him a lot" Grace pretends that these details are in the letter she received today and not from the one she received at the beginning of May, the details she gives to Alice are the truth, but from several weeks ago. "You must read your other letter before we write back to the boys"

Alice picks up her second letter, she is distracted when Grace suddenly stands and goes to the window,

"Who is that in your garden Alice?"

The letter is put down and Alice joins Grace at the window, she looks down the garden, the vegetable patch is as it always is, in need of a little attention, the water pump is still there and the Yew tree is ever present, someone is standing under the tree, Alice recognises him immediately, it is John Freeman. He is standing under the tree, staring directly at them, his army cap sits untidily on the back of his head, the mass of vivid red scars can be seen on his face, he is wearing his green army shirt and tunic, both are not buttoned up and flap in the light breeze, the sleeve on his right side flaps back and forth with ease without a limb to prevent this movement, his white undershirt is dirty, he has his army trousers on without a belt, they seem wet at the bottom, his boots are not tied and the laces are hanging on either side of each one.

"What on earth is he doing here?" Alice speaks, Grace then asks,

"Who is it, Alice?"

"That is Private John Freeman, from East Hyde"

Grace gasps, "Is that Janice's brother?"

Alice nods, Grace speaks again,

"She said that her brother was injured and not well, but I wasn't expecting this, what is he doing here?"

Shaking her head Alice moves toward the door, "I don't know, but he has been leaving the ward recently and has been found near here at the railway station, his family received a telegram about John's older brother, David, he has been killed in action"

She turns to Grace, "Can you run to the East station please, speak to the soldiers there and explain that one of the patients from the Institute has got out and will need to be returned"

"What are you going to do Alice?"

"I am going to speak to him, he knows me, it will be fine, he has never been aggressive before, I promise it will be safe" Grace doesn't move, "Please Grace, go and fetch the soldiers, I will be alright with John"

Grace nods in agreement at the words Alice is telling her and makes her way to the station, Alice walks slowly down the garden path, past the vegetable patch, she steps off of the path to the right and stands next to the water pump, John Freeman is a few yards to her left.

"John" she says gently, "Are you alright"

He does not answer, he moves his head to look at her, his body remains unmoved, he has tears in his eyes, they roll slowly down his ferociously scarred cheeks, he is silent, she takes a few steps toward him, her hand out in front of her, "John, I heard about your brother, so very sad" she pauses for a second and takes a step or two nearer to him, "Will you come indoors with me, we can have a hot cup of tea and then I can get you back to the ward?"

She is standing almost next to him, he has not moved, his head still turned in her direction, she leans forward and takes his left hand in her right hand, he does not resist, "Come on John, come with me inside the cottage, it is safe there, I promise you, we will just sit and have a tea, how does that sound to you?"

The soldier does not move, Alice pulls very gently on his hand, he steps and follows her, they walk, slowly, up the garden path to the cottage, she lets his hand go as they reach the door, it is not wide enough for both of them to pass through together, she turns back and takes his hand again and guides him into the cottage, she takes off his cap and sits him on the bench seat under the window.

Silent tears fall from his eyes as he sits.

* * *

Sunday morning arrives, it is the second Sunday of June, Alice wakes up early in her room at the pub, she is meeting Grace this morning at the cottage, they are to write the letters to Martin and Charles that they had intended to yesterday but when John Freeman turned up at the cottage and all thoughts of writing had left their minds. John had been collected by the soldiers posted to the East station, they stayed with him until Pete arrived in his ambulance a couple of hours later and took John with two soldiers to escort him back to the ward. Uncle Pete, Aunt May and the girls had been in the pub last night to share the meal of rabbit pie served with vegetables, also to joyfully eat the best sponge cake Mary had cooked earlier that day, Alice overheard a conversation when Pete told Mary and May that Private Freeman was to be taken to an asylum on Monday morning, she is so sad, not for herself but for John Freeman, a young man who had volunteered his service for his country and after only a few days on the Western Front, was severely injured, his physical wounds have healed but Alice fears his mind may never be well again and he will spend much of his remaining life in mental asylums. She descends the stairs slowly, still in her nightgown and without slippers on her feet, as she steps into the kitchen, she hears Mary,

"Good morning Alice, what have I told you about wearing slippers, if you are having tea could you make me a cup, please, I am gasping"

Alice takes in everything her Grandmother has said to her, she lifts the kettle, it needs filling, taking the three steps from the stove to the sink, she turns the tap, it squeaks as it is opened, water gushes into the kettle and it gets heavier in her hand as it fills, the tap is turned off silently, strangely it only squeaks when it is being opened, Alice puts the lid onto the kettle then takes a few steps and puts the kettle on the hotplate. She goes into the narrow hallway and looks around on the floor, she spies a pair of Marys clogs and puts her feet into them, she has no idea which clog is left and which is right, they both seem exactly the same, her silent footsteps are replaced with the obvious sound of wooden clogs on a wooden floor, as she enters the bar Mary is wiping tables and emptying the ashtrays, she is wearing a brightly coloured head scarf, her brown dress is protected by an apron, in a lighter shade of brown, her sleeves are rolled up past her elbow,

"A charwoman gets ten shillings a week for this work, I have to do it as part of my job, the place is filthy this morning"

Alice does not think the pub is at all dirty, but she knows that Mary has high standards and set herself strict daily routines to ensure the pub is always up to scratch,

"Was it a busy night then Granny?"

"It was Alice, did you not hear the men singing in here?"

Alice shakes her head, "I was exhausted after what happened with John Freeman yesterday"

She looks up as she hears voices of women talking as they pass by the front of the pub, Mary does not look up,

"That's the Methodists off to the early service" Mary stops for a moment and looks at Alice, "That man did not hurt you, yesterday, did he?"

"Oh no Granny, John is not aggressive, he is just not very well, I think it is very sad indeed"

Mary moves onto another table, she tips the ashtray into the bucket on the floor, wiping the clear glass clean with one cloth and then wiping the top of the table with another, the ashtray is returned to its original place, cleaned and ready for use.

"Kettle young lady"

Alice takes a few seconds to register what Mary has said to her, she stands still for a few seconds and then moves off toward the kitchen, the clogs making a racket as she does so,

"And take my blooming clogs off will you!"

Alice smiles as she enters the kitchen barefoot, the clogs now back in the hallway, the brick floor feels cold on the soles of her feet and she likes it, the kettle is steaming, she takes a thick cotton cloth and removes it from the hot plate and puts it on an iron stand next to the wash tub lid, she looks around for the teapot, she locates it and pours a little hot water into it, putting the lid back on and swilling the hot water around inside it. The loose tea is in a tin in the cupboard under the sink, it has a tight fitting round lid that sits firmly on the lip of the tin, an oriental scene is depicted in bright yellow and red on each side of the tin, the black background makes the dragons and oriental men stand out in an almost lifelike manner, the leaf tea inside the tin is probably Lyons, Granny buys it loose from the grocer who has a large silver coloured scoop that he gathers the tea in and then, with some drama, pours it into brown paper bags from a height, all part of his sales and service. Alice takes the small silver spoon from inside the tin, then remembers she has to empty the water from the pot, she does this and puts three spoonful's of tea into the teapot and pours the still very hot water on top of the tea that now nestles in the bottom of the pot, she fills it about three quarters full and gives the liquid a little swirl to encourage the tea to mix with the water, the lid is replaced on the tea pot, putting it onto the kitchen table, she takes the hand knitted tea cosy and puts it over the top of the pot. Alice opens the large door on the left of the sink unit and bending down takes the bottle of milk that is stands on slab of marble to keep it as fresh as possible, the bottle with the name of the dairy embossed in the glass, is half full, taking off the cardboard lid she smells it to make sure it is not sour, it isn't, the bottle is placed next to the teapot containing the stewing tea. On the other side of the kitchen is a small sideboard, it is from there that Alice takes two cups and saucers and puts them next to the milk bottle, she pours a small amount of milk into one of the cups, she prefers the milk to be put in first, Granny is against this practice and always puts the tea in first, adding the milk afterwards, she thinks it is 'barbaric' to put milk in first.

"Granny!" she shouts, "Tea is ready"

She hears a reply from the bar but has no idea what words are spoken by Mary, she opens the cupboard door again and takes out a loaf of bread, or what is left of yesterday's loaf, it is wrapped tightly in brown paper, placing it on the slate next to the sink she takes the bread knife and begins to cut herself a slice of bread,

"What have I told you about using the wooden bread board?" Mary scolds as she enters the kitchen, she sits and pulls a cup and saucer toward her, she peers into the cup and sees milk in the bottom, she tuts and swaps it for the other one, she pours the hot brown liquid from the pot into her cup and then fills the other cup for Alice who is now cutting a slice of bread on the inch thick wooden bread board, the single slice is then put into a long handled wire mesh toaster, it is opened up and the bread placed in it and it is then closed, Alice puts the secured slice of bread above the glowing wood of the stove fire,

"Butter and jam are in the sink cupboard" Mary tells Alice, who retrieves both items and sits at the table, almost immediately getting up again to turn the mesh toaster over on the fire so as to brown both sides of her bread.

"You look tired Granny" Alice sounds concerned, Mary smiles,

"I am fine love, just a bit old to be running a pub" she points at the stove and just says "Toast"

Alice jumps up and rescues her toast before it burns, turning the warm toast onto a plate she butters it quickly, she loves the taste of the melted butter on her toast, she adds a spoonful of strawberry jam and greedily eats her breakfast, Mary sits and slowly drinks her tea, she declines the offer of toast from Alice. Two short chimes from the clock on top of the shelf tell them both that it is half past the hour, Alice looks up and sees that it is only half past eight, she clears away her breakfast crockery and puts it all away neatly after cleaning them in the sink using the still warm water from the kettle, she leaves Mary still drinking her tea and goes up stairs to get dressed, she doesn't hear Mary mutter,

"The girl will have indigestion, guzzling her tea and bolting her toast" She tuts again and finishes her tea.

Alice is tying a ribbon into her hair when she hears the front door of the pub being knocked firmly, a few seconds later she hears Mary calling up the stairs,

"Alice, Grace is here"

She finishes tying the bow and hopes that Grace is not this early because she has to cancel their arrangement to meet at the cottage later to write their letters, she runs down the stairs and into the bar, Mary and Grace are talking, both look very serious,

"Is everything alright?" Alice asks both of them,

"Grace is here to tell us that smoke is coming from the chimney at the cottage"

Alice is confused, she certainly ensured that the fire in the cottage range was out yesterday before they left, even so, if it had been lit it would have burnt out by now.

"The fire was certainly finished when Alice and I left yesterday evening" Grace says and Alice quickly agrees with her,

"Right then" Mary speaks in a no nonsense manner "We had best go and see who is in our cottage then" She takes off her pinney, takes the keys for the cottage from behind the bar, walks across to the door and opens it, she stands holding the door open, "Come along you two" she hurries Grace and Alice along, they both leave the pub, Mary shuts the door behind her without locking it, they all look across at the cottage,

"I did lock up yesterday Granny" Alice says,

"She did Mary, I saw her" Grace defends Alice,

Mary nods and the three of them walk toward the cottage, they can all see smoke gently spiralling from the chimney, when they reach the gate, Alice and Grace hesitate, Mary is less fearful and opens the gate and walks into the garden, they can all see that the back door to the cottage is open, wood splinters lie on the ground, the door has been forced open. Mary shouts, "Come on out of there, whoever you are!" She is met with silence, "I won't ask you again, get out of our cottage!" Silence again. Mary takes a garden fork that has been left at the vegetable plot, the three iron prongs leave the soil easily as Mary pulls it clear, she walks toward the cottage with the fork in front of her, Grace and Alice follow uneasily behind her. As they reach the open door, they can see a figure inside sitting at the table, "Who are you?" demands Mary, she is angry and aggressive.

Alice peers into the cottage, "Granny put the fork down" she steps inside the cottage "John, what are you doing here again?"

Private John Freeman is seated at the kitchen table, the fire in the range is roaring making the kitchen almost unbearably hot, the kettle is sitting on the hot plate, no steam is rising from its spout, it has boiled dry, Mary steps over, puts a cloth over the handle and lifts it from the heat, she looks at the bottom of it, it is black and scorched,

"That won't be any use again" she takes the hot empty kettle outside; they all hear a hissing sound as she pours cold water from the bucket outside onto it to cool it down.

"John, what are you doing here?" Alice asks again.

He has a maniacal grin on his scarred face, he is holding a mug in his left hand, a tea pot is on the table next to him, he does not answer, he continues to smile, it makes both Grace and Alice feel uneasy, Mary comes back into the room and demands to know what is going on, Alice looks at Grace who takes Mary back outside promising to tell her what is going on. Alice takes the cup from John, it is still warm, she looks into it and does not recognise the slightly green liquid at the bottom of the cup, she knows that there is no tea or coffee in the cottage as she has to bring loose tea and milk with her whenever she meets Grace,

"John, what are you drinking?"

He does not answer and hardly moves, she notices that he is sweating profusely, she puts this down to the extreme heat in the kitchen from the fire that John had earlier prepared and lit, she stands up and opens a window, Mary and Grace are outside, she tells them that she is safe and will be fine with John, she asks if they can go to the railway station and get the soldiers again, she will stay with John. They both leave and Alice sits down again, John has drool forming and dripping from the left side of his grinning mouth, she takes a handkerchief from her dress pocket and gently wipes his mouth, his face feels very hot, and it is obvious that he is sweating heavily, she can see that his unbuttoned shirt and undershirt are soaked through, he does not appear to have his tunic with him this time,

"John are you sick?" she asks him, he does not respond, his breathing becomes rapid, and he appears to be struggling to breath properly, she takes his hand in hers, his fingers are very cold, he passes out. Alice jumps up and shakes the slumped figure of the soldier who has fainted in front of her, she shouts his name several times, he opens and closes his eyes but appears unable to stay awake, he suddenly opens both eyes wide, takes his hand from Alice's grip and puts it to his chest, Alice can see his chest muscles spasming, John looks her in the eyes, his are bulging, almost coming out of his head, he smiles a wide and odd smile,

"Thank you" he struggles to say the words, his voice is raspy and dry, he slumps back into the chair, eyes closed, his chest moves up and down very quickly, she can hear him gasping for breath, Alice is stunned, these are the first words she has heard John speak,

"John!" she screams, "What have you done?"

She looks around and Uncle Pete and Dr Blake are entering the cottage,

"Uncle? Doctor? what are you doing here?"

"Private Freeman was reported missing again this morning, we have soldiers and nurses out looking for him everywhere" he points at Dr Blake "I grabbed the Doc from Bowers house and drove here in the ambulance, I had an inkling that he might be here, as he was found in the garden yesterday, we have just passed Mary, Grace and four soldiers on their way here"

Dr Blake is trying to rouse John, without success,

"Will he be alright Dr?" Asks Alice who is now standing next to her uncle, he has a protective arm around her shoulders, Blake looks at them,

"He is alive, but barely, it looks like poisoning to me, but quite what, I don't know"

Alice points at the mug on the table,

"He has been drinking that"

Dr Blake picks up the mug and smells its contents, putting the mug down he lifts the lid on the tea pot and peers inside, "Oh dear" the Doctor sighs,

"What is it Doc?" asks Pete.

Dr Blake puts the lid back onto the tea pot, "Alice, I think I am correct in saying that there is a Yew tree in your garden"

She nods a response,

"The teapot if almost half filled with the needles and bark from the tree, the Private here has made a home brew tea from it"

Both Alice and Pete look confused, the doctor continues, "Taxus Baccata, the Yew tree to you and me, is poisonous in fact every part of the tree, with the exception of the red flesh that covers the berries in spring, is highly poisonous" He points to the unconscious figure of Private John Freeman, "I believe that the Private has ingested quite a quantity of the brew he made from the bark and needles, taxine alkaloid ingestion is fatal"

Alice and Pete are both shocked,

"What can be done for him Doc?" asks Pete

"Nothing" is the straightforward reply from Dr Blake "The ingestion of Yew tree poison is usually fatal within five or six hours after taking it, so it depends on when this young man started to drink and if he has taken enough to poison himself" he looks at the other two, "I really think he has taken enough to do the job"

Grace arrives with four soldiers, they have been running and are all out of breath, Mary is not with them, Alice runs into Grace's arms, "Oh Grace, it has happened again"

Grace does not reply, she gently strokes Alice's hair,

"Peter" asks Doctor Blake, "Could you and one of the soldiers fetch the stretcher from the ambulance, we should get young Freeman back to the institute and make him as comfortable as we can"

Pete nods and he leaves with one of the soldiers, the other three take a step outside of the kitchen, Grace is not sure if it is out of respect for their wounded and dying colleague or because of the stifling heat inside, she remains with Alice in her arms.

Pete and the soldier return, "Doc, can you go outside and see to Mary, she seems to be taking a bit of a turn"

Alice makes a run for the door, Grace keeps a firm hold on her, "Alice, slow down now, let Dr Blake see to your grandmother, I am sure she is fine"

Pete indicates with a nod that Grace should take Alice outside, she does this,

"Come on in you fellas" Pete shouts to the soldiers outside "Give us a hand to get him onto the stretcher, the three soldiers wait for Alice and Grace to leave before entering.

Dr Blake is talking to Mary at the gate, when Grace and Alice arrive, they both hear Mary say, "I am fine William, really I am, I am not as young as I used to be, all this nonsense this morning and running to the station has made me out of breath, that is all"

Dr Blake insists that he accompany Mary back to the pub just to check her over and to make sure she is well, they both leave and walk slowly toward the pub,

"Is she OK?" Pete asks

"Dr Blake is checking her over at the pub, but it seems she is just out of breath" Grace answers him,

"I think it best that you two go as well, we are bringing Private Freeman out"

"I am staying" Alice says "He is my patient"

Pete nods and indicates into the house for the soldiers to bring the stretcher out, the four soldiers have one corner each, John Freeman lies seemingly lifeless on the stretched canvas, Alice steps forward and puts her hand onto his scarred cheek, "I will be in early tomorrow to see you John"

Grace gently pulls her back to let the stretcher pass, Pete speaks to them,

"I will be back later to fix that latch on the door"

As the stretcher is put into the back of the ambulance, Private Freeman will be protected by the thick canvas cover on the back of the vehicle, its huge red cross symbol is above the words '*St Johns Ambulance*'

The corporal speaks to Pete, "My lad, Jimmy can do that" he indicates to one of the privates "He was a chippy back in the real world"

"If you are sure" Pete says, "There does not seem to be much damage, just a bit of frame broken"

"That won't be a problem Sir" one of the privates says, Pete presumes this must be Jimmy, Pete thanks the soldiers for their help, he takes the keys from Alice and hands them to Jimmy,

"That is very decent of you, young man, my thanks to you"

"I will get the keys back to the pub when I am done if that is alright" Jimmy says

Pete agrees with him, Dr Blake is walking back toward them, Alice looks scared,

"Your Grandmother is just fine Alice, all this excitement and running about is not good for a lady of her years, a few hours rest, and all will be good"

He looks at Pete, "The mug and teapot will need to be destroyed, to be on the safe side"

The Corporal steps forward, "Leave that to us Doc, we will get rid of them both"

With a nod of his head, Dr Blake gets back into the open front section on the passenger side of the ambulance, Pete does likewise on the driver's side, he tells Alice he will be back later to see her.

They drive off, the Corporal looks at Alice and Grace,

"Ladies" he says "If it is in order, we will be getting on with fixing the door"

Grace takes Alice gently and moves her away from the cottage, as they walk away, they hear the Corporal barking orders,

"Fred and Charlie, back to the station, me and Jimmy will sort the door and the tea stuff"

Grace is still with Alice in the kitchen of the pub when Pete returns, Mary is upstairs having a rest, Walter is working at the bar, he is happy as he will get to sup a few free pints,

"A pint please Wally" they both hear Pete speak to the barman, he enters the kitchen, takes off his cap and sits in the chair nearest to the door, they both look at him,

"Your beer Pete" Walter hands him a foaming pint of beer, he thanks him, and Walter goes back to the bar, it is a quiet Sunday in the pub and there are about ten or twelve men drinking at the tables. Pete takes a long pull from his pint; he puts the glass down on the table "I am sorry ladies, but Private Freeman was dead by the time we got back to the institute"

Alice puts her head onto the table, resting it on her crossed arms, she is not crying aloud but tears fall freely from her eyes, Pete puts his hand on her shoulder, "I am so sorry Alice; Doc Blake says that there was nothing that anyone could do for him"

She sits up and looks at both of them, eyes red and full of tears, "I am never going back in that cottage ever again"

She puts her head back into her arms on the table, Pete and Grace look at each other, Pete shrugs his shoulders, he picks up his pint and take another drink.

* * *

It is Friday 5th August, Alice has walked to work from Maple Cottages, she has not been back to the cottage since John Freemans death, she is walking as it is Uncle Pete's day off, he is back working on the estate, it is his day off from driving the ambulance, a bright morning, the sun is steadily rising, and it is going to be a blisteringly hot day. Alice enjoys these early morning walks to the Institute, her route takes her across the common, she is alone for most of the walk, the grass on the common is still a little damp from the early morning dew, she walks along the horse racing track, it has not been used for over a year since war was declared, she walks along the track, the common opens up on either side of her, Limbrick hall is to her right, as she passes it she sees the sun has risen from behind the building and is just crowning over its roof, she carries on walking over the top end of Cravells Road and onto the footpath, she remains on the racetrack as she passes the Brickwell Dells on her left, known locally as the 'Brickle Dells' although some of the boys refer to it as the 'Ups and Downs' as it is an area of land that has been dug out for gravel and clay for the local brick making industry and deep pits and dips have been left behind, St Johns wood is on her right. A little further on she passes the 'pool', a former small gravel pit opposite the Silver Cup public house used in the summer by the children as a paddling pool, she passes under the Baa lamb trees, the shade bringing a coolness against the warmth of the early morning summer sun, she pauses for a moment and looks across at the Institute, already she can see activity in the front of the building, the patients are being escorted or wheeled outside to take advantage of the warm morning. Feeling better than she has done for a few weeks, she steps out of the shade and walks to the Institute with the sun on her back.

Alice is getting changed when Joan puts her head around the door, "Morning Alice, could you do four breakfasts today, we have a new soldier on the ward, he arrived late yesterday evening"

"Of course, Joan"

With that Joan is gone, Alice makes her way to the small kitchen and prepares her trolley, the cook has a tray of sausages just out of the oven and some scrambled eggs, with her four covered plates and a rack of toast on the top of her trolley, the lower shelf has butter, jam, and marmalade on it, she enters the ward. Joan is handing out the medication to the men, none of them are in bed and two of them are sitting outside smoking cigarettes, she can see Lieutenant Guy Dodgson, a twenty year old soldier from the Hertfordshire Regiment, he has a chest wound, he was hit with red hot shrapnel, he is with Private John Cook from the Royal Bucks Hussars, he is twenty three years old and is still hobbling on crutches, his leg injury received only two weeks ago, several machine gun bullets hit him, all in his right leg, he and Guy, despite being of different ranks have become great pals and are a force to be reckoned with, they are both inside the ward sitting on chairs by Johns bed, outside is Private Joseph Cooper from the Royal Berkshire regiment, he is fully recovered from a shrapnel wound in his back and is leaving the ward tomorrow to go back to his regiment at the western front in France, he is sitting in a chair talking to the new soldier, she cannot see either of them as they are deep in conversation with their backs to him. She smiles brightly and serves breakfast to John and Guy, they both flirt with her and she ignores their weak advances toward her, she pushes her trolley toward the open double doors, Joan is finishing handing out tablets to Joseph and the newest arrival,

"All yours" she says to Alice,

"Good morning gentlemen" she says to both men, Joseph turns and says,

"Hello Alice, as always you bring brightness to my day" she hands him a plate, he takes it and puts it on a small table next to him, making no attempt to begin to eat it as his is still smoking his cigarette, the new arrival turns to face her, he speaks directly to her,

"Good morning Alice"

She lets out a little shriek of recognition, RSM Westerman is sitting in the chair,

"Eddie!" she shouts, she bends down and takes both of his hands in hers, he moans in pain, it is only then that she sees that both of his hands are bandaged, she lets go quickly,

"Oh, I am so sorry if I hurt you"

He laughs, "No, you are fine Alice, it is lovely to see you"

She begins to cry tears of happiness,

"Good God Regimental Sergeant Major, do you have this effect on all the women you meet!" Lt Dodgson laughs as the speaks to Eddie, who laughs in return at the young officer,

"I met this beautiful young lady a long time before any of you did, let me be clear" he smiles at all of them, "If you upset her, you will have me to deal with' he looks at Guy Dodgson, "Officer or not!"

They all fall about laughing, Joseph has finished his smoke and is buttering a piece of toast,

"Can I help you with your breakfast Eddie?" he asks

Alice steps in, "Certainly not Joseph, you eat your food, and I will take care of the RSM"

Eddie raises both his bandaged hands, "I can manage, honestly I can"

Alice puts his plate on the table next to him, he manages to pick up his cutlery and begins to eat his breakfast, "I have duties to attend to Eddie, but can I come back and speak to you after breakfast? I am desperate to hear how everyone is"

Eddie looks at the ground, "Of course, you can lass, before you go, I must ask after Mary, is she well?"

Alice thinks about her grandmother and how tired she has been and how Dr Blake had to attend to her after John Freeman had been found in the cottage, she replies,

"She is just fine"

Two hours later Alice, with Joan's permission, is sat outside with RSM Westerman, she has served him tea in a mug with a straw,

"Can I ask how you got injured Eddie?" He is quiet, she speaks again, "I don't mean to pry, please, if it is too hard to tell me, then don't"

He puts a bandaged hand on her arm, "Of course, I will tell you Alice, it's just that I don't know where to start"

He thinks for a moment, sips tea through his straw and begins. He tells her that he was with the 5th and the 8th Sherwood Foresters near to a town called Hooge in Belgium, the fighting with the Germans had been fierce and it was in early June that the Germans got their first breakthrough, they took an area of ground around the Château from the Allied troops, the German bombardment that day had been so brutal, only two walls of the old Château remained standing but they had taken it from the Allies and it was a position of great advantage to them. For the next two weeks the battles to retake the Château were ongoing, many hundreds of men from both sides were killed or injured, during this time the incredibly brave men from the 175th Tunnelling company had dug a huge gallery under the fortifications near to the Château, at 7pm on 19th July they detonated 3,500 lbs of explosives. It created a crater one hundred and twenty feet wide and over twenty feet deep, the lip of the crater rises fifteen feet above the ground, many Germans were killed because of this action, it was then that two companies charged the German lines but were unsuccessful, no ground had been gained or lost, but there is a huge hole in the middle of the battlefield. He pauses to drink more tea, Alice remains respectfully quiet, the three other soldiers are also listening, he carries on and tells them that in the early hours of the 30th July a huge German bombardment commenced, details had been passed through the trenches that a nearby wood was on fire, a detachment from the 8th Rifles was sent to investigate, they met with ferocious resistance from the Germans and had to retreat when all their grenades had been thrown, the wood was still burning at this time. The rest of the 8th Rifles had to retreat to the lines and trenches where the Sherwood Foresters were, they had been easily overrun by greater numbers of enemy infantry soldiers, this was when the Germans pursued and continued to attack, a retaliation to the explosion two weeks earlier, with a new weapon, the flame thrower. The containers on the back of the user are filled with gas and oil, when a lever is depressed, the mixture flows through a long tube and is ignited by a simple wick at the nozzle, the resulting flame is instant and has a useable distance of twenty yards. Although the Germans were beaten back on the first attempt at using this tactic, they broke through the allied lines on the second attempt, using the flamethrower with great effect, they took over 600 yards of Allied land, those Allied soldiers that remained became involved in heavy and prolonged hand to hand fighting.

RSM Westerman stops talking and sits quietly, no one else speaks, they all wait for him to continue,

"It was an immediate deluge of fire, everything was alight, we were all ordered to withdraw back to Sanctuary wood or to Zouave Wood, we call it retreating, the officers call it 'taking support positions'" He looks at Guy, "No offence Sir" he says quietly.

"None taken RSM" the Lt responds gently.

"I took up a position at a machine gun, and let them have it, I used all the ammunition we had left in that position, when I was out of ammo, I ran, with all the others, away from the flames and the Germans"

He raises his hands, "It was only when we got to our '*support positions*' that I realised that my hands were in this mess"

"Eddie" exclaims Alice, "That is so barbaric, using fire like that"

"It is lass, it certainly is, anyway, I was sent to the casualty clearing station and then back to Blighty, I had no idea that they would send me back to this town, but it seems that as my regiment were originally stationed here for training, this is the nearest base hospital for me"

"Bloody hell" says Joseph, "I am going back to that madness tomorrow"

"You will be fine mate" Eddie assures him. Alice looks at Eddie,

"What about the boys that stayed in our cottage? Have you seen any of them at all?"

Eddie looks at the three soldiers in turn and then at Alice,

"Bob Beeson was badly injured during the fire attack and bombardment; he is in a hospital in France somewhere" Alice is waiting for him to finish,

"Sorry Alice, but Jake Stevens and Abe Bragg were both killed during the fire attack, I wasn't with them, so I have no details, but I am very sorry to tell you that they didn't make it"

Alice slumps in the chair she is sitting in,

"Will Bob Beeson be alright?" she asks hurriedly,

Eddie shakes his head,

"I don't think so, he is in a bad way"

Alice remains slumped in the chair, Joan enters the ward and calls her name, she does not move, Guy quickly intercepts Joan and whispers the story to her, a graphic but shortened version, she nods and leaves the ward. Putting her head onto Eddies shoulder, she is silent and stares across the common, he puts an arm around her and gently pats her upper arm with his bandaged hand.

She is not crying; she has no more tears to give.

1916

CHAPTER SEVEN

The end of 1915 has been a quiet one for the men of the 2nd Battalion Bedfordshire's, billeted at Fourdrinoy until the week before Christmas, many of the men are glad for the break away from the mud and hell of the war, many yearn for the boredom to pass and for a hasty return to the trenches they have all been told to expect a few weeks rest away from the front line, a boxing competition and a football league has been organised to encourage them to remain active. The Battalion has had a huge change of officers since the beginning of December 1915, many officers being allowed home on leave prior to taking up new posts either with another Battalion within the regiment or being transferred to a new regiment, either way, the rank and file are unhappy that the 'Ruperts' seem to be getting preferential treatment to them.

The 20th December 1915 bought with it changes, the Battalion leave the 21st Brigade and become part of the 89th Brigade, under the command of the 30th Division, Martin has no idea why the 7th Division has been disrupted and the regiments that have fought side by side since the beginning of the war in the 21st Brigade are all being broken up, the other change is that they are moving from Fourdrinoy to Ribeaucourt, 16 miles to the north of their billet. This news is met with moans from the men, these increase to complaints when they are told they are to march the whole way from Fourdrinoy to Picquigny, once a delightful town, now a mass of rubble, mud and corpses, from there to La Chaussee to Bois du Gard, stopping for a rest at Saint Ouen. The 2nd Bedfordshire regiment sit at the side of the road and eat cold rations in a town that has ceased to be, all the inhabitants left during the bombardment from both the Allied army and from the Germans, not one building is left standing whole, trees lie dead on the ground and as far as the eye can see the landscape has been destroyed, the road they are sitting by seems to be the only survivor of the war. Moving onto St Leger, to Domart where the Battalion is divided for billeting, some in Barlette and some a mile to the north in Ribeaucourt. Martin is in a converted farm building, rough wooden bunks, five high, have been constructed inside, he takes a top bunk, although difficult to get to, it is the safest place to be. Many of the men have dysentery symptoms and being in the bunk below a man with sickness and diarrhoea is not a good place to be, he doesn't throw his stripes around very often but if it means getting a good bunk, then he will.

There has been much talk of a Christmas truce being organised between the British and German soldiers at the front as there had been in 1914 but all units at the front have been ordered by the Allied commanders not to repeat the truce of 1914, every unit had been encouraged to mount raids on the German positions on Christmas morning after a lengthy artillery barrage from the Allied cannons and guns carefully aimed at the German trenches. All the officers and the NCO's have been ordered by the Commanding officer that no raids will be taking place, but a truce is not in place so any friendly contact with the enemy is forbidden. Christmas dinner is served, it isn't a lot of food but so much better than the bully beef or Maconochie's beef and vegetable stew in tins that the lads in the trenches will be eating, no one asked where the chickens came from, but a meal of chicken stew, potatoes and vegetables is welcomed by the whole regiment, they each get a small piece of Christmas pudding from the commanding officer, again, no one asked where it came from. Parcels and gifts arrive from home, some of the lads who transferred in from the 1st Battalion tell the others that they had all received a tin from the Royal Family, known as Princess Mary tins, they contain cigarettes, loose tobacco, sweets, chocolate and a card from the Royal Family stating, '*May God protect you and bring you home*'. None of the 2nd Battalion had received any such gift last year as they were in the trenches, cold and wet, so even though there was no gift from the Royal Family, at least this year they are dry, lice free and eating reasonable food.

All Martin hopes is that Grace, Alice and Granny got his Christmas cards in time, John Marrables had drawn on some card for him, lovely Christmas scenes, he has no idea how the man can be so seemingly festive when all around them is death and chaos, they are superb, and he is very thankful to the man from his platoon.

The Battalions all gathered on the 28th of December 1915, the RSM demands quiet as the CO reads the Christmas message from King George V,

"*Another Christmas finds all the resources of the Empire still engaged in war and I desire to convey my own behalf and on behalf of the Queen, a heartfelt Christmas greeting and good wishes for the New Year to all, who on sea and land are upholding the honour of the British name. In the officers and men of my Navy, on whom the security of the Empire depends, I repose in, common with all my subjects, a trust that is absolute. On the officers and men of my armies whether now in France or in the East or in other fields, I rely with an equal faith, confident that their devotion, their valour, and their self-sacrifice will, under Gods guidance, lead to victory and an honourable peace. There are many of our comrades now, alas, in hospital and to these brave men, also I desire with the Queen to express our deep gratitude and our current prayers for their recovery. Officers and men of the Navy and the Army, another year is drawing to a close, as it began, in toil, bloodshed and suffering, but I rejoice to know that the goal to which you are striving draws nearer to sight. May God bless you and all your undertakings"*

George R.I

Three cheers for His Majesty the King and a large rum for each man follows the reading.

* * *

New Year's day 1916 arrives, Martin is lying in his bunk writing another letter to Grace, over the past few weeks he has written every other day, the lack of fighting and days away from the trenches has given him time to do this, he has just finished todays letter he hopes that his declaration of love for her in his last few letters will not put her off writing to him, he has not had any mail for a few days so he is in the dark as to whether his words have been accepted and responded to in a similar way or they have scared the daylights out of her and she will never write again, he has not had any mail this week from Granny or Alice, so he is not concerned as much as he was. The letter is sealed in the addressed envelope, the postal regiment tent is not far away, he is about to climb down from his top bunk when he hears a familiar voice,

"Gilson, you are a horrible man, you need a wash lad, I am certain you could grow spuds in your ears, and I am currently standing on your bloody hair!"

Staff Sergeant Oakes voice carries throughout the billet, some of the soldiers, no doubt in need of a haircut themselves, move quickly out of sight, Dan Gilson stands up from his bunk, 23 years old of large build and several inches taller than Oakes,

"Yes Staff, I will see to it today"

Oakes looks him up and down, "Be sure you do lad, I will be back to check, remember, short and neat, back and sides, whatever is under your cap is yours" he looks up at Gilson, "But in your case we don't have caps big enough to get that mop of yours underneath, so can I suggest you go and see Jimmy Janes, he was a barber and has some clippers, he can help you"

"Yes Staff" Gilson starts to move off, Oakes has not finished, "Gilson, have you seen your Corporal?"

Gilson shakes his head, Martin sticks his head out of his bunk,

"Up here Staff"

Oakes tells Gilson to 'bugger off" and looks at Martin,

"Jump down lad, sharpish now, the Lt Col needs to see you"

Martin is surprised, what does Lt Col Hugh Stainton Poyntz want with him, their latest commanding officer is a bit of a star, as well as a full time soldier he is a first class cricketer with Somerset, a reliable right handed bat and a steady right arm leg break bowler, he even played three times for the Orange Free State in South Africa when the Battalion was stationed there in 1913, sadly, the matches were played over a hundred miles away from Pretoria so none of the regiment got to see him play, his brother Edward 'Massey' Poyntz, was the Captain of Somerset before the war and is now a Captain with the 3rd Battalion, currently on home defence duty.

"Come on Martin, let's not keep the man waiting"

"Any idea what he wants with me Staff?"

Oakes shakes his head and tuts, "No idea son, not a clue" he points at Martins head "Don't forget your cap Corporal"

Martin reaches into his bed space, takes his cap, jumps down and puts it on his head, he follows S/Sgt Oakes through the mud as they walk toward the Battalion HQ. Martin is surprised to find that the HQ has been constructed within a trench system, they are a few miles away from the front line and the building has been constructed out of wooden pallets, tarpaulin and corrugated sheets, Oakes raps his knuckles on the frame of the doorway,

"Enter!" a voice from inside responds to the knock, Oakes pulls aside the heavy tarpaulin 'door' and Martin walks in. The inside is remarkably large, it is warm and dry, unlike many of the local billets, an army cot with rumpled blankets on top of it sits in the corner, Lt Col Poyntz has the trench phone to his ear, he covers the mouthpiece and waves his free hand at Martin and Oakes, indicating that they should sit on the chairs in front of his desk. He is a dapper looking man in his late thirties, his sandy hair is short and immaculate as is his trimmed full moustache, his tunic is on the chair behind him and his tie is tucked into the front of his shirt, he speaks into the phone,

"I am being busted again, back to Major and off to the 1st for a bit" he listens and nods a few times, "Roche is having a spell of leave, so old Onslow is coming back to the 2nd for a couple of weeks to cover for me" he listens again, "Well, stay safe Brigadier, good luck and I hope to have a drink with you before this is all over"

He puts the phone down, he addresses Oakes and Martin,

"Brigadier Charles Richard Jebb Griffiths, formerly of the 1st Battalion and now with the 108th Division in the 36th Ulster Division" He smiles and pauses before he says, "How that man is still alive I will never know, always leads from the front, he has a charmed life gentleman, a charmed life" He addresses Oakes, "Is this the Corporal we discussed Staff Sergeant Oakes?"

"It is Sir" Oakes nudges Martin, who stands and gives Poyntz his name, rank and number, the Lt Col looks at him without speaking but indicates that he should be seated again, Martin does as he is told, more confused than ever.

"Yours I believe Corporal" the Lt Col opens his desk drawer and hands Martin two sets of Sergeant stripes, Martin takes them,

"I don't understand Sir?"

"You told me this chap was the man for the job Oakes, now he doesn't understand, are you sure he is bright enough?" Poyntz leans back in his chair, his hands across his midriff with fingers interlocked,

"I believe we may have taken the Corporal by surprise Sir" Oakes says.

Poyntz nods, "I don't have time for parades and other nonsense" he looks at Martin, "We are three senior NCO's down, one dead, one wounded and back in Blighty and one other with appendicitis of all things, the Staff Sergeant and I thought you would be the man for the job"

"Sir, I am only a Corporal, not even a Lance Sergeant" Martin stammers

"Well, I am in charge and if you want to be a Sergeant then, as I said, the job is yours"

"Yes Sir, thank you Sir" He looks at Oakes, "Will I be moving from my current platoon?"

"No lad, if the truth be known, you have been carrying out the role of Sergeant for months, you stay where you are"

Poyntz stands up and puts his hand toward Martin, they shake hands, "Bloody well done Sergeant, now sod off the pair of you, I have a war to win!" They both stand to attention, "Dismissed Sergeants" the Lt Col says with a grin on his face, Martin and Oakes step toward the tarpaulin door, Poyntz speaks again, "Oh Sergeant"

Oakes turns and says, "Sir"

"Not you Staff Sergeant, the other Sergeant"

Oakes steps back and Martin steps forward, his new stripes held tightly in his left hand,

"We are to be visited by Brigadier General Stanley at some point in the near future, March is rumoured, but our former Regimental commanding officer, General Curties, left me the sum of five pounds before he moved on, it is to be awarded to the NCO or private who has performed most gallantly without receiving citation, medal or recognition"

Martin looks at Oakes, the Lt Col continues, "It seems to be the opinion of the senior NCO's that Private George Freshwater might be the man to get the prize after his heroics with Capt. Foss at Neuve Chapelle last year"

"I couldn't agree more Sir, George is a fine soldier, I have known him since the battalion was in Bermuda and South Africa"

Poyntz nods, "Keep it to yourself Sergeant, but when the General eventually gets here, we will be inspected, and Freshwater will get presented to the General and get his money"

"Yes Sir, of course Sir"

Martin can see Oakes grinning like a Cheshire cat, the officer continues,

"Also, Sergeant, on that day, you will be presented with your Distinguished Conduct Medal, for your gallantry at Estaires in April last year"

Martin shuffles his feet and can feel his face turning red, "It was nothing really Sir"

"Lt Col Thorpe and Captain Shearman disagree Sergeant, you have read the citation I presume?"

"I have Sir"

"Nothing more to be said about it then Sergeant" the Lt Col stands up again, "Get those stripes sewn on today Sergeant, see the company clerk about your promotion, a rise in pay always helps, and finally" he points to the two stripes on Martin's tunic, "When you take them off, give them to Private Freshwater, he is your new Corporal"

Martin is just about to tell the Lt Col that George Freshwater is only a private and not yet a Lance Corporal, Oakes digs him in the shoulders,

"Will that be all Sir?" Asks Oakes

"Apart from wishing you a happy New Year, that will be all thank you Staff Sergeant" Poyntz says as his phone rings, he answers, "Ah, yes, Albie, we need to have a bit of a chat…"

Martin and Oakes leave the HQ,

"Well done lad, you deserve it" Oakes and Martin shake hands,

"Thanks Staff, it is a bit of a shock" Martin responds,

"Ralph" says Oakes

"Who is?" asks Martin

Oakes laughs long and loud "I am" he says between laughs, "Ralph is my name, and I think that as we are now the same rank, you can drop the 'Staff' or the 'Sarge', Ralph will suffice"

“Thanks Ralph” Martin looks around where they are standing, “I had better go and find George, break the news to him that he has made Corporal”

Oakes takes out his pipe, “Then pack your kit Martin”

Confused, he asks, “Why?”

“Sergeants have their own billets, there will only be five of us including you, we have a small cottage on the other side of your billet in the corner of the field”

“Who else is in there Ralph?”

Oakes lights his pipe, taking a deep inhale of smoke and blowing it out, he smiles, “Wait and see lad, wait and see”

The two Sergeants part, Martin is pleased with his promotion and the recent promotion for Ralph Oakes to Staff Sergeant, he wants to find George Freshwater but he needs to take his corporal stripes off of his tunic and his shirts first so that he can give them to George, he also plans to go and see ‘Sew Sew’, a soldier with one of the Indian regiments, an enormous man that is a dab hand and as delicate as a spider’s web with his needle and cotton, he is cheap and very quick.

Martin is dressed only in his green undershirt braces and trousers, his shirts and tunic are with ‘Sew Sew’, he is lucky to have found him, the Indian battalion are moving out in the morning, the Indian tailor has promised a quick job. He arrives at his new billet, a small single storey cottage a hundred yards behind the barn where he had been living on the top bunk with eleven others in the small, allocated space. Len Hubbocks is sat outside and sees Martin arrive,

“How are we to know that you are Sergeant without your stripes?”

“I thought I wouldn’t bother wearing stripes Len; I just needed a better billet!”

“I bet you have seen the company clerk to get your wages sorted though” Hubbocks points at him.

Martin laughs out loud, that was the first thing he had done, Len stands up and takes Martins large backpack and ushers him into the billet.

“It isn’t much mate, but it is home for now and better than most have got, lucky for us Hutch is one of the billeting officers”

“Hutch?” Martin asks, as he does, Company Sergeant Major Edward Hutchinson walks in, he is dressed in his under shirt, his braces are not over his shoulders and they hang limply at either side,

“Me” he says, ”Congratulations on the promotion Martin”

Before Martin can answer, Hutch starts to cough and cannot stop, his breathing seems difficult and his chest is rattling as he does so, in between coughs he says, "Sorry lads, here we go again" he leaves the room and goes through a doorless doorway and out of sight,

"Poor sod has bronchitis; the MO is on about sending him home it is so bad"

"Where am I sleeping Len?" Martin asks Hubbocks

"Through there" Len points to another doorway without a door,

"All the doors have been removed in here, we have no idea why, but it is dry and warm with the fire going"

Martin has an inkling where the wooden doors may have been used, but he keeps it to himself,

"Thanks Len, who else is with us"

Len tells him that as well as himself, Martin, Hutch and Ralph, that Bill Peggs had moved in yesterday and that their new home is now full, Martin walks into his new space, it was almost certainly a former food larder, it is not very big but big enough for him, it has a single wooden shelf, sturdy and fixed both to the wall and to the floor by two stout and plain wooden legs, atop it is an old mattress stuffed with straw, it has one small window that is currently closed and Martin thinks that it may not have been opened for at least a century, but as it is January he does not care. The room is warm as it is next to the kitchen, he has seen an army camp bed in there but the occupant is unknown to him, putting his kit bag down on the floor he tests the mattress, in comparison to the hard wooden board he has been sleeping on, this is pure luxury, he looks up as Ralph appears at his doorway,

"Here you go lad" Ralph puts two grey blankets down on the mattress, he puts his right index finger to his nose and says, "Don't ask where they came from"

"I won't and thank you" Martin replies

"The others will be back in a while, we usually sit in my room" he puts a thumb over his shoulder indicating toward the kitchen, "Bill has found some Frenchie beer in bottles, so we can sit and have a drink" Ralph finishes talking and is gone, leaving Martin to his own space. He stands on tiptoe and looks out of the window, it is opaque with dust, but he can see a large house in the distance, remarkably still in one piece, it has a few of its grey roof tiles missing and a couple of broken windows, but for such a large place, it is in good shape,

"I bet the officers are in there" he mutters to himself.

He opens the blankets on his mattress, creating a decent bed for himself, then he leaves his little room, goes through the kitchen, it is empty and steps outside into the fresh January day, he takes a cigarette, lights it and looks around his surroundings, he walks as he smokes. The village is tiny just a few houses and barns, most have been destroyed, a church that only has half a steeple, its grey tiles fragmented and sticking out into the sky lie a row of hideously broken teeth, the château has ornate iron gates with a huge, sturdy brick support on either side, there are a couple of larger houses situated close to the château, Martin presumes that they were for the more senior members of the community, the remainder living in the small cottages and houses that are damaged beyond repair. He walks into the graveyard, it has obviously suffered a hit from a high explosive shell, many of the grave markers and stones are missing or destroyed, there is not a blade of grass to be seen in this area, but there are signs of recent reburial or covering up of the exposed graves, the soil is level and a healthy brown colour in comparison to the greyness of the French winter. He lights another cigarette from the nearly finished butt of the one he is smoking and makes his way back toward the cottage, he spies an old farmhouse that is sitting behind a group of trees, both the building and the trees as yet untouched by the war, it is a two storey building with a steep sloping grey tiled roof, the brick of the building is the same delicate light shade that sandstone is, but the bricks are huge and very sturdy looking. A tall chimney, reaching higher than the pointed apex of the roof stands at one end of the house, Martin stops and stares at the dovecote, it has white walls with strong black timbers supporting its sharply pointed roof, again finished in grey tiles, it seems serene and lonely amongst the chaos of the war and the destruction of this and all the surrounding villages. He walks toward the road that they marched in on days ago, Martin imagines that it would have been a beautiful road, trees lining each side, gently concealing the wide open countryside behind them, now the countryside has nothing to conceal it, the trees are just stumps, their huge trunks lie dead and lifeless at the side of the road and in the ugly muddy fields, he flicks his cigarette into a water filled ditch, turns away from the scene of devastation and man-made disturbance.

The cottage he is now billeted in also has grey tiles but they are a different style to the farmhouse he has just seen, the tiles on the cottage are smaller and the roof has a large deep dip in the centre where the where the hidden timber supports have dried and settled over the many years they have been in place, it has a large chimney, tall with a red slate cap, the windows are all shuttered, they could do with a lick of paint to spruce up the fading and flaking grey colour that they are now. He steps inside and the warmth of the fire hits him as he enters, he closes the door quickly, momentarily he is transported back to the kitchen of his cottage, visions of Grace fly through his mind, just for a second he can smell the soap on her skin and feel the softness of her hair brushing against his face, then it is gone, Len, Ralph and Bill are sitting on aged stools at a rustic wooden table, Ralph is leaning on the table with both his elbows, his lit pipe held firmly in the corner of his mouth, Len and Bill are smoking cigarettes, Len has a pack of cards in his hand and is trying to persuade Bill to play a few hands of poker, Bill is having none of it,

"Have a seat lad" Oakes points at an empty stool,

"Is that not for Company Sergeant Major Hutchinson?" asks Martin,

"No lad" says Oakes, "He is having a kip in his room, he is not feeling so good"

Martin takes his seat and lights another cigarette, as he inhales, he feels a slight tightness in his chest, he has been telling himself for weeks that he should cut down on the amount he is smoking, but as yet he has not succeeded.

"Now then Martin" says Len, "Are you a gambling man?"

Martin looks at him, takes a big draw on his cigarette, blows the smoke out toward the heavily beamed ceiling, "Bugger off Len!"

Len puts the cards down onto the table heavily, "I might have to apply for a change of battalion if you lot won't play with me anymore" They all smile, Oakes takes his pipe out of his mouth and points it at Len,

"That is because you are a bloody cheat Len, don't get me wrong, you are a good one, but a cheat none the less!"

Len Hubbocks fanes shock and distaste at Oakes words to him, he points at himself,

"Me? Cheat? Never Ralph, that is slander or something like that, I am sure!"

Oakes puts his pipe back into his mouth, "You can't even spell slander Len, let alone know what it is"

Hubbocks puts on a dramatic display of being offended,

"Beer anyone?" asks Bill.

It is just getting dark, the time in the winter between the sun setting in the early afternoon and the darkness of the night taking over, the residents of the small cottage are all sitting around the fire drinking the beer that Len swears blind he won in a card game, it is a dark, almost black, Belgian beer, it has a lovely bitter taste and is very strong,

"Who broke 2nd Lt Grovers leg?" asks Hutch lighting a cigarette, he coughs heavily as he inhales the smoke,

Oakes nearly chokes on his pipe smoke,

"Not really funny Ralph, the young lad has two breaks, it happened in the last minute of the game" Hutch scolds Ralph,

"Not laughing really Hutch, it's just that he is a good lad, he has been on the battlefield, in the trenches and on the front line, all without a scratch, he plays a game of football and breaks his bloody leg!"

Hutch nods in agreement, "They were tough opponents" Hutch looks at Martin, "A lot from Liverpool I think, wasn't it?"

"It was, the 17th Kings regiment from that city, to be fair, the Lt went in for a tackle on their centre half" he smiles, "Honestly, he was so big, I wouldn't have tackled him even if I had a bayonet!" The rest gently laugh with him, "Lt Grover ran straight into him and came off second best, poor sod"

There is a knock at the door, all of the senior NCO's are still sitting in the kitchen in front of the very hot fire, they all look at Martin,

"Oh, I see, the new boy gets to answer the door"

They all answer "Yes" at the same time, Hutch breaks into another coughing fit, he looks at his half smoked and glowing cigarette and throws it into the fire,

"I'm off for a lie down in the cool of my room fellas, I will get the door on my way"

Martin thanks him, he hears the door open, and a familiar voice says,

"Sorry to disturb Sir, I am looking for my Corporal" he corrects himself, "my Sergeant"

"Come in son" says Hutch, "Martin, Private Freshwater is here to see you" he calls to the other side of the room, he is struggling to get breath and coughs without breathing in, his face is very red, he eventually stops, "Fresh air for me" he leaves, closing the door behind him, George Freshwater is standing just inside the cottage, Martin beckons him over,

"Come in George, take the CSM's chair" he points to the vacant space, George sits, he seems a bit uncomfortable with all the Sergeants looking at him, "Ignore them George, something is afoot I guarantee it, I am just not in on it as yet!"

"What can I do for you Martin" he looks at Oakes and quickly corrects himself for the second time, "Sorry Sarge"

Martin looks at Ralph, Bill, and Len, they are staring at him without saying anything, he has no idea what is going on,

"Martin is just fine with me George" he turns to the back of his chair that his tunic is hanging on the back of, three new stripes perfectly sewn on each arm, a cost of two packets of cigarettes for two shirts and one tunic, Sew Sew has done a superb job, "As I have been promoted" the other three Sergeants whistle and cheer, he looks at them and mouths 'Sod off!' to them, much to their amusement, the strong beer has given them all a festive mood, "I need a full Corporal for the platoon"

George looks bemused, "Who's getting the job then Sarge?"

Martin takes the three pairs of double stripes from his tunic and hands them to George, "You are mate, congratulations"

George takes the stripes from Martin, he stares at them, "Thanks Martin" he looks up and Len, Bill and Ralph are looking at him, both he and Martin are confused, before they can be told to leave George alone, he speaks, "I don't get it Martin, I am a private, I haven't made Lance jack yet, so how is this happening?"

Martin starts to answer but Bill and Ralph are screaming, cheering, and poking Len with their fingers, George looks at Martin and shrugs his shoulders,

"What is going on chaps?" Martin asks, Len is looking very down in the mouth,

"We had a little wager between us, as to whether Freshwater here will question his promotion and say words similar to, "But I am not a Lance Corporal yet', Len said he wouldn't and that he would take the stripes without question" they are all laughing, except Len when Hutch comes back in, the coughing seems to have abated,

George stands,

"Sit down lad" instructs Hutch, "I get the feeling that you may have just won me five bob from Sergeant Hubbocks here!"

George sits holding his stripes, Martin leans over to him, the others are hassling Len for their five bob winnings, Hubbocks is not happy, he has just lost fifteen shillings!

"The Lt Col made the decision to promote you, no one will question it, this is war and things are being done differently" Martin tells him, "Do you know where the Indian lads are billeted?"

George replies that he does,

"Nip down there now and ask for a lad called 'Sew Sew', he is expecting you, I know you don't smoke so I have given him a couple of extra packets to sew your stripes on, I have also told the company clerk, so your money will go up as well!"

"Strange name that Martin, 'Sew Sew'?"

"Not his real name mate, but everyone knows him by this nickname, even the lads in his own regiment don't know what his real name is!"

"How will I recognise him?"

Martin pats him on the shoulder a couple of times, "He is well known, but if you can't find anyone to help you, just look for the biggest man you have ever seen, that will be him!"

George stands up, nods at all the Sergeants, Len, straight mouthed, looks at him and says, "You have cost me Freshwater; you have let me down lad" George has not a clue that Len is joking with him and looks terrified, Hutch steps in,

"The thing is George; you have made three sergeants very happy here and only upset one. It also happens to be a fact that one of the happy Sergeants is the CSM" He looks at Len, "So the unhappy Sergeant had best not step out of line" He winks at Len, he turns back to George "Go on Son, get those stripes sorted"

"Thank you, Sir" he turns to Martin, "Could I have your empty top bunk Martin, I am fed up with being trod on by bloody Freddie Pearce and Larry Wignall"

"You are the Corporal now George, take which bunk you want!" He hands George a bottle of the French beer, "Don't get caught with it!"

With George gone, Martin sits at the rough table in the kitchen, his light provided by a small candle, before starting he had ensured that all the shutters on the outside of the cottage were closed tight, he takes an unfinished letter to Grace, he opens it and reads the words he had written that very morning,

My darling Grace

As this New Year begins, I truly hope and believe that we will be together again before 1916 is over, I miss you more each day and it is difficult to imagine being alone with you when I am surrounded by chaos…

He tells her about his promotion and that they are on a long leave behind the lines, so he is safe at this time, Grace often asks about the war in her letters, he understands it is because she fears for his life, but he has no inclination to share the horrors he has seen with anyone, he keeps his comments about his situation very general and certainly without description. He thanks her for her Christmas gifts that had arrived just over a week ago, the socks are a Godsend, his feet get so cold in the trenches at night, he thanks her for the bars of chocolate and the cigarettes, the letter very soon drifts back to how he wants nothing more than to be alone with her in the cottage, as always he tells her his best memories ever are when he and her were alone. He writes for another quarter of an hour before sealing the letter in an envelope, he writes three postcards, all depicting different images of France that he picked up en route to Ribeaucourt, one for Granny, one for Alice and the last one for Pete, May, and the girls.

"I'm off out to deliver these letters to the postal lads, I hope I am not too late to get them sent"

"I'll come with you Martin" Bill Peggs pipes up, "I have a couple to post home as well"

The men leave the cottage, Martin is happy with his new home, albeit a temporary one, he looks forward to a good night's sleep and hopes that nice dreams will keep him that way and not the nightmares that wake him up.

* * *

The time Martin gets to spend in the dry and warm billet is short lived, at 0915 hours on Friday January 7th, the Battalion is formed up and the few weeks behind the lines is now over, the trenches they are heading for are at Suzanne, a long march that is expected to take two or three days dependant on terrain and enemy contact, the soldiers are unhappy at having to move after spending nearly a month in billets and over three weeks at Ribeaucourt, a stint in the trenches will be starting again in three days and they have to march at least ten miles on each of these days to get there. The column of men set off, the senior officers on horseback, Lt Col Poyntz is at the head of the three long lines, they set off, Martin can see that Hutch is struggling with his breathing, Oakes speaks to Hutch and insists that he wait for the ambulances to arrive tomorrow and he can travel with them, Hutch puts up a bit of resistance but Capt. Beal also insists that Hutch step out, he is prepared to order him to do so but does not have to,

"Company Sergeant Major Hutchinson, step out and report to the M.O, I am on leave in two days and will not be traveling with the battalion today, you can stay here with me and a few others that are sick, lame or lazy, a bit of comfort in that bloody huge Chateau might do you the world of good"

CSM Hutchinson waves feebly at them as they leave, Martin thinks that he looks very ill and that a three day march might just have killed him.

The march takes them along the far Western edge of the battle lines, moving South on the road, once a decent solid road but now a muddy mess of rocks and puddles, they reach the Hamlet of Barlette, a huddled collection of four houses and a farmhouse, all are undamaged, but the residents have long since left, although the war is concentrated further East, it is still close enough for the residents to lock up and leave. Moving East on through Berneuil, then South again to Canaples, then Southeast to Haverness, East to Wargines then into Naours for an overnight stop, far enough behind the lines to be safe but near enough to hear the artillery, the war is never far away. Martin and a few of his platoon, along with Ralph Oakes take a quick visit to the underground city at Naours, a former Roman limestone quarry that over the centuries has been excavated and the caves and tunnels used as hiding places against invaders, there are twenty eight galleries and over three hundred chambers, stables and bakers ovens have been introduced over time, Martin is pleased to see a lot of soldiers taking the time, and possibly as a distraction from the war, to look around the amazing underground city. The following day they march from Naours to Pont-Noyelles, through Molliens au Bois and Saint Gratien, the Château at this location is a hive of activity, Allied army personnel are using it for logistics and administration, they carry on, arriving at Pont-Noyelles just after 2pm, it is a small village, most of the residents seem to have stayed, they are only 5 miles to the North East of Amiens, and like this city, the village and villagers have escaped any huge damage from the war, Martin is sure it will not last, the front is only a few miles away and towns in and around the front line have all but been destroyed, the battalion billet for the night.

The following day, the 9th of January is spent marching into the town of Chipilly, the Battalion split here, with two companies remaining and the remaining two moving a short distance to the town of Etinehem. As they march into Chipilly the route takes the men along the side of the marshland of the River Somme, evidence of the war getting closer can be seen, abandoned German field artillery guns and artillery trucks on the side of the road are stark reminders that the enemy are not far away. The billet for the senior NCO's is a thatched cottage, so far undamaged, the walls have all been reinforced with sandbags, another indication that the trenches and the war, are getting closer, they all need a wash and a shave, having been unable to do either with any satisfaction since they left Ribeaucourt. Len finds an old mirror and nails it to the outside wall, and they take it in turns to shave in the hot water that they are boiling on the open fire inside the cottage, they all clean their weapons as they wait their turn for the hot water and the mirror to be free to use. Ralph Oakes is temporarily promoted to CSM in the absence of Hutch, there is no news of how he is doing, Ralph had tried to ask 2nd Lt Lawrence for any details, he replied, rather angrily,

"Do I look like the bloody medical officer Company Sergeant Major?"

Oakes, respectfully and professionally, tells the young officer exactly what he thinks of him and gives him some suitable advice, what he is suggesting the young officer does is physically impossible, but he gives the advice anyway.

It is a quiet evening for all of the men, even the front lines are unusually quiet, they all eat, drink some wine that Len has 'found' and then sleep anywhere they can find a space.

The following day, Monday 10th January, the Battalion remain in billets at Chipilly and Etinehem, a welcomed rest day for all, some of the NCO's and soldiers are given permission to visit Bray sur Somme, a nearby town, some four miles to the Northeast, this is where the 1st Battalion are currently billeted, many of the lads want to reacquaint themselves with pals they have not seen for nearly two years. Several lorries are making the journey to Bray sur Somme, and the chance of a ride is taken by a lot of the lads, including Martin. The town is only a few miles from the front, the trenches at Fricourt are rumoured to be taking a hammering from the German artillery almost every day, Martin bumps into a few soldiers he knows and he is informed that the 1st will be leaving the town at just after six this evening for a four day stint in the trenches, they are relieving the 1st Norfolk regiment who have had a hard time, snipers have been a problem and several young men have fallen victim to them. Martin makes enquiries to locate 2nd Lt Charles Gray, he is sent to three or four different places, Charles is not to be found at any of them, fed up, he sits outside of the church of St Nicholas in the centre of town, his back is resting against the cool yellow limestone brick, he is finishing his cigarette when he sees an officer enter the church through the large vaulted wooden door, just for a second he thinks the man may be Charles, he is of similar build, but all young officers look the same to him, he puts the cigarette out under his ammo boot and walks toward the church door, he can see that most of the stained glass windows are missing, as is the top of the bell tower, evidence of shell damage, he presumes German shells as the Allied army have had Bray under their control for several months.

"Worth a look" he mutters to himself as the enters the church, he removes his cap and has to wait a few seconds for his eyes to adjust to the gloomy light inside the building, it is cold inside and Martin rubs his hands together to warm them. The church is quiet, a beautiful wooden statue of the Virgin and child dominates one section of the church, an oil painting depicting the denial of St Peter hangs proudly on another wall, the wooden confessional is seemingly empty, the pulpit is one of the most ornate Martin has ever seen, made of a very dark wood it has steep straight stairs that lead to the circular pulpit, it has a wooden bas relief sculpture of a salamander behind it, the canopy above it is also made of dark wood and atop this is an angel standing on a crown, it is a stunning piece of furniture, he stops staring at it when he hears,

"The Salamander is the emblem of King Francois the first of France, he reigned in the mid sixteenth century"

Martin turns and sees a Lt Col standing close to him, Martin recognises him but cannot remember where from, he is certainly an officer from the Bedfordshires, although he has a slight Irish accent,

"Thank you, Sir, it is truly magnificent"

"What brings a Sergeant from the 2nd Battalion to Bray sur Somme?" he asks. Martin shuffles his feet a little,

"We are billeting at Chipilly Sir and as we have a rest day, some of the lads wanted to come up and see pals from the 1st, it has been a while since we all left Bedford"

"A bloody lifetime Sergeant!" agrees the Lt Col, he introduces himself, "Lt Col Benjamin Roche, C.O. of the 1st"

The penny drops with Martin, he introduces himself to Lt Col Roche,

"Who are you here to see then Sergeant, I am certain your visit was not just to see the church"

"No Sir, a friend of my sisters is a 2nd Lt with your Battalion, I just wanted, if possible, to see him so I can write to my sister to assure her that all is well"

Lt Col Roche nods as he says, "Jolly decent of you Sergeant, may I ask who the 2nd Lt is, I may be able to help you"

"Of course, Sir, 2nd Lt Charles Gray is the gentleman I want to find"

"I know the chap" the Lt Col nods as he speaks, "Recently promoted to Lt." He looks at his watch, "He is due back in the trenches this afternoon, so I know where he will be" He puts on his cap and walks toward the door, "Come along Sergeant"

Martin is confused, he follows the officer anyway,

"He will be at operations HQ getting details of his taskings for the next few days"

"Sir?" Martin questions,

"Put your cap on and follow me Sergeant, no more than a five minute walk, it is on my way" he steps off, his brass tipped stick taps on the ground with every other step he takes, Martin puts on his cap and follows behind. "Keep up Sergeant, I may be getting on in years, but I can still set a bit of a pace"

Martin picks up his pace and walks alongside Roche, who, true to his word, sets off like a greyhound. The streets of Bray are cobbled, they are active with many hundreds of soldiers who appear to be lining the streets, then Martin sees the line of German prisoners of war, walking slowly behind six horses that are pulling a large trailer, it is filled with injured men, blood stained bandages cover wounds recently made by British and French bullets or artillery, they are very quiet and subdued,

"Where will they be kept Sir?" ask Martin

"Bloody huge prisoner of war camp at Amiens, probably better than being at the front, but these men will be made to work for us, digging trenches and such" He stops walking, turns to Martin and says, "The camps in England are bursting, Dorchester, Southend and Holyport, all full to the brim, best to keep the buggers here and set them to work"

He sets off again, soldiers step out of his way when they realise who he is, he marches past the Ecurìe barn on his left, the shop next door to it has an ornate balcony, three English soldiers are lounging about with two Frenchmen, they have glasses of red wine in their hands, all are smoking, Roche looks up and the soldiers all stand to attention, this makes the Frenchmen laugh, the officer continues toward a three storey building, it looks intact to Martin, the top two floors each having six windows, all with white frames, the ground floor only has a door in the centre of the front, it is guarded by two soldiers from the 1st Battalion, Martin knows one of them, Charlie Simms, a 20 year old lad from Bedford who had joined the Regiment just as war was declared, he had been at Kempston Barracks when Martin had arrived back from South Africa, they had travelled, with others from the barracks to Southampton, Martin has not seen him since they boarded the S.S. Winifredian, Charlie, who had been posted to the 1st Battalion went his separate way on board, both Charlie and the other soldier stand to attention as their C.O. approaches, Martin, upon seeing the young man with Charlie does not believe him to be old enough to be in the service, he looks about fifteen.

"Sir" Martin says, "If it is in order, I will find Lt Gray inside, it is just I know this private and haven't seen him since leaving Southampton"

"As you wish Sergeant, I will be in the ops room" he points inside the building with his stick, "Take the left corridor, third door on the right"

He is gone without another word,

"Hello Martin" says Charlie "Who have you been kissing to make Sergeant!"

Martin smiles "The Kaiser mate"

The men shake hands, Charlie looks across at his young colleague,

"Bloody hell Ernie, relax will you"

The young soldier is still stood bolt upright with his rifle in the position of attention, he is not moving but Martin sees the soldier's eyes moving and looking at him,

"At ease soldier" he says to him

The young soldier relaxes and puts his rifle over his shoulder using the sling,

"Thanks Sergeant" he speaks with a very strong country accent, Martin cannot place it, Charlie helps him out,

"Sergeant, meet my young mate, Private Ernest Cook, Ernie to you and me, I have taken him under my wing"

Martin shakes Ernie's hand,

"How old are you lad?"

"Eighteen Sergeant" replies Ernie, Martin nods,

"Where are you from?"

"East Fenn Common, Soham, Cambridgeshire Sergeant" he nervously replies

"Nice part of the world so I hear" Martin says, even though he has no idea where Soham is, he turns to Charlie, "I have to go in and see Lt Gray, I will only be an hour or so at most" He looks at his pocket watch, "Any chance of a beer and a catch up before I leave"

Charlie looks at his watch, "Possibly, we are due off from this boring duty in forty minutes, we are off to the trenches tonight, but my billet is just across the street" He points to the balcony where the four soldiers are still drinking and smoking, he notices Martin looking at the soldiers,

"They are not ours Martin, they are from the 1st Norfolk regiment, they all took a direct hit in a trench last week, how they survived I will never know, another four of their mates were killed, anyway, these lads have been given a few days off to recuperate" He looks at Martin, "They are certainly making the most of it, anyway, I am on the ground floor with Ernie and two other lads from the battalion, we are sharing a half decent room"

Martin tells him that he will find him later, he says cheerio to Ernie and steps into the building, he approaches a desk that is set in the centre of the room, a Lance Corporal is sitting behind it, he looks up, Martin introduces himself,

"The Lt Col is in the ops room Sarge; he says you can find it"

Martin thanks him and takes the corridor as instructed and smiles as he finds the door he is going through, someone has chalked '*Room 40*' on the door, this being the room at the Admiralty in London where the Royal Navy intelligence teams work, he opens it and enters. It is busy, he can see maps on the walls and on the huge table in the middle of the room, the telegraphists from the battalion are hard at work, headphones on to listen to the Morse code and radio signals as they come in from the front line and from other places, at the table are a group of officers and two NCO's he knows from barracks back home, RSM Bill Bartlett and Sgt. Albert Higgins, they are studying the maps on the table with Charles, the Lt Col is also standing at the table, he addresses Charles,

"Lt Gray, you have a visitor"

Charles looks up, as does Bill and Albert, almost as one they say,

"Martin?"

The officer and NCO's look at each other and then laugh, Charles steps away from the table approaches Martin and they shake hands, Charles pats him on the shoulder,

"I take it you know RSM Bartlett and Sgt Higgins?"

"I do Sir, from Kempston"

Charles appreciates Martin being formal, especially in the ops room where there are lots of senior officers' present, Martin shakes hands with both men,

"Congratulations Sergeant" Bill says to him, Martin lifts his left arm and looks at the stripes on his sleeve,

"I was in the right place at the right time Bill, seem you have done alright, RSM and all that"

"Only acting Martin, but for how long? Who knows?"

"What's it like to be in the papers?" asks Albert

Martin tells him that he has no idea what he is talking about, they see the confusion on his face, Lt Col Roche steps forward,

"You made the New Year's honours list Sergeant; your DCM is listed"

Martin blushes, applause breaks out in the room, he is embarrassed and does not know what to say or do, he is again saved by the Lt Col,

"Lt Gray" he looks at his watch, "Back here in an hour, take the Sergeant to the mess for a coffee"

Charles looks at the Lt Col, as a Sergeant, Martin should not be allowed into the officers' mess,

"My orders Lt, if we can't buy a coffee for a man awarded the DCM, and a Bedfordshire to boot, then the civilised world is at an end!"

Both men leave the room, Martin follows Charles up a steep staircase situated toward the back of the house, they reach the first floor and Charles opens a door and they step inside. Several officers are sitting around in armchairs and two are sat at a table, cigarette, and pipe smoke floats in the air, seemingly unsure as to whether it should sink or rise, Martin follows Charles to a small hatch in the wall, he can see a young woman behind the hatch,

"Bonjour Celeste" Charles speaks to her "Deux cafés, s'il vous plait"

Although Martin does not speak French, understands, Charles turns to him, "Milk and sugar?"

"Neither thanks"

"Deux café noir" he says to Celeste.

Whilst they are waiting a voice shouts across the room,

"I say old man, what is going on here"

Charles looks over at the captain who is addressing him,

"What do you mean Bertie?"

The captain puts his cup of coffee down,

"Lower ranks in the officers mess, come on now Charles" he looks at the other officers, "Standards and rules should be met"

Charles steps forward to confront the captain,

"Look here Bertie"

He is cut off by the senior officer,

"It is *Captain* in front of the enlisted men Lieutenant"

Martin can see Charles getting angry, he pulls him back a little, "Charles, don't worry, I will leave, I am not very comfortable in here anyway"

The captain turns on him, "Sergeant, you will address an officer by his rank, or you will call him Sir, do I make myself clear?"

Martin feels anger rising in his throat, he is just about to give the snotty officer a piece of his mind when he hears his name being called, he looks up and sees Lt de Buriatte talking to him, he is sat next to Lt Shaw, both are formerly of the 2nd Battalion but had left last month to lead a sniper and machine gun team, Martin nods to both of them,

"Gents, how is the team going?"

"Bloody well Sergeant, congrats on the promotion by the way, damn fine work" Shaw speaks to him.

The captain becomes apoplectic with rage, "Have you all gone stark staring mad?" he looks around the room at his fellow officers, "Enlisted men are not allowed into the Officers mess, I don't care if he knows you" he points at Charles, "Or you and you" he points at de Buriatte and Shaw, "I am the ranking officer her and I say he leaves!"

The officers suddenly stand, Martin sees Lt Col Roche enter the room,

"At ease chaps" he says, he turns to the captain,"

"Bertingham, do you have a gallantry medal?"

"No Sir" Captain Bertingham replies to his commanding officer, Roche pauses for several long seconds"

"The Sergeant here has, in fact he is in the New Year's honours" Roche looks at Martin, "What gong did you get Sergeant?"

Martin holds back a smile, Roche knows full well what medal he has been awarded,

"I haven't got it yet Sir, but it is the DCM"

Roche takes a step toward Bertingham, "The Distinguished Conduct Medal, a medal you can never get as an officer Captain, a medal of gallantry, a medal of exemplary service to our King and it was I, your Commanding Officer, that invited the Sergeant into *my* mess for a cup of coffee with one of our officers that he knows from home!" His voice is raised as he finishes the sentence, Martin thinks about correcting the Lt Col, he and Charles had never met before the war, he decides against it. There is silence in the room, the Lt Col has his arms folded across his chest, he is staring at Captain Bertingham,

"Congratulations Sergeant on your medal" the captain is speaking quietly, "Please accept an apology for my impertinence"

"No need Sir, really" Martin replies graciously.

Roche opens the door and stands by it, "Bertingham" he says and nods his head toward the corridor, Captain Bertingham puts his coffee down and walks out of the mess, Roche addresses Martin,

"Congratulations again Sergeant, enjoy your coffee" he looks at his watch again "Forty five minutes Lt Gray" He nods at the other officers and is gone, closing the door quietly behind him.

Applause breaks out in the room, the officers are clapping Martin for his citation, he is again hideously embarrassed, he thanks them all and he and Charles take a small table by the window.

"It is good to see you Charles"

"And you Martin" he pauses and as he opens his mouth to speak, Martin beats him to it,

"You must look after her Charles, especially if I don't make it"

Charles bows his head, "Nothing will give me greater pleasure Martin, although it would be decent if you were around to see it!"

"I hope to be, but you never can tell in this war can you" He looks at Charles,

"Promise me Charles, promise me that you will not hurt my little sister and that you will always be there for her"

Charles smiles, "I want nothing more than to spend the rest of my life with her"

Martin raises an eyebrow, "That sounds like a bloody bad attempt at asking my permission to marry her!" Charles smiles and says nothing, "Bloody hell, you are asking me aren't you" Martin exclaims.

"I am" Charles answers, "I know she is only sixteen, but this mess isn't going to be over anytime soon, so I was just planning ahead, I wanted to wait to speak to you and then wait a little longer, perhaps until summer, so that I can say the words to her that I want to"

"Seventeen" Martin says,

"What is?" asks Charles

"Alice is, in fact she is seventeen today"

Charles looks stunned,

"I completely forgot what day it is, I should write to her and explain how busy and mad it has been here"

Martin puts his hand on Charles forearm, "Calm down Charles, I bet you write to her at least once a week, so in your next letter wish her happy Birthday" The men look at each other, "You can also tell her that my permission is granted if you want to"

"I want to ask her myself, so as I said, summer I hope, please keep it to yourself for now old man"

Charles lifts his coffee cup, Martin does the same, they touch the cups in a 'cheers' motion,

"Thank you, Martin, you have my word that I will always look out for her"

Martin takes a swallow of coffee, "All we have to do now is to survive this mess"

"Amen to that" replies Charles

"Now then" Martin leans back in his chair, "Tell me how you 1st Battalion boys are doing in this war, it has all been a bit quiet over here hasn't it!"

"I bloody heard that Sergeant!" the voice of Lt de Buriatte carries across the room, "Get old Bertie back, he can throw the nasty NCO out of here for us!"

Martin raises his hands in a mock surrender, he hears de Buriatte and Shaw giggle, he turns to Charles,

"How bad has it really been Charles, if your war is anything like mine, then you are having a damned awful time"

The two men sit and chat quietly for the next half an hour before Charles has to go back to the ops room, Martin is cheered out by the officers from the mess, he, and Charles leave and a few minutes later they are stood outside of the ops room,

"Be safe Martin" Charles says

"I will" he replies, "And you, keep your head down"

They shake hands again and part, as Martin is walking away, he calls back,

"Charles" he waits for him to turn around, "I can't believe I am going to be related to an officer!"

Charles salutes him and goes through the door to the ops room, Martin leaves the building and makes his way across the street to go and see Charlie.

* * *

June begins and continues with overcast and wet weather; a brisk Northerly wind means that almost everyone is dressed in warm winter clothes rather than the light and free flowing summer clothes expected to be warn during this month. Alice is walking home from her volunteer duties, she has been working at a house called 'Rosemary' at 28 Milton Road, the Institute patients have all been transferred to this large house, a mass exodus during the middle months of 1915 and the building has been returned to its pre-war status. 'Rosemary' has been loaned to the VAD by Mr Hodgson, it has been lying empty since he had it built some years previously, Alice, with the other volunteers helped the VAD nurses to transfer all the remaining equipment from the Institute to Rosemary Hospital, although there is not a great distance between the two buildings, they sit almost on opposite sides of the railway lines, the equipment is heavy and cumbersome and even loading it into Uncle Pete's' ambulance was strength sapping work. Rosemary Hospital is large and spacious in comparison to the Institute, it has three floors so it can accommodate many more injured men than the Institute, it only having a single room at either side of its structure above the first floor, Alice had been sad to leave the Institute, but all the staff from there had moved across to the Rosemary hospital.

Now the Rosemary stands empty again, all soldiers have left the town and have been sent to various parts of the world to fight in the War, both the town and Rosemary Hospital seem eerily quiet since the departure of the military men, Alice has been told by the VAD commandant, Dr Kelynack, that there are no plans in the very near future to take in any more injured servicemen, they are all being sent to larger hospitals. Dr Kelynack also dropped the bombshell that she is leaving town in September to work in a larger hospital in London, the VAD will continue in town and will be led by Mrs Oakeshott, who will become the new Superintendent, sadly there will be no further need for volunteers and Alice is still too young, at seventeen, to join as a nurse.

Today has been her final duty at the hospital, the last week has been taken up with cleaning the hospital, there have been no patients at all to look after since the first week of the month, both her cousins finished their volunteer duties over a month ago when their services were no longer needed, there are no more wounded soldiers being transferred to the town at all. She is glad of the drizzling rain and the cold wind, it gives her an excuse to cover her head with a scarf and to hide the tears that she cannot stop, she keeps her head down not wanting to speak to anyone, she heads up Shakespeare Road across the junction with Cowper Road and past the water works, she turns left onto the footpath that will take her to Station Road. Stopping on the footpath, she looks across the open land in front of her, she cannot shake the sadness she feels about no longer being needed to work at the hospital, she had even offered to travel to the military hospital at Blackmore End, it had been set up by the Federated Malay States in October of last year, but they don't have volunteers working there in any role, so her time as a volunteer to the VAD has come to an end. She follows the footpath onto Station Road, turning right and walks down the slight incline toward the Malta, Alice is now living with her grandmother, this had been her choice although Aunt May and Uncle Pete were insistent that she stayed with them they are all aware that the cottage isn't really big enough for her to stay for an extended period of time. Only stopping at Fred Hitchcock's dairy shop to buy butter, she continues her walk toward the footpath that leads across to the river, it seems to be taking an age in the very wet weather, Alice is soaked through, the drizzling rain has penetrated through her coat and her clothing, she does not care, she has no drive to walk faster to get her home quicker, she looks up when she hears a horn honking, a motor vehicle has pulled into the side of the road, it is the delivery van for Rowes Bakers on the High Street in town,

"Alice!"

She looks again when she hears her name being called,

"Get in the van young lady, you look soaked through"

As she walks toward the delivery vehicle, she can see the ornate signwriting on the side panels,

'*Rowes Bakery est.1907*',

The owner of the bakery, Benjamin Rowe is waving at her out of the window, she reaches the vehicle, Mr Rowe speaks again, he has a gruff voice and still has an accent from his origins in the East End of London, he has lived in town for nearly a decade with his wife Clara, Alice knows him very well as his Wife and Aunt May are good friends,

"Come on young lady, be quick and get in will you!"

Alice walks around the vehicle and opens the door on the passenger side, she has been in a motor car before, but only a few times, she is a bit scared of them.

"Thank you, Mr Rowe" she says,

"Blimey girl, you are soaked through"

Alice looks at her dishevelled coat and dress, she then looks over at Mr Rowe, he smiles,

"I will have you at the pub in a few minutes, my Clara and your Aunt May are with a group of women who are meeting in the kitchen"

Alice has no idea what he is talking about, but she nods politely,

"It is kind of you to stop Mr Rowe, I was certainly getting more drenched by the minute"

"Lovely June weather!" he exclaims with a laugh.

In only a couple of minutes, Mr Rowe is parked outside of the pub,

"Thank you again Mr Rowe, will you be coming into the pub?"

He nods, "You go in, I will follow shortly"

It is obvious to her that he does not want to be seen to enter the pub with a younger lady, or with any lady come to that, Alice gets out of the vehicle and climbs the steps to the pub door, as she opens it she is met with a cacophony of noise. The bar is busy, the usual noise and smells surround her, pipe and cigarette smoke create a false fog inside the lounge bar to the left of the bar and the public bar to the right, men's voices can be heard talking to one another, she cannot make out any individual conversations, but she catches words as she passes,

"Jutland, what a bugger..."

"Warm beer..."

"Irish rebels..."

"Bloody women...."

Regardless of content, these are regular sounds and words to her, there is a new sound, that of women's voices, they are coming from the kitchen area behind the bar, she looks at Walter, who is again covering the bar for Mary.

"Don't ask young Alice, just don't ask"

She asks anyway, "What is going on Walter?"

He rolls his eyes, "Bad business, women in a pub and in numbers" he nods to the men in the bar, "Many are not pleased I can assure you"

Alice smiles, the men may not be happy, but none are brave enough to confront her Granny about their moans and groans, she responds politely to a few of the men who say, "Hello young Alice" to her, then makes her way around the bar and into the kitchen. There are at least ten women in there, she knows some of them, but others are new faces to her, Mary spots her and waves at her to come into the kitchen, Alice moves through the crowded small room and stands in front of Mary,

"Granny, what is going on?"

"A rebellion if we are not careful!" she laughs as she speaks,

"These ladies are all working for the war effort, some in munitions, some in administration, some on the land and others are driving vans and delivering"

Alice is slightly shocked, she knows that some women are working in industries that have typically and historically been for men only, the war has changed this drastically even in a town as small as theirs, the conversation seems to be about the difference in wages between these women and the men who work, or worked, in the same industries. Alice nods at a few of the women, Aunt May is sitting at the table, the others include Clara Rowe, Mrs Wilson, Graces Mother, May Austin from East Common, Maggie Munday from Belmont Cottages, just past the Gibraltar Castle pub and along from the Cottage. Her Husband Edward had been seriously injured during the retreat from Mons at the first battle of Ypres, he has only recently returned home after a long spell in a London military hospital and then at the Rosemary hospital in town, he has been discharged from the army because of his wounds, Maggie points to Alice and speaks to Mary,

"Alice could come and work with me at the munitions factory now the hospitals in town are all finished"

"Don't be daft Maggie" Mary is quick to answer, "She is just a child"

Alice is offended by this remark, "I am seventeen Granny and I have seen much over the past few months, many my age would certainly not have coped" she looks around the now silent room, "I am very sad that the hospital work has finished"

"At least I get paid for my work" Maggie says,

"Leave her be" chides Mary.

"I have been working there as well Mrs Spratley" May Austin speaks to Mary, "Two smaller munition workshops are being set up behind the George in town and behind the Silver cup and I will be working as supervisor at one of them" Alice looks at her, keen for more information, May continues, "Everyone has to start at the factories in Chaul End or Luton for a few months, to get experience, Maggie and I have been there for nearly a year now"

"I am staying there as well" says Maggie, "The train from East Station takes me direct to Chaul End, the factory is two minutes' walk from the station" She takes a large gulp of tea from her mug, "That is much better than a half hour walk to town every day"

Alice hears her name called out again, she turns and sees Grace coming into the kitchen,

"Grace!" Alice runs and hugs her friend, who responds with a hug back,

"I haven't seen you in ages!" Alice exclaims,

"Two weeks Alice, it has only been two weeks!"

Grace turns to speak to her mother, "Father heard you were here and has stopped off in the bar for a pint, I thought I would come in and see Alice"

"Shall we go upstairs Grace? I need to change out of these wet clothes" she looks at Mary, "Will that be alright Granny?"

Mary smiles, "Grace is always welcome here, you both know that"

Alice walks toward the staircase, she turns and addresses Carla, "Mrs Rowe, your Husband was kind enough to pick me up in the delivery van, he is also in the bar"

"Thanks love" says Carla, "I hope there is enough room for May, I have promised her a lift back to the common, Aunt May speaks up,

"Pete is coming to collect me shortly Carla, we can take May in the ambulance" she looks at the other women, "Pete is still driving for the hospitals in St Albans and Napsbury, so he still has the ambulance"

Alice and Grace leave the women in the kitchen and go upstairs to the front room, Grace sits in the armchair, Alice changes her clothes and then sits on the old settee,

"Alice, I am sorry it has been a couple of weeks since I last saw you, but with the soldier's leaving town, we have been busy changing the rooms they were using at Highfield Oval back to their proper use" she blows out her cheeks, "It has been so crazy, I have not had a day off for nearly two weeks!"

Alice replies, "Are you off this weekend?"

Grace nods, "In fact, I am off tomorrow as well, a long weekend is very welcome"

Alice claps her hands, "Would you be free tomorrow? I have so much to tell you"

Grace leans back on the armchair, she suddenly leans forward making Alice jump, "Shall we stay at the cottage tomorrow night? We could cook a meal and sit and chat, I have three letters from Martin to tell you about, just you and me, would you like that, Alice?"

Alice is visibly very happy, "I would very much like that, I have letters also, from Charles, one I received this morning, I haven't opened it yet, I will save it for tomorrow, only one from Martin though, what shall we eat?"

They both know that food has become less easy to get recently, the war is having a serious effect on what is available and what is not, Grace has a glint in her eye,

"If you have vegetables in the cottage garden then I might have a nice surprise for us!"

"What is it? Grace You must tell me!"

Grace shakes her head, "Certainly not! You will have to wait"

Alice crosses her arms and pretends to sulk, Grace laughs at her,

"You look ridiculous when you pull that face!"

Mrs Wilson shouts up to Grace, "I am off home now Grace, are you coming now?"

"Yes Mother, I am" Grace stands up and hugs Alice, "I will come to the pub just after lunch tomorrow, then we will have all afternoon and evening together, I was going to write back to Martin tonight, but I will save it for tomorrow"

Alice follows Grace down the stairs, the kitchen is almost empty only Mary and Maggie are left, Mrs Wilson has made her way into the bar to encourage her Husband to finish his pint,

"If you are interested in working at the munitions factory, let me know Alice, I can have a chat with the recruitment and welfare lady, Miss Hammond"

"Thanks Mrs Munday" she looks at Mary, who has her arms crossed and looks stern, "I don't have a job now, so I would appreciate it if you could speak to Miss Hammond on my behalf, please"

"I will do it tomorrow, you will need to have a medical" Alice looks horrified, Maggie smiles at her, "Don't worry love, they look in your throat and your eyes and pass you fit for work!"

Maggie moves from the kitchen and into the hallway,

"Could I walk with you Mrs Munday, I would like to know a little more about it"

Maggie nods and walks into the bar, Alice turns to face Mary, who says,

"I suppose I will be making the steamed bacon pudding myself then!"

Alice runs and hugs her Granny, "You are the best!" she says, then turning around and following Maggie out of the pub for the short walk to Belmont cottages.

The following afternoon both Grace and Alice are sat in the kitchen of the cottage, the range fire is burning white hot, it is another wet and dreary day, the fire makes them both feel warm and safe from the weather outside. Grace stands and looks out of the window, "We will need to pick some vegetables for this evening's meal soon"

Alice looks excited suddenly, "You still have not told me what we have for tea tonight Grace"

Grace walks away from the window and picks up her willow cane basket, made and purchased locally, she puts it on the table and takes one corner of the linen cloth that covers the contents, she pauses,

"Don't tease Grace!" says Alice.

The linen is removed, and a brown paper parcel sits at the bottom of the basket, Grace takes it out and opens it on the table, Alice gasps

"Pork chops! Where on earth did you get them Grace?"

They both know that pork, and most meat, has become more difficult to purchase and that the price of many foodstuffs has risen dramatically, there are rumours of rationing, but nothing has happened as yet. Grace covers the meaty chops, both have thick white fat across the top of them and will not take long to cook through in the old black pan that hangs above the range,

"When the army left for good yesterday, the catering Sergeant that has been working at the NCH gave them to me as a gift"

Alice reaches across the table and pulls over a round tin, she lifts the lid and inside is half a Walnut cake that Mary had baked that morning, Grace takes a deep smell of the contents,

"Delicious! We shall eat like Royalty tonight" she faces Alice, "Now, tell me about this dangerous job you will be taking"

Alice leans back into her chair; she tells Grace about her talk with Maggie yesterday evening.

The work is filling explosive fuses and working at the munition's factory in Chaul End, the other factory at Biscot Road is smaller so most of the workers end up at Chaul End, Maggie takes the train daily from East station which takes her to Chaul End, only stopping at Luton Hoo and Bute Street before arriving at the station, which is very near to the station. The Biscot road factory belongs to George Kent, a man from the East End of London who in 1908, moved to Luton and opened his factory and manufactured water meters but at the outbreak of the war he offered to make his factory capable of making armaments, in 1914 the changeover was completed and they now make over a dozen different types of fuses for shells and other artillery, a second site was built at Chaul End in 1915, financed by the ministry of munitions, this site is purely a fuse filling factory and George Kent had built, staffed and continues to manage it on behalf of the ministry. The starting pay is one pound a week, the hours are long, on Mondays, Wednesdays and Thursdays are 12 hours shifts including an hour break for lunch, starting at seven in the morning, on Tuesdays, Fridays and Saturdays, the shifts are eight hours long, again starting at seven but finishing at three, no lunch break is taken on these days, Sundays are a day of rest, many factories in the country run twenty four hours a day, but George Kent's Munitionettes currently finish over one hundred thousand completed fuses a week, so, for now, it is day work only.

Maggie told Alice that the company supply a train ticket, valid for one week, for all workers that do not want to take advantage of local lodgings, again organised by the company, she takes the five thirty in the morning train from Harpenden East, until last month the train stopped at a temporary halt right next to the factory, allowing all the women to get off and have a very short walk to work, this has now stopped and they have to walk from Chaul End station. The girls are known as 'Mutionettes' but they call themselves, 'Kent's Canaries' , this is because the TNT high explosive that is packed into the fuses by the ladies, turns their skin yellow and their hair ginger! The TNT has to be packed very tightly into the fuses, if there are any voids it could cause the fuse to explode prematurely when inside the barrel of the field guns. Grace is concerned and tells Alice that it sounds like a very dangerous job for anyone to take, Alice seems excited by the challenge,

"Will you tell your cousins about this new job; I presume that they have both had to leave the hospitals as well?" Alice shakes her head,

"Jenny starts a new job on Monday, she is only the second girl in town to be given the position of postal delivery boy" She stops to have a mouthful of tea, "Catherine has been working in the fields at Rothamstead for a couple of weeks now"

"Would you not prefer to take a job like theirs, much safer I think"

Alice screws up her face, "Not for me, working outside in this weather" she points outside, "Does not look like fun at all"

"We must go and pick the carrots and greens, regardless of the bad weather"

Alice does not move,

"Come along Alice!" Grace speaks firmly to her, Alice gets out of her chair, "The rain seems to be slowing, if we are quick, we won't get too wet"

They both take their overcoats from the hook on the back of the door, putting them on they step outside, Grace is wrong the rain is as heavy as it has been all day, when half a dozen carrots have been pulled and enough leaves cut from the stems of the greens, they rush back inside to the warmth of the kitchen. Shortly after five that evening, they are getting the food ready to cook when there is a knock at the door, they look at each other, neither is expecting a visitor and only Mary knows they are here, Alice opens the door, Maggie Munday is standing in the rain,

"Come in Mrs Munday, please get out of the rain" Maggie steps inside, her coat is dripping water onto the stone floor, she looks and is very apologetic,

"Don't worry Mrs Munday, take your coat off and have a warm by the fire" Grace says.

Maggie takes off her coat and accepts the offer of a cup of tea from Alice, a chair is put in front of the range for her to sit on,

"Alice, I have spoken to Miss Hammond, she was a bit off about you being only seventeen, but I have explained your experience working at the hospital and she has offered you a starting date of June 19th"

Alice works it out quickly in her head, "A week on Monday?"

Maggie nods and takes a sip of tea from her mug that is clasped in both her hands,

"The first day is to have a medical, to be issued some uniform" she snorts, "They call it a uniform, it is a cap to cover your hair, a pair of overalls and a pair of rubber boots or clogs with a rubber sole" More tea is noisily sipped, "Then you will be shown around the factory by one of the staff members, you will probably get May Constable, she is near to your age but has been at the factory for the longest, she will show you what job you will be allocated, it will be filling the fuses, I almost guarantee it"

"Thank you so much Mrs Munday, will it be alright if I travel with you on that day?"

Maggie reaches into her bag and hands Alice a small envelope, "Your train ticket for the first week, I will call for you on my way to the station, it will be early, about ten past five" she looks up at the ceiling, "That reminds me, I must get old man Pellant down to change the clocks, I don't understand why they had to be put back an hour, anyway, my Eddie can't do it and I certainly can't so it will have to be Mr Pellant"

Alice smiles, "The daylight saving time was changed in April Mrs Munday!"

"I know Alice, and if we are to be working together you had better call me Maggie, don't you be late on the 19th"

"I will be ready, and thank you again"

Maggie finishes her tea, takes her coat from the hook on the back of the door, "Stay indoors tonight ladies, daylight saving or not, the rain is not going to stop"

Maggie leaves and Grace congratulates Alice on getting a job so very quickly,

"Promise me you will be careful Alice; I couldn't bare it if you were hurt"

"I will be fine Grace; I will be around to pester you for a very long time"

Grace fries the pork chops and Alice boils the carrots and greens, the meal is a huge success, not a scrap of meat is left on the chop bones and all the vegetables have been eaten, the dishes are washed and cleared away and the two of them sit near the range, still very hot with some newly added logs burning well, to keep out the early evening chill.

"It has stopped raining, listen" Alice says quietly,

"So, it has, let's hope for a dry day tomorrow" Grace replies, "Did Martin or Charles have any news in their letters?" she asks Alice

"Martin eventually told me about getting his medal presented to him, I had to ask twice, he ignored my question in one letter, so I had to ask him again!"

"I think he is embarrassed with all the attention, I sent him a clip from the local paper when it was announced, it was only then that he told me about the presentation in front of the Battalion"

"I know" Alice says, "But that was in March! A high ranking officer gives him a bravery medal in front of all of his pals and he doesn't tell us!"

Grace had known about the medal ceremony, Martin had written to her shortly after he had received it, it was him that had asked her to keep it to herself, he doesn't want any fuss about it at all. Grace starts to write her reply to Martin, Alice is reading her latest letter, she has just opened it, she looks up at Grace and screeches,

"Charles is coming home on leave!"

Grace stops writing and smiles at her young friend, "When?" she asks

"He thinks in late August all being well" she reads on, "He has ten days at home!"

She holds the letter to her chest and smiles at Grace, "What is the matter, Grace?"

Grace loses her smile, "Martin has not had any leave at all since he left, every time he gets it authorised, it gets cancelled" she looks across to Alice, "Lovely news about Charles though"

Alice stands up and goes to Grace, she puts her arms around her,

"I am so sorry that Martin has not been allowed home, I shan't mention Charles leave again"

"Don't be silly Alice" both are now crying "I look forward to seeing him, after all, he was the last of us to see Martin when they met a few months ago, I should like to know how Charles thinks that Martin is coping"

Alice wipes her eyes, she moves away from Grace, "I will turn the bed down for us"

She leaves the kitchen and goes into the 'living room', the large wooden double bed with its new sprung mattress stands alone against the wall, it is the only piece of furniture that has been moved from the back room, Alice has been meaning to stay at the cottage more often, but tonight will be the first time she has spent the night since her parents were found dead under the tree in the garden, she thinks about them and about David Shefford and how she found him dead hanging from the Yew tree, also John Freeman, the soldier she cared for, died from drinking a hot brew made from Yew tree bark and needles.

She looks down the garden, forcing herself to look at the tree, "That Yew has enough now" she whispers to herself, "No more ghosts"

They are awoken the following morning with bright light pouring through the window of the living room, Alice and Grace slept 'top and tail' and both had slept very well,

"Sunshine at last" Alice declares,

Grace has a look out of the window, it is bright and dry but certainly not sunny, she looks down the garden, the familiar water pump and Yew tree, seemingly unchanged for as long as she can remember and the stream at the bottom of the garden, it is part of the River Lea and due to the amount of rain over the last few days, it is swollen and has taken several feet from the garden and large swathes of the water cress beds on the other side. Grace stokes the fire, adding soft wood for a quick burn and Alice collects water in two wooden buckets from the water pump, a kettle is put onto boil for tea and for a wash in the back yard, bread is toasted in front of the fire, both have the thick and creamy butter that Alice had purchased from Fred Hitchcock's dairy shop on the corner of Station Road and Manland Avenue on her way home yesterday, a second round of toast is eaten and both have a mug of tea. Hot water is put into a large bowl and the pair of them have a quick wash in the back yard, the weather is still dry, if not a little overcast, it is just after nine in the morning and both of them sit in the kitchen enjoying the heat from the range.

"Come on Alice" says Grace "We can't stay in here all day" she stands and goes to the window that overlooks the garden, "I know what we can do!" she says suddenly excited, Alice does not answer, she seems a little confused at her friend's excitable mood, Grace continues, "Let's climb the tree!"

"Tree? What tree?" questions Alice,

Grace laughs as she says, "The tree in your garden silly"

Grace loses her smile, "The Yew tree?"

"Of course, the Yew, it is the only tree in your garden"

Alice looks through the window at the huge, old, gnarled Yew tree, she has always been a little afraid of it and has hardly been near it since David died in its branches, even collecting the water this morning had given her cold shivers. The huge trunk has the beginnings of a split in the middle of it, rising from the ground to several feet up and into the huge trunk, it looks like the tree is silently screaming, its huge branches stick out from the trunk like yellowy brown arms and legs, the massive canopy currently has a mass of green needles, and it blots out a large amount of sky to the South of the cottage,

"I don't know Grace" she puts her hand on the glass in the window, "I am a little afraid of that tree"

"I will go first; you can watch and see how easy it is" she points to the tree "That branch is so low it will be easy to get onto it"

"It isn't very ladylike is it, Grace?"

Alice feels Grace put an arm around her and guide her toward the door,

"We spend our whole lives being ladylike because that is what society says we must do" She opens the door, "Anyway, when I take Patrick to the woods for a walk, we both climb trees, ladylike or not!"

Grace links arms with Alice and takes her down the garden toward the Yew tree, ignoring Alice when she says, "You are older than me and supposed to be responsible"

They reach the tree, as they are taken in by its shade, the temperature around them drops suddenly, Alice shivers, Grace laughs.

"Shall I go first?" she asks Alice, who nods in reply.

Grace takes off her outer jacket, grey in colour in a single breast style with a belt around the waist, she hands the jacket to Alice who folds it neatly over her arm, she then kneels down and re ties the laces on her black boots, she is wearing a plain grey skirt, it reaches almost to her ankles and is flowing enough for her to move with ease through the branches of the huge tree.

"Ready?" she asks Alice,

"No" is the plain reply.

"Watch and see how easy it is"

With these words, Grace moves to the lowest branch and easily climbs onto it, putting her hand against the trunk to steady herself, she balances and reaches for the next branch, situated about shoulder height, she grabs this branch, using it she pulls herself up the short distance, pushing with her feet on the trunk, Alice puts her hand over her mouth,

"Be careful Grace, please"

Grace has climbed another level and is sitting comfortably on a sturdy branch, she is at least ten or twelve feet above the ground, Alice feels excited, her fear forgotten for now, another climb and Grace is so very high up that Alice has to crick her neck and look upwards, Alice calls up,

"What is it like?"

"Marvellous" shouts Grace, "Absolutely marvellous"

Alice wants to climb as well, she puts Grace's jacket over the handle of the water pump and puts hers on top, she moves nervously toward the lowest branch, looking up she sees that Grace is still on the same bow but now has her legs either side of it, Alice feels this position is defiantly very unladylike, Grace is slowly shifting up the length of the huge bow. Alice slowly gets onto the low branch, she believes it feels safe and strong,

"Wait for me Grace" she calls up,

"Slowcoach!" Grace playfully calls back.

Alice is feeling nervous about the climb, but excited at the same time, she looks up, the clouds are turning black and it feels like it might rain, Grace is reaching up and trying to grab the branch above her, it is just too high, Alice watches as her friend lifts her right leg over the branch, she is now sitting on it with both legs dangling, she lifts her left leg up and puts her foot on the branch, she pushes upwards and stands as she does so, reaching up for the branch and missing. Her right hand grabs at thin air,

"Grace!" screams Alice, "Stop!"

It is too late, Grace topples forwards and as she tries to counter the forward motion her feet slip off of the branch, she falls.

Alice watches as Grace falls and bangs her head heavily on a lower branch as gravity takes her, the sound is sickening,

"Grace!" Alice screams again, she hears another loud thud as her friend hits the ground hard, she slowly gets down off of the low branch and runs to Grace. She kneels next to her and takes her hand in hers,

"Oh my, are you alright!" she whispers.

Grace has her eyes closed and does not respond, Alice shakes her gently, "Wake up, wake up now please"

Tears fall from Alice's' eyes, she smiles when Grace moans and opens her eyes,

"What happened?" Grace asks groggily

"You fell, you fell such a long way, I was so scared"

Grace puts her hand to her head and winces as she touches it,

"You banged your head so hard, I thought you were hurt or worse"

Grace manages a smile, she puts her hand to one of her ears and as she takes it away, fresh blood can be seen on her fingers, Alice is scared again,

"Grace, you have blood coming out of your ear" she cries, then looking at the other ear, "You are bleeding from both ears"

Grace seems to be staring but not focusing, "I'm fine, I feel a little groggy Alice, could you help me to the tree, I need to sit and rest against it"

Alice struggles with Grace as she is now semi-conscious, the bleeding from her ears is not stopping,

"Grace, I must go for help" Grace tries to stand, Alice puts a firm hand on her shoulder, "Stay here, don't move I will run to the pub and get Granny, she will know what to do"

Grace nods almost imperceptibly, Alice runs from the tree and up the garden, it is beginning to rain again, she goes through the gate and onto the road, she looks left and right, Mr Scott is pruning the roses in the gardens of the Methodist church opposite, he was the church steward for many years and still likes to keep the gardens looking nice, he looks up when Alice calls to him as she crosses the road, he puts down his secateurs,

"Alice? Whatever is the matter?"

Alice is sobbing, "Mr Scott, help me please Mr Scott"

He gently, but with firmness in his grip, holds both her shoulders, "Now calm down child, tell me what is wrong"

"Grace fell from the tree, she was climbing and fell, she banged her head and I think she is badly hurt"

"Oh my, where is she?" he asks calmly

Alice points to the cottage, "In the garden, under the tree"

Mr Scott looks up and sees a horse and cart pull up outside of the Malta pub, he calls over, "Jack, Ernie, can you help!"

Both men climb down from the cart and walk with haste toward the Church,

"Now George" says Jack, "What is all the fuss about"

George Scott points at the cottage, "Alice says that Grace Wilson has fallen from the tree and is hurt, can you help?"

"Of course we can, George, can you take Alice to the pub and get Mary" he nods at his brother,

"Ernie and I will go and take a look"

George guides Alice toward the pub as the Almond brothers cross the road toward the cottage.

Mary comes to the door of the pub when George knocks, he quickly tells her what has happened and she grabs her coat and puts it on as the three of them walk quickly toward the cottage, Mary holding onto Alice tightly to stop her from running,

"Slow down Alice, Ern and Jack will be with her."

But they are not.

The trio enter the garden, Ernie walks toward them, shrugging his shoulders,

"She is not here, wasn't here when Jack and I arrived, we have looked around the house and in the back yard, nothing"

He is disturbed by his brother shouting at him and the sound of water splashing, "Ernie! Ernie! She is in the river!"

They run quickly down the garden, Ernie jumps into the swollen stream and runs as fast as he can in the water to where Jack has stopped, Alice screams. In the stream, about twenty or so feet upstream is the body of Grace Wilson, face down with her arms floating out to the side, she is caught in the reeds at the riverbank on the far side, the swollen stream has taken her from where she entered the water to where she now lies. Ernie and Jack lift her out of the water, her body is limp and lifeless, they struggle to get her to the side of the stream, but they manage, and she is put gently down on the bank on the opposite side of the garden fence,

"Jack, Fred Dowty was having a cuppa at the East station when we left, go get him if you can, take the horse so if he has gone you can get after him"

Jack nods and runs off toward the pub, Alice cannot take her eyes off of Grace who has been laid on her back, her head is tilted backwards, her eyes and mouth open in a ghastly image, her skin is grey and her body lifeless,

"Grace!" Alice shouts from the garden, Ernie looks up and shakes his head at George and Mary, Alice sees him do this, she screams,

"No! no! no!"

Mary has to grab her again and hold her firmly in her grasp, "Stay with me Alice, it won't do any good now"

"Mary is there a sheet or a tarpaulin in the cottage?" Ernie asks, Mary tells him that there should be a tarpaulin in the back yard, he looks at George who moves away quickly and returns shortly with a green tarpaulin, the men cover the body of Grace, Alice cannot bear to look. Minutes pass by until the sound of horse hooves at the gallop breaks the silence, Jack is back with Pc 137 Fred Dowty, both men join Ernie and George, they lift the tarpaulin to show Pc Dowty the corpse he shakes his head, and the men talk for a minute before he comes over to Mary and Alice,

"Alice" she does not look at the police officer, he repeats, "Alice, I need to know what happened, just briefly so that I can tell Mr and Mrs Wilson, can you tell me please" he speaks in a soft and gentle manner, Alice tells him what happened,

"Well done, Alice, I will need to speak to you a little later" he looks at Mary, "Perhaps at the pub?"

"We will be there Fred" Mary responds, she takes Alice away toward the pub, they both hear the constable say to the other men,

"I have to go to Salisbury Road to tell the parents, we will need a doctor and an undertaker" One of the men responds but Alice and Mary can't make out who it is, the constable continues,

"Thanks Jack, Reeves the undertaker is working today, and we will have to get Dr Blake here from Bowers house"

The rest of the conversation is lost to both the women as they are too far away, Mary takes Alice into the pub, she bolts the door behind her, the pub won't be open today.

* * *

The iron framed church at the National Children's home certainly isn't the prettiest in the land, but today, Friday the 16th of June 1916, is the funeral of Grace Wilson, much loved daughter, sister, teacher, and Alice's greatest friend. Grace arrives in the back of a horse drawn hearse, it has beautiful decorative roof finials, sparkling clear glass that is etched at the edges and white metal fittings, both the coachmen are turned out in full black livery with black silk top hats, both horses are jet black and their black leather harnesses can only just be seen against their skin, the collars are black with white metal fittings, matching the funeral hearse. The coffin is plain dark wood with gleaming silver coloured handles, two simple wreaths sit atop it, Mr Reeve has certainly given Grace a fine final journey from her home in Salisbury Road to Highfield Cemetery.

Rev Wesley Woolmer from the Methodist church gives a short sermon, not an overly religious affair at the request of Henry and Mrs Wilson, Grace wasn't particularly religious, the church at the NCH is a Wesleyan chapel, so they asked Rev Woolmer to say a few words. Grace will be buried, in the quiet and beautiful Highfield cemetery that is in the secluded North West corner of the site, her plot is, somewhat ironically, underneath a Yew tree, but this is a fine, young tree and not as frightening or ugly as the tree in the cottage garden, the corner plot is protected by the serenely pretty Westfield Woods on two sides, her grave will be marked with a simple wooden cross, no names or dates will be displayed, no stone will be put above her as a permanent marker.

She lies with the few children and Sisters from the NCH that have also lost their lives since the home opened in 1913, the cemetery is quiet, only disturbed by the occasional rumble of a train slowly passing by on the Nickey Line.

* * *

Alice is waiting outside of the pub at five fifteen the following Monday morning, she feels empty, her tummy feels heavy and her heart empty, she sent a letter to Martin last week, telling him about the death of Grace, Charles will also receive a similar letter, it was easier writing to Charles than it was to Martin, she feels the warmness of tears as they fall gently down her cheeks,

"Morning love" Alice looks up and through bleary eyes she sees Maggie, she can't speak she is so choked up with emotion, "Come here my love"

Maggie puts her arms around Alice and holds her very tight, "Now then young lady" Maggie says "We have work to go to" she pulls away from Alice and holds her upper arms in her hands, she looks directly into her eyes, "It will be fine Alice, everything will get better, I promise"

Alice mumbles "Thanks" through her sobs, Maggie steps back,

"Do you have your train ticket?"

Alice wipes her eyes and face with her handkerchief, "Yes, thank you I have it in my purse"

"Come on then, let's get you to work"

They walk the short distance to the East station, they only have to wait a few minutes until the train arrives, pulling into the station with clouds of white steam rising from underneath the engine, the funnel has a veil of black smoke rising from it and there is a loud hissing as the train comes to a halt, they both get on board, the train has a few bleary eyed passengers already seated, Maggie nods at a few of the women she knows from the factory, she takes a seat on the platform side of the train, Alice sits opposite her next to the window. The train slowly chugs out of the station, the veil of black smoke becomes thicker as the engine demands more heat and steam, the driver hoots the whistle with a short sharp blast causing white steam slowly rises from underneath it, the train picks up momentum and Alice listens to the sound from the funnel, it gets slowly faster, then faster still until it is one continuous mesmerising sound, she stares out of the window in a world of her own.

"Here we are Alice" Maggie puts her hand gently on Alice's knee

"Is it far from the station?"

"No, only a couple of hundred yards, I will take you to Miss Hammond for your medical and introduction" Maggie sees the worry on her face "Don't worry, it will be fine"

They get off of the train along with a dozen or more other women, Alice presumes they are all heading for the factory, Maggie and Alice follow on in the crowd, a large industrial area opens up in front of them, the buildings seem to be fresh and new, only a couple of years old at most, the main factory building is huge, they walk up a gentle slope toward the building, Maggie tugs on Alice sleeve and takes her away from the crowds of talking women,

"They are off to the changing rooms, work starts at seven sharp; we have to go in here" she is walking toward a green painted wooden door, "I will leave you in the capable hands of Miss Hammond, if I don't see you at lunchtime we can meet here when we finish, we have to be swift though, the train leaves at seven twenty tonight, so it's a quick change and a dash for the station"

Maggie goes through the door and tells Alice to wait for a few minutes until she finds Miss Hammond, Alice is left alone in the corridor as Maggie goes through a door at the end. Alice looks around at the plain magnolia coloured walls, a few old paintings and prints are haphazardly hung in different places, the door opens behind her and a young woman, aged about twenty enters the building, they look at each other,

"Good morning" the lady says brightly to Alice,

"Hello" Alice replies nervously,

"You must be Alice" she says

Alice looks at her, unsure of how she knows her name, the lady giggles infectiously,

"Don't look so shocked, I am May Constable, Miss Hammond has attached you to my team for this week, I also had a chat with Maggie last week who told me you were joining us"

"I have to have a medical first, don't I?"

"Yes, but a little later on this morning, first we have to..."

They are interrupted by Maggie calling them into the office,

"Morning May, come along please, Miss Hammond will see you now Alice"

May sets off and Alice follows, Maggie speaks to them both,

"I am off to get changed, May will see you right Alice, I will see you later"

Maggie leaves through the door that they had come in through a few minutes earlier, May holds open the door to the office and nods that Alice should enter, she does and sees a middle aged lady seated at a large desk, she is smartly dressed in a plain white blouse with a delicate lace edge that covers the buttons, a black waist length jacket that has a beautiful green and gold brooch on the left lapel, she stands and Alice can see she is wearing a high waisted black skirt, her hair is salt and pepper grey and tied in a bun at the back,

"Good morning Alice, I am Miss Edith Hammond, and I am in charge of recruitment and welfare" she indicates that Alice should sit in the high backed chair in front of the desk, May remains standing by the door, "Firstly, I must pass on my condolences to you for the loss of your friend" she pauses "A terrible business indeed, Maggie told May and I about it last week, we are all very sad for you"

Alice looks at the floor, desperately trying not to cry, "Thank you, Miss Hammond, that is very thoughtful of you"

"Right then" Edith brightens up "Shall we start"

Alice smiles, "Yes please"

"I see you have already met May Constable" she nods toward the back of the room, Alice turns and smiles as May,

"I have"

"May will be your shadow for the week, and also your Inspector, we have three more new joiners this morning" she looks at her watch, "Let's hope they are not late on their first day"

Alice is told that she will be issued with a uniform to wear, it has to be worn at all times when on the factory floor, Alice is handed a grey coloured heavy linen coat, almost like Grannies housecoat but with long sleeves and large buttons at the front, in addition to this she is given a white linen cap with an elastic edge, she is told this must be worn at all times when in the factory, all hair needs to be put under the cap and to remain covered throughout the day. Alice confirms to Miss Hammond that she will not need lodgings and is told that she will need to collect her weekly train ticket on Fridays during her lunchbreak, wages will also be collected at the same time, there is noise and chatting coming from the corridor,

"May, will you see to that please" instructs Miss Hammond.

May opens the door and politely asks those talking in the corridor to do so quietly and that they will be seen in a few minutes, she thanks them and closes the door.

"The other three new starters are here Miss Hammond" she says

Edith tuts, "So I can hear, anyway Alice, whilst I introduce myself to the other three, they all need lodgings so it will take longer, May will show you around the factory and take you to your locker so that you can get changed, you will find a pair of rubber soled clogs in the locker, they are all the same size so you will have to make the best of them, your medical will be at eleven sharp, May will bring you back to my office for that"

"Thank you, Miss Hammond"

"Do you have any questions at this time Alice?"

"Only one, I have no idea what job I will be doing here"

Miss Hammond giggles, "May will talk you through it all, but you will be putting detonators into the fuses, they will already be filled with high explosives, all our new girls start on this line"

Alice thanks Miss Hammond again and leaves with May to be shown her locker, they exit the building and begin to walk around it,

"How old are you, Alice?" asks May,

"Seventeen" she replies

"You are joining at the right time, there is talk about making the minimum age eighteen to work in munitions factories, but nothing has happened as yet, you are here now so you will be alright"

They reach a door at the end of the large factory building, "Here we are" May opens the door and she and Alice go into a long corridor, each side is lined with small lockers, "Find one with just a pair of clogs in, that means it is not being used by anyone"

May opens a locker, Alice presumes is hers, she finds one with only a pair of clogs in it,

"Will this one be alright for me to use?" asks Alice, May walks down toward her as she puts on her factory coat, she only has her underwear on underneath it, Alice looks away,

"That will do just fine" she looks at the number on the locker, "I will let Miss Hammond know that number 49 is yours, you need to put your factory coat on, they are not the height of fashion, but it will protect your clothing" Alice takes her factory coat and puts it on, May stops her, "If I can offer a little advice, take off your outer coat, even on the coldest winter day it is hot in the factory, the furnace is next door, so you won't be cold"

Alice takes off her outer coat and puts on the factory coat, she removes her boots and puts on the clogs and then the linen, elasticated cap,

"You look just lovely Alice, you will be in underwear only before we know it!" exclaims May,

Alice looks at her drab work uniform and then at May, the both collapse into fits of giggles,

"It is so much better to see you laugh Alice, but I need to cover a few things with you first"

Alice nods and pays attention, "Now that you are dressed, I have to ask you if any of your clothing has any metal clips or wires" Alice blushes a little, May continues, "Any corsets or any type of underwear with metal clips cannot be worn inside the factory, a spark from any metal in there is dangerous"

"I don't wear a corset, only a slip" Alice is still blushing

"Any hair clips?" Alice shakes her head, "Good, I would hate to have to make you strip off now you are fully dressed!"

"Has that happened before?" asks Alice

"Only on first days, many of the new ladies turn up in their best clothes, hair clips and corsets, all have to be taken off or they don't work" Alice can't imagine having to strip off in front of others, May helps Alice's obvious embarrassment by saying, "One lady was caught out on the factory floor when a match fell out of her pocket! Can you believe that"

Alice looks surprised, "What happened to her?" she asks May,

"Sacked on the spot and charged in court, she got a prison sentence for endangerment"

"Oh my!" exclaims Alice, May continues,

"She never got over it and died in prison, she was twenty"

Alice doesn't say anything, there is a moments silence for them both to reflect on this information, May breaks the silence,

"None of the men who work here are allowed in this area, you do get used to dropping your own clothes and putting the factory coat on over your undies"

"Oh, I can't imagine doing that" Alice can feel her face turning redder and redder,

"You will Alice, in a day or two"

Alice smiles, May carries on with her introduction, "The cloaks and lavvies are behind this block, toward the Dunstable road entrance, the canteen is behind them" she stops for a few seconds,

"There are other lavs nearer to the factory floor, but the ones by the cloaks are the best, we also have a small hospital facility, that is situated behind Miss Hammonds office"

Alice looks dumfounded, "A hospital? Do people get hurt?"

"I shan't lie to you Alice, yes they do" May looks at the look of shock on Alice's face, "I think it fair to tell you that your skin will turn yellow and your hair ginger!" she smiles as she says this,

"Yellow and ginger!" exclaims Alice, the nodding May carries on,

"Yellow, the Trinitrotoluene is yellow and being near it stains your skin, your hair can change colour depending on what colour it is naturally"

"What is…" Alice cannot remember the long word May used,

"Trinitrotoluene, TNT to you and me, a high explosive that we pack into the fuses, it does fade after a while, but as long as you work here you will have a yellow tint to your skin, in fact, Dawn Jacobs had a baby two months ago and the baby was born bright yellow!"

Alice puts her hand to her mouth to try to cover a giggle, "No? really?"

May laughs very loudly, "So, unless you are planning on having a baby Alice, you only have to worry about yourself!"

Blushing again, Alice replies, "Certainly not!"

"Well, although we are officially known as Munitionettes, we are known as the Canaries, because of the yellowness of the skin"

Alice looks at May, "Your skin is not yellow"

"I am one of the Inspectors" she points at Alice, "Your Inspector actually, so I don't have prolonged exposure to the TNT"

"What about the job I am to do?"

"Not much exposure Alice, when the fuses arrive at your section on the line, the TNT is already packed into the fuse heads, the detonators are filled in another section, so although you will be close to the explosive, you should get away with a bit of staining of your fingers" Alice has no answer to this, "Finally, before we go and have a look around, I must warn you that working with explosives is dangerous, there is a danger of burns, lost fingers or hands and blindness, sometimes permanent"

"Has that happened here?" asks a frightened Alice,

"No, we have been lucky, but I have heard horror stories from other factories, we wear caps to tuck all of our hair in, then it can't be caught in a lathe, press or one of the belts that drive them"

"Is this a safe job"

"No, but we do our best to make it as safe as we can" Alice is checking that all her hair is tucked inside the linen cap, "Your section doesn't have any machinery in it, so if you have a stray hair or two it won't matter, but remember what I said, the TNT in the air will turn your hair ginger!"

Alice checks the cap again, May laughs at her, "Shall we go and have a tour of the factory?"

Alice follows May to the other end of the corridor, as she opens the door the high level of noise hits Alice like a thunderbolt, inside this part of the factory there are long lines of belt driven machines, the rubber belts are attached to a small spinning wheel at one end of the machine and they stretch out to the ceiling where the belts are attached to a central rod being turned by a steam driven engine, behind each machine stands a woman, all are working swiftly and with precision, May indicates that Alice should put her fingers in her ears, as she does this she is able to hear May shouting over the noise,

"Lathes and presses, for turning the brass and copper to make the casings and component parts for the fuses"

May can see two men working in this section of the factory, one is wearing a long brown work coat and seems to be the supervisor, the other is a young man with scars on his face, he is the only man working behind a lathe, May waves at the man who waves back, they then walk the length of this section and through a door at the far end. It is quieter here than in the main factory, dozens of women are seated on high backed wooden chairs, all sat in front of long workbenches that are lined with crates that are filled with brass dome shaped objects, May tells her that these are the fuses and that this is the assembly room, where all the component parts are put together, but not fully finished as the fuse has to have the TNT packed into it, Alice follows May through a door and into a short corridor and through another door, heavier than the last,

"This is the fuse filling magazine" May tells her, "This is where the Canaries work!"

They enter through the heavy door, some of the women, there are at least twenty in this room, look up and say hello to May, Alice is shocked, every single one of them has yellow skin and the smell in the room is vile.

"I should have mentioned the smell Alice, you sort of get used to it"

"No, you bloody don't love" shouts one of the women, "Don't listen to her"

They all start laughing, Alice is amazed to watch them work, some don't even seem to be looking at what they are doing, she watches as a hot thick liquid is poured into the fuse heads,

"What is that?" asks Alice,

"That is the TNT" replies May,

"I thought it was a powder" states Alice, clearly confused,

"It will become solid as it cools, it has to be hot and melted to be able to use it as the girls are here"

They leave the women to their work, Alice is shown other departments, the pellet room, the bond room, the main fitting shop, the furnace, and the magazines where the finished products are safely stored, finally she is taken to workshop number seventy,

"This is where you will work Alice"

Alice looks around the room, there is a similar number of women in here as there was in the fuse filling room, it smells of TNT but not anywhere near as strong as it was in the filing room,

"Kate, could you show Alice what is done in here please, she is starting today, you and her are the same age"

"Of course, hello Alice, I am Kate Tomkins" she pulls a chair over to the workbench next to her, "Have a seat, this is an easy job, but we have to be very careful" Alice sits next to Kate,

"I have to show the other new girls around now, so I will be back later"

"Where are they going to be put, not in here I hope, there is not enough room for anymore" one of the ladies speaks to May, another of the workers, a lady in her thirties answers before May has a chance to,

"Bloody hell Elsie, leave May alone, if we need to make room then we will, the more the merrier I say"

"Alice will be the last in here for a while, until Kate leaves to go and work in the filling rooms"

With a wave of her hand, May is gone,

"When are you moving to the filling room?" asks Alice,

"Sometime this month" replies Kate "More money for me!" Alice looks confused, "The work filling the fuses with TNT is paid a little better than other departments"

"Wont your skin turn yellow?" Alice seems concerned,

All the women in the room stop what they are doing and show Alice their hands, all have tinges of yellow on their fingers, they look like some of the men from the pub who smoke too many cigarettes, Alice nods politely and the women return to their work. Kate explains that when the crates of fuses arrive in their work area, the TNT is already in place, she shows Alice inside one of the fuses, the TNT is easily identified inside the brass fuse as it is bright yellow, Alice can see a hole in the middle of the now hardened TNT,

"Why is there a hole in them?" she enquires,

"When the TNT starts to solidify, the girls in the filling rooms push a small metal tube into the mixture, creating this hole" she points at the TNT, "When it hardens it leaves the space for us to put the detonators into" She takes a small, cylindrical metal object from another crate, "This is the detonator, also filled with TNT, we don't do that here, it is done in another of the filling areas, we take the detonator like so" she carefully and gently inserts the detonator into the solid TNT,

"You are being very careful, is it dangerous?"

"We have to be careful Alice, any friction could cause the TNT to explode, so we work carefully and gently but with efficiency" Kate puts the fuse with its new detonator back into the crate, "May will come and inspect our work before the crates are sent next door" she points her thumb over a shoulder to another door, "That is where the final construction of the fuses is completed, a spring and screw thread needle are inserted above the detonator and a brass cap fitted to hold it all in place" Alice is nervous and it shows, "Don't worry Alice, as long as we are careful in here, then all will be well, anyway, May has to check to make sure that the detonators are correctly placed, if they are too shallow then there is a risk of explosion in the next room when the cap is screwed on, if they are in too deep then the fuse may malfunction and the shell it is inside may not explode"

"I check them all before May comes in"

Alice looks up and sees an older lady, she has a tool in her hand, and she is measuring the remainder of detonator that sticks out from the TNT.

One of the ladies begins to hum a tune, Alice recognises it, Uncle Pete had played in on his gramophone, at Maple Cottages, one of the girls begins to sing, very quietly, others join in,

"Jeremiah Jones, a lady's man was he..."

They are singing, "Hello, hello, who's your lady friend" by Ted Yorke, Alice smiles and listens.

Kate hands her a fuse head and then a detonator, Alice gently puts the detonator into place, assisted by Kate, who says to her,

"Welcome to George Kent's fuse filling factory Alice"

Alice takes another fuse head and puts in her first solo detonator as she listens to the quiet singing all around her.

* * *

It is nearly the end of June, Martin and his platoon are in support trenches at Maricourt, they are all very nervous, having been in these trenches for fourteen days now and waiting for the order to 'advance', Operation order number 76 is to be put into action sometime today, when instructed the men will climb out of the trenches and advance in support of the 17th and 20th Kings Liverpool Battalions, who are in the trenches next to and just in front of them. All battalions will be moving from the British and French held lines and toward the German lines and trenches, heavy casualties are expected, mainly from the Allied soldiers as they will be the ones advancing toward a multitude of firing German machine guns, the men are scared, so is Martin. The support trenches are uncomfortable and open to the elements, sandbags are piled high on both sides but they do not stop the trenches from flooding, the rain mixes with the loose mud on the floor and creates a thick and immovable mass, all the soldiers have previously spent four or five days living in this mess but the last two weeks have been real hell on earth, hot food and hot water are in short supply, mainly due to the weather making any delivery of sustenance almost impossible. The almost constant bombardment from the Germans means that the British Artillery replies in kind, sleep is fitful and disturbed by the huge guns.

It is dry today, but the trench Martin is in is mid-calf deep in mud, he and his platoon have spent the last forty eight hours in these conditions due to the constant wet weather, many of the Sergeants and Corporals have reported cases of trench foot in their platoons, they all believe that it is the newly issued gum boots that are causing the problem, the mud is so deep and thick that the boots fill up with it and the men's feet become like boiled puddings, Martin has ordered his platoon to wear the issue ammunition boots and not the gum boots, it does involve a lot of kit being dried out when they are relieved but he knows that untreated trench foot could mean losing it in the hands of a surgeon. Another new trench system built by the enemy had been sighted and reported last night, it is very close to the allied trenches and after a day of heavy bombing by the Germans the 17th Kings Liverpool regiment report that they had one hundred and twenty casualties just that afternoon, a huge mine explosion had been heard from the enemy lines, it had not been initiated by the British or the French, so its origin is still a mystery. Because of this increased activity, CSM Chandler had taken a patrol out after dusk and had noted that the enemy had moved several machine gun platoons from their trenches and into shell holes, from these they have a good, clear line of sight and fire toward the Allied lines and as the enemy are away from their main trenches, this gives the Allied soldiers two areas that need covering rather than the one. They also received a report that a glint of light has been seen from the top of a damaged church, when they are sent forward to investigate, they find a German spy, a long way behind the Allied lines, he is dressed as a priest and has been signalling to his colleagues across the battlefield, they have to presume that their positions have now been correctly reported for the enemy to hit them with more accurate artillery fire, this seems to confirm why the Kings Liverpool lads are having a terrible time in their trenches.

The enemy spy refused to come quietly and when he tried to signal more messages, he was shot dead.

On the way back to the Allied lines, the platoon is fired upon by German machine guns from an unsighted shell hole, Sgt 'Robbo' Robinson and CSM Percy Chandler are both wounded, Chandler very seriously. At five in the evening news is passed along the line that the advance has been postponed, Martin thinks it is because the weather over the past forty eight hours has been so bad that the ground will be turgid with rain and not conducive to advancing quickly and attacking the enemy, the men all breathe a sigh of relief, but it is short lived, they are all to move to the forward trenches occupied by the 17th Kings Liverpool Battalion, they are being moved back because of their losses, the Bedfordshire men move forward, knowing that the enemy has been very accurate with their artillery in the positions they are moving to, they are all nervous again.

Orders are passed down to Martin that he is to take a platoon, with 2nd Lt Walker leading, to carry out reconnaissance of the enemy lines, they are to move as soon as it is dark, the artillery begins to fall around them, very close to the trenches, they all sit low down in the trenches, in the thick wet mud, hoping that a shell does not hit them directly. It is after eleven that night when A/CSM Oakes appears in the trenches with 2nd Lt Walker, a Lance Corporal that Martin has met a few times and two privates,

"Hello Ralph, what brings you to our delightful home?" asks Martin,

"I'm fed up sitting in the HQ dugout, in front of a burning brazier and drinking hot tea, so I thought I would come down here for cold bully beef, tea that tastes of petrol and to sit in the mud"

Oakes calls over to George Freshwater to join them, he speaks to the officer,

"Sir, if I may take a few moments to give Freshwater new orders"

Walker nods and remains silent whilst Ralph speaks to George,

"Sir" he says as he stands with Martin and Ralph,

"As we are a couple of Sergeants down" he turns to Martin, "Robbo is on his way to a casualty station and Percy died this afternoon from his wounds" The men all stay silent for a few seconds, Oakes continues, "I am now no longer acting CSM, Hutch has been sent back to Blighty, so I get the honour of being the newly promoted Company Sergeant Major" The men all congratulate him,

"George lad, you are now an acting Sergeant, you are to move trenches and take over Robbo's platoon, you won't have a corporal, but I will find you one"

George does not move,

"Are you still here lad?" asks Oakes

"No Sir, I am not"

George turns to Martin, "See you later Martin, be safe out there tonight

"He certainly will be safe tonight, acting Sergeant" Oakes looks at Martin, "I am going with him and his platoon"

Martin laughs as George makes his way through the trenches to his new platoon,

"Sir" Oakes stands back, "Thank you for that, we are all yours"

Walker steps forward, he is hunched over as he is well over six feet tall, Martin thinks him to be roughly the same age as him but at least five or six inches taller,

"Thanks Company Sergeant Major, with these two NCO's" he points at Martin and Ralph, "I am sure we will all be in safe hands tonight, I will need all of your names to register with HQ before we leave" he sees Oakes nod at a private to complete this task, he turns to the men, "All eight of you will be coming with us across the open land in front of us" he takes out a map and illuminates it with a red light torch,

"Not sure how much use this map will be in the dark, but we are to head from our position on the far right of our lines, here" he points and then moves his finger to a trench that is coloured green, meaning it is an enemy held area," This is our nearest German line, we are to move through the Dublin trench, quietly, then on toward the village of Montauban de Picardie and carry out reconnaissance of the artillery, trenches and machine gun points that we can see, I need not remind you gentlemen, silence and no lights" He looks at Ralph and Martin, "Eleven thirty kick off Sergeants, please have the men ready"

"Sir!" they say together, 2nd Lt Walker, takes a piece of paper from the private, a list of all the names of the men that will be in the patrol tonight, he thanks the soldier and is gone.

The Lance corporal turns to Martin, "How are you doing Sarge?"

"Good thanks Nobby, I presume you and your lads from D company did not volunteer for this tonight?"

Lance Corporal Charles 'Nobby' Clark smiles,

"I did actually, when the CSM told me that George was being moved to act with another platoon, I realised you would be without a Lance Jack, so I foolishly volunteered!"

Martin looks at the other two men from D company, Nobby introduces them,

"Private George Gilbey and Private Frank Cann"

Martin does likewise with his five privates,

"Henry 'H' Jarman, Alfie Bean, Dennis Waldock, Eric 'Sharpie' Sharp and John Marrables"

Most of the men are known to each other in one capacity or another,

"If you girls have finished making friends, then listen in" Oakes speaks quietly,

"The Sergeant" he nods at Martin, "Is by far the most experienced man here in relation to working in and near enemy trenches" He points at each of the privates, "If he says its Christmas today, then its bloody Christmas today, do you all understand, what he says, goes" They all nod, "Lance Corporal Clark will lead the platoon, the Sergeant will be in charge of the operation and I will look after the 'Rupert'" he looks at his watch, "Ten minutes lads, go and hide away from view and grab a quick smoke, then back here quick sharp"

The seven privates all scuttle off for a smoke,

"Do we know much about the 2nd Lt?" Martin asks Oakes and Nobby,

"I have heard that he was an enlisted man, one of us, a Trooper with the King Edward Horse Cavalry regiment and that he was discharged to be able to take a commission with the Bedfordshires" Nobby answers "Brave as a lion so I have heard and a dab hand with a grenade"

A voice from behind them takes them by surprise,

"I don't know about brave as a lion Lance Corporal, but I can chuck a bomb fairly well"

Nobby attempts to stammer an apology to the officer,

"None taken Lance Corporal, after all, I was once '*one of us*', I am sure that is how you put it"

Nobby continues to try to apologise, both Ralph and Martin have covered their mouths so as to muffle their laughter, Nobby looks at them,

"It had to be me that got caught out didn't it"

"Nobby lad" Ralph has controlled his giggles, "You must learn, look around you before speaking about others" he looks at Walker, "Especially about a fine young man like 2nd Lt Walker here"

"Bugger off Company Sergeant Major!" Walker retorts.

The seven privates return,

"Sir, if you are happy, I will take front point" Martin suggests, the 2nd Lt nods in agreement, Martin continues, "Nobby, you take the back point behind the lads, the CSM and the 2nd Lt can fit in behind or alongside you, it will give them an overview" He looks at all of them, including Ralph and the Officer, "If any of you see anything, anything at all, do not shout out, not unless our lives depend on it, put your hand firmly on the shoulder of the man in front and when it gets to me, I will stop and one of you can report to me or to the Lance Corporal, silence might just keep us alive"

Martin climbs the ladder and when he reaches the top of the trench, he takes a low squat position and moves a few yards in front of it, to give the others room to move, he is thankful that there is no moon tonight, it is cloudy and all heavenly bodies are covered, he looks out in front of him, darkness takes over and his view is curtailed to just a few yards. He hears a whisper from the back of the line,

"Move off"

Martin stands up into a crouched position, he waits for the expected sound of a machine gun from the enemy trenches, when it remains silent, he moves off slowly, he tries to recollect the layout of the ground in front of him from when he has been looking at it in daylight, nothing seems familiar, he continues to move off. At about the halfway point, Allied artillery begins to bombard the German positions, Martin is pleased as the noise enables him to talk to the platoon and he hopes it will keep the enemy busy so that they can move swiftly and undetected,

"Take a sharp left turn Sergeant" 2nd Lt Walker shouts at him over the bombardment, "I can see the main road, or what is left of it to my right, this means we are a tad off course"

Martin has no idea what a 'tad' is, but he understands that he has drifted to far to the right, he changes course and sets of at a fast pace. A further half mile in and Martin indicates for everyone to stop and to move into cover at the roadside, they do so silently and Nobby makes his way forward to Martin,

"What have we got Sarge?"

Martin points into the darkness, "Germans, on our side of the road, they don't seem very interested in anything but watching the shells bursting on the village" he pauses to take a breath,

"About five yards in front of us is another road, can you get the 2nd Lt to join me here"

Nobby is gone without an answer, he returns thirty seconds later with Walker and Oakes, the four men get into a huddle, Walker takes a large cape from his backpack and covers their heads with it, he takes out his red light and map, the NCO's cover the dim red light so as not to give away their position, Martin explains what he has seen. Using the map Walker believes that they are still to the right side of the village and that the road that was on their right flank a while ago has taken a left turn,

"Lance Corporal, take two men and go here" he points to a crossroads on the map, "I think we are a short distance from there, have a look and if you can see a wooded area on the far side of the crossroads then I know where we are, we can move away from the enemy without being detected I think"

They all have to hit the ground hard as a stray shell explodes fifty yards to their left, close to the German positions,

"Sir, if we go to the edge of the road and wait in the ditch, then Nobby will have more chance of finding us"

Nobby moves off tapping the shoulders of the two lads from D company to go with him, Martin leads the rest of them to the road, there is a deep ditch, possibly an old trench system, it affords them cover from view and from the hellish number of shells being sent to the German lines, they are landing close to them so they all know that they are deep behind the enemy lines, they all lie in the bottom of the ditch and gather their thoughts and their breath.

They don't have to wait long, Nobby returns on his own, "I have left Gilbey and Cann at the crossroads, the wood is on the other side and as far as we can see, it is unguarded at this time"

"That makes sense" Oakes replies, "The Hun are not expecting any of us to be this far forward tonight, the shelling of their front line is keeping them busy" He looks at Walker, "Sir?"

"Let's move into Bernafay wood, I hope that we may have a vantage point overseeing the German trenches"

Martin indicates that Nobby should lead, and he follows him, they reach the crossroads in under a minute and using the loud explosions they cross the road and get into the wood without any enemy contact. Martin sets his soldiers out along the Western edge of the wood, in front of them is an open area, it gives them a view toward Montauban de Picardie, the shells are landing only a few hundred yards in front of them, Walker takes out a pair of binoculars and has a look over the scene in front of him.

"I can see the front line trenches, we are definitely deep inside the German territory, getting back might be difficult"

"How the hell we got across Dublin's trench without firing a shot is beyond me Sir" Ralph says,

"I agree Company Sergeant Major, I have to believe it is because of the bombardment, anyhow, here we are, and we need to sort out a plan to gather information"

Martin suggests that he take a small patrol to check out the woods immediately surrounding their current position, just to ensure that there are no Germans posted nearby, Walker agrees, and Martin, Oakes, Alfie Bean and Henry Jarman are to go, Martin wanted to take John Marrables as well, but he has confessed to being an artist and Walker is keeping him close by to sketch out any details that they can make out using the flashes of exploding shells to obtain details. Martin takes the lead and Ralph is at the back, Bean and Jarman are in the middle of the sandwich, it isn't long before Martin stops suddenly and takes cover behind a large gorse bush, he points in front of his position, the shelling is so loud and so close that spoken communication is almost impossible. Not thirty yards from their original position on the edge of the wood is a track through the trees, it is a stone and dirt track and on the other side of it is a German gun point, a huge gun with heavy metal tracks to get it through the terrain with ease, it is situated on a high point in the wood and in a clearing and just off of the track, backing onto the woods. They can all see that the gun is mounted in front of a huge number of sandbags, Martin believes that there must be a trench dug behind the sandbags as he can only see the helmet of one German soldier, from experience he knows that this point will have four, or even six men in it. He moves next to Ralph and shouts,

"We need to move around the back of the gun point, if we can get behind them undetected, we may have a chance to attack it, we can use the artillery as cover"

Ralph nods, the CSM points at both privates and indicates that they should follow Martin, they follow their Sergeant, he remains inside the cover of the wooded area but follows the track back to the road they crossed earlier, they are about twenty or thirty yards to the East of the crossroads, as shells explode to the West of their position they use the distraction to cross the track and get to the other side of the wood, Martin turns to the men and puts his finger to his lips and he slowly makes his way back toward the gun point, again following the track but on the opposite side, he uses the thick woodland as cover.

The enemy gun is in view, from their position they have a view of the back of it, just as Martin thought, the front is made entirely of stacked sandbags and the rear has a trench and a firing point built into it, two Germans are on the gun and four others are sitting in the bottom of the trench smoking cigarettes, huge shells are stacked up neatly in the bottom of the trench, Martin knows that they need to be closer to mount a surprise attack. He gets the men into a close huddle, he uses the continued artillery to cover his words to the men,

"There are six enemy" he puts up six fingers to confirm this, "Two are on the gun, Alfie, H, I want you to take a position behind them and when the CSM and I take on the other four, I need you to shoot the gunners" He looks at Ralph who shrugs his shoulders, "Don't miss fellas, the CSM and I need you to be able to back us up quickly" Both men nod enthusiastically, H points to an area on their right, he points at Alfie and then at himself and then again at the point he has chosen for the attack, Martin nods and they move off quietly,

"Ralph, we will do the same, but we might have to be quick off the mark with our shots"

Ralph nods again, he takes his bayonet and puts it on his rifle, he mouths the words "Just in case"

Martin does likewise, they move carefully forward until they only have a few slight bushes for cover, Martin nudges Ralph, the bombardment is almost continuous from the Allied lines, he puts up one finger, then two and finally three. They both break cover and stand on the back edge of the trench, Martin points his rifle without aiming, points it at one of the Germans in the bottom of the trench, he hears a rifle crack to his right and almost immediately another, he fires and sees one of the Germans fall to the ground, the bolt action on his rifle is cocked in seconds, he hears Ralph fire and in his periphery vision another German falls, he has no idea about the two enemy gunners, he moves his rifle and finds the second German on the far right of the trench, he is picking up his rifle, Martin hears another crack from a rifle to his right, he hopes that Alfie and H have finished off the gunners, he hears Ralph shout, "No, you don't you bastard"

This is followed by a scream, he knows it is not Ralph screaming and presumes the enemy soldier has been bayonetted by the CSM, who by now must be in the trench, Martin can see the German does not have his rifle in a position to fire it, he pulls his trigger, nothing happens, his rifle has jammed, a quick look tells him that the bolt action has jammed, there must be something in it, the German has a grenade in his hand and is going for the pin. He throws his rifle at the enemy soldier, it spins as it moves through the air, the heavier stock end giving it momentum, the German lifts his rifle to protect himself, dropping the grenade, now without its pin, the German scrambles for the side of the trench in an attempt to get out, if this grenade goes off, Martin knows it could set off the live ordnance in the trench and will wound or kill him and possibly Ralph, who is scrabbling like hell to get out of the trench. Martin runs and jumps into the trench, it is about four or five feet deep, he grabs the grenade and throws it over the sandbags, it explodes harmlessly on the other side, he then runs and jumps forwards, he lands on the German, who is still attempting to get out of the trench, the sandbags are too high for an easy escape. Martin sends him sprawling, the soldier drops his rifle, Martin picks it up and shoots the man in the face with his own weapon.

The six German soldiers are all dead.

Martin hears H and Alfie returning to where he and Ralph are positioned, he is still in the trench and Ralph is helping him to climb out,

"That was insane Martin, you could have been killed by that grenade" Ralph says,

"Thanks all the same, it would not have done me any good if it had gone off"

"How in God's name did you miss with your first shot Alfie?" H asks

"I did not miss, I hit the bugger as he turned and my bullet must have ricochet off of his helmet" He nudges H, "I didn't bloody miss with the second one, did I?"

Martin is used to such loose and easy talk about taking another man's life, he has said words similar himself, they still sound unfeeling and harsh when said out loud.

"Good work lads" says Ralph, "Let's go"

Martin jumps back into the trench,

"What the hell!" exclaims Ralph

Martin jumps onto the firing point and pulls open shell hatch of the gun, a live shell is in place, and it falls to the bottom of the trench, it lies in between two of the dead Germans, he takes two stick grenades from one of the dead men's belts,

"Move lads, I am destroying the gun"

He pulls the pin on one of the grenades and puts it into the barrel of the huge gun, he slams and locks the shell hatch, he then clambers out of the trench, on his own this time, the others have already begun to move, taking the pin out of the grenade he throws it into the trench, he doesn't hang around to see the effect it will have on the dead bodies and the deadly gun. A few seconds later the first grenade explodes in the breech of the gun, the second goes off with a dull thud, the live shells do not explode but at least they can't be used in this gun anymore. Martin re-joins his mates, and they move away from the destroyed gun, the artillery is still being fired at Montauban de Picardie, although slower than earlier in the day, they are back with 2nd Lt Walker and the remainder of the patrol in under five minutes, Oakes takes Walker to one side to debrief him about the German gun point. Martin is called over to them, as is John Marrables who is carrying a notepad with him,

"Martin did you know that Marrables is an artist?"

Martin shakes his head, "I found out tonight, the same as you Sir"

"He has completed a thoroughly excellent map and plan of this area and the area in front of us, the bursting shells and fires have been a great help to him" Walker says

Martin has a look at the sketches that Marrables has completed, he and Ralph show him on the map where the track is and where the machine gun post is, he adds it to his sketch plan.

"The others have completed a check of this side of the wood, there are several unoccupied trenches a couple of hundred yards to the North" he shows the NCO's the point using the sketches, he points into the darkness across the field,

"Lance Corporal Clark and Privates, Sharpe, Waldock, Cann and Gilbey went across there, bloody brave of them, they almost reached the outskirts of the village, they have been able to get great details about the German defences over there, all without being seen"

Martin speaks to the officer, "Sir, if we have got what we need, shall we get the hell out of here"

Walker thinks for a few seconds, Clark joins them as Walker answers

"Yes Sergeant, but if you are all up for another bit of an adventure, I would like to go back this way" he points at his map, Martin has to lean in as the red light being used by the officer does not give off much illumination, he smiles,

"Are you sure Sir, that takes us right through the tiny village of Briqueterie" Walker is about to pick Martin up and tell him that '*Briqueterie*' on the map is French for a brickworks, he doesn't have time as Martin continues, "We know that the Germans have a lot of soldiers on that side of the road and that there is absolutely no cover at all as the landscape has been levelled by ours and their artillery" He runs his finger down the right side of the road, "If we travel on the other side, it might be lower and we could get through without an issue, but we would have to move fast, no creeping about"

"So be it Sergeant, get the men together and we will be off"

The officer moves away,

"Told you he was as brave as a lion" Nobby says to Martin and Ralph,

"Or bloody nuts" Oakes replies.

The platoon is all together, and they all know the plan and the route back to their lines at Maricourt, as they reach the edge of the wood, H, who is at the front suddenly drops to the kneel and moves behind a tree, the others follow suit,

"What have you seen H?" asks Martin

"A patrol on the far side of the road, I think they saw us as well as they have dropped into the ditch?"

"Germans?"

"I don't know Sarge, I only got a glimpse, but they could be ours, I am almost certain I saw khaki green uniforms rather than German grey"

"Sergeant, can you see anyone?" asks Walker

"No Sir, I am sure they can't see us either"

2nd Lt Walker scratches his chin, "Rifles up men, aim for the top of the ditch, if we get any hostility, shoot at it" he commands

They all do as instructed by the young office, Martin wonders what the Lt is about to do, he almost laughs out loud when the officer shouts,

"2nd Lt Walker, 2nd Battalion Bedfordshire regiment, we can see you and have rifles pointed at you, step out now"

Martin looks at Ralph, who says, "If they are German, I hope they speak English Sir"

Walker turns to Oakes, "Good point Company Sergeant Major, but we can't sit here with a damned stalemate all day, can we?"

A voice is heard shouting from the ditch,

"2nd Lt Charles Rothon, 1st Battalion Dorset regiment, I bloody well know you can't see us because we are six feet below the ditch!"

Loud laughter can be heard from the ditch and from the treeline, Walker turns back to Oakes,

"Mighty good English speakers these Germans don't you think Company Sergeant Major?"

Oakes ignores him and orders the men to lower rifles, the men in the ditch come into view, as they reach the road, a volley of shells lands only yards behind them,

"Run!" Walker shouts at them.

The men from the Dorset regiment don't need to be told twice, they run and dive unceremoniously into the bushes and trees, one private nearly lands on top of Martin,

"Steady on chum!" Martin says to him, the Dorset soldier is picking himself up from the middle of a bush,

"Sorry and all that mate, but I am in the middle of a bloody thorn bush, so pardon me for living"

He looks up and sees the stripes on Martin's tunic, "Sarge" he adds quickly.

Martin is laughing again as he helps the private out of the bush, Walker shouts at him,

"Sergeant, this barrage is a bit close, I say give it fifteen minutes and then they should change their aim a bit, we should be able to move then"

"Agreed Sir" Martin shouts back

The Dorset soldier is picking thorns out of his arms and face, "Bloody hell these sting a bit" he exclaims

"Smoke?" Martin asks him,

"Are we safe to light up Sarge?" he asks

Martin points at the scene in front of them, shells are landing and exploding with vivid and bright light,

"I think we will be alright Private don't you!" Martin responds, he can smell pipe tobacco from Ralphs's pipe, so he knows he won't be the only one having a smoke, the Dorset man happily accepts a cigarette from Martin,

"Thanks, Sarge, I am William Albert James Samways by the way"

Martin nearly chokes on his cigarette, "Bloody hell that is a proper mouthful!"

William smiles as he smokes,

"My name is just Martin, nothing as fancy as yours William!"

William shrugs as he smokes, "Where are you from Sarge?"

Martin tells William where he grew up, including a description of the cottage,

"I don't know it Sarge, but before this war, I had never been outside of Dorset, although your cottage sounds like nearly every house in the street where I come from"

Martin asks where he lives, William explains that his father, George, is a shepherd, so the family, his Mother Rosalie, and his eleven brothers and sisters move around a lot. Martin chokes again for the second time in a few minutes,

"Eleven brothers and sisters! I only have one sister"

William nods and continues to tell Martin that for the past couple of years they have lived just outside of Bridport, an area to the West of the town called West Allington, they all live in a small cottage at Gresham Place, near to the rope works, he had worked in the rope industry before the war, his job had been 'laying' out the rope, Martin does not know what this means, but listens on with interest. Martin starts to giggle when William tells him the name of the village he was born in,

"You are pulling my leg mate"

"No" William says, not understanding why Martin is giggling, "Piddlehinton is the name of the place I was born"

Martin apologises for his laughter, the shells are still landing around them but as predicted by Walker, they are moving to the West.

"I didn't know that the Dorset's are fighting in our sector?" Martin says,

"We aren't Sarge, we are further North, just outside of Albert, a village called Aveluy, we are on a patrol, we were heading toward the German lines at Thiepval and Authuille, that is where we will be headed when the push forward is eventually called" he pauses to finish his cigarette, "Our Lt Col wants to know what we might be walking into and sent us out on patrol, we knew that there would be artillery, but nothing like this, we had to change direction and ended up here"

"You are a few miles out of your zones now mate"

Martin is interrupted by Ralph,

"Martin, the Dorset lads are coming with us back to Maricourt, they can get transport to their positions from there" Martin puts out his cigarette, Ralph finishes his sentence, "It sounds like the Dorset's senior officers are as bloody useless as ours, it's a shambles"

The weather is bad as they move off, torrential rain and heavy wind, although this helps the two platoons make it back to Maricourt without any contact with the enemy, they are given an hour in the reserve section to have a cup of tea and for Marrables to finish his sketches. The Lt Col is over the moon with the information and intelligence that 2nd Lt Walkers platoon have returned with, he is even happier that none of them were killed or wounded,

"A miracle 2nd Lt, a miracle considering the artillery being lobbed in that direction"

"I doubt there will be much left of Montauban de Picardie when we get there"

"If we get there, 2nd Lt, I have grave doubts about the plan to go over the top and charge at the German lines" Lt Col Poyntz puts his pen down and leans back in his chair, "It's bloody suicide Walker, but with your new information we might just avoid a massacre by nipping and tucking a few of the orders that are coming down to us"

"Any news on when the Advance will be Sir?" asks Walker

"It is supposed to be in a few hours, at seven thirty this morning, but word has been sent that is has been postponed again due to the weather, so, probably tomorrow, depending on the blasted rain"

Walker forces a smile, "A grand way to start July Sir"

Poyntz is just about to dismiss Walker but stops when the young officer speaks to him again,

"Sir, could I suggest to you that some of the chaps might deserve a commendation of sorts for their work today"

"Go on Lt"

"Well Sir, the CSM, the Sergeant and two of the privates found, destroyed and killed six enemy soldiers in a huge gun point that we had no idea was there, from what I can tell the Sergeant jumped into the trench and killed one of the German soldiers who had dropped a live grenade, the CSM is certain that both of them would have been killed or wounded without the Sergeants actions"

"Put it in writing Lt and I will review it" Poyntz says

"Also, Sir, Lance Corporal Clark and four privates made a daring and brave reconnaissance of the enemy positions close to Montauban de Picardie, they also could perhaps be mentioned"

The Major puts down his pen,

"Anybody else Lt? Yourself perhaps?"

"No Sir, I just supervised Private Marrables doing his sketches"

"Put it all on paper Lt, including your splendid artistic supervision"

Walker suppresses a smile, "Thank you, Sir, I will"

Martin is having a very welcome cup of tea with William, they have exchanged addresses and Martin has promised to visit Bridport when the war is over as he has never been to the coast, the men shake hands and wish each other luck.

"Be safe Sarge, keep the Hun in front of you!"

"Always William, good luck, see you by the seaside one day!"

"Sarge" William speaks as he leaves, Martin looks up, "If you happen to hear I haven't made it, me and my mates are in the first wave, visit Bridport anyway, find my old Mum and tell her about how we met, she will laugh and laugh at me falling into a thorn bush on the battlefield"

"Bloody tell her yourself William"

William looks at Martin, who then says, "Ok, I will, but when you are there, and you will be there, you had best be buying the beer!"

"A deal Sarge, Palmers Bridport beer is the best in the world" He licks his lips, "So very dark and sweet"

The lorry taking the Dorset's back to their trenches sets off in a cloud of fumes and several hard jolts that cause the men to hold on tight, Martin walks back toward his platoon,

"Come on you lot, back to the trenches for us" they all look tired and gloomy, "What is wrong with you lot, anyone would think that there is a war on!"

"Lt Finks patrol didn't go as well as ours Sarge, they were looking at the German front lines to the West, Corporal Thurgood and six others are still missing, they got separated when the artillery shelling landed very close to them"

"Who are the six missing?"

Oakes appears,

"Palmer, Sutton, Humbles, Gray, Bacchus and Childerley"

Martin nods slowly, "Not good news, but there is hope lads, they might be out there and unable to get back, Phil Thurgood is a good NCO, he will know what to do"

"Gilbey, Cann, back to D company" Oakes gets the men moving, "Lance Corporal Clark, you are to remain here with this platoon, you are their new Lance Jack"

Martin is pleased, Nobby is a good soldier and a fine leader,

"My platoon, let's take Nobby to our trench and show him what this war is all about shall we!"

"Yes Sarge!" they all say, including Nobby.

* * *

The morning of the 29th of June 1916 is dry, but it has been raining for most of the night, Martin and his platoon are soaked to the skin, the only good news for them is the advance has been postponed yet again, they are all set for another day, their fourteenth, in the trenches.

"Any chance we can brew up Sarge?"

Martin looks up and down the long line of the trenches the men from the 2nd Bedfordshires are in, he can see a few are using the trench stoves and mess tins to boil water for a brew, these thin trenches are not ideal for boiling water or cooking meals, the reserve trenches are better as they are bigger and have areas build into them for the soldiers to stow kit, to cook or even grab some sleep in, some have decent dugouts, although these are only used by the officers, it isn't unknown for the men to brew up in these areas as they are dry and warmer than being outside. The front line trenches at Maricourt are not very wide and are nearly always wet and muddy, today isn't any different, the rain from last night has not helped the situation with the mud, but Martin could do with a decent brew, he now refuses to drink any hot brew that arrives in an old petrol can.

"Crack on H, make sure there is enough for the whole platoon to have at least half a cup"

"Great, thanks Sarge"

H Jarman takes off his knapsack and removes his trench stove, it is in a red cardboard box, Martin notices that it isn't the issue stove, the *Tommy Cooker*, a small tin of fuel with a metal ring on which to place your tin or kettle to boil water, many of the men don't use them as it can take over an hour to boil a half pint of water,

"What have you got there, H?"

"It's the latest kit for cooking in the trenches with"

He lifts up the box to show Martin, a small cardboard box with the words 'Anglo's Trench Fires' emblazoned on the top and the sides,

"These were issued late last year, but as per usual the blokes at the front had to wait for them to get here, a bit like the new Brodie helmets"

Martin understands his frustration, the '*new*' helmets are a design upgrade on the old style Brodie helmet, the latest version has had the liner re designed to make them a bit more comfortable to wear, in Martins opinion the small change makes no difference, the leather chinstrap is either too tight or too loose when in position, so much so that he rarely wears his with the chinstrap on, preferring to put the leather strap over the back rim of the helmet. The modified version had been introduced in Spring this year, but the Bedfordshires had only go theirs a few weeks ago, each man had to swap his old helmet for a new one, the steel from the old helmets will be melted down and used as part of the ongoing war effort. Alfie, John, Dennis, Sharpie and Nobby appear in the trench just as H is lighting the solid fuel block on the burner, the metal support is in place and ready for a tin or kettle to boil the water in,

"That's the barbed wire checked and a new roll of about fifty yards has been laid by us and by George Freshwaters lads in the front of our trenches"

"Good work Nobby, any issues out there, I didn't hear anything, so I presume that all went well"

Nobby nods, "Not a peep from the German trenches, in fact the only person we saw moving was Sergeant Laycock who is out and about visiting the Lewis gunners in the West trenches" he looks at H who is blowing gently on the solid fuel as it catches alight "Good effort H, a brew is needed, its bloody parky for June in France"

"Alfie, have you got the old helmet?" asks H

Alfie throws H an angry look, Martin tries to hide his smile,

"Helmet?" he asks H

"Well, Sarge, it is like this, I, well, I" He gives up trying to make up an excuse, "I kept my old helmet; I took out all the gubbins inside and it is great for brewing tea in"

"Best you get on with it then H" He looks at the rest of the lads, "Has anyone got any Oxo left?"

"I have Sarge, you want one?"

"Yes, please Nobby" Martin replies with a tired smile. Nobby reaches into one of the side pockets of his knapsack and takes out a small red Oxo tin, he opens it and hands Martin a small foil wrapped block of Oxo, he takes one for himself,

"Anyone else? I have got two lumps left"

The others all refuse and state they will have a brew of tea, Dennis wants coffee, but no one has any, Alfie sheepishly hands H the old Brodie helmet, it is filled to the brim with water from H and Alfie's water canteens,

"Give me that H, I will go and refill them at the water point, anyone else?"

"I will come with you Alfie, I need a trip to the latrines" John Marrables says,

"Again John? Have you got dysentery?"

"I don't think so Corp" he answers Nobbys question,

"It might be worth a trip to the docs dugout mate, get some jollop for your guts"

"I will be alright Corp" he assures the NCO.

Alfie and John take all the water canteens for refilling, at least the water here is piped, the engineers have done a great job of fitting piped water from the outskirts of Maricourt to the trenches, sadly, some idiot has dug the latest latrine within yards of the stand pipe, but having water from a tap is much preferable to the water delivered to those in trenches without water, like the tea, it is delivered in old petrol cans and the recent addition of chloride of lime to the water, to keep it as clean as possible makes it taste vile, the mixture of petrol fumes and chloride of lime has driven many to use water from the trenches and shell holes. Martin has seen this happen throughout his time at the Western front and has seen many men get sick and some die from dysentery, so although they all joke with John about his frequent visits to the trench toilet, he knows it will need addressing when they get back to the reserve section, whenever that will be. The last two weeks in the front line trenches is taking its toll on the platoon, a diet of cold bully beef and stale bread is getting boring, even when they get the opportunity to fry some bacon, it is gristly and unappetising, the rain over the past week has stopped nearly all cooking and boiling in the trenches, without any overhead cover it has been impossible to keep anything dry, including the stoves.

Martin looks up and down the trench system, they had been unlucky to get a section of the trench that has no overhead '*bridges*', planks of thick solid wood that enable men and vehicles to move over the trenches to get to the opposite side if needs be, the platoons near to these locations are able to take it in turns to cook a mess tin full of hot food, even the hated Maconochie would be welcomed by Martins platoon today, as long as it Is hot they would not mind, but their section is open and the walls of the trenches are so soft that digging into them to create a '*cave*' or sleeping area is too dangerous, the lads are sleeping standing up or in a crouched position with only a thin waterproof cape to protect them from the elements. Machine gun fire is heard from above the trench coming from the German trenches, Martin hears the Lewis gunners return fire,

"Front positions!" Martin yells at his platoon; similar orders are being shouted up and down the trenches by nearby platoon commanders.

Martin throws himself against the front wall of the trench and slowly crawls up the incline to the top, Nobby, Dennis, Sharpie and H have followed suit, their Lee Enfield rifles are held in front of them, these will be the first thing to clear the summit of the trench, Martin hears Oakes shouting,

"I want reports and I want them now!"

Martin looks over the edge of the trench and waits for the expected hail of bullets to land in and around his location,

"Look!" yells Dennis

Martin sees that his private is pointing to his left, he sees five figures running toward the trench system, they are dragging another figure, seemingly lifeless,

"Hold fire!" Martin shouts as loud as he can both ways into the trenches, "It is some of our lads!"

Oakes is now in Martins section of trench, the five soldiers dragging the lifeless soldier between them reach the top of the trenches and all throw themselves over toward safety, none caring how deep the drop is on the inside, the Lewis gunners are still firing toward the German positions, and this has slowed down their returning use of their machine guns.

Martin looks around quickly, H appears to be hit, he is hunched over,

"H!" he yells, "Are you hit?"

"No Sarge" H replies, "I am protecting the stove and the water, it is nearly boiled, and I didn't want it knocked over"

Martin laughs, a thankful laugh, he moves over to the five men who are all lying in the bottom of the trench, caring not if they are lying in the cold, wet mud, Martin recognises one of them as Corporal Phil Thurgood, he also recognises the dead soldier, Sergeant Augustus Henry Laycock and he is certainly dead, his eyes are open and he has the thousand yard stare that the dead sometimes have,

"Nobby, get two others, get a stretcher and take Sgt Laycock to the padre" Oakes commands,

"Where is he Sir" one of them asks,

Oakes looks over his shoulder, "A hundred yards or so back there in the reserve trenches, he will be in the trench HQ, Augustus will need to be registered"

Nobby sends Dennis away for a stretcher and he and Sharpie move the lifeless body to the far side of the trench before lifting it, somewhat unceremoniously, onto the edge of the back wall.

Martin is helping Phil to his feet,

"You missed a great dinner party last night Herb, where were you?"

Herb Thurgood does not smile, "I tell you Martin, we have been to hell and back, I am still not sure how we got back here" he looks at his patrol, they are getting themselves back to their feet and leaning against the front wall of the trench,

"Smoke 'em if you have 'em lads" Oakes says quietly to Herb's patrol, he turns to Thurgood, "Who is missing Corporal?"

Thurgood hangs his head, then looks up, "Privates H Bacchus and A Childerley Sir" he takes a deep breath, "Bacchus was killed yesterday, our hiding place was discovered by the Hun, he charged them, firing his rifle as he did so, we all got away because of him"

"You saw him go down Corporal?" Oakes asks

Thurgood nods and again hangs his head, "Also private Childerley, he was with us up until we ran across no man's land in front of this trench, we saw Augustus get taken down by the machine gun, I saw Paul turn and begin to fire his rifle at the machine gun post, it's in a shell hole about sixty yards from here" he accepts a cigarette from Martin, he lights it from Martins match, "When we picked Augustus up and dragged him, I thought we were all here until just now"

"He got hit Corp, I heard him shout and when I turned, he was down and not moving"

"What's your name son?" Oakes asks the private that spoke up,

"Private Humbles Sir, Ernie Humbles"

"Good lad Ernie, who are the other lads with you?"

Ernie Humbles looks around to see his mates' smoking cigarettes and accepting a hot drink from H,

"Private's 'Dolly' Gray, sorry Sir, I don't know his real name, Private F Sutton, and Private 'LG' Palmer"

"Patsy's younger Brother Ralph" Martin then adds, "Dolly's first name is Arthur"

Oakes acknowledges Martins comments, he addresses Herb,

"Corporal, when you lads have finished your brews, come to the dugout in the trenches behind this one, the Lt Col will need a report"

"We will Sir, I have lots to report about the German positions, they are much stronger than we have been led to believe" He looks at Oakes, "When is the big push going to be Sir?"

Oakes smiles, "Not today lad, not today" he nods at Martin and leaves, making his way along the trenches, everyone knows Company Sergeant Major Oakes, and everybody gets out of his way.

Martin hands Herb a hot drink, who accepts it and smells it before taking a sip,

"Oxo, bloody lovely, thanks"

Martin looks across at H, who shrugs his shoulders,

"I will put another helmet of water on Sarge" he says

Herb begins to talk, and Martin listens to him as he explains why they did not get back yesterday after the patrol. He speaks highly of the 2nd Lt that they were on patrol with,

"2nd Lt Fink is pretty new to this war, he only arrived with us late in March, I thought he was just some posh kid from London, but he was born in India, went to some private school in West Kensington, he went back to India to work on a rubber plantation and then volunteered for this mess last year" He takes out his cigarettes and gives one to Martin, they light it from the butt of Martins cigarette he is just finishing, Herb continues, "He led from the front mate, in the trenches we came across a German patrol, he was the first to react and shot two of them before we could join in, it wasn't his fault that we got separated" he takes a large gulp of hot Oxo and two pulls on his cigarette "We were making our way back and we were in an area being shelled heavily and we lost touch with him and the others, this was when Bacchus got it in the trenches, he saved us all mate, I will have to get it reported" A sip of the hot drink and then another, "We had to back track and ended up spending the night in a trench" He gently laughs, "As it turns out the enemy were about ten yards away in the same bloody trench, I had to order Dolly to stop laughing, the stupid sod was going to give us away!" Martin looks at Dolly Gray and raises his eyebrows, the private raises his mug of tea,

"Everything alright Sarge?" He asks,

"Just hearing from your NCO about your fit of giggles this morning"

Dolly turns his attention to Herb, "Sorry about that Corp, I just found it amusing that we had spent the night in a trench only feet away from the Germans and neither of us knew about the other"

Herb tells him not to worry and that he is glad he managed to stop laughing, or the situation may have been much worse.

"He is a good kid Martin, but his biggest problem is his lack of fear, he is not frightened by anything" Martin does not answer but let's Herb continue, "When we got to the edges of the German lines" he looks Martin directly in the eyes "And they are much bloody closer than any of us think, they have machine gun posts all over the place" he leans in and whispers, "There are thousands of them mate, I do mean thousands" he leans back and finishes, "We saw our chance as the Germans were brewing up and eating sausages, over the top and we just ran, the rest you know"

"Finish your Oxo mate, then go back a few trenches and report to the Company Sergeant Major, he will take you to see the old man" Martin stands up, he looks straight at Dolly, "Don't forget to leave our mugs here"

Dolly raises his mug again, "Nearly done Sarge, thanks"

The following morning is the last day of June, the sun should be shining but the ever present smoke from the continuing bombardment hangs heavily in the air, both the Germans and the Allied guns are really throwing a lot of artillery this morning, the noise is deafening, Martin has lost John Marrables, the M.O insisting that he leave the trenches to get some treatment for his obvious case of dysentery, in fact, over a dozen officers and soldiers have been taken off the line because of this. In the two weeks that the Bedfordshires have been in the trenches at Maricourt, ten of the regiment have been killed in action, 2nd Lt

Hankinson is the only officer to have lost his life, six soldiers have been killed on the battlefield and in the trenches, one man died of accidental wounds, two other soldiers made it to the hospital but soon died of their wounds, two are missing, presumed dead, three are in the hospital with wounds inflicted accidentally, three are in the hospital with self-inflicted wounds, they will all be court martialled, almost certainly found guilty and will face long prison sentences for " *Wilfully maiming himself with intent to render himself unfit for service* " an offence under section 18 of the Army act 1881, nine poor souls are suffering with shell shock. Martin has seen a few cases of shell shock and does not follow or agree with the normal chatter in the trenches that the sufferer has 'lost his nerve', he knew of one soldier, a regular and long serving private who has been decorated several times for bravery, both in the Boer War and in this war, one afternoon at the beginning of June after a particularly bad day of being shelled and having to run across barbed wire, then jump over the corpses of your countrymen and kill other men for no other reason than they are on the other side and will kill you if they can. This soldier sat in the bottom of a trench, took of his helmet, and refused to speak, Martin recalls clearly that he was staring ahead just like a dead man, then he began laughing and he would not stop, he laughed maniacally for over an hour before he was taken to the casualty clearing station. Martin had heard a private soldier, new to the battalion, say to his mate,

"Lost his bloody nerve that one", and he had exploded in anger at the young soldier, it was the young soldier that seemed to have lost his nerve, both during and after Martins vociferous rant at him. Shell-shock and shell concussion cases could have the letter '*W*' prefixed to any official report on the casualty, if the shell shock was due to being in action or from other enemy actions, the patient will be entitled to be ranked as 'wounded' and to wear on his arm a 'wound stripe' on his uniform. If, however, the man's breakdown does not follow a shell explosion or any recent enemy contact, it is not thought to be 'due to the enemy', he will have the prefix '*Shell shock*', or the letter '*S*' for sickness, will be prefixed to his casualty report, these men are not entitled to wear a wound stripe or entitled to any pension. Martin finds this harsh, he has at many times, and he knows others feel the same, not wanted to go into battle, not wanted to climb over the trench, not run at the enemy and most certainly not wanted to kill another human being. Something keeps him going, his will to survive is strong and he knows it is only the thought of spending the rest of his life with his Grace, to feel her arms around his neck or the softness and warmth of her body when they lie together, that he is still in all this madness, it is all for her, not for the King or the country, those thoughts left him many months ago, it is all for her, she is his life, and she is keeping him alive.

The morale of the men is low, they all yearn for a properly cooked meal and a hot drink that doesn't taste of petrol, they also need a mail delivery, his last letter from Grace had been delivered a day before they came into the trenches, it had been written on the 8th June and had arrived with him by the afternoon of Wednesday 14th June, only a couple of weeks ago but it seems like a lifetime to Martin. He has read the letter more than half a dozen times, feeling elated by the words of love and affection and feeling saddened by the distance that separates them, he is pleased to read that Grace and Alice are still meeting regularly but due to being busy at work, it had been a week or so since they had last met but she is hoping to get a few days off the following weekend and to spend it with Alice, as always she signed off using words that he cherishes every day, "*Yours forever, Grace'*, even thinking of these words makes him smile. Mail delivery to the front line had been stopped due to the conditions in the trenches and because of the enemy shelling, it is impossible to get through safely, the men of the 2nd Bedfordshires had been told that they should be relieved after the big push, then mail would be available to them.

"Martin"

He looks up and sees a fellow Sgt, Percy Compton, also a fellow holder of the DCM, he had won his by running out into no-man's-land on no less than six occasions and under horrendous enemy gun fire he dragged six men from the battlefield to the trenches,

"Morning Percy, how goes it?" Martin greets him,

"Not bad" he takes a piece of paper from his tunic," All NCOs on my list have to meet at the HQ dugouts at the Chateau in an hour for a briefing" he puts it away "Me and you are on it mate"

"Any idea what it is for Percy?" asks Martin

Percy shakes his head, "To do with our push over the top I would suppose"

Martin nods, "Is Nobby on the list?"

Percy takes out the piece of paper again, he runs his finger down the list,

"Lance Corporal Clark is on my list, but I have no idea if it is your lad"

Martin gives Percy Nobbys army number,

"Best bring him with you Martin" the paper is put away again, "Must get on, I have to find a few more, any idea where Henry Nicholls and his lads are?"

Martin points to the trench running adjacent to this one, "In there mate"

Percy thanks him and is gone, Martin calls over to Nobby,

"We are needed at the Chateau, a briefing in an hour"

"That can't be good news then Sarge"

Martin agrees, "Let's get the lads ready for the off, it will be happening soon"

Just under an hour later, Martin and Nobby are standing with a dozen or so other NCO's, he can see two 2nd Lt's standing by the dugout with Oakes and the Lt Col, Martin nods at some of the soldiers he hasn't seen for a while, he is pleased to see that all are uninjured and still in good health, Lance Sergeant Levi Smith, of course known as Smudge or Smudger, pats Martin on the back and shakes his hand, Phil Thurgood is there as well, he is taking a lot of stick from Lance Corporal Arthur Mee of the 1st Battalion and on loan to the 2nd, and Lance Sergeant Sam Simons, Martin gets a bit of their conversation as he passes by,

"Herb, make sure you don't get lost and end up camping out again" Andy says

"I don't want to be anywhere near your platoon mate, spending the night with the Kaiser is not my idea of fun!" Sam Simons joins in.

As Martin walks by, he hears Herb laugh and reply with a volley of abuse at both men.

He nods at Lance Corporal Fred 'Boycee' Boyce and Nobby stops for a few seconds to chat with Acting Corporal Ernie Cannon, they all stop talking when Oakes calls them to attention, the Lt Col stands them at ease and begins his briefing.

The Battalion will be advancing on the German line's tomorrow morning along with over one hundred and twenty thousand Allied troops, some will lead the initial assault, some will be in immediate support roles to those leading, others will be in secondary advance and reserve roles, to ensure continued pressure is put on the German lines. The 2nd Bedfordshire men will be in support of the 17th and 20th Battalion Kings Liverpool regiment, who will lead the advance, two officers and sixty other ranks from the Bedfordshires will remain behind and be the third line of attack, to clean up and deal with any enemy soldiers left behind by the first two waves of advancing Allied soldiers. Martin, Nobby and their platoon, along with a platoon led by Lance Sergeant Smudge Smith and acting Corporal Alfred Howard, they will be on the far right flank as part of a team led by 2nd Lt Anstee, their role is to follow behind the 17th Kings and assault the far German positions at Dublin trench, from a point at the redoubt to a point four hundred yards to the West at the boundary with the Briqueterie, when this area has been taken, a strong point is to be established immediately and they will be assisted by one platoon of the Battalion pioneers. The establishment of a strongpoint will make that sector a key point in any further defensive fighting and will anchor the overall defence line taken during the Allied attack, Martin remembers a large redoubt with heavily fortified bunker in it, he will mention this to Lt Anstee because when it has been taken the platoons and the Pioneers may not have much to do to ensure it remains as a good and advantageous position for them to consolidate.

The 17th Kings will advance in four lines, with approximately one hundred yards between each line, the companies from the Bedfordshires will follow immediately behind the last wave of soldiers from the 17th, Martin's platoon will be part of this team. Each platoon will have intervals of fifty yards between them and one hundred yards between each line, the first two lines will advance into Faviere trench, then into Casement Trench, with the 17th and the last two lines will remain in the Casement trench system until the 17th and the two lines of Bedfordshires have advanced again into the Dublin Trench system, when this has been completed the last two lines will advance from the Casement Trenches and into the Dublin trenches, they are to remain there and not move until instructed, these trenches must be consolidated and remain under Allied control, the 19th Kings will be the reserve battalion. Martin's platoon will be in the first line of Bedfordshires, directly behind the 17th Kings. When a strong point has been established on this side, the 20th Kings will advance, when instructed from Dublin trenches, go through on the opposite side of the newly taken strong point and attack La Briqueterie, Martin now knows that it is not a village, but a brickwork and he feels a little stupid. They are told that the areas they take up to and including the Dublin trench, and the strongpoint, will need to be held until other Allied soldiers from the third and fourth armies, move in to take Montauban from the Germans, when this is done, the advance on La Briqueterie will go ahead.

Lt Col Poyntz tells them he is going to alter the advance plans he has received from Army command; he gives thanks for the information received from the two patrols that went out overnight on the 28th into Bernafay Wood and into areas of the Casement and Dublin Trench systems, Poyntz tells the men that because of this information he has been in contact with the commanding officers from the 17th and 20th Kings Liverpool regiments and passed the information to them. It has been agreed that a charge toward the German positions will be nothing short of suicide, so the Kings soldiers will advance slowly, crawling if they must, the artillery support will continue for fifteen minutes after the advance begins, before moving forward toward other German positions, this should give them and the Bedfordshires a chance to take the Faviere and Casement trench systems without huge loss of life. The final words from Poyntz are,

"Loss of life is a certainty, we must advance and take these positions, failure to do so will affect the whole attack if any part of the advancing line fails to take their area" he pauses and looks at his men, "We will take our assigned areas, but charging over the top is not an option for me, so, men of the 2nd Bedfordshires we have a job to do tomorrow, we must do it"

Oakes instructs all NCOs to have their platoons mustered and ready by 0130 the following morning, the advance, or Zero Hour, will be called and all platoons will advance as instructed by Lt Col Poyntz. Martin and Nobby hang around after they have been dismissed to look for Smudge and Albert, they find them and the four of them move away from the front of the dugout and find a quiet place to have a cigarette,

"I am bloody glad that the Old Man has his head screwed on" Albert says, "Otherwise we might all be dead in a few hours"

"You have to feel for the poor sods that don't have our information or because it has been ignored by high command" Martin agrees with Albert,

"Any idea who is further up the line from us?" asks Smudge.

Martin tells him he knows that the 1st Dorset's are advancing toward Authuille through an area known as 'Sausage Alley', moving from trenches just outside of the village, the German army also has a huge presence in both Fricourt and Thiepval, none of it will be good. The men all shake hands before they leave to prepare their platoons for the advance, it won't be easy, nights in the trenches are bad enough but knowing you are to climb out of your trench, climb over the top and to move forward, the only good news Martin can give them is that it will not be a charge into a hail of machine gun bullets, it will be slow and careful, he doubts this will be enough to calm his men.

The artillery bombardment starts before it is light, Martin has never heard such a noise, over the past few days there has been hundreds of thousands of shells sent across to the German defences, but not like this, he is unable to distinguish one shell being fired to another, the sound of firing is continuous, it is now light and the view across the trenches is hazy with the early morning mist and smoke from the exploding shells, to his left and to his right he can see his friends and colleagues from the 2nd Bedfordshires lying on or standing by the front trench wall, all ready to move off when told to do so, he knows that the 17th and 20th Kings Liverpool lads are ten yards in front of them in trenches at a right angle to the open battlefield, they are to go first, Martin and his platoon are to follow on. He hears the artillery move position, he can tell by the sound of the explosions, they have certainly moved a little away from their front lines.

He looks at his pocket watch, it is seven twenty five in the morning.

Seven thirty is zero hour.

"Steady lads, five minutes and we will be ready to move, remember, don't run, I am ordering you all to hit the ground if you hear machine gun fire, do not, I repeat, do not carry on walking toward it"

They all mumble that they understand.

Seven twenty six.

"Check your kit lads, make sure you know where everything is"

He knows that they already know, they have been wearing the same kit since this began.

Seven twenty seven.

2nd Lt Anstee arrives, "Morning chaps, remember, steady as you go, remember what your Sergeants and Corporals have told you"

Seven twenty eight

The artillery barrage moves yet again, Martin believes that it has moved from aiming at the German positions at Faviere trench to their positions at Casement trench.

Seven twenty nine.

The men are silent, some have their eyes closed, some are staring at nothing in particular and others have a tight grip on their rifles.

Seven thirty.

Whistles are heard from all along the trench system, Martin hears the shout,

"Advance!"

From the trenches in front of his, the Kings Liverpool lads are climbing out and moving forward,

"Advance!"

The command is given by 2nd Lt Anstee, to his credit he is first over the top, Martin can hear the chatter of machine gun fire from further along the line to his left, the artillery continues to pound the German defences, he stands up and climbs over the edge of the trench, he is met by a wall of smoke, he is pleased as this will afford them some cover, he takes a steady step forward, then another, then two more, he makes good ground and moves onward, forward, toward the enemy. The smoke clears a little and he can just about make out the 17th Kings final line, it is in front of him, not the one hundred yards as designated, they are much closer, he continues forward, his platoon is either side of him, they step through reams of barbed wire, the artillery has successfully destroyed most of the first line of the German defences, including the masses of barbed wire and wooden staves. The first line of trenches they come to is the Faviere Trenches, Martin watches on, the Kings are advancing over the top of the trenches, he realises that they must be empty or with very little enemy activity,

"Check the system lads, mop up any enemy" 2nd Lt Anstee shouts,

Martin points to where he wants his platoon to go into the trench, they are led in by Nobby, Martin remains at the top of the trench with his rifle in a position to fire if needed, it isn't, the trench has been abandoned by the Germans, they press on toward Casement trenches, the 17th Kings are now the designates100 yards in front of them. The artillery has moved to a more forward position, nearer to Dublin Trench and Dublin redoubt, Martin knows he has now been advancing for about a quarter of an hour, he hears a voice shout,

"Casement!"

They have arrived at Casement trenches and have, so far, met very little resistance, he arrives at the top of the trench system and looks in, the artillery has also successfully cut a huge amount of the German wire that had been in front of this trench system. Most of the German soldiers had been taking cover in their dugouts at the base of the trenches, they have been caught out and are now prisoners, there are dozens of them, Martin can see the lads from the 20th are remaining with the prisoners, all of whom have their hands in the air and their rifles at their feet. The German lines in front of Montauban de Picardie are well structured and very strong, even the front line defences at Casement trenches are better than most of the hastily dug Allied trenches he has been in, the steep wooden steps from the top of the trenches have been built by craftsmen, they are solid and become wider toward the base of the trench, there is mud in these trenches, but, as Martin has seen before, the German engineers have put in a wooden planked raised floor, enabling the men to walk without having to be ankle or even knee high in wet mud. Every five yards there is compartments built into the trench walls, these compartments have been lined with planks and have supported wooden roofs, these are also solidly built, some even have tarpaulin covers to completely enclose the soldiers inside, this enables the men to shelter from the elements, the dugouts are purpose built, most of the Allied dugouts have been hastily built using wooden pallets and tarpaulin. It is in these where most of the enemy had been when the 17th arrived, they surrender without any resistance at all. It seems a shame to move out of such good trenches, but the 2nd Bedfordshire soldiers follow on behind the 17th, as they step out of Casement trench machine gun fire can clearly be heard from their left, Martin is certain that it is not within the boundary of their attack area, he believes it to be the attack on Glatz redoubt, a few hundred yards to the West of their position, the 21st Brigade, also part of the 30th Division and the 2nd Bedfordshires old brigade before being assigned to the 89th brigade, are taking on this area, Martin hopes that the machine guns he can hear are British, but he has his doubts. The 19th Kings arrive and take charge of the prisoners, the 20th Kings move forward alongside the 17th Kings and the 3rd Battalion from the 153rd French regiment, they have just joined on the east side, they have also not encountered a great deal of resistance from the enemy, the 89th machine gun company are also with the 2nd Bedfordshires, they will establish a machine gun at the Dublin Trench strongpoint when it is taken. Martin takes a look at his pocket watch, it is eight thirty, they have been advancing for an hour and so far, no casualties from the 2nd Bedfordshires, the 17th and the 20th Kings are moving off, Martin can hear machine gun chatter in front of him again, this trench might not be as easy as the first two, smoke candles have been lit by the 17th Kings, this is the cue for the Bedfordshire men to move,

"Advance Bedfordshires!" the order from Anstee is heard, even above the artillery and the fighting going on all around them. Martin is out of the trench and looks ahead, the smoke is clearing, and he can see the Liverpool men are making good ground, a few have been hit and are on the ground, they move on, they have orders that no wounded man will be escorted back to Allied lines by an unwounded man, he hears a scream to his left, he looks as he moves. He hears,

"Fred! Fred! Are you hit?"

He cannot make out who is shouting or who has been hit, he had seen Fred Feast at Faviere trench, it might be him, Martin pushes on regardless, he sees Richard Beswick and Richard Ball both fall, both are dead before they hit the ground, he hears a shout from the 17th or the 20th lines,

"Dublin!"

They have reached Dublin trench, he can just make out, to his right, the French infantry are entering the Redoubt, he hears shots fired, but not many, then a cheer from the French soldiers, it seems as if Dublin Redoubt has been taken,

"Move on men!" Anstee encourages them all to move into line with the Kings Liverpool soldiers,

"Orders are to remain at Dublin trench and defend and consolidate" Anstee speaks to Martin and Smudge, "The 17th and the 20th will remain here and keep the trench nearest to the Redoubt, we are to enter the trench system and clear up any further enemy and deal with any resistance"

Martin and Smudge are to split up and take their respective platoons into different areas of the trench system, other teams from the Bedfordshire regiment will be doing the same all along the Dublin Trench. Martin can hear noise from the redoubt, he looks up and sees the lads from the 89th Machine gun company setting up their weapons, it is obvious that very little needs to be done to this strongpoint, only that losing it is not to happen. The redoubt is a huge area of sandbags, barbed wire, huge wire obstacles, dugouts, and tunnels, all reinforced with heavy wooden beams and staves, the Pioneer team are moving in, they will reinforce the few areas that need it, but all in all it is in very good shape.

Martin and Smudge are ready to move off,

"Remember lads, there should not be any British or French soldiers in the sections we are going into" Martin looks at all of them, "If you see a man and his hands are not high in the air, shoot him"

Anstee puts the map on the trench wall,

"These are our areas, one team led by Sgt Smith will go this way" he runs his finger along a red line on the map" he looks at Martin, "You and your chaps will obviously go the other way" he pauses and points behind himself, to areas either side of the traverses in the trenches, "We can see the machine gun points from here" he points again, "So, the entrances to them must be in your areas, be careful"

Martin says good luck to Smudge, and he leaves with his platoon,

"Nobby, are we all ready?" he asks his Corporal,

Nobby looks at the platoon,

"H?" Jarman nods back

"Alfie?" who replies

"Yes Corp"

"Dennis?" another nod, this time from Waldock

"Sharpie lad?"

"All good corp"

Martin asks, "Who has the bombs?"

Dennis puts up his hand, "Got three Sarge"

Most of the men have a couple of hand grenades with them as well, as far as he knows, none of them have yet fired a shot during this attack, each man should have the one hundred and seventy rounds issued to each of them last night. Martin and his platoon set off, starting at the front line trenches then moving back into the German support trenches, after only ten yards Martin stops, there is an opening to his left, he points at Nobby and Sharpie to move past the gap and cover as he intends to take the others into the unknown area, he nods, Nobby and Sharpie move quickly across the gap, no shots are incoming from the gap, Nobby has his gun pointed down the trench and Sharpie has his aimed into the area now in front of them. Martin enters the gap and follows the new, thinner trench, it turns sharply to his left, and he is facing a blind corner, he indicates for the others to stop, he lowers his body to a crouch position and slowly puts his head around the corner. He breathes a sigh of relief, it is an abandoned machine gun nest, he hopes it is one that he could see from the front line trench, the gun is still in place as are boxes of ammunition,

"Clear!" he shouts, the others join him,

"Bloody hell!" exclaims Dennis, "Look at all this ammo, can we use the gun Sarge?"

Martin raises his eyebrows, "Which way is it pointing Private?"

Dennis realises he has asked to fire a gun pointing at the British rear lines, he rolls his eyes,

"Sorry Sarge, I wasn't thinking"

Martin tells him that the support teams from the 17th Lancers, who are the 30th Divisions 'runners', will be told about the gun and if it is needed to be taken, they will do it, if not it will be destroyed.

They move back to the main trench, Martin nods at Nobby who moves off with Sharpie, rifles held high and fingers on the triggers, they reach another gap on the right side, Nobby tells Sharpie to run to the other side, as he moves, they all hear a shot fired, Sharpie is on the ground, they know he is alright because he keeps rolling away from the gap and is shouting,

"Shit! Shit! Shit!"

Martin takes a hand grenade from his webbing, Sharpie stops him,

"He has gone Sarge, further back into the trench"

"Just one?" asks Martin

Sharpie nods,

"You stay here Sharpie, Alfie will stay with you" He looks at the others, "Let's go"

Martin turns into the gap, it is clear, but just ahead he can see another blind point, this one turns right but it also has another gap at on the left side, he has two areas to cover, slowly moving forward into the gap, he takes two steps when he sees a German soldier run from the blind spot and into the gap on the left side, he is quickly followed by another and then another, the third enemy soldier is firing a pistol, but he is not aiming he is firing to get away. Martin and the others hit the floor of the trench, no one has been hit, he calls Dennis forward,

"Den, I think that gap on the left might be a bunker, the blind turn on our right must lead to another machine gun nest" he points at the gap on the right, "Put a bomb in there will you"

Dennis nods and slowly moves forward, taking a bomb from his webbing, it is primed, and he is ten feet from the gap, Martin has his rifle pointed at the gap, if anyone comes out, he will shoot them, Dennis is five feet away, his step has slowed somewhat, Martin thinks this is understandable, why run toward at least three armed enemy soldiers. When he is about a yard from the entrance, the bomb is primed and he throws it into the gap, it is a dark tunnel with a roof, unlike the rest of the trench system that is open to the elements, he runs and throws himself into the dirt and mud next to his Sergeant.

Martin shouts at the top of his voice, "Bomb!"

The bomb explodes, there is as huge rush of air from inside the tunnel, Martin feels the pressure change in his ears slightly, he stands up and shouts, "Clear!"

The shouting is for the soldiers outside of this trench, he does not want any Allied soldiers standing on the edge of the trench above them with guns pointed and primed ready for use.

Nobby is on his feet and has run to the blind corner, he puts his head around and shouts,

"Another machine gun, no enemy though"

Martin is on his feet also, he checks everyone is uninjured, they are, and he moves into the gap on the left,

"It is a dugout or a bunker, there are steps going down" he turns to the platoon, "Alfie, can you go back out and see if 2nd Lt Anstee has a trench torch we can use"

Alfie jumps up and is gone,

"What can you see Sarge?" asks Nobby,

"Not much, a huge set of wooden steps leading down into the darkness, the walls are supported by wooden beams and planks are on the wall, it looks like a garden fence" He listens, "I can't hear anything, they must all be dead"

A minute later, Alfie is back, Anstee is with him, Martin looks at the young officer with a confused face,

"Sorry Sergeant, one of you buggers will lose this torch" he lifts up the torch, it is a Orilux trench torch, its main body is made of metal and is the shape of a hip flask, it is covered in dark red leather and has a large bull's eye style glass lens protruding at the front, it has a hinged lid and eyelets on the back, it is powered by three small batteries, "Are we going in here?"

Martin nods and Anstee turns on the torch, its light is not very bright, but it will be fine in the bunker, he puts the torch in his left hand and takes out his revolver with his right, "Shall we Sergeant?"

Martin moves to the front of the gap, Anstee has to bend down to get through the opening at the top of the stairs, the torch light creates shadows on the walls and ceiling of the tunnel, giving the impression of movement, the stairs, six of them, lead to a small area and another entrance on the right. The wood on the walls and ceiling are badly damaged and burnt, evidence that the bomb exploded the other side of the entrance, Anstee steps in, torch held high and revolver in front of him,

"No one here Sergeant"

"I saw three run into here Sir"

They move through a small room, light can be seen from inside the next room, Anstee steps in, Martin follows him, they are now several feet underground, the light they can see is from the far end of this room, another set of steps leading out can be seen in the dimness,

"Here Sergeant!" Anstee suddenly says,

Martin turns, his rifle in his shoulder, finger on the trigger, he knows that there is a round in the chamber as he cocked it before he came into the trench, he can see three German soldiers, all are badly burnt, one is obviously dead, he is face down and lying in an unnatural position, Martin moves his rifle to one of the others, Anstee has the torch held high and his gun on the third German,

"Do you speak German Sergeant?"

"Not a word Sir" Martin replies,

"Hands up" Anstee says to the two surviving enemy soldiers, he lowers his arms to indicate that the men should bring up their arms, the moving torch creates further shadows, Martin sees the other soldier, the man that he is not covering, lift a pistol toward his officer, he turns his rifle and shoots the man, the noise is deafening in the small room, he cocks and reloads and quickly covers the remaining soldier, he hears another shot and realises that Anstee has fired his revolver, he has killed the final soldier.

"The bugger has a grenade in his hand Sergeant, I think I got him before he pulled the pin"

Martin looks at the young officer,

"I bloody hope so!" Anstee laughs, Martin speaks to him, "Thanks Sir, if that had gone off, we would all be mincemeat"

Anstee puts his revolver away, "Thanks to your reflexes, I don't have a bullet from his pistol in me" he nods, "Thanks Sergeant"

They both hear Nobby shout, "Are we all OK down there?"

"Yes, we are fine, we are just going to check another machine gun nest at the other end of the bunker"

Anstee tilts his head and looks at Martin, "Machine gun nest?"

Martin points his gun at the entrance at the far end of the bunker, "After you Sir"

Anstee points the torch at Martins face, "Thank you, Sergeant, ever the gentleman"

They both move toward the light coming in from the steps leading out, both have their guns held high.

By 1230, the trenches have all been searched and cleared, over 300 German prisoners have been taken by the Bedfordshires and the Kings Liverpool soldiers, several dozen have been killed for not complying with the requests of the allied men, four working machine guns and thousands of rounds of ammunition have been also been seized, the prisoners are marched away, only the German officers are allowed to keep their sidearms, this to keep their own troops in order, the 19th Kings take them toward the advanced collection station on the Maricourt to Briqueterie Road, a detachment from the 13th Corps Cyclist Battalion will take charge of them and deliver them to a designated camp. At this time, news reaches them that Montauban has been taken and consolidated, the 4th Company from the 20th Kings is ordered forward to take La Briqueterie, this is where the HQ for the 6th Bavarian Infantry is based, reports suggest that it is being abandoned by the enemy, they are believed to be running toward Bernafay Wood, three platoons of bombers from the Kings and from the Bedfordshires are sent along what is left of the road to cut them off, artillery starts again to support the taking of this area, the 20th Kings soldiers move in. In less than five minutes La Briqueterie is taken, no loss of life on either side as the Germans surrendered.

The advance is completed, the Bedfordshires are ordered to remain in trenches, the engineers and the Pioneers have already started fixing the road that has been all but obliterated by the shelling, by 6pm, the road is fixed and runs over two hundred yards into what was enemy held territory.

All the objectives set out for the soldiers of the 30th division have been met.

During the early part of the evening, two companies from the Bedfordshires are ordered by Brigade HQ, to drop back into the old front-line trenches, these are now for the Divisional reserve soldiers, Martin and his platoon remain in a forward position at Dublin trenches. Smudge and his platoon are sent back with the reserves, Smudge tries to complain that he wants to stay 'at the front', his words are ignored, 2nd Lt Anstee knows that Smudge has lost three of his platoon when a bunker they entered had five Germans in it, Privates Jimmy Liston, Ernest Holden, and Richie Ball all paid the ultimate sacrifice, all five of the Germans are also dead.

Martin is having a cup of hot coffee, coffee that his platoon had found in a bunker, he is with Nobby and Lt Anstee, the officer having just returned from Battalion HQ, which is now situated in the old front lines along with the Divisional reserve, his news is not good.

"All objectives have been met today, but at a high cost" he stops to sip his coffee, he pulls a face, the German coffee is very strong, he continues, "Thousands have been killed today from the Allied forces, God only knows how many Germans are dead" He looks at Martin and Nobby, "Rumour has it that we may have lost up to twenty thousand men this morning"

"Bloody hell" Nobby exclaims,

"Any news on how our other Battalions got on Sir, I know the 7th were involved somewhere on the Somme"

Anstee lets out a huge breath,

"Again, not good news Sergeant, at least a hundred of our 7th Battalion colleagues are dead, and at least double that are injured, the casualty transport stations are full to bursting, it is carnage, the casualty clearing stations behind the lines are already full to bursting as well"

They all stand in silence, a Captain from the 17th Kings Liverpool regiment enters the bunker they are in, they all stand straight,

"No need chaps, no need" he says, he looks tired and drawn,

"Coffee Sir?" Nobby asks "Its bloody lousy but it is hot"

The officer accepts the offer and takes a mug of coffee, he sits in an old wooden chair,

"Sir, are you well?" asks Anstee

"No Lt, not really, I have just heard that the 18th Kings, who were fighting in the next sector to ours have been almost wiped out, it was a sodding massacre." He sips the coffee and lights a cigarette, offering them around, Martin and Nobby take one and light up,

"Have you heard that we took everything we wanted?" he asks

"Yes Sir" Martin replies, "But we also hear losses and casualties are high"

The captain blows out smoke, "Very high Sergeant, I hear that your 7th lads took a hammering, also the Green Howards and the 1st Dorset's didn't fare well"

Martin looks up, "The 1st Dorset's Sir, do you know what happened?"

"Almost wiped out Sergeant, from what I hear, only a handful made it across no man's land, and they were from the final wave, the first five or six waves were machine gunned and massacred"

He puts out his cigarette on the floor, he stands up to leave, "Alright if I borrow this mug?"

"Take it Sir, it is one we found in this bunker, along with the coffee" He thanks them and leaves.

Martin can only think about William Samways, he was in the first wave, Martin is sure that is what he said, he remembers the conversation they had only days ago, the words haunt him,

"If you happen to hear I haven't made it, me and my mates are in the first wave, visit Bridport anyway, find my old Mum and tell her about how we met, she will laugh and laugh at me falling into a thorn bush on the battlefield"

"Bloody hell" he mumbles to himself,

"What's up Sarge?" asks Nobby

"Nothing mate, just thinking out loud" he finishes his cigarette, puts it out on the floor,

"Come on Nobby, let us get back to the lads" he turns to his Corporal," And Nobby, it's Martin, please call me Martin"

Nobby nods and they both leave the bunker, it is dark outside in the trenches, but it is dry, artillery begins to land all around them, the Germans are responding to today's loss.

"Here we go again Martin; here we bloody go again"

* * *

During the night of the 1st and the early morning of the 2nd July the Germans counter attack the trenches and strong points they lost earlier on four separate occasions, heavy artillery followed by infantry assault, the fighting is heavy at times but all the allied trenches and strong points are consolidated, Martin and his platoon had been fighting all of yesterday afternoon and evening, during these battles, on three separate occasions, a truce had been agreed by both sides, men are sent from the trenches to recover the wounded, the dead are to stay where they lay. Martin and Smudges platoons are sent to an area to the East of their position at Dublin trench, to search a location where the 21st Brigade had advanced and had lost many hundreds of men to the German shells, mortars, and machine guns, they recover dozens of injured British soldiers, this task, at times, is more traumatic than the hand to hand fighting they endured during the past day or so due to the horrific injuries sustained to their fellow soldiers. Martin, on more than one occasion moved his platoon past a severely disfigured man, believing than no one could have survived the injuries they are witnessing, but then the soldier will groan, a noise that is not only a cry for help, but a true indication that the injured man is still alive. On one occasion the platoon are walking slowly through the carnage left behind on the battlefront, the terrain is full of shell holes and not a single tree has survived, the occasional shattered tree trunk stands alone sticking out of the ground like an eerie grave marker, Martin and Nobby are paired up and the others from the platoon are nearby, they step over the destroyed corpses of their fellow soldiers, limbs are missing, shrapnel wounds to their bodies revealing internal organs to the world, arms and legs lie alone ripped from their rightful place and dumped in the brown, wet earth, there are rats everywhere, huge beasts with a taste for rotting human flesh.

Martin turns to Nobby when he hears his name called, "What's up Nobby?" he asks

"Nothing Martin, why do you ask?" Nobby seems confused by the question,

"You called my name, didn't you?"

Nobby is shaking his head when they both hear, "Martin" the voice is clear and loud, they both look around and behind them, in the shell hole they have just cleared is where the voice is calling him from,

"Bloody hell Nobby, we have left one for dead!"

Martin jumps back into the shell hole, it is littered with the corpses of British soldiers, he looks around and can see nothing that has the semblance of being alive, he hears it again,

"Martin"

Clear as day, a firm voice and not seemingly that of an injured man, then he sees a movement to his right, amongst three other dead soldiers he can see the face, or what is left of it, of a soldier, his left eye is open and blinking very quickly.

"Nobby over here!"

Nobby yells for Alfie and Sharpie to join them with their stretcher, the three men join their Sergeant who is kneeling next to the body of the soldier, a man who now has half of his face missing. A terrible wound, flesh from the top of the man's nose to his right ear and from his lower right jaw to the top of his right eyebrow is missing, a view into the mans' mouth shows that his teeth, both upper and lower, are missing. His right eye and most of the jaw and skull are missing, an odd sight is that his nostrils have survived but the upper part of his nose is gone and is just a gaping wound, he is able to speak as his upper and lower lip have survived the impact of whatever hit him, there is no blood and the wound appears to be clean and dry, the smell of burnt flesh coming from the man is horrific.

"Martin"

The man says again, weaker this time, as he speaks the grotesqueness of his wound is further enhances as the loose flesh where the cheek used to be moves as he talks, because of the wound, 'Martin' sounds like 'Marshin',

"Good Lord Sarge, this fella knows you" Alfie is taken aback by the horror of the mans' wounds and also that he seems to know Martin, "He is a Sergeant as well, is he one of ours?"

Martin shakes his head, "He does seem to know me" Martin replies, "He is not one of ours, this is the wrong sector, I don't even know what regiment he is from" He looks at the epaulettes on the man's shoulders, "Yorkshire regiment, must be from the 2nd Yorkshires if he is with the 21st Brigade"

"Blimey Sarge, we were with the 21st until a few months ago, that could have been us!" H observes

Nobby moves in next to Martin, he speaks to the Yorkshire Sergeant, "We will get you back to the casualty transport station mate, all will be well"

The man grabs Martin by the arm, "You mean you don't recognise me?"

The man tries to laugh but the noise he makes is horrendous,

"At least you have got your humour mate" Martin responds, "But, sorry, I don't recall you"

The man manages to sit up, he is uninjured anywhere else on his body apart from his face,

"Archie, Archie Basher" Martin must listen carefully as the man's words are slurred and there is a whistling noise as he talks, he is still none the wiser, Archie continues, "2nd Yorkshire regiment" he pauses as he struggles to get the words out, "We met and had a smoke in Belgium, near to a town called Arsehole Brook"

Martin laughs out loud, "When we were in bivvies at Klemskerke!" he remembers "You were the Corporal I met first thing in the morning"

"You must recognise me now Martin, even with this shaving cut I seem to have sustained" Archie points weakly at his wounded face,

The platoon cannot believe how the man is managing to speak, let alone make jokes about his wound,

"Let's get you out of here Archie" he turns and speaks to the platoon, "Stretcher lads, nice and easy now"

"It don't hurt at all" Archie slurs

"Really Sarge?" asks Sharpie

"It was a bloody red hot lump of shrapnel lad, I felt it hit me, it stung for a bit but no blood at all"

Archie attempts to stand but his legs won't allow him, Martin and Nobby grab him and hold onto him,

"Steady Archie, it might not hurt, but your body won't let you move very well, let us get you on the stretcher, you stay still"

Archie allows the men from the Bedfordshire regiment get him onto the stretcher,

"How did it all go Martin? Did we get what we wanted?" Archie asks

Martin instructs the other three to grab a handle of the stretcher, he also takes one and they lift Archie and begin to carry him out of the shell hole,

"We did Archie, but at a huge cost mate"

Martin looks down and Archie's good eye is closed, he is breathing noisily, it can be heard clearly on the strangely quiet battlefield as the air from his lungs leaves his body through the hole in his face, he has passed out. The four men carry the badly wounded Yorkshire soldier to the casualty transport station situated near to the chateau at Maricourt,

"Take a smoke break, then we had best be getting back" Martin instructs his platoon, they move out of the casualty transport station, Martin stays with Archie, who is still unconscious, a soldier with a red cross on his arm walks by,

"Excuse me" the young soldier stops,

"Yes Sarge, what can I do for you?"

"Where are the wounded being taken to?"

"The nearest casualty clearing station is at Corbie, about 15 miles behind the lines" he looks into the distance and at the smoke and the battlefield, "It is the safest place to be I reckon"

Martin nods in agreement and thanks the young medic, he puts his hand on Archies' chest,

"The war is over for you now old man; I hope Blighty is everything you remember it to be"

He walks away leaving the man he has only met twice and on both occasions for only a short period of time, he hopes that Archie will be alright and is shipped home soon.

He lights a cigarette and moves off to find his platoon.

The following two days are spent in the trenches, German artillery and attacks continue throughout both days and the trenches taken on the 1st of July are still under their control, the digging of a new trench, running East from Dublin trench to Briqueterie Road, has assisted with free movement, soldiers can now get to the road without having to leave the trench and exposing themselves in open no man's land. The Germans still have machine guns placed at nearby Bernafay Wood, Martin and his platoon assist with putting out hundreds of yards of barbed wire along the length of the new trench and atop Dublin trench, replacing the German wire destroyed during the artillery bombing, this work keeps them busy, and they are all happy to be relieved, albeit at ten at night on the fourth of July, the 3rd South African Infantry replace them in the front line. The Bedfordshires withdraw to Bois des Tailles just North of the Etinehem, a small town on the banks of the River Somme, Bois des Tailles translates as 'Wood of sizes' and the area is a good as its description, a large area of woodland that, at its edges, is full of tents that are the billets for the battalion, all the men are exhausted, their casualties have been light in comparison to other battalions, including the 7th Bedfordshires, who have had over one hundred of their number killed and at least three times this amount are wounded, the 2nd have had eight killed, fifty six wounded and eight are still missing, one of the dead is a friend of Martins, Henry Barnes, who was killed by German machine gun fire on the third of July. Martin finds his tent, he is sharing with Nobby and Dennis, they all collapse into their army cots and almost immediately fall asleep without changing out of their filthy battledress and without washing or eating.

The morning of Wednesday 5th July 1916 is dry and sunny, Martin is sitting outside of the tent smoking a cigarette, he is dressed only in his trousers, his tunic is hanging up outside and his shirt and undershirt are both on the ground beside him, he hears the tent flap open,

"Morning Sarge"

"Morning Dennis, sleep alright?"

Dennis pulls a face, "Sort of, how about you?"

"It was fine to begin with, but as soon as the sun came up, I was awake"

Dennis stretches his body and yawns, "I could do with a bath and to get my clothes washed"

Martin agrees, he picks up his shirt and undershirt, "Let's go and find out where we can get clean and wash our clothes, I will just grab my knapsack, it has my wash kit and my clean clothes in it"

Dennis does the same, Nobby is still sound asleep, they leave him and walk from the tent village toward a small cottage at the bottom of a gentle slope, they meet Ralph Oakes coming the other way, he is clean and shaved,

"Morning men!" he says happily

"Morning Sir"

"Morning Ralph" Martin replies, "You look better than both of us, where is the wash area?"

Oakes points behind the cottage, "In the barn behind that cottage, there is four huge half barrels and a massive coal boiler in there, the water is bloody clean and bloody hot, it is quiet in there now but won't be for long" Martin lifts up his filthy clothes, Ralph understands, "Yes, you can wash your clothes as well, we should get two or three days' rest, so get them all cleaned up"

"Sir" asks Dennis, "We left all our remaining kit at the Chateau before we went to the front line, do we have to go and retrieve it?"

"No lad, it is all here, find the marquee, it is all in there with the company clerk, take what you need only, it will be going back to the Chateau in a few days"

Ralph turns to Martin, "You can share a tent with another Sgt if you wish"

"No thanks Ralph, there is only three of us in ours anyway, thanks"

Oakes walks toward his tent, Martin and Dennis run toward the barn, not wanting to have the dirt and stink of the trenches and the dead on them for a second longer than is necessary.

They enter the barn and Ralph was right, the half barrels are absolutely enormous,

"Morning Martin, Dennis"

They both look over and see George Freshwater and Andy Mee, in the same barrel of steaming hot water, the other three barrels are not currently in use,

"Who was snoring in your tent last night, we are next door, and the noise was worse that the artillery last Saturday!" Andy Mee laughs as he speaks to them both,

"Pull that hose over to a barrel and pull the lever on the side, bloody hot water will just appear like magic!" Andy tells them, "This is an old brewery shed, sadly no beer but the boiler is great, and the water is just fantastic"

Martin pulls the hose over to the barrel nearest to him, he pulls the lever and hot, steaming water begins to gush out into the barrel,

"It won't take long to fill Martin", says George, "That hose used to be used to wash the grain and mash to make the beer, I think the water for the boiler must be piped in from the river"

The barrel is half filled in just a few minutes, the water is very hot, Martin takes off his trousers and underwear, he ties his thin towel around his waist and looks around for an area to wash his filthy clothes,

"Just around the corner Sarge" Andy Mee points around to the side of the bar, "There is carbolic and everything you need there"

"I want to kill the bloody lice that have made my trousers their home!" Martin laughs. He walks around into a smaller barn, there are tin baths lined up against the wall, he drags one to a point below another pipe hanging from the roof of the barn, a lot smaller and newer than the one in the main barn, he presumes that the engineers have put this pipe in, he fills the tub and throws in his clothes, shirts, undershirts, underwear, socks and trousers, they all go into the same tub. He takes a bar of carbolic soap from a wooden shelf and puts both his hands into the water, he vigorously rubs the soap and creates a huge amount of suds, he pushes his clothes up and down a few times and then leaves them to soak in the hot carbolic suds. When he gets back into the larger barn, Dennis is already in the huge barrel, steam is rising,

"Bloody lovely Sarge, get in before it goes cold" Dennis shouts at him,

"Not much chance of that Dennis, the steam tells me it is still hot"

He hangs his towel up and walks naked across the cold stone flagged floor of the former brew house, he stands on a bench and climbs into the hot water, enjoying the immediate feeling of heat, of beginning to be clean, of not being in a shitty mud filled trench, he hears a noise and realises it is him making a sound of utter pleasure, he lets his body and head sink below the water slowly, enjoying every second of the feeling of solitude as he sinks to the bottom of the barrel. As he surfaces the cooler air inside the barn hits his skin, he takes the bar of carbolic soap and cleans every inch of his body scrubbing the dirt away that has almost become a second skin, he climbs out of the barrel when he is done, Dennis is still in and refusing to get out, George and Andy are out of their barrel and a huge bung has been removed from the side of it and filthy, but still hot water pours from the barrel into a large drain, obviously there for a similar use when it was a brewery, he puts the towel around his waist and feels his face, a shave is certainly needed,

"In the clothes washroom Martin" George is walking toward the smaller room, "There are a few old mirrors nailed to the wall above a trough, I had my shave before getting washed, can't stand having a beard"

Martin follows George and Andy into the small barn, he tips the dirty water from his tin bath and adds a little fresh hot water and then covers the clothes with cold water from a tap and hose, he rinses all his clothes, they are so much cleaner than they were, he wrings them out gently and hangs them on a line that someone has put up just outside of the side door. He dries off and puts on clean underwear, trousers and undershirt, his braces hang down at his side and he has no intention of putting a shirt on or socks and shoes, he shaves and as much as he hates the shaving process, he feels human again when all the bristles have been removed, he cleans his razor and brush and stows it all away in his wash bag, which in turn is put inside his knapsack, he picks up his boots, puts his towel over his shoulder and decides to come back for his uniform later when it is drier than it is now, he hears George Freshwater shouting his name from outside, he thought George had left a few minutes earlier.

"Martin!"

"In here George, I will be out in a minute"

George appears at the doorway to the smaller barn,

"What on earth is up George?" asks Martin

George points outside, "There are two Lt's asking for you outside mate, one if from our lot but not our battalion and I have no idea who the other one is, but he is the oldest Lt I have ever seen!"

Martin is confused, he thanks George, who face is a deathly grey, gathers his kit and follows him outside, as he leaves the main door to the barn, he sees Charles standing with another Lt, he recognises him but can't recall why.

Then it hits him, the older Lt is Eddie Westerman, who was, when Martin last saw him, an RSM with the Sherwood Foresters, he has obviously been given a commission, he feels elated for one second at seeing them both, then his stomach drops as he knows they must be bringing bad news, is it Granny? Alice, Pete or May? Not the twins, surely not. He drops his knapsack and boots onto the ground, he remembers that there are other soldiers about, both George and Andy are standing close to him, so he keeps it formal,

"Lt Gray, Lt Westerman, what brings you here?"

Martin's heart is beating almost out of his chest, Charles steps forward and shakes Martin's hand, Eddie follows suit, Martin is sure he hears Eddie say, "He doesn't know Charles"

Martin is so confused as to why the two men are here in front of him,

"Martin, have you had any mail, letters from home" asks Charles

Martin shakes his head, his mind spinning, and he is becoming frightened,

"No, not for two weeks, we have been at the front and no mail has got through, I should have letters from Grace, Alice and Granny waiting for me, I hope to get them today"

He looks at Charles, then at Eddie and then back to Charles, before he can speak, Charles says,

"Grace is dead Martin"

Martin stares at Charles, he is sure he has heard him wrong, "What?"

"Grace is dead" It takes a few seconds to register what Charles has said to him,

"Dead" he says, "No, you have that wrong Charles"

"I'm sorry Martin but he hasn't" Eddie speaks gently to Martin, "We are both so very sorry"

Martin looks at the officers, he closes his eyes, balls his fists, and can feel rage burning inside him, he explodes in anger, as he does so he hears Charles say,

"Now please Sergeant, Corporal",

George and Andy have been asked by Charles to stay, he has already told them why, Martin feels strong arms around him holding him up, he tries to fight them off but both George and Andy have a tight grip of him, he screams and struggles until all the fight he has leaves him, he collapses into Georges arms,

“What the fuck!” Dennis has appeared and thinks that Martin is being attacked “George, what the fuck are you doing?” He moves menacingly toward George and Andy who still have a tight grip on the now limp body of Martin, Dennis stops when Eddie growls at him,

“Stand down private”

“Sir?” Dennis says, his fists clenched tight, ready to defend his Sergeant “That is my Sergeant”

“Dennis” George says “Martin has just had some bad news, the worst news from home, help Andy and I get him back to your tent”

Dennis drops all his kit onto the ground and rushes to help out, speaking as he moves,

“Sorry George, Andy, sorry” he turns to the two Lt’s “Sorry Sir, Sorry Sir, I didn’t know”

The three men have Martin in a safe grip, he is completely limp, tears fall slowly and quietly down his cheeks,

“No need for an apology private” Charles speaks, “Can you get the Sergeant back to his tent” he looks at Eddie, “Lt Westerman will accompany you; I will have to report to the C.O and explain what has happened and why I am here”

As the three men help Martin, who is walking slowly and needs propping up, Eddie calls to Charles, “You don’t know where his tent is Charles, how will you find us?”

Charles stops, George answers first, “Sir” he says to Eddie “If you can help us with Martin, I can send Dennis, Private Waldock, with the other Lt” he looks at Charles, “He can take you to the Old Man’s tent, apologies, the commanding officers’ tent and then can accompany you back to Martin’s tent”

Charles nods, Eddie steps in and helps to hold Martin as Dennis steps out,

“Come on lad” Eddie speaks to him “Let’s get you back and sorted”

He nods at George and Andy, and they slowly take Martin toward the rows of white pointed tents, Nobby, Alfie and H are walking down the gentle slope from the tents toward the barn, they see Martin being held up and run toward the men,

“Martin, what the hell….” Nobby sees that one of the men holding up his friend is an officer, “Sir?” he says as Eddie, George and Andy continue forward,

“Bad news from home Corporal” Eddie tells them, “Go for your bath lads, you will find out soon enough”

“Yes Sir” Nobby says, he looks at George who nods at him to carry on, Nobby, Alfie and H walk toward the wash area, George whispers in Nobbys ear and tells him about Grace,

"Shit!" is all that Nobby can think to say.

When they reach the outside of Martins tent, Eddie turns to George and Andy,

"Thanks, Sergeant, Lance Corporal, I have it from here" he looks around at the busy tent village, the tired men from the 2nd Bedfordshire regiment are waking up, "Do me a favour, keep anyone out of here for a bit, I think the lad will need a break"

"Yes Sir" they both say and move toward their tent, they both remain outside, so as to stop anyone else going into the tent with the Lt and Martin.

Inside the tent, Martin allows himself to be seated on a cot, Eddie sits opposite him,

"Why are you here Eddie?" asks Martin weakly.

Eddie explains to Martin that he is now with the 1st Battalion Sherwood Foresters, he joined them late in 1915, the Battalion had returned from duties in India and were sent straight to the Western Front, he explains how at the start of the war he was with the 5th and 8th Sherwood Foresters and had been injured at Hooge, both his hands had been burnt, how he was sent home and that he ended up at a hospital in Martins hometown and that Alice had been caring for him, Martin manages a smile. Eddie takes out a packet of cigarettes, he lights one and hands it to Martin then lights one for himself, he continues with his tale.

"After I was passed fit for war duty again, I was offered a commission, lots of young, brave officers had been killed in several battles and the regiment needed officers and quickly, I along with several other RSM's and CSM'S accepted the chance to be an officer, I finished training, it was completed very quickly, and I was posted to the 1st Battalion"

He stops to take a couple of deep drags from his cigarette, Martin has not touched his and the ash hangs precariously on the end, Eddie explains that after the first few days of the battle of the Somme, he was promoted from 2nd Lt to Lt in the field by his Lt Col, when the Battalion was relieved yesterday, he had to go to Allied HQ at Albert to be promoted officially. It was here that he bumped into Charles, who was at HQ, not only to find out where the 2nd Bedfordshires were to be billeted, but to collect orders for his C.O. for the 1st battalion, Charles had received his letter from Alice last week and heard the news about Grace, obviously before Martin. Eddie catches the ash from Martin's cigarette in his hand and throws it outside, Martin takes a very long draw on his and exhales the smoke, he looks at Eddie,

"Why was Charles looking for me?"

Eddie realises that the news of Grace's death has confused him, he explains that Charles Battalion are currently on Divisional reserve duties at a place called Givenchy le Noble, he believes it is about 30 miles from where they are now, Charles has been excused from bayonet training to visit Martin by his C.O., Lt Col Onslow, who was also Martins C.O. for a short while and remembers him. Charles travelled to Albert to collect some papers for Lt Col Onslow, and this is where they met. Charles had told Eddie about Grace and they had agreed to travel together to Bois des Tailles, he tells Martin that the 1st Sherwood Foresters are in trenches just outside of a town called Poziers, they have moved forward from Ovillers la Boiselle, he has witnessed as much slaughter as Martin has, they are now on a few days off just outside of Ovillers la Boiselle.

"Don't get in trouble for being here with me Eddie" Martin says,

"I have left word where I am, don't worry about me"

Martin flicks his cigarette through the tent flap, "Eddie, what happened, how did Grace die, I don't understand?" Martin appears to have come to a little, he is sat bolt upright and staring at Eddie,

"Charles is the best man to tell you lad, I only know the basics, I just wanted you to see a couple of familiar faces here when you got the news"

Martin remains quiet,

"Have you had any leave home at all since you got here?" he asks Martin,

"No, we have had a few weeks behind the lines, but the only time we were given home leave it was cancelled with short notice" he looks at Eddie, "I have been here the whole time"

Charles enters the tent with Dennis,

"You alright Sarge?" He asks

Martin forces a small smile, "Not really Den, not really"

"Sorry and all that Sarge, shitty news" He looks at Charles who moves his eyes toward the tent flap, "I am going to see Nobby and the others, catch you in a bit"

He is gone, Charles sits next to Martin,

"I have told him why we both happen to be here Charles" Eddie tells him, "Martin asked about Grace" The two officers look at each other, "I have suggested that the details are best coming from you as I don't really know" Charles takes a letter from inside his tunic,

"Alice tells me all about it in here Martin, do you want to read it?"

Martin slowly shakes his head, Charles puts the letter away and quietly tells Martin the details of how Grace had fallen from the Yew Tree, banged her head and drowned in the swollen stream in the garden of the cottage. When he finishes Martin looks up suddenly,

"I have to get home, I have to see Alice, poor Alice" He stands up, Charles tells him to sit down,

"They won't let you go home" Martin stares at him with an open mouth, Charles continues, "Grace wasn't family, so the Army will not let you home, the grounds for compassionate leave are not met, I have tried with your Lt Col, but his hands are tied and as much as he wants to grant it, he can't"

"What about Alice?" Martin asks, his eyes are again filled with tears

"Alice is fit and well, so the grounds are also not met for her either I am afraid" he looks at Martin and takes him by both arms, "Listen to me mate, don't do anything stupid, if you bugger off, they will catch you and you could be shot, going AWOL is not tolerated, you know that"

"I know" he says "I won't, no point in letting our side get me, I will leave that to the Germans"

There is a silence between them, "When was the funeral?" Martin asks weakly

"A week after her death" Charles tells him. Charles takes a small pile of envelopes from his tunic pocket, "I took the opportunity to collect your mail"

He hands Martin five letters, he looks at them, two from Alice, one from Granny and one from Grace, he takes the envelope from Grace and puts it to his nose and inhales deeply, he hands the letter to Charles, who takes it from Martin, "Keep it Charles, I don't want to read it"

Eddie leans in, "But it is her last letter to you lad, do you not want to read it?" he says as Charles tries to hand the letter back to Martin,

Shaking his head, he replies, "No Eddie, I can't read her beautiful words knowing she is dead, I just cannot, I would not get to the end" He looks at both men, "My Grace always signed off her letters the same way" he pauses and covers his face with his hands,

"You keep those words for yourself lad" Eddie says "We don't need to hear them"

Martin says in response, "I don't want to read her words, it will be too much" he looks at Charles, "Please keep the letter"

Charles nods, he says to Martin, "I am going home on leave in a few weeks, I will ensure that Alice is fine"

Martin thanks him, sick to his stomach that he can't get leave, officers get leave, not a lot, but they do get it, but the enlisted men are only supposed to get leave every fifteen months, he has now been in France for nearly two years and hasn't been home.

"It's not fair!" he shouts,

"No lad" Eddie says as he rests his hand on Martin's arm, "It isn't"

* * *

Monday 7th August 1916, a newly promoted Captain Charles Gray arrives at Victoria Station in London shortly after one in the afternoon, he is stiff from sitting in a cramped first class carriage with two other officers and three enlisted men, Charles, much to the chagrin of his fellow officers, had asked the sergeant and two privates to join them as they were without seats and standing in cramped corridor, the leave train is packed and the nearly four hour journey has been uncomfortable for all of them.

"Thank you, Sir, for the seats, my lads and me very much appreciate your kindness"

Charles shakes hands with the Sergeant from the 1st Norfolk's, "It was nothing Sergeant, we have fought alongside each other for a while and let's face it, the last couple of weeks have been a bit intense" The Sergeant laughs as he says,

"You are right there Sir, this leave is just what we needed, ten days at home" he nods at one of the privates, "Billy is not heading to a happy home, he lost his brother, George, a private in the 8th Norfolks, he was 21 years old and his cousin, Sidney, aged only 20, a 2nd Lt, also with the 8th, both on the first day of the Somme, and then his Father died, so he is heading home to much sadness I am sorry to say"

"Oh, how dreadful, has he far to go?"

"His Mother lives in Swardeston, near Norwich, so he has a couple of hours to go when he gets the connecting train"

"And you Sergeant"

"I am off to Kings Lynn, the Wife and baby, who I haven't seen yet, are waiting for me, so my leave will be better than Bill's"

"What about the other chap?" asks Charles

The Sergeant looks over at the other private, "One of mine from the Norfolk 7th Service battalion, we have all been at the front since May last year, I am a regular, but all my lads are Kitchener's new army volunteers, young Tom Perry there, has the heart of a lion, you wouldn't know it, but he lost a huge chunk of his left thigh on the second day of the Somme, a lump of shrapnel hit him"

The Sergeant coughs and bangs his chest, "Excuse me Sir, anyway, Tom is only home on leave at the insistence of one of the Doc's, he wanted to stay and carry on fighting"

"Brave or stupid!" Charles laughs

"A bit of both I think Sir, he is travelling to Stoke Ferry, so we are all going the same way" he looks around, "I do hope I haven't put the other two officers' noses out of joint or put you in a spot Sir, for offering us the seats"

"I don't know them Sergeant, so I don't really care, we are all scrapping in the same fight, if they didn't like it, they should have spoken up"

"Sarge, we have to go like!" Tom Perry shouts at him,

"Off you go Sarge, and good luck"

"Thanks again Sir, good luck to you and yours"

The three enlisted men move off into the crowd of hundreds of soldiers and officers, all leaving the train,

"I say old man"

Charles turns to see one of the officers, a 2nd Lt, that had been in the carriage with him and the three enlisted men, "Yes" Charles is curt with the young officer,

"It's just that we thought you inviting the Sergeant and privates into our first-class carriage was a bit, well you know" The young officer looks over to the other 2nd Lt that travelled with them, he is standing some distance away and making no attempt to join in the conversation, Charles puts his bag down and stands in front of the officer, he is at least four inches taller than the younger man,

"No, I don't know 2nd Lt, I don't know what you are referring to"

"Well, it is fine fighting alongside them, but do we have to travel with their type when home on leave?"

Charles feels anger rising in his chest, he moves his nose to within an inch of the man speaking to him, "Fuck off 2nd Lt"

The young man is taken aback, "Excuse me?" he says quietly

"Excuse me, Sir" Charles insists

"Is everything alright here gents?"

They both turn and see a Regimental Sergeant Major from the Military foot police standing in front of them, he is older than both of them, his uniform is immaculate, from his cap with its red cover, his tunic, complete with red armband emblazoned with 'MP' in large black letters, he is wearing the DCM ribbon, amongst many others he has emblazoned on his tunic, his trousers are pressed and his boots glinting as they are so shiny,

"Everything is fine R.S.M" Charles assures him

"Is it really?" the young 2nd Lt pipes up

The R.S.M. just looks at him and then turns his attention back to Charles,

"The 2nd Lt was attempting to berate me because I let three enlisted men sit with us on the train"

The 2nd Lt attempts to speak, the R.S.M. does not look at him but raises his index finger at the officer, insisting on silence, the young man decides not to speak, Charles continues, "I was only educating the young officer about the rules of war, share and share alike and look after each other"

"Now look here, I was only suggesting that the Sergeant and the two private soldiers should mix with their own kind and not with us"

The R.S.M. turns on his heels and faces the 2nd Lt, "Where is your cap Sir?"

"I beg your pardon?" he replies

"R.S.M."

The 2nd Lt looks dumfounded,

"You will address me as R.S.M."

"R.S.M., I assure you that my cap is with my bag over there with my fellow officer" He turns and points to his bag, his colleague, seeing that a confrontation is happening, has slipped away.

"You are not dressed correctly then, are you Sir?"

"Now look here R.S.M., I am an officer and..."

"And I am a Regimental Sergeant Major in the Military Foot police, and I am telling you that you are out of uniform"

Charles bites his lip; he is beginning to really like the R.S.M.

"I am home on my first leave R.S.M., so a bit of slack would be appreciated" the young officer stammers,

"I agree Sir, a bit of slack would be appreciated by all of us, especially when a Sergeant and two privates, who are fighting the same war as you and me, are invited to sit with you by an officer of a Senior rank" He nods at Charles, who can't speak as he fears he will burst out laughing,

"Look here R.S.M., I have been on the front lines for over three months now and your tone is not acceptable"

The R.S.M. raises an eyebrow, he points to the DCM ribbon on his chest, "Battle of Neuve Chapelle, March 1915, I got this alongside my Captain, a bloody fine officer, who also got a gong for his troubles that day" he pauses, "As it happens, it is the same medal the Captain here is sporting" he points at Charles medal ribbon, "The Military Cross lad, they don't give those away" he turns to Charles, "May I ask when you were awarded this Sir?"

"Of course, R.S.M., a bit of a dust up at Messines, early 1915"

The R.S.M. speaks quietly to the 2nd Lt, "Now, we are all in the same scrap, I thank you for your service to His Majesty the King, but don't you dare throw your three months at the front at me, or at the captain here, we have both been over there since the start" he takes a deep breath in, "Can I suggest you do exactly as the captain told you to do"

"R.S.M.?" The 2nd Lt is confused,

"Fuck off Sir"

Charles burst out laughing, he manages to make it short and controls it,

"Excuse me R.S.M.?" The officer asks

"You heard me Sir, now fuck off"

The 2nd Lt does not know what to say, he turns and walks toward his property,

"Sir" The R.S.M. calls after him, the young man turns, "Put your cap on please"

Charles laughs again, this time he cannot control it,

"Sorry R.S.M., but that was bloody funny"

The R.S.M. winks at him,

"Can I be of any further service to you Sir?"

"Actually, I have to get to Kings Cross, any idea of which tube I need to take?"

"Avoid those underground menaces Sir, they will be packed, if you walk to the end of this platform and enter the street, the bus station in front of you is what you need, the 390 will take you to St Pancras, Kings Cross is just over the road from there Sir"

"Thank you R.S.M., you have made me laugh more than anyone has for the past two years"

He puts his hand out and as they shake hands he says, "My name is Charles"

"David Charlton Norcross" says the R.S.M.

Charles laughs again, "I think David will have to do for now!" The men shake hands and Charles picks up his kit, "Good luck David"

"And to you Charles, see you over there, I am back in a month or so"

The R.S.M. walks away, shouting as he does so, "Corporal, if you don't dress correctly then I will have to assist you"

Charles smiles and makes his way to the bus stop to get the 390.

The bus stop is crowded, as the 390 appears on Victoria Street, a mass of people begin to bustle to get to the front of the queue, Charles stands back and lets them get on with it, he feels overwhelmed by the crowded street after his time in France with the huge, destroyed, and open spaces of the Somme, the impatience of the crowd annoys him, it obviously annoys a lady selling flowers nearby, she shouts at the crowd,

"Oy! Will you unhelpful and ungrateful bunch of heathens step back and let one of our brave soldiers onto the bus" The hustling slows down but continues as the bus pulls in at the stop, the lady pushes her way to the front, she puts her arms in the air and shouts, "Now!"

The crowd, unsure of what to do, stop jostling, "Step back and let the lad on the bus first, he ain't got all day to wait for you lot, he is too busy fighting for us" She looks at a man, about the same age as Charles, smartly dressed in a suit and tie, she says to him, "Unlike you love"

Charles is a bit taken aback by the comment she makes to the man, who is obviously embarrassed, but he thanks her as he passes, he buys a rose from her, tells her to keep the change and gets onto the bus,

"On you get Guvnor, no charge for our lads in uniform" the driver says

Charles is again taken aback by the generosity, "If you are sure"

"I am Guv, my lad is over in France somewhere, so on you get" Charles moves onto the bus, the driver turns to him, "Where are you going to?"

"Kings Cross" Charles answers

The drive nods, "When I shout, ' St Pancras', that will be your stop" Martin thanks him again and climbs the short spiral staircase to the upper deck, it is empty, and he takes a seat at the front, he watches out of the window as the bus pulls out of Victoria Street and London begins to pass him by, he listens to the driver as he shouts, loudly, as they approach each stop,

"Grosvenor Place!"

"Hyde Park Corner!"

"Piccadilly!"

"Park Lane!"

"Cumberland Gate!"

"Marble Arch!"

Charles is not fully listening as they enter Oxford Street, he is daydreaming as the driver continues to shout at the four stops, he makes on this Street, Duke Street, Hanover Square, Soho and Charing Cross, the bus turns a sharp left and the driver shouts, "Tottenham Court Road"

He continues to stare out of the window, admiring the architecture of the London buildings, old and new, it seems strange to him that only a day ago he was in France where all the towns around him, and their buildings have been all but annihilated, London looks untouched, he is aware that East London and the docks has been attacked by Zeppelins and one aeroplane, all dropping large bombs during 1915, but this area of London is untouched. He hears,

"Euston Road! Next one is your Guvnor" Charles stands as the bus turns right onto Euston Road, he slowly walks down the staircase with his kitbag, "Two minutes Guv and we will be at St Pancras" The bus pulls over and Charles moves forward to leave, the driver points across to the other side of the road, "Cross St Pancras Road here Guv, King's cross is right in front of you"

"Thank you" Charles replies

He steps off of the bus, there are plenty of men in uniform milling about, he makes his way through the crowd, he enters the main causeway at Kings Cross and looks at the departure board, he needs the train to get to Wheathampstead, he sees the train he needs and it leaves in under five minutes, the board says he needs to change at Hatfield for the connection to Wheathampstead, he needs platform 11 and he is standing by platform three, he walks quickly through the crowds, it is very busy, he reaches platform 11 with a couple of minutes to spare, he moves toward the platform entrance and realises that he doesn't have a ticket, he approaches the ticket collector,

"I am sorry, but I have not had time to get a ticket to Wheathampstead, could I possibly get one on the train from the conductor?"

The elderly ticket collector has faded medal ribbons on his uniform, he smiles at Charles,

"No charge today Sir, I am a former army man myself, step through and be quick the train is about to depart"

Charles thanks him and begins to run down the platform,

The ticket collector shouts after him, "Don't forget to change at Hatfield!"

The noise from the train, it is hissing steam, tells him that it is getting ready to leave, he climbs aboard and sits by a window, the grimy city passes by slowly, the train never really gets going to full speed as it stops at Holloway Road, Finsbury Park, Hornsey, Alexander Palace, Oakley Park then through a tunnel before stopping at Hadley Wood, then onto Potters Bar and South Mimms going through the long tunnel at Enfield chase, the final station is Hatfield. Getting off of the train is certainly less stressful than it was getting onto the last one in London, the station is busy, not as busy as its London cousin, but busy none the less. Martin walks underneath the covered platform and looks across at the trains coming and going, there are five different tracks that he can see from his position,

"Can I help you Sir?"

He turns and the elderly Station Master is standing next to him, immaculate in his blue uniform, he has a shock of pure white hair and a huge white moustache, like his colleague at Kings Cross, he is wearing medal ribbons, a lot of them.

"I am changing here from Kings Cross; I need to get to Wheathampstead please"

The Station Master points a bony and bent finger toward the covered overbridge,

"Take the bridge Sir, the small connecting platform in the middle is the one you need, the Luton and Dunstable branch line" He takes out a huge silver pocket watch, "Best you get a hurry on lad, it leaves in a couple of minutes"

Charles thanks the man and not for the first time on this day, he is running to get a connecting train, he takes the steps up the overbridge as quickly as he can, he runs down the opposite set for the platform he needs, he is on the platform, the train is readying itself to leave, he moves quickly toward a door of the first carriage he comes to.

"Charlie!" He stops at a carriage as he hears someone calling, he looks along the platform and hears the voice calling out again, "Charlie boy!"

He recognises the voice, but can't quite put a face to it, a scruffily dressed man in his fifties appears through the smoke,

"Uncle George!" he cries out, dropping his belongings he hugs his uncle,

"Gerrof you stupid bugger!" George says and responds with a hug back for his nephew.

"What are you doing in Hatfield Uncle? I am supposed to be on this train, but I can get the next one"

"No matter lad" George puts his pipe into his mouth, "This here train won't leave without me"

Charles is not following, the last he remembers, George was working for the railways but as a labourer, "I'm doing a bit of subbing, the company is short of fireman, all the fit young lads have joined up, so every now and then I come aboard and shovel coal to get this big bugger going"

Charles retrieves his kit, "Come with me Charlie" George sets off down the platform toward the engine, Charles follows,

"Come on George, we are about to be late!" the driver is shouting from the engine cab,

"Now calm down Sidney, meet my nephew, Captain Charles Gray, back home from fighting in France"

Charles steps forward and shakes Sidney's very grubby hand,

"Nice to have a fighting lad on my train, do you fancy a ride up here with George and me?"

All of Charles boyhood dreams have come true at once, he has always wanted to ride in the cab of a mighty steam train,

"I really would love that Sidney thanks"

He still has his kit in his hands,

"George, take his kit and give it to Jim" he looks at Charles, "He is the guard, he will put your kit in his van" he sticks his head out of the cab,

"Bloody hurry George or I will get a real fireman to do this work" He turns to Charles,

"Would you like a job, Charles?"

"I am a bit busy at the moment, but maybe when all this is over!"

George clambers into the cab, "It gets a bit dirty up here Charlie lad"

"Oh, I don't mind one bit Uncle George"

George starts to shovel coal into the furnace, it is glowing white and spitting out a huge amount of heat, the smoke from the stack fills the cab and Charles uniform is covered in soot, as the train gathers pace the smoke lifts, and he can see the light brown wispy trail behind them. It is noisy and Uncle George and Sidney are shouting at each other and laughing, Charles cannot make out what they are saying but he doesn't care, he sees the countryside open up around him and the warm wind blows through his hair, it seems no time at all when the train starts to slow down, they are approaching Ayot station. It is a small station with two platforms that has a pair of tracks and a small loop line, the platform on their left side has a canopy over it and the station house with its two large chimneys is directly behind the platform, he can hear the loud steps of people rushing for the train as they run over the wooden boards that make up the platform, the other, on the opposite side, also has a wooden boarded platform, it has a smaller canopied area and no house behind it, the whistle blows and they set off again. The train passes a landscape that Charles knows very well, his Parents house at Cherry Trees is only three or four miles from the Ayots, he sees Long Spring Wood on his left, then toward Ayot St Peter the mighty Sauls Wood, Little Hocket Wood is on his left as the train continues to move, he moves to the other side of the train to see the huge quadruple woods of Fish, Bladder, Warren and Dowdell, the train moves on past Three Groves Wood and Coneydell Spring, then Cherrytree Spring and the fantastically named, Scratching Grove. They pass Robinsons wood which lies right next to the railway line, past Black Bridge on their right and through the gravel pits and into Wheathampstead, Charles shouts at his Uncle,

"How do I get all my kit?"

"Stay where you are lad, Sidney will drop you at your door!"

Charles does not understand but remains in the cab as it pulls into the small, single tracked railway station at Wheathampstead, the platform canopy with its decorative edging covers the whole of the platform, it is not busy here, they don't have to wait long before they hear the shrill whistle of the station master, giving them the all clear to move off. The train is not moving very fast and appears not to be gathering momentum,

"Get ready Charlie" shouts Uncle George.

The train pulls out of Wheathampstead station, the Railway Hotel can be seen from the train and as it leaves the small village, Mags Pond comes into view, Charles smiles as he remembers swimming in this section of the River Lea as a child, as they approach Leasy Bridge, the train slows almost to a halt,

"Off you get lad, I will see you later, when I finish"

Charles thanks Sidney and shakes his hand, he steps down from the still moving train,

"Uncle George!" he shouts "My kit"

As he says this, he can see the guard leaning out of his carriage with Charles kit, it is dropped gently into his arms as the train passes, it begins to pick up momentum and Charles gets out of the way, he can see the footpath from Leasy Bridge that will take him to Cherry Trees.

He is home.

* * *

Alice steps off of the train at the East Station, it is just after 8 in the evening, the air is warm, and the sun is beginning to drop in the West, she says goodbye to the other women, also from the Chaul End factory, she steps away from the platform with Maggie Munday, they set off along Station Road, toward the footpath that will take them toward the bridges across the river and then to the Lower Road to Luton, Maggie stretches her arms upward and makes a screeching noise as she does so,

"That was a bloody long twelve hours in that factory Alice, I am fair tired I can tell you"

Alice laughs, "Maggie, don't make such a spectacle of yourself, people might be looking!"

"I don't care" Maggie replies "Are we not serving our King by making these bombs that kill and maim" Alice nods. "Well then, I am entitled to a stretch and a yawn after such a long day!"

Alice laughs again, she looks at her hands, "It has been a long day today, my hands are so sore from putting fuse after fuse into the shells, my fingers are yellow, and I cannot seem to shift it no matter how hard I scrub"

"You won't shift it by scrubbing, you have seen the girls in the TNT section, yellow all over, everywhere, if you get my meaning"

Alice puts her hand to her mouth, "Maggie!"

They both laugh and take the left turn onto the footpath,

"How did you find the nightshifts last week Alice?"

Alice groans out loud, she started her first ever set of night shifts last week, finishing at seven on the Saturday morning, "I hated it Maggie, I could barely keep my eyes open, I slept on the train every morning and more than once had to be woken up by one of the girls!"

"My turn next week, I am getting used to them now, although I sometimes wish that I had taken the job in the shed behind the Silver cup when May Austin offered it to me!"

"I am so glad you didn't take it Maggie" Alice puts her arm through Maggie's "I would hate it if you left Chaul End"

Maggie pats Alice's hand gently, "Don't you fret young lady; I am staying put for now"

They walk toward the bridges in silence, as they cross the second and larger bridge that takes them over the River Lea, Maggie says quietly,

"How is Martin getting on? Have you heard from him?"

Alice stops and looks at the slowly moving river, the sun casts the shadows of the reeds across the glinting surface of the water, she sighs, "Only once since Grace died" she puts her hand to her mouth and tears fill her eyes, Maggie puts her arm around her shoulder, Alice continues,

"The letter was short and to the point to say the least, he thanked me for writing to him and telling him about Grace, he told me that Charles and Eddie Westerman had found him before my letter did" she turns toward Maggie, "Charles has written to me and told me all about how he and Eddie met and broke the news to Martin" she stops again to sob gently as she stares back at the water, "But Martin did not say much more at all, he said he was as well as could be and that he hoped I was fine and that he loves Granny and I very much" She turns to Maggie for a second time, "I am so scared that he will do something stupid, I can hardly bear the thought of him being all alone"

Maggie pulls Alice toward her with a comforting hug,

"You listen to me Alice, Martin will be fine, it is so sad that he has lost Grace, but he has you, he has you and Mary to come home to, he will be fine, I am sure of it"

Alice is thankful for the comforting presence of Maggie, she dabs her eyes with her handkerchief, she looks at her yellow fingers again,

"Just look at them, horrible, what would Charles think if he could see me now?"

Maggie sets off across the bridge, Alice has to follow as Maggie has linked arms with her again,

"On the subject of Charles" she looks playfully at Alice and winks as she says, "How is all that going"

"Maggie!" exclaims Alice "Charles and I are not…" she looks at Maggie who has her eyebrows raised "Charles and I are most certainly not, well you know"

Maggie laughs out loud, "I do know, I am a married lady, so I do know"

"How is Mr Munday?" Alice asks, then takes a sharp breath in, "I am sorry Maggie, I shouldn't pry"

"That all right love, he is doing well considering, there is a little improvement every day" she smiles and unlinks her arm from Alice's "Night-time is the worst for him, he doesn't get much sleep because of his injuries, they are healed but still cause him great problems, we are together and that is all that matters" She steps away from Alice, "Here I am, home again, see you in the morning, usual time?"

"I will be waiting for you Maggie, as usual, have a good night"

They part company and as Alice walks away, Maggie calls back after her, "Alice?"

"Yes Maggie"

"Edward and I still manage occasionally" Alice looks at her, confused, Maggie continues, "We manage to…, well you know!"

Alice, a little shocked by Maggie's candid comment, opens her mouth wide, she doesn't reply as Maggie is walking toward Belmont cottages laughing very loudly as she does so, Alice turns and walks toward The Malta, passing the cottage as she walks on the Lower Road, she quickens her pace as she passes it, only brave enough to turn her head quickly for a look in the garden, the ever present and looming Yew tree is very much alive and glowing in the late evening sun.

Alice feels a shiver rip through her body and even though it is very warm, she pulls her jacket around her body and walks on.

The pub is busy as she opens the door and enters, the familiar sound of men talking in low voices fills the air and mingles with the tobacco smoke that hangs silently in the air,

"How are you, Alice?"

She turns and sees Jack and Ernie Almond sitting with a couple of other local men she knows, it is the former that has spoken to her,

"I am fine thanks Mr Almond"

Jack smiles at her, "Good girl, how is that job of yours going on?"

She tells him that the job is fine,

"Hello young lady" Mary has entered the bar from the kitchen,

"Hello granny" Alice smiles at Mary "Is there any tea left for me please?"

With a smile Mary says, "Of course," she nods toward the kitchen "In the oven, shepherd's pie with some greens, it should be fine and warm"

Alice thanks her and walks behind the bar and into the hallway, she hangs her coat on a hook, takes of her heavy work boots and sighs, "Oh, my that feels good" she says as she rubs her stockinged feet

"I bet is does" a voice speaks from the kitchen.

Alice looks through the kitchen doorway and sees Charles sitting at the old wooden table with a half-finished pint of beer in front of him, his uniform seems to hang a little looser on him than it used to, he looks tired but also very dapper,

"Charles!" she screams and runs into the kitchen, she runs into his arms as he stands and throws her arms around his waist, he gently takes her in his arms,

"Hello Alice" he whispers "Surprised?"

She cannot answer him as huge, heavy sobs have taken over her body, Charles looks and sees Mary stood in the doorway,

"That's enough of that" she says sternly

Charles releases Alice from his arms, she continues to hold onto him very tightly, her head buried in his chest,

"Alice" Mary speaks again "Shall we release Charles from your grip now?"

Charles sees a small smile form on Mary's face, he gently puts his hands on Alice's shoulder and moves her away from him,

"Alice, you are squeezing the very life from me!"

She wipes her eyes and turns to Mary, "Granny! You should have told me Charles was here" she looks at her drab work clothes "Look at the state of me!"

Mary wipes her hands on a bar cloth, "Perhaps" she says and turns back to the bar, a wry smile on her face.

Alice looks at Charles and moves in close to him, she takes his hands in hers, she looks him directly in the eyes, stands on tiptoe and they kiss, slowly and gently, they only part when Mary shouts from the bar,

"I can hear what's going on in there with you two!"

They both laugh and Alice hugs Charles again,

"Alice, eat your tea before it burns in the oven, I can finish my beer"

Alice opens the door to the oven, Mary shouts again, "There is enough for two if Charles hasn't eaten"

Charles nods at Alice and puts his beer glass to his lips, Alice smiles, all her recent troubles and sadness evaporates there and then, she takes the food from the oven, gets two plates, and puts the hot food onto them, she sits at the table, putting a plate in front of Charles,

"Thank you, Alice" he smiles and her heart flutters "It is so good to see you Alice, so good that I just can't tell you.

They eat in near silence, only briefly broken by Charles, who when asked by Alice, tells her that he has seen his parents and they are both well, the food is finished, and Alice clears the plates and cutlery away. Mary comes in holding a full beer glass, she puts it on the table in front of Charles and picks up the empty,

"Thank you, Mrs Spratley, how much do I owe you?"

"You are alright Charles; I think the house can afford a couple of pints for one of our fighting lads"

"Granny" Alice says, "Could Charles and I go upstairs to the living room?"

Mary frowns at her Granddaughter, "Certainly not young lady"

Alice looks crestfallen,

"We are fine here Mrs Spratley, I honestly can't move after the lovely plateful of your Shepherd's pie" He looks at Alice and winks,

"Bloody young love!" Mary exclaims as she leaves the kitchen.

"Don't be sad Alice, just being with you, no matter where it may be, is all I ask"

The pair chat, at ease with each other's company, only when Alice asks Charles what the war is like, does he become very serious and insists that they change the subject, they briefly discuss men and boys that they both knew that have perished in the war recently, Charlie Bigg, who died whilst serving with the 1st Battalion Hertfordshire's on the fourteenth July, a hand bomb had exploded prematurely as he held it, Charlie had survived the blast and was taken to a casualty clearing station, it was there that he was killed when a shell landed directly in the area he was being treated in, his parents, Thomas and Rhona, live only a few minutes' walk from the pub.

Henry Barnes from Kinsborne Green, aged 24, killed on the first Monday of July at Maricourt, he had been a school friend of Martins, he was also in the 2nd Battalion Bedfordshire regiment.

Percy Burgess, only 19 when he was killed in the Balkans, he was serving with the 10th Battalion Hampshire regiment, having joined them from the 3rd Bedfordshire's early in 1915, his mother and two younger brothers are still in shock and have hardly left their cottage near to the East station since getting the news of his death in December of last year.

Albie Clarke, originally from Warwickshire, had been living at Kinsborne Green and worked at the Childwickbury estate with the hounds from the hunt, Uncle Pete knew him well. Albie had been killed on the 22nd of April on the Western front, he had served with the 8th Battalion Bedfordshire regiment. They speak about Martin, Alice cries as Charles tells her how he and Eddie Westerman had broken the news to him about the death of Grace, he tells her that Martin had taken it as well as he could have and was in reasonable spirits when Charles had returned to the 1st Battalion, he did not tell her how devastated Martin had really been, she did not need to hear it.

They both looked at the kitchen door when they heard Mary shout, "Time gentlemen please, come on, time to go home to your poor wives and families"

Charles stands up, "I had no idea how late it was, I should be going back to Cherry trees" Alice moves her chair out to stand, Charles shakes his head, "Stay seated dear Alice, I saw that Robert Izzard was in the bar with some of the railway lads, I am sure he can take me on his cart"

"Have you heard how his son is getting on?" asks Alice, Charles shakes his head,

"Last I heard, Horace was in France with the Duke of Wellingtons and was still with us, I have to presume that all is well, or my parents would have told me"

Mary appears in the kitchen, "Charles, Rob Izzard is asking if you want a ride back to the Folly"

Charles smiles and looks at Alice, "Can I see you tomorrow?"

Alice bursts into tears,

"I am working till seven again, and all this week!"

"No matter, I will meet you at the East station tomorrow evening, I have ten days leave, including today, so we have plenty of time"

She nods her head; he thanks Mary again for the beer and food and is gone.

Mary steps into the kitchen and puts her hand on Alice's shoulder,

"Come on now Alice, give me a hand clearing up in the pub"

True to his word, as Alice steps off the train the following evening, Charles is there to meet her, he is in full uniform and steps forward and offers his hand to her as she steps onto the platform, some of the ladies' cat whistle, Charles takes off his cap and bows toward them,

"Thank you, ladies" he says to all of them

"I suppose I am walking on my own tonight then?" Maggie pipes up, Charles replaces his cap,

"I wouldn't dream of it Mrs Munday, I will be happy to walk both you ladies home"

Alice can see all her work colleagues looking at her, she blushes and stands next to Charles, he offers one arm to her and the other to Maggie, they both accept and prepare to set off with Charles in the middle,

"Shall we?" Charles asks both of them with more than a small amount of theatrics, they both nod and the trio set off.

They stand in the shade of a large and old oak tree opposite the Gibraltar Castle pub, Maggie's cottage is just along from the pub, she seems a little sad,

"What is wrong Maggie?" asks Alice

"Nothing really love" Maggie tries her hardest to smile "Ed is having a bad time at the moment, nothing I do or say can get him out of it"

"What seems to be the problem?" asks Charles, Maggie has a glint of tears in both eyes,

"He seems scared Charles, of what I have no idea, but he seems genuinely scared, we have times like this since he came home"

"Would it help if I came to see him, you know, soldier to soldier and all that?"

"I would not want to take your time" she looks at Alice "I am sure you would like to spend your short time at home with loved ones"

"That is true" he also looks at Alice "But what sort of man would I be if I can't try to help a fellow soldier" Alice tells Maggie that she should take Charles up on his offer, and that she will go home, freshen up and see Charles later,

"I have managed to get a day off tomorrow" she says to Charles

"That is wonderful Alice, how on earth did you manage that?" Alice smiles at Maggie,

"Someone had a word with Miss Hammond at the factory and I have been given a whole day's leave!" She looks at Maggie,

"I need a break from you Alice, nothing to do with Charlie boy being home, I want some peace and quiet!" Charles steps forward and kisses Maggie on the cheek,

"Thank you, Mrs Munday, thank you so much"

Maggie blushes, "You sure you want to meet the old man?"

"Yes, he does" Alice pushes Charles toward the road "Go on, but don't you dare go home without calling into Grannie's pub" Charles tells her that he would not dare go home without seeing her first, Alice watches as he walks across the road with Maggie, she hears him say,

"Now Mrs Munday, quickly tell me about Edward, rank, regiment and where he served"

Alice walks away, not stopping at the cottage but, as usual picking up her pace as she passes it.

Belmont cottages are small terraces, the thatch on the roof is wearing thin but the walls are made of good solid stone and look as strong as they did on the day they were built. Maggie points to a small alley to the right side of the terrace,

"I always go through the back door; Ed won't answer the front door anymore" She seems embarrassed and walks into the alley, followed by Charles, they walk through the back yard of the first cottage and Maggie stops by the door to the second, "Are you sure Charles?"

He smiles and nods, "After you Mrs Munday"

Maggie puts her thumb on the door latch and after a second's hesitation, she pushes the latch open and enters the house, "Ed, it's just me love, hope you have cleaned up, we have a visitor"

They both walk through the small but very clean and tidy back kitchen and enter the compact living room, as with the kitchen it is tidy, it is a bright room as it has windows at either end, Edward is sitting at the small wooden dining table, occupying one of the two plain but serviceable chairs.

"Ed, this is Charles, he is home on leave from the war and wanted to introduce himself to you"

Edward does not move, his hands are balled into tight fists on the table, he is staring straight ahead, "Ed love, did you hear me?" He slowly turns his head toward his wife, Charles can see scarring to his jawline and neck, he turns his head back to its original position and continues to stare, Charles has seen this before,

"Hello Edward" He steps forward with his hand outstretched "My name is Charles Gray, home on leave from France, I live at the Folly, just up the road" Edward does not move, he continues to stare but his eyes have changed, Charles can see genuine fear in them, he lowers his hand, "Not to worry old man" He nods toward the kitchen and he and Maggie leave the living room,

"I am so sorry Charles" Maggie has both her hands on her face, Charles can tell she is desperately holding back floods of tears.

"I have seen this many times Mrs Munday, not just on wounded men but on men that a few seconds before were perfectly normal, we call it the thousand-yard stare" The tears begin to fall onto Maggie's cheeks, she does not cry, he continues, "His fists are clenched, is he, you know, ever aggressive toward you?"

"Oh no Charles, he has never raised a fist to me or anyone that I know, this is a new thing he has started doing over the past days" They stand in silence for a few moments, Maggie speaks first,

"Thank you for trying Charles, I will just have to wait it out as usual, he will be fine in two or three days"

"Nonsense, if you are prepared to let me try again, I am happy to" She nods, "Mrs Munday, it may seem a little unusual what I am about to do, even cruel, but please bear with me, I am sure Edward is actually missing the war, he feels as though he has let his colleagues down and that he is scared about is failing you" Maggie breaks down in tears,

"Why scared of me? He has no need; I am so proud of what he has done"

"I know, but I don't think he does" She wipes her eyes,

"But I tell him every day that he is my man and that I will always love him and that everyone around here is proud of his service and sacrifice, especially me!" She becomes angry with herself for letting Charles see her like this, he looks at her, "Go on then soldier boy" she smiles "Give it a go if you must"

Charles nods and steps into the living room, Edward has not moved, he still has his fists clenched tight and is staring at the wall, Charles stands up straight and in the attention position,

"Edward, my name is Captain Charles Gray, 1st Battalion Bedfordshire regiment" Edward does not move position, Charles continues, "I was also at Mons when we had to retreat, bloody awful"

Nothing again from Edward, Charles looks at Maggie who shrugs her shoulders, Charles takes a step forward and stands to attention again, "Private, I am a Captain and I do not wish to be ignored!" he raises his

voice, Edward does not move, Charles shouts so loud it makes Maggie jump, "Do you hear me private!"

She is more shocked when Edward stands to attention so quickly, the chair he is sitting on falls with a clatter to the stone floor, his arms locked tightly into his sides, chin up and chest out,

"Private 39574 Munday, 1st Battalion Gloucester regiment" he pauses before shouting "Sir!" Charles smiles and nods at Maggie, "Thank you private, stand at ease"

Edward relaxes his shoulders and lowers his chin slightly, Charles continues, "Now then private, I am home on a bit of leave and find myself at a loose end" Edward, looking straight ahead, says,

"Sir" Charles slowly paces around the room,

"How about, you and I, a couple of soldiers, go for a pint or even two?" Edward smiles and turns his head slightly toward Charles,

"As long as it ain't the Gib Sir" he turns his head back to face the front, "Beer is bloody awful in there" Charles nods,

"The Malta it is then, are you alright to walk there?" Another smile from Edward,

"Yes Sir, I have been carried home from a pub, but never toward one!" Charles turns to Maggie who is still crying but also has a huge smile on her face,

"Mrs Munday, a cap and a jacket for Private Munday please" Maggie leaves the room, Edward is smiling, "Something amusing you private?"

"Yes sir" he looks toward the door that Maggie left to get his jacket and cap, "My Mrs would never let me talk to her that way!" Maggie returns with a jacket and cloth cap, Edward does not move, she is confused,

"Stand easy private, get your gear on, we have beer to drink"

Edward says "Yes Sir, thank you Sir" as he takes the clothing and accepts a wooden walking stick Maggie has retrieved from its home next to the fire.

"We won't be long Mrs Munday" Charles says as he lets Edward walk in front of him and through the back door, "Oh, Maggie" she smiles as Charles uses her Christian name, "Make sure you have the man's dinner ready for when he comes home" He leaves and follows the very loud laughter from Edward as he hobbles across the yard, Charles turns and winks at Maggie,

"Bloody cheek!" she says.

Alice is behind the bar talking to Mary when the pub door opens and Charles holds it open for Edward to walk through, she makes her way to the end of the bar to walk toward him, he catches her eye and quickly shakes his head at her, she understands and moves back behind the bar, Mary has her mouth open,

"Granny, what is it?"

Mary whispers "Edward Munday has hardly left their cottage since he came back home"

Edward, leaning on his walking stick and breathing heavily, approaches the bar,

"How do Edward" Mary says, He turns to look at Charles, his eyes showing the return of fear,

"Don't ignore the lady Private Munday" Edward forces a smile,

"Hello Mary, it's been a bit of time, hasn't it?"

She nods, barely able to speak, she notices Alice looking at her, obviously surprised to see her grandmother lost for words, she quickly gathers herself,

"I don't want any trouble from you soldier lads" she points at both of them, "Do you understand me?" Both men nod, both men are smiling. Alice hears a noise in the pub, it starts quietly but it is getting very loud, she looks around, all the men in the pub are standing and applauding the ex-soldier and the serving soldier, she hears comments from the locals,

"Nice to see you Edward"

"Mary, put one behind the bar for the boys"

"Can I buy you fellas a pint?"

"You look just fine Edward"

"Bloody well done lads"

Charles once again sees the look of fear return to Edward's face, the loud noise of the clapping is obviously getting too him, he puts his hand on the former soldiers' shoulder and says to him, very quietly,

"Get the bloody beers in private"

The clapping stops and the regulars sit down and tell each other that it is 'bloody great' to see Edward out and about again,

"Two pints of pale please Mary" Edward speaks to the landlady, she pours the beer and puts the foam topped pint mugs on the bar, Charles steps forward,

"I will get these Mary"

"I don't think either of you will have to pay for a pint tonight" He looks around and half a dozen locals lift their pint pots in a salute to him and to Edward, he picks his pint up and returns the salute to them,

"Sir" Edward asks Charles

"Yes private" he answers, firmly believing that Edward is about to ask him if they can leave the pub,

"Would you mind carrying my beer, I can't manage with this stick"

Charles picks up both pints and nods toward a table by the window, Edward hobbles his way toward the table, he is patted on the back by several of the patrons and he nods and speaks to several of them, he sits down with his back to the window, Charles puts a pint in front of him,

They both lift their beers and take a long, slow draught of the bitter liquid, Edward puts his pint down on the table, has a quick look around his immediate surroundings,

"Thank you, Sir" he says to Charles

"You are welcome Edward" he lifts his pint toward his drinking companion, "Drop the Sir, Charles is my name" Both men drink their pints, talking quietly about their experiences in the war, Alice looks over toward them, a little jealous because she wants to be with Charles, but very pleased and proud that he has managed to help Edward, who, it seems, just needed the company of another soldier to share stories with.

She hopes it will last, for Maggie's sake.

* * *

"Morning sleepy head"

Alice holds a mug of hot steaming tea in front of Charles face, he opens his eyes, confused and unable to work out where he is,

"Alice?" She smiles at him, he is lying on a bench seat in the bar of The Malta, a brightly coloured crochet blanket covers his body, he can see his uniform tunic on the back of a chair and his boots are on the floor, he is fully clothed apart from these items. A searing pain hits him, from the back of his head and across his forehead,

"Oh God, how much did I drink?" Alice laughs,

"Lots and lots, Granny thought it would be unsafe for you to walk home, so you stayed here for the night"

"Edward?" Alice laughs again,

"He was so drunk and funny, he even started singing at the end of the evening" Charles looks around the empty bar,

"Where is he?"

"Ernie and Jack took him home; they only live a few doors down from the Munday's"

Charles sits up and holds his head with both hands, Alice leans in and kisses him gently on the lips,

"You did good work last night soldier" It is Charles turn to smile,

"I am sorry that I could not spend the evening with you Alice" They both look over toward the bar as Mary enters, she is carrying a glass, half full of a red liquid,

"What on earth is that Mary?" asks Charles

"Best you don't know lad, just swallow it in one go, it will help with your hangover" He looks at her quizzically,

"Don't deny you have a hangover, I have been a landlady for a long time, I know a hangover when I see one" She hands the glass to Charles, who smells it and pulls a face,

"Don't smell it lad, get it down you" orders Mary.

Charles puts the glass to his mouth; he tips his head back and swallows the liquid in one go.

"Blimey Mary! What the devil is in that?"

She thinks for a few seconds,

"Tomato juice, the yolk of an egg, black pepper, salt, hot pepper sauce, vinegar and Worcester sauce" He puts his hand to his mouth as a burp escapes,

"Do excuse me ladies" Both the women look at each other and both raise their eyebrows,

"Bacon and eggs in five minutes" Mary says as she leaves the pair alone in the bar, she shouts back at them, "I also sent word to your poor Mother last night that you were here, just in case she was waiting up for you?"

"Are you feeling better after Grannie's remedy?"

"Honestly?" asks Charles

"Of course," replies Alice

"Then no, not at all!" Charles says as he stands up, he steadies himself on the table, Alice laughs,

"We should go and see Maggie and Edward today, to see if their marriage made it through the night!" Charles nods in agreement,

"Would you like to come and meet my parents after that?" he speaks quickly

Alice stands close to him, he bends down, and they kiss, a passionate, long, and lingering kiss, Alice pulls herself away, "Go and wash sir, you are a disgrace to the uniform!"

He throws a mock salute at her, they walk from the bar toward the kitchen, Mary points at Charles,

"There is a sink in the yard, a tap as well" She points at the kettle "It has just boiled, I have a pot of tea on the go, use the rest if you wish" He thanks her, finishes his mug of tea then picking up the kettle, he leaves the kitchen through the small back door that takes him to the yard.

"You can sit down young lady, there will be no watching that young man take his shirt off"

"But Granny, I wasn't going to…"

Alice does not finish as she can clearly see that Mary has the 'I know best' look on her face, she sits and pours herself and Mary a cup of tea.

"Granny"

"Yes love"

"Charles has invited me to go and visit his parents today"

Mary wipes her hands on her pinney,

"And?"

"Well, what should I do?"

"What do you want to do?' Mary replies

Alice sighs, "You are not helping me Granny!"

Mary takes a pan from the stove and puts two large pieces of bacon on each of the three plates, each already has a fried egg on it,

"Charles!" she yells "Breakfast!"

They both hear a muffled reply from the back yard, Mary puts a plate in front of Alice,

"If you like him, then you should go and meet his mother and father"

She kisses her Granddaughter on the top of her head, Alice, not used to such a show of affection from her Granny can only say,

"Thank you"

"That has made me feel better" Charles speaks as he comes in through the back door, his hair is wet, his undershirt is clinging to his damp body, he is carrying his shirt in his right hand,

"Why did you not ask for a towel Charles?" scolds Mary

"Didn't want to cause a fuss" he says as he runs his left hand through his hair to flatten it, he rubs his chin, "I don't suppose I will get caught out for not shaving today"

Mary point at a chair and puts a plate down on the table, he nods his thanks.

"Martin got caught out once" Alice giggles as she speaks, "He came into the pub, his uniform a mess and unshaven, Eddie Westerman was here, and you should have seen the look on his face!"

"It was nice of Eddie to go and see Martin with you" Alice looks at him, he nods without reply as the bacon he is eating is still being masticated, he finishes his mouthful and excitedly speaks,

"Oh my! I forgot to tell you both" he rubs a small amount of bacon fat from his chin, "Martin is up for another gong!" Both Mary and Alice put their cutlery down, they both speak at the same time,

"He hasn't mentioned it"

"How wonderful!"

Charles goes on to tell them that Major Poyntz has recommended Martin and others for medals after they had been on a patrol and had met with some German resistance, Martin is being recommended for a bar to be added to his DCM and the rest of the patrol will all get mentioned in despatches for their part.

"What does mention in despatches' mean" asks Alice, before Charles can answer, she has another question, "Why is Martin only getting a bar?" Charles laughs,

"Firstly, a mention in despatches is for officers and men that get mentioned in official reports and whereby their conduct is deemed to be gallant or meritorious in action in the face of the enemy, each will eventually get a silver oak leaf that they can attach to their service medals at the end of this war"

"Martin did not get a mention?" asks Mary, Charles knows better than to laugh at Mary,

"No, but he has been recommended for a second Distinguish Conduct Medal, instead of giving the soldier a second medal, they get a rosette for their DCM ribbon bar and a laurel spray for the medal ribbon, it used to be a silver bar, but it changed only a few months ago." Mary and Alice look at each other,

"You should both be very proud of Martin; they don't give the DCM to just anyone"

"Do you know what he did to earn it?" asks Mary, Charles shakes his head and lies,

"No Mary, I don't, but whatever it was it was bravely done." He does not mind the white lie, he does know how Martin earned his second DCM, but does not want to worry either Alice or Mary with tales of Martin taking on an armed German gun battery, he will tell them himself if he wants to. Breakfast is finished and Charles stands to help with the dishes,

"Leave them to me Charles, you and Alice had better go and see if Edward is still alive!" Mary allows herself a little giggle.

"Then shall we go and see your parents, Charles?" A huge grin forms on the young officers' face,

"Thank you, Alice, nothing would make me happier"

He stands next to Mary, who has her hands in the sink washing the pots and dishes, he leans in and kisses her on the cheek,

"Thank you for breakfast Mrs Spratley"

Mary blushes, much to the amusement of Alice,

"Get out of here, the both of you" Mary tells them.

Charles now has his uniform on and looks as smart as ever, he and Alice are walking toward Belmont Cottages, Alice feels a tingling throughout her body as he takes her hand as they walk past the cottage, she even manages to look at the Yew tree and smile a little.

Maggie answers the door, she sees Alice and Charles and throws her arms around Charles neck,

"Thank you, thank you, thank you" she exclaims Charles is stunned by the reaction,

"Lord! Maggie, what have I done?"

She opens the door for them to enter,

"Go inside and have a look"

Charles takes off his cap and enters the kitchen, as he did yesterday, a couple of steps further takes him into the kitchen, Edward is seated in the same chair as he was yesterday, but the change in him is amazing, he looks up.

"Morning Sir!" he stands and speaks in a clear, strong voice, "You need a shave Captain!"

The men shake hands and Edward speaks first,

"Thank you, Charles"

"What for? All I got out of it is a huge hangover!"

Edward sits down, Charles follows suit,

"I have been down and lonely since I got back, especially about the injuries and the scars" he looks at Charles "I love my wife, but I miss my mates" Charles nods,

"I get it Edward, but, as I think we discussed last night, you have done your bit, others continue what you and yours started for us all" Charles looks over his shoulder, Maggie and Alice are standing by the door, Maggie has a handkerchief to her mouth,

"When are you back Charles?"

"Just over a week, then it is back to France to try to get this mess finished so I can come home and get on with my life" He looks over his shoulder again as he finishes the sentence, nodding at Eddie, who says.

"Will we be able to have another pint before you go back Charles?"

"I damn well hope so Edward" he stands "Don't you have a hangover at all?" Eddie shakes his head,

"Woke up feeling just great" It is Eddies turn to look across the room, he smiles at Maggie, he speaks without breaking his gaze,

"We both thank you Charles"

"No bother at all, but next time, could we drink a little less?", Edward throws his head back and laughs loudly,

"Not a bloody chance Sir!" The men shake hands again,

"Charles, I know there will be bad days, but I really hope that there will be many more good days than bad"

"You will be fine" Charles puts on his cap "Can I ask one more thing?"

"Go ahead" Edward says

"Did that woman of yours have your dinner ready when you got home last night!"

They both laugh, they promise to have another drink later on in the week, Charles leaves the room and nods at Maggie, she kisses him on the cheek,

"Now get out of my kitchen"

Alice and Charles leave and start the walk toward Cherry Tree cottages at the Folly, they walk arm in arm, Alice feels very happy. The morning sun is warm on their faces as they walk past the Mill, the thatched cottages and the Smithy, Alice waves at a lady who is standing in the doorway of the first cottage,

"Morning Annie" she shouts and gets a similar reply, they walk on. The fields open on both sides of the road that leads to the Folly and then to Wheathampstead, they both shorten their step as the track they are walking on steepens slightly, the top of the incline gives them both a wonderful view, of the fields and farm buildings to their left and the upper watercress beds and Causewell Farm on the right, Charles stops and looks at Alice,

"Beautiful" he says, she giggles,

"Do you mean the scenery or me Captain Gray?"

He leans his back against a two bar fence, putting his right heel on the lower bar,

"Both" he replies "But in very different ways"

She takes a similar position on the fence next to him and so close that their bodies are touching,

"What on earth do you mean Charles?" Alice asks, he turns to face her,

"Should we get married Alice?" she does not reply, her mouth is open slightly,

"I know you are seventeen, but I am only twenty-one and I love you more than all of this beauty that surrounds us", She stammers a reply,

"But Martin and Granny, I have to ask…" He stops her by taking her hands in his,

"I have spoken to Martin, when we met in France, before Grace died, I talked to Mary yesterday before you arrived at the pub", she looks into his eyes but does not speak,

"I told my parents yesterday; I want to marry you Alice" she smiles at him,

"It seems everyone knew about this proposal, all except me!" he squeezes her hands gently,

"I had to get Martin's permission, I dare not ask you without Mary knowing and I was bursting to tell my parents all about you", Alice loses her smile,

"But Martin is in France?"

"I know, when I spoke to him, I suggested that if I was lucky enough and you say yes, that we could get married next year, after you are eighteen and hopefully Martin can be here to give you away" Alice is still leaning against the fence,

"What do you say Alice?" she playfully tilts her head to one side,

"I can't say anything as you haven't asked me anything yet, if that was a proposal to me then it was a jolly bad one." He leans in and kisses her on her forehead, he then stands back and drops to one knee, he takes of his cap and looks her in the eyes,

"Alice, I love you more than you will ever know, will you please marry me?" The smile is back on her face, and she whispers,

"Yes, yes of course", Charles stands, and they embrace each other tightly,

"Shall we go and introduce me to your mother and father now?"

He stands away from her, puts on his cap and offers her is arm, she accepts, and they set off toward Charles family home,

"They are going to love you Alice, I just know they will."

1917

CHAPTER EIGHT

The final few months of 1916 and the beginning of 1917 are a blur to Martin, the battalion spend a lot of time in trenches at Givenchy, Berles, Agny, on the Hindenburg line at St Martin sur Cojeul then into Belgium at Observatory Ridge near to Zillebeke, bombardment is a daily occurrence at these locations.

George Freshwater had been killed just three days after Martin had received the news about Grace's death.

The days, weeks and months pass by battles are fought, some won, some lost, men from many different countries die in their thousands, time in trenches and time on rest behind the lines moves slower with each passing day. Some days seem to be easier to recall than others, 19th September 1916 the Battalion received notification about all the men that had been awarded medals, Martin is one of these, his second DCM, he couldn't have cared less about it.

2nd Lt Walker is killed during a charge toward bayonette trench during the battle of Translov on 12th October '16, he and others all cut down by machine gun fire.

The 2nd Battalion C.O. Lt Col Poyntz is wounded during a briefing on the same day.

15 officers and 242 men died during this battle, many hundreds are wounded or missing.

The Christmas period arrived and finished, the cold sleet turned to snow and then to rain making the trenches and the surrounding areas muddy swamps, almost impossible to make your way through.

The 2nd Battalion, and the other battalions of the 90th Brigade, are not in trenches on the day the Christian world celebrates the birth of their saviour, the billets at Humbercamps, a town Southwest of Arras, are basic but dry and warm. Christmas dinner and gifts are sent to the battalion from the 'Women of Bedfordshire Comfort Fund', from Colonel Coates and the Liverpool City Battalions Comfort fund, Christmas puddings are received from the Daily Telegraph and the Daily News, a football match between the Sergeants and the officers takes place on Christmas Day afternoon.

Martin did not play or watch the game.

The trenches at Berles au Bois are completely mud bound and waterlogged, but they are a welcome sight for Martin, the New year of 1917 is brought in quietly, the bombardment from both sides has stopped, for now. The Battalion only has 1054 officers and men left alive and in the trenches.

The early part of the New year starts much the same as the previous one finished, the trenches at Berles au Bois are no different to any of the others the Bedfordshires have been in, only the landscape between the allied and enemy trenches has changed, it will not change again as there is nothing left to destroy, houses, barns, farmland, trees and fields have been replaced with barren open spaces, full of shell holes and the dead and dying.

January sees the Battalion medal presentation ceremony; Oakes, now fully promoted to Regimental Sergeant Major, has to order Martin to attend and to smarten up, his bar to his DCM is presented to him by the General officer commanding 30th Division, Major-General Sir John Stuart Mackenzie Shea, he accepts the medal ribbon and then leaves the presentation, not wishing to be part of the celebrations.

April sees them fight in the Battle of Arras, a complete disaster for the allied troops, enemy wire and guns stopping the advance very quickly, the Germans had learnt from the heavy losses they suffered during the fighting on the Somme battlefields. The German high command takes the decision to shorten their defensive lines, they use Russian prisoners of war to build a fearsome and strong defensive line called 'The Hindenburg Line', they cleverly began to withdraw from their old defences and by mid-March they have completed the withdrawal to behind the Hindenburg Line. This withdrawal had drawn the Allied high command into a false sense of victory and security as the German trenches are found to be deserted. Most of the land around Arras is flat, so advancing across it is fraught with danger, the higher ground at Vimy Ridge, is held and dominated by the German army. It is deemed a strategic success when the allied armies take Vimy Ridge, but the battle rages on for another six weeks with little gain for either side. Allied soldiers killed number over one hundred and fifty thousand, the German army have lost a similar number of men.

During this offensive, between the 9th and the 12th of April, the 2nd Bedfordshires have 13 killed on the battlefield, a further 4 men died from wounds received and over 80 wounded, most are severely wounded.

* * *

Since hearing about the death of Grace, Martin has become a different man, where previously he had been a dynamic and friendly leader of his platoon, he now keeps himself to himself, he still cares deeply for the men under his command, but he no longer spends time with them when they are not at the front or in trenches. It has been nearly a year since she drowned in the garden of his cottage, but he cannot lose the feeling of loss or the emptiness in his heart, he doesn't want to go home, in fact he has recently refused to spend time with the battalion during a rest period away from the trenches, telling his adjutant that he would rather have the ten days at the front line, this was refused and he had spent ten days with the rest of the battalion, but remaining on his own.

June arrives and the trenches are thankfully drier now due to a spell of good weather, the Battalion are in trenches at Observatory Ridge near Zillebeke having moved into Belgium on the 27th of May from trench positions in France. Martin is called to a briefing late evening on Monday 4th June, he is to take his platoon, along with three others and join 2nd Lt Jones at 0130 hours the following morning for a reconnaissance patrol, to gather information about the strength of the German defences nearest to their position. He gathers his platoon together,

"What have we got Martin?" asks Nobby, Martin looks up at his Corporal,

"If you listen in, you will find out"

The other lads in the platoon, Sharpie, H, John Marrables, Alfie, and Dennis all look at each other but don't speak, they have become used to their Sergeant being surly toward them, but they all agree that it is because of his skill as a soldier and as a leader that they are all still alive, Nobby is the only one who has concerns. Martin, in his opinion, has become reckless with his own life and this puts all their lives at risk, they all feel obliged to follow him into battle, but Nobby firmly believes that as Martin does not care about his own life, he is putting the other lads lives on the line, he has tried to speak to Martin about his attitude, about Grace and about how the platoon feels, each time he is met with hostility and ignorance. The men all listen without questions,

"We are forming at 0130 hours and will make our way across the open land toward the German front line trenches, this is an information patrol only, we go in, we look, and we leave" he looks at all of his patrol "Am I understood?"

They all reply, "Yes Sarge" Martin looks at his pocket watch,

"Have everyone ready in thirty minutes Nobby"

Before Nobby can answer, Martin turns his back on them and leaves,

"Good Sergeant or not, I am not taking much more of this" Nobby says to the others, "I know he is still mourning Grace but, bloody hell it has been nearly a year" The others all nod in agreement, Nobby continues, "I am not putting up with it much longer, any more madness from him and I will go to the R.S.M. and get moved" He gets no reply from any of the others, "This war will probably kill us all anyway, but the way he is going on death will bite us all on the arse very soon" He sighs, "Come on lads, get your kit sorted, we have to be ready to move, we don't want to upset him anymore now do we?"

2nd Lt Jones has twenty four soldiers under his command for this patrol, he doesn't need to ask for a volunteer patrol to be at the front as Martin tells him that he and his men will take the lead,

"As always" moans H

"I told you" Nobby speaks "He will get us all killed"

It is exactly 0130 hours and the patrol set off, Martin at the front, his patrol right behind him, they have only gone about fifty yards when Martin indicates for them all to stop, 2nd Lt Jones moves up to the front,

"What is it Sergeant?" Martin points through the darkness,

"Trench, about ten yards in front of us, I can hear movement"

"Let me get the remainder of the patrol informed and then we can advance slowly"

Martin nods, "Me and my lads will take the trench first if that is in order with you Sir"

Jones agrees, the platoon silently curse their leader. Jones returns,

"Move off please Sergeant"

Martin sets off with Nobby and H at his side, Sharpie, Dennis, Alfie, and John are right behind them, they reach the edge of the trench system without detection. Martin jumps into the trench without warning, he lands on a German soldier,

"Fuck!" Nobby shouts

All the Germans in the trench turn toward the noise of the Corporal shouting, they are taken by surprise, and all turn their guns toward the men from the 2nd Battalion Bedfordshires, Martin's platoon jump into the trench to help their Sergeant restrain the struggling German he landed on top of. Lt Jones, with Corporal Charlie Jeeves, Private Harry Medcraft and Lance Corporal Henry Preston run forward and jump into the trench firing at the Germans as they do so, the remainder of the patrol form a defensive area around the front edge of the trench. Martin has hold of the German soldier, H and Nobby are providing covering fire at the other end of the trench, the racket has bought more enemy soldiers toward them, the fire from Nobby and H is keeping them at bay, for now. The Lt and the two corporals have managed to make the Germans at their end of the trench retreat due to their ferocious attack, Martin takes the German soldier to the trench and Alfie and Dennis pull the prisoner out of the trench,

"Get him back to our lines!" shouts Martin, who then turns to join Nobby and H in firing toward the Germans in the trench.

"Everyone out!" the order comes from 2nd Lt Jones, "Back to our lines"

Nobby and H leave the trench and realise that Martin is still in the enemy trench and is still firing toward the Germans,

"Martin! Get out of there!" Nobby shouts at him.

Martin looks up at his corporal but continues to fire his rifle, he runs out of ammo and reloads from his webbing, Jones appears and shouts at Nobby,

"Corporal, did you hear my order?"

"I did sir" he points into the trench "My Sergeant has decided to take the Germans all on his own"

"Sergeant!" the officer shouts at Martin "Get out and get out NOW!" Jones is angry "That is an order Sergeant"

Martin finishes firing when his magazine is empty, he allows H and Nobby to pull him out of the trench, the Germans are nowhere to be seen, Jones shouts at all of them.

"Our lines, and now!"

They all make their way back to the allied trenches, it is 0137 hours, the patrol has been out for just over seven minutes, enemy soldiers have been killed and a prisoner has been taken, Martin is walking away from the rest of the patrol when he hears his name being called, he turns, Corporal Alf Howard is storming toward him,

"What the fuck was that all about Martin?" Alf is fuming, he is stopped from grabbing Martin by his Sergeant and John Marrables,

"What is your problem Corporal?" shouts Martin, Alf is being restrained and is raging toward Martin,

"You are you maniac; you jump into that trench without a care for your own self but also you don't give a shit about the others that have to jump in after you!"

Sergeant Smudge Smith pulls Alf away, he points at Martin as he drags his Corporal from the others,

"Martin, next time you are on a patrol, remind me to take my lads away from you"

Smudge and Alf walk away, Nobby turns to Martin,

"Are you alright?" he asks

"Why shouldn't I be?" screams Martin, Nobby steps back as 2nd Lt Jones approaches,

"Lance Corporal Clarke, you are dismissed I need a word with the Sergeant" Nobby nods and walks away, Jones turns to Martin, "It seems your German prisoner is singing like a canary, I already know his name is Neumann and he is an N.C.O from 5 company, 2nd Battalion, 58th German infantry Regiment, it appears he has had enough of the war and will tell us what we need to know" Martin nods, the young officer steps in close and speaks to Martin quietly so that no one else can hear, through gritted teeth, "What you did today Sergeant was reckless, stupid and dangerous, you put the lives of all of us at risk, just because you got a prisoner and we all survived don't think we had a good day" He pauses, "Four of the lads got wounded helping you out if you give a damn about any of them" Martin opens his mouth to give a retort, Jones won't let him, "Button it down Sergeant, I am speaking and you will damn well listen" he lowers his head before saying, "Some might think what you did today was heroic and soldierly, I don't, I think it was headstrong and the actions of a man who has lost the will to live" He steps in very close to Martin, "If I have the displeasure of having you on my patrols again, and you do something like you did today, it might not be the Hun that shoots you" he stands back, "Am I clear Sergeant?" Martin is stunned,

"Yes" Jones stands up straight,

"Yes, what Sergeant?"

"Yes Sir, Sir" Martin replies. Jones turns when he hears the R.S.M

"Is everything alright here Sir?"

"Yes, thank you R.S.M, I was just discussing the finer points of this morning's short, but very effective patrol" Oakes raises his eyebrows,

"Really Sir, anything I should know?" Jones shakes his head,

"Not at all R.S.M, I believe the Sergeant and I are done" Jones walks away without another word, Oakes turns to Martin,

"I hear on the grapevine, that young Lt Jones and a couple of N.C.O.'S had to bail you out on the patrol?" Martin snorts and shakes his head,

"That will be the day" he says angrily, Oakes stands, almost to attention,

"Now you listen here Sergeant, you are not fucking invincible, now get away from here, get away from me and have a damn good think about your actions"

"I got the enemy prisoner, so that ..." He does not finish as Oakes stops him,

"Martin" he says quietly "I am not used to repeating myself, don't make me start now"

Martin walks away leaving Oakes shaking his head.

That afternoon Martin hears Nobby and H talking, H sounds excited,

"I can't believe it Nobby, home leave for us, bloody hell" Nobby replies to H,

"The C.O. was so pleased with our result last night that he has not only put us up for a bloody gong, but we are to get ten days leave at home!" Martin steps around the corner of the trench and angrily shouts,

"No one gets leave from my platoon, not without my say so"

As Martin looks up, he sees that Nobby and H are not alone, 2nd Lt Jones is with them and has obviously been the bearer of the good news,

"Oh, really Sergeant? And on who's authority might you be refusing these fine soldiers their leave?" For once Martin is lost for words, Jones continues, "For your information Sergeant, I have also been given ten days leave, as has Corporal Jeeves, Lance Corporal Preston and Private Medcalf" he snorts a laugh "Unbelievably Sergeant, the C.O has seen fit to give you ten days home leave as well, for taking the German prisoner who has given lots of valuable information"

Martin sneers at the officer,

"I don't want it and they can't make me take it"

"Indeed, they cannot" Jones replies, he shakes Nobbys and H's hand, "Enjoy Blighty lads" he looks at Martin and walks away from the trench system.

"Ten days home leave Sarge, you can't be serious about not taking it" H says

"Am I not?" Martin barks back "I don't need to go home to some bullshit hero's welcome"

Nobby interjects,

"And nor do we, this is not about heroics it is about a bit of recognition for a job well done" he stops for a moment "A job incidentally that you nearly screwed up for all of us"

Martin turns to Nobby,

"If you don't like it Corporal, find another patrol to join, I don't need whiners and heroes in my team"

"I have done Martin" he replies

"You have what?" Martin asks confused

"I have asked for another patrol, to get away from you, in fact it would be easier if you left this patrol and we got another Sergeant, one who can lead us like you do but not want to kill us like you do"

Martin is about to protest that he does not wish to get any of them killed and that Nobby needs to wind his neck in, he is stopped by the booming voice of the R.S.M

"Sergeant!" The platoon becomes silent, as does all the others in the nearby trenches, "Trench HQ, now!" Oakes turns on his heel and heads toward the trench HQ. Martin turns to Nobby,

"This will be finished later Nobby"

Shaking his head, he replies,

"No Martin it won't, I am going to take the ten days leave and when I get back, I will be posted to a new platoon" He looks at the others "If they have any sense, so will they"

Martin leaves the platoon and makes his way toward the trench HQ, a small structure built out of wooden pallets and sandbags, he knows better than to barge in, he stands outside and knocks on the wooden frame,

"Enter"

He hears the familiar voice of Lt Col Poyntz from inside, it seems the wound the C.O. got a few days ago has not stopped him from remaining at the front, Martin steps in. Ralph Oakes is in the room with another officer, Captain Oakley, Martin stands to attention in front of Poyntz desk, the officer looks at him,

"I hear you have refused to accept my home leave offer Sergeant" Martin just replies,

"Sir" Poyntz stands,

"You are an idiot Sergeant, a fine soldier, but an idiot" he looks across to Captain Oakley,

"Robert, shall we take a tour of the trenches and leave the R.S.M to his business?" Oakley nods and both men leave the room. Martin has no idea what is going on, especially when Oakes takes him by the front of his tunic and pushes him onto his back, sprawling across the desk,

"Ralph, what the hell?" Martin shouts, he tries to stand but Oakes is extremely strong and holds him down,

"Shut up and listen to me Martin" he keeps a firm grip on the front of Martins tunic, "I hear you nearly got a bunch of lads killed yesterday, taking the prisoner was your only saving grace, your actions caused at least five other men to jump to your defence" Martin tries to speak, Ralph Oakes tightens his grip and lifts Martin slightly and then pushes him hard onto the desk, "Not your time to speak lad!" Martin decides to remain silent; Oakes releases his grip slightly but keeps Martin on the desk, "You have gone from the best Sergeant in the Battalion to the worst, your Corporal has asked to be moved to another platoon, your lads don't trust you anymore and I think they are only staying with you because you have always had their backs, loyalty Martin, loyalty!" he spits the last word into Martin's face, he keeps his firm grip on Martins uniform, "I know you lost your lady, that is sad, it is hell on earth to lose a woman you love, but you have to move on, you have to get over it" He slackens his grip slightly, "Grace is dead lad, and we are all sorry for you, but after nearly a year of your near suicidal behaviour, I have had enough" Ralph stands up releasing Martin from his grip, Martin does not move, "If you want to kill yourself Martin then so be it, but I won't let you get those lads killed because you are hurting inside" He rubs his face "We are all hurting in one way or another" he points at Martins face "You need to get your shit together Martin, I am taking your platoon from you, Nobby can take over as acting Sergeant and you.." he points again at him, "You Sergeant, if I can sort it, will be getting a shitty desk job behind the lines, sadly, you cannot be trusted anymore" Ralph Oakes looks down at Martin who has his hands over his face, and he is sobbing uncontrollably, Ralph moves toward him and grabs him by the shoulder, "Up you get lad, come on now"

Martin stands, his hands still covering his tearstained face,

"Ralph, I am sorry, Grace was everything to me and I could not even be there for her" Martin seems to slump, his knees buckle, and Ralph grabs him and supports him,

"I know lad, I know" Ralph puts his arms around the sobbing Sergeant and holds him tightly, Martin regains the strength in his legs but lets the R.S.M continue to hold him, "Martin, no one wants to send you away from your platoon" Ralph is speaking very quietly, "But you need to get over Grace, you don't have to forget her, but you need to get over her, it is nearly a year now lad, many of the lads have had personal and family bereavement and it is difficult" Martin stands up and Ralph lets him go,

"They all got to go home Ralph, they all got to go and say goodbye" Tears still fall freely from his eyes, he has anger and sorrow in his voice, "I didn't, I wasn't allowed to go and see my Grace for the last time, to see her put into the ground" Ralph nods,

"I know Martin, but it is time to let go son, to move on, we have to win this war and we have to survive, we have to go home to our loved ones" he grips Martins shoulders, "And you have to go and say goodbye to Grace"

"I still don't want the leave I was offered"

Ralph laughs a little, "The old man won't give it to you now, you refused and that is that as far as he is concerned"

"Quite right R.S.M" Both Martin and Ralph turn to the doorway as Lt Col Poyntz enters, "Any chance I can have my office back now?"

"Yes Sir" Ralph speaks to him. Poyntz looks at the mess on top of his desk,

"What the hell happened here R.S.M?"

"It was me Sir, not the R.S.M, I fell Sir, please let me tidy it up" Martin turns to sort out the mess on top of the desk,

"No Sergeant leave it alone; you have made enough mess in one way or another today" Martin stands aside to let his Commanding officer pass him, Poyntz sits in his chair and looks at both,

"All sorted R.S.M?"

"I think so Sir" Ralph looks at Martin, who confirms

"All good Sir"

"Good" Poyntz says "Now bugger off and leave me alone" Both men stand to attention,

"Sergeant"

"Yes Sir" Martin replies

"Take twenty-four hours leave, no arguments, sod off to some Belgian town and get drunk, take the remainder of your platoon with you and for God's sake sort out whatever needs to be sorted out" Martin nods,

"I will Sir, thank you"

"One more thing Sergeant"

"Sir"

"I presume you still want the leave in August?"

"Sir?" Martin has no idea what the Lt Col means, Ralph steps forward,

"For your sister's wedding Sergeant, the C.O. is not usually of a mind to offer two lots of leave in one day"

Martin knows that Alice and Charles are getting married in August, but he has not put in for any leave for it,

"Captain Gray and I took the liberty on your behalf Martin" Ralph tells him. Poyntz stands up,

"This is all very nice and fluffy, but the war is not yet won, so you" he points at Martin "I don't want to hear another shitty report about you, sod off for a day, take your lads in your platoon and come back refreshed and ready, your ten days home leave in August is granted"

He sits down and begins to tidy his desk, both Martin and Ralph look at each other, they have not been dismissed by the Lt Col. Poyntz looks up,

"Are you both still here?"

They both say, "No sir" and leave the small dugout. Once outside Ralph turns to Martin and says,

"Lt Jones, Corporal Clarke, Corporal Howard, Corporal Jeeves, Lance Corporal Preston, Privates Medcraft and Jarman"

"What about them?" asks Martin, Ralph leans in and whispers in his ear,

"You owe them all an apology for your antics this morning and for the past few months" Martin nods,

"On your way lad" Ralph instructs "You should get them all before they get on the lorry"

* * *

Martin arrives back at the front lines after lunchtime the following day, Wednesday 6th June, he along with John, Alfie, Dennis, and Eric have spent the last twenty-four hours together, away from the front lines, they only got as far as Brandhoek, a small hamlet to the West of Ypres, it is where the nearest casualty clearing station is and the base station for the field ambulance units. They arrived and it wasn't immediately obvious if they were going to be able to get a drink anywhere, all they could see was pointed military tents set in very straight lines and surrounded by sandbags with sturdy wooden walkways between each one so as to be able to move the injured men from one place to another without having to walk in the mud. All of them are pleased to see nurses, clean and tidy women with bright white starched uniforms, they in their filthy combat uniforms looked out of place, all of the nurses and medics were lifting and carrying wounded soldiers from lorries and carts, the injured men had been on board a supply train bringing much needed ammunition to the Western front, it had been attacked by enemy aircraft and the train, its cargo and many soldiers had been destroyed, these men had survived but were all seriously injured. Martin and his platoon forgot about their 24 hours leave and got stuck in assisting with the movement of the injured men from transport vehicles into the tented casualty clearing station, when all the wounded had been successfully moved and were being cared for, Martin was approached by an orderly from the hospital, a small Belgian man named Lukas who spoke superb English, he invited them to attend a bar with him for a drink, they all accepted. The bar turned out to be in the front room of a local house, one of the few still standing, the English soldiers were treated well and were plied with strong, dark Flemish beer and fed with warm bread and 'Waterzooi', a local stew made with chicken, butter, and eggs, they all managed to forget the war for a few hours and after enough strong beer were all able to tell Martin what they needed to.

Martin needed to hear it and listened intently to all the comments.

Being back in the trenches feels good to Martin, but he does have a hangover, as does all the lads, they are welcomed back by Ralph Oakes,

"Well look at these ladies returning back after a night on the town"

They all nod at the R.S.M, Martin walks over to speak to Ralph,

"Looks like you all had a good night Martin"

"We did Ralph" he puts out his hand and Ralph takes it, as they shake Martin says, "Thanks"

Ralph nods, "Best you get some terrible scran, coffee or tea inside you, we are attacking Messines Ridge in under twelve hours"

Martin is aware that this attack has been many months in planning, the miners, and sappers from the Royal Engineers tunnelers have been in this area for nearly two years. He has got friendly with a miner, Pete Hawthorn, he met over a rare hot dinner, he told Martin that the tunnels were nearly one hundred feet deep in places and, if successful, the mines, all containing ammonal, a mixture of ammonium nitrate and aluminium, would devastate the German lines, he said that all the mines would have a total weight of several hundred thousand pounds of explosives. Mines and tunnels have been dug at several locations, two have been placed beneath Hill 60 on the Northern flank, this will be the nearest to the Bedfordshires, one at St Eloi, three at Hollandscheschur farm, two at Petit Bois, one each at Maedelstede Farm, Spanbroekmolen, Ontario Farm and Peckham House, there are two tunnels at this. A further four mines have been placed under Kruisstraat and four at the German strongpoint, known a Birdcage, this is at Le Pelerin, a short distance from Ploegsteert Wood, two mines have been placed on the southernmost flank, under trench 122 and trench 127. The large mine at St Eloi has been charged with 95,600 lbs of ammonal, Maedelstede Farm has 94,000lbs and Spanbroekmolen has 91,00lbs, this mine is placed at a depth of 88 feet below the highest point on the Messanines Ridge, this has the largest gallery and longest tunnel, a total distance of 50 yards. Martin and Pete met several times over the coming weeks, then a mine, known as Peckham two, suffered a tunnel collapse, Pete and three other miners were buried and a rescue mission for them is impossible, they are all listed as missing presumed dead.

Brigadier Charles Harington-Harington, known as '*Double H'* to the troops, has given a quote to the press, all the men have now heard of it,

"*Gentlemen, we may not make history tomorrow, but we shall certainly change the geography*"

Zero hour is to be 0310 on the 7th June, Martin and his platoon are to be in the front lines with the rest of the 2nd Battalion, it is not known if they will form part of the initial attack, yet another rush across no-man's-land toward the German trenches, the 8th Battalion of the Kings Own Yorkshire Light infantry, from the 23rd Division, are to the immediate right of the 2nd Bedfordshires, the defensive flank formed by both battalions is to provide cover for the main attack, further round are the 8th Battalion Royal Irish Rifles, their position tells Martin that they will be the first to advance.

At 0300 hours Martin and his platoon are in position, word has been passed down the line that up to 25 mines will be detonated, followed by a huge artillery barrage from the howitzers and the 'eighteen pounders', this is when the order to advance will be given, they wait for the sound of the mines exploding.

At just after 0309 hours there is a huge explosion to the southeast of Martins location, the advance is called, the 2nd Bedfordshires are told to '*hold fast*', meaning they are to remain in position and not advance with the first wave, Martin can see, in the distance, that the 8th Royal Irish Rifles are moving from their trenches and advancing,

"Why has only one mine exploded?" asks Dennis

"Because it has been set off early, now the Germans know we are coming, and the Irish lads will be out of cover when the rest go off"

They have no more time for conversation as the other mines explode within seconds of each other, but not simultaneously as was planned, debris, earth, steel, and concrete can be seen being blasted high into the night sky, the whole scene is lit up with the orange and white flames of the explosions, the mine at Spanbroekmolen, fare to the southeast of their location is by far the loudest and biggest explosion of all,

"Get down!" Martin yells to his platoon, his words are swallowed by the cacophony of sound emanating from the explosion all around them, he hits the bottom of the trench hard covering his ears from the noise, the others all do the same. The artillery begins and is a heavy and constant barrage, the Germans, seemingly recovered from the initial blasts, send a hostile barrage of artillery back toward the Allied trenches, many of the shells are landing close to the Bedfordshire positions. Martin gets up slowly, his body pushed firmly into the sandbags that line his trench, a shell lands in front of his position and he is thrown backwards to the back edge of the trench, he looks up and the top of the front edge is damaged,

"That was fucking close!" yells Alfie, Martin looks to check on his men, he knows Alfie is alive as he is shouting, Sharpie and John are covered in sand and mud, but are both uninjured, Dennis is lying on the floor of the trench, Martin fears the worst but breathes a sigh of relief when he hears Alfie again, "Bloody Hell Den, that is a huge splinter in your arm!"

Dennis retorts, "Don't stand there looking at it, help me up and get the bugger out"

"Everyone, to the front wall, get in the sandbags!" Martin yells above the noise,

Alfie is helping Dennis to his feet, both are covered in mud, they are not quick enough to get to the front edge of the trench, another shell lands and they are both knocked off their feet, Martin, and John run to them and get them to their feet, Dennis screams as John grabs his arm that has the large wooden splinter in it. The whole platoon are standing against the sandbags and Alfie is taking the large splinter out of Dennis's arm as John holds him very tightly, a grubby bandage is put on directly over the top of his tunic. Martin looks to his left and sees Sergeant John McPheat, a 36 year old regular army man, he gives Martin the thumbs up, standing next to him are privates Edward Odell and Ernie Dockring, the latter is obviously wounded and scared, the former has his arm around him, supporting and encouraging him. Martin returns the thumbs up just as a shell lands in the trench, there is a flash of brilliant light and an explosion, mud, wood, and sand are sent in all directions, including hitting Martin and his lads, a stinging sensation hits Martin on his face and he puts his hands up over his eyes to protect them, he can feel the detritus from the trench hitting his hands, it stings but he leaves them in place covering his eyes. The shelling continues but is moving away from their location, he uncovers his eyes and looks across the trench to where John had given him the thumbs up, there is nothing there, the area of trench where his three comrades had just been standing in is gone, there is a huge hole in the trench system, through the ringing in his ears he can hear his name being shouted, he looks at the hole in the trench and can see Sergeant Alf Howard waving at him, he can just make out what he is saying,

"Martin, are you and your platoon alright?"

He stands up and replies, "All good here Alf, where is John and his lads?"

"Dead mate, all dead, a direct hit"

Martin doesn't reply, instead he turns to his platoon and tells them to remain close to the front wall of the trench, he knows that if they get hit there is a chance of being buried but surviving.

By daylight the main attack is over, from what Martin can ascertain it has been successful, it is rumoured that over ten thousand Germans were killed by the mines exploding, some of the mines at the southern end of the battlefield had not been detonated as the Germans had made a tactical retirement after the first detonation, a total of nineteen mines had been successfully detonated, the others either abandoned or left for another day, the loss of enemy life has been huge, Martin knows they will regroup very quickly and retaliate.

At 0930 hours, 2nd Lt Joyce and twenty soldiers leave the trenches and make their way across no-man's-land, Martin, and his platoon for the first time since the explosions, look over the top of their trench and see the raiding party move across toward the enemy lines, the devastation is amazing. Hill 60 is now a crater but not as big as the crater formed at Spanbroekmolen, it can clearly be seen by Martin and his position is at least 4 miles to the North, he gazes across the battlefield, it is barren, apart from matchstick like tree trunks that stand upright having survived the war so far, not one of them has a canopy, no branches or leaves, just jagged remains and stumps of their trunks. The battlefield is littered with huge shell holes, some filled with water, some dry, small artillery cannons have been left, half sunk into the mud, bodies lie everywhere, for the first time in a long while Martin can smell the rotting corpses of the dead, the sweet, sickly, and unmistakable smell wafts across the land and into the trenches. He is aware of shouting coming toward them,

"Arms up men, the Boche are coming across!" he yells

He is stopped from putting his rifle over the top of the trench by John,

"It's ours Sarge, it's the raiding party returning, and bloody quickly"

They all duck down as machine gun bullets hit the earth in front of their trench, seconds later, five or six Bedfordshire men land heavily in the trench. Martin looks left and right, the same is happening all around him, he sees a man he knows well, a man he has known all his life at home, Charles Henry Crumplin who worked at the mill by the river before the war.

"You in a hurry Charlie!"

Crumplin looks over toward Martin, "I bloody am young fella"

The two men shake hands, Charlie is fifteen or so years older than Martin and has lived close to the cottage and the Malta his whole life, he is laughing as he tells Martin about what happened,

"We advanced toward the Hun trenches, Lt Joyce at the front, we get to the enemy trenches without a shot being fired by us or at us, we were getting into the trenches when Joyce shouts for us to retreat" he takes a deep breath in, "I look into the trench and it is packed full of Germans, there were hundreds of them"

"What did you do Charlie?" asks Martin

Charlie laughs again, "I followed the order and ran like buggery!" He looks up and down the trenches, "I think we all got back, which is a bloody miracle considering the machine guns shooting at us"

Martin hands Charlie a cigarette, they light up,

"Could I bum one from you Sergeant please" Lt Joyce is walking toward them, he is covered from head to toe in mud and is soaked through, Martin takes a cigarette and lights it for the officer from his cigarette, "Much obliged Sergeant, that was bloody close!" he moves to the front sandbagged wall and finishes his cigarette in silence, throwing the butt into the water gathered at the bottom of the trench, "Private Crumplin, I am taking a walk down the line to gather our platoon, you should come with me"

Charlie nods, "See you later Martin"

Martin nods and watches as they walk away, Lt Joyce collecting his team as he goes through.

The shelling continues from both sides but with less ferocity than at the beginning of the attack, it is about an hour later when a cry of "Attack right!" is heard, Martin sticks his head over the top of the trench, about three hundred yards to his right he can see several hundred Germans advancing toward the Bedfordshire and Yorkshire trenches, the bark of the Vickers guns begins,

"John, get the Lewis up here!" he orders

John Marrables is next to him in a flash, the Lewis light machine gun is quickly set up despite it weighing in at twenty eight pounds, its familiar inverted V shaped legs placed firmly on the ground and John starts to fire into the advancing Germans. This gun has a ninety six round pan magazine, the .303 ammunition firing from its wide muzzle at over five hundred rounds a minute, Dennis is next to him and reloading the gun at a fast rate, it has an effective range of just over eight hundred yards, so it will hit the advancing Germans easily, many are killed quickly, some turn and run back toward their lines, a yell goes up,

"Enemy in the trenches!"

A handful of enemy soldiers have entered the Bedfordshire trenches through a gap caused by the earlier artillery bombardment, they are heading toward Martin and his platoon.

"Mind out there!" a voice commands,

Martin can see 2nd Lt Searle running toward him from the other end of the trench, he is followed by Wally Battams, George Kempson, Daniel Flynn and Edwin Thorn, the battalion bombers, behind them are a handful of Canadian Tunnelling company soldiers, all explosive trained soldiers. The men in the trenches stand back and let the bombing crew go past, a few minutes go by, then muffled explosions are heard from further down the trenches, John Marrables shouts from the top of the trench,

"They are getting out of our trenches and running back toward theirs Sarge"

"Fire at will" Martin commands with quiet menace in his voice.

The Lewis gun springs into life, he hears the empty click of the pan magazine emptying,

"Cease fire lads, cease fire" Martin says "Let's not waste any more ammunition"

John and Dennis return to the bottom of the trench, the Lewis gun is still on top, it needs to cool down before it can be moved.

"Not a bad morning's work, thank you men" Martin tells the platoon "Must be time for a brew"

The battlefield is quieter, and it remains like this until early evening on the 8th June when the Germans counter attack again, they are very quickly stopped and all ground is held by the allied soldiers, the only further casualties for the Bedfordshires is when the British artillery starts again, firing 4.5 inch howitzers and the 18 pounders, sadly their aim is off and all the shells land short, landing in the allied trenches, the Bedfordshire soldiers are being shelled by the enemy and by their colleagues, two officers are wounded, one seriously, seven ordinary ranks are killed and nearly thirty are wounded, some seriously, no one really knows if the men have been killed by friend or foe. It takes a lifetime for word to get to the artillery men that they are killing their own soldiers, the barrage stops then re starts when the aim has been adjusted, the battalion is due to be relieved in less than twenty-four hours, the wounded are taken to the casualty clearing station at Poperinghe. Martin and his platoon, and one other platoon, are tasked with collecting the dead, taking them to the burial area, situated just behind the firing line, they dig a mass grave for the bodies, as deep as the ground will allow them, the ground is soddened, and the grave soon begins to fill up with water. They collect the seven dead soldiers and lay them out, each with a grave marker, which is a basic wooden cross, a strip of tin with the name of the deceased, his regiment, army number and the date of death are roughly scratched into the soft metal, it is attached to the centre of the cross with a single nail.

The dead soldiers are.

Sergeant 10221 Frank Whiddett, 30 years of age from Eaton Socon, Cambridgeshire

Private 9787 Ernest Kedge, 24 years of age from Bedford

Private 2447 Ernest Purkiss, 36 years of age from Thornton Heath, Surrey

Private 28838 Henry Harmer, 34 years of age from Stalham, Norfolk

Private 200920 David Hall, 19 years of age from St Neots, Huntingdonshire

Private 39811 Edward Bishop, 36 years of age from Long Buckby, Rugby

Private 202802 Bertram Poulton, 27 years of age from Dunstable

Each man is laid gently in the muddy grave, their first identification tag has been taken from the body, the second tag is left with the body for later identification if required, the cross with the tin plaque attached to it is placed at the head end of the grave and the heavy, wet spoil is put back into the graves covering the bodies. All the soldiers remove their helmets or caps as the Chaplain stands over the buried men and says a few appropriate words. The Chaplain attached to the Bedfordshire regiment is Reverend P.H. Turnbull, he is unwell, so another Chaplain attached to the Regiment is attending the burials, Padre Phillip Thomas Byard Clayton, known to everyone as 'Tubby', a meek looking bespectacled man, he is a familiar face to the men and popular member of the Royal Army Chaplains department. Tubby arrived at the Western front in 1915, at the town of Poperinghe, an allied held area and just out of reach of the German artillery guns, the town is popular with the soldiers when they are not on the front line. As the ongoing stalemate between the Germans and the Allied forces continues, this town is the closest 'safe' place, because of this it has become the centre for military operations, everything military that is headed for the Ypres Salient passes through the town, it is known as 'Pop' or 'Little Paris' by the visiting soldiers, numbering around a quarter of a million men, most of whom are in billets and camps outside of the town in the small villages surrounding it. The town has grown due to the influx of soldiers, cafes, bars, concert halls, brothels and even a cinema are available for the soldiers to enjoy during their break from the front lines. Because of this 'debauchery', a senior Army Chaplain, Padre Neville Talbot, instructed Tubby to start a club that offers another side of life to the soldiers, a building is rented and both men initially wanted to call it "The Church Club', but this was frowned upon by the Army hierarchy, so it was named 'Talbot House', in honour of Padre Talbot's brother, Lt Gilbert Talbot of the 7th Battalion Rifle Brigade, who had been killed at Hooge in July of 1915. It is a popular place with officers and men who shorten its name to T.H., this has become TocH, this being the phoneticized words used by signalmen, Toc for T and Aitch for H. The TocH has no room for rank, in fact, above Padre Claytons door is a sign that reads, '*Abandon Rank All Ye Who Enter Here*', the top floor is now a chapel, but the house is not primarily a religious bolt hole, it has other rooms for billiards, chess, table tennis and reading. Poperinghe is only nine or ten miles from Observatory Trench so a visit from Tubby to see the men or to bury the dead is not unusual, when the burial is completed, Martin sends the platoon off to get a decent hot drink and a meal if they can find one, he remains and stands in front of the freshly covered cadavers and lights a cigarette,

"Did you know these men Sergeant?"

Martin turns and sees Tubby standing a few feet away from him,

"I am sorry Padre, I thought you had left"

Tubby shakes his head, Martin thinks the chaplain is a very unlikely military man, his round spectacles and fresh complexion are the opposite of most of the men here, he has on his army tunic and cap, with its badge, a blackened bronze Maltese cross with the points of all its arms just touching, atop the cross is a small Imperial Kings crown, under his tunic his thick white collar of his religious office can be clearly seen.

"I always like a few moments to myself after burying our dead" he says

Martin nods and takes a draw on his cigarette, offering one to Tubby, he refuses and takes a short wooden pipe from out of his tunic pocket, he puts it in his mouth without lighting it, "Did you know these men?" he asks again

"Some, not all" Martin answers without giving further detail

"It is still a loss is it not Sergeant, whether or not we knew any of the dead" Martin agrees but can only nod his head, "You have known loss I presume Sergeant?" Tubby lights his pipe,

Martin can feel tears welling up in his eyes, his throat becomes tight, and he can only, again, nod his head, Tubby puffs out smoke and speaks quietly to Martin,

"In war Sergeant, loss of comrades is to be expected, so are feelings of guilt and sadness"

Martin, for reasons unknown to himself, blurts out,

"My loss was at home Sir"

He regrets saying it almost instantly, Tubby can see the pain on Martin's face, he walks toward him and puts his hand on Martin's shoulder,

"If you are in Poperinghe, come and see me at Talbot House, you lads call it the TocH club, if you want to" Martin nods and smiles at the chaplain, "Sergeant, my name is Phillip, everyone calls me Tubby"

"I know who you are Sir" he pauses "We all know who you are Sir!"

Tubby coughs out pipe smoke and laughs,

"Fame and notoriety at last Sergeant!"

"My name is Martin Sir, and we are in Pop in a few days, I might take you up on your offer"

"You will be welcome Martin, everyone is welcome"

The Chaplain walks away without another word, Martin stands and finishes his cigarette, he is only disturbed when Dennis shouts at him,

"Sarge! we have decent tea here; do you want a mug before we go back to the trenches?"

"Go on then Den, no sugar for me"

Dennis laughs,

"There ain't none, so you wouldn't get any"

* * *

The battalion are relieved at ten in the evening of the 9th June, the full battalion relief is finished by two the following morning, the 2nd Battalion Yorkshire regiment now have control of the Observatory trenches, the Bedfordshire men are exhausted and withdraw to the town of Vlamertinghe five miles from the trenches, here they get a train for a short journey to the town of Poperinghe, arriving at six in the morning, the wounded, nearly seventy men, are the first to alight from the train and they are taken to the casualty clearing station, during this period in the trenches, eleven more Bedfordshire men have become, and will forever remain, part of the Ypres landscape. News passes through the train that some of the battalion are to be given awards for gallantry for their part in the Battle of Transloy in October last year during the Somme offensive. Capt. Oakley is to get the Military Cross, Sergeant Alf Howard, and Sergeant Albert Mason both get the

DCM, this news lifts the Battalion, and a spontaneous round of applause begins around both of the Sergeants, this becomes quite boisterous until R.S.M Oakes arrives and calms things down,

"Get off the train" he looks at Sergeant Alf Howard "Heroes as well" a cheer erupts around Alf, "Your billets are approximately two miles southwest of here, so, N.C.O.'s, get the men formed up, there are dozens of London omnibuses on the road, ready to take us all to our camp"

Martin and his platoon wearily get on board a large London Omnibus, climbing the gently curving staircase to the open top deck, the bus sets off with a jolt and in a huge cloud of smoke, it is an uncomfortable ride as every inch of the bus has been filled with soldiers, Martin closes his eyes and remains this way until the bus jolts to a stop, he looks around from his elevated position and all he can see for hundreds of yards, are white tents, this is to be their home for the next ten days. As he gets off of the bus, Ralph calls him over, he tells his platoon to see the clerk and get their billet sorted out, then get some food, a bath, to de louse and to find the laundry, he has heard that this camp has a laundry run by French ladies that have crossed the border, it being only a few miles away, to help the soldiers, he walks over to Ralph,

"No tents for the likes of us Martin, I have arranged for a bit of comfort for you, me and a couple of others for a few days"

Martin can only smile, Ralph always finds a decent billet if there is one to be found,

"Where are we off too?" he asks the R.S.M.

"Patience lad, I am just waiting for a couple of familiar faces to join us"

Martin can only see a mass of filthy soldiers slowly making their way toward the tented area,

"Here they are" Ralph seems pleased with himself; Martin still can't make out who Ralph is talking about, then he recognises two faces,

"Bloody hell, I thought at least one of you buggers was dead!"

Sergeant Bill Peggs says to Martin and Ralph, beside him is Sergeant Len Hubbocks,

"Len, how are you? I haven't seen you for a few weeks" Martin says

"Not bad Martin, I had a spell in hospital with a bit of a nasty wound, but all is well now?"

"Right lads" Ralph instructs them "Follow me"

"It's a shame Hutch isn't with us" Len speaks as they walk

"He is the CSM at Bedford, I hear he is being moved to be CSM at Ampthill in a few weeks, he won't be back over here, his chest is too weak after the bronchitis" Ralph tells them as he strides on through the crowds. The three sergeants follow the R.S.M. as the mass of soldiers begins to thin out, they pass the officers tents and Ralph takes a sharp left turn, they all follow toward a small grey slate roofed building,

"Here we are chaps" They all look at the small structure, Ralph turns to them, "It is warm, dry and has beds, they are all in one room, but this old building has a fire and a stone floor, no mud for us for ten days or so"

All four of them enter the building through a heavy wooden door, a door that is almost certainly older than all of them combined, they each take a bed and put their kit by their chosen billet,

"I need to get clean" Martin tells them, they all agree

"A communal bath house has been set up by the engineers not far from here, there is also a Heath Robinson contraption that supposedly steam cleans the lice from clothes " Ralph tells them

"What are we waiting for!" Bill stands up and grabs his knapsack

"It is not open yet Bill" Ralph tells him

"How do you know that?" asks Bill

A killer grin forms on Ralphs's face, "Because I have not given the order for it to be opened as yet!" he exclaims

"You're a sly old sod Ralph" Martin laughs

"I think you will find Sergeant, that my title is Regimental Sergeant Major sly sod!" They all laugh "Shall we ladies?" Ralph says with a grin.

They all get up, grab their knapsacks, containing what little wash and shave kit they have left,

"If you have money, take it with you" he adds, the three sergeants look at him with confused images on their faces, "Come on, you will see"

The 'Battalion Baths' have been set up about a quarter of a mile from their billet, they arrive at an old barn, the doors are shut, Ralph nods at the Royal Engineer Sergeant and the two of them shake hands,

"All ready for you Ralph, it is a Frenchie style shower system, they call it a *doosh* or something like that"

"Good man George, we don't care as long as the water is hot" he turns to face a Lt standing nearby, the officer has a severe limp, George introduces them to each other,

"R.S.M. Oakes this is Lt Marsh, the officer in charge of laundry and bathing"

"Thank you for this Sir" Ralph shakes the officer's hand,

"Think nothing of it R.S.M" he taps his left leg "Best I can do these days"

"We appreciate it none the less Sir" Ralph turns to George,

"Where did that come from?" he points to a large circular contraption that is on the back of a lorry, it has a small engine attached to it, Lt Marsh speaks up,

"Borrowed from our New Zealand comrades R.S.M" He smiles "Best not to ask too many questions, but this is a mobile disinfector, shifts the lice from clothing"

"Do we have laundry facilities Sir?" asks Martin

"Yes Sergeant, around the back of this barn, you will find a group of French ladies, who, for a few coins, will wash just about anything you have"

They all thank the officer and George opens the barn doors and they enter, inside there is lengthy system of pipework running in rows across the barn, home-made shower heads hang from the pipework, at the far end of the barn there are four mobile bathing units, huge machines that run similar to a steam locomotive, the fires heat the water and the pressure from the heat pushes it across the network of pipes, the water will be one temperature, hot.

"What the bloody hell is that?" asks Bill as he points to the other end of the barn, he is pointing at what seems to be a large market stall, it is stocked with food, drink, soap, razors, shaving sticks, socks, and lots of other items,

"That is François stall, he is a local man and has taken it upon himself to set up a canteen, he knows that the small battalion canteen is usually sold out, he is usually set up outside of the camp, but when the wash facilities were fitted, he set up in here, we didn't stop him" George informs them

"Nor do we ask questions about where his stock comes from" Lt Marsh has joined them inside.

"Understood Sir" Ralph nods at the officer. "Shall we gents?"

The four men strip off very quickly and stand under the very hot water, they all scrub and clean their filthy bodies, when they are clean, they step to the far wall and fill old, scarred tin bowls with water and shave in front of small mirrors that have been nailed to the barn wall,

"Ralph, can I open up? There is a bloody log queue forming outside" George shouts across, he is told he can let the masses in, as soon as he opens the door, a rush of soldiers enters the building, the four of them are surprised when they hear Lt Marsh shout very aggressively,

"Slow down and form an orderly queue or I will shut this facility down!"

The freshly shaven quartet of N.C.O's spend some of their money at François stall, Martin buys socks, razors, soap and two bottles of Belgian beer, the other three have purchased similar items, they take their dirty laundry to the French ladies, who also have a couple of huge boilers for cleaning the filthy uniforms of the soldiers, they have what seems like hundreds of yards of washing lines, all filled with shirts, vest and trousers, the four again part with a small amount of money for this service, they all feel better than they have done for weeks.

Back in their somewhat comfortable billet, a fire has been lit, it is roaring hot, even though it is a warm June night they all want a fire, beer and wine bottles have been opened, Ralph has his eyes closed is smoking his pipe sitting next to the fire, Len is shuffling a pack of cards, moaning as no one will play poker with him, Bill, spectacles perched on the end of his nose, is reading a battered book and Martin is writing to Alice. He wants to tell her how desperately sorry he is for his lack of contact since Grace died, he wants to tell her how proud he is of her and that his leave has been granted, that he wants nothing more than to come home and to be by her side and to give her away when she marries Charles, he has so much to say but does not know where to start.

Alice

My darling Sister,

It has been many months since I last wrote anything worth reading, for this I am truly sorry.

I must firstly tell you that I am well, better than I have been in many months and that I love and miss you and Granny more than these words can ever say…

* * *

Alice is looking at the cottage; Martin is due home tomorrow for his ten days leave, to give her away when she marries Charles on Monday 6th August, she forces herself to keep calm although the excitement she feels at seeing Martin is ready to burst from her body. Alice had not been inside the cottage for over a year, since Grace died, she has feared entering the garden or the house, the ghosts in her mind play tricks with her every time she passes by, the Yew tree that still dominates the garden had begun to scare her so much that she cannot even look at it, until today. Granny has been pestering her to go to the cottage to have it ready for when Martin arrives home, he will have to stay there as the pub will have no room, May, Pete, and the twins will be staying there for a few days before the wedding and after the wedding reception, Alice has been putting it off because she is still scared of her own experiences both within the garden and inside the cottage. Earlier this morning, Mary had been so cross with her for not getting to the cottage, to air it and to clean it up, she was so insistent that it must be done that Alice has stormed out of the pub, before having any breakfast and has walked with great haste toward the cottage, as she gets closer, her steps faulter and her pace slackens, firstly to a walk and then she finds that she has stopped altogether, she is now standing outside of the Methodist Chapel, where she is to be married. Staring at the cottage over the road, the cottage where her parents had lived, and died, seeing its dark thatch roof, becoming bare in places, the privy can just be seen outside of the back yard, worst of all she can see the Yew tree, the tree where her parents had been found dead and the tree that killed her best friend, the tree where David took his own life and the tree that poisoned John Freeman, it stands so tall and so proud with the ever moving almost silent stream behind it. Alice has to catch her breath, her heart is pounding heavily, and she begins to feel faint,

"Good morning Alice dear, you are up and about early"

The voice comes from behind her, she looks over her shoulder to see the Reverend Wesley Woolmer standing inside the blue railings of the chapel garden, easily recognisable with his pure white thin hair and large side whiskers, his black waistcoat bulges at the buttons and his white cloth collar is as clean as newly laid snow, he has heavy gardening gloves on and is holding a pair of secateurs,

"Are you quite well?" he asks

"Yes Reverend, I think so" she stammers

He steps from the garden and onto the thin path that leads to the church door, he takes off the gloves and gently places them on the wall with the secateurs, he reaches the gate, which is closed, and he leans onto it,

"Well now, something tells me that statement is not quite true"

She turns to face him, he can see the glisten of the beginning of tears in her eyes,

"Martin is home tomorrow, I have to prepare the cottage, but I cannot face it, I see Mother, Father Grace and the boys everywhere and the Yew tree terrifies me!" she says very quickly.

Wesley Woolmer smiles gently at her, he puts his arms out toward her, she steps into him, and he embraces her over the gate,

"Child, blessed are those who mourn, for they will be comforted." he says quietly "The cottage is the same as it always has been, a home and a place of warmth and love" he puts his hands on her shoulders and looks directly at her "As for the tree" he looks across the road "It is just another tree amongst many" He releases her from his hold, and he opens the gate, "Come along" he says in a jolly manner, Alice hesitates, he puts his hand out toward her and she takes it, they cross the road and stand outside of the cottage by the garden gate, he grips her hand ever so gently, he raises his free hand toward the cottage,

"You may not be religious Alice, but the Lord knows you"

He stands with his eyes firmly closed.

"Lord, O that we could begin this day, in devout meditations,
in joy unspeakable, And in blessing and praising thee, who hast given us such good hope and everlasting consolation. Lift up our minds above all these little things below, which are apt to distract our thoughts;
And keep them above till our hearts are fully bent to seek thee every day,
In the way wherein Jesus hath gone before us"

He turns to face Alice, who says to him, "Thank you, Reverend, how clever you are to be able to say those lovely words just like that" Reverend Woolmer chuckles,

"Don't tell anyone Alice, but that is the Methodist Morning prayer! I thought it apt as we are here and welcoming a new morning and a new start"

"Thank you anyway"

He chuckles again, his large jowls jiggle as he does, "God grant that I may never live to be useless!" Alice looks at him again, "I can't claim that phrase either Alice, those are the words of John Wesley himself" he opens the gate "Shall we?"

They both enter the garden, Alice is surprised when the Reverend turns left toward the tree and not toward the cottage, she follows as fear rises in her throat, he ducks down under a low branch and places his left hand on the huge trunk, moving his fingers over the gnarly bark, he seems thoughtful,

"Ancient, morbid and toxic, a long lived beast that has become a symbol of doom and death" He beckons Alice closer, she does not move, he continues, "But this terrifying beast provides shelter and food for many animals, keeping them safe and alive" He turns and leans his back against the tree, "Romans believed that Yews grew in their hell, they have been associated with the Church in this country for hundreds of years, growing in churchyards for all of this time"

Alice, listening to the Reverend, has forgotten her fears,

"Why is that Reverend?"

He shakes his head, "No one really knows Alice, but it is thought that the Yew tree was planted on top of the graves of the victims of the great plague" he looks at her as he places his linked hands across his ample belly, "To protect and purify the victims in death, so you see, it was, and possibly still is, a belief that this tree is a protector of the dead rather than being a symbol of it" He chuckles to himself as he says, "Of course, the clergy of the past also liked to plant them in churchyards to stop the common man from grazing his livestock on Church ground, the Yew is extremely harmful to livestock" He looks up into the branches and to the thick canopy, the early morning light barely piercing its dark core, "Symbols of immortality and omens of doom, for centuries Yew branches were carried at funerals and on Palm Sunday" He looks back at Alice, stands up and pats the bark, "After all this, it is just a tree, a living, breathing tree, it means no harm to anyone" He walks away from the tree, guides Alice up the path toward the cottage, "Are you ready for the wedding? I am quite excited as it shall be my last offering as the Methodist minister in the chapel"

Alice looks stunned, "I did not know you were leaving Reverend?"

"Not leaving Alice, moving on, Amelia Ann and I have taken a position in Woolwich, we will be living in Plumstead, the Chapel here will have a newly ordained minister, a good man, Reverend Clarence Cartwright"

They enter the cottage, Alice feels an overwhelming sense of calm, she believes it is the presence of the Reverend that is helping her, "How long have you been married Reverend?"

"Amelia Ann and I have been married for over thirty-two years now, it was my father, also a Methodist minister, that married us!"

Alice sits next to him on the window bench seat, "Really? Your own Father married you?"

"Yes indeed, a good and thoughtful man was my father" He turns slightly in the seat to face her, "Alice, marriage is an important part of life, the ceremony, although a moving and vital part of this institution, is only a tiny part of the ongoing union"

He emphasises his point by making a small gap in the air with his thumb and index finger, "The partnership, the friendship and the trust are very important to a happy and fruitful marriage, responsibility for each other and for your children"

Alice blushes and the Reverend chuckles again, "Children are an important part of married life, I myself have six children!"

Alice looks shocked, "Six!"

This time he laughs out loud, "Yes, indeed we do!" he begins to count off using his fingers, he looks up as he speaks, searching his memory for the correct details,

"Margaret Amelia is the eldest, she married the Reverend Harold Jolly in January of this year" he looks stern for a second, "Amelia Ann was not in favour of the union initially, but she is warming to Harold"

He points to a second finger, "Florence Mary, or Florrie, is next, she is an English mistress at a boarding school in Luton"

Finger number three, "Shirley Beaumont is our first son, he is a manager of a hat factory in Luton, then comes Frederick Charles, he is a senior bank clerk"

He counts silently to himself, Alice smiles as she can see his lips mouthing the numbers,

"Geoffrey Challener is next" He closes his eyes as if in prayer "He is away fighting in the war, he is a 2nd Lt with the Tank regiment"

He opens his eyes and smiles, "Finally, our youngest, Ellen Beatrice, or Nellie as we call her, she is newly qualified as a teacher of Physical Education" he frowns

"What is it Reverend?" asks Alice

"Young Nellie is quite taken with a young army officer we have lodging with us at this time, 2nd Lt John Newton Hudson, he is in training with the Royal Horse Artillery, I noted that the pair of them were quite chatty at Margaret's wedding, Amelia Ann is not excited by the potential pairing I can assure you!"

Alice and Reverend Woolmer remain silent for a few minutes,

"Reverend, how do you feel about your son being at war" she pauses "I only ask because I am so scared for both Martin and Charles that I can hardly sleep"

Wesley Woolmer again looks to the heavens as he answers her, "As a minister, I cannot justify war, but reluctantly recognise that this violence being used, may bring an end to tyranny and bullying from the supposed enemy"

He pauses again, "The Church will uphold the rights of individual members of our congregation that conscientiously chooses to take a position whereby the fight is deemed appropriate"

He slowly stands, pushing his hands on his knees to help himself to get up,

"As a father of a serving soldier, I am terrified for him each and every second of the day"

He steps toward the door, "I hope to see you, Charles and Martin at the Sunday service"

With a nod, he is gone, leaving Alice to her thoughts and with her ghosts, spectres that no longer seem to have control over her fear, she stands and takes an old broom that stands next to the even older range in the fireplace, she begins to sweep the stone floor that lies thick with dust.

* * *

Martin is having a heated discussion with Ralph, it is nearly one in the morning,

"I am going on leave in less than twelve hours, authorised by Lt Col Poyntz as from 12 midday today!"

Ralph shrugs, "Sorry Martin, but Poyntz is in the hospital, Lt Col Bunbury took over command five days ago, he has been our relief C.O before, you know he is a stickler for the rules and because of the impending attack on the plateau and Pilkem Ridge, he has cancelled all leave"

Martin explodes in anger, "But my sister is getting married next week, I am giving her away for fucks sake, I haven't been home since this began in 1914!"

Ralph is about to remind Martin that he refused home leave last month, but decides against this, he puts his hands up in mock surrender, "I know lad, but what can I do, you and a dozen other lads have got to stay"

"I bet Charles isn't having a problem, I bet he is already on his way home!"

Ralph nods, "The 1st Battalion are front of the line at Arleux" he pauses "But, as an officer, I have to presume that his leave is going ahead, especially as he is the groom"

An officer approaches them,

"R.S.M, Sergeant, I think it will be better if you keep your voices to a mild scream, your *conversation*" he emphasises the word "Can be heard for many a mile and I think our positions have been compromised as I am certain every single Bosch soldier has heard you!"

Ralph turns smartly on his heel to face the officer, he sees which officer it is and realises that it isn't some young smartarse Rupert, it is Major Wynn and he is not happy,

"My apologies Major, young Martin here is supposed to be on leave today, he is still here, so you can imagine how he feels"

"Sacrifices R.S.M., sacrifices, we all have to take one on the chin at times, now be ready, we are off shortly"

Major Wynn makes his way down the line, telling all the platoon commanders to have their soldiers ready to move off at a moment's notice.

"I will be staying then" Martin looks at Ralph, who nods,

"Looks like it son, get your team ready, I will find you later"

Ralph also moves off down the line, Martin turns to his lads and gets them to check all their kit, to be ready for the off. At 0350 hours the Fifth army attack begins, the Bedfordshires are being held in reserve, the four battalions from 53rd Brigade of the 18th Eastern Division have joined the 30th Division and orders are, that the division will move forward and advance across the Gheluvelt Plateau toward Glencorse wood. There is confusion as the attack begins in the dark of the early morning, it is also raining heavily, it is quickly reported that the 21st Brigade, who are to the North of the Bedfordshires and the rest of the 30th Division positions, has lost its way during their advance through the chaos and wreckage of Sanctuary wood, the sound of heavy German machine guns can clearly be heard, also the 90th Brigade are trapped at Chateau

Wood to the North of Sanctuary wood, they are taking a battering from German artillery, the Battalions of the 30th Brigade in the furthest Northerly positions of this sector, are instructed to move across the Menin road, south of the dog leg and advance toward and to take Glencorse Wood. Martin's platoon and the rest of A company, along with B company are told to remain in their front-line positions, they are to be ready to attack Jargon Trench, held by the Germans and in a position just West of Glencorse wood. It is just after 0545 hours when R.S.M. Oakes calls all the Sergeant and Corporal platoon leaders from A and B companies to a briefing to update them, Martin knows it has not gone well when Ralph begins his briefing with the words,

"Gentlemen, this is an absolute cluster, a proper mess"

He tells them that other battalions from the 30th Division, their Division, have made a mistake whilst manoeuvring in the dark, they have inadvertently crossed the Menin Road in a position to the north of the dog leg in the road instead of to the south, they are reporting that they have taken their objective, Glencorse Wood, without any resistance at all but it is believed that they are in the southern point of Chateau Wood, close to the soldiers from the 90th Brigade. The remainder of the 30th Division is to prepare to move off shortly to attack Jargon trench, they can't move off until the attached Battalions from the 53rd Brigade of the 18th Eastern division have been stopped from advancing across the Menin road with the mistaken belief that Glencorse wood has been taken and held by the Allied troops. The sound of heavy machine gun fire tells them that it is too late, the lads from the 53rd Brigade have a fight on their hands, they advanced believing that the areas would be undefended, and they find the opposite, the Bedfordshires get ready to move in to help. At 0600 hours they are all told to 'move out', instead of moving forward they are marched away from the front line to Chateau Segard near to Voormezeele, no sooner than they arrive they are marched away again, this time to Promenade Trench, immediately South of Zillebeke Lake, here they take up defensive positions and have time for a brew and a smoke. Sanctuary wood has been taken by the 21st Brigade after being subjected to several hours of artillery and fighting against heavy German machine gun fire.

At 4.15 that afternoon they are moved again, marching for another half an hour to a position north of Maple Copse, heading back toward the front lines, here they wait in file for orders. Orders arrive, the Bedfordshires are to advance toward Jargon Trench taking the left advancing position, the Kings Liverpool Regiment are to be on their right, rain is cascading down the men are all soaked through and the ground beneath their feet is a river of mud and sludge, they can hardly move as the mud is so thick. The soldiers stand in file for over an hour and a half, eventually at 5.50pm, the order is sent through to cancel the attack on Jargon Trench due to the awful weather and the boggy conditions, it is also obvious that many of the German machine gun positions have not been destroyed as they are still spewing out their murderous bullets toward the Allied positions. The division is yet again told to move back and away from the front lines, to a field 300 yards to the East of Dormy house, shelling begins again, it is heavy and continuous, the Bedfordshires take cover in adjacent trenches as the Allied artillery responds by firing their 5.9's toward the German lines that are not very far at all from the trench where Martin and his platoon are lying as flat as they can in the mud and rain. Here they stay until a reconnoitring party let by 2nd Lt Methuen are sent toward Jackdaw trench, this had been held by the Germans until they had been driven from it by the men of the 90th Brigade in a vicious hand to hand fight , the patrol returns just over an hour later to confirm that Jackdaw Trench is in the hand of the Allies, the worst of the fighting is over for now and small parts of the main objective to the North, a German observation area on the high areas of Pilckem Ridge, has been taken from the Germans. The men of the 30th Division are again sent forward, the Bedfordshires are heading for Jackdaw trenches, 50 yards from Sanctuary wood, the Battalion have been moved in circles all day and have not fired a shot in anger. The night is dark and wet when they set off for Jackdaw trenches, arriving just before eleven that night, relieving the soldiers from the 16th Manchester regiment, who are very pleased to see the Bedfordshires, they have been involved in heavy fighting and many of their number have been killed. Martin gets his platoon sorted, it is too wet to brew up and no one wants to eat any cold bully beef, the men have stiff muscles, they are cold, soaked through, hungry and most are very miserable indeed, none more than Martin,

"I am never going to get home" he mumbles to himself.

* * *

Charles has been away from the front line for four days; his leave is being allowed even though the 1st Battalion are back in front line trenches at Arleux, his C.O., Lt Col Percy Worral informed Charles that he had, again, been '*Gazetted*', a citation for his second Military Cross award, has been published in the latest London Gazette, published on 17th July 1917, this citation relates to his actions during the Battalions attack at La Coulotte on 23rd April 1917.

Capt. Charles Gray, M.C., and Bar

1st Battalion Bedfordshire Regiment

'For conspicuous gallantry and devotion to duty by rushing to a dug-out in which men had been buried by shell fire and digging out the men, aided by two other N.C.O's. He himself was wounded and in a state

of collapse but insisted on helping to carry the wounded to a dressing station under heavy machine gun and shell fire, returning on two more occasions to evacuate the wounded.

He displayed the greatest courage and ability and is an inspiration to all ranks.

(M.C. Gazetted 2nd April 1915)

Charles and his unit are alongside another unit commanded by Capt. William Chirnside, both had reached the furthest objective, crossing open land, this despite this first wave from the Battalion suffering many casualties, Charles is aware that at least eight of his men have been killed, heavy fighting with the enemy ensued and a shell exploded close to both units. William is nearly completely buried by the explosion and many of his men are also buried and seriously wounded, Charles unit also had many wounded due to this shell exploding, he himself took a piece of shrapnel in his shoulder but he remained on scene with his Sergeant and Corporal and helped to dig out the buried men, William Chirnside helps. Some of the men are already dead, probably killed by the shell exploding, but several are found alive, most have serious wounds, William insists on remaining in position to establish a strong point to maintain security of the ground taken. Charles organises the safe evacuation of the wounded, both from his unit and from Captain Chirnside's. Charles returns to the front line from the rear lines and the relative safety of the dressing station on two further occasions, on this final trip, he had been instructed to take four platoons to maintain the strong point, this is when he insisted that William Chirnside return with him to get checked over. Their positions are being constantly shelled and attacked by large numbers of the enemy, due to the actions of both Charles and William, the strongpoint is maintained, and many men survive their injuries.

Lt Col Worral has only been the C.O of the 1st Battalion for a little over three weeks at this time, he admires the tenacity and bravery of both men, William had been recommended for a D.S.O. but as this decoration is usually only given to those of the rank of at least Major, so he was awarded the M.C and promoted in the field to Major, Charles had been recommended and receives, a bar to his first M.C. The C.O. likes Charles a lot and authorised his leave despite intelligence suggesting that another big push is being put forward by the British Army high command. The battalion is back in the trenches just South of Arleux on the 28th of July, Charles is given special dispensation not to go forward, even though his leave does not start until today, he had led and completed the night training exercise on the 27th of July, whereby the battalion had to complete a night march to Ecurie Station, every man wearing his box respirator for the whole march, it was after this that Lt Col Worral told him to remain in camp rather than travel to the front lines at Arleux, Charles has spent the few days working with the Lt Col on Battalion orders. It is just before nine in the morning and Charles is ready to leave, transport to Vimy, recently taken from the Germans, has been organised and he will take a train to Choques, then change trains to get to Boulogne, then a ferry to Folkestone, the 'leave' train to Victoria will depart at eight tomorrow morning, he should have plenty of time to make it, the ferry should get him into Folkestone this evening, giving him time to be ready for the train tomorrow morning, there will be thousands of others travelling for home leave, he is prepared to sleep on the platform if he can't get a hotel or a room.

He presents himself to his C.O. before he leaves,

"That's me Sir, thanks again for sorting my leave, it means a great deal to me"

"Of course, Captain, I hope the wedding is all you wish it to be, it is a damn shame that you will only get a few days with your new bride"

"I am grateful for any time I get to spend with her Sir" The Lt Col stands up and offers his hand to Charles, who accepts, "Sir, any news on the 2nd Battalion, my future brother in law is a sergeant with them and is giving the bride away"

Worral sits down and rubs his chin,

"Sorry old man, but they are in the thick of it, battle orders first thing this morning, the whole lot of them are in it, Charlie Bunbury has cancelled all leave"

Charles is lost for words for a few moments,

"Where are they Sir?"

"The main offensive is an attack on Pilckem Ridge, but there are offensive attacks all through the Gheluvelt plateau" he looks directly at Charles "I have already heard this morning that the initial attack, although successful so far, has been costly, many men injured and killed I think" Charles is quiet "Captain, there is nothing to be done, I know what you are thinking, and I won't allow you to traipse halfway across France and into Belgium on some bloody goose chase" Charles remains quiet "Do you hear and understand me Captain?"

"I do Sir"

"Good, now get home and marry that bride of yours"

Charles salutes his Commanding officer and leaves the room, making his way outside he sees the lorry that will be taking him on the short journey to Vimy,

"All your stuff is aboard Sir"

Charles thanks the private and gets into the back of the lorry, there are several other soldiers already seated, both officers and enlisted men, all are going on home leave.

The lorry sets off in a cloud of smoke, most of the men cheer because they are going home for a few days, many for the first time since the beginning of the war.

Charles does not join in.

* * *

Alice wakes up early again this morning, she finished cleaning and tidying the cottage yesterday afternoon and feels so much better about everything, she misses her parents and Grace dreadfully, but she has been able to face her demons, both in the cottage and the garden, especially the Yew Tree, that for so long has been her nemesis, she smiles as she recalls the words of Reverend Woolmer.

"*After all this, it is just a tree, a living, breathing tree, it means no harm to anyone*"

She now believes this, it is just a tree, a huge living beast, but a tree none the less.

She is excited because Charles is due home today, his train from London is due in at one thirty three this afternoon, she has arranged to meet him from the train at East station, she hears Granny calling up the stairs,

"Breakfast is ready!"

Alice steps from her room, it will only be her room for another five days, and goes down to the kitchen, "Morning Granny" she says happily

"And to you Alice" She sounds grumpy

"Is everything fine with you Granny?"

"Just dandy, I have a busy day today and don't really know where to start"

Alice giggles, "What can I do to help? Charles is not due at the station for a few hours, so I can do just what you want me to do"

Mary frowns, "Is that cottage neat and tidy?"

Alice tells her that it is.

"Fresh linen on Martin's bed" The same response from Alice, "Have you been and had the dress adjusted?"

"Maggie is finishing it today; I will try it on later" She stands and hugs Mary, "It is so nice of you to give me your old wedding dress Granny, it is so pretty"

"Less of the old if you please, Maggie will need paying for her time"

Mary puts her arms around her Granddaughter for a second or two,

"Your Dad and Grandad Ted would be so proud of you" she whispers, standing up straight she smooths her apron, "You could tidy the bar and glasses if you would not mind, it was busy last night, those lads from the North Staffordshire's were in again"

"I will do that for you Granny, what have you got to do today that is making your life so busy?"

Mary looks at Alice,

"Mrs Ackroyd needs me to see the cake, it is nearly done" she rolls her eyes, "That will need paying for, I bet she has put too much fruit in it" she adds, Alice takes a bite of her fried egg sandwich, Mary continues, "Mrs Ackroyd is kindly lending me one of her fancy dresses for the wedding, she is so busy as Thomas has purchased the empty house on Station Road right on the corner with Victoria road, they are closing the bakery in Flamstead and having two here" she looks at the floor, "The dress is lovely, but it needs a bit of adjusting and that girl that works in the bakery" she pauses "You know the one that is dating young Ernest"

Alice smiles, "Olive is her name Granny"

"That's her, well she is a bit of a seamstress and is adjusting it for me, I have to go for a fitting this morning" Mary rolls her eyes skyward; Alice fails in her attempts to stop laughing, "What is so funny my girl?" Mary asks crossly

"Nothing Granny" Alice stands and hugs Mary again "You are the greatest and I love you very much"

Alice sees Mary smile, just a little.

"Now Alice, Walter will be in before lunchtime to open up, he is working every day this week and is behind the bar for your reception, did you tell me how many of the munition's girls will be coming?"

"Five not including Maggie, she and Edward have separate invites"

Mary looks at her, "Were any of the girls close to those killed in the accident in January?"

Alice shakes her head, "Olive Andrews from Coldharbour lane is the only one I know a little from around here, her 17-year-old brother was killed, but she doesn't work with us"

"I know her Mother, Elizabeth and her Husband Thomas, bad business for them, don't they have two other children?"

"Yes" says Alice "Edwin and Reginald, both overseas in the war with the 1st Battalion Hertfordshire regiment"

"Thomas does not come in here much nowadays, since the lad died"

Alice nods again, she has just started her last mouthful of sandwich, but she has also not seen Mr Andrews for some time,

"I must be off, get that bar cleaned and don't be late for the train, tell Charles that everything is in order, I have even spoken to his mother"

Alice stands and puts her hands on her hips, "Granny, what have you been speaking to Mrs Gray about?"

Mary folds her apron and puts it across the back of a chair,

"Your wedding night" Mary answers bluntly

"Granny!" Alice begins to blush

"Hush child, I was just confirming that Charles and you can stay there after you are wed, I have a pub full so there is no room here"

Mary leaves the kitchen without another word, Alice picks up her grandmothers' apron and puts it on, she enters the bar and begins to collect glasses and empty the ashtrays.

At one thirty exactly, Alice is standing on platform one of the East station, waiting for the inbound train from London, she has butterflies in her belly and has a smile that won't leave her face, she can see the smoke from the train engine in the distance, she resists the temptation to jump up and down like a child, she has to force herself not to do this and to behave like a woman, a soon to be married woman. The train pulls in and stops with a squeal of its brakes and much hissing of steam, she watches impatiently as the doors open from the carriages and the passengers begin to get off, Charles is nowhere to be seen, she turns around and waits for the steam to clear so she can get a view toward the front of the train, she can hear doors slamming closed in front of her and behind her, the steam clears,

"Next stop, Luton Hoo!" she hears the station master shout, and this is followed by a shrill blast of his whistle, she hears the pressure building up in the engine, more steam is released, and the huge engine and carriages begin to slowly pull away. The passengers that have left the train have nearly all cleared the station, leaving Alice standing all alone with tears running down her cheeks, Charles is not on the train.

* * *

The first day of the eight month begins in the rain, the Bedfordshires have spent the night in Jackdaw trench, Martin and his platoon and the rest of A company and the lads from D company are side by side, C company are about three hundred yards behind them in Jam Avenue trenches, B company are missing and cannot be found. Their C.O, Lt Col Bunbury has been through and visited each of the platoons in the trenches. Martin has a silent admiration for the man although he ruined his chance to get home, he is dressed in his smart officers' uniform and was wading through the same mud and water that he and his platoon are currently in and did so without batting an eyelid. H is standing on a shelf made from sandbags and wooden pallets, he has his head inside an area that has been dug out from the wall of the trench, it even has a tarpaulin cover over the top of the shelf, it makes Martin think of the butcher's shop in town,

"I'm brewing up here Sarge if you want a Bovril or something?"

"What's the water like?" asks Martin

"Wet Sarge" H smiles

"I think what the Sergeant is asking you private" Nobby pipes up "Is if the water is clean or the usual filth we get in trenches?"

"I was only joking Corp, the water is from mine and John's canteens, so it is as clean as we can get around here"

"In that case, two Bovril's please H"

H turns around, Nobby speaks to his back, "When you have done that, there are several trench latrines that need clearing out"

H turns back quickly to face his Corporal, Nobby puts his hand up to silence the private, "Only joking H! Get them brews made"

"Very funny" grumbles H as he turns back around.

They all hear the familiar sound of artillery incoming toward them, every man takes cover as huge explosions happen in quick succession all around them, Martin hears men crying for help and shouts for a medic, he can see that trenches have collapsed, and he can smell the obvious destruction of human bodies. Every time he and his platoon try to move out to help their colleagues, the shells exploding stop them in their tracks, to leave their position will mean certain death. It seems like a lifetime, though in reality it is only minutes, until the home artillery responds and begins to fire back, this moves the enemy attack away from Jackdaw trenches.

"Let's go!" shouts Martin

The platoon follows him toward the nearest site of destruction, a shell has hit the top of the trench, almost right on top of the men in it, Martin cannot see any soldiers but in front of him is a mass of broken wood, lying around like huge, discarded matchsticks, the now split sandbags have done nothing to reduce the impact of the shell and it is quiet, no screaming, no shouting, all the yells he had heard only minutes before from this location have stopped. Further up the line, the picture is the same, he can hear screaming, crying men, he can hear orders being shouted, but here, where he is, there is nothing but a screaming deathly silence. He sees movement in the liquid mud in front of him,

"Alfie, H, John, get in there and get that man out!"

The three of them move as quick as they can through the mire, they delve into it and pull out a man, he is unidentifiable as he is covered in brown slime, the crimson of fresh blood on his head stands out easily against the dullness,

"I think it is Lt Shaw" H yells.

The popular young officer is attached to the 2nd Battalion from the 3rd, his brother is also an officer with the 2nd but is currently back home after being wounded, sadly his wife died whilst he was in hospital.

"Is he alive?" asks Martin

"Barely" H replies

"Get him out and get him on a stretcher to the dressing station"

"Martin!" Nobby screams "Got one here!"

Martin turns to see Dennis, Nobby and John pulling a man from underneath a huge, wrecked pile of wood and metal sheeting,

"Shit!" John has cut his hand badly on a torn piece of corrugated iron

Martin orders him out of the way and jumps into the area to help Nobby and Dennis, he is shocked, almost to tears, when he sees who the man is that has been pulled out of the shell hole, so very obviously dead. Ernie Harris from Kinsborne Green, Martins friend from home, they had been at St Nicks school together, they had been fishing together at weekends and both had played football and cricket on the common with the other boys from town. Martin takes Ernie's body and sits on the edge of the trench, Ernie's head lies limply in his lap, Martin has his hands on his dead friend's face, gently clearing the mud away from his dead staring eyes and his limp mouth,

"Sarge" Martin does not hear Dennis address him, "Sarge" Dennis tries again

No response. Nobby steps forward, firmly he says, "Martin"

He looks up at Nobby, "Ernie was my pal from school Nobby, one of my oldest mates"

Nobby kneels in the mud, "Let us take him Martin, we can get him registered, we have to get him registered and then he can be buried" Nobby nods at the other two.

Dennis and John, who has a filthy bandage tied around his cut hand, assist Nobby to take the body of Ernie Harris from Martins gentle grip, they carry him away, leaving their Sergeant sitting, looking emotionlessly across the open derelict land in front of him, he pays no mind to the exploding shells that continue to destroy the already smashed landscape in this area of hell.

Ernie is dead, will he be next?

Early evening arrives and it is relatively quiet, Lt Shaw died from his wounds an hour ago, Ernie Harris was dead almost immediately the shell hit, Privates Douch and Reynolds died in the same attack as did Billy Marston and Granthby Painter. All the remaining men from the 2nd are lined up, ready to move from Jackdaw trenches to the front line, to relieve the lads from the 17th Battalion Kings Liverpool Regiment, when given the order to move off they only manage to get a few yards, the ground is sodden, deep mud everywhere and impossible to move across, the field guns are stuck, as are the horses that are dragged in to pull the guns out, Major Wynne orders them all back to Jackdaw, he disappears to report that it is impossible to move. The battalion are told to remain in Jackdaw but to prepare, certainly within the next forty eight hours, to carry out the attack ordered yesterday; Glencorse Wood needs to be taken from the enemy.

Martin has a feeling that he will never get home, he hopes that Charles is having more luck.

* * *

Charles is at Folkestone station at seven o clock on the morning of the 1st of August, he has spent the night on a bench outside of the station, he gave up looking for a hotel or a room after being turned away on five different occasions, everywhere is full.

"Could I get a light from you please Sir"

Charles takes out his matches and lights the cigarette being held by a young Corporal,

"Would you like a smoke Sir?" the Corporal asks

Charles declines, thanking him for the offer,

"It's a bugger about the leave train ain't it Sir"

Charles turns to the lad, "What do you mean Corporal?" he asks

As he blows smoke out of his mouth, the Corporal answers,

"The eight o clock has been cancelled, it never left London last night, it's still there as far as I know"

Charles cannot believe his bad luck, "What time is the replacement Corporal?"

A shrug and a "Don't think there is one"

This means Charles is stuck here and there is nothing he can do about it. He takes a cigarette from the packet in his pocket, takes off his cap, lights his cigarette and tries to remain calm, he finds this very difficult as he can feel disappointment and anger welling up inside of him, his ten days of leave is now at least one day short. He finishes his smoke and sets off to find a member of staff to get details of the next leave train, there must be one as thousands of troops are milling about waiting to get to London. When he finds an elderly station master, he asks him about the leave train, the old man only answers,

"Tomorrow"

"What do you mean tomorrow, are you saying that there are no leave trains today at all?" Charles is trying to keep his anger in check, the old man looks at him and repeats,

"Tomorrow"

Charles climbs aboard the leave train, it is six thirty in the morning, he has spent a second night sleeping on the bench, thousands of other uniformed men have done the same, he takes a seat in a first class carriage with four other officers, he leans back, puts his cap over his eyes and sleeps, last night's rest was fitful at best, it was a warm and dry night, and he is thankful for that, the train sets off, its gentle rocking motion helps to keep Charles asleep.

"Sir" Charles hears a voice "Sir"

He feels a gentle shake on his shoulder, he takes his cap off of his face and looks directly at a Lt,

"Victoria Station Sir, you have slept all the way from Folkestone"

The officer seems pleased with himself,

"Did I miss much on the journey Lt?"

"No Sir, it was tedious"

Charles smiles at the officer, "Glad I managed to sleep all the way! I thank you for waking me up Lt"

"My pleasure Sir, do you have far to travel?"

"Kings Cross first, then just a half dozen or so stops and I will be home"

Charles stands up, "What about you Lt?"

"St Pancras for me Sir"

Charles pats the officer on the shoulder, "Follow me Lt, avoid the tube at all costs"

"Really Sir, I thought the tube will be quickest"

Charles laughs, "Lt, if you wish to take the tube and join the long lines of other soldiers queuing to get across London, then be my guest, if you want to sit and watch the city go by, then follow me to the bus stop!"

Charles sets off followed by the 2nd Lt, they arrive at the bus stop and again as before, the locals let the army lads on first, the driver of the 390 bus won't take a fare from them and they get a seat.

"What is your name Lt?" Charles asks,

"Frank William Curtis Sir"

Charles shakes his hand and introduces himself,

"Is this your first leave Sir?"

"No" he says shaking his head "My second, I am on my way home to get married in a few days!"

"Congratulations Sir"

"Please, call me Charles, I will be off to see my young lady this evening, I should have been there yesterday, but the train was cancelled"

Frank nods, he was supposed to be on the same train, "I only have ten days leave and one of them has already gone"

"Where have you travelled from?" asks Charles

"France, I was sent to Salonika in January with the Shropshire light infantry, but I contracted malaria and was sent back home to England, I went to join my new unit, the 6th Battalion Leicester regiment about eight weeks ago and no sooner had I arrived than leave was authorised, so here I am!"

"Bloody hell Frank, you have been about a bit, I take it you are back to France after this"

Frank nods,

"Do you live far from London Charles?"

"Not really, a small place called the Folly"

Franks eyes light up, "The Folly just outside of Wheathampstead?"

Charles looks shocked, "Indeed yes, it is, how do you know it?"

"Football, we played the Folly many times"

Charles is amazed, "Which team did you play for?"

"The town first eleven, I live with my mother at Longcroft avenue up behind the Old Church of St Nicks"

Charles claps his hands, "My brother-in-law to be played for them as well, I think we must all be about the same age"

"What is his name?"

Charles tells him, a huge smile appears on Frank's face,

"Martin, yes, a very good player, we went to St Nicks together, I was the year above him, I haven't seen him since about 1910 when he joined the army"

"Well," Charles says, "He still is in the army, and I am hoping he will be able to get home as he is giving his sister away to me!"

"Are you marrying young Alice, Charles?"

"I am, so nothing bad must be said about her in my presence!" Charles jokes

"Not at all, she was only a young girl when I last saw her"

Charles rubs his head, "I met another chap from town, he knows Martin and Alice, he is a footballer as well" Frank stays quiet as Charles thinks, "Bertie something"

"Not Bert Weston!" exclaims Frank

Charles points at his new friend, "That's him, he is a private with the... bloody hell I can't remember"

"The 7th Battalion East Surrey regiment, I saw his mother at her home at Coleswood Road when I was back with the Malaria, he is also a fine footballer"

Charles turns to Frank, "Will you be available on the 6th?"

Frank nods, "I should think so, may I ask why?"

"Well, as I said, I am marrying the lovely Alice, I have a surprise guest attending as my best man and it would be great to have another fellow officer there, how about it"

"I would be honoured Charles, if you are sure, we have only just met after all"

"I am certain, do you know the Methodist chapel?"

"In town, near Leyton Green or the Bowling Alley?"

"Neither, do you know the Malta pub near to the East Station?"

"I do, I forgot about the little Chapel there"

"Monday 6th, Midday in the pub, a few chaps will be having a drink before the ceremony at two"

"In uniform I presume"

Charles nods, "Not full dress, I don't have mine, but tunic shirt and tie, you know the form"

"I will be there, thank you again"

The driver yells up the stairs, "St Pancras!"

"That's us Frank"

They both get off of the bus, Charles points over the road to Kings Cross,

"I am over there" the men shake hands, "Damn fine to meet you Frank, see you on the 6th"

"The Malta, Midday, I will be there, so nice to meet you Charles"

They part and Charles makes his way toward Kings Cross station, he is in luck the train he needs is standing at the platform and he makes it aboard with plenty of time before it leaves, he takes a seat, opposite him sits a lady, in her late forties he guesses, she is smartly dressed and is staring at him, he ignores her apparent rudeness, he takes his newspaper and begins to read it, as the train moves off he hears a female voice,

"I suppose you love the uniform, the war and all don't you?"

Charles lowers his newspaper and realises it is the lady sitting opposite him that is talking,

"Pardon me Madam?" he says politely

"You heard me, you lot in your uniforms, glorifying war and killing"

Charles folds his newspaper, "Madam, you don't know me, I don't know you and I would appreciate it if you would refrain from talking to me in that manner"

She carries on, obviously not listening to Charles,

"You lot had my lad killed"

Charles looks around the carriage, most of the men are ignoring the angry woman, heads buried deeply into their open newspapers, Charles sighs,

"I am sorry your son was killed, I presume by 'my lot', you mean the army?"

"Yes!" she almost spits the words at him, her vitriol is clear to anyone listening, "He was a family man was my Richard, Lily and his two children are now all alone, and you lot are to blame!"

Charles begins to say,

"I assure you Madam, that..."

She shouts over him, "Killed in a place I have never heard of, by people I have never met, all I get is a letter, not even his body"

Another man in uniform wearing a red cap walks down the carriage and stands in front of Charles and the angry lady,

"Would you like me to escort this woman off of the train for you Sir?"

Charles looks up at the Military policeman,

"That won't be necessary Sergeant, the lady is bereaved, her son was killed, I understand her anger"

The Sergeant nods, "I'm just back here if you need me Sir"

"Thank you, Sergeant, I will be fine"

Charles looks across at the lady, she is sitting bolt upright, her teeth clenched, Charles can see the tension in her jaw, she is crying silently, he takes a handkerchief from his pocket and hands it to her,

"Tell me about your Richard Madam, I am truly sorry that he was killed"

She takes the handkerchief from him gently and dabs her eyes, although upset, she has calmed down considerably.

"He was a painter and decorator, only twenty five, married with two lovely kids" She looks at him with anger back in her eyes "He had no interest in fighting in a war or the army, and before you say or think it, he was no conchie!"

"I have no issue with those who don't or didn't want to fight, I have no problem with conscientious objectors either" She still looks very angry, and her jaw is still tightly clenched, "I chose to join the army and serve, but I understand those that don't feel the need to do as I have"

"Richard had no choice!" she says with venom, Charles remains calm,

"Conscripted?"

She nods several times as she wipes mover tears from her eyes,

"They changed the rules in May last year, married men were included in the call up and his letter arrived soon after, he was dead less than four months later"

"I am sorry he was killed; do you know where he was?"

She nods,

"Some place called Transloy, or something like that" Charles is aware of the battle of Le Transloy "He was with the London regiment, joined them in September after his training and was killed on October the first, I have no idea where, or even if he is buried"

"Madam, nothing I can say can change what has happened, but I can say with confidence, that he would have had a decent Christian burial, his mates will have seen to that" Charles really has no idea if this is true, many men lie dead on the fields of France and Belgium without a burial or a marker,

"All I got was a lousy letter from some Colonel or another telling me that His Majesty sends his sympathy on the loss of my boy" She sits bolt upright, and speaks in a clear loud voice, "What a load of bollocks!"

Charles fights to conceal his smile as he notices that most of the men hiding behind their newspapers are making tutting sounds or looking around their papers at her, Charles also speaks in a loud voice,

"Here, here!" She now smiles in surprise at his reply "At least he did his bit, whether he wanted to or not, he went over to France, which is more than I can say for some of these, paper shaking, tutting men that we all seem to meet on a daily basis"

She lets out a little laugh, she holds out her hand,

"Mrs Elizabeth Robinson from Willesden Green"

He gently shakes her hand,

"Charles Gray, The Folly"

"Where on earth is that?" she asks

"Near to Wheathampstead, if you haven't heard of that, I suppose St Albans is the nearest city to me"

"I know both, my sister lives in the Ayots, that is where I am travelling today"

"If it is in order with you, I would like to keep you company on the journey"

She agrees and they talk about her son until they reach Welwyn where they both must change trains, as they stand, one of the men who was hiding behind his newspaper approaches Charles, extending his hand to shake with Charles,

"I heard what this woman said to you Sir, and I am disgusted that she feels she can talk to a serving soldier like that" the man looks at Elizabeth "And using such language"

Charles does not shake the man's hand,

"I presume you have served Sir, wounded, or injured in battle?"

"No" the man says confused "I am a civil servant, I am needed here, I serve my King in my employment"

"Interesting" says Charles "What do you do exactly?"

"I teach English"

"So, you are a schoolteacher?" Then man nods, "Many former teachers are fighting in this war" Charles tells him,

The man becomes very defensive, "My role in educating the young is an important one, as important as all the young men being killed in France and Belgium"

Charles laughs out loud, "Sir, if I may quote this lovely lady who has been sitting with me, who incidentally has lost her son fighting in the war" he pauses before saying. "What a load of bollocks!" He offers his arm to Elizabeth, "Mrs Robinson, if you would be so kind as to let me escort you from the train"

Elizabeth takes Charles arm, and they step off of the train, the man is angry with Charles, he turns to the soldier in the red cap,

"You are an army policeman; did you hear what this man just said to me"

The Sergeant stands from his seat very slowly and stands next to the man, he stands a good four inches taller than the teacher,

"Are you talking to me" he growls

"Yes, indeed I am" the teacher cowers a little as he is spoken to by the soldier,

"Well, I am Sergeant Butler of the Corps of Military foot police, I am aboard this train to ensure that good discipline is maintained by members of His Majesties armed forces, also to look for deserters and those absent without leave" He takes a step closer toward the teacher, he is very close to him, "I don't think you fit any of these descriptions" he turns to Charles

"Have a good day Captain" he touches the front of his cap as he addresses Elizabeth, "You too Ma'am"

Charles and Elizabeth walk across toward platform 3, this is where the Dunstable branch line is and will take them to their destinations. As they travel the short distance from Welwyn to Ayot, Elizabeth asks Charles what being in the war is like, Charles does not want to instil vivid images of pain and death in her mind, she will always relate these to her son, he tells her it is ninety five percent boredom, sometimes wet and cold in the trenches, but mostly it is quiet, sometimes during attacks or advances, men are killed, it is a sad fact about the nature of conflict.

"I didn't really mean to blame you for Richard's death, I know it isn't your fault, but I had to vent off and when I saw you, well, I lost my temper"

The train pulls into Ayot station, Charles stands as Elizabeth gets up to leave,

"Elizabeth, I am truly sorry that Richard was killed, many have died, and I am afraid that many more will die before this is sorted"

She leans in and kisses him on the cheek,

"I hope one of them isn't you Charles"

She waves goodbye to him and is gone. Charles, for the first time in a long time, feels empty about the death of a stranger, an odd feeling because he has been involved in the killing and wounding of hundreds of enemy soldiers, all of whom are strangers to him, he is saddened for the Mothers, Sisters and wives that have, and will, lose their nearest and dearest, as he sits back down for the rest of the journey, he thinks only of Alice and how he must do his absolute best to stay alive, for her so that she does not have to go through what poor Elizabeth Robinson and thousands of others are having to go through every day of their lives.

* * *

Mary is sitting at the kitchen table with Alice,

"I am sure everything is fine with both of them, just delayed that is all"

Alice is sitting with her chin resting on both her hands, with her elbows on the table, Mary scolds her,

"Sitting like a sulking child is not a good look for a woman who is to be married in a few days!"

"I know Granny, but not hearing anything is the worst"

"Did you try your dress on at Maggie's?"

Alice nods, "It is stunning Granny; Maggie has done an amazing job"

A voice calls out from the bar, Mary turns and answers,

"I will be there in a minute Walter" she looks at her watch and calls back to him "Open up, it's about time" Mary takes off her apron, "I have to go and work the bar with Walter, lunchtimes are busy, these farm lads start early and finish late, so they all want a couple of pints at lunchtime"

Alice nods glumly, her head looks up suddenly when she hears a voice from the bar,

"A pint of pale please Walter"

She looks at Mary,

"Charles?" she whispers

Mary stands out of the way as Alice jumps up and runs toward the bar.

Charles is leaning against the bar, pint in hand and cap on the bar top,

"Charles!" Alice shouts, she runs, tears falling down her cheeks and puts her arms around his waist and hugs him, he hands his pint quickly to Walter,

"Charles, oh Charles, I thought something awful had happened"

"It did" Charles tells her "The leave train was cancelled, and I had to sleep on a bench!"

"Alice" Mary sounds stern "Not in the public bar please"

Alice takes her arms away from Charles waist, Mary nods toward the kitchen,

"Go in there, the pair of you"

He picks up his pint and lifts it toward Mary,

"Good to be back home" he says

"It's good to see you Charles" Mary replies "Now get in the kitchen before my Granddaughter bursts!"

* * *

"Have you heard Sarge"

Martin shakes his head at Dennis, who has returned from the trench latrine and is climbing into the 'den' that has been created in the side of the front wall of the trench. It is no more than a man dug hole that has been lined with corrugated sheeting and sandbags,

"We are being relieved tonight; it has just come across the wire" Martin looks at Dennis and raises his eyebrows, "Honest Sarge, 'Flinty' is a mate of mine and works the radios, he reckons about three this afternoon"

Martin looks at his pocket watch, it is just after one thirty in the afternoon, the rain is pouring down and thankfully, their section of trench has decent dug outs so shelter can be taken by those not on watch.

"I will believe it when I see it Den" Martin flicks his cigarette butt into the bottom of the trench, "Come on mates, it's our turn inside" He shouts to John and H to get their bodies out of the dug out to relieve them "Don't mention about the relief Den, I hope it is true, but if it doesn't happen again then its misery all round"

Dennis nods as John and H wade through the mud, avoiding the deepest by walking on half submerged wooden planks, and climb up onto the firing platform, the dugout is just big enough for two to sit in, so Martin and Dennis vacate the dryness of the dugout and get out into the rain,

"At least we get a couple of hours in the warmth" he can see that there is smoke coming out of the makeshift chimney that leads into the dugout and to a small home-made wood burner, made from an old oil drum with a section at the front cut out, the fire isn't really needed for warmth, but the men are wet from the trenches and the incessant rain, therefore they feel cold, the small fire is a Godsend for them. The dugout, although not very big, is usually filled with men from the Bedfordshires who are in nearby sections to this bolt hole, Martin and Dennis go inside and the heat and smell of cigarettes and pipe smoke hit them immediately,

"Over here Martin" Nobby shouts across the throng of soldiers trying to keep dry,

Martin and Dennis move over toward the wood burner, it is obvious that the wood being burnt has been taken from the trench supports, there are several thick pieces of wood drying out near to the open fronted fire, Martin can feel the heat emanating from it, he nods at two N.C.O's he knows from the Battalion, Corporal George Sturdey and Lance Corporal Tommy Harman,

"How are you fellas?" Martin asks as he accepts a mug of tea from Nobby and a cigarette from Alfie,

"Good Martin, can't complain really" George says, his Lance Corporal does not agree,

"Bloody hell George, its August, in Belgium, it is pissing down with rain and the trenches are eight inches deep in sloppy mud and sewage, can't complain? I have loads to complain about!"

George moves away from the front of the fire, giving Martin, Dennis and two other lads from another section that have just come in from the rain, room to sit and get dry, he leans back against the flimsy corrugated iron wall of the dugout,

"Tommy lad, I agree, our accommodation is not the finest, the facilities are not what a British man expects when on a foreign trip, even the weather is not what we need" He leans forward and pokes his Lance corporal playfully in the chest with his pipe, "But we are sat inside a warm, dry dugout, drinking tea" he looks into his mug "I think this might be tea, and we only have to go outside for an hour at a time, some poor buggers are right up at the front in four foot deep filthy trenches without cover, they have something to moan about Tommy, but not us matey, not us"

Martin smiles at the positivity George is exuding, he agrees with Tommy, the place is a hell hole, he takes in the warmth of the fire, smokes his cigarette, and sips his hot tea. The man sitting next to Dennis, who came in with Martin and Dennis, is very quiet, he is on the floor hugging his knees and staring into the fire, he nudges Dennis and nods at the man,

"You alright chum?" Dennis asks him, the man just nods and attempts a smile, his face is filthy, and Martin can clearly see the clean trails that tears have left on his face, cutting through the dirt like a reminder of how scared this man is,

"What's your name mate?" asks Martin

The man looks across at the Sergeant talking to him, Martin guesses that they are about the same age,

"George Wooster Sarge" the man says, he has a thick accent

"That is not a Bedfordshire accent George, where are you from?"

George smiles, "Originally from Preston in Lancashire Sarge"

Martin looks at Nobby and Alfie, "How about a brew for our Northern friend here Alfie?"

"On it Sarge" Alfie reaches behind him for a mug and takes the huge teapot from the top of the oil drum wood burner, he pours out a good measure of tea and hands it to George,

"Thanks mate, I appreciate it" he says to Alfie

"Tough day George?" asks Martin

"Tough year Sarge, I find the quiet days like this one, the worst" he sips his tea "We are all sitting around waiting for something bloody awful to happen and we don't know when, who or why" he throws his cigarette into the fire "And to be honest, I have had enough of it"

"We all have" John Marrables pipes up from the corner "Stick with it mate, all will be well"

Someone from the crowded room says, loud enough for all to hear,

"Anyone got a white feather for the bloke at the front!" he laughs but no one else laughs with him, Martin stands up, "Who said that?" The room is quiet, Martin explodes, "Who was it that said that!"

No one answers but several men look at a soldier who has gone red in the face, Martin pushes through the crowd, Nobby shouts after him,

"Leave it Martin!"

The man with the red face is grabbed firmly by his tunic by Martin, who is raging,

"Say it again" The man is silent, Martin screams into his face, "Say it again!"

The room is quiet, shells and machine gun fire can be heard getting louder outside.

"Sarge, I didn't mean no harm, I was just having a joke"

Martin shakes him, very firmly, "You think accusing a man of cowardice is funny? Your words could have a man shot for an accusation like that"

The man is scared and is shows,

"Sarge, please, leave him be"

Martin looks round and it is George asking him to leave the man alone, George continues,

"If everyone here wants to know if I am scared, then yes I am, do I want to be killed here, no, certainly not, the fear of being shot, shelled or machine gunned lives with me every day, every second I am here" Martin still has a firm grip on the soldier, George speaks to the crowd, "If any of you say you are not scared, at all, at any time, then I am calling you a liar" He turns to the man Martin has gripped up, "I am not a coward, I have been here since 1914, since the beginning, I have just had enough of this"

The tarpaulin door opens, and Regimental Sergeant Major Oakes is standing there,

"Sergeant put that man down now and don't make me ask you a second time"

Martin throws the man away from him and into the crowded room, Oakes continues,

"It seems as though the Bosch have woken up, so all you ladies, get out of here and take up your defensive positions"

The men all move toward the door, Oakes stands to one side, as the man Martin had hold of walks past, Oakes puts out his arm and says,

"Over there, sonny" he points to a corner in the room. "Sergeant, you stay as well"

Martin nods, he smiles at Nobby,

"I will get the lads set up Martin, see you in a bit"

Nobby and H escort George out of the room, he is protesting as he wants to defend Martin's behaviour,

"He will be fine George, he is a big boy now, no point in everyone getting a bollocking is there"

George thanks them and disappears into the trenches to join his platoon, the dugout is empty apart from the three men, Martin, Ralph, and the soldier, who identifies himself to the R.S.M as private Phillip Starley, he looks more frightened of the R.S.M than he was when Martin grabbed him.

"Why did the Sergeant feel the need to grab you Starley?" Phillip looks at the floor, "Well man?" Oakes is getting annoyed

"I was joking Sir; it was only a joke"

Oakes bends down to put his face in front of Starley's,

"What was so funny to you son?"

"That lad at the front by the fire had been crying, we all saw it, I just asked if he wanted a white feather"

Oakes looks at Martin, "Thank you, Sergeant, you are dismissed, re-join your platoon"

As Martin leaves the dugout, he hears Oakes fearsome venom pour from his soul and onto the unsuspecting victim that is Private Phillip Starley, who, Martin has no doubt, will feel like crying himself after Ralph has finished with him.

As Martin approaches his platoon and their section of the trench he ducks as machine gun fire chatters and bullets thud into the top of the trench only a foot or so above his head, he hears shouts across the trenches.

"Get down!"

"Attack on the right!"

He runs in a crouched position and arrives at his section, H and John are on the firing trench with their rifles over the top and they are firing at will,

"What is happening Nobby?" he shouts over the noise

"Germans advancing on the trenches, both here and to our right, they seem to have a large attacking force to the right"

Martin shouts at Alfie, Sharpie and Dennis,

"Lewis gun, go to the right of H and John and lay down fire, if they get into our trenches then we will have a proper scrap on our hands"

Other platoon commanders have had the same idea, the sound of Lee Enfield rifles and Lewis guns are constant, when a much louder sound begins, they all know that the Vickers gun crews are in action, teams of six men operate this amazing piece of machinery, a solidly reliable weapon that can work continuously for hours if required, one man fires, one man feeds the ammunition and the remainder carry the large amounts of spare .303 ammunition needed as this gun fires over four hundred and fifty rounds per minute. The jacket that sits around the main barrel holds a gallon of water, to stop the weapon over heating with constant use, a rubber hose is attached to the jacket to ensure that the steam produced is condensed, although not accurate, the amount of ammunition it fires across this battlefield makes up for this, Martin can see the enemy falling as this machine gun sprays death toward the enemy. The platoon all hears explosions in the trenches around them, the enemy have got close enough to throw their stick grenades,

"Fix bayonets!" Martin yells, both he and Nobby put bayonets on to the rifles belonging to Alfie and Dennis as they are still busy with the Lewis gun, Sharpie has his fixed, he is handing the ammunition to Alfie at the top of the trench, explosions continue around them, men are screaming in pain and fear, no one knows if it is German or British screams, they all sound the same when in pain.

"Here they come!" H shouts down at Nobby and Martin, H and John are firing and reloading as much as they can, until H shouts,

"I'm out!"

Martin realises that John won't be far behind H in being out of ammunition, Nobby and Sharpie join him at the top of the trench as H and John slide down and fix on their bayonets,

"Bloody hell" Nobby shouts, the Germans are only fifteen yards away, many are being cut down by the Lewis gun fired by Dennis, the Vickers gunners are killing many, but some are getting through, closer and closer as the seconds tick by.

"Bomb!" Alfie shouts down to John and H who are in the bottom of the trench, they move in time as a stick grenade lands in the very bottom of the trench, it falls into mud and water, at least three feet deep and explodes with a dull thud, covering John and H with filthy liquid mud, Martin aims his rifle, pulls the trigger and shoots and kills the enemy soldier that has thrown the grenade, the charging Germans are nearly on top of them, Alfie and Dennis stop firing the Lewis gun and take their rifles and get ready to use the bayonets.

All seven men of the platoon are at the top of the trench and meet the incoming enemy with bayonets, bullets, and vicious and violent anger. Two German soldiers jump over the top of the trench, over Martin's head, they land in the bottom of the trench, one of them has very obviously broken his leg in the fall and the other is stuck with both legs deep in the mud, both put their hands in the air to surrender,

"Nobby, Sharpie, get down there and disarm them"

The two men move from the summit of the trench, rifles up toward the Germans, Martin hears Nobby shout,

"Don't you dare!"

He turns and sees the German with the snapped leg lift his rifle toward Nobby, he is dead in less than a second when Nobby shoots him from close range, Sharpie shoots the other man, who still has his arms raised in surrender, a look of shock appears on his face.

"It was automatic, I heard Nobby shoot so I did the same"

Martin nods at Nobby and indicates that Sharpie needs to be shaken out of his shock at shooting dead a man who was surrendering, he is needed and he is needed now. Martin stands up and faces a quickly advancing German infantryman, Martins bayonet finds its target and easily pierces the belly of the enemy soldier, Martin twists the bayonet and hears the German scream in agony, Martin pulls the trigger and a bullet blasts into the impaled man at very close range, he falls to the ground and Martin turns to face any more attacking men, he is very pleased to see that the Germans are retreating, he can see scores of dead and wounded German soldiers lying on the barren field of battle, his platoon stop firing, the Vickers machine gunners continue to fire at the retreating Germans, many are killed as they run for safety, Martin slides down the trench, Nobby has hold of Sharpie and is shaking him violently, the Vickers guns become silent.

"Enemy is the enemy Sharpie, sometimes prisoners cannot be taken, it is too dangerous, his mate was going to shoot me, how do we know that your man wasn't about to do the same!"

"He had his hands raised Corp; I shot a man who was surrendering"

Martin calls him over, "Sharpie, come look at this"

Martin points to the left hand of the dead German, in his tightly clenched dead hand is a luger.

"Sharpie lad, I think you might just have saved at least one of our lives, surrendering men don't have pistols in their hands"

"I didn't see it Sarge, I just fired when Nobby did"

Martin points at Sharpie, "I don't care if you saw it or not, have no doubts Sharpie, this man was going kill you or one of us" he pats Sharpie on the top of his helmet "Good lad, this is war and he knew that, if he was going to surrender then he would have chucked the pistol"

Sharpie nods slowly,

"Thanks, Sarge"

"Right, you lot, get the Lewis gun down and get down the lines to see if any of our lot need help, I presume we are all uninjured?"

They all nod and climb down the trench and make their way to the right to check on their colleagues, Nobby and Martin are left in their section of trench, they are standing on wooden planking to avoid standing in the mud, they both light cigarettes,

"That German did not have a pistol when I saw him Martin, he was carrying that rifle" He points to a Geweher 88 rifle lying next to the dead man

"Really Nobby, are you sure?" Martin says with a wry smile, Nobby takes a long drag on his smoke,

"You took his pistol and put it in his hand didn't you" Martin nods, "To make Sharpie feel better I presume?"

"We both know he fired automatically when you did, we were in no position to take prisoners mate, so it was the best thing to do, I can't have any of my platoon mulling over a dead German"

"My lips are sealed Martin" Nobby flicks ash from the end of his cigarette, "Good decision, Sharpie is a good lad, and we can't have him losing his edge"

"Agreed" Martin replies "Between you and me though mate, not a word to the others"

They look along the trenches as their platoon returns,

"Most are OK Sarge" John says "George Sturdey and Tom Harmon are dead, most of their platoon didn't make it either, further down took a hammering, that Northern lad was killed"

"Not George Wooster?" Martin jumps in

John nods, "Yes Sarge, apparently he jumped over the top of the trench and killed half a dozen enemy before he got taken himself"

H joins in the conversation, "Oddly enough, the man standing next to him and fighting with him was Phillip Starley"

"The soldier that made the 'white feather' quip?" asks Nobby

"That's him" H says "He didn't make it either"

"Bloody hell, how many did we lose?" asks Martin

None of them know, Martin looks at his pocket watch, it is nearly three in the afternoon,

"No rest lads, we all stay in the trenches for the foreseeable"

They had all been expecting this,

"Shall I brew up Sarge?" asks H, he is already in the process of setting up the small fuel stove in the trench dugout,

"Bloody great idea H, Bovril for me if we have any?" Martin replies.

At 7 in the evening the 12th Battalion Middlesex regiment arrive to relieve the Bedfordshire men from their position in the front line trenches, as usual it is a slow process and the Battalion do not arrive at Micmac camp until past 2 in the morning of 3rd August.

The camp, next to railway sidings between Dickebusch and Ouderdom, consists of lines of wooden huts that are now the billets for the soldiers of the 30th division, they have been built by Engineers and the first residents were Canadian troops and they named it in celebration of a tribe of Native Canadians, the Mi'kmaq tribe from various regions across Canada. It is not a popular place with the soldiers, although the billets are dry and warm, the food and sanitation throughout the camp is less than perfect, but mildly better than the trenches, many of the men use a local café on the far edge of the camp where they can get cooked eggs and half decent coffee, the other issue is that many locals are less than friendly toward the Allied troops, a large amount of them are of a Flemish background and have more than a little sympathy for the advancing German troops. Martin does not care, he is exhausted and wants to find his billet and to go to sleep, this is the start of nearly three weeks away from the front line, the next few days are to be here at Micmac camp, and he intends to get clean and sleep.

"Martin, the C.O. needs to see you"

Ralph is standing beside him as he queues with the others to find out where his billet is

"Now?" asks Martin

"Now" replies Ralph

"I will sort your billet Martin, you ok bunking with me and the lads?"

Martin nods, he doesn't care where his bunk is as long as he can sleep, he steps out of the line and makes his way toward the far end of the camp, where the Battalion HQ is, Ralph hangs back, and Martin sees him talking to Nobby before catching him up.

"What was that all about?" Martin asks

"Nothing lad, a small bit of admin that Corporal Clarke needs to see to"

Ralph steps off with Martin now behind him, he is so tired that putting one foot in front of the other is difficult. They reach HQ and Martin can see light from a lamp inside through the dirty window, Ralph knocks the door,

"Enter" a voice from inside commands, Ralph stands aside,

"You not coming in?" Martin asks him

Ralph shakes his head and opens the door for Martin to enter.

Sitting at a desk is Major Wynne, he looks up at Martin,

"Ah, Sergeant, thanks for coming"

Martin is confused, "Sir? I was expecting Lt Col Bunbury"

Wynne looks up at Martin, "Well Sergeant, the old man is indisposed for a few days, so I have the Battalion command"

"Sir"

"Bunbury, if he were here, would not be giving you leave for your sister's wedding would he"

"Sir?" Martin questions, still confused

"If I were you, I would bugger off on your ten days leave" he looks at his watch "Starting now, and I would do it before the old man comes back"

"Now sir?"

"Yes, now Sergeant, I will deal with the Lt Col when he returns, leave that to me"

"I will Sir, thank you Sir"

"Two things for you Sergeant, firstly, the R.S.M has organised transport for you to the train station, I believe you can get a late train to Calais and then onto Blighty"

"Thank you, Sir"

"Secondly Sergeant, I am very, and I do mean very, partial to decent wedding cake"

"Of course, Sir" Martin is no longer tired and has a huge smile on his face,

"Sergeant, you look like the bloody Cheshire cat, now get out of here and give my regards to England"

Martin salutes and leaves the hut, Ralph is outside, Martin shakes his hand,

"Thank you, Ralph, I presume you had a hand in this"

"I did, when Bunbury buggered off for a few days, I approached the Major and he is more forgiving than the old man"

Ralph points to a lorry, "Your transport"

"What about my kit?"

"Nobby has already sorted it, that is why I spoke to him"

"But I am filthy, and I stink"

"Your choice Martin" Ralph smiles, "A bath or home leave"

"I am going to smell then!" Martin says

He walks toward the lorry,

"Sergeant" Ralph calls after him

"Yes R.S.M" Martin replies

"I am also very partial to wedding cake!"

"Yes Sir!"

Martin climbs into the back of the lorry, his kit bag and knapsack are already there, he is not alone, there are several injured men who are being taken to the casualty clearing station.

He is going home for the first time in nearly three years.

* * *

Charles has been trying to find out about the movements of the 2nd Battalion Bedfordshires, so that he can hopefully find out about Martin and that he is still alive and unwounded, this might placate Alice who is still distraught that her brother won't be there to give her away, she refuses to name anyone else and has told him that she will walk down the aisle on her own. Charles is hoping that news of her brother being safe may change her mind, but he is having no luck at all, red tape and classified movements of troops are stopping him getting any information, he is pleased that the wedding is still going ahead, another problem is that his best man has not, as yet, arrived and he has not a clue who could replace him, all his mates from the Folly are either serving overseas or have been killed. Mary and Charles's mother have all the food sorted out and the reception will be held at the Malta straight after the ceremony, Charles and Alice will then stay at his Parents cottage for the night, they will only have three days after this to enjoy each other's company before he has to set off again for France, Alice has refused to discuss his return to the front at all, he will try again today. As he walks toward the cottage, he can see smoke coming from the chimney, crossing the road the opens the garden gate,

"Hello" he calls

Alice comes out through the kitchen door, she smiles when she sees Charles,

"Morning" she says cheerfully "I am just warming the cottage through, just in case Martin gets home"

He smiles, "It is August, and it is very warm today Alice"

"I know, but this range has not had a fire in it for months, so I thought I would light one"

Charles knows that she is finding things to do to pass the time whilst they all wait for Martin to arrive, if he does arrive.

"Are you going to be here for a bit?" he asks her

"Yes, why?"

"I have to go and see Mary and sort out some money for her, you know to go toward the reception"

Alice laughs,

"Good luck with that, you know how proud she can be"

He nods, Alice puts her arms around his neck and kisses him on the lips,

"What was that for?" he asks

"For being a very nice man!"

He pulls her gently toward him and kisses her,

"Three days to go Mr Gray"

"That is Captain Gray to you, young lady" he jokes

She flicks a tea towel at him and tells him to go away, he leaves and heads toward the Malta pub.

As he walks in through the pub door, he hears Mary shout,

"We are not open yet!"

"It's only me Mary"

She appears in the bar from the kitchen,

"If it is Alice you are after, she is at the cottage"

He shakes his head, "No, it is you I have come to see"

She rubs her hands on a bar cloth, "Sounds a bit ominous Charles" He invites her to sit in the bar with him, he declines her offer of a drink, "Well, what's this all about then Charles?"

He puts an envelope on the table, she looks at him in an old fashioned way,

"Charles?"

"I know you won't like this, but my contribution toward the wedding"

Mary stands up indignantly, "I don't need your money Charles, I will pay for my Granddaughter to be married, if my Ted or Victoria and Jeramiah had been alive, they would almost certainly be paying for the day, as tradition dictates it should!"

Charles asks her to sit down, she does but she sits bolt upright and will not look at Charles,

"I mean no offence Mary" Mary opens her mouth, but Charles stops her, "Please Mary, let me finish"

She nods but her lips are pursed as if she is sucking something sour,

"I would like to give you some money, it isn't a lot, my parents don't have a great deal, but this is my army pay, or some of it" he pauses "I know how hard you work in this pub and how much you have done for Alice since her parents died"

"Don't forget our May and Pete, they looked after Alice when the war started"

Charles raises his hands as a gesture of peace, "I know that Mary and I am certainly not stating otherwise, what I am talking about is you, Mrs Mary Spratley, landlady and Grandmother, who never has five minutes to herself and, I am certain, doesn't make a fortune from this pub"

He looks at her,

"Well," is all she can say

"So, I know you are paying for the dress to be adjusted, for the cake and the food for the reception, although you and my mother tried to keep that from me, I have my spies!" He looks at her and she doesn't deny anything, he continues "I bet you don't accept any money over the bar that day either"

She snorts, "Mrs Ackroyd has very generously given the cake as a wedding gift, Maggie won't take any money for adjusting the dress, even though it has taken her hours and hours, my dress is lovely and the girl, I forget her name, would not even take a penny for her work, so I haven't paid for anything yet"

He pushes the envelope toward her, "You have paid for Alice's clothes, her food, her keep and everything since she was fifteen, I would like to pay toward the food and the beer for the reception"

"It's only a small buffet and a few pints Charles"

"Even so, please take this as a small contribution toward everything"

She stares at him for what seems a lifetime, he sees a small smile appear on her face for a second or two,

"You are a very decent man Charles Gray"

He nods, "So I have heard" he smiles,

"Thank you" Mary says as she places her hand over Charles, she removes her hand, taking the envelope with her and puts it in the front pocket of her apron, she stands,

"I have to get this place ready for opening"

"Can I help at all?"

She looks at him, she smiles, a proper, big and happy smile,

"No Charles, go and see that Granddaughter of mine and make sure she gets to Maggie's for the final fit this morning"

Charles stands and salutes Mary, "Yes Ma'am"

"Get out, you silly bugger"

Charles leaves the pub and heads back toward the cottage to see Alice, he is happier than he has been in a long time.

Mary is serving the 'last orders' drinks to the few remaining customers, it is nearly ten thirty, she has heard that some pubs in Luton and other larger towns are now closing early, local magistrates have cut the licencing hours, pubs to be closed between nine in the evening and ten the following morning, but the local magistrates in the village and town haven't sent any notice, so all the publicans are carrying on as normal. Mary is putting glasses onto the shelf behind the bar when she hears the pub door open, she speaks without turning around,

"We are closed, last orders have been called and I want these men to go home!

She hears a few murmurs in the pub from the men, as she reaches up to put a pint pot on the top shelf, she is spoken to by the visitor that has just entered her pub,

"Some things never change, glad to see you are still a welcoming host Granny"

She turns, drops the pint glass, it hits the wooden floor but does not break, Martin is standing at the bar in front of her,

"Pour me a pint Granny would you"

She puts her hands to her mouth and takes a huge breath, she wipes her hands on her apron and moves, swiftly, around the bar and almost falls into the arms of her Grandson, for the first time in the memories of every man in the pub, their landlady is sobbing and sobbing and sobbing as Martin holds her very tightly.

"It's alright Granny, I am alright" He looks around the pub, "I suppose I better buy you lot a drink for looking out for my Granny whilst I have been away"

A cheer erupts from the men and Mary regains her composure,

"Last orders are cancelled I presume?" she says wiping the tears from her cheeks,

"It would seem so" he turns to the bar "Pints all round gents?"

Martin joins Mary behind the bar and serves fresh pints to the half dozen or so local men still in the bar, Martin puts a band new ten shilling note in the till, the large note with bold red print is easily identified,

"Take that back young man!" Mary insists

Martin hugs his Granny again, "The army graciously pays me 2s 4d a day, and I really don't get to spend it, so I am buying the beers for these lads"

She has her hands on her hips, "Seven or eight pints is less than 3s and you know it"

He smiles, "That '*Bradbury*' note is for you Granny, a bit of housekeeping as I will be home for a week or so"

She looks at him,

"We will discuss this later"

"Is Alice in bed?" he asks

"She has been staying at the cottage every now and then, she is there tonight"

He finishes his pint with a large gulp and moves toward the door,

"Martin, let her be tonight, she will be asleep, she has been working so hard at the factory and at the cottage, she needs rest"

"Is she working at the factory tomorrow?"

Mary shakes her head, "She finished yesterday and has a week off for the wedding"

Mary turns to the locals "Come on you lot, drink up, get home the lot of you!"

The men all finish their pints, all of them pat Martin on the shoulder and tell him it is good to see him looking so well.

Martin bolts the door to the pub and walks over to Mary,

"Cup of tea Granny"

"You need a bath and a change of clothes young man"

She nods and throws her arms around him and begins to cry all over again.

* * *

Alice sits bolt upright in bed, she must have been dreaming, the loud hammering has stopped, so it must have been a dream, then she hears it again, Bang! Bang! Bang!

Someone is banging on the front door of the cottage, she has no idea what time it is and no idea who it can be, her head is still fuzzy with sleep, and she swings her legs out of the bed and slowly walks toward the door, she ignores her slippers and her dressing gown, the banging continues,

"Enough!" she shouts angrily "I am coming!"

She walks past the window and ignores the figure standing at the door, she reaches up and unbolts the top slide bolt and does the same at the bottom of the door, she puts her thumb on the latch and opens the door quickly, intending to be angry with whoever is at the door. As the door opens outward, she sees a figure in uniform take a step back, for a split second she thinks it is Charles, she screams when she sees who is standing at her door in his clean army uniform,

"Martin!" she jumps into his arms, her arms around his neck and her legs wrapped around his body, "Martin!"

"Blimey little Sister, anyone would think that you haven't seen me for years!

She untangles herself from him and hits him in the chest,

"I thought you were not coming or…." She does not finish her sentence as the words will not come out, he hugs her again as she sobs into his chest,

"Let's get you inside before you catch your death, the neighbours will talk if they see you in your nightdress!"

They go inside and the door is shut behind them, Alice hugs and kisses her brother,

"Alice, go and get dressed and I will stoke the fire, I am gasping for a cup of tea, Granny was too busy in the kitchen this morning to get me one"

Alice turns to him sharply, "When did you get home?"

"After ten last night, and before you say anything I was going to come and call on you, but Granny asked me not to, it was very late, anyway I am here now"

He ushers her out of the kitchen, and she goes to the living room to get changed, Martin puts soft wood on the fire and gently blows on it until it catches fire, he smiles as he completes the task, he has done hundreds of times before and has never really thought he had missed it, until now.

Alice re appears ten minutes later, looking every inch the lovely young woman, she has grown to be, Martin pours two cups of tea and they both sit at the old wooden table, she takes both his hands in hers,

"Martin, I was so scared when you did not turn up, I thought, well you know what I thought"

He smiles at his sister,

"I have no idea what you are talking about Sis"

She punches him playfully, "You are a rotter Martin, Charles was late home as well, so I thought that I would be getting married on my own"

Martin looks at her and narrows his eyes, "And how would you have done that, without a groom and me to give you away"

Alice bursts into tears, Martin moves his chair closer to hers and puts his arms around her,

"Alice, I was only having a bit of fun, everything will be great, I promise"

"It's not what you said, I was thinking about Grace and how I wish she were here as well"

Martin pulls his sister tight to him,

"So do I Alice, so do I"

They remain in each other's arms in silence.

It is mid-morning and Alice has gone to Maggie's for her final dress fitting, Martin finds himself standing under the Yew tree staring into the slow moving stream, he thinks about his Parents, about the baby he buried here and of his Grace, he looks up into the huge canopy of the tree, it gives him no answers, certainly none that he wants to hear.

"You have taken so much tree, and given so little, yet you continue to thrive, nothing changes with you"

He mumbles as he looks up, he has a lump in his throat and the beginning of tears are forming behind his eyes,

"Talking to yourself again Sergeant, they will lock you up for that"

He looks up and sees Charles coming down the garden toward him,

"I do hope so Sir then I won't need to go back to the madness we have just left!"

He walks toward Charles, his hand outstretched,

"Hello Charles"

Charles shakes his hand firmly,

"Hello Martin; bloody good to see you" Charles points at the tree," Asking the old girl some questions, were you?"

Martin smiles, "Something like that" Martin manages a smile

Charles realises that this is where Grace died and that Martin may have been having a private moment,

"Sorry if I interrupted you"

"No, you are fine Charles, in fact, if I get my tunic, do you fancy a pint?"

Charles agrees and waits whilst Martin collects his tunic from inside the cottage, he is surprised when Martin turns right toward the river instead of left toward the Marquis,

"Not going to the Malta?" he asks Martin

Martin shakes his head,

"No, I want a bit of privacy to speak to you"

Charles stops walking,

"Sounds ominous"

Martin laughs,

"Not at all mate, I just want to speak to you without my Granny nosing around!"

"The Gib then?"

Martin pulls a face,

"Don't like the beer, the Marquis of Granby is a short walk, shall we go there?"

Charles knows the pub, many of the Folly lads that worked over this way stopped off on the way home at the Marquis for a beer or two, they walk on Charles waves at a man sitting outside a row of thatched cottages,

"Come and meet Edward, Martin, his Wife works with Alice at the munitions place in Luton"

"I know Ed, from years back"

They cross the road,

"Morning Captain" Edward shouts at them

Charles raises his hand, Edward struggles to his feet,

"Bloody hell, is that young Martin with you"

"It is Ed, how are you?"

Charles looks at Martin and shakes his head very gently, hoping that Edward would not see it,

"It is fine Charles, really, much better" He looks at Martin "Took a bit of a beating in France and had to come home"

Martin nods,

"Will that duff leg of yours make it to the Marquis, we are off for a pint"

Edward grabs his walking stick,

"Watch me! Glad you are still avoiding the Gib; the beer is still bloody awful"

Edward hobbles down the steps to the pavement and the three of them walk along the left side of the road, they all see a man standing in a garden of a house on the road junction of the lower road to Luton and Ford Road, Martin, and Edward both know him, and both say,

"Morning Mr Drury"

Mr Drury puts a pipe in his mouth,

"Where might you lads be off to then?"

They tell him and he nods, Martin asks him,

"Mr Drury, how is Ernie, he was with the 6th battalion when he got hit, I heard he had been sent home to recover?"

Edward looks at Mr Drury and then at Martin,

"Martin, Ernie died a few weeks ago"

Martin faces Mr Drury,

"Sir, I am so sorry I had no idea"

Mr Drury wedges his pipe in the corner of his mouth,

"Don't fret lad, it was awful, he came home all battered" he looks at Edward "Just like this 'un, but he recovered really good, but he got the TB and it took him on 13th May just past"

The three men remain silent, Mr Drury acknowledges them all and says,

"Enjoy your beer lads" he walks slowly up the garden toward his little cottage

"Buggered that right up didn't I"

Both Edward and Charles tell him that it is just one of those things, especially in this time of war, they walk on, they are just about to cross the road and are stood outside number 28,

"Now then, what have we here?"

They all turn and a middle aged man, in decorators' overalls is closing the front door of number 28,

"Morning Fred" Edward says,

Martin looks at Fred for a few seconds and then realises who it is,

"Mr Warwick, how are you, still chucking paint everywhere!"

"It looks like it, Martin, you are home then?"

Martin finds this a strange question as he is stood in front of the man,

"Yes" he replies, it becomes clear when Fred continues,

"My lad is with your lot and I ain't seen him for well over two years"

Fred is pointing at Martins cap badge,

"Do you mean Bert is with the Bedfordshires, I had no idea, do you know which regiment?"

"I do" says Fred "The 1st Battalion, has been since he went over there"

Martin looks at Charles, who steps forward and offers his hand to Fred, who accepts,

"Sir, I am Captain Charles Gray, I am with the 1st Battalion, and you need to know that your lad, Bert, is a fine man and a fine soldier"

Fred stands tall,

"You know our Bert?"

"Everyone in the 1st knows Bert Sir, he is quite the character"

Fred seems very pleased,

"He joined the 1st Bedfordshires with another lad, Henry Worral, I work with his Father"

Charles nods,

"Please tell Mr Worral, that his son, Henry, is also a fine man and soldier and you should both be very proud of them"

They leave Fred with a huge grin on his face as they walk away, as they head toward the mill, Edward says to Charles,

"You have no idea who Bert Warwick or Henry Worral are do you?"

"Not a bloody clue about either, I have probably seen them, but the battalion has a lot of people in it!"

They all laugh as they walk, Martin suddenly stops and looks at the gates to the Mill,

"Lads, can I meet you at the pub, I need to have a quick chat with Mr Fisher"

Edward knows the man that Martin has seen,

"William Fisher? Why do you want to speak to him?"

"His son, Len, was in my battalion and was killed last year, I wrote to him"

Martin steps ahead of the other two, William Fisher catches sight of the soldier walking toward him and hurries to meet him and as they do, he puts his arms around Martins shoulders and hugs him, a most unlikely thing to see from a tough Mill worker, Edward and Charles walk by,

"William" Edward says as they pass, not stopping to spoil the man's moment with Martin.

"So good to see you lad" William Fisher says to Martin

"You to Mr Fisher, you look well"

William stands back,

"I am lad, doing as well as I want to"

Martin pauses,

"I was so sorry to have to write to you about Len, but I thought I had to, he and I grew up together, so I wanted to tell you, the army can be a bit slow about that sort of thing"

"It was very decent of you lad, both me and Emily were right happy that it was you that let us know" he stands back and looks at the sky,

"He died doing his duty a brave and noble lad. We reached a part of the trench we were fighting for, and it was while holding on to that piece of ground that your son was killed. He was hit in the head by a bullet and died an almost painless death. On behalf of the company and myself I extend to you our heartfelt and deepest sympathy" he looks at Martin, puts his hand on Martins arm,

"Your words lad, I have remembered each and every one of them"

Martin is astounded that the man has remembered more about the letter than he has,

"A brave man, Mr Fisher, a very brave man"

"You look well Martin"

Martin nods, "Not so bad Mr Fisher, it is nice to be home for Alice's wedding, you will pop into the pub for a beer after the ceremony on Monday, won't you?"

William Fisher tells Martin that he will be there,

"How are the rest of the family?" Martin asks, "I have been away for so long that they must be all grown up now?"

William raises his eyes toward heaven,

"We lost Lucy in 1914, she was only fifteen and then our Anne in '15, she was nineteen"

Martin had known both girls before he left to join up, he is shocked and gives his condolences to Mr Fisher, who continues,

"I am still the foreman here" he nods toward the Mill, "Emily and me still live with the family in the Thatch cottage by the forge, she is still as lovely as ever, our eldest, Bill is overseas fighting, Alice, who is now fifteen and Arthur is nine, they both are just grand"

William turns when his name is called,

"I have to go and sort this out Martin, I will see you on Monday afternoon for a pint"

Martin nods and smiles at Mr Fisher, he walks on, turning right to go over the ford bridge, he passes Mr Fishers cottage and the forge, he can hear the clanging of hammer on metal from inside, he stands on the bridge for a few moments and then goes over to the Marquis pub to join the others.

He enters the pub and sees his two companions at the bar, the landlord, whom Martin does not know, is talking to them, Edward does the introductions,

"Martin this is George Parsons, licensee and patron of this public house!"

They nod to one another,

"Nice to meet you George, last time I was in here, Lizzie Martin was in charge after her husband had passed"

George holds his belly as he laughs,

"Well Martin, customers like you I can do without! Lizzie left this pub when I took over in 1912!"

"Martin has been a bit busy George" Edward tells him,

"I know his grandmother very well indeed; she is a fine publican"

Martin thanks him and asks if he knows anything about the family of Liz Martin, he used to play in the river with Alice and Edith, the younger lads were always told by their bossy sisters to stay at home!

George tells him that both of the 'girls' still live locally, both are '*finishers*' for the local straw hat business, the boys, now own and run an ironmonger shop in town, Lizzie has retired and lives quietly in Wheathampstead with her widowed Sister. The three men leave the bar, pints in hand and take a seat next to the fire, currently unlit, in the small bar of the pub, it has one table and a semi-circular bench seat that gives a view through the small window over toward the river with its beautifully gentle Weeping Willow trees just moving in the whisp of a summers breeze.

"I think I know that chap you were talking to outside of the mill Martin"

Charles says, Martin puts his pint down on the table,

"William Fisher, how do you know him?"

Charles drinks from his pint pot before answering,

"I might be wrong, I was just a boy, but I recall, many years ago, must be toward the end of the last century, Victoria was still on the throne, I do remember that"

"Bloody hell Charles, get on with it!" Edward exclaims impatiently

"Alright, alright!" Charles says with a smile, "Well, I must have been four or five years old when that chap you were talking to, turned up at our house"

"Whatever for?" asks Martin

"My Mother is literate, which back then was rare in the Folly, or anywhere, especially for a country woman, anyway, Mr Fisher needed a letter for his sister in law, her husband, they lived at Nomansland common, had drank water from the river on the common on one hot summers day and consequently died of typhoid fever!"

"Bloody hell!" Edward says

"That's not all" Charles continues, "I remember my father telling us later that all the family bedding had to be burnt on the common and when the poor man died, he left a Wife and seven children"

"Charles, telling a good story is not your forte, what the hell happened and why was your mother involved"

Charles finishes a mouthful of beer, "The family needed a letter outlining the family circumstances to take to a Magistrate to be signed, when the letter was done and signed, the family were legally allowed to beg for money, which they did and eventually had enough to buy the widowed lady a treadle sewing machine, she was a superb seamstress by all accounts, and this enabled her to work from home"

Martin puts an empty pint pot down on the table, "Terrible tale Charles, for that you must get more beer in for us"

Charles protests but gives up when Edward agrees with Martin, he returns after a few minutes with three full pints of beer, he sees a sealed envelope on the table,

"What is this then?" he asks

Martin leans back in his seat after pushing his pint away from the edge of the table,

"It is a letter for you Charles, but only to be opened in the event of my death"

Charles puts his pint onto the table, a little too heavily, he spills some,

"Now look here Martin, you can't expect me to carry any sort of burden like this around with me"

"Charles, I promise you, the letter contains nothing startling or strange, just a few requests should the jolly old Bosch get me before it is all over"

Charles is playing with the small puddle of beer on the table,

"What the hell is in it?"

"Let's hope you never have to read it and find out; it is just a few minor requests and a will of sorts"

"Give it to Alice or to Mary" Charles says quickly

Shaking his head, Martin replies, "No Sir, I want you to have it, I trust you not to open it until I am dead and if I survive the war, you can give it back to me" he looks at Edward "Ed here is my witness"

Charles thinks for a few seconds, he then picks up the envelope, puts it inside his tunic,

"You can bloody well have this back when we meet after the war Martin, I will take it, but I don't like it one little bit"

He finishes the rest of his beer in one quick swallow,

"Now it is your turn to get them in" he slides his empty pot toward Martin, who looks over at Edward who is also quickly finishing his beer,

"Yes Sir" Martin mocks as he stands up to go to the bar.

* * *

The bar of the Malta pub is packed, it is the day before the wedding of Alice and Charles, Alice is sensibly staying at Maggie's for the day, and the night, because all the men, the locals, Martin, Charles, and Edward are celebrating the last night of freedom for Captain Gray,

"Why is it called a stag night?" asks one of the Almond boys, a rifleman with the Kings Royal Rifle Corps, who at this time has the duty of guarding prisoners of war in France and had been escorting over five hundred German POWs to Alexandria Palace in London, he is also home on leave for a few days before going back to France. No one knows the answer, a loud voice, not a local accent speaks above the crowd and noise,

"You Southerners know nothing" they all turn to look at the man in uniform who has entered the pub and is standing behind them, "It has been suggested that the term 'Stag' dates back to the fifth Century in Sparta, when a Spartan soldier was to be wed, there was always a feast the night before to toast the Groom to be, the term 'Stag' has strong male connections and is probably associated with fertility, if you get my meaning" the soldier points at Charles, "So you, young man, had best be prepared"

Lt Edward Westerman stands still as the pub becomes quiet, a few locals recognise him,

"Eddie! Great to see you"

"You owe me a beer or two Edward!"

Charles steps forward, "About bloody time Westerman!"

They shake hands, Charles calls for silence, "Gentlemen" he looks at Mary who is behind the bar, "And Lady, most of you probably know the former R.S.M. that stands before us, can I introduce my best man, Lt Edward Westerman"

He stands back and the pub begins to clap as Eddie makes his way toward the bar and greets Mary, she puts a pint in front of him"

"On the house Eddie, this is the only one though!"

He raises his mug toward her,

"Hello sir"

Eddie turns and sees Martin standing in front of him, caring not who sees him, he hugs Martin very tightly,

"Hello son, how are you doing?" he asks letting Martin free from his grip

"All good now Eddie, I had a rough few month" he looks across at Charles who has his eyebrows raised "Well, the truth is, I had a rough year or so after Grace, but I have moved on, I had to"

"Good lad, I knew you would, you can remember her without fear of being upset and angry at the rest of the world you know, war has taught us all that"

Edward Westerman is introduced to Eddie Munday and then he makes his way around the pub, renewing old acquaintances from his days when his regiment was stationed in town, Martin nudges Charles,

"You're a sly old sod, how did you find Eddie and how did he get leave?"

Charles grins, "Since we met on the fateful day when we had to tell you about Grace" both men lift their mugs in salute, Eddie Munday joins them "Old Westerman and I have kept in contact, as for getting leave, I have no idea, he promised me that he would be here and here he is"

"He was very tough and resourceful as an R.S.M, so I will bet he is the same as an officer, getting leave for this would have been a doddle for him!"

The three men clank their mugs together and drink from them, Eddie Westerman is standing on a chair, Mary shouts at him,

"Ed, get off my bloody chairs!"

"I will Mary, I will" he has lost his hat and a local is wearing it, "But I would like you all to charge your glasses and raise them to Captain Charles Gray, the man of the hour!"

As he gets down from the chair to go and apologise to Mary for standing on it, the whole pub cheers,

"Captain Charles Gray!"

It is at this point when the door to the pub opens and a young officer walks into the cheers for Charles, he is handed a pint of ale and he raises it along with the others in the pub,

"Who is the young Rupert?" Martin asks

Both Charles and Eddie look at him,

"No offence meant Sirs!"

"Frank, over here man!" Charles is waving at the officer, who sees him and makes his way through the crowded pub

"Bloody hell, its Frank Curtis!" Martin exclaims "And an officer at that"

Frank shakes Martin's hand,

"Hello Martin, so good to see you, it has been a few years I feel"

Martin nods and tells him that it must be over seven years, Martin introduces Frank to Eddie Westerman,

"I am surrounded by officers; this just isn't fair!" Martin laughs

"You need close supervision Sergeant; you are a rogue at best!" Charles tells him

"Don't forget me Martin, us rank and file must stick together!" Edward Munday pipes up, "Who's round is it?" he asks

They all point at Frank and say,

"His!"

The celebration for the stag has begun.

It is just before midnight, four men sit in front of a blazing fire in the grate of the huge black range, they are all drinking tea with a healthy slug of Whisky in each mug.

Captain Charles Gray, 1st Battalion Bedfordshire Regiment, the Stag and tomorrow's groom, Lt Edward Westerman, 6th Battalion Sherwood Foresters who is the best man, Lt Francis Curtis, 6th Battalion Leicestershire Regiment and Martin, Sergeant with the 2nd Battalion Bedfordshire regiment who is proud to be giving away the bride. Edward Munday has to be taken home, the four of them left him slumped on his doorstep, they banged the front door very hard and all ran away like scared children!

"So" Charles says slowly and with a slight slur to his voice "I am the youngest here and the first to be married?"

They all lift their mugs of tea, at least two of them spill some onto the stone floor,

"Charles, I think you need looking after, so being married will suit you" Eddie says as he points to the others with his mug "We are all independent souls, so we are just fine" he smiles before adding "Just don't tell my wife!"

Frank asks,

"What is your story Eddie, you must be a career soldier?"

"I am Francis" Eddie replies, "I joined in 1891, before any of you young men were even born!"

They all cheer, he continues

"I was a young Private with the 4th Nottinghamshire Militia, part of the Sherwood Foresters, in October 1891 and my service number was 1479, I made Lance Corporal and was in the 2nd Battalion Sherwood Foresters by 1897 and we were fighting in the Tirah campaign" he looks at the other men "That is in India lads, anyway, I was at the front line at a place called Khorappa, this is where I got shot"

The other three all sit up,

"What!" Charles says

"You have been shot?" Martin joins in

"Where were you shot Eddie?" asks Frank

"I just told you lad, India"

Frank is confused, "I know that, where on your body where you shot?"

Eddie, now understanding the question, lifts up his shirt to reveal a huge and obviously badly stitched scar,

"Just here" he points and then puts his shirt back down to cover it, his audience are transfixed,

"I got promoted to full corporal in May 1900 whilst stationed in Malta, stayed there until March 1902 when South Africa beckoned, I had a few decent run ins against the Boers I can tell you" He sips his tea, "Then after that I went to China for a year and a bit, made Sergeant and returned to HQ Garrison services at Normanton, Derby where I remained for a decade on the instructional team until I made R.S.M and joined the 6th Battalion, it was when we were posted to this town for training that I met Martin, Mary and the rest of the lads in the pub, until we went to France early in 1915"

"When did you get a commission?" asks Frank

"Early 1916, I think so many young officers had been killed or wounded, that they needed to offer the commissions to some old soldiers to get a bit of experience at the front, so I took it, having fought in India and South Africa I suppose I had the experience they needed" He takes a long drink from his mug, finishing it and then adding neat whisky to it, "Let me tell you, no experience can get anyone ready for this type of trench warfare, this is brutal and unforgiving"

"You have a few medals Eddie" Frank observers, Eddie nods,

"India medal, with two campaign clasps, the Punjab Frontier and Tirah, the Queens South Africa medal, with the Cape Colony clasp, the Transvaal clasp and the 1902 clasp, and my long service and good conduct that I got in 1910"

Frank looks at the ribbons, the India campaign ribbon has five equal stripes, three of red and two of green, the South Africa medal has red and blue stripe on each side with a yellow stripe separating them, the Edward VII Good conduct medal ribbon is crimson,

"The ribbon changed in 1916" Eddie tells them "It is now used for the Victoria Cross; the new V.C. ribbon has a cross on it to distinguish it from old soldiers like me that have the old, good conduct ribbon"

Frank looks at Charles, "You have the Military Cross Charles"

Charles nods and smiles as both Eddie and Martin shout, "And Bar!"

"Don't forget the Sergeant" Charles slurs "He has a D.C.M"

Eddie and Martin again shout "And Bar!"

Frank looks gloomily at his fellow soldiers, "I appear to be the only one that does not have a gong"

"Don't worry young Francis" Eddie says to him "That just means you haven't done anything stupid, yet"

"Or been shot"

"Or wounded"

The other two join in laughing as they do so, Martin reaches over and puts his hands onto Franks shoulders,

"Frank, there is plenty of time yet my man, this war won't be over anytime soon"

Martin falls drunk onto the floor and remains there for a few seconds, he starts to giggle, he slowly gets himself up,

"Why are you not married Martin?" asks Frank

Martin slumps into his chair, he takes a poker and jabs it at the fire a few times,

"I was to be married" he looks at Eddie and Charles, both smile gently at him "But my lady died last year whilst we were all in France or Belgium"

"Oh, I am so sorry Martin, I would not have said anything had I known"

"Think nothing of it Frank" Martin stands and goes to the window, he looks out over the dark garden, he can see the silhouette of the Yew tree, "In fact she died in this very garden of mine"

There is a silence in the room, only the crackling of the fire can be heard, Martin turns and claps,

"I have an idea!" he grabs the coal bucket, it has no coal in it, he puts a small amount of kindling wood into it and a few large pieces of wood, he lights a piece of kindling from the fire in the grate,

"Come on you lot, bring the Whisky"

He opens the door and carefully carrying his piece of lit wood, he makes his way to the Yew tree, when under its dark canopy he takes more kindling and lights it all, when it is burning enough, he puts the smaller wood on it and then the larger pieces until he has a decent fire burning. The four men sit around under the huge canopy of the tree, staring into the fire, Martin stands,

"A toast to the groom" he lifts his mug of whisky, the others follow suit, he takes a large gulp of the fiery spirit, again raising his mug to the fire,

"To all the ghosts and secrets held by this Yew Tree"

The others silently raise their mugs, Martin, still standing, stares into the fire and whispers,

"Goodbye Grace, I love you"

* * *

Martin can hear his name being shouted, he opens his eyes and is looking directly up into the branches of the Yew tree, he sits up and cannot get his bearings for a few seconds, then he remembers, he looks at the remains of the fire he started last night and at his three drinking comrades, all of whom are asleep on the ground.

"Martin!" He looks up the garden toward the house and sees Mary standing in the doorway of the cottage, he raises a limp arm in a gesture of greeting to her, "Camping out, are we?" she asks

"Yes Granny" he replies and as he does, a pain shoots across his forehead and behind his eyes, he puts his hands to his head, he can hear his grandmother laughing,

"Serves you right"

"What time is it?" he asks feebly

"Breakfast time" is all she replies

"Morning Mary" says Eddie, who is standing and seems unaffected by last night's drinking, Mary nods at him,

"You feel alright Ed?"

He nods back, "Just dandy, did I hear someone mention breakfast?"

"I have stoked the fire on the range, there is a pot of bacon and sausages I cooked at the pub, they will keep warm until you are ready to eat them, a loaf of bread is on the table"

She walks away without another word, Martin hears moans from behind him, both Frank and Charles are awake, both look dreadful, Eddie laughs at them,

"The youth of today, can't handle a little drink or two"

"Eddie, if you feel so good, go and put the kettle on will you"

Eddie strides up the garden, looking as fresh as a daisy, the other three slowly get to their feet,

"Bloody hell, it is only seven o clock" Charles says

The trio slowly walk up the garden toward the cottage, they can hear Eddie whistling some tune or another from inside.

Just after one in the afternoon, the four men are in the pub bar, three of them are nursing their first beer, Eddie is getting ready for his third. They have all spent the past few hours getting their uniforms ready for the wedding, the officers have clean tunics, shirts, and ties on, the groom has his medal ribbon, complete with the new silver rose in the middle of it, showing he is the holder of the Military Cross and Bar, they all have their Sam Browne belts on, all clean and with shiny buckles, all three are wearing gleaming boots and clean, shiny leather trench gaiters.

Martin has a clean and pressed tunic on with shiny buttons a neatly pressed collar, all thanks to Mary, his medal ribbon has a rosette in the centre of it, showing that he holds the Distinguished Conduct Medal and Bar, his puttees are gleamingly clean and his boots shiny, all his own work.

"Feeling better lads?" Mary asks, she looks at Eddie "Not you Ed, you have hollow legs"

Charles looks up at Mary, "Thanks for the early breakfast, it is just what was needed" Mary pushes a brandy glass toward him, "No Mary I can't" She crosses her arms and stares at him, "Really, I am just beginning to feel human again, this will kill me"

Mary again remains silent,

"Best do as you are told" Martin tells him "Granny won't take no for an answer"

Charles picks up the glass and downs the large brandy in one gulp,

"That will make you ready for the wedding Charles, now finish your beers and get to that Church"

"Granny" Martins speaks

"Yes" she replies curtly,

"You look absolutely amazing in that dress"

"Here, here!" the others all join in, she blushes

"Get to the church, I will be along shortly" she leaves the bar.

"You ready Charles" Eddie asks him

"Never felt better Eddie" he replies

The two men finish their beer and leave the pub,

"Frank and I will catch you up in a minute" Martin says.

He turns to Frank, "Will you sit with me and Granny up the front, apart from Aunt May, Uncle Pete and the twins, there will be no family with Alice, I would be grateful if you would join us"

"I will be honoured" he looks at his watch "Better go now, the bride will be here in half an hour or so"

They get up and leave the pub and walk to the church.

* * *

The small Methodist chapel is full to bursting, all the locals have turned out to see Alice marry Charles. The sides of the church are panelled in light oak and the walls are all painted pristine white, on the back wall above the small altar, a basic crucifix is attached, standing at the front is the Reverend Wesley Woolmer, Charles and Eddie standing on the right side of the church in front of the Gray family and Frank is sitting with Mary, Pete, and May on the front row seats on the left.

"I presume an amount of the demon drink was consumed last night?" Woolmer gently jokes with Charles and Eddie

"I have no idea what you mean Reverend" Eddie responds

"You should not lie in my church Lt; you may just go to hell!" Woolmer smiles at Eddie,

"We have already been in hell Reverend, and we all have to go back very soon"

Woolmer smiles at both of them, "I wish you well on your journey, I will pray for your safety as I pray every night for the safe return of all our fighting men"

"Thank you, Reverend" Eddie says

Woolmer looks at the back of the church and nods at the man who has been waving to get the attention of the minister, "Ladies and Gentlemen, if you can all stand, I believe the bride has arrived"

The congregation stand and all look at the man standing at the entrance to the chapel, he is also wearing a white collar,

"May I introduce the Reverend Clarence Cartwright, as most of you know, I am leaving for pastures new, Clarence will be taking control of your souls" he smiles and whispers to Charles and Eddie "May God help him"

A piano strikes a chord and all the congregation again look to the door as the Bridesmaids enter the church, Catherine and Jennifer look delightful in light blue dresses, both are carrying a small pose of roses, behind them Martin enters with Alice on his arm, she looks stunning.

Marys wedding gown has been adjusted to perfection, it is pristine white silk cloqué with a delicate floral pattern around the top with a plain white wide brimmed skirt with a small train silently flowing behind, her waistline is shown off with a beautiful silk wrap, her bridal veil is delicate and covers her face from the congregation as she walks slowly toward the front of the church, her wedding bouquet is a small bunch of white lilies, Martin, beaming a huge smile, walks with pride by her side. They reach the front of the Chapel and Martin hands Alice to Charles, Wesley Woolmer smiles at Martin, it was he that had only recently told Alice the act of 'Giving the Bride away' had only been restored in the Methodist churches in 1862, Martin stands with his Grandmother, Auntie, Uncle and Frank.

The Reverend Woolmer spreads his hands to the congregation, he begins the service.

"Marriage is a divine institution..."

At the end of the service, as the bride and groom leave the chapel, there is a guard of honour standing at the doorway, on the left are six ladies from the Munitions factory and on the right are six soldiers from the North Staffordshire Search light division, they are based in town and on his way through, Eddie had visited the C.O and the R.S.M and requested the guard of honour, the R.S.M from the North Staffordshire's is part of the guard, he has been promised free beer all night by Eddie!

Charles is holding onto Alice's arm tightly, he doesn't ever want to lose the feeling he has right now, he hopes she knows how much he loves her.

The pub is full of cheering locals, the Bride and Groom are seated at a bench table under a window near to the far left side of the bar, Martin is standing up and calling for silence,

"Firstly, raise your glasses for Charles and Alice, the Bride and Groom!"

Everyone in the pub stands up and as one they say, "The Bride and Groom!"

Martin looks at Mary, "A toast to the best Landlady, best Granny and the best woman in my life now that Charles has married my sister" He raises his glass toward her, and Charles also stands and does the same, "Finally, a toast to those who are not here, for those whom we all miss every day and those have given their lives so that we may be here today"

He raises his glass toward William and Emily Fisher and to Henry, Mrs Wilson and young Patrick, all of whom are standing quietly by the bar, William nods knowingly at Martin, Henry Wilson raises his glass in silence.

"Now, I am not going to make a long speech, there is food to be eaten and drink to be taken" Everyone cheers "I have to thank the Munitionettes and the lads from the North Staffs regiment for forming the guard of honour" he looks at Eddie "I presume you had something to do with that, and we all thank you" He takes a sip of his beer "I would like to thank you all, on behalf of the Bride and Groom for your gifts, each and every one will be cherished" he pauses "I have not had time to purchase a gift, as most of you know, I was a bit late getting here, so I was unable to get anything for them" he looks at Charles and Alice who both are telling him that it does not matter, he continues "I do have something for them" he reaches into his tunic and takes out a large key that has a white ribbon tied around it in a bow, "This is my key to the cottage, to our family cottage and I want Charles and Alice to have it, as the eldest child of our parents it has come to me and I am now giving it to Captain and Mrs Gray as a wedding gift" he looks at both Alice and Charles, his Sister has her mouth covered with her hand and Charles has his mouth open, "There will be no arguments, the cottage is yours" he hands the key to Charles,

"Ladies and Gentlemen, may I present, Lt Edward Arthur Westerman, the oldest best man in our recent history!"

The clapping continues as Eddie stands up and using his best R.S.M voice he shouts,

"Silence!"

The room quietens for him, "Unaccustomed as I am to telling tales on a fellow officer, I was once of course a Regimental Sergeant Major and I wasn't fond of officers, so here are some tales, believe them or believe them not, about Captain Charles Gray M.C...."

* * *

Alice wakes up in familiar surroundings but in unfamiliar circumstances, she feels comfortable and warm, the old bed, that is probably as old as the cottage, it is easily big enough for two people, she knows this because Charles is lying behind her with his arms draped over her naked body, the design of the bed is like a huge cot, with deep raised sides and a headboard that is unusually not as tall as the foot board. She can feel a small amount of heat from the fire in the living room, Charles had made it up last night before they went to bed, to spend their first night together, she pushes her body into Charles and smiles as she remembers how good he made her feel last night, every part of their wedding day had been perfect. She manages to untangle herself from Charles and gently takes herself out of bed, covering Charles with the thick eider down, she shivers just a little and hugs herself, rubbing the outside of her upper arms with her hands, she feels a little strange standing in the room naked, she takes her dressing gown from the back of the door and puts it around herself tying the cord tightly around her waist. She opens the door quietly and enters the kitchen, the stone floor is cold on her bare feet, the range fire is glowing red, barely alive, she quickly adds small pieces of kindling and in just a few minutes the fire is jumping alive again and will provide hot water very soon, the kettle is already on the hot plate and thankfully full of water, she does not have to walk down to the pump in just her dressing gown. Whilst the water is heating, she puts on her shoes and opens the back door, taking the short walk to the privy, her need to pass water is great, the sun is creating light to her right but has not yet crowned the top of the cottage, the privy is cool as she takes off her dressing gown, realising that she has never been naked in the privy before, she lifts the lid and sits on the worn wooden seat. Once she has urinated, she notices a small amount of blood on the small squares of toilet paper she has cleaned herself with, she blushes as she remembers Maggie telling her that this may happen after the first time, she takes the jug of water from the small shelf in the privy and gently cleans herself, then pouring some of the water into the privy pit, closes the lid, puts on her dressing gown and makes her way back to the cottage. The kettle has boiled, and the morning tea is brewing in the pot, Alice smiles as she hears Charles call sleepily from the living room,

"Morning Mrs Gray" She walks to the door, opens it a small way and looks around it into the small room, Charles pats the empty bed next to him, "Come back to bed my Wife!"

"Charles!" she exclaims "Whatever for?" she adds playfully

She moves away from the door and pours two mugs of tea, taking them into the bedroom, Charles sits up as she opens the door, she feels a tingle shoot through her body as she sees his naked upper body, she hands him a mug and he reaches over the headboard and puts it onto the thick wooden windowsill behind his head, he reaches to her and puts his hands around her waist and gently pulls her toward him,

"I need to put my tea down or I will spill it on you!" she scolds

She reaches over him and leaning over the headboard, she puts her mug next to his on the windowsill,

"Oh dear, this seems to have come undone" Charles says as he pulls the cord on her dressing gown, she makes no attempt to cover up as it opens up revealing her nakedness beneath, he moves his hands to inside the dressing gown, gently pulling her even closer to him, she slips off the gown and it falls to the floor, he lifts up the eider down and she climbs in next to him.

* * *

Martin wakes up in the small front room of his Grannies upstairs rooms of the pub, he is on the small settee, and he looks across at the armchair his Granny usually sits in, Eddie Westerman is snoring loudly, he has a blanket tucked under his chin, but Martin can see he is still in uniform as he can see his boots sticking out from under the blanket. He sits up and rubs his eyes he is also fully dressed, his tunic is lying at the end of the settee, on the floor, also with a blanket over him and a small cushion under his head is Frank, he opens his eyes as Martin stands up and stretches,

"Bloody hell that was a good night" Frank says

Martin nods in agreement, the door to the living room opens and Aunt May sticks her head around the door,

"Do you heathens want tea?"

"Yes please" Frank says, Martin nods and with his eyes still shut, Eddie says

"Me as well please", the then jumps up and again looks as though he has had a teetotal night, although nothing is further from the truth, "Morning soldiers!" he says happily, Frank and Martin look at each other, Eddie smiles, "You bloody youngsters are soft when it comes to having a few beers, at least Edward Munday and that lad who is the prisoner of war guard can sink a few pints"

Martin pulls his braces over his shoulders, he looks at his pocket watch, it is just after eight,

"Why are we up so early!"

Eddie answers him, "I have to get back today lad, duty calls and all that"

"So soon Eddie, you only got here on Sunday"

"I know lad, but even getting these few days was tricky, I am getting a ride with some of the Staffordshire lads this afternoon"

The three of them make their way downstairs, Mary is in the kitchen with May, Catherine, and Jennifer,

"Get in the bar the lot of you, I don't want any of you in the kitchen" Mary tells them

"Morning Granny" Martin laughs as he says this,

"Don't you 'good morning' me Martin, my bar is in a right mess"

"Mary, we will have it sorted before we leave, I promise" Eddie tells her

"Is Pete here May" ask Martin

"No" she answers "He is driving the ambulance today for the Rosemary Hospital, he set off early"

Martin had forgotten that Pete had told him the night before, that the house in Milton Road had reopened in March to treat wounded soldiers and he was back driving the ambulance for them,

"Morning lads" Eddie speaks in a loud voice to the men sitting at seats in the bar, it is where the five soldiers and the R.S.M from the North Staffordshire searchlight team have spent the night,

"Morning Eddie" the R.S.M says to him "Did I hear tea being made"

Mary shouts from the kitchen, "You did John, and it won't be a moment"

He whispers, "How the hell did she hear me?"

"Granny doesn't miss anything John, did you all have a good night?" Martin tells him.

All agree it was a brilliant night,

"I think we should help the landlady out by clearing this bar up, what do you say?" Eddie asks them all,

"Jump to it lads" John tells his crew of soldiers, who all begin to put the dirty glasses on the bar, John and Eddie roll up their sleeves and begin to rinse the glasses out in the small sink behind the bar, Martin and Frank get the bin from behind the bar and empty all the ashtrays and wipe the tabletops.

"I can do that" Mary says as she brings in a tray with huge teapot, mugs and milk on it,

"I won't hear of it" John says to her

"Have some tea first, I have bacon on the range, will a bacon sandwich be alright for all of you?"

They all say 'Thanks' to Mary, no one asking, or caring, how she happens to have enough bacon for nine soldiers,

"You look tired Granny, are you alright?" Martin asks

She forces a smile, "It has been a long few days Martin" she turns toward the kitchen, stops and turns back to him, "Giving them the cottage was a very decent thing to do Martin"

"You might not say that when the war is over Granny"

"Why would you say that?" she asks

He puts his arm around his grandmother, "Because I will have to live here, or I will be homeless"

"I had not thought about that, but you can have Alice's old room when you come home"

He kisses her on the cheek, "Now, did you mention bacon sarnies?"

She walks away tutting to herself, one of the soldiers begins to whistle 'Pack up your troubles in your old kit bag', the song written two years ago by George Asaf and recently recorded by Helen Clarke, they all join in whistling,

"I saw Florrie Forde sing this in 1916 when I was back in Derby for a few short days to take my commission, I was with and old friend, R.Q.M.S Harry Petrie, who was being forced to leave the army as his full time had been served, we went to the Derby Castle ballroom and saw her on stage, a marvellous show"

The whistling continues as the men clean up.

* * *

Eddie has gone back to war, he had seen Charles and Alice before he left but did not want any fuss, he spent a few moments alone with Mary with whom he has forged a great friendship and he visited Edward Munday before jumping into a battered old army lorry that was taking the lads from Staffordshire back to their billets in town.

"If I never see any of you again, let me tell you, it has been fantastic to meet and to know you" Eddie's parting words are said with genuine feeling as the lorry pulls away from the front of The Malta. Martin has turned down an invitation from Alice and Charles to eat lunch with them at the cottage, both are so happy with their gift from him, but he has a promise to keep and is on his way to Cravells Road in the Bowling Alley to visit the Father of a 2nd Battalion colleague that had been killed on the Western Front in August 1915, he has always intended to keep his promise to Corporal Ernie Haines, so he has turned down lunch and is walking from the pub to the Bowling Alley. As he walks up Crabtree Lane, he does not recognise much of it, the first houses were built on this steep hill in 1906 and when he had left in 1910 only a few were finished, there are many more now, he passes Topstreet Farm and just after the junction with Milton Road, he climbs up onto the railway line and walks toward the Bowling Alley. He can see the gas works to his left as he passes over the local landmark known as Skew Bridge, only a few minutes' walk from the bridge he clambers down the shale and onto Cravells Road, he walks up the hill and after a short distance he stops and walks down a very short front path to the house that Ernie Haines had grown up in. Martin has not seen Mr George Haines for over eight years and doesn't expect, the now late middle aged man, to recognise him, he knocks on the door and stands back as he hears the latch being opened, he recognises Mr Haines, a little older, a little thinner and with less hair,

"Martin lad, how have you been" George Haines has recognised him,

"I am well Mr Haines, home on leave for my sister's wedding and have taken this opportunity to visit" he shuffles his feet, "I promised Ernie I would come and see you"

"It is good of you lad, come on in, you are welcome"

Martin steps into the dark, thin, hallway, musty, stale air can be smelt, Martin can smell that no windows in the house are open, they enter the small front room to the right, a small fire is burning in the grate, the room is tidy, shabby but tidy. Martin sits in an old, battered armchair, George sits opposite him on two seater settee, covered with an old blanket.

"Mr Haines, my condolences for the loss of your Wife, Ernie told me about her passing"

"That is very nice of you lad" tears form in the older man's eyes, "I won't say that the past few years have been easy"

"I understand that Sir"

George looks at him, "Do you fancy a pint at the Engineer Martin?"

"I never say no to a pint Mr Haines"

"Come through to the kitchen whilst I get my outdoor shoes on"

Martin follows George from the front room to the kitchen, it has a single window that is closed, the fireplace is cold and unlit, the range has a small fire on the go, Martin can see the red glow from the heated coal, the old wooden kitchen table sits under the window and one place has been set for a meal, the knife fork and spoon set perfectly in front of the single chair, a lonely and half-filled bottle of HP sauce stands upright in front of the cutlery and next to the sliver salt and pepper pots. George sits in an old, small armchair in the corner of the kitchen, placed comfortably next to the range, he puts on an ancient pair or black boots and slowly ties the laces, he stands and looks at his guest,

"Shall we?" he asks Martin nods and they leave the kitchen and George pulls the door to as they get outside, "I never lock it; I always forget the bloody key"

They walk up the hill a short distance into Upper Cravells road, the pub sits on the corner of a dirt track that leads across the common,

"When I was a boy, this pub was called the Bird in Hand, it changed name when the railway was built" he pauses for a moment "Sometime toward the end of 1868"

"Is this your regular pub Mr Haines?"

"It is, I used to go to the Carpenters arms, but a chap, Arthur Kingham, calls himself a beer retailer, took over late in 1912 from Mr Olney and he immediately put the price of his beer up" he shakes his head "I haven't been in since"

They walk toward the door of The Engineer, George stops,

"I do pop into the George IV occasionally, I have known the landlord, James Giddings for many years and his good lady, Annie" he looks at Martin and points his finger to his nose, "Don't mention to old Frank Sanderson in here that I have a pint in the George occasionally, he likes his regulars to be regulars, if you know what I mean"

Martin nods in agreement, and they enter the pub.

"George, the usual?" the man behind the bar asks

"Please Frank, Martin what do you drink?"

"I will have the same as you Mr Haines"

Two pints are put on the bar and Martin pays for them, George does not argue with him, the take a bench seat in the far right corner of the pub, giving them a view over the common,

"That's a place that doesn't change much over the years" Martin says

"True" George says, "Been much the same since I was a lad, me and the gang spent every summer evening over there, climbing trees and running up and down the holes in the Brickle Dells made by the clay digging in the 1850's"

Martin smiles as he recalls doing exactly the same with his pals,

"Ernie and I used to climb a huge conker tree at the top of Upper Cravells road, opposite the track to Limbrick hall and next to the public well, it was a beast of a tree"

"It still is local lads still climb it and get their conkers from it"

George takes a pull on his pint, he is staring over the common toward the Brickle Dells,

"Did he suffer?" he says without averting his eyes "Did Ernie suffer?"

"I wasn't directly with him Mr Haines, but what I can tell you is that we were in trenches and the enemy artillery was very heavy" he takes a deep breath "The section of trench Ernie and his patrol were in took a direct hit" he looks at George who is still staring over toward the common "In my experience, when this happens, it is quick, instantaneous, so, no, Ernie did not suffer Mr Haines"

"Thanks lad, that means a great deal to me" George sips his beer, "All I got was some army letter, a couple of months after he was killed, that was it, nothing more, not even a telegram, I thought I would get a telegram"

Martin knows that only the death of an officer is reported to the next of kin by telegram, he also knows exactly the form that George had received, Army form B 104-82, a pre-printed form whereby the records officer from the dead soldier's regiment will hand write the deceased's name, rank and number, regiment served, date and place of death, underneath this section are the words.

The report is to the effect that he…

The reporting officer will, almost without exception, write next to this, in neat script,

'*was killed in action*'

George reaches into his pocket and takes out a folded envelope, he takes out the letter from inside it, it is the Army form B 104-82 reporting Ernie's death, he hands it to Martin,

"Read that bit below where the words 'killed in action' are written for me will you" he asks Martin,

"Are you sure you want me to Mr Haines?"

George nods, Martin takes a swallow of beer and reads aloud,

"By his Majesties command I am to forward the enclosed message of sympathy from Their Gracious Majesties the King and Queen. I am at the same time to express the regret of the Army council at the soldier's death in his Country's service. I am to add that any information may be received as to the soldier's burial will be communicated to you in due course. A separate leaflet dealing more fully with this subject is enclosed, I am Sir, your obedient servant"

Martin folds the letter and hands it back to George,

"I can't make head nor tail of it lad, do they know where he lays or not?"

"Mr Haines, this is a delicate subject, but when a British soldier is killed, he is buried on the battlefield, the reporting officer or the Padre will note the death, where he was killed and where he lays"

George turns from gazing out over the common to Martin,

"Have you had to bury some of our lads?" Martin nods and does not answer, "Well, my Ernie wasn't the first and he won't be the last man from this town to be killed"

"True, sadly true" Martin agrees

"Do you know who the first was?"

Martin does not understand the question, George continues,

"The first from our town to be killed"

Martin tells him that he has no idea, he tells George again that this is his first time home since war began,

"Wilf Franklin, did you know him?"

"I don't think so" Martin replies

"He was a bit older than you, but his parents, William and Alice live down your way"

"Don't think I knew him Mr Haines"

"Holly Cottage, Willoughby Road, do you know where that is?"

Martin nods, "Off the bottom of Ox Lane, after the railway bridge by the nursery"

George nods, "Well, he was the first, September 1914, he was with some Welsh regiment I think"

He looks again across the common,

"I am grateful you came to see me lad, but the town just isn't the same without my Mary Ann and our Ernie" He turns and looks at Martin again, "It just isn't the same, but I don't have any other place to go, I was born in the house I live in, as was Ernie, and I will die there"

"I will come back and see you Mr Haines, when I am home next or after the war, whichever comes first"

"That is good of you lad, so very good of you"

Martin stands and shows George his empty pint mug, "Shall I get us another pint Mr Haines?"

* * *

Martin knows today will be a tough one for Granny and Alice, Charles leave is over, and he has to return to France, back to the front line trenches, he has told Martin the 1st Battalion are at Arleux, and he knows, from experience, that the enemy artillery is almost constant at this location, Charles has not told Alice this and Martin won't tell her either.

"You coming with me Granny?" Martin shouts up the stairs of the pub,

"No Martin, I will stay here and mind the pub" Mary replies

Martin knows the pub does not need minding, but also that Granny wants to stay out of the way,

"I will be back soon, I am going to see Charles and Alice, to say cheerio"

He gets no reply so he walks through the empty bar, it is an hour or so until opening time, he leaves the pub and walks the short distance to the cottage, the warm, mid-morning sunshine feels good on his face, they have been lucky with the weather, August has been unseasonably chilly with a good amount of rain, but for the wedding and the few days following it has been dry and sunny.

"It's only me!" he shouts as he goes through the gate of the cottage, he can see Charles suitcase and kit bag by the front door,

"Down here Martin" Charles returns his greeting,

Martin turns away from the cottage and can see that Charles and Alice are sat on a bench underneath the shade of the Yew tree, the bench that had been against the front wall of the cottage for as long as he can remember, Charles has his arm around Alice's shoulders.

"Morning all" Martin tries to sound cheerful "I like the bench being here, it suits the garden"

"We put it here the first morning after the wedding, we like looking into the stream and across the watercress beds, we have done it every morning" Charles says, also trying to sound positive.

"Alice" Martin says to his sister "How are you?"

She turns to face him, her eyes are red from crying and she cannot speak,

"She will be fine Martin; I have told her to move back into the pub if she wants to"

"I won't" Alice says in a croaky voice "I want to stay here in our cottage" She manages a smile to Martin "Our best wedding present"

Martin changes the subject, "Did you manage to visit your Parents yesterday Charles,

"We did, we had a lovely time" He looks at his Wife "They have promised to come and see Alice every week whilst I am gone"

Alice breaks down in tears again,

"I will go and wait in the cottage, if that is alright with you" Martin says to them,

Charles nods and Martin takes a slow walk up the garden, past the familiar water pump, he stops at the vegetable patch, it is empty as no one has planted any vegetables this season, he sighs, walks to the front of the cottage, he does not go inside but leans against the wall and lights a cigarette. Charles and Alice walk up the garden, arm in arm, a few minutes later,

"Martin, Alice will be staying here when I leave, do you fancy a walk with me to the station?"

"Of course," he turns to Alice "Will you be alright here whilst I go with Charles"

She nods and runs into the cottage,

"I will be a few minutes Martin, I just need to say goodbye to Alice, she wants to come to the station, but I have told her it will be better if she stays here"

Martin nods, "I will meet you on the road"

Charles goes inside and Martin walks back toward The Malta, he can see Granny in the top window, obviously looking out for Charles leaving, he waves at her, she opens the window,

"Has he gone?" she asks sternly

"No Granny, he is saying goodbye to Alice, I am walking to the station with him, Alice is staying at the cottage"

"Wait there" she says, the window if firmly closed and less than a minute later, she is coming out of the front door, "Come on, I will wait with Alice"

They walk to the cottage, Charles is picking up all his kit, Martin steps in and picks up the army duffle bag,

"Mary, what brings you here?" Charles asks

"Tea" she says

He looks at Martin who shakes his head just a little, Mary stands in front of Charles,

"Be safe Charles and make sure you come home"

He leans forward and kisses her on the cheek,

"Anything you say Mary"

She walks into the cottage and Martin can hear Alice sobbing as Mary walks in,

"Come on Charles, let's get you out of here"

"A good batman would carry my suitcase as well" Charles jokes with Martin

"Don't push your luck Sir" Martin replies with a smile

They walk in silence until they get to the bottom of Station Road, they turn left,

"I am going back tomorrow Charles" Martin blurts out

"What? Why? You have a few more days yet"

"I am due back on the fourteenth, but I am going in the morning"

Charles is astounded, "I don't understand, why would you rush to get back?"

Martin stops and takes a cigarette from his packet, Charles declines the offer, Martin lights it and leaves it hanging out of his mouth as they set off again,

"I miss it, there you have it, I have said it, I miss being in the war"

"I would do anything for it all to end tomorrow" Charles says

"I agree, but whilst it is on, I want to be in the thick of it, my mates are still out there whilst I am here, I am glad I was home to see you and Alice married, but I need to be back with my platoon"

They are outside of the station,

"My train won't be more than a few minutes" Charles says, he takes his kit from Martin,

"Make sure, if I don't see you before we are home, that you will take care, you will come home"

Martin smiles and shakes Charles hand,

"Yes Sir" Charles walks away, "Oh, and Sir"

Charles turns, "Yes Sergeant"

"If you don't come home to look after my little Sister then I will not be a happy N.C.O."

Charles laughs out loud, "Nothing worse than an N.C.O that is unhappy, good luck Martin"

"And to you Charles, keep your bloody head down"

The whistle of the train arriving takes Charles onto the platform and out of sight from Martin.

Hands in his pockets, Martin walks toward the river, he needs half an hour on his own, just staring into the River Lea from the bridge, maybe for the last time.

* * *

Mary is not happy; Martin has his kit bag and knapsack packed,

"But you have three days left of your leave, you told me so yourself"

Martin has explained at least three times to his grandmother,

"I have to get back Granny, another three days won't matter"

Mary goes from being unhappy to angry in an instant,

"You can't win this war on your own! We haven't seen hide nor hair of you for three years and you spend a week with us and want to go back"

She sits down on one of the seats in the bar, Martin sits next to her,

"I know the war won't or can't be won by me alone, but I have spent those three years with a bunch of men, most of whom are now dead, I have to go back to honour those that gave their lives" He sees that Mary has tears running down her cheeks, "Oh Granny, I am sorry, but this will be over soon, and I will be home and you will be sick of the sight of me!"

She turns on him, "Will you be home? Can you promise that? Because we both know that you can't and there is a high chance that you might not get back at all!"

The pub door opens and before Mary can shout that the pub is not open, Alice walks in,

"You are going then?" she says to Martin, he nods in reply

"He is a bloody fool" Mary wipes her eyes with a tea towel.

Alice smiles at Mary and sits the opposite side of her to where Martin sits,

"He needs to go back Granny, no matter how horrible it is for us, he has to go back for his own sanity"

"I don't know what you mean Alice, you can't mean that this war is good for him"

"No, I don't mean that, but staying here is not good for him either, because it is still going on, it is an unfinished job"

Mary dabs her eyes again, Alice puts her hand on her grandmothers' knee,

"Look at the mess Edward Munday was in when he got back, his injuries healed but his mind did not, because he felt like a failure and that he had not finished the job that he went out to do, Maggie told me that"

"Even if it gets him killed!" Mary explodes in emotional anger

"Yes" Alice says quietly as she looks across at her brother.

Mary pulls Martin toward her and hugs him, a rare and unexpected show of emotion from her, she kisses the top of his head,

"Don't make this the last time we see each other" She lets go of him and stands up, "Do you hear me, Martin?"

As she walks away toward the kitchen, he replies,

"I do Granny, every word" Alice hands Martin a brown paper wrapped parcel, "What is this then?" he asks

"Wedding cake for your man in charge and your R.S.M, you promised them"

Martin laughs out loud, he does this to try to cover the huge lump he has in his throat,

"Thank you, Alice, thank you, I would have been in trouble had I forgotten this for Ralph and Major Wynne"

She puts her arms around her brothers' shoulders and hugs him tightly,

"Please be careful Martin, no heroics or idiotic behaviour, I need you home, Granny needs you home"

On his face he can feel the wetness of her tears as they hug,

"Don't worry little Sister, my days of craziness are over, I learnt a lot in the year since Grace died"

They separate, "I really would not have cared if I had been killed after she died you know"

"I do, but that is really selfish Martin"

He looks stunned, "Selfish?"

She nods "You would have solved your sadness but made mine and Grannies a whole lot bigger"

He hugs her again and whispers,

"When did you grow up so fast?" He stands, ready to leave,

"Martin, if you get the chance to see Charles, please do, I am so worried about both of you"

He assures her that he will get together with his new Brother in law as often as the situation allows. He picks up his kit,

"Tell Granny that I will be fine and that I love her Alice"

"I will"

She kisses him on the cheek,

"I love you too Alice and I will miss you every day"

She wipes her eyes, "Get out of here you!"

He walks to the door, before he steps outside, he shouts at Mary,

"See you soon Granny, I know you will miss me really!"

Alice laughs. Mary is standing in the kitchen, she has both hands on the back of a kitchen chair, she has a huge headache, she feels dizzy because of it and her vision is blurred, she can't form words and is crying without making a sound, after a few seconds she manages to say to herself,

"Goodbye Martin, I will miss you every day"

* * *

Martin's journey has not been an easy one, troop movements from London to the ports on the South coast are constantly busy with trains to Southampton, Dover, Folkestone, Newhaven and Richborough, this last port being where Martin has eventually been sent to. After arriving at Dover, but unable to get across the channel, he is sent inland to get across to France. Richborough 'port' is still under construction, building of this port is to support and to release the pressure on Dover, it had begun in 1916 and the building still continues, a new channel has been cut into the land to create a new wharf and to divert part of the River Stour, huge cross channel barges are loaded here with heavy military equipment, new railway tracks and massive sheds are under construction but the barges are in operation and it is on one of these that Martin crossed over the sea and landing at Dunkirk.

It is late on Saturday afternoon when they eventually land at Dunkirk.

He learns, from a company clerk of the Berkshire regiment, that the Bedfordshires have moved out of Belgium whilst he has been at home, they left Micmac camp only three days after he had himself left, they entrained at Reninghelst arriving at Caestre in France the following day, a one day stop they then moved to Meteren and the whole of the 2nd Battalion Bedfordshires are now at Saint Jans Cappel, only a short distance, 30 miles or so from Dunkirk. He is directed by a very grumpy Lt from the Royal Engineers to board a London Omnibus, it leaves for Saint Jans Cappel at first light, it has been painted khaki to make it seem military, he takes a seat on the lower deck as it is raining, his seat is just big enough for him and his kit, he makes himself as comfortable as he can, lowering his cap over his eyes he tries to sleep.

He hears and feels the bus start up, the whole body of it shakes as the engine jolts to life, he realises that he has been asleep for a few hours in the relative comfort of an old London bus.

"Excuse me Sergeant" A voice speaks in front of Martin, he ignores it hoping whoever it is, is addressing someone else, "Sergeant"

Martin sighs out loud, he is tired, "What" he says without moving the cap from his eyes,

"Sergeant, my name is 2nd Lt Leonard Agar, if you wouldn't mind taking your cap off your face for a few minutes"

Martin, realising he is being spoken to by an officer, takes the cap from his eyes and sits up, he sees two young officers sitting on the seats in front of him, both are turned to face him,

"Yes Sir, what can I do for you, apologies for my rudeness, I am very tired"

"Not a problem Sergeant, could I ask if you are with the Bedfordshire Regiment?"

It is a fair enough question, even though the regimental badge is on his cap, soldiers can be moved about.

"I am Sir, have been since 1910"

The other officer, also a very young man, asks Martin,

"Do you have any idea where the 2nd Battalion might be? the logistics officer at Dunkirk was less than helpful"

"Sir, the troops move about a lot over here" Martin is presuming that both officers are on the bus heading towards the front and that they are straight out of training,

"I myself was intending to go back toward Ypres, as that is where the 2nd were when I left them just over a week ago"

"You are with the 2nd?" asks the officer that has not introduced himself,

Not such a fair question as he has just told the officer he is,

"Yes Sir, I have been told that they are in camp just outside of a small village called Saint Jans Cappel, right on the French Belgium border"

"Any idea where it is Sergeant?" Lt Agar asks him,

Martin smiles, "Not a bloody clue Sir!" Both officers seem concerned with Martin's response, "But I am sure we will find it without a problem, I have been moved about a fair bit with the Battalion and have always found my way home"

The officers relax, Martin introduces himself, 2nd Lt Agar introduces himself again,

"I am 2nd Lt Gilbert Manners, nice to meet you Sergeant"

"Likewise, Sir, I think the journey will take a couple of hours in this old bus, so make yourselves comfortable Sirs and when we get to the village, we can get ourselves sorted"

Both men thank him and turn around to face the front, Agars turns back quickly,

"Sergeant, what is it like?"

"You will be alright Sir, it's a bit like being at home with a large family, some good days and some bloody awful ones"

He pulls the cap back over his eyes and tries to sleep.

It is just after eight in the morning when the rattling bus pulls into the small village of Saint Jans Cappel, Martin gets off and stretches his stiff and aching bones, taking a cigarette from the packet in his tunic pocket, he lights it and has a look around his surroundings. He is at one end of the village, or what is left of it, the church, with its pointed spire protruding from a square tower looks battle weary at best, it is standing but has suffered at the hands of artillery probably from both sides of the war. The main street has a few buildings left standing, but most are bomb damaged, a few have their roof beams intact but all the slates having been blown off, they look like a line of macabre spider webs, there are soldiers everywhere, seemingly from every part of the British empire, English, Scots, Irish, Indian, ANZAC's and a large contingency of French infantrymen, all from the camp and all having a few days away from the front line trenches.

Martin sits on his kit bag and finishes his cigarette.

"Sergeant, glad we found you, any idea where we have to go?"

Martin looks up at 2nd Lt Manners, "No Sir, I haven't asked yet, do you have any idea?"

The officer seems taken aback by Martin's lack of enthusiasm,

"Well, would it not be a good idea to do that Sergeant?" Manners says indignantly,

"What I think Gilbert is trying to say Sergeant, is that we are new here and like ducks out of water and would appreciate a bit of a helping hand" 2nd Lt Agar steps in.

"Certainly Sir, give me but a minute"

Martin stands up, he sees a private from one of the Yorkshire regiments walking out of the village smoking a cigarette,

"Excuse me mate" Martin stands in front of him, the private looks up and sees the veteran Sergeant and two officers standing near to him,

"Shit" he whispers under his breath,

"Don't worry lad" Martin nods toward the officers "They are new and if you put that ciggie behind your back you won't have to waste it"

"Yes Sergeant, thank you Sergeant"

"Can you point me in the direction of the camp"

A huge smile appears on the man's face, "Sergeant, if you walk through the village, you will smell the place before you see it, you can't miss it, pointed white and brown tents and shitty huts as far as the eye can see"

Martin thanks the Private and tells him to disappear and to finish his smoke, he turns to the officers,

"Gents, if you would follow me"

He picks up his kit, throwing his duffel over his shoulder and begins to walk up the dusty road, he holds in a laugh as he hears 2nd Lt Agar speak to his colleague,

"For Christs sake Gilbert, pick up your bloody kit, this is not training college and you do not have a batman to do everything for you"

Agar catches up with Martin,

"Everything alright Sir?" he asks, Agar smiles at him,

"This might take a bit of getting used to for some of us Sergeant"

"Indeed, it might Sir"

They walk through the village, there are many soldiers just milling around, some relaxing on their own, reading a book or having a smoke, others are hanging about in groups, chatting, although all are in uniform, some are informally dressed.

"Soldier, do up your tunic and put on your hat" he hears Manners talking to an obviously battle hardened Corporal,

"Don't say a word Corp" Martin says with authority to the soldier "Stand easy and carry on"

He turns to Agars, "You deal with him Sir" nodding at Manners, "I will stop the Corporal from punching him out"

"Really Sergeant?" Agars seems astounded,

"Really Sir, these lads have been on the front line, some for weeks at a time, they are tired and angry, the last thing any of them need is a rollocking because their tunic is undone"

He steps over to the Corporal and has a quiet conversation with him, they shake hands and Martin walks back to the officers, he gives Manners a filthy look,

"Let's get there shall we" he says as he picks up his kit and starts to walk in the dusty again.

It only takes a few minutes to walk through town,

"Bloody hell" Martin says as he sees the camp.

Rows and rows of tents, almost all the same shape and size, each one having a pointed canvas roof, Martin thinks it looks like hundreds and hundreds of witches' hats, all lined up in military fashion, every few hundred yards of so there is a few short lines of wooden huts intermingled in the sea of canvas.

"Welcome home" he says to the officers, both look stunned at the scene in front of them, the smell of human sewage is almost overpowering. "You gents should be in a hut, not under canvas" he looks at both of them "I spent my first winter under canvas, bloody freezing, to be fair to the army, they don't get much right, but after that, in Winter they sorted billets in local towns for us, either in barns or with the locals" he points across to the tents "But in summer, especially in training camps like this on, this is how we live"

It takes Martin nearly half an hour, with several wrong directions and advice, before he sees Ralph walking toward him,

"Are you early or are you fucking late Martin?" he growls, smiling as he does so,

"Due back tomorrow Sir, missed you all so much I came back a bit early"

Ralph appreciates the formality in front of the young officers,

"What do we have here then?"

"2nd Lt's Manners and Agar Sir"

Ralph looks the young men up and down, "Come with me Gents, I will get you to the billeting office"

"What about me Sir?" Martin enquires

"Hut seventeen Sergeant, I will meet you there is a short while" he turns to the officers "Follow me gentlemen"

The trio set off, Ralph stepping off at a fast pace and the young officers struggling to keep up as they are carrying all their kit, Martin shakes his head and sets off to find hut seventeen.

The hut is full of N.C.O's, mostly Sergeants but a couple are Corporals, he sees Nobby in the far corner, who waves when he sees Martin.

"Welcome back Martin"

Martin nods, "Busy in here isn't it Nobby?" he asks.

There are at least twenty of them billeted in this hut, wooden and canvas cots line each of the four walls, each has blankets stacked on them.

"It is not so bad really, everyone here is glad to be away from the front line for a bit, officially it's a training camp, but we have mostly been playing football" He stands up "In fact, we have a game this afternoon if you are interested"

"No chance, who are we playing?"

"The 20th Kings Liverpool again, it was a bit of a bloodbath last time!"

"Is this my bedspace?" Martin points at the tidy space next to Nobbys

"Yes, you are registered already, we had to get you on the list otherwise you would be in one of those tents again"

Martin thanks him and puts his kit down, "Is the R.S.M in here as well?"

Nobby snorts, "Not a chance, he, and the other R.S.M's, C.S.M's and Staff Sergeants have their own hut next door, not quite as crowded as this one!"

Martin makes the space his own, he hangs his coat and tin helmet on nails in the wall, each space has a few nails banged in behind them, so he supposes, correctly, that these few are his, as he and Nobby have their beds on the back wall, they have a shelf behind them, he takes out his mug, his washbag and shaving kit, his uniform and boot cleaning kit and puts them in the space that has been left for him.

"How was the wedding?" Nobby asks

"It was good mate, but after it, when everyone else had come back over here, it was a bit boring to be honest, I could not wait to get back"

He reaches inside his knapsack and hands Nobby a bar of chocolate, a packet of 'civvy' cigarettes and half a pound of loose tea that he had purchased in town before leaving,

"Ta Martin" he smells the loose tea in the brown paper bag "My God that smells decent, shall we have a brew?"

Martin nods in agreement, he asks, "How are the others in the platoon, all fit and well and no bits missing I hope?"

Nodding, Nobby replies, "All good, apart from the odd bit of violence on the footy pitch, we have been away from the front since you went"

"I have some ciggies and chocolate for them as well, any idea where they are billeted"

"Under canvas, not far from here, let's have a brew first"

They both look up when they hear the voice of Ralph across the room,

"Brewing up Corporal, what a splendid idea, I do hope there will be enough for this R.S.M.?"

Martin and Ralph shake hands,

"Everything alright in Blighty lad?"

"All good Ralph" he reaches into his knapsack and hands the R.S.M a parcel wrapped in brown paper, "As promised, it should be alright it is a fruit cake"

Ralph takes it, "Thank you, Martin, I shall have it later with a drop of beer"

Nobby brings the tea over,

"Have you told him Corporal?" Ralph asks Nobby, who shakes his head,

"Told me what?" Martin quizzes them, Ralph's face breaks out into a rare smile,

"The old man went haywire when he came back and found that Major Wynne had authorised your leave to go home"

Martin nearly chokes on his first mouthful of tea, "Blimey, what went on?" he asks

"It was all behind closed doors lad"

He looks playfully at the Sergeant and Corporal,

"But as R.S.M. I had to remain in the area to ensure good discipline all round"

Martin and Nobby both nod in agreement, both have wry grins on their faces, Ralph continues,

"The old man really wasn't happy, he started off berating Major Wynne for such bad judgement and undermining his order that no man was to have leave" he pauses "I wish I had been in the dugout to see the old man's face when Wynne said to him,

'Sir you left me in charge when you were taken elsewhere, as the man in charge I was the man to make the decisions and the orders, if that is not to your satisfaction then next time, find some other poor bastard to do your job', the old man must have just sat there as it was silent in the room for over a minute" he takes a sip of his tea, a huge smile appears on his face, "Bloody hell this isn't army tea, it actually tastes like tea, anyway as I am standing outside the door of the dugout, Wynne suddenly leaves and I am caught with my pants down, listening in" Both Nobby and Martin laugh,

"The Major just looked at me and said, 'Is everything all in order Regimental Sergeant Major?', I told him that it was and off he went" he points at Martin "Hence I got young Nobby here to register your billet and I have registered you back from leave so that you can avoid the old man for a few days"

Nobby laughs so hard he nearly spills his tea,

"Sod off Nobby, you know what the old man is like, he will have something to say about it when he sees me!" Martin says

"That is what I am laughing at mate, there is nowhere to hide, even in this massive training camp!"

They finish their tea and Ralph excuses himself, Martin and Nobby also leave to go and see the platoon, they are walking toward the tent that houses the rest of the platoon when Martin hears his name being called,

"Sergeant, bloody fine to see you back from Blighty" it is Major Wynne, standing with another Major and a Captain, both from the 20th Kings Liverpool regiment,

"Thank you, Sir, you off to see the game?"

"I'm the bloody ref worst luck, and these two are only coming to make sure I am fair and show no bias toward the much more skilled team that the Bedfordshires are putting forward"

"Yes Sir" Martin replies, Wynne looks at his watch,

"Kick off is not for a couple of hours and I might have a coffee beforehand" he stares at Martin, who for a moment has no idea what is going on, then the penny drops

"I seem to recall you are quite partial to wedding cake Sir?" he says as he reaches into his knapsack,

"Well, I have no bloody idea who told you that Sergeant, but yes I am!" Wynne replies with a very straight face, Martin hands him the cake wrapped in brown paper,

"Thank you so much Sergeant, very decent of you"

"I do hope that you have not had no issues with my being on leave Sir"

It is Martins turn to keep a straight face,

"Bugger off Sergeant" Wynne says to Martin

"Yes Sir" is the reply.

Wynne and the Kings Liverpool officers walk away, Martin can see that Wynne has already opened the parcel and is sampling the cake,

"You got any more of that cake in there, Martin?" asks Nobby

"Bugger off Corporal" is the reply he gets.

The football match is a success for the Bedfordshire soldiers, a win against the 20th Kings Liverpool lads, a single goal scored by Private Willie Williamson, a big man from Kings Lynn, vey nimble on his feet for a man of his size and it was a goal to be remembered according to him! He scores twice the following day when the Bedfordshires beat the 19th Battalion Kings Liverpool regiment 3-1, the Bedfordshire men celebrate by organising a sing song and a campfire, authorised by Major Wynne, Martin is bored already, he wants to get back to the front.

It is days before he gets to leave the camp, this time as part of a large group led by Capt. Beal and a Major from the Royal Engineers, they get taken about eight miles northeast by lorry directly back into Belgium to help with the work on the ridge defence in the Vierstraat area, the work is mind numbingly boring but it gets him and the platoon out of camp, there is a small piece of brightness at the end of the day when the Royal Engineers Major gathers the working party around the back of a lorry and when he opens the canvas flaps at the back, there are at least twenty crates of bottled beer inside, he addresses Martin,

"See the men get one bottle each Sergeant, if any man asks where it came from, don't give him a bottle!"

* * *

The days and weeks seem to drag by the Battalion have moved out of camp at Saint Jans Cappel and are now in trenches at the front line near to Wytschaete, Martin is happy to be back at the front line, the battalion have spent a few days as reserve Battalion in camp at a place known as the Chinese Wall, because of the very lengthy communication trench that runs for miles, this is called the Great Wall of China due to its length.

On Tuesday 11th September the Battalion are moved again, this time to a trench system known as Estaminet Corner, but they are put in a support role so although on the front line they are not at the front, although ten men have been sent to a casualty clearing station having been exposed to gas when a surprise attack caught them all out. A week later Martin is happy to be called to a briefing given by Lt Col Bunbury, whom Martin avoids at all costs, he and his platoon are to be part of a raiding party that will advance across toward the German lines, supported by a barrage of artillery and smoke cover, when they are in reaching distance of the enemy wire and trenches, reports are to be sent back for artillery to attempt to destroy the wire and German defences to give access to the raiding parties, it is hoped that the 89th and 90th Machine gun companies and the 89th trench mortar company, who will be concentrating their fire to the East of the raiding parties, will occupy the enemy enough for the raiding parties to get into and capture the enemy trenches and any enemy that may be there. Once this has been achieved a very white light will be illuminated, this will be the signal for the Royal Engineers to then join the men from the 2nd Bedfordshires and they will quickly advance into the trenches, escorted by an officer and Martin's platoon, enemy dugouts are to be destroyed by the sappers. Once this is completed a withdrawal is to be made using the same route as the soldiers entered the area, again protected by machine guns and trench mortars. The 19th Battalion Kings Liverpool regiment will be carrying out a similar raid at the same time, at a location a little further to the southeast, every soldier is to wear light battle dress, service belt, water bottle (full), to be issued fifty rounds of standard army ammunition and four bombs per man, each soldier is to be in possession of a box respirator in case of gas or poison attack.

Zero hour and Z Day will be posted shortly, these raids will take place in conjunction with the advance of the 2nd and 5th armies on the Menin Road, in positions further East than that of the Bedfordshires. It has been drilled into all the officers and platoon commanders that the main event is the advance on the Menin Road, infantry will advance to agreed positions and then stop and consolidate the ground taken, the minor raids to be carried out by the Bedfordshires and the Kings Liverpool soldiers are purely to gather intelligence, to capture prisoners and to destroy enemy dugouts in specified sections of the trenches. Martin knows that he cannot return to the mindset he was in before going on leave, he knows he put his platoon and other colleagues in situations of high risk when he did not care what happened to himself or to anyone else, but he does want to lead from the front for the rest of the war but in a controlled manner, this raid, he hopes will give him the opportunity to reaffirm his devotion to his platoon, to the Battalion and to the Regiment.

It is five thirty on the morning of Thursday 20th September, Z day, Martin and his platoon are ready to move off, they are one of three platoons under the command of Lt Searle, Martin knows him well as he used to be an enlisted man who had joined the regulars only a few months before Martin in 1910, he and Martin were in different Battalions, Martin has always been with the 2nd, Thomas started with the 1st Battalion but was promoted to acting Sergeant with the 3rd Battalion in September 1913. Thomas was promoted to Lance Sergeant at the outbreak of war, he joined the 2nd Battalion in December 1914 and he and Martin became mates, although of different ranks, they shared a hard working ethic and a will to serve, Thomas was posted to Brigade HQ when he made full Sergeant, rejoining the 2nd Battalion in July 1916, a brave and hard soldier, he was awarded the Meritorious Service Medal for gallantry, this is a medal for rank and file only. Martin was not surprised when Thomas was commissioned in the field, staying with the 2nd as a 2nd Lt.

It was in June of this year that he was awarded the Military Cross, Martin remembers the day well, although not in the same section as Thomas, it was during these raids that he captured a German prisoner, his actions nearly cost the lives of his platoon and Lt Jones had torn him a strip afterwards, then Nobby had also had a go and then Ralph, days like that one he needs to remember. It was on this day that Thomas had stopped a large number of German troops advancing into their trenches when he led a bombing party to drive out the enemy, his citation had been published only a month ago. A feeling of sadness takes over him for a few seconds as he remembers the reason why he was almost suicidal with rage for over ten months, Grace, his Grace, and her untimely death.

"You and yours ready to move Martin?" Lt Searle brings him back to the war,

"Yes Sir" Martin replies

"Good man, no heroics today, let's get in, get the job done, let the engineers have the glory of blowing up a few dugouts and then we leave" he slaps Martin on the shoulder,

"See you later for tea and biccies Martin"

He is gone, moving down the line to speak to all under his command,

"First real action for a while Martin" Nobby says

Martin agrees and checks that all his platoon is in order and ready to go.

The orders of the commanding officer have made it clear; each platoon must only be a Sergeant and three men, Martin chose Nobby and left it to him to choose the other two, he knows that Dennis and Sharpie will be behind him all the way and that the others, H, John Marrables, and Alfie will be unhappy at the patrol going out without them, but they will all get their chance another day.

At precisely five forty, the signal is given for the patrols to advance, Martin can see Thomas is at the front of the platoons he is leading, as he gets out of the trench, he can hear the machine gun and trench mortar companies hard at work, creating a small diversion for them to, hopefully, advance without meeting much of a challenge from the enemy. The land in front of them is heavily clouded with smoke and the artillery are now launching their death and destruction toward the enemy lines, hopefully destroying much of the wire, making the final advance into the enemy trench, a smooth one.

As they move slowly through the open land, shielded by smoke, it becomes obvious that the Germans have many machine guns themselves in this area, many more than had previously been reported,

"Objective in sight!" Lt Searle shouts to his platoons, he then shouts "Wire!"

Martin knows that the artillery support has failed to cut the German fortification made up of wire and huge wooden X shaped crosses,

"Get down, get down!" Martin yells at his platoon, he can hear other platoon commanders giving similar orders, he can also hear men screaming in pain and dying.

The enemy fire is so intense that not one of the platoons can move from the positions they have taken up in a shell holes, they cannot advance because of the continuous fire from the Germans, they also cannot return to their trenches for the same reason, the sun isn't fully up yet, and they are stranded in no man's land with no way out. As the sun sets, the platoons from the Bedfordshires, with the eight men from the Royal engineers are still in the shell holes, they have hardly moved all day and the enemy fire has not stopped; at

9pm the firing from the German lines slows enough for the platoons to retreat back to the relative safety of the allied lines. Other raids had been more successful, B company, further on the left flank, managed to advance three hundred yards and joined up with the advancing 6th Battalion Wiltshire regiment, the line has extended as far as the canal.

Lt Col Bunbury proclaims that the operation is entirely successful, seven are injured, eight are dead most have got back safely after a long day in the shell holes. Not so for Lt Thomas Searle, it is known that he was wounded by machine gun fire early in the advance, he is missing presumed killed in action.

Back in the trenches it is just after midnight, Martin is trying to get as far inside his waterproof cape as he can to escape from the incessant rain, the bottom of the trench is filled with water, it has been for the two days they have been here, even the new duckboards that have been supplied are slowly but surely being covered by the stream of thick brown mud that is building up by the minute, Nobby, H and Dennis are in the relative dryness of the dugout shelter, the tarpaulin roof is heavy with water but if they empty it, the contents will only add to the mud and water already in the trench, so it is left as it is, looking like the belly of an expectant Mother, the dugout shelter is not an officers dugout, this is a hole that the previous occupants had dug into the side of the trench and lined with bits of wood and corrugated iron, the tarpaulin is held up by two pieces of wood that both have burns and bullet holes on them, it has been made big enough for two men to sit in it comfortably or three men, not so comfortably.

"Glad we are only here for two days Sarge" Sharpie says, John Marrables nods in agreement, Alfie, who is lying at the top of the trench on watch, says nothing.

"We should be relieved soon; we only came into the trenches for the raid" John says to anyone that will listen. Martin looks at his pocket watch, it is so wet and dark that he cannot make out the time,

"It is ten after midnight Martin" Nobby tells him from inside the dugout shelter, they all hear a voice carry down the trench,

"Prepare for relief, the 17th Manchester Regiment are here, when relieved form up at the far side of the support system trenches"

They all know from experience, that handing over the trenches to the incoming regiment, is not a quick process, it can take hours to get it done safely.

"Get in here Martin, I can take your stag for half an hour, you don't have to be out there" Nobby says to Martin,

"Stay inside mate, these boys have another half hour to go, I will stop out with them" Martin says as he nods to Nobby,

"I would have gone in for a bit" moans John

"Luckily for me, I am in charge, so you stay out to finish your hour"

John doesn't answer, he knows that Martin is correct, the other three in the shelter, have done their time in the rain. They turn as group of soldiers approaches from the rear of the trench,

"Much going on chum?" the Corporal from the Manchester's asks Martin,

"Just rain mate, rain and more rain, the Bosch have been keeping dry and staying in tonight, I hope it continues for you" he points to the shelter "It's not so bad in there, we have been doing an hour about"

The Corporal thanks Martin and puts three of his lads into the shelter, telling one of them to 'get a brew on', H, Nobby and Dennis get out of the shelter, letting the men from the Manchester regiment take their places,

"Alfie, come on down" Martin instructs their man on watch, as he gets down a gloomy looking soldier replaces him, Martin nods at the Corporal relieving him,

"Keep your head down mate" he says as they leave and make their way toward the support trenches at the area known as Estaminet corner, only a ten minute walk from the line, but now, as the support Battalion, they will get to sleep in huts, with beds and a wood burning stove.

Martins platoon line up with the rest of their colleagues, Ralph shouts at them,

"Moving camp again lads, a nice march in the rain at night will do us all the world of good!"

"You must be fucking joking" John says quietly, Martin looks at him and he doesn't speak again.

"Any ideas where we are going Sarge?" asks Alfie

Martin shakes his head,

"No, could be anywhere, but it won't be too far as we are on working party duties for the next few days, so we need to be within reach of the front line"

They all moan, everyone hates the working party duty because it means going out in front of the line to mend any shell damage to the front walls of the trenches and other defences, they will have to carry the barbed wire and corkscrew pickets for any repairs that will need to be done to the huge belts of wire that protect the front line, they all know that it has to be done, they have all come across wire when attacking the Germans and it has always stopped them in their tracks, with the only choices being to cut the wire, which leaves you all standing or lying exposed for the enemy to shoot you or move back and hope that the artillery will hit it and destroy it. So, they all appreciate that it is a job that has to be done but none of them like being so very exposed when out of the trenches.

The R.S.M is walking up the line of Bedfordshire soldiers,

"How was it out there?" he asks Martin when he reaches the platoon,

"Just wet Ralph, nothing at all from the Germans, but the trenches are all flooded again"

They both look up into the night sky,

"This rain ain't going to stop anytime soon Martin"

"Any idea where we are going Sir?" Nobby asks the R.S.M

"To the big city Corporal, Ypres in fact, a bit of a march but the billets will be warm and dry"

Martin turns to the platoon as Ralph walks up the line, he tells them that the billets in Ypres are going to be better than the dugouts, tents, and huts they have been in.

The billets in Ypres are invariably in houses, buildings or barns that have either been taken over by the army or have suffered bomb damage, the windows that have been blown out will have been replaced with sandbags and all will have a roof, even if it is only a ceiling above and the main roof of the building is gone. The platoon seems happy enough with this, Ralph is back talking to Martin,

"Change of plan lads, they want us nearer to the front line, we are off to Bedford house camp"

They all moan, Bedford house camp is shelled regularly by the enemy, the main buildings have all been virtually destroyed, the cellars and underground tunnels are used by the medical corps to treat wounded soldiers coming off of the line before they are sent back or moved to a casualty clearing station, the billets for the resting soldiers will be the old wooden huts, a bit draughty but on the whole, dry and there is a large stream toward the back of the grounds, so if it stops raining, they will be able to wash themselves and their clothes if there are no proper facilities available for them to use, Martin is sure that there won't be any due to the artillery activity by the enemy.

"One good thing lads, we should be there in under an hour, it is only just a bit further down the canal"

They set off as the rain slows to a drizzle, none of them notice the change.

* * *

The early morning fog of Sunday 4th November has cleared, and a light drizzle carries the light from the cloud covered sun across the garden as Alice looks out over the garden, it is chilly enough for the range fire to be fully burning and a small fire in the living room will be kept going for the whole day. Alice moves across the room when she sees Mary come through the garden gate, she is carrying a reed basket and is not wearing a coat or a head scarf, she opens the door and hurries her grandmother to get inside in the warm,

"Granny why on earth have you not got a coat on?"

She shuts the door behind Mary who puts the basket onto the table,

"It is fine love, really"

Mary sits and seems out of breath,

"Are you poorly Granny?" asks Alice

"Certainly not!" Mary replies "I am getting a bit old to be running a pub on my own that is all, it will pass, anyway I have this lunchtime off, Walter is opening up for me"

Alice checks the kettle that is on top of the stove, Mary stands to go and get the cups, saucers, and the teapot, she seems unsteady on her feet

"Sit down Granny" Alice commands "I can get them; this is my cottage after all!"

Mary reluctantly sits back down, she is feeling unusually dizzy,

"I hope this will do us" she says as she takes a recently plucked chicken from the basket,

"Granny, that is wonderful, enough for three meals at least"

"You should see my back yard, all feathers and blood!"

Alice screws up her face,

"Granny!"

Mary manages a smile, "I have some potatoes and some winter greens..." she pauses and seems momentarily confused, then she remembers and finishes the sentence "that Walter gave me yesterday"

She hopes Alice has not realised she stammered and forgot her words for a second or two,

"A feast for us today then Granny, I have some carrots that Mr Almond gave me this morning, he was on his way to church I think"

"We need to get this chicken in your oven sooner rather than later Alice, do you want me to peel the potatoes?"

Alice tells Mary to stay sitting down, she pours hot water into the teapot, swills the contents around and empties them into the bucket next to the range, she adds three spoons of loose leaf tea, she knows Mary likes her tea strong, more hot water on top of the leaves and a hand knitted tea cosy is placed over the top of it, she takes the potatoes from Mary and peels them,

"Cut them in half and put them in with the chicken Alice" Mary instructs, Alice looks at her grandmother but does not speak, Mary smiles, "I know I am an interfering old so and so, but I can't help it"

"I will put them in the roasting pan all together if it will please you Granny"

"It will, shall I pour"

Alice nods and Mary pours the tea into the cups, after a final swill of the contents just to make sure it will be strong, Alice prepares the greens and the carrots and they are put in pans of cold water and left on the table, they will only be put on the heat when the chicken and potatoes are done.

"That is the last of the water, I will get some after we have had our tea" Alice tells Mary, who lifts her cup to her lips and takes a small amount of tea, she immediately feels it dribbling from her mouth,

"Granny, what is wrong?" Alice looks worried

"Nothing child, I just took too much tea, and it is hot, have you never dribbled tea before" Mary seems angry

"As long as you are sure Granny"

Mary tells Alice not to fuss and asks if she has heard from 'the boys'

"Charles writes every week, I had letters yesterday from him, Martin has not written for a week or so, but he said in his last letter that it may be a couple of weeks before we hear from him again" She puts her tea down on the table "I have to presume that he is back on the front line, I wish they would tell me"

"They can't tell you" Mary says "They are not allowed"

Alice knows this but as Mary seems a little out of sorts, she decides to play dumb on this occasion, she stands and looks out of the window,

"It seems to be brightening up Granny"

Alice looks across at Mary who is looking directly at her but seems to be having difficulty understanding her, she looks confused, Alice feels concerned and a little scared,

"Granny" No reply from Mary, Alice tries again, "Granny"

No reply again, Alice steps forward and shakes Mary on the shoulder,

"What are you doing child!" Mary shouts, her words seem slow coming from her mouth

"I couldn't get you to answer me Granny, you were miles away"

Mary rubs her face and then pats her hair gently,

"I was thinking about something else, now what did you say?"

"I said, the rain seems to have stopped and it is brightening up"

Mary leans and looks around Alice and through the window,

"Yes, so it does" she sits back up straight in the chair, her hands are in her lap and her left hand is clenched tightly "Are you going to put that roast in the oven, or will I have to do it?"

Alice smiles, that is much more like Granny she loves,

"I will do it, finish your tea, you haven't touched it"

"I will in a moment"

"Granny"

Mary looks slowly toward Alice,

"Yes Alice"

"I need to go and use the privy"

Mary looks disapprovingly at Alice,

"I am sure I don't need any more details thank you"

Alice manages a little laugh,

"What I mean Granny is that whilst I am gone, you stay sitting and finish your tea" Mary shuffles in her seat, Alice puts her hands on her hips, "I mean it Granny"

Mary puts her right hand on Alice hip,

"Grandchild, I will sit and do not an ounce of work whilst you are gone" She moves her hand and picks up her cup, "I will finish my tea" Alice leaves the kitchen through the door to the back yard,

"The cheek of the child" Mary says to herself.

She sips her tea but for some reason she cannot swallow properly, "Do nothing indeed" she says out loud.

With a struggle she stands up and takes the empty bucket and shuffles toward the front door, she cannot understand why she feels so tired, the latch on the front door opens easily and it swings opens outwards, Mary breathes fresh, clean November air into her lungs,

"That feels better, it is too hot in that cottage, fresh air is all I needed"

She sets off, slowly, down the garden toward the water pump. Instead of putting the bucket down on the ground below the spout, Mary drops it on the ground, she bends down to set it right and suddenly cannot focus or get her hand to do as she wants it to, she feels dizzy again and very uncoordinated, she takes a deep breath,

"It is too hot in that cottage; it has given me a turn" she tells herself off.

She manages to right the bucket and it now sits below the spout, using her right hand, her left seems very tired and useless to her, she begins to push the handle of the water pump down, it will not move, she does not have the strength to push it. She suddenly puts her right hand on her forehead a severe and blinding pain shoots across the inside of her head, this is pain like she has never experienced before, unusually for her she tries to cry for help but cannot form words, her left hand and now her left arm hang uselessly beside her, she cannot move it. Standing up straight she looks around and can just about focus to see the huge trunk of the Yew tree a few yards to her left, stepping away from the pump she moves toward the tree trunk, she will be able to support herself on that and sit down if she needs to, she almost falls as she steps away, her left leg will not do as she wants it to, it is almost being dragged as she moves. She can no longer swallow at all, the pain in her head brings tears to her eyes, confusion takes over her every being, she looks at the Yew and cannot remember why she needs or even wants to go near the old horrible tree, as she takes a step with her right leg it is not followed by her left, she stumbles and falls to the ground, she is lying on her side, the tree trunk is only a yard or so in front of her, if she can only move that short distance she can sit up, she tells herself this several times as she can no longer speak, the left side of her face feels odd and as she touches her cheek there is little or no feeling there. She can hear the old branches of the Yew moving in the breeze, they seem to be screaming at her, attacking her senses with their noise, Mary is sure she can hear laughing from the huge bows above her, she can no longer move, her left side is paralysed, she is sure she can hear someone calling her, but she cannot be sure, a gust of wind moves the lower and upper branches of the tree in one movement, the noise of this is the last thing she hears before darkness takes her.

"Granny!"

Alice is running down the garden, she has returned from the privy and immediately sees that the front door is wide open, and Granny is not in the kitchen, she has looked and seen Mary lying on the ground under the Yew tree and begun to run toward her,

"Granny!"

She carries on running, Mary is completely still, lying on her side with her face toward the tree, she has not replied to Allices screams, she slides to a halt and falls to her knees next to Mary,

"Granny" she says quietly.

Alice rolls Mary onto her back, she can see that her grandmothers' eyes are open but are not looking at anything, just staring upward, the left side of her mouth is drooping lower than her right, Alice does not know what to do, she sits next to Mary and puts her Grannies head in her lap, she gently runs her hand over Mary's face and smooths over her hair,

"Oh Granny" she cries "Whatever shall I do?"

Alice is sat in the pub with Walter, the pub has not been opened, when May, Pete and Catherine enter the bar, Alice jumps up and falls into May's arms,

"Auntie May, I couldn't do anything, I didn't know what to do, it's all my fault"

May hugs her niece, "Hush now Alice, it is not your fault at all"

Alice feels safe for the first time for hours, she hugs her Auntie and will not let go,

"Where is she?" Pete asks Walter

"In the kitchen Pete, the lads didn't want to risk taking her up the stairs, you know, the coffin and everything, it could be a bit tight" Pete nods quietly, "Dr Blake from Bowers house has been" Walter then changes his voice to a whisper "Stroke he says, he will do the certificate and get it to Friday Thorogood by tomorrow morning"

Pete knows that Mr H. Thorogood, known locally as 'Friday', has the undertakers shop in Redbourn

"Thanks Walter, thanks for sorting this out and thanks for staying with Alice"

Walter stands up to leave,

"Walter, can you open up for the rest of the week, lunchtimes and evenings please"

Walter touches the front of his cap and leaves the family in the bar, May gently seats Alice on a chair, Catherine sits with them,

"I have sent a telegram to Martin and to Charles, Jenny sorted it out at the post office for me" May tells Alice "I just told them Mary had died suddenly"

Alice sits up, "Oh my, what about the pub?"

"Walter will sort it this week Alice" Pete tells her.

There is a light tap on the door of the pub, Pete moves across the bar and opens it, they all hear him say,

"Hello Henry, you on your own?"

Alice hears a voice outside say,

"My lad got called up a while ago and is away fighting"

She recognises it as Mr Harry Reeve, a local cabinet maker, upholsterer, and undertaker, he has a small shop on the Wheathampstead road and a workshop up on West Common, he is collecting Mary's body to take it to the undertakers in Redbourn, Pete and Henry know each other well,

"Come on in, I will give you a hand"

Harry enters the pub and nods at the ladies,

"My condolences to you all" he looks at Pete and quietly says, "Might be best if the ladies were not here Peter"

"May, can you take Alice and Catherine to the cottage" Pete is nodding at her as he speaks, "I will join you in a while"

May nods and stands up, both Alice and Catherine are looking at her, avoiding any eye contact with Harry or Pete, both are crying quietly,

"Come on ladies, let us leave the men to work"

"No" Alice says,

May is insistent, "Yes Alice, none of us need to see this" She stands in front of Alice and Catherine, "My Mother, your grandmother has died and she needs to leave the pub, I need you to be with me and not here"

Alice looks at May and then to Catherine, both have red eyes and tears running down their cheeks,

"Alright Auntie May"

The three ladies leave the pub, Pete and Harry carry an empty, plain coffin into the pub, Mary's body is removed from the kitchen table, placed in the coffin and Harry puts on the lid, the now full box is carried out to Harry's horse and cart and the two men load it onto the back, Harry closes and secures the back flap of the cart.

"Condolences again Peter, I will get her to Friday's place for you without any bother"

"Thanks Harry, I will drop in tomorrow to sort the funeral details, can you tell him that please"

Harry nods, climbs aboard his cart, and nudges his horse to move forward, as he passes the Bakers, Mr and Mrs Ackroyd are standing outside, heads bowed and silent.

* * *

Mary's funeral is a quiet affair, St Nicholas Church is just over half full of locals from the pub and friends who knew and loved her.

Alice stands at the front with Pete, May, Jennifer, and Catherine, she is with family but feels all alone.

Charles sent her a telegram of condolence and Alice also received a letter from him on the morning of the funeral, he explained, as much as he could, why he was not allowed to attend he tells her that his friend, Albert Munt, serving with the Hertfordshire regiment, who's family live next door to his parents at the

Cherry Trees, has been killed on 31st July 1917, he signed off telling her that he loves her more than anything else.

Martin has sent a telegram.

It just said "NOT COMING"

1918

CHAPTER NINE

The war drags itself into 1918, leaving the dead of the previous years to lie in the ground in foreign lands.

The 2nd Battalion Bedfordshires spent the final month of last year in trenches, six days in and four days out, finally being relieved at ten in the evening of Christmas eve, Forrestor camp is to be their billet for the Christmas period. The day itself arrives and nothing is celebrated, the men are tired and need to get their bodies and their kit clean. Christmas is celebrated by the Battalion on Boxing Day, Martin attends the festivities but does not enjoy himself and early in the evening he makes his excuses and goes back to his billet, Nobby finds him an hour later and has a bottle of Jenever, a gin like drink, they sit in front of the fire talking and drinking until the early hours.

They are in trenches again as the New Year is bought in, Martin and the platoon are in Jackdaw tunnels and it is cold and wet, they try to make the best of their situation and Lt Col Thorpe has authorised fires to be lit in the trenches as it is so cold, the enemy has been quiet and they are certain to be just as cold as the Bedfordshires and the other battalions in trenches.

The first week of the New Year is not a good one, many men are killed and wounded by artillery and trench mortars, the second week arrives, and the Battalion are moved from Belgium and into France by train, firstly to Battalion HQ in Amiens and then to trenches at Viry Noureuil, South of Amiens.

Rumours of a big push from both sides are rife throughout the Battalion, Martin has heard such tales before, tales of the final big push to end the war, he heard this in 1914, 1915, 1916 and 1917, he sees no reason why 1918 should be any different, the war drags on and drags him and his lads along with it

* * *

"Morning Sarge"

Martin looks up from his seat outside of one of two dugouts he, Nobby and the rest of the platoon are sharing, the Battalion are currently on support duties, only a short distance from the current HQ,

"Morning Nobby, nice for it not to be wintry again"

The weather for the past few weeks has been cold with wintry showers, some heavy, the temperature has barely reached past freezing, today is warmer and dry

"Who are you writing too this time?"

Martin chuckles, "You say that as if I am an avid writer! Just a note to Alice, letting her know that I am doing alright"

Nobby sits down next to his Sergeant, "How is she now, you know after your grandmother died?"

Martin puts the pen and paper aside, "Doing alright mate, I think it was hard for her when neither Charles nor I were allowed home leave for the funeral"

Nobby has a wry grin on his face,

"Sod off Nobby, I know what you are thinking, you all thought I would go off the rails again, but although I was really very angry at the time, I sort of accepted it"

"Not what I heard Martin and you have never told me what happened when old Wynne took you to see the Major General?"

Martin picks up a mug of lukewarm tea, and he, for the first time, tells Nobby what happened the day his grandmother died.

Ralph had been the one to break the news to him, Martin did not even try to hide his sadness at the passing of Mary, Ralph took him directly to see Major Wynne, who was once again the Battalion commanding officer as Lt Col Poyntz was, again, in hospital. Wynne had been very sorry for the loss of Martins Grandmother, but he was not authorised to allow any leave, for any reason at that time even though the Battalion was only in a support role in trenches at the Chinese Wall. Martin had asked to see the Major General to request to go home for a short leave to bury his grandmother, Major Wynne agreed to this and arranged it for that afternoon.

Things did not go well when Martin was kept waiting for nearly two hours by Major General Williams, when Major Wynne returned for his fourth visit to the Major Generals office, he left Martin alone for a few minutes, when he returned, he stated that the meeting would be in a couple of minutes, he looked angry, but Martin did not ask the reason. They were both called into the Major Generals office, Martin remembers it being bigger than the cottage at home, Wynne had told him to remain silent and to let him talk to the Major General. They had both been standing for over a minute in front of the Major Generals desk, he had not even looked up from a document he was reading, Martin had to stop himself from balling his fists, eventually Major Wynne coughed,

"I know you are there Major" Williams said without raising his head "Wait until I am ready"

"Sir" Wynne replied.

Another long minute passed in silence, Major General Williams eventually lifted his head and looked at Major Wynne, he ignored Martin completely,

"Get on with it Major, I don't have all day"

"Sir, the Sergeant here has received a telegram today telling him of the unexpected death of his grandmother, this is an application for short leave for the Sergeant to attend the funeral"

"Denied" Williams replies without thinking

"Sir?" Wynne says

"Denied Major, at this time it is impossible for anyone to have leave and that is that"

The Major General put his head down and continued to read the document on his desk, he still had not looked at Martin. His fists balled and tight, Martin takes a step forward, Wynne turns and stands in front of him, whispering he says to Martin,

"Sergeant, if you have any respect for me, any at all, you will salute the General, turnabout on your heels and leave this room" Martin has his teeth gritted so tight his jaw is hurting, Wynne continues, "Sergeant do as I say and wait outside for me"

Martin does not move, Williams talks without looking up,

"Are you still here Major?"

Wynne steps very close to Martin,

"Now please sergeant"

He steps aside and Martin salutes the Major General, who is still ignoring him, turns on his heels and leaves the room, slamming the door behind him.

He waits outside and a few minutes later he is joined by Major Wynne, who closes the door quietly.

"A subtle exit you performed just then Sergeant"

"I am sorry Sir; I couldn't help myself"

"I can't say as I blame you, I am genuinely sorry about not sorting the leave for you, but you saw what he is like"

"I did Sir, thank you Sir"

Wynne tells Martin to walk with him, as they leave the HQ building, Wynne starts to chuckle,

"Are you quite well Sir?" Martin asks him

"Indeed, I am Sergeant" he stops walking and turns to Martin "Although my hopes of promotion may just have been dashed"

"May I ask why Sir?" Martin is intrigued

"Best not Sergeant, let's just say that when the old man asked me why the door had been slammed, I told him, and in no uncertain terms!"

"I do hope you are not in trouble Sir, but thank you"

"No more than usual Sergeant" the Major looks around where they are standing,

"There it is" he says "Follow me Sergeant"

Martin walks alongside the Major and he enters the wireless telegraphists office, the Lance Corporal on duty stands up immediately,

"Morning Sir, Morning Sergeant"

The small room is jammed with electronic equipment, most of which Martin has never seen, he recognises the wireless that the operator is sitting in front of, although he has no idea how it works.

"Lance Corporal, the Sergeant needs to send a telegram home immediately"

"Sir, I am under orders not to send any communications of a personal nature, I …" He does not finish his words because Major Wynne talks over him,

"Lance Corporal, I will say this just once more, the Sergeant needs to send a telegram home immediately and I am authorising it"

"Yes Sir, but..."

Wynne stares at the wireless operator, who visibly slumps in his chair,

"Yes Sir"

Wynne claps his hands together, "Splendid, Sergeant, once again, my condolences"

Wynne leaves the room,

"Can I have the details then Sarge, can we make it quick, if my Captain catches me, I am for the high jump, regardless of the order from the Major"

Martin takes the telegram he received earlier that day, he hands it to the Lance Corporal,

"Can you send an answer to this telegram mate"

Looking at the details, the Lance Corporal nods, "What is the message Sarge?"

"Not coming"

"Is that it?"

Martin nods,

"No problem I will do it now"

He hands the telegram back to Martin,

"Keep it or bin it will you mate"

Martin turns to leave,

"Thanks for this"

He leaves the wireless office and walks back to his platoon.

* * *

"Do you have any idea what Wynne said to the General?" Nobby asks

"None at all mate, but I don't think it would have been words of love if you understand me!"

Nobby laughs out loud,

"Don't think any of us will be laughing later on Corporal"

Sergeant Percy Compton has walked into the trench,

"Morning Percy, I see they eventually got around to giving you your D.C.M" Martin acknowledges him, "Do you want a brew?"

Percy shakes his head,

"Can't Martin, thanks anyway, I am here to tell you all to get your kit together, we are off again at some point today"

"Where to this time Sarge?" Nobby asks

"Some shit hole between Etreillers and Savy, looks like the Hun are getting ready for another scrap"

Percy waves as he makes his way toward another dugout to break the news to another platoon.

"Come on Nobby" Martin says as he puts his unfinished letter into his knapsack "Best we get on"

They both walk into the dugout, both have to duck down to get under the beam of wood that forms the roof of the open fronted dugout, it has been cut into the end section of their trench, the wall at the back is lined with old, thick wooden boards, sandbags and the trench wall form the other two sides, the roof is bowing under the weight of several sheets of corrugated iron, more sandbags and lots of earth, both have make shift, home-made wood burning stoves, Martin and Nobbys dugout even has a table and benches that John Marrables put together for them. Martin kicks the feet of H, who is lying on one of the benches,

"Time to get up mate, we are on the move again"

"Blimey Sarge, I was on a beautiful beach with a beautiful young lady, the sun was shining, and we were going in for a swim, you woke me up at a very crucial part of the preparation"

"Get up H, I reckon I have just saved your soul" Martin tells him.

Nobby has roused the rest of the lads from the dugout next door, slightly larger to accommodate the remaining four members of the platoon,

"They are getting sorted Martin"

Martin nods and packs his own kit, it doesn't take long, he is wearing most of the clothing he owns to keep the cold out, even though it is warmer today they all have several layers of clothing on, most of it dirty, smelly and lice ridden.

In less than half an hour they are all waiting for orders to move off,

"This could be a long day" Martin observers, he throws his finished cigarette butt into a puddle,

"Shall I brew up Sarge? If it's going to be a long day, best we grab a tea whilst we can"

Martin agrees and tells the lads to get back into their dugouts to keep warm, no point in standing in the freezing cold waiting for information to arrive that might not be sent for a few hours yet, the army can wait the extra minute it will take them to get ready.

It is past three in the morning and very dark when the order 'standby' comes through for the battalion and the rest of the 90th Brigade, the 2nd Bedfordshires having joined the 90th from the 89th in February 1918, the men form up, it is very cold and there are clouds of white frozen air surrounding every section of the Battalion as they all huff and puff with nervous energy, men are stamping their feet and rubbing their hands together to keep warm, none of the N.C.O's berate the soldiers for moving whilst in formation.

Finally, the order to "Move out" is given and the men march from their warm dugouts and damp trenches firstly to the outskirts of the village of Savy only a short distance from where they were when they started, leaving this village behind the Battalion march on, following the road toward Etreillers, heavy enemy artillery begins to land all around them, some of the men, mainly the newest arrivals, are obviously scared and begin to panic, all the senior N.C.O's tell them to 'be steady', Martin has an experienced platoon, he has no need to say anything. The order to keep marching is given, it is only when Martin hears someone shout 'Gas! Gas! Gas!" That he gets his platoon and the others immediately around them to stop and to put on their Mark II gas mask, made by the French and used by the Allied soldiers since early 1916, it is more of a hood than a mask, Martin has always thought that it looks just like the nose bags the horses on the farms at home are given to eat from. This hood is one piece of material that covers the whole face of the wearer and additional straps are tied around the head, the hood has two eyeholes, made of cellophane glass and secured in place by a metal ring, vision is obscured when wearing it and if worn for any length of time, condensation builds up inside and the hood has to be removed to clear it out. The chlorine gas, although present in the air is mainly concentrated on the front line trenches, so the Bedfordshires are getting the far edges of it as it drifts toward them on the early morning breeze, explosions up and down the front line can be seen and heard, the Battalion have been marching for just over an hour when the order to "stand to" is given, they are right in the battle zone between Savy and Etreillers, it is just getting light and still only a few minutes before five on the morning of 21st March 1918. D company are sent back to HQ at Stevens Redoubt, B company are put in counter attack positions in a North to West trench system to the East of Entreillers, A company, including Martins patrol, are to remain as '*stood to*', C company are alongside them in these shallow trenches to the West of Savy, the whole of this front line, situated to the South West of St Quentin is taking huge hits, over 40 miles of trenches, wire defences, shell holes and shattered buildings form the Allied front line and the Germans are obviously preparing for a big push, the artillery is incessant and none of the soldiers have a second to think as the shells burst all around them. As the sun rises the battlefield is shrouded in morning fog, this is made all the thicker by the smoke from the ongoing bombardment, visibility is less than ten yards, Martin knows that mist and smoke can give cover to them from the Germans, it can also cover any advance made by the enemy, they could be on top of them before they know it. Word is passed down the line the front line has been badly damaged and that communications to the rear and to HQ have been disrupted as the front line communication wires have been cut. It is nine thirty when the barrage from the Germans stops, many of the men breathe a sigh of relief as the horrendous noise has stopped and the risk of a shell landing on them has drastically reduced, from the screams they can now hear, they know that men are injured and dying around them.

"Be ready lads, we all know why they have stopped the artillery, expect an infantry assault at any time"

As he says this to his platoon, a soldier falls over the top of the trench and almost on top of H and Dennis, it is a young soldier from the Kings Liverpool regiment,

"Sorry Sarge, I am the runner for my Battalion, and I have been running round in circles in this fog and smoke, I need to get to HQ because the Germans have defeated our front line, communications are down as they have cut all the wires and I hate to tell you this, but they are coming your way"

"Good lad, HQ is back at Stevens Redoubt, if you go to the support trenches, they will direct you, give them plenty of warning you are coming and tell them to get up here to support us"

With a nod, the runner is gone, out of the back of the trench and toward the location of B company,

"Nobby, get up the trench and tell the next platoon that we are going to get hit very soon, H, you go the other way" Martin looks at the others, "Keep watch lads, these trenches are shallow and don't give us much cover, if you see the Bosch, shoot at him, don't wait for orders"

Martin has been staring so long into the fog and smoke, when he sees the Germans advancing through it doesn't register with him straight away, it isn't until another platoon to the right opens fire that he realises that the enemy are less than ten yards away. He shoots quickly, in his peripheral vision he can see German infantrymen falling dead and wounded in front of him, he has no idea if he is hitting any of them, but he must be with his rate of fire and reloading. The immediate enemy attack withdraws very quickly, the Bedfordshires have fought off a much larger number of enemy soldiers,

"In the trench, they are in the trench!" Someone shouts,

Martin hears the screams of men being wounded, he hears gunfire, lots of gunfire, the Germans have infiltrated the trenches to his right, he can't see because of the hanging smoke, but if he moves his platoon in to help the others to his right, it leaves their section wide open.

He sees movement to his right at the rear, he is pleased to see that B company have moved forward, he shouts at the officer in front to get further right, which he does, for now they are all safe. The war rages on all around them, on all sides, it has also become clear that the enemy have established themselves firmly on both sides of the Savy road, many allied soldiers are dead and many more have been taken prisoner, there is no word from HQ about what the plan is, they have to stay in place until they hear.

It is early afternoon when word reaches them that defences to the North have been defeated and the Allied troops have retreated to avoid being attacked on three sides, to the South, the Germans have penetrated at least two miles South of Esigny, deep into former territory held by the French and the British, the Bedfordshires and the rest of the 90th Brigade are holding fast, for now.

As dusk begins to fall the stalemate continues, the Bedfordshires and the other Battalions are outnumbered and certainly outgunned by the Germans,

"Movement Sarge, here they come again" Alfie tells Martin, who whistles to his colleagues in platoons further down the trenches.

Suddenly the air around them is hot, boiling and seemingly burning,

"Fuck!" yells Nobby "I am on fire!"

Martin grabs Nobby and throws him to the floor of the trench and rolls him around on the damp muddy bottom,

"Thanks Martin, I would have been a goner"

Alife and H despatch the Germans with the flamethrower, the enemy both fall dead from very quick shooting from the pair, around them are sporadic attacks by the Germans, with flame and with bombs, the 90th Brigade are holding out, but they are taking a severe beating.

Martin's hands are very painful, they are burnt from putting Nobby out when he was on fire, it is dark so he cannot see how badly they are damaged,

"Sarge, another runner is coming" Dennis informs him

Martin moves along the line to meet the runner,

"Sarge, you have orders to withdraw to Stevens Redoubt immediately"

The runner is gone, carrying his message to those still fighting on this line,

"You heard the man, move back"

They climb out of the trench and in less than two minutes they are on the main road from Savy to Entreillers, there are a lot of soldiers in retreat and a huge amount of them are injured, many being carried by friends and colleagues, Martin and his platoon join in and carry stretchers for the wounded, Martin struggles because of the blisters on his hands.

Martin and Nobby are carrying Captain Hobbs, who initially refuses to get on the stretcher and has to be put on it by both men, C company remain in the forward most position, just East of Entreillers, the Germans have thankfully stopped for now.

All the men are exhausted, they have been fighting without sleep for over twenty four hours, every one of them is too fearful of counter attacks to even consider shutting their eyes, Martin never ceases to be amazed how the human body can keep going, especially if death is ever present.

Shelling has continued all night and C company have taken losses, both wounded and killed, it is just after two in the afternoon when C company are forced to retreat as their positions are overrun by the enemy, an amount of them have been killed or taken prisoner, A and B companies are ordered to stand their ground, but in under two hours both companies, and what is left of them, are almost fully surrounded by the advancing Germans, who have moved forward in large numbers.

At five in the evening the Bedfordshires receive the order to withdraw further, the German army have now surrounded the fortress that was Stevens Redoubt and will overrun it very soon, it means losing a valuable position but if they stay, they will all be killed, the withdrawal starts immediately. Martin leads a large group of Bedfordshires across open ground, avoiding main roads and trench systems, they pass through

Germaine, Foreste, Villers St Christophe and Ham, all villages and communes that show the signs of the war having visited them recently, some properties are still smouldering, all the locals have left. They arrive in Verlaines after a trek of over ten miles across fields, open ground and through empty villages, they use the cover of darkness as their friend, this friend probably saves their lives, billets are allocated when they arrive, they all grab some hot food and then all get some sleep. The Battalion has lost a lot of men, six officers from A company are wounded or missing, no one knows how many ordinary ranks have been killed or taken prisoner. Martin does not get to eat or sleep immediately, he visits the dressing station to have his burns treated, they are nasty but not bad enough to get him sent back to a casualty clearing station, Nobby refuses to eat or to bed down, he stays with Martin as he feels a little guilty about his Sergeants injury, also he feels very thankful that he has a Sergeant like Martin who will put himself on the line for his platoon, they get to their billet at a few minutes after midnight on the 23rd March.

Just four and a half hours later, they are all woken up and told to 'stand to' yet again, the 89th infantry brigade had taken up positions in the town of Ham overnight, but have been ordered to retire as their defences are now being overtaken by the enemy, the Bedfordshires are ordered to take up positions near a commune called Esmery Hallon, two miles behind their current location, whilst the 2nd Battalion Royal Scots Fusiliers are ordered forward to cover the retirement of the 89th Brigade. The Germans are really pushing this attack and they are beating the Allied soldiers at every turn. Upon arrival at Esmery Hallon, the Battalion form up on the road that leads back to Verlaines, Martin and his platoon are led by 2nd Lt Parker, they have orders to advance into the village to ensure that no Germans are there, the C.O. does not want to be facing Verlaines and then be attacked from the village behind them.

The sun is rising as they enter the village, the first building they see is standing proud, except for its roof, which is completely gone, carved into a huge stone beam, that is now the top of the building, the words '*LIBERTE EGALITE FRATERNITE*' stand out against the red brick and three large windows, all without glass, the double wooden front door is untouched and both are closed, no other buildings around remain fully standing,

"Liberty, equality, fraternity" 2nd Lt Parker translates the words,

"Any idea what it means Sir?" Alfie asks

"The motto of the French Republic" he replies, they are all listening,

"Liberty, the state of being free as a society from oppressive restrictions imposed by an authority on ways of life, behaviour and political views"

"Well, I can see how well that is going for them at this time Sir" Alfie responds with a hint of sarcasm.

"Equality" continues the officer "Of being equal, in status, rights and opportunities"

Alfie nods but does not answer as Nobby tells him to be quiet,

"And Fraternity, meaning a group of people sharing a common interest"

"That sounds more like the Germans than the French to me" Alfie can't resist the urge to answer,

"Let's hope not private, for the sake of the French" the young officer says quietly.

The village is small and deserted, Martin does not think that any more than two or three hundred would have lived here, the Church, at the far end of the village, seems remarkably untouched, its grey roof and tall pointed spire with vented bell windows on each side is a little battle scarred but still standing, it is empty, the whole of the village is empty.

2nd Lt Parker takes the platoon back to the Battalion positions outside of Esmery Hallon, some of the Battalion have been moved forward to support the 89th Brigade as the enemy has now stopped outside of Ham and the 89th are resolutely remaining in place. Martin is told to take his platoon to a trench position on the left side of the road, along with about half of the Battalion, the remainder are put on the other side of the road, although this spreads the Battalion out, they can at least remain in cover should the need arise, and they are in a good position to attack the enemy if they approach on this road.

Martin looks at Alfie, he is dragging a rusted and well used brazier into the trench system,

"Have you got any dry wood nearby Alfie?" he asks

"Yes Sarge, there is a lot stored in a dry hole over there" he points up the trench, Martin can also see that other platoons are taking old braziers, metal bins and anything that can hold wood,

"Light up then Alfie, we are far enough behind the 89th for them not to be seen, and we need to keep warm" Martin looks up at the lead grey sky, "And I think we might need it, I reckon snow before the day is out"

Lt Parker arrives,

"Damn fine idea, I think it is going to be a cold day"

"I am going to brew up in a minute Sir, do you want a tea or a Bovril?" H is taking the brewing up kit from his knapsack

"Tea would be excellent, thank you Private"

"Are we staying put for a bit Sir?" Martin asks Lt Parker

"I think we may be here for the whole day Sergeant; the fighting is going on at Ham, but as far as I know the 89th along with some of our lads and some to the Scots Fusiliers are holding their own"

"We shall know soon enough if it isn't going to plan" Martin replies

"Yes Sergeant, I think we will, so best we have a cuppa before it happens"

Both Martin and Lt Parker stare at H,

"On it now gents, on it right now" he says to them

Martin and the platoon manage to keep the brazier going all day and into the evening, they expect to be told to put them out as it gets dark, but no such order is forthcoming, so Alfie keeps theirs going, burning whatever wood he can find, it is needed because it is very cold and sleeting heavily. Apart from John, who is on watch lying on the front bank of the trench with his rifle pointing along the road, they stand around it keeping their hands and bodies warm, they all have their backs away from the heat, each and every one of them has a scarf on under their tunics and collars on great coats turned up.

Every fifteen minutes they take a turn on watch, although only a short time, it is freezing cold, even lying on a sandbag in an attempt to keep dry, doesn't really help, the cold creeps in from the ground and is exacerbated by the biting wind and stinging sleet.

It is past one the following morning when the Battalion receive orders to move, reports have been sent back that it is believed, 2nd Lt Shaw has been killed and Captain Parker, no relation to 2nd Lt Parker, has been taken prisoner after being wounded.

The men all feel cold and vulnerable, cold, because they have all been taken away from their hot burning fires in the trenches, most of which they left burning and vulnerable because they are formed up in the open on the main road facing toward Verlaines. They finally set off into the dark cold night, marching in silence, knowing that either side of them across the open, barren fields, are the enemy in huge numbers. Verlaines comes into sight, parts of it are burning, the tell-tale glow of fire can be seen from some distance, it appears that the fighting has been severe in the town, but as they are marching toward it and not away or round it, they can only presume that it is being held by Allied troops. The line of soldiers is taken from the road and across fields, following the river until they reach a dirty and muddy track, Verlaines is now to their left and the village of Villette to their right, machine gun fire can be heard, and it is very close, the men are nervous, tensions are high, fear can be felt in the air. The 2nd Battalion Royal Scots Fusiliers are also at this location, the Bedfordshires have been sent here to support them as they have been forced back by the enemy, who are flanking them and the 89th Brigade from the left. The Bedfordshires are all told to take up defensive positions on the road, there are no trenches here, so ditches and any remaining bushes and tree stumps are used, they can hear the enemy working their way around on the right flank, the Bedfordshires and the Fusiliers fire at them, the returning fire is heavy and without cover both Battalions risk losing lots of men.

"Enemy on the left flank!" is called out by an unknown soldier,

"Shit" Martin says out loud, "They have tricked us, we are being attacked on both flanks" he turns to the platoon, "Get ready to retreat lads, I assure you it is coming"

"Martin!" he looks up the trench, Percy Compton is shouting at him,

"We are surely going to retreat, if not we are sitting ducks here and we will all get killed!"

Just at that moment the order comes in for both Battalions to withdraw, back toward Esmery Hallon, the enemy have made it as far as Golancourt, a tiny village but is strategically important in this small area of the war, it is clear that they have gone right around the positions held by the Bedfordshires and the Fusiliers without meeting much resistance. As they begin to retreat, the attack by the enemy on the left flank intensifies, the withdrawal is ongoing and the soldiers are making their way across country toward Esmery Hallon, it is muddy underfoot and because the artillery has destroyed all buildings and trees, there is no cover, as a group they run toward the village in an attempt to get into some sort of cover. Martin can see the still burning braziers in the trenches to his right on the outskirts of Esmery Hallon, it has been hours since they left this location and the fires should have burnt themselves out by now.

"Stop" he orders, all the men around him stop and get as low to the ground as they can, Martin can feel water oozing through his boots, it is cold and his socks are wet,

"What is going on over there?" a voice through the darkness asks, Martin has not idea whom it belongs too, but it sounds like an officer,

"Sir, our fires are still burning in those trenches, they should have gone out hours ago, someone is in the trenches and has kept them going or re lit them"

The lines of men are silent, movement to the left gets Martin's attention, it is Capt. Pares and 2nd Lt Carpenter,

"Who called the halt?" he asks

"I did Sir" Martin tells him,

"Good work and a fine assessment Sergeant, are we to presume the Germans are there?"

Martin nods in the darkness,

"I think so Sir, if it is true that they have gone around our right flank and taken that town..." Martin pauses,

"Golancourt" the captain confirms, Martin nods again,

"Then it must be a fair assumption that they have moved further round on our left flank and taken the trenches outside of Esmery Hallon that we had last night"

"Agree" the senior officer says, "Shall we go and have a look?"

Martin looks at his platoon, "Two with me and the officers"

Nobby steps forward,

"No, not you Nobby, if this line moves off and we are not back, then you take the platoon"

"Understood" Nobby says.

John Marrables and Dennis step forward and take a position behind Martin,

"Follow me lads" The Captain sets off with the Lt next to him, Martin, John, and Dennis move as quietly as they can behind them. Heavy machine gun fire from the right of their position takes them by surprise, Martin, Dennis, and John lie flat on the ground, caring not about the mud and cold,

"Sergeant!" Lt Carpenter calls through the darkness "Both the Captain and I are hit, move back to the line and tell the Major to avoid the village and to move off"

Martin looks at Dennis and John, all three of them stand up, the machine guns are still firing in their direction, they reach the two officers who are a few yards in front of them,

"Didn't get to ground quick enough" Carpenter says, he has a wound to his right arm,

"What about the Captain?" asks Martin

"I wasn't bloody quick enough either Sergeant, got one or two in the leg"

Martin quickly assesses the situation, ignoring Carpenter who is attempting to rollock him for disobeying an order to retreat,

"Dennis, take the 2nd Lt back and do it now"

Dennis takes the protesting officer, who wants to stay with the captain and the others, Dennis has no problem moving him away.

Martin nods at John, who says to Capt. Pares

"Bite down on something Sir, I think this might just hurt a bit"

They grab the officer and taking one side each, they lift him under his armpits and run back toward the position of the other Bedfordshires, Capt. Pares barely makes a sound as they drag him over the mud and dirt.

Capt. Anstee appears at the end of the file of soldiers,

"Private" he points to a soldier from another platoon, "Fetch a stretcher for Capt. Pares" he turns to Martin "Fine work by you and your platoon Sergeant" he then turns to 2nd Lt Carpenter "Walter, how bad are you hurt?"

"Enough to take me out of the game for a couple of days, bullet in my arm, I think it has gone right through"

Anstee nods and sends him to find the medical officer,

"How about William" he stops and then carries on "I mean Capt. Pares?"

"He has taken a few hits Sir ,he is conscious but in a lot of pain I think" John tells Anstee

"We will continue to move back, the Hun are almost surrounding us here, I have looked at the map and we can move back to the canal, there are, or were, trenches in that area, hopefully we can get some communication with HQ"

He moves off back down the line, the private returns with the medical officer, he quickly looks at Capt. Pares,

"William, you will survive old man, but we need to get you to a dressing station" he stands up and quietly says to Martin, "Sooner rather than later"

Capt. Pares is taken away by two privates and they follow the medical officer.

Machine gun fire continues from the German positions on the Esmery Hallon road to Verlaines.

The two Battalions make it to Buverchy Bridge without any further enemy contact, the wounded, Pares and Carpenter are not the only ones, are taken away from the line and to the nearest dressing station, the officers will both be assessed, and both be taken further away from the front to a casualty clearing station. The remainder of the 90th Infantry are spread out along this new line, as far as Lannoy Farm Ridge, the enemy seem to know that the regrouping of the 90th has been successful, and the rest of the day is quiet.

The Battalion are responsible for the security of the sub sector of Buverchy Bridge, the trenches here are deeper than those at Esmery Hallon, they are also better constructed with corrugated iron walls and duck boarded walkways, there are more dugouts for the men to use, fires are again lit, and again, no one tells them to put them out when it gets dark.

The following morning, artillery from the Allied forces is attacking the Germans at Arvillers, reports suggest that the enemy are massing for another attack. The soldiers take the chance to change their socks and to dry their feet, a routine that is supposed to be carried out daily but very rarely is, the past three or four days have made it impossible for any of the soldiers to check their feet.

Martin is insistent that his patrol carry out a foot check on each other,

"Come on lads, you know the drill, get your foot partner" he looks at H, John, and Sharpie, "You three in this case, get your boots off, your feet checked by your mate, oil them up and then put on dry socks" he looks menacingly at all of them "You do all have dry socks?"

They all state that they do, Martin sits down and takes off his muddy and wet boots, his socks are sodden, so much so that he has a problem getting them off of his feet

"Bloody hell Martin, how long since you last checked these"

"You did it before the fight at St Quentin"

Nobby looks up and counts in his head, "That was five days ago, your feet are alright, but they need to be dried and left to air a bit"

Martin looks down, the skin, especially on the heel and ball of each one, has become so wrinkled and white in colour, he is surprised that he does not have the tell-tale blisters or open sores that trench foot gives a man,

"Your turn Nobby" Martin, in bare feet and on dry ground, inspects Nobbys feet, "Not bad mate, give them an airing and then we can get some whale oil on them, I might leave it as long as I can so that my boots might dry out a bit"

It is another cold day, but it is dry, and they have a fire burning in the trench, not in a brazier this time but on a large bent sheet of corrugated iron. Martin can hear a mild altercation going on between John, H and Sharpie, he calls over,

"What is the problem over there?"

He sees John Marrables throw H and Sharpie a filthy look,

"John won't take off his boots Sarge, says that his feet are in good order"

"You know the rules John, daily checks must be carried out by you and your foot chums" he waves the three of them to come toward him, H and Sharpie both are barefoot and place their boots next to Martins on the far edge of the corrugated sheet, John is moving toward him very slowly,

"Move your backside John and get over here and get your shoes off!" Martin commands,

"But Sarge…" John begins, Martin stops him,

"Now John, that is not a request"

"I can't Sarge"

Martin looks at H and Sharpie, who both confirm that is what John had told them as well, Martin looks knowingly at John,

"Won't or can't John?" Martin asks

John has his fists clenched, trying to control his temper,

"Can't Sarge"

Martin realises that John's feet must have swollen inside his boots, and it will not be easy and very painful for them to be removed,

"They have to come off mate, you know that" Nobby joins in, John does not move, "When were they last checked?"

"Same as all of us, before the St. Quentin battle" John says

Martin and Nobby don't say anything, John waits a few moments before adding,

"It is only today that I realised my feet hurt more than normal, I can't get the boots off"

"Go find the Doc John"

"I will be alright Sarge, I can check them later, we are out of the mud and water now"

Nobby, who has been putting whale oil onto his feet is now putting dry socks on,

"Pass my boots will you Alfie" he asks

Alfie walks slowly on the wooden duck boards, although dry they do have splinters sticking up and he is barefoot, he collects the Corporals boots and gives them to him,

"Come on John, I will come with you and find the doc or the medic"

John, knowing that he has no choice, moves with Nobby away from their section of the trench and along the line,

"I will be back in a bit" he tells the others; Martin has his doubts.

Nobby is gone for nearly an hour, he returns with news that John has been taken off of the front line by the medical officer, they had to hold him down when his boots were taken off at the aid station, his feet are a mess, Nobby tells the others that he had to '*put the medical officer right*', when he accused John of neglecting his feet and disobeying the direct order for daily checking of each other's feet,

"What did you say to him Nobby?" asks Martin,

"I knew he has been with us all of the way since St Quentin and that unless he took his boots off in the freezing cold nights to check them, he is in the same boat as all of us and hasn't done his feet for nearly a week"

Martin smiles and takes a long mouthful of warm Bovril, "Go on" he encourages Nobby

"I just asked him when the last chance was that he had chance to look at his feet"

"Bloody hell mate, how did that go?" Martin asks, he is dipping a chunk of not fresh but not very stale bread into his hot drink,

"He got a bit shirty if truth be told, but I must have been right because he immediately orders John off of the front line and he is being taken to a clearing station for treatment"

"How bad are his feet Corp?" Alfie asks

"A bit of a mess, swollen badly and I have never seen skin so white, he has them red blisters and some open cuts, poor bugger"

"I checked his feet when we all did it, when we were in support duties, his were better than mine then" Dennis says and Alfie agrees with him,

"Well, they won't send him home, unless he has gangrene" Martin says and looks at Nobby for a reply, Nobby shakes his head,

"I don't think so, they didn't smell like some of the feet I have seen over here"

"He will get a bed and have his feet cleaned three or four times a day, have talc put on them to dry out the skin" Martin tells them,

"Moving out in thirty minutes Sarge" A runner arrives and speaks to Martin,

"Where are we going?" he asks the runner

"They don't tell me that Sarge, I just get to be the bearer of news"

He moves on and the remaining five of them, four currently without footwear or socks on, get ready for the off.

The sound of incoming artillery is unmistakable,

"Take cover!" is shouted all the way along the line as the shells hit the bridge nearest to Martin's platoon, many shells are being fired over the top of the Bedfordshires toward the town of Moyencourt,

"We could be in a bit of bother here; we can't go forward without getting most of us killed and the town behind us is being shelled to hell and back!" Nobby shouts over the noise.

A shell lands to the right of Martins platoon, thankfully this section of trench is unmanned, Martin feels pain on his face, he puts his hand up to his cheek and blood covers his hand,

"Bloody hell, something has hit me" he shouts

"Stand still Sarge" Alife yells over the scream of incoming artillery,

"What is it?" he asks Alfie

"A bloody huge splinter in your cheek"

Martin puts his tongue onto the inside of the cheek that is bleeding,

"I can't feel anything sticking through inside my mouth" he tells Alfie

Nobby comes over and has a look at the splinter,

"It has gone in at an angle, it is just in the skin" he looks at Martin "It will have to come out"

"Well, take the bloody thing out then!"

Martin sits down on the back edge of the trench, Alfie stands in front of him and pulls the skin taught around the splinter, Martin winces, Alfie gets his fingers on the end of the large piece of splintered wood and pulls it out without giving his Sergeant any warning, blood continues to seep from the wound,

"You need to get that looked at Sarge" Alfie tells him

"No, it's a bloody splinter and it is out now" he turns to the others, "Get your boots on whilst you can, pass me mine will you H"

"Go and get a medic will you" Nobby asks Dennis and before Martin can speak Nobby tells him, "It's either that or you will be taken off the line when that gets infected"

Martin sighs and agrees with his Corporal. Dennis is putting his dry socks on, his boots follow immediately after, he sets off along the trenches. A few minutes later he returns with a medic, easily identified by the white armband with a red cross in the centre of it,

"Alright Sarge" the medic says "Let's have a look at this splinter"

Martin lets the medic have a look at the hole in his cheek,

"It ain't gone through, but there are a few little bits still in there, I will get them out and put a covering on it"

Martin nods, the medic takes out a small bottle of tincture of iodine and dabs it on the wound, it stings but Martin stays still, a few smaller fragments of wood are removed with a pair of tweezers and the medic puts a small dressing on the cut and secures it with a few strips of zinc oxide plaster, Martin thanks the medic,

"No worry Sarge, have you heard, we are being withdrawn again"

"Any idea where to mate?" he asks the medic

"Apparently, toward that town the bosch are currently bombing the shit out of" He puts his medic bag over his shoulder, "Should be fun for us all" He leaves the platoon and heads off back down the trenches,

"Get ready to move out lads" Martin tells his platoon as more shells land nearby and they all have to dive for cover as mud sprays over them all.

At six in the evening, the Bedfordshires withdraw again, this time toward the town of Moyencourt, the enemy have broken through the French lines, they turn West before getting into town and move onto another town, Solente. They are all pleased to see rows and rows of buses, they are ordered on and shortly after embarking, they move off, stopping a short while later for a break in the village of Roye, some take the opportunity to sit inside the church to get a short escape from the freezing weather. The buses set off again and eventually arrive in the town of Arvillers, about twenty miles West from their original location at Buverchy, it is quieter here and they are ordered to eat and to grab a few hours' sleep wherever they can.

The next morning Martin returns to the billet he is sharing with the platoon, he has been trying to find out about John Marrables but due to the chaos involved in withdrawing and the communications lines still not being fully restored, it is impossible to get any details, Martin is sure that he will find them when his feet have healed. Alfie and H are stoking wood onto the fire they have built outside in the yard of the billet they are in, it is a bomb damaged wooden and brick built small house, the whole town is smashed, wooden barns now lie like broken matchstick models, the church, once magnificent, is a mass of rubble, only the spire and part of the roof stand defiantly against the war.

"Just getting ready to cook breakfast Sarge" Alfie says happily

"I am sick of Huntley and bloody Palmers number four biscuits, my teeth hurt eating them even when I have dunked them" Martin answers

Alfie smiles, "We do have biscuits Sarge, we also have some tea, sugar, eggs and bacon"

Martin looks surprised,

"They are dishing out rations this morning" H says "I got one loaf of bread and a bit of butter"

"Good work lad!" Martin says enthusiastically "It must be two weeks since we had bacon and bread"

"Shall I cook it all and have it in bread?" Alfie asks

"I don't care mate, I will eat it however it is served, but a sandwich might be easier"

Alfie turns around and picks up a large black frying pan, Martin does not ask how or where he came to have such an item,

"Are the rest up and about?" Martin asks

He is told that everyone is awake, it seems that they all had a reasonable night, the shelling was minimal from both sides, so a well-earned sleep was had by all, Martin could not sleep to begin with so he finished his letter to Alice, he found a clerk to give it to for posting when he went to enquire about John, he walks into the shattered house he and the platoon have slept in, Nobby is cutting slices of bread as best as he can with a long knife,

"No need for finesse Nobby, you hack at that loaf!" Martin jokes

Nobby turns around and smiles, he has the long knife in his hand,

"I am sorry the French family that lived here got bombed out, but they could have sharpened their knives before legging it"

The other two members of the platoon are sitting on old barrels and boxes, Dennis is eating an apple and Sharpie is barefoot, his boots and socks are in front of the damaged fireplace in which a small but warm fire is burning, an old black kettle hangs above the flames, water heating for their mugs of tea.

By lunchtime, the men of the 2nd Bedfordshires are again in position on yet another road, this time on the Bouchoir to Rouvroy road a short distance North of Roye, to their left are the Battalions of the 89th Brigade and to the right are the depleted numbers of the 2nd Battalion Royal Scots Fusiliers. It is unusually quiet, heavy enemy movement can be seen from their position, huge numbers of soldiers and lots and lots of artillery, all moving through the village of Le Quesnoy, a few patrols are sent out to gather information about these troop movements, all return safely despite a few skirmishes on the outskirts of the village, it is dark when they pull back toward Arvillers but safely take up positions in trenches on the outskirts of Bouchoir.

The hot breakfast seems a lifetime ago as they all sit down in the chill of the evening, eating cold bully beef straight from the tin and soaking the dreaded number 4 biscuits in hot tea. No further rations or water has been delivered to these trenches; this could be their last cuppa for a while.

Shortly after ten the following morning, the enemy attacks again, both flanks are subjected to heavy machine gun fire and trench mortars, the 89th are holding out well but the Germans have got through on the right side, cutting straight through the Royal Scots Fusiliers, the fight continues for a couple of hours but at half past twelve, all Allied troops are withdrawn to trenches on the Arvillers to Foiles road, the enemy continue to attack but the new position gives the Allied men a minor advantage and the Germans move back to the trenches they took earlier in the day. As dusk arrives, the Germans attack again, and again the position is consolidated by the Bedfordshires, the 89th and the Fusiliers. Darkness falls and the promise of relief by French troops does not materialise, the promise of fresh water and hot food also does not happen.

The men sit in trenches, without shelter against the cold wind, no water to make tea and no food left. Each and every one of them knows that the Germans will attack again, they sit in silence and wait.

* * *

Shelling of the Allied positions starts at first light on the 28th of March, it has stopped sleeting, but it is still very cold, the Bedfordshires suffer several casualties during the shelling, all the men are thirsty and hungry, air shells begin to burst above them, spraying the trenches with red hot metal balls, direct from hell, that spread out rapidly over a large area. The shouts of "Keep down!" are mixed with men screaming in pain and fear, the longer ranged artillery can be heard with its distinctive popping sound as it is fired from distances of five miles or more, five to six seconds later the shell hits the ground and explodes in a mass of flying earth, barbed wire, and the bodies of soldiers. Shells are landing very close to the Bedfordshires positions, Martin and the platoon are regularly covered in flying debris, all six of them are lying as flat as they can against the front edge of the trench; machine gun fire rattles to the left of them, from the village of Folies,

"Who has the village?" Nobby shouts at Martin over the hellish noise, Martin shrugs

"No idea mate, the 89th were on our left last I knew"

They both push their faces into the mud of the trench as a shell lands only yards in front of them,

"I think the Scots lads were heading into Arvillers last night, so it must be the 89th" Martin adds.

2nd Lt Pennington arrives in the trench, he is covered in mud from head to feet,

"Orders Sergeant" he shouts at Martin "The Hun have attacked on both flanks again and have got into Arvillers and Folies"

Another shell explodes, landing in the trench less than twenty yards to the left of where Martin and his platoon are, the Lt is thrown off of his feet, Martin and Nobby reach down and drag him up again,

"Bugger!" the officer shouts, he has blood coming from his forearm and it is obvious that he has taken a piece of shrapnel into his arm. Martin grabs the officer and puts him firmly against the front edge of the trench, Lt Pennington is holding his damaged arm,

"The enemy are coming Sergeant, they are only a few hundred yards away, we are retreating again" Martin is tying a field bandage around the officers' arm, he pulls it tight, ignoring the obvious pain the young Lt is in, "Sergeant, I have to go up the trench line and tell the rest of ours to get back"

Martin looks up the trench line, most of it has been smashed to a pulp, the last shell that landed close to them has made further travel up the trenches impossible,

"You are not going anywhere Sir, look"

Martin points along the trenches and the officer sees the devastation,

"Come on then Sergeant, get your lads together and get out of here"

Martin points at Dennis,

"Den, get the 2nd Lt out of here and to the advance dressing station" Dennis protests, Martin claps him on the shoulder "We will be right behind you, now move!"

Dennis takes the officer away from the trench and Martin orders the others to get ready to move, they wait for a shell to land and then they make their move. As they step out of the trench, moving back toward the road, Arvillers is now on their left and Folies on their right, Martin can see many soldiers retreating away from his left and his right, soldiers cover the fields around them, once green and plentiful, but now are bogs of mud and shell holes, the dead lie unburied and at this time, dead and uncared for.

An air burst shell explodes near to them, Martin feels hot bullets hitting his back, he falls to the ground,

"Sarge!" he hears Dennis shouting at him from the other side of the trenches,

"I am alright I think Den, now get out of here with the Lt"

Dennis finally leaves his view, and he has his arm around the young Lt, who seems to be coping well with his injury. Martin is not sure how badly he has been hit, his knapsack and thick coat may have taken some of the velocity out of the traveling bullets, he manages to stand with H helping him, he looks across and sees Alf and Sharpie crouching over Nobby, they move away toward Martin and H, shells are now landing all around them,

"Nobby, what about Nobby!" H shouts at Alf and Sharpie,

"Dead, nothing we can do for him"

Martin moves off, walking toward his Corporal, he is grabbed by Alf and Sharpie, he turns on them,

"That is our mate, that is Nobby!" he screams at them, they hold onto him tightly,

"Sarge, he is a goner, he is dead!" Sharpie shouts above the noise.

"Sarge" H stands in front of Martin and is calm "Let's go Sarge, Nobby is dead, you are injured and if we don't move now, then the shells or the bloody Germans will get us.

Martin knows they are right, but his heart is crying for his fallen friend, the whining of an incoming shell wakes Martin up,

"Move lads!" he yells

As he sets off, he can feel blood running down the inside of his shirt and also down his right leg, he has taken hits to his back and to his leg and although it hurts he moves off with the others, every step he takes is becoming harder and harder, waves of pain make him cry out in pain,

"Sarge, come on keep up" Alfie shouts at him and he manages to increase his pace a little,

"Are you alright Sarge?" Sharpie asks him, Martin nods and moves off, just ahead of the other three,

"Come on!" he yells

Platoons from all along the trenches are moving back, Martin has no idea where they are retreating to, they can't go to Arvillers or Folies as they are almost certainly in German hands, he hears H call out,

"Bloody hell Alfie!"

As Martin turns around, he can hear the three men laughing, Alfie has slipped and fallen over and is covered in mud, as he stops, he looks toward the three of them, H and Sharpie are helping their mud covered mate to his feet, all three are laughing maniacally.

As he is waiting for his three soldiers who are only yards away, he hears a very loud sound as shell lands almost on top of him, seconds before he is blown off of his feet, he sees H, Sharpie and Alfie obliterated from the face of this earth by the landing shell. He tries to scream but his throat is burning, he opens his eyes, the skin around his eyes feels sticky, he can see the sky above him, he is lying on his back and cannot move, the small blots of beautiful blue are quickly obscured by smoke and explosions. He tries but can't move, he can't feel his left arm and leg and his face is on fire, he relaxes and looks for more blue sky, for a little piece of normality amongst this unnatural and hell like situation, just above him a patch of blue opens up and he tries to smile, his face will not move, he hears someone shouting,

"Sarge! Sarge!"

He recognises the voice but does not see the caller, he knows the voice but cannot call back,

"Sarge, bloody hell Sarge"

Martin sees Dennis looming over him seconds before the world becomes black and silent.

"Hold on Sarge, we are nearly there!"

Martin is lying on his back, still looking up at the sky, he is being bounced about, he can see two men in front of him, he can hear Dennis talking behind him,

"The advance dressing station is just ahead of us Sarge, hang on in there"

Martin realises he is on a stretcher being carried away from the front line, he looks to his left and can see many injured men, some walking, some being carried on stretchers, but all moving away from the explosions that continue around them.

"Medic! Over here!" Dennis shouts at an R.A.M.C Corporal as they put the stretcher down,

"Alright mate, calm down"

The medic looks down on Martin,

"He took an airburst to the back as well Corp, I saw him go down"

"His face is burnt mate, this ain't no airburst"

"Corp, I have no idea how he got burnt, but I did see him get hit just before I bought that officer here"

The medic nods,

"Nice and easy Sarge, I will have a quick look at you"

Martin feels his blanket being lifted off of him, he feels cold hit his naked skin,

"Where is my jacket and shirt?" he mumbles

"Probably blown off you Sarge" the medic tells him

Martin sees the medic nod at Dennis, they roll him gently onto his side, pain thrusts through his left leg, he screams in agony, they roll him gently onto his back.

"Leave him with me lad, you were right, he has shrapnel balls in his back and his legs, I also think he has an open fracture of the left lower leg"

Dennis kneels next to his Sergeant,

"The others Sarge, what about the others?"

Martin manages to shake his head gently, he tries to say 'all dead' but his throat is on fire, he feels a single tear fall across his burnt face, Dennis nods,

"I understand Sarge, I understand"

Dennis is moved out of the way by a medical officer who has arrived, he takes one look at Martin and orders him to be taken inside,

"I will catch you later Sarge" Dennis calls after him.

Martin is taken a short distance and into a dark room, he realises he is in an underground dugout, he can still hear the war, but it seems a long way away.

"Sergeant, you will need to be sent out to the casualty clearing station, but until this shit stops you are with us for now"

The medical officer is in shirtsleeves and has blood covering his lower arms, it is not his blood, someone puts a cigarette into Martin's mouth and lights it, he inhales, feeling pain as he does so, he coughs and reaches his right arm up to take the cigarette out of his mouth.

He feels a needle go into his right arm; it tingles as the drug is administered.

He feels bandages being put around his head, also on his left arm and his legs are bound tightly together, he can see wounded men all around him, blood on each and every one of them, the medical officer is examining the man next to Martin, he is also without a shirt, a tunic, or a jacket, he has his right arm raised,

"I think it went right through Sir" Martin hears him say.

The man has iodine put on the entrance and exit wounds, he is also given a cigarette as the wound is bandaged, he is pointed toward the far end of the dugout and he moves out of Martins sight.

"Sergeant, Sergeant"

Martin opens his eyes,

"Thank the stars, I thought you had gone on me Sergeant"

He turns around, the medical officer is standing over him, he has no idea how long he has been passed out.

"Here Corporal, this man needs to go now, I have given him a few more grains of morphine so it should be enough to get him away from here at least"

Martins sees the same Corporal that treated him outside,

"Hello again mate" the medic says happily "You are off for a ride in an R.A.M.C ambulance, not the best I'm afraid but it will take you to the C.C.S, the main dressing station is nearer, but you need a bit more treatment I'm afraid, it will get you away from this lot"

Martin sees the Corporal nod at the man standing behind him,

"Careful now lad, the Sarge has taken a bit of a hammering"

Martin feels himself being lifted up and carried over uneven terrain, as they leave the dugout the bright light of the day causes Martin to be momentarily blinded, he feels himself being lifted up and then slid onto a shelf inside the ambulance, he is surrounded by other men lying on stretchers.

He closes his eyes and feels the drug slowly creep over his body, taking some of the pain with it, he breathes deeply, and darkness takes him again.

* * *

Alice stops for a break, it is mid-morning, and the sun is shining on this bright April day, she checks the kettle to see if it is boiling, it isn't, she sits down on the old bench seat under the window and looks over the garden, spring blooms are moving slightly in the breeze and the whole place looks alive with daffodils and crocus, she has even planted vegetables in the allotment, carrots, parsnips, onions, greens and lettuce, the tomatoes are in pots outside of the house.

So much has happened in the past few weeks, it has been a whirlwind for Alice since receiving two letters, one last week from the British Army, a standard military form informing her, as registered next of kin that her brother has been injured in France and will be sent to a UK hospital for treatment. No further information is given to her, then a second letter arrived, the following day, in handwriting that she did not recognise, when opened she realises it is from Martin, but it has been written by someone else on his behalf, by the neat writing she believes that a woman is writing it for him. It briefly explains to her that due to his wounds he was taken from the front line to a casualty clearing station, then almost immediately transferred to a base hospital in Amiens, here he received treatment and surgery for wounds to his back, both legs, the left is far worse than the right, and to his face and neck. Alice clearly remembers feeling lost, lonely, and useless as she read the letter, her husband is still away fighting in France somewhere and now Martin is badly wounded, she contains her mild panic and walks to the Malta that is still being run by May and Pete, her Auntie, as usual, is the voice of reason and manages to calm her down. May is running the pub mostly on her own as Pete has continued working at Childwickbury, they still have their home at Maple Cottages, they are unsure as to whether the brewery will keep them on or will put a new landlord in, but for now the brewery are happy for May and Pete to carry on. Alice has no idea where Martin is or when he will be home, but she is getting the back room ready for him, he will have to come and live with her and Charles, living at the pub is not appropriate, especially as no one is sure who the brewery will grant the licence to, so without the room at the cottage he will be homeless. She has written to Charles explaining all the details, she has not heard back from him yet but she is certain he will be fine with her decision, it will be strange for everyone, Martin giving the cottage to her and Charles as a wedding present, and then coming back to live with them, she is just pleased, that although injured, she has no clue how badly, he has survived the war and will be coming home.

She stands up when she hears a knock at the door, looking round through the window she can see Maggie standing there,

"It's open Maggie, come on in"

The door opens and Maggie steps in,

"Morning love, how are you?" she asks Alice

"All good Maggie, do you want a cup of tea, the kettle is ready"

Maggie tells her that she would love a quick cup of tea and Alice sets about making up a pot as Maggie takes off her headscarf and sits down at the kitchen table.

"You back at work tomorrow Alice?"

"I am, days for this week, what about you?"

Maggie takes the cup of tea from Alice and puts it on the table,

"Thanks love, I am also on days, shall we meet as usual?"

Alice agrees with Maggie and they both sit, waiting for their tea to cool a little,

"It's not the same at work since the explosion is it, Maggie?" Alice says

Maggie slowly shakes her head, "No, it's all a bit quiet isn't it, although I have never been to a funeral like May's, blimey she got a good send-off"

Both pick up their cups and take a sip, Alice thinks about May Constable and the other three girls that died when an explosion ripped through part of the factory on 1st March this year, Lillian Harris, Kate Tomkins, and Florrie Warnes, all badly injured at the time of the explosion and all taken to Bute Hospital, May being the last to die 6 days later from her burns. May had lived in the village of Fenny Stratford, some 16 miles from the factory in Luton, she had been living locally whilst working but her home village gave her a hero's funeral, Maggie, Alice, and many of the Munitionettes attended, transport was laid on for all of them by Mr Kent. Her coffin was placed on a gun carriage, supplied by the Royal Engineers Depot, drawn by four stunning horses, and accompanied by soldiers from the Royal Engineers, who formed the bearer party. The coffin was draped in the Union Flag, covered in wreaths and messages of love from her family and friends, including the Mutionettes, over sixty attended and all were in factory uniform, they had led the cortege from May's family home to the cemetery, all wanting to show support to her family and to show respect to their comrade.

"You know what sickened me about that incident?" Maggie asks Alice, who shakes her head,

"The way it was reported in the papers, or should I say, not reported"

Alice puts her cup onto the saucer, "You know why Maggie, reporting news of this type is deemed to have a negative effect on the readers, it's all to do with the Defence of the Realm act, Mr Kent told us all this"

Maggie snorts, "I know, but when four women are killed serving their country then are basically ignored, it gets my back up"

Alice starts to giggle, "Nothing funny about this young lady!" Maggie scolds her.

"I am sorry" Alice says "I was thinking about that poem from the Telegraph"

"Since when do you read the telegraph?" Maggie smiles at her

Alice rolls her eyes, "I don't, but the MP for St Albans was in the pub a couple of Saturdays after the explosion, I forget his name, Hilda or something like that, there is some election or other coming up and he is visiting all the local business"

"Hildred" Maggie pipes up, Alice looks confused, "His name is Sir Hildred Carlile"

"How do you know that?"

Maggie sits up straight in a mocking manner, answers in her best upper class voice,

"Because I get to vote in them up and coming elections and I have been doing a bit of reading"

Alice is open mouthed, "Really?

Maggie nods, "Since they changed the law in February, I fit the bill to vote" Alice does not reply but looks, again, confused. "I am over thirty years old and as Ed and I are registered property occupiers, I meet the property qualification, so I get to vote" She pauses as she drinks her tea, "Not sure I will bother though"

"You must!

Maggie ignores Alice, "Anyway, this poem"

Alice stands up and walks to the ancient Welsh dresser and opens one of the smaller draws, she has to tug it as it always sticks a little,

"He saw me in my work uniform and called me over, he showed me the article in the paper and some journalist has written a poem about the explosion, as many of his readers contacted the paper, wanting to know about the incident at the Chaul End factory" She continues to rummage for a few seconds,

"Here it is, I cut it out to keep as it had to do with the factory"

"In your best voice please Alice" Maggie mocks gently as Alice clears her throat,

"When your favourite paper you search, For special latest news
And find you have been left in the lurch, Don't start to us abuse

All we have heard, or all we've seen, Must not be told to you
For D.O.R.A. is the ruling Queen, Of press and public too

A King may come, a Queen may go, By thousands recognised
But just why so we cannot show, Until we've been advised

Explosions, strikes and kindred things, Apt to engender woe
Must wait until the press wire sings, Released by Press Bureau

Maggie stands and claps as Alice takes a theatrical bow,

"None of this will ever help May and the other girls that died, will it?"

"No, it won't" is all Alice can think to answer. Maggie finishes her tea,

"Thanks for the brew" she says as she ties her headscarf back on "What are you doing for the rest of the day?"

"Getting the back room ready for when Martin comes home" Maggie puts her hand to her mouth,

"Oh my, I have not even asked how he is, forgive me Alice"

Alice tells her not to worry and explains that Martin, she thinks, is back in England in a military hospital, he is badly wounded, but he is alive and will be home when he is fit enough to do so, Maggie asks about Charles, Alice tells her all she knows, which isn't a great deal.

"See you at five fifteen in the morning then Alice, I am off to get a bit of bacon for our lunch"

"Best be quick Maggie; I hear rationing will be coming in for all of us soon"

Maggie closes the door quietly behind herself and Alice returns to her chores in the back room.

Alice receives another letter from Martin a week later, this time it is in his handwriting, she hurriedly opens it and digests the words quickly.

My dearest Sister,

I hope this letter finds you well and that you have heard nothing but good news from Charles.

I am well and back in England, I eventually got sent to the Royal Victoria Military Hospital in Netley, this is just outside of Southampton, after being sent to three hospitals in France, they eventually put me on an ambulance train, and I arrived here two days ago.

How odd it is that my journey to war started and finished in Southampton.

The hospital is vast, a huge and grand frontage with lovely gardens, I am currently on a ward in a wooden hut in the rear grounds of the hospital, I am receiving tremendous care from the British Red Cross, despite my feelings about living in huts similar to those we sometimes billeted in when overseas.

I am recovering well, my broken leg has been set and I am still in plaster cast and will be for the next few weeks, I was unlucky enough to have over a dozen bullets in my back and legs, all but one has been removed, one at the top of my back is too dangerous to have it taken out.

My darling Alice, I have to tell you that my face and neck are hideously burnt, and I fear I will be unrecognisable when I eventually get home, I am receiving treatment for these injuries, but scarring will be extensive and although they may fade with time, they will be easily noticed by all.

I will be in hospital for several more weeks and I will write again to keep you informed of my recovery.

Many here have horrific wounds and injuries.

I am one of the lucky ones.

My love to you,

Your Brother

Martin

Alice holds the letter to her chest; she then reads it again and then for a third time,

"You are alive Martin, you are alive" She whispers to herself.

Taking paper and a pen she immediately writes a response, telling Martin that he is to move into the cottage with her and Charles, both of them are in agreement on this and that she loves him, and he will always be her big brother, bullets, broken bones, scars and all, she tells him to come home as soon as possible as she firmly believes that the army will not send him back to the war with the injuries he has suffered. Once finished, she puts the letter into a white envelope, writes the address of the hospital under Martins name and army number, and puts a penny stamp in the top right corner, she walks out into the sunshine to go and post the letter, she pops into the pub to let Aunt May know that Martin is alive, and is as well as can be, Alice is surprised when May becomes very emotional when told this news, she wants to know when Martin will be home, Alice is unable to confirm a date but they both agree that they hope it will be soon.

"Have you heard from Charles?" May asks

"Not for a few days, I have to presume that they are back at the front lines again, so I hope to hear from him soon"

They hug and Alice leaves the pub to walk toward the post box, as she approaches the bakers, Mr Wilson walks out, he sees her and stops,

"Good morning Alice, how are you?"

"I am fine, thank you Mr Wilson, I hope you and Mrs Wilson are fine"

He nods and tells her that they are both in good health,

"I presume young Patrick is keeping you both busy?"

He laughs, "That boy ages me every day! But he is doing just fine" There is an awkward silence between them, Mr Wilson breaks it, "How is your Husband and Martin faring over in France?" he asks, Alice takes a deep breath,

"Charles is fine, I have no idea where he is, Martin is in hospital near Southampton, he was seriously wounded a few weeks ago"

"Oh Alice" he exclaims "I do hope he will be well and that his injuries are not too bad"

"He got shot in the back and legs, he has a broken leg and burns to his face and neck, but I had a letter from his yesterday, and he seems to be in reasonable spirit"

"Glad to hear it, will he be home anytime soon?" Alice shakes her head,

"I don't think so Mr Wilson, a few months to rehabilitate I think"

"Well, be sure to pass on our thoughts to him from all the Wilson family, I will say a prayer in Chapel for him on Sunday"

He touches the front of his hat and walks away, Alice walks on, meeting Mr Wilson has given her a tremendous feeling of guilt, she has not been to visit Grace's grave for a few months, she hopes that Grace doesn't think she is forgotten, wherever she may be now, because she isn't, she reaches the post box and posts the letter to Martin, turning back toward the cottage she decided to spend the rest of the day weeding the vegetable plot.

Toward the end of the month, Alice receives another letter from Martin and has written back to him, his words comfort her, but she senses that he is unhappy, he tells her that most of his wounds are healing nicely and that he is being treated very well but she detects an underlying sadness, she cannot be sure but although his letters are trying to be positive, they feel very flat to her.

"Morning Alice"

Alice looks over the fence to see the postman, John Buttress walking toward her gate, she walks down the path to meet him,

"Good morning Mr Buttress, do I have letters today?"

She is hoping to hear from Charles, she has not heard from him for well over a week, in fact, she realises, Charles has not written for nearly a fortnight, the postman hands her one letter, he smiles and walks away.

The envelope is plain with the familiar army 'REGISTERED LETTER' stamp on it, the post mark states, 'Army Post Office'.

She feels her hands shaking, she opens the envelope as she walks to the cottage, removing the letter from inside, she sees the words 'Army form A 6' and immediately knows it is a notification that Charles has been wounded, it is the same letter that she received when Martin was injured. It is a usual army form, printed lines with spaces for details to be written, she reads quickly and takes in the information.

Capt. Charles Gray , 1st Battalion Bedfordshire Regiment, Wounded in action, 22nd April 1918, in hospital at St Omar.

Waves of fear and panic run through her body, her hands are shaking and her heart beating so strong she can feel it in her chest, the letter does not tell her what injuries her husband has or how bad they are, she fears for the worst,

"Why did you not send me a telegram?" she shouts angrily, no one hears.

She feels utterly useless, she enters the cottage and sits at the kitchen table and sobs and sobs, even though she knows that both Charles and Martin are alive, she has never felt so scared or alone before.

* * *

Martin has been told that he is to be discharged from the army, he has been in the Military hospital at Netley for over three months, he even received the Bar for his D.C.M. in a ceremony in the courtyard of the hospital in June, he did not want to attend the ceremony at all, but as some of the other lads were getting their medals presented, they persuaded him to take part. It felt strange being back in uniform, having lived in hospital pyjamas since arriving, also that his uniform is clean and not lice ridden is a very distinct change for him, so he, on crutches and alongside the others, hobbled up to the General, saluted and took the bar for his medal from him.

The 'King thanks you for your sacrifice and service' is the remark the senior officer makes to each and every man, it is meaningless to Martin.

The leg he broke has caused him a lot of issues as the bones mend and some of the bullet wounds in his back refuse to heal, they keep bursting open and becoming infected, the left side of his face and neck are a mass of bright red scars, he has been sent out to smaller hospitals on at least three occasions but has always been sent back for more surgery, because of serious infection or because the smaller hospitals are purely for recuperation and not treatment.

It is now the first week of July and he is finally heading home, to the town anyway, he is to spend a few weeks in the military hospital, it is still at 'Rosemary' on Milton Road, Alice, and Uncle Pete, who still have friends in the VAD, have somehow managed to get him a bed in the hospital, so he will still be in the army but near to home, the feeling of having to leave the Colours is not one he likes, he has a constant, heavy and empty feeling in his belly that just won't go away. He regularly thinks about his 'lads', Nobby, H, Sharpie and Alfie, all dead, Dennis and John Marrables, as far as he knows, are both still fighting the Germans, although John was in hospital with trench foot when he was injured by the shell exploding almost on top of him.

He knows he is not the only man in the hospital that silently cries himself to sleep at night, if sleep comes at all, he also knows that he is not the only one to lie awake, looking into the darkness, sometimes all night, a few of the men in the hut he is in are not coping, they have been known to shout and scream all night as the terrors they witnessed come back to haunt them. Martin is in pain, but not in the same way as these poor souls, they spend their days scared and, in some cases, unable to move or walk, the worst affected are being taken away from the main wards and huts at Netley to be sent to Napsbury military hospital, as well as being a temporary military hospital, it is a lunatic asylum where most will likely spend the rest of their days.

The day arrives for him to leave Netley, an ambulance train will take him to London and then another will take him to the railway station in town, not the East station, but the 'New' station in town as the locals call it even though it has been built for nearly fifty years, he is in uniform, he is now classed as 'walking wounded', he has crutches and a walking stick to get around on, the crutches cause excruciating pain in his upper back where he still has the bullet lodged, but on most days he is unable to use the stick as his damaged leg is not yet strong enough to carry his body weight, so he will be transported in a chair to the train where he will be given a bed to lie on.

He is longing to see his sister who has been a tower of strength to him, writing to him every week, even when Charles was injured and hospitalised in France, she told him that Charles has shrapnel wounds to his legs and was gassed during defence of Nieppe Forest. He has written to Martin, who hasn't mentioned this to Alice, he tells him that the enemy fired gas shells at them directly into the trenches he and many others were caught out by the use of gas, although they all had masks, they were not quick enough to prevent exposure to the poison, Charles describes feeling 'as though his body were on fire' as the gas penetrated through his uniform. Whilst blinded, thankfully only temporarily, he and the others were being led out of the trenches, toward the rear lines, when the enemy fired trench mortars at them, he was hit by fragments of metal as one exploded nearby. He is thankful that the shrapnel wounds are not serious, the effects of the gas eventually wore off, although he tells Martin of a sharp pain in his lungs, he has not mentioned this to the army, the wounds to his legs are clearing up nicely and the best news of all is that he is to spend the rest of the war at the Number nine regimental command depot, known amongst the men as the 'Ampthill Command Depot', so he will be much closer to Alice, and he tells Martin that it is a joy to spend a great deal of time with her. The depot was used, from 1914 to train new recruits up until mid 1916, then, it ceased to be a training facility and at the request of the Duke of Bedford, a Colonel in the Regiment, it became a depot for nursing wounded soldiers back to health, Charles had been sent there initially to recuperate and, when fit, is to be posted to the depot. Martin laughs out loud at the end of the letter when Charles states that he has met 'an old friend' of Martins at the depot. Charles passes on a message to Martin from Company Sergeant Major Edward Hutchinson; the message is so rude and insulting that Martin is surprised Charles has even included it in his letter! He is even more surprised when he is told by Charles that he has signed on to remain in the army, to continue his service as Adjutant, Martin, knowing that his career is over, is pleased for Charles, but jealous that he has the opportunity to remain in the Colours.

"Sergeant, are you ready?"

Martin sees Sister Lovell from the Red Cross VAD, one of the hard working and seemingly tireless nurses on the staff at the hospital,

"Yes Sister, I think so"

Martin picks up his walking stick and tries to get up, as soon as he puts weight on the injured leg, he stumbles, Sister Lovell helps him back into his chair,

"Stay in the chair Sergeant, one of the orderlies will take you to the transport for the short journey to the hospital train"

He nods and relaxes, annoyed that his leg has defeated him yet again,

"I know the hospital you are going to Sergeant" she tells him

"How so Sister?" he is suddenly interested,

"Actually, I don't know the exact hospital, but I was senior training Sister at the Institute in the town when it first opened in 1915, I worked with Dr Kelynack who was the Superintendent then Commandant at that time"

Martin smiles, perhaps for the first time in a while,

"Go on, I know the building, but it wasn't a hospital when I left the town in 1910"

"Well, I went in to train the St Johns V.A.D. staff and the R.A.M.C orderlies, I was there until the first troops" she stops to think for a few seconds, "I recall it was the Sherwood Foresters that were first in, I also recall the arrival of a spotlight and the anti-aircraft gun they placed on the beautiful common land"

Martin starts to laugh, it feels good, so he continues, Sister Lovell breaks out a stunning smile,

"What is it Sergeant?"

Martin controls himself, "The world is a mad place Sister, firstly you were posted to my hometown, then I end up in Southampton in the very place I set off from in 1914 to go to Belgium" he looks at her "I would like to bet that you knew R.S.M Edward Westerman?" It is the nurses turn to laugh,

"My word, we all knew the R.S.M., I wonder what happened to him?"

"I can tell you that he took a commission and is now an officer with the same regiment, and last I heard, he was doing just fine over in France"

"Small world Sergeant"

Martin suddenly sits up, "Hang about, my little sister worked at the institute"

"Really? Was she a St Johns V.A.D. nurse?"

Martin shakes his head, "She would have liked to have been, but she was too young, so she volunteered, you know serving breakfast and reading to the injured men"

"We had a few really decent young ladies working as volunteers, their title was actually General Service Members, but we liked to include them as V.A.D.'s, what is her name?"

Martin tells the sister who claps her hand in delight,

"Of course! Alice is wonderful, I moved on in late 1915, to a hospital in France, Alice was still there then"

Martin tells her that she is now married to a Captain, who she met at the Institute, he tells her Charles full name, but the nurse cannot recall him in her mind,

"I saw so many men go through that place, I am thankful and pleased to say that the majority of the men were fit and well when they left"

"Fit enough to go back to war Sister"

She nods slowly, "Anyway, I know the current Commandant at 'Rosemary', she is a strict lady, but she has a very soft spot for you injured types"

"What is her name, I will find her when I get there?"

"Mrs F M Oakeshott, tell her I send regards and love"

Martin assures her that he will do that for her, an orderly arrives,

"You ready for the off Sarge?"

Martin nods, he stops the orderly for a second as he speaks to the sister,

"What was it like?" he asks her

"What exactly?" she replies, not understanding the question

"The hospitals in France, what were they like, I was in a few but I can't remember?"

She pauses for a few seconds,

"Every day was different, and the following day was always worse than the day before" she puts a hand on his shoulder "But all of our days combined were not as bad as one day on the front line Sergeant"

He puts his hand on hers,

"It wasn't all that bad really, not every day anyway"

He nods at the orderly and he is pushed from the hut and out to a waiting ambulance.

* * *

As the train approaches the main station in town, Martin is unusually nervous, he has butterflies in his stomach and very sweaty palms, he is glad to be going 'home', albeit not to his home, as he really doesn't have one, he thinks about the lads still fighting and feels sad that he now knows that he will not return to fight with his comrades again, he will be discharged from the army within the next month and is really unhappy at the thought of having to change from a life the has known for over eight years, the train stops gently with a hiss of brakes and in a cloud of steam.

He is home.

He is helped from his bed and into a chair by a young nurse who introduces herself as 'Miss Day',

"Welcome Sergeant, I will get you off of the train, although it is only a short journey, we might have to wait for the ambulance, we only have one and there are a few of you being transported to the hospital, but the Salvation army have a tea stand, so we can get a hot drink"

Martin nods and thanks the nurse, she pushes him from the train and onto the familiar platforms he remembers from his youth, a lump forms in his throat,

"Won't be too long Sergeant, shall I get you a tea?"

He nods, unable to speak, he looks around and takes in the view, the same gas lamps still hang from the covered areas of the platform, the waiting room still has the same horrible blue painted window frames, he is smiling to himself when he hears,

"Hello son"

He looks up and Uncle Pete is standing in front of him, he tries to get up, but his leg won't let him, he falls back into the chair, Pete bends down and puts both arms around Martin's neck and hugs him tightly,

"Welcome home Martin" he says

Martin puts his arms around his uncle and begins to sob, big heavy sobs leave his body, four years of war and nearly eight years since he left town and he is so very glad to see his uncle.

Martin is one of forty two soldiers being cared for at Rosemary, most are nearly as fit as they are ever going to be, this time spent convalescing is just what most of them need, they are all 'ordinary ranks' and they spend the days dressed in uniform and not in hospital clothing, so they still get a little bit of the military lifestyle they are accustomed too, but they are treated as patients and not as soldiers. Martin has found himself to be somewhat of a good listener, he spends a lot of time talking and listening to his fellow soldiers, some of whom are suffering great mental trauma because of what they have seen and what they have done, none have shell shock or 'the wind' as it is known by the soldiers, but some are severely disturbed by their experiences, Martin, although sad at the loss of many of his pals, has learnt to keep his feeling inside himself and his happy to be able to help his new mates in any way he can, he always deflects any questions about his time on the Western Front, he does not want to share his experience with anyone just yet. The staff are brilliant, very strict with the soldiers, but brilliant none the less, the Commandant, Mrs Oakeshott, who is so very happy to hear that Martin had met Sister Lovell, then there are the nurses, the Divisional Superintendent, Mrs Rowley, then the Sister in Charge, Sister Sprawson and all the nurses, Miss Kay, Miss Low, Miss Spear, Miss Peirson, Miss Fowler, Miss Corbett, Miss Day, Miss Jones, Miss Ince Jones and Miss Cost, the General service ladies are Miss Knowles, Miss Garland, Miss Constable, Miss Walthem and, much to Martins joy, his cousin, Catherine, is back as a volunteer at Rosemary and she fusses over him almost every day.

Martin is visited by a Captain, a clerk, and an R.Q.M.S from the regiment, they confirm that his discharge date from the British army is to be the 1st August, in just two days' time, he will need to relinquish his uniform and all his military kit, what he has left of it, much of his stuff was left in France when he was injured, the R.Q.M.S is unusually pragmatic about not getting everything back. Martin opts to keep his army greatcoat, a cost of one pound, which will be deducted from his final pay packet for this, he is told that he will be advanced two pounds in cash, this will also be deducted from the same pay packet. He fills out forms with the clerk, form Z22 to claim for disability due to a wartime injury, form Z44, the plain clothes claim, or 'civvy clothes' cash, as the soldiers call it, a certificate of employment it given to him showing his rank, name, army number and dates of service, February 10th, 1910, to August 1st, 1918. On the Disposal certificate, containing his military details, his new 'civvy' address, he signs to confirm the two pounds advance, Martin is given a copy, which he signs again,

"You will need this to present to any unemployment benefit, including the unemployed soldiers and sailor's donation" The clerk tells him.

The captain presents him with a *Kings Certificate on discharge*, he says to Martin

"Sergeant your service has been graded exemplary, it is my sad duty to tell you that your time in the Bedfordshire Regiment is to finish because of wounds sustained on the battlefield, your discharge from the service is honourable and under Kings Regulation sixteen, you are no longer fit for war service"

He hands Martin the certificate, it again has his number, rank, name, and regiment written on it, below the neat handwriting are the words,

"*Served with honour and was disabled in the Great War. Honourably discharged on 1st August 1918*"

The signature of the King is printed below this.

The captain continues,

"Army Order 316 of 1916, His Majesty the King has approved the issue of the Silver War Badge to officers and men of the British, Indian and Overseas Forces, who have served at home or abroad since the 4th August 1914, and who on account of age, or physical infirmary arising from wounds or sickness caused by military service have, in the case of officers, retired or relinquished their commissions, or, in the case of men, been discharged from the Army"

He hands Martin a small silver badge, he is aware it is the Silver War badge, known amongst the men as the 'Silver Wound badge'

The captain stands back and salutes Martin,

"The King thanks you for your service Sergeant"

Martin has no idea if he should salute back or not, so he doesn't, he thanks the three soldiers, they hand him an envelope with all his relevant documents, and they leave.

He looks at the envelope, even the bloody envelope has a document number, Army form Z82, he can see the ink stamp below it from the Regimental records office, it says on the front, in bold print.

Cover of certificate and other documents of soldiers on transfer to reserve or discharge

He looks at the small Silver War Badge, intended to be worn on civilian clothes to identify the wearer as a former serviceman and as a man who has served and was injured in a time of war. It had been the practice of some women to present white feathers, as a sign of cowardice, to able bodied young men who are not in the Kings uniform, it is always to be worn on the right breast of any jacket, medals are worn on the left side.

He reads the wording on it, around the rim are the words, '*For King and Empire*' around the top edge, and '*Services Rendered*' around the bottom, the Kings cipher of GRI is set in the centre, on the reverse is a unique number, the badge is registered to Martin, the Captain told him that if it ever gets lost and is handed in to the police, it will be returned to him, but if he ever loses it, replacements will not be forthcoming from the state. Martin puts the badge into the envelope, if anyone looking at his scarred and burnt face cannot see that he has served in the war, then the badge is not worth having, he swears never to wear it, he has said the same of his medals, his D.C.M. and Bar sit in the bottom of his suitcase, the clerk tells him that if any more medals or citations are forthcoming, they will be sent to the address he has supplied them, the clerk also added, excitedly, that he has heard that every soldier will get a war service medal and perhaps some campaign medals. Martin cares not for medals; his life has just been pulled from under him with a salute and the presentation of a silver badge.

He opens his suitcase and throws in the envelope.

Two days later Martin is standing outside of Rosemary, Uncle Pete is picking him up in the ambulance to take him home to the cottage, he has on his own clothes for the first time in many years and he feels naked without his uniform, which is all bagged up in his kit bag, to be collected by the army from the QM at the hospital, Mrs Parker, who has told him not to worry about any kit that may be missing, she will sort it out for him. Nearly eight years of his life has been dedicated to the army and to serving his country, now it is over and all he is left with is scars on his face and neck and a limp, he is now walking, slowly, with a stick.

"You don't have your medal ribbons or your silver badge on Sergeant" Sister Sprawson says to him,

"By choice Sister, and I am sad to say that it is no longer Sergeant, just plain old Martin from now on"

The ambulance pulls up and Pete shouts over the engine, "If you are ready Martin can we make a move, I have a couple of new lads to collect" Martin climbs aboard the ambulance, Pete shouts to the sister, "I have three to collect in an hour or so, I will spin by after dropping Martin off to pick up the nurses"

Sister Sprawson waves as the ambulance pulls away from outside of the hospital in a cloud of smoke, Pete looks at him and smiles,

"It is bloody good to have you home son, so bloody good"

Martin nods but cannot reply, he turns and looks out of the window as Station Road passes by on their way to the cottage.

"How is the pub doing Pete?" Martin asks, more to have something to say than to sit in silence,

"Not bad, but I don't think we can keep it up forever, not with my job on the estate and the ambulance driving, poor old May runs it on her own mostly"

"Could you not jack in the job on the estate?"

"I could" Pete replies "But I have been there since I was a lad and the cottage is tied with it, I don't think we can risk it to be honest"

Martin understands but is sad because his Granny had run the pub on her own for so long, but he realises the life of a licensee is not for everyone,

"I will drive past the cottage and turn around at the Gib, that will upset that miserable bugger Arthur Bruton if he sees us using his pub frontage" The manoeuvre is complete without the landlord seeing it done, Pete pulls up outside of the cottage, "I can't stop Martin; as you heard, I have to collect some more wounded, will you pop in for a pint later"

"Thanks for bringing me here Pete, you have gone above and beyond"

The men shake hands, Martin picks up his suitcase and after shutting the door he walks the short distance to the gate, Pete pulls away with a hoot of the ambulance horn, putting down his suitcase he looks at the cottage and then the garden. The cottage looks in good condition, tidy and clean on the outside, the garden is also looking good, the vegetable patch is flourishing and has obviously been tended well by Alice, the water pump looks like it could do with a touch of paint, the stream trickles on as it always has done, then he looks at the tree, the massive old Yew tree, he shares a secret with this tree, the secret burial of a long dead child that only he and the Yew know about, he smiles until he remembers it is also where Grace died, with a shake of his head he opens the gate, just as the front door of the cottage opens,

"Martin! Martin you are home" Alice shrieks and begins to run down the path, Martin closes the gate behind him, Alice almost runs into him and puts her arms around his neck, he has a suitcase in his right hand and a walking stick in his left, his injured leg gives way as Alice hits him and he falls to the ground, his sister on top of him,

Alice is horrified,

"Martin, I am so sorry I completely forgot myself, are you hurt?"

Sitting up on the path he dusts himself down,

"No more than I was when I arrived! Lovely to see you little sister"

He manages to get up and hugs Alice who is now in floods of tears,

"Come now Alice, if you can take my case then I can lean on you for a bit of support to get in"

Alice picks up the suitcase and Martin puts his right arm around her shoulder,

"That was a right proper welcome home, Alice!"

She apologises again for knocking him over, as they move toward the door, he begins to laugh, she joins in and they both stand at the doorway laughing at each other,

"Any chance of a cup of tea?" he asks her as they both enter the kitchen, and the door is shut behind them.

Martin sits at the kitchen table, resting his stick against the wall,

"How is Charles?"

"He is doing great actually; I think he is enjoying his new job at Ampthill"

"What about his wounds?" Martin asks

"All healed, thank the Lord, his lungs are a bit sore still, he coughs a lot, he did breathe in a lot of gas"

Martin has experience of gas, but only on the periphery of any gas attacks, he is glad that he hasn't had it like so many others, including Charles,

"Lucky really, it killed a lot…" he stops himself saying the rest of the sentence,

"It is fine Martin, I understand that lots of men were killed, I am just thankful that you and Charles are not amongst them, I am happy you are both back in this country"

Martin realises that although his younger sister is only nineteen years old, she has had to grow up very quickly with everything she has had to deal with since he left to join the army. Their parents dying, Grace was killed and then Granny died, all of which she has dealt with almost on her own, he is so proud of her,

"Alice, I don't want to be in the way here, I will get a job and I will move out as soon as I can"

"Charles said you would say something like that, he told me to give you a message"

"And the message is?"

"Shut up and stop being so stupid sergeant!"

Martin smiles, salutes at his sister,

"Yes Sir"

"Do you want to see your room?"

"Yes please"

Alice opens the old door to the living room, where she and Charles sleep, it resembles a building site, wooden frames have been built and filled with wooden laths, they have been put up, making the room smaller, to create a walkway to the back room, the old bedroom door that opens into the kitchen is still in place but a new door, leading to Alice and Charles room, has been put into the new wooden frame.

"Blimey, you have been busy" Martin exclaims

"We both thought that you might find it a bit uncomfortable having to walk through our room every time you need to go to the kitchen or to the privy"

"Such a kind thought, I hadn't even contemplated it" Martin tells her honestly

"Charles is going to horsehair lime plaster the first coat this weekend, he got the wood from Arthur Putterill, in fact when he delivered it, Charles managed to get Arthur to show him the best way to join the wood then to put in the laths, poor old Arthur got roped into helping him"

Martin walks through the narrow corridor created to give all house members privacy, it takes him along the wall on the right, where his mother used to have her wardrobe and then, turning left at the back wall, walking toward the door to his new room. He enters and it looks so very different to the last time he was in here, it was Alice's room then, it was pretty and functional and a huge change from when it was their childhood room they shared. Alice has changed it slightly to make it less feminine and more neutral for her Brother, the metal frame bed is still in place but the eiderdown is plain dark blue instead of the floral design he recalls, the wardrobe is still in place, this means that Mothers old wardrobe has been put in Alice and Charles room, the white wooden fireplace and mantle are clear of any items owned by Alice, the floral tapestry screen has been removed from in front of the small fire although the brass fender remains in place, the floral wall paper he remembers has been painted over in a light green, the blue curtains have been replaced with a green pair, all in all the room is very light and warm.

"Thank you, Alice, it is perfect"

"I have decided that I am never painting any wall ever again, it was a horrible experience"

He hobbles over to her and kisses her on the cheek, "I love it, thank you"

"It will be better when Charles finishes the plaster on those wooden slats, they can then be painted as well"

"I can do that Alice; I can help with the plastering as well" She puts her hands onto her hips,

"You will do no such thing Martin; you are still recovering, and you will be taking it easy"

"How did my nineteen year old little Sister turn into such a strict woman!" She tries to hide a smile but fails,

"Charles was just as bad when he came home, wanting to do this that and everything else, he still has some small pieces of metal in his legs you know"

Martin puts his hand onto the back of his neck and feels the scar near to his shoulder blade, a scar made by a bullet that is still lodged in his body,

"Charles is lucky the army kept him on, especially as a regular now"

"I think because he agreed to stay in England and to take on the Ampthill Depot, they had no choice, nearly everyone else is in France"

Martin knows that most of the Regiment are in France, the 1st and 2nd regular battalions are on the Western Front, the 4th, 6th, 7th, and 8th Battalions are posted across France and Belgium, the 5th Battalion has been divided, some remain in the UK as the home Battalion, the others had been sent to Egypt in 1915 and still remain fighting on that front of the war. The 3rd reserve Battalion are posted to Landguard Fort as part of the East coast defence team, numbers in this territorial unit have been hugely depleted with many men being sent to France to join one of the two regular Battalions on the front line. Charles had spent a few days with the 3rd for training and medicals when he was injured in 1915 and before he was sent back to the front. Charles decision to remain in the army and accepting the responsibility as adjutant at Ampthill has certainly kept him from being sent back to France, a decision that may well have saved his life.

Martin is walking to the pub later on that evening, it is still warm and light, the walking stick in his left hand to support his weakened left leg, it is over four months since he was injured and the leg wounds have healed, leaving extensive scars, but it is so weak and does not seem to be getting any better. He has an old cloth cap pulled far down on his forehead, in an attempt to cover the scars,

"Martin? Is that you?"

He looks up and sees Edward Munday walking on the opposite side of the road, he also has a stick and is waving it at Martin,

"Eddie, how are you doing?" Martin asks

"Not so bad, good days are better than the bad one's mate" he turns to his friend walking with him, "Do you remember Henry?"

"Hello Martin, how are the injuries these days?"

Henry Shadbolt from St Georges Cottages, Martin knew him before he joined up, they used to play along the river with all the other kids,

"Shaddy, is that you?"

"It is mate"

Martin crosses the dusty road and meets up with them outside of the Methodist chapel, they all shake hands,

"I thought you were with the 1st Bedfordshires?" Martin asks Henry, who nods his head and then shakes it,

"I was, went over in '14, got a bit busted up at the end of '15, then again in September '16 and finally I got clobbered at Cambrai in November last year, went to hospital for a bit, I eventually got home just before Christmas, it was all very quick for me, and I was discharged wounded in February"

Martin understands as he has been through almost the same process, although his wounds have seemingly taken much longer to heal.

"You lads going for a pint?" Martin asks

"We are now!" Eddie says looking at Henry.

The three men, two walking with sticks and the third with a heavy limp, get to the pub and Henry goes in first, followed by Edward and then, very slowly, Martin, the pub is very busy, Martin can see that Edward and Henry, or Shaddy as he remembers him, are regulars and most of the patrons acknowledge them, Martin hobbles into the bar, cap pulled down low, but he is seen by Walter, who shouts out,

"Martin's home!"

May looks up from the bar and tears well up in her eyes, Martin makes his way slowly though the crowded bar, he is patted on the back and shoulders, everyone is pleased to see him. He has a sudden overwhelming feeling of panic rushing through his body, a feeling he has not had since being in the trenches, Edward notices how pale Martin has become,

"Come on Martin, let's sit over here"

He nods at Henry, who pulls a small round table out from the corner and Martin sits on the bench seat, Henry and Edward take chairs and sit opposite him,

"You will be fine Martin, that feeling you have, the same feeling you had over there, will go away, you are not used to being around civilian folk yet mate" Edward tells him

May has made her way round from the bar and she sits next to Martin and throws her arms around him,

"So nice to have you back Martin, we have all missed you and were worried sick when we heard you had been wounded"

"I am fine May, honest, it is nice to be back" He looks around the pub and realises it is his first visit since Alice's' wedding, and his first time back without Granny being here, May seemingly reads his mind,

"She is still here you know" May is smiling

"Who is?" Martin asks confused

"My Mother, your grandmother, I can feel her in every part of this pub" she hugs her nephew "Don't be sad Martin, be happy you are home" Pete arrives and puts three pints on the table,

"These are the only free buggers you lot are getting!"

They all thank him; Pete and May go back to work and the three former soldiers drink quietly.

"I see you are not wearing your silver war badge Martin; I presume you did get one"

He nods as he takes a mouthful of lovely bitter beer,

"I did, it is in my bag somewhere" he looks at Edward,

"Mine is at home on my good jacket, took me long enough to get the bloody thing"

"When I got discharged, they were a new thing, I had to apply for mine" Henry says

"I think they came in in 1916 mate, the backlog for those wounded in 14 and 15 must have been huge" Martin tells them

"As you know, my third and final wound was in 1916, I got one anyway"

"You must have served with Martins brother in law, he was an officer in the 1st Bedfordshires" Edward says

"Not anymore" Martin intervenes "He is at the depot at Ampthill, got wounded a while back and got a nice job to see the war out"

"I know that Martin" Ed says with sarcasm "I wondered if Henry knew of him in the regiment"

"I did" Henry tells them "He was an acting Captain when I got injured and sent home, a good officer and we all know there ain't many of them about!"

Martin is feeling relaxed as he finishes his fourth pint, Edward and Henry are also finishing,

"One more lads?" Martin asks, they both agree, Martin struggles to his feet, Pete tells him to sit down and that he will bring the beers over.

"Table service at The Malta, now that is new!" Henry laughs

"Granny would not have done that Shaddy, we all know that!" Martin joins in the laughter, it feels good.

Pete puts three beers down on the table and refuses the shilling that Martin hands him,

"Pete, I insist, this is part of your work now, you can't afford to give beer away" he puts the shilling in Pete's hand,

"Leave the change in the till Pete, I am sure we will be having another"

Henry and Edward both cheer and lift their pints in the air.

"So, Martin" Edward has begun to slur his words "Did you get any gongs for your bit of service?" he puts his pint down "I got sod all" he points at Henry "Military medal over here Martin, the bloody Military Medal"

Martin lifts his pint glass toward Henry,

"To you Shaddy" he says

"I got mine, it was introduced early in 1916 I think, mine was given to me when I left" Henry tells them

"Well?" Henry asks Martin, who picks up his beer and drinks it,

"Do we have to do this chaps?" he asks. Both Henry and Edward laugh,

"Come on Martin, play the game! I don't have any medals, just a couple of wound stripes and one overseas stripe" Edward tells him

"I have three wound stripes, four overseas and one good conduct badge" Henry offers

"And the Military Medal" Edward reminds him

"And the Military Medal" Henry adds quietly. Martin sighs,

"I have seven overseas stripes, three in red for before the war and four blue ones for during the war" The other two look at him in silence. He continues, "Two wound stripes" he pauses "Hang on, I might have three, I don't remember, also I have two good conduct stripes for eight years undetected crime!"

"And?" Edward pushes him, Martin looks uncomfortable,

"You bloody know Edward!"

"I know I do Martin, but Henry here doesn't"

Martin turns to Henry,

"I got the D.C.M." he then turns to Edward, "The M.M. is a higher award anyway"

Henry shakes his head,

"No mate it isn't, the M.M. is a level three award and the D.C.M. is a level two, so yours is higher my friend, well done indeed"

"He got two Henry" Henry looks at Martin,

"You got a bar for your D.C.M.?" Martin nods,

"But only one of us here has two service numbers don't they Eddie"

Edward stands and takes a bow,

"Private 3252 Hertfordshire regiment and Private 39574 Gloucestershire regiment" Martin and Henry clap as Edward sits down, "It was nothing really, serving the King in two regiments in less than a year, you can keep your Military medal and your two Distinguished conduct medals, serving two regiments is the bravest thing any soldier can do!"

The three of them clink their glasses together, an older man approaches their table, he is wearing a brown coat, tied around the waist with an untidy length of rope, his hat is old and his trousers tatty, he is wearing bicycle clips even though he is inside and has a battered pair of brown shoes on, Edward speaks to him,

"Evening Horace, is everything all right?" All three of them know Horace Gunnel from Coldharbour,

"Glad to see you lads all here and safe" They raise their pints toward him, and he lifts his pewter mug toward them, "It is really good to see you all, you are the lucky ones you know" Horace says

Martin puts his pint down on the table so heavily he spills some over the top of the mug,

"I beg your pardon Mr Gunnel?" he says quietly

"I was just saying that you three are the lucky ones, you know, you got out and got home safe and well"

Martin explodes, he stands with difficulty and faces the old man, he tears off his cap and throws it onto the seat, he points at his face,

"Safe and well? Safe and bloody well, look at my face!" he is so angry that he ignores the protestations of the older man "Do you want to see the bullet holes in my back, one is still in there, just next to my shoulder, they could not get it out, how about my leg, plenty of scars there if you want to see them" he sits down "Safe and well indeed" he looks at Horace "How dare you"

Horace tries to speak

"I meant no offence, my lad didn't get home, that's all I meant"

The pub is suddenly quiet, Pete comes to Martin from behind the bar,

"Horace, go and get a pint, on me" Horace looks at Pete,

"Go on, May will pour you a beer, we are all sorry about young Ed not making it Horace" He looks sternly at his nephew "I do mean all of us" Horace steps away,

"Bloody hell Martin, what was that all about?" Edward asks him.

Martin does not answer,

"Son, are you alright?" Pete asks him "Horace meant no harm or offence, he lost his lad in July last year, his only son, young Edward, the boy didn't live round here anymore, he had moved to Stafford after he got wed up there" he looks across at Horace "The poor bugger didn't get to see Ed before he joined up, there is also his sons' young widow up North that he hasn't met either"

Martin hangs his head, Pete carries on talking, "Ed joined up in Leeds and never came back home before he went over to France, Horace told us all about it" he picks up the empty glasses,

"Just thought you should know lad; he meant no harm" Martin looks up at his uncle, "Are you sure you are all good lad?" Pete asks him, Martin looks at Edward and Henry,

"I'm scared" he whispers

"Of what Son?" Pete asks him

"Of everything and everyone Pete, everything" his words can hardly be heard

Martin gets to his feet and picks up his walking stick, he hobbles to the bar, watched by Edward and Henry, Pete moves forward to intervene, Henry puts his hand on Pete's forearm and shakes his head. Martin stands next to Horace, who turns toward him when he feels Martin's arm around his shoulder, they watch as Martin speaks quietly to him, Horace nods and smiles in return before wiping his eyes with the cuff of his old coat. Both men leave the bar and walk back to the table, Horace with his freshly filled pewter mug,

"Grab Horace a chair will you Shaddy?"

Henry takes the free chair and Horace sits with them; Pete goes back to the bar.

"I have apologised to Horace for my outburst, and I accept I was out of order" he looks at his two former soldier friends "Fear can be horrible, it takes over your every being, I should be sorry for being scared of everything since I came home, but I am not"

He picks up his cap and lifts it to put it back on his head to shield his scars, with a sigh, he stops and puts it back on the seat, he turns to Horace,

"Horace, tell us everything you know about Ed and his service abroad for King and country"

Horace smiles, leans forward , puts his elbows on the table and begins to talk to the three soldiers.

The pub returns to its normal gentle noise level as others get on with their conversations.

* * *

The weeks pass by and soon it is September and Martin has settled into his new surroundings, the corridor separating the bedrooms has been finished, Martin did persuade Charles to let him do a little work, he had to do it whilst seated as his leg, although slightly stronger is still weak and standing for any length of time causes pain and collapse of the limb. Charles has insisted that Martin stay living with them despite Martins private protestations, Charles tells Martin that he is likely to be away for periods of time as he is remaining in the army and that it will great knowing that Alice is not on her own again. They find out that Lt Frank Curtiss, who had been at Charles and Alice's' wedding, was killed during the second battle of Passchendaele, not long after he returned to the Western Front, along with three others, when a shell hit their trench, he was only 26 years old when he died on 4th November 1917, strangely the same day that Mary had died.

The weather for August and the beginning of September has been changeable with unseasonable rain and chilly wind, there has been very hot days but not the summer that any of them wants, today is hot, Martin is sat on a deck chair in the shade of the Yew tree, any chance he gets, he leaves the cottage and sits in this location, he feels safe and close to Grace when he is here, also he does not want to be in Charles or Alice's way, Charles is home for a few days and Martin has no desire to interfere with their personal time. Charles looks out of the kitchen window at Martin who is sitting in the shade of the tree, he is in shirt sleeves, his tie hangs loosely below the open top button on his shirt, his Captains tunic is hanging on the back of a kitchen chair.

"How has he been Alice?"

Alice puts down the knife she has been peeling potatoes with and dries her hands on a towel,

"Thoughtful and quiet, but I think he is coping, he sits out there every chance he gets, he has become mildly obsessed with reading the newspaper reports on the war"

"Has he mentioned Mary or Grace at all?" She shakes her head,

"Hardly and when I bring either of them up in conversation, he will politely listen to me and then change the subject" Charles rubs his chin,

"Has he been to visit their graves?" Alice again shakes her head,

"No, every time I ask, he tells me his leg won't take the walk and he doesn't want to use the bus because of the scars on his face" Charles continues to look down the garden,

"How about we go today, I have the staff car, so he won't have any excuse not to come with us"

She agrees and Charles leaves the cottage, taking two cups of tea with him as he walks down the garden toward Martin,

"Tea Martin?" Martin turns around,

"Yes, thank you Charles"

He takes the cup and saucer from Charles, who sits on the grass next to Martin,

"I often wonder what secrets this tree holds, I mean, it must be a couple of hundred years old" Charles says as he looks up into the canopy of the Yew,

"I don't suppose we, or anybody, will ever know" Martin replies, hiding a wry smile.

"Martin, Alice and I are visiting the graves of your Parents, Mary and Grace today, just to put some flowers on each of them" Martin remains silent and drinks his tea, "Won't you come with us?" Charles asks him

"I won't" Martin snaps back at him, Charles puts his cup and saucer on the grass,

"Steady on mate, no need for that" Martin nods and apologises to Charles, "We are taking the staff car I have assigned to me"

"That beast must save you a fortune in train fares"

"I suppose" Charles replies "But as I have to travel between Kempston and Ampthill when I am at work, it makes life easier for me and for the army" Charles looks at Martin who is very obviously ignoring him,

"Well?" Charles asks Martin

"I can't Charles, I just can't" Charles does not answer, he waits for Martin to carry on, "We have both seen death up close and accepted it, but that was war, I don't know how I will be feeling when I see the ground where they are buried, how I wasn't here for either of them or how Alice was left to deal with all of this on her own"

"I wasn't here either remember" Charles adds quietly

"I know Charles, and I meant nothing by what I said, certainly no slur on you at all, but I was away when my Parents died as well, Alice has attended every funeral without me, so I am not sure I need to or want to disturb memories that are as settled in me as they are going to be"

Charles finishes his tea, he stands up,

"Martin, I am taking my Wife to visit the graves of your parents, your grandmother and Grace, I think you should come with us, as a show of support to your sister" He pauses for a few seconds before adding, "Strange that all three of the graves don't have stones on them, unmarked so to speak, you will never find them without Alice"

Although Martin has been to his Parents burial plot, he has no idea where Grace or Granny are buried, Charles begins to walk up the garden,

"Charles" Martin calls after him

"Yes Martin"

"Can you help me up if we are going in that damn motor car" Charles smiles and walks back,

"Of course," he helps Martin out of the deckchair and hands him his stick "How does it feel?"

"How does what feel?" Martin questions

"Having an officer taking orders from a former Sergeant!"

"I could get used to it....Sir!"

Alice calls from the cottage, "What are you two laughing at?"

"Nothing really" Charles tells her "Get your coat on, we are going for a ride in the car"

Alice clasps her hands together and smiles at both of them, "Martin, you sit in the front, it terrifies me"

The army staff car is a Vauxhall D type, painted army green of course, the reclining roof is down and Martin holds open the rear door for Alice and puts his hand out to steady her as she steps up onto the running board and then takes her seat on the green leather, Charles is already in the driver's seat and is preparing to start the huge engine, as Martin gets in Charles gets out and when he is at the front of the car, he places the crank handle into the crank shaft and on the second turn, the engine jumps to life. As he climbs in, he says to Martin,

"It takes a bit of getting used to, the gearbox is a bit of a bugger, and this thing has no brakes on the front wheels" Martin looks amazed and terrified all at the same time, Charles continues, shouting as the car is now moving, "It has an engine transmission brake and I have a small foot pedal to press when we need to slow down, let's hope it works!"

Martin is not comforted by this, he has travelled in army lorries and on omnibuses, but this is his first time in a motor car, he really is not sure if he likes it at all, and turning around to look at his sister, he confirms it is not just him, Alice looks very grey and pale.

"Let us see what this old girl can do!" Charles shouts, he is having the time of his life.

They turn off of the Lower road to Luton and left onto Station road, over the river bridge and then Charles takes a right turn onto Coldharbour lane, he does not stop or slow down for the turn, he drives past the Almagam rubber works then a left onto Ox Lane, past the Nursery, both Martin and Alice are pleased that the steep lane slows the vehicle down and Charles has to change gears a few times, each time with a crunching sound from within the engine. They get to the top of the lane and Charles throws the car onto Sun Lane with a turn to the left and drifts downhill toward the town, he slows and stops at the junction of the High Street, taking a left turn and then shortly after a right turn and parks outside of St Nicholas Churchyard.

"That was fun!" Charles exclaims, Martin and Alice look at each other and raise their eyebrows.

"Granny is next to Mother and Father Martin; do you recall where they are buried?" Alice asks her brother.

"I do" he says "Are you coming"

Alice smiles at him, "In a minute, you go on"

Martin gets out of the car and slowly walks, aided by his stick, into the Churchyard through the old, battered gate, the white fence around the yard could do with a new coat of paint, walking under the arch of trees he turns left before getting to the door of the church and can see the huge Yew in front of him, his Parents are buried on the far side of the huge tree. His progress is slow because his leg is causing him great pain, as he approaches he can see where his parents are buried in their unmarked plot, he is pleased that on the grave next to it is marked with a new, small wooden cross, he stands in front of the grave and can read the slightly tarnished brass plaque on the wooden cross,

'*Ted and Mary Together Again*'

He smiles weakly and stands and stares at the cross,

"I made it home Granny, just like I said I would" he says to himself very quietly, he moves his head slightly and looks at his parent's grave, he nods in the direction of their burial plot. After a few minutes Alice and Charles arrive at his side, they are arm in arm and Alice is carrying two small bunches of flowers, Martin recognises them as being from the garden at the cottage, she hands one of them to him and he places it gently on Mary and Ted's resting place, Grace does the same on the grave of Jeremiah and Victoria, "Thank you for bringing me here" Martin says

"My pleasure" Charles replies

Martin looks up at toward the sky, his view is partially blocked by the bows of the Yew tree,

"This is certainly different to the last graves I stood next to" he points at the cross with the brass plaque "The grave markers are similar though"

Charles puts a hand on his shoulder, "Come on you two" he says, "Shall we go and visit Grace?"

Martin feels panic beginning to surge through his body,

"I will be at the car in a moment or two" he says to Charles and Alice, who walk away from the graves and back toward the car.

"I'm sorry Granny, I'm sorry Mother and I am sorry to you Dad" he takes a deep breath,

"I wasn't there when Alice needed me, I am sorry that we never had the chance to say goodbye"

He turns and makes his way toward the car.

"Alice has told me to slow down a bit with my driving" Charles tells Martin

"Thank the stars for that!" Martin grins as he gets into the front passenger seat, "Come on then Charles, move along man!"

"Bloody cheek" Charles says as he puts the car into gear and it lurches away from the church, he turns a half circle and goes back to the main road where he turns left onto the High Street but this time he drives past Sun Lane, onto the Upper road to Luton and heads toward the West side of town, as he approaches the large railway bridge he turns right onto Hollybush Lane, changing up a gear he puts his foot down on the accelerator and the engine noise changes pitch as it fights against the upward incline. Toward the top of the Lane, past the Alms houses and the old Convalescent home, Charles swings the car to the left and onto Ambrose Track, a dusty road that leads toward the National Children's home, Charles accelerates as he approaches the small bridge over the Nickey Line, when the old chalk pit comes into view in the distance on the left Charles turns right into Highfield Oval, the Chapel is at the far end of the circular inner road of the home, hence the name, Charles pulls up outside and brings the car to a halt. A few of the young residents come to see the motor car and Charles is more than happy to let them sit in the driver's seat and play with the steering wheel, Alice and Martin, his cap pulled down over his scars, walk to the rear of the Chapel, Alice stops and hands him a small bunch of flowers, she points toward the tiny and peaceful cemetery,

"In the far corner Martin, underneath the Yew tree, not a big gnarly beast like ours or the one at St Nicks, this is a young and fine looking tree" she pauses "Grace is buried underneath it, you will see Mr and Mrs Wilson have marked her resting place with a simple cross"

She turns and walks back toward Charles who is having a good time with the youngsters from the home, Martin hobbles across the grass, it is quite dry and firm, so his stick does not sink, he is thankful for this as he is finding the short walk difficult.

Most of the grave stones are lined up against a hedge on his left, he looks at them as he walks, small stones for the children and stone crosses for the Sisters who cared for the children, he then sees the Yew, Alice was right, it is a much younger tree than the one at the cottage and it stands in the far corner, upright and green in the morning sun, it doesn't yet have the huge boughs the older trees have, he can see a small wooden cross in the ground just in front of the tree, he is holding his breath as he approaches. Then he is standing at the far end of Graces burial place, there is only a small mound on top of the grave now, the earth has settled in the two years since she died, he steps forward and places the flowers in front of the cross, next to another fresh posey, he reads the clean and shiny brass plaque.

"*Grace Wilson*

b 24th December 1892

d 9th June 1916

Aged 23 years"

He takes off his cap and falls to his knees, he puts the palms of his hands into his face, covering his eyes as he begins to sob uncontrollably, he has seen death, he has seen suffering, he has witnessed horrors no man should, he has buried friends on the battlefield. This is his worse day, none of his previous experiences come close to how sad and lonely he feels right now, he is alone and knows he will be alone for the rest of his life. The walk back to the car seems to take an age, he has to lean heavily on his stick to even move a small pace, Alice sees him appear from behind the Chapel,

"Martin!" she shouts as she runs toward him, "Are you ill or hurt?"

As she reaches him, he accepts her arm to support him as he walks,

"I am fine, just a bit tired"

"Is the leg causing you pain?" she asks concerned as Martin is pale and gasping for breath,

"No" he lies "It is fine" he looks for the car "Where is Charles and the motor car?"

Alice sits Martin on a bench at the front of the Chapel, she laughs lightly,

"He is driving the children around the Oval, much to the disappointment of the sister over there"

Martin can see a lady, aged in her mid to late twenties, standing at the side of the Oval, she has on her uniform cap and a plain navy blue, calf length coat, her gloves and stockings are also dark blue, the collar of her white blouse is fastened tightly at the neck.

The children at the home are cared for by the sisters, all of whom are part of the Sisterhood Order of the Children's Home, their official title is, Christian Deaconess of the Children's home, Martin calls over to her,

"All will be well Sister"

She is rubbing her hands together and as she walks toward them, "Such fearful noise from that mechanical beast!" she exclaims

They both agree with her, Martin introduces himself and Alice,

"Nice to meet you, I am Sister Joan and some of my boys and girls are with the captain" she looks at Martin, "Are you a soldier as well?"

"Not any more Sister" Martin tells her

"Well, we all must hope that the war is over soon, we have many of our former boys serving at this time and sadly some have been killed"

As she speaks, the roar of the D type engine can be heard, as can the screams of joy from the children in the motor car with Charles, he pulls up next to the awaiting trio as the children shout for more and all are thanking Charles,

"Captain, if I may have my children back now, please" Sister Joan mildly scolds Charles,

"Certainly Sister, no harm done, but they might be a bit excitable!"

"I can see, remind me to thank you for this another time" she calls the children to her, "Line up in front of me please"

She claps her hands, and it is only then that Charles, Alice, and Sister Joan notice that all the children have become quiet, and all are staring a Martin.

"Children, don't be so rude, stop staring and line up here at once"

Martin slowly puts on his cap to cover the scars on his face, he turns away from the children and begins to walk slowly away, his stick bearing most of his weight,

"Martin" Alice calls after him

"Leave him be Alice" Charles says quietly "We can pick him up on the way out"

"Captain, I must apologise for the conduct of these children, such rudeness" She is obviously upset and cross with the children,

"Don't be too hard on the Children Sister Joan, seeing an injured man like Martin is a new experience for many, not just them"

"Will he be alright; I feel he is offended" The Sister adds quickly

Charles shakes his head, "He will be fine, he is not used to the way he looks yet, but he will be fine"

Charles and Alice bid Sister Joan a good day and as they get into the car, they can hear her remonstrating with the children

"They are really for it!" Charles says with a laugh

"It isn't funny Charles" Alice says sharply "Martin must be devastated"

Charles turns and takes Alice hand in his, "My darling, he is a soldier, a tough one at that, he walked away to give himself some space, come on, let's go and get him"

He pulls the car away and they catch up with the hobbling form of Martin very quickly,

"Get in old man, you look just about done in" Charles tries to sound happy

"Thanks" Martin struggles to get into the car but refuses any help, Charles speaks to him,

"Everything alright mate?"

"It is, I just forgot about my face for a moment, must have scared those kids half to death"

"To be fair Martin, you would have scared them before you had the scars, you were a very ugly man!"

Alice is about to give her Husband a piece of her mind but stops when she hears Martin roaring with laughter.

"Bloody cheek!" Martin says as he wipes tears from his cheeks, his tears of laughter are hiding the huge tears of sadness that are slowly tearing his soul apart.

Charles drives back to the cottage in a more sedate fashion that he did on the outgoing trip, he takes a route back to the High Street, taking his time through the town, eventually turning left onto Station Road, under the Midland railway bridge, driving past Milton Road on the right, Martin has not ventured to town since leaving the Rosemary Hospital, it is still being used by the military and is full of wounded soldiers. At the crest of the incline, Charles cannot resist, and he puts his foot down as Station Road begins to go downhill, he only slows down as he approaches the railway bridge, knowing the road turns sharply left just after the Great Northern Inn and then toward the railway station, Martin is beginning to enjoy the speed in the motor car, Alice certainly isn't. Charles keeps the speed down as he takes the gentle right curve in the road and then over the river bridge, turning right they pass the bakers and the wheelwright shops, The Malta is coming up on their left, as they pass it seems to be closed, it should be open for the lunchtime trade, Charles gets to the cottage and swings the car over the road and parks next to Uncle Pete's ambulance that is parked next to the cottage. The three of them get out of the motor car and see Pete and May sat on the bench by the front door, Alice calls to them,

"The door is not locked; you should have gone inside"

Martin, Charles, and Alice go through the old garden gate and as they get to the cottage, both Pete and May stand up,

"Is everything alright with you?" Martin asks, his Aunt and Uncle look at each other but don't speak, Martin turns to his uncle, "Pete, what is it?"

"We have left the pub Martin" he puts his hands up in front of him, palms facing the three arrivals, "Before you say anything, let me explain"

"Come inside" Alice tells them both "At least then we can have a cup of tea"

They all go inside, Alice puts the full kettle on the hot plate, the fire is still burning in the grate but needs a little attention, Martin sees to this, Charles takes the large bucket to the water pump to fill it, May and Pete sit at the table.

"It is just too much for us, what with Pete still working on the estate and driving the ambulance for the hospital, I am here nearly every day on my own" she looks at Pete and smiles at him "By the time he gets home he is exhausted, the girls are both living at Maple Cottages, Jenny works long hours at the post office and Catherine is still volunteering at the hospital, so we need to be at home, the pub is not making any money really, not enough for us to stay" she looks at Alice and Martin, "We are so sorry" she continues, she takes a hankie and dabs her eyes "I am sad, the Malta was my Dads pub and when he passed, my dear old Mum took it on and she ran it alone, God only knows how she did it, but when she died, I think I moved in and took over out of respect and to keep her memory alive"

Alice steps over and puts her arm around May's shoulder,

"It is fine May, honestly, you certainly must do what is best for you"

"Agreed" Martin says as he struggles to his feet, Pete stands to help him "I am good thanks Pete, so who is taking over the licence, I presume the brewery have someone in mind?"

Pete nods, "Some chap by the name of McCable, from St. Albans we believe, he has it as from midday tomorrow, but we are not opening" He looks at his Wife "We are going home"

Charles can be heard putting the bucket outside of the door, he enters the kitchen,

"Is the kettle nearly done Alice?" he asks, she puts her hand on the side of the kettle

"A few minutes yet Charles"

"How is the war going for you lot then Charles?" Pete asks

"Well, it depends on how you look at things, the lads are consolidating the ground taken recently, but the losses have been terrible, the 1st Bedfordshires lost ten officers, including the commanding officer, and nearly two hundred men in the last two weeks of August alone"

There is a short silence, broken by Martin, "Who was the C.O. that copped it?"

"Lt Col Courtenay, a good chap, during a scrap at a place called Achiet le Petit, he was wounded and died of his injuries, I have no idea who will be put in charge of the 1st now"

"Any news on my old lot?"

Charles shakes his head, "Nothing specific, but the 1st and 2nd are fighting in the same area, so probably not that great I am afraid"

Martin, a little pale in the face, nods and makes for the front door,

"Martin?" Alice is concerned for her brother

"Just going outside for a smoke Alice, I am fine"

"Can I join you, Martin?" Charles asks

Martin opens the door and waves Charles to go past him,

"You are a Gent" Charles tells him.

Once outside, Martin, who is leaning against the wall of the cottage, gives Charles a cigarette, once lit and both men are smoking, Martin asks,

"Do you really not know what is happening to my lads?"

Charles inhales deeply and blows the smoke from his lungs before answering,

"I am not sure it good for you, or me for that matter, to dwell too much on what is happening, I get messages through my office daily, so I struggle to avoid it and if I am truthful, I only really look out for how the 1st Battalion are doing"

"Don't try to tell me you ignore what is happening to the other Bedfordshire Battalions"

"No" Charles says truthfully "I don't"

Martin flicks the ash from the end of his cigarette,

"Well then?" Charles just looks at him, "Come on Charles, I am not going to go to the Yew and string myself up if the news is not good!"

He instantly regrets his choice of words, the Yew has enough association with death in this family without him adding to it,

"Fair enough Martin, I honestly don't know a great deal more, but I know whilst my lads were being battered at Bapaume, your lot, on the same day, were close to Albert fighting another battle, then your lot went into Bapaume a week later and again held the ground but with losses"

Martin continues to smoke his cigarette in silence, Charles continues,

"One officer and six other ranks killed in the battle, but nearly fifty wounded and most of those did not, or will not survive"

"Any more to tell me?" Martin asks blankly

"A few days later, they were at Sunken Road, I believe you were in trenches there at some point, weren't you?"

"A few times" Martin answers

"Reports suggest that during enemy artillery attacks and machine gun attacks, one officer and thirty two men were killed"

Martin whistles through his teeth, "Bloody hell"

"Before you ask Martin, I don't have any details of any of the men who were killed, we only get figures not details"

Martin flicks his finished cigarette into a puddle, he raises his eyebrows and lets out a huge sigh,

"Come on Charles, let's go have a cup of tea and forget all this for a few moments"

Charles laughs, "I made Major by the way"

Martin hobbles over to him, "Congratulations old man, when did this happen?"

The men shake hands,

"I get the promotion next Monday"

"That is some good news at least"

"Can you really do that?" Charles stopes before he enters the cottage

"Do what?" is the reply

"Forget about it all, if only for a moment?"

"No" Martin replies "But I can pretend"

* * *

September finishes and Martin has become quiet and lonesome, spending more time in his room, or sitting under the yew tree if the weather allows him to, since May and Pete left The Malta, he has not been into the pub, or any other, Ed and Henry occasionally call on their way to the Malta, but Martin has always made an excuse, or gets Alice to do it for him, just so that he does not have to go. He has applied for a few jobs, the rubber factory turned him down because they 'Don't have facilities for the handicapped', Martin suspects the others turned him down for similar reasons or because of the way he looks. Charles continues on in the army and is now a Major, he tells Martin and Alice that he is hopeful that the end of the war is near, Alice is overjoyed, Martin says he won't believe it until it happens.

Alice is taken ill toward the end of October, Dr Blake tells Martin that it is probably 'Spanish Flu', he sends her to bed for a week and as Charles is away, Martin looks after his sister, she only gets her out of bed to use the privy, he has to carry her, a task he finds very difficult as his leg is still unable to take much weight and using his stick to keep upright, he holds Alice in his right arm and almost drags her to use the toilet. For three days she is almost incoherent, so much so that when Charles comes home, he considers putting her in the motor car and driving her to hospital, she is through the worst of it by then and manages to convince him that she is getting better and that a trip to the hospital is not needed. After five or six days she is well enough to get out of bed, both Martin and Charles are relieved, it has done Martin some good, he has been unable to spend most of his days locked away because Alice needs almost constant attention, he secretly enjoys the responsibility and the feeling of being needed again.

He and Charles are sitting by the fire one evening, it is the last day of October, Charles tells Martin that the war is going well for the allied troops,

"Menin has been recaptured, that was a huge blow for the Kaiser, more areas of France and Belgium are being recaptured every day, I have heard that the Belgian army firstly retook Zeebrugge and then Bruges, then the following day they continued to fight and retook every inch of the Belgian coastline back"

Martin sips his beer, "All looking good, and they did it without either of us being there!"

"They could not have done it without any of us mate, still a few hurdles to get over though, I know we got Armentieres back earlier on in the month" he stops and thinks for a moment, "I think we both went there or near it at some point" Martin agrees and Charles continues, "The best news so far is that I heard today that the Turkish army have surrendered at the River Tigris, it is expected that they will accept defeat and cease hostilities tomorrow"

Martin raises his bottle and Charles touches his bottle onto Martins

"We can then get on with our lives hopefully" Charles says "Thanks for caring for Alice whilst I was at work, I could not get away, you know how it is"

Martin nods "She is my sister, so it was my pleasure to look after her, and as for knowing how it is with the army, I wish I still did, I really do"

Charles nearly spits his beer out when Alice shouts from the living room,

"Will you two stop patting each other on the back for a moment, I could do with a cup of tea"

They both look at one another and at the same time, they say,

"She is feeling better!"

* * *

Martin is sitting under the Yew tree, it is a cold and sunny November morning, and he sits alone in his deckchair, his army great coat with its collar up high on his neck and all the buttons done up tight.

On his lap is the Daily Mail, dated today, 11th November 1918, the headline screams at him,

'GERMANY WAVES THE WHITE FLAG'

His hands are shaking as he stares at the front page of the newspaper, Charles had hinted a few days ago that it seemed that Germany were willing to surrender and sign the Armistice, and at eleven this morning, all fighting had stopped a few minutes ago, no more death and destruction across the world, he is pleased that the war is over, but he has a feeling deep inside himself that he cannot understand, but it just won't leave him. There are not many families across the country that have suffered the sacrifices of loved ones or friends, is the feeling he has sadness? grief? hatred? or a combination of all three, whatever it is it is with him always and he cannot control it.

He looks up into the tree, as he has done so many times before throughout his life, it seems different today, darker, and more joyless than it has ever been, he thinks that he knows this tree, the secrets they share and the grief he feels that was caused by the tree, but the truth hits him as he stares up into the green canopy, the tree is the secret, the tree is knowledge and the tree is life and death, none of which he can control.

Charles pulls up outside of the cottage in the Vauxhall staff car, he is out of the driver's seat seemingly as the car is still moving,

"Alice!" he calls "Alice, where are you?"

Hearing the mild panic in his voice, Alice leaves the kitchen and meets him at the door,

"Charles, whatever is wrong, please tell me that the war is over, and the fighting is finished?"

He takes his Wife into his arms and hugs her very tightly, "Charles, you are scaring me now, what is it?'

He pulls away from her, "Frankie was killed"

For a moment Alice cannot place who Frank is, then she realises,

"Your Cousin Frank?"

He nods, it is obvious to her that he if fighting back strong emotions,

"Oh Charles" Alice says, she knows how close they were "I am so sorry"

His shoulders slump and he leans against the frame of the door,

"He was killed at a place called Haussy, on the 24th of October, eleven days before the war ended, eleven bloody days"

"How are his parents?" she asks

"Devastated, they only found out yesterday, Frankie's Wife received the telegram a couple of days ago, but with the children to care for she struggled to get up to see them straight away, taking the train from Caversham only yesterday"

He looks down the garden to where Martin is sitting, "He must be freezing sitting out there" Charles says

"I have asked him to come inside but he refuses, he was shivering this morning, but he told me he was hot, he hasn't eaten since yesterday morning, he has a hacking cough as well"

"Do you think he has that Spanish flu that you had?"

"I hope not because it is the worst I have ever felt, but I did not have that cough and he doesn't have the two brown spots on his face that I had, the Doctor told me this was a sure sign"

She puts her hands onto the stone windowsill and looks at her brother,

"All he will say is that he wants to finish the paper, but he has not even turned a single page yet"

Charles takes in a deep breath,

"I have news for him as well Alice, news that I fear he will not take well"

"What news Charles?" she asks

"The only two members left of Martins last platoon were killed last week, we got the names through this morning, I asked the C.O. if he wouldn't mind letting me go, he was fine when I explained my reasons for leaving work so soon after arriving"

"This is supposed to be a day of celebration" she leans into her husband and kisses him gently on the lips "It certainly is nothing of the sort, is it?"

Charles shakes his head and nods toward Martin, "Wish me luck Alice"

He steps away from the door, Alice goes inside and closes the door quietly, she can feel the heat from the range quickly replacing the cold air from outside, she stands and looks through the kitchen window as Charles approaches her brother. Martin can hear someone approaching him, he had heard Alice and Charles talking at the door but could not make out what was being said, he looks up when Charles arrives, Martin speaks to him,

"Something must have happened for you to be home from work, you only left here at six this morning and although the War is supposedly over, I doubt whether the Regiment has sent you home to celebrate, has it?"

"No, they haven't" Charles answers him

"I don't think it will ever be over for some, perhaps including you and me Charles, what do you think?"

Charles takes a cigarette and lights it; he hands it to Martin who thanks him, he lights another and takes a deep drag from it,

"Martin, I have news from the Regiment"

"I am presuming that none of it is good news" he replies without emotion

"No, none of it" Charles says quietly "Martin I have some names of lads from the 2nd that were killed during an attack on a place Preux au Bois on the 4th of November"

Charles waits for Martin to ask him the names, he doesn't and just keeps on staring at the newspaper, Charles clears his throat, Martin has a coughing fit.

"One officer and seven ordinary ranks killed; I believe two of them are from your last platoon"

"John and Dennis?" Martin says in a matter of fact manner.

Charles takes a deep breath,

"Martin, John Marrables and Dennis Waldock were killed along with five others"

He looks down at Martin, who's head has dropped deep into the collar of his coat, his chin sitting on his chest

"I am sorry Martin" is all he can think to say, Martin mumbles something, "Say again Martin, I didn't catch what you said"

Martin sits bolt upright in the deck chair,

"Just me Charles, I am the only one left of that platoon, just me"

"Don't be sorry that you survived it my friend"

Martin wipes his eyes with the sleeve of his great coat, "I am not sorry for surviving Charles; I am sorry that I didn't die with my lads over there in that mud and lice infested shit hole"

"I for one am glad that you are here, for my sake and for Alice"

Martin manages a weak smile, "Thanks Charles, that means a lot to me, how did your lot get on in the end?"

"At the very end they were off of the front line, but in the couple of weeks leading up to it, they took a bit of a kicking"

Martin finishes his cigarette and flicks it toward the stream, it lands short, Charles puts his out under his boot, he finishes his sentence,

"On the 23rd of October, whilst capturing a tiny village, Beaurain, from the Germans the chaps from the 1st were hit with heavy machine gun fire as they went over the top, one officer killed and another eight wounded" he stops for a moment,

"One is a former R.S.M. that you may have met, Henry Trasler"

"He got his D.C.M. posted in the Gazette on the same day as mine, I met him a couple of times, I had no idea that he had taken a commission"

"Sadly, fourteen of the men were killed by the machine gunners, over a hundred were seriously wounded"

Marin shakes his head, "How the hell are we supposed to forget about this and get on with our normal lives?"

"I have no idea, if I am honest, that is one of the reasons I am staying in, to be with others who know about it" Charles speaks quietly.

"Lucky you" Martin responds

Charles knows that Martin means no harm or spite with his words, he knows that Martin would do anything to get back into the army.

"My cousin was also killed a couple of weeks ago"

Martin turns to Charles but remains seated, Charles can see beads of sweat on Martin's forehead.

"Not Frank Gray?"

Charles nods, "He was with the 2/4th Battalion at somewhere called Haussy, West of Le Quesnoy, during the German retreat, all I know is that he was killed on the 24th of October"

Martin shakes his head and lets out a loud sigh,

"Sorry mate, I am sorry for you, for me, for the Regiment and for every single man that didn't make it" He hands Charles the newspaper, "Take that away will you Charles, nothing but bad news in it"

Charles takes the newspaper,

"Have you even read it?"

"No" replies Martin "But there won't be anything good in it"

As Charles walks away, he hears Martin coughing, a dry hacking sound erupts as he coughs almost uncontrollably, Charles turns around,

"Martin, you should get inside, I think you have a cold, I can see you are sweating"

Martin shakes his head, "I am fine, I am so hot that I need the fresh air, I will come inside in a bit"

He turns his head and stares back at the stream

"Charles" he says

"Yes Martin"

"I am really glad the fighting is over, and I am so sorry about Frank"

He turns his head away again and does not see Charles nodding at him.

Charles gets back inside the cottage and shuts the door, rubbing his hands together he looks at the fire in the range grate, it is burning very well, the kitchen is cosy and warm, Alice is sitting at the kitchen table, she puts down her embroidery,

"How did he take the news?" she asks

"Better than expected, but I agree with you Alice, he is not well, he is shivering in the chilly air and sweating a lot, I asked him to come inside but he refused, stating he will come inside shortly"

Alice picks up her embroidery but does not continue working on it,

"I will make a pot of tea in a while and I will go and see him, and I will make sure he comes inside to drink it"

Charles sits on the bench seat, crosses his right leg over his left and opens the paper and begins to read,

"I am so pleased that the war is over Charles, I cannot tell you how scared I was the whole time"

He lowers the newspaper and smiles at her,

"All is well Alice"

He lifts the paper and carries on reading,

"Not knowing where you were or what you were doing was just intolerable" she continues, Charles again lowers the newspaper and smiles at his Wife, he lifts the paper for a second time and starts to read again, "When you did not write I always thought the worst had happened, I feel silly now for thinking like that"

Charles closes the newspaper, folds it in half and puts it on the windowsill, he stands and walks over to Alice, he bends down and kisses her on the head,

"Shall I make the tea Alice?" he asks her

She nods and Charles puts the kettle full of water onto the range.

Twenty minutes later Charles is pouring three cups of tea for them all, he hands Alice hers,

"I will go and get Martin first Charles; I won't be a minute"

"Wrap up Alice because it is colder out there than it looks"

"Do you think there will be celebrations in town today?" she asks as she stands at the door

"Oh, I should think they are already happening Alice, perhaps we could drive up this afternoon, take Martin with us, it might make him feel better"

Alice opens the door and steps outside, she shivers as she closes the door behind her, wrapping her arms around her body she begins to walk down toward the Yew tree where Martin is sitting, she calls his name,

"Martin, come inside please, Charles has made tea" He does not move, his head is down on his chest, deep inside the upturned collar of the great coat, she giggles, "Are you asleep Martin? How can anyone sleep in this chill!"

He does not move; she reaches his location and gently shakes his shoulder. It is then that she sees the trickle of blood coming from his right ear,

"Martin?" she says anxiously and shakes his shoulder, his head lolls a little and she can see that his eyes are closed and the skin on his face has turned a shade of blue,

"Martin!" she says again but now with an anxious tone to her voice. She touches his hand, and the skin feels cold, he makes no response, she kneels beside him, she realises that he is not breathing, he is silent and still. "Oh Martin" she says quietly, she keeps hold of his cold hand and squeezes it gently,

She looks up toward the cottage when she hears the door open, Charles, who has been watching through the window stands in the doorway, he looks at his Wife crouching next to his brother in law,

"Alice" he calls to her

She looks up at Charles, she has tears freely falling across her cheeks, Charles and Alice lock eyes and she gently shakes her head at him.

Charles closes the door and slowly walks toward Alice.

* * *

Charles is at his desk at Ampthill Depot, he is preparing to hand the site back to the Duke of Bedford, the War office no longer has any need to use it, at the end of this week the last soldiers will leave and all head home for Christmas.

Charles will come in once more toward the end of December to make sure all that needs to be done has been completed, he wants to be sure that all t's have been crossed and i's dotted before the site is vacated by the Regiment toward the end of January 1919, over ten thousand troops have passed through this depot since the Regiment moved in, new recruits and injured soldiers, many of whom are now dead Charles starts a new job at Kempston Barracks in the new year, he is to command a unit of the 1st Battalion, he knows that the numbers of officers he will command will be greatly depleted, many were killed in the war, he will have the responsibility to ensure his officers and soldiers are trained correctly, that their welfare and administration is up to scratch and the management of all the equipment they will need. He opens his briefcase, then checks all the drawers in his desk, he has left a few items that he will not need in his new post, something catches his eye at the back of the top drawer on the left hand side, he opens the drawer to its fullest extent and can see an envelope has been caught on the back edge of the drawer. He gently pulls it and sees his name written in script that he recognises, this is the letter that Martin gave to him in the Marquis of Granby pub when he, Martin and Ed went for a drink one August afternoon last year just before he married Alice. He has forgotten all about it and had always intended to give it back to Martin, just as it is now, unopened, and unread. He sits down at his desk and puts the envelope in front of him, Martin had asked him not to read it until he was dead, he picks up the envelope and looks at it,

"You are dead now my friend, so here goes"

He opens the envelope and takes out the letter from inside, it is set out in an informal fashion, he begins to read.

Charles,

If you are reading this then the War has managed to finally get me.

This letter is to tell you how happy I am that Alice has you in her life, she has always been the single most important person to me, and I know, now I am dead that she is in the safest of hands.

I have 3 requests for you to consider, I will understand if they sound strange to you and that you cannot fulfil them on my behalf.

1. *I promised a dying friend that I would name my first child after him, his name was Walter Dennis and he was a fine soldier, he died in my arms at 0730 on the morning of the 12th March 1915, before he deployed that day, he asked if he would be safe on the raid, I told him he would be fine, his last words to me were to the effect of, "If I am not, will you name your first child after me?"*
   I told him to bugger off, these were my last words to him.
2. *At the end of June 1916, I met a fine young man named William Albert James Samways of the 1st Battalion Dorset regiment, he fell on top of me after falling into a thorn bush, later, later we had a cup of tea together, he asked me to visit his mother should I hear of his death, he believes his mother will laugh and laugh when she hears how he fell into a thorn bush. He died, along with thousands of others on the Somme on July 1st, 1916.*

I don't remember her name, but she lived in a place called West Allington near to Bridport, I am presuming in Dorset, I agreed to do this.

3. *Bury me under the Yew tree*
4. *Alice need not know about this letter*

Martin

Charles folds the letter and leans back in his chair, he digests the contents of the letter, one of the strangest he has ever received, he smiles as he says aloud,

"No Son of mine will ever be named Walter!"

Martin is buried next to his Parents and Grandparents at St Nicholas church, the plot is under the ancient and huge Yew tree, Charles opens the letter and reads point three again,

"You did mean the Yew tree at St Nicks didn't you Martin?

END OF BOOK I

My thanks to the Methodist church for granting permission for the use of the Morning Prayer.

The Yew Tree Book II will follow

Part three - 1939-1941

Part Four - 1970

Printed in Great Britain
by Amazon

86255181R00394